"The thought strikes me I ought to be happier than I am," declares Judith Gill, the heroine of Carol Shields' deft first novel, *Small Ceremonies*. In this exclusive Quality Paperback Book Club edition of three early novels by the Pulitzer Prize-winning author of *The Stone Diaries*, we meet a host of like-minded characters whose desire for certitude, order and stability leads them only further into a tangle of illogic. Judith is a biographer, mother, and would-be novelist whose failed attempts at fiction writing take her on a labyrinthine path to determine if, as a friend confides, "writers are no more than scavengers and assemblers of lies." *The Box Garden* continues with the story of Judith's thwarted poet sister, the "half-educated, half-old, half-married, and half-happy" Charleen Forrest, who disdains pretentious "pome" people and resists marrying a genial middle-class orthodontist after she is taken with the ascetic charms of a reclusive admirer. And Shield's *Swann* unfolds with considerable depth and humor as a ragtag group—a feminist historian, a frustrated biographer, a devoted librarian, and an urbane publisher—orbits around the slowly rising star of the deceased poet Mary Swann, each finding in her spare, trenchant verse a piece they would like to claim. *Swann*'s central question—who has stomping rights to the story of any person's life—is fundamental to these three novels, in which characters come to realize that half-truths and contradiction are the only constants when searching for a true identity. Cast in Shields' wryly penetrating prose, the women of *Small Ceremonies*, *The Box Garden*, and *Swann* are humorous, hopeful, and fiercely intelligent above the restless tide of their divided selves.

Carol Shields, recipient of the 1995 Pulitzer Prize for *The Stone Diaries*, was born in 1935 in Oak Park, Illinois. After graduating from Hanover College in 1957, she married a Canadian, Donald Shields, and in 1971 became a citizen of Canada. Now the author of some sixteen works of poetry, drama, literature and criticism, Shields' first publication was a revision of her master's thesis for the University of Ottawa, *Susanna Moodie: Voice and Vision* (1972). (In 1976, she incorporated her remaining research on the Canadian poet into *Small Ceremonies*.) Shields has taught English at the Universities of Ottawa, British Columbia, California at Berkeley, and Manitoba, where she currently lives and writes. The recipient of numerous awards for her novels and short story collections—including a National Book Critics Circle Award and a Governor General's Award—Shields' other works include *Others, Intersect, Happenstance, The Republic of Love, Various Miracles,* and *The Orange Fish.*

small ceremonies

the box garden

swann

By Carol Shields

POETRY
OTHERS

INTERSECT

COMING TO CANADA

NOVELS
SMALL CEREMONIES

THE BOX GARDEN

HAPPENSTANCE

A FAIRLY CONVENTIONAL WOMAN

SWANN

A CELIBATE SEASON
(WITH BLANCHE HOWARD)

THE REPUBLIC OF LOVE

THE STONE DIARIES

STORY COLLECTIONS
VARIOUS MIRACLES

THE ORANGE FISH

PLAYS
ARRIVALS AND DEPARTURES

THIRTEEN HANDS

CRITICISM
SUSANNA MOODIE: VOICE AND VISION

CAROL SHIELDS

:

small ceremonies

the box garden

swann

QUALITY PAPERBACK BOOK CLUB

NEW YORK

CONTENTS

∵

small ceremonies

For Inez
1902-1971

September

Sunday night. And the thought strikes me that I ought to be happier than I am.

We have high tea on Sunday, very Englishy, the four of us gathered in the dining ell of our cream-coloured living room at half-past five for cold pressed ham, a platter of tomatoes and sliced radishes. Slivers of hardboiled egg. A plate of pickles.

The salad vegetables vary with the season. In the summer they're larger and more varied, cut into thick peasant slices and drenched with vinegar and oil. And in the winter, in the pale Ontario winter, they are thin, watery, and tasteless, though their exotic pallor gives them a patrician presence. Now, since it is September, we are eating tomatoes from our own suburban garden, brilliant red under a scatter of parsley. Delicious, we all agree.

"Don't we have any mustard?" my husband Martin asks. He is an affectionate and forgetful man, and on weekends made awkward by leisure.

"We're all out," I tell him, "but there's chutney. And a little of that green relish."

"Never mind, Judith. It doesn't matter."

"I'll get the chutney for you," Meredith offers.

"No, really. It doesn't matter."

"Well, I'd like some," Richard says.

"In that case you can just go and get it yourself," Meredith tells him. She is sixteen; he is twelve. The bitterness between them is variable but always present.

Meredith makes a sweep for the basket in the middle of the table. "Oh," she says happily, "fresh rolls."

"I like garlic bread better," Richard says. He is sour with love and cannot, will not, be civil.

"We had that last Sunday," Meredith says, helping herself to butter. Always methodical, she keeps track of small ceremonies.

For us, Sunday high tea is a fairly recent ceremony, a ritual brought back from England where we spent Martin's sabbatical year. We are infected, all four of us, with a surrealistic nostalgia for our cold, filthy flat in Birmingham, actually homesick for fog and made edgy by the thought of swerving red buses.

And high tea. A strange hybrid meal, a curiosity at first, it was what we were most often invited out to during our year in England. We visited Martin's colleagues far out in the endless bricked-up suburbs, and drank cups and cups of milky tea and ate ham and cold beef, so thin on the platter it looked almost spiritual. The chirpy wives and their tranquil pipe-sucking husbands, acting out of some irrational good will, drew us into cozy sitting rooms hung with water colours, rows of Penguins framing the gasfires, night pressing in at the windows, so that snugness made us peaceful and generous. Always afterward, driving back to the flat in our little green Austin, we spoke to each other with unaccustomed charity, Martin humming and Meredith exclaiming again and again from the back seat how lovely the Blackstones were and wasn't she, Mrs. Blackstone, a pet.

So we carry on the high tea ritual. But we've never managed to capture that essential shut-in coziness, that safe-from-the-storm solidarity. We fly off in midair. Our house, perhaps, is too open, too airy, and then again we are not the same people we were then; but still we persist.

After lemon cake and ice cream, we move into the family room to watch television. September is the real beginning of the year; even the media know, for the new fall television series are beginning this week.

I know it is the beginning because I feel the wall of

energy, which I have allowed to soften with the mercury, toughen up. Get moving, Judith, it says. Martin knows it. All children know it. The first of January is bogus, frosty hung-over weather, a red herring in mindless snow. Winter is the middle of the year; spring the finale, and summer is free; in this climate, at least, summer is a special dispensation, a wave of weather, timeless and tax-free, when heat piles up in corners, sending us sandalled and half-bare to improbable beaches.

September is the real beginning and, settling into our favourite places, Martin and I on the sofa, Meredith in the old yellow chair and Richard stretched on the rug, we sit back to see what's new.

Six-thirty. A nature program is beginning, something called "This Feathered World." The life cycle of a bird is painstakingly described; eggs crack open emitting wet, untidy wings and feet; background music swells. There are fantastic migrations and speeds beyond imagining. Nesting and courtship practices are performed. Two storks are seen clacking their beaks together, bang, slash, bang, deranged in their private frenzy. Richard wants to know what they are doing.

"Courting." Martin explains shortly.

"What's that?" Richard asks. Surely he knows, I think.

"Getting acquainted," Martin answers. "Now be quiet and watch."

We see an insane rush of feathers. A windmill of wings. A beating of air.

"Was that it?" Richard asks. "That was courting?"

"Idiot," Meredith addresses him. "And I can't see. Will you kindly remove your feet, Richard."

"It's a dumb program anyway," Richard says and, rolling his head back, he awaits confirmation.

"It's beautifully done, for your information," Meredith tells him. She sits forward, groaning at the beauty of the birds' outstretched wings.

A man appears on the screen, extraordinarily intense,

speaking in a low voice about ecology and the doomed species. He is leaning over, and his hands, very gentle, very sensitive, attach a slender identification tag to the leg of a tiny bird. The bird shudders in his hand, and unexpectedly its ruby throat puffs up to make an improbable balloon. "I'd like to stick a pin in that," Richard murmurs softly.

The man talks quietly all the time he strokes the little bird. This species is rare, he explains, and becoming more rare each year. It is a bird of fixed habits, he tells us; each year it finds a new mate.

Martin, his arm loose around my shoulder, scratches my neck. I lean back into a nest of corduroy. A muscle somewhere inside me tightens. Why?

Every year a new mate; it is beyond imagining. New feathers to rustle, new beaks to bang, new dense twiggy nests to construct and agree upon. But then birds are different from human beings, less individual. Scared little bundles of bones with instinct blurring their small differences; for all their clever facility they are really rather stupid things.

I can hear Meredith breathing from her perch on the yellow chair. She has drawn up her knees and is sitting with her arms circled round them. I can see the delicate arch of her neck. "Beautiful. Beautiful," she says.

I look at Martin, at his biscuity hair and slightly sandy skin, and it strikes me that he is no longer a young man. Martin Gill. Doctor Gill. Associate Professor of English, a Milton specialist. He is not, in fact, in any of the categories normally set aside for the young, no longer a young intellectual or a young professor or a young socialist or a young father.

And we, I notice with a lazy loop of alarm, we are no longer what is called a young couple.

Making the beds the next morning, pulling up the unbelievably heavy eiderdowns we brought back with us from

England, I listened to local announcements on the radio. There was to be a "glass blitz" organized by local women, and the public was being asked to sort their old bottles by colour—clear, green and brown—and to take them to various stated depots, after which they would be sent to a factory for recycling.

The organizers of the blitz were named on the air: Gwen Somebody, Peg Someone, Sue, Nan, Dot, Pat. All monosyllabic, what a coincidence! Had they noticed, I wondered. The distance I sometimes sensed between myself and other women saddened me, and I lay flat on my bed for a minute thinking about it.

Imagine, I thought, sitting with friends one day, with Gwen, Sue, Pat and so on, and someone suddenly bursting out with, "I know what. Let's have a glass blitz." And then rolling into action, setting to work phoning the newspapers, the radio stations. Having circulars printed, arranging trucks. A multiplication of committees, akin to putting on a war. Not that I was unsympathetic to the cause, for who dares spoof ecology these days, but what I can never understand is the impulse that actually gets these women, Gwen, Sue, Pat and so on, moving.

Nevertheless, I made a mental note to sort out the bottles in the basement. Guilt, guilt.

And then I got down to work myself at the card table in the corner of our bedroom where I am writing my third biography.

This book is one that promises to be more interesting than the other two put together, although my first books, somewhat to my astonishment, were moderately well received. The press gave them adequate coverage, and Furlong Eberhardt, my old friend and the only really famous person I know, wrote a long and highly flattering review for a weekend newspaper. And although the public hadn't rushed out to buy in great numbers, the publishers—I am still too self-conscious a writer to say *my* publishers—Henderson and Yeo, had seemed satisfied. Sales hadn't been bad, they explained, for biography. Not everyone, after all, was fascinated by Morris Cardiff, first barrister in Upper Canada, no matter how carefully researched or how dashingly written. The same went for Josephine Macclesfield, prairie suffragette of the nineties.

The relative success of the two books had led me, two years ago, into a brief flirtation with fiction, a misadventure which cost me a year's work and much moral deliberation. In the end, all of it, one hundred execrable pages, was heaved in the wastebasket. I try not to think about it.

I am back in the good pastures of biography now, back where I belong, and in Susanna Moodie I believe I have a subject with somewhat wider appeal than the other two. Most people have at least heard of her, and thus her name brings forth the sweet jangle of familiarity. Furthermore Susanna has the appeal of fragility for, unlike Morris Cardiff, she was not the first anything and, unlike Josephine, she was not aflame with conviction. She has, in fact, just enough neuroses to make her interesting and just the right degree of weakness to make me feel friendly toward her. Whereas I had occasionally found my other subjects terrifying in their single-mindedness, there is a pleasing schizoid side to Susanna; she could never make up her mind what she was or where she stood.

The fact is, I am enamoured of her, and have felt from the beginning of my research, the pleasant shock of meeting a kindred spirit. Her indecisiveness wears well after the rough, peremptory temper of Josephine. Also, she has one of the qualities which I totally lack and, therefore, admire, that of reticence. Quaint Victorian restraint. Violet-tinted reserve, stemming as much from courtesy as from decorum.

Decency shimmers beneath her prose, and one senses that here is a woman who hesitates to bore her reader with the idle slopover of her soul. No one, she doubtless argued in her midnight heart, could possibly be interested in the detailing of her rancid sex life or the nasty discomfort of pregnancy in the backwoods. Thus she is genteel enough not to dangle her shredded placenta before her public, and what a lot she resisted, for it must have been a temptation to whine over her misfortunes. Or to blurt out her rage against the husband who brought her to the Ontario wilderness, gave her a rough shanty to live in, and then proceeded into debt; what wonders of scorn she might have heaped on him. One winter they lived on nothing but potatoes; what lyrical sorrowing she might have summoned on that subject. And how admirable of her not to crow when her royalty cheques came in, proclaiming herself the household saviour, which indeed she was in the end. But of all this, there is not one word.

Instead she presents a stout and rubbery persona, that of a generous, humorous woman who feeds on anecdotes and random philosophical devotions, sucking what she can out of daily events, the whole of her life glazed over with a neat edge-to-edge surface. It is the cracks in the surface I look for; for if her reticence is attractive, it also makes her a difficult subject to possess. But who, after all, could sustain such a portrait over so many pages without leaving a few chinks in the varnish? Already I've found, with even the most casual sleuthing, small passages in her novels and backwoods recollections of unconscious self-betrayal, isolated words and phrases, almost lost in the lyrical brushwork. I am gluing them together, here at my card table, into a delicate design which may just possibly be the real Susanna.

What a difference from my former subject Josephine Macclesfield who, shameless, showed every filling in her teeth. Ah, she had an opinion on every bush and shrub! Her introspection was wide open, a field of potatoes; all I had to do was wander over it at will and select the choice produce. Poor Josephine, candid to a fault; I had not respected her in the end. Just as I had had reservations when reading the autobiography of Bertrand Russell who, in passages of obsessive self-abasement, confessed to boyhood masturbation and later to bad breath. For though I forgive him his sour breath and his childhood excesses, it is harder to forgive the impulse which makes it public. Holding back, that is the brave thing.

My research, begun last winter, is going well, and already I have a lovely stack of five-by-seven cards covered with notations. It is almost enough. My old portable is ready with fresh ribbon, newly conditioned at Simpson-Sears. It is ten o'clock; half the morning is gone. Richard will be home from school at noon. I must straighten my shoulders, take a deep breath and begin.

Far away downstairs the back door slammed. "Where are you?" Richard called from the kitchen.

"Upstairs," I answered. "I'll be right down."

At noon Martin eats at the university faculty club, and Meredith takes her lunch to school, so it is only Richard and I for lunch, a usually silent twosome huddled over sandwiches in the kitchen. Today I heated soup and made cheese sandwiches while Richard stood silently watching me. "Any mail?" he asked at last.

"In the hall."

"Anything for me?"

"Isn't there always something for you on Mondays?"

"Not always," he countered nervously.

"Almost always."

Richard dived into the hall and came back with his airletter. He opened it with a table knife, taking enormous care, for he knows from experience that an English airletter is a puzzle of folds and glued edges.

While we ate, sitting close to the brotherly flank of the refrigerator, he read his letter, cupping it toward him cautiously so I couldn't see.

"Don't worry," I chided him. "I'm not going to peek."

"You might," he said, reading on.

"Do you think I've nothing to do but read my son's mail?" I asked, forcing my voice into feathery lightness.

He looked up in surprise. I believe he thinks that is

exactly the case: that I have great vacant hours with nothing to do but satisfy my curiosity about his affairs.

In appearance Richard is somewhat like Martin, the same bran-coloured hair, lots of it, tidy shoulders, slender. He will be of medium height, I think, like Martin; and like his father, too, he speaks slowly and with deliberation. For most of his twelve years he has been an easy child to live with; we absorb him unthinking into ourselves, for he is so willingly one of us, so generally unprotesting. At school in England, when Meredith raged about having to wear school uniforms, he silently accepted shirt, tie, blazer, even the unspeakable short pants, and was transformed before our eyes into a boy who looked like someone else's son. And where Meredith despised most of her English schoolmates for being uppity and affected, he scarcely seemed to notice the difference between the boys he played soccer with in Birmingham and those he skated with at home. He is so healthy. The day he was born, watching his lean little arms struggle against the blanket, I gave up smoking forever. Nothing must hurt him.

Absorbed, he chewed a corner of his sandwich and read his weekly letter from Anita Spalding, whom he has never met.

She is twelve years old too, and it was her parents, John and Isabel Spalding, who sublet their Birmingham flat to us when we were in England. The arrangements had been made by the university, and the Spaldings, spending the year at the English School in Nicosia, far far away in sunny Cyprus, left us their rambling, freezing and inconvenient flat for which we paid, we later found out, far too much.

To begin with our feelings toward them were neutral, but we began to dislike them the day after we moved in, interpreting our various disasters as the work of their deliberate hands. The rusted taps, the burnt-out lights, the skin of mildew on the kitchen ceiling, a dead mouse in the pantry, the terrible iciness of their lumpy beds; all were linked in a plot to undermine us. Where was the refriger-

ator, we suddenly asked. How is it possible that there is no
heat at all in the bathroom? Fleas in the armchairs as well
as the beds?

Isabel we imagined as a slattern in a greasy apron, and
John we pictured as a very small man with a tiny brain
pickled in purest white vinegar. Its sour workings curdled
in his many tidy lists and in the exclamatory pitch of his
notes to us. "May I trust you to look after my rubber plant?
It's been with me since I took my degree." "You'll find the
stuck blind a deuced bother." "The draught from the lava-
tory window can be wretched, I fear, but we take comfort
that the air is fresh." Even Martin took to cursing him.
(These days I find it harder to hate him. I try not to think
of John Spalding at all, but when I do it is with uneasiness.
And regret.)

If nothing else the Spaldings' flat had plenty of bedrooms,
windy cubicles really, each equipped like a hotel room
with exactly four pieces; bed, bureau, wardrobe and chair,
all constructed in cheap utilitarian woods. It was on a bare
shelf in his wardrobe that Richard discovered Anita's letter
of introduction.

He came running with it into the kitchen where we stood
examining the ancient stove. At that time he was only nine,
not yet given to secrecy, and he handed the letter proudly
to Martin.

"Look what I've found."

Martin read the letter aloud, very solemnly pronouncing
each syllable, while the rest of us stood listening in a foolish
smiling semicircle. It was a curious note, written in a
puckered, precocious style with Lewis Carroll overtones,
but sincere and simple.

> To Whoever is the Keeper of This Room,
>
> Greetings and welcome. I am distressed thinking
> about you, for my parents have told me that you
> are Canadians which I suppose is rather like be-
> ing Americans. I am worried that you may find

the arrangements here rather queer since I have seen packs and packs of American films and know what kind of houses they live in. This bed, for instance, is rotten through and through. It is odd to think that someone else will actually be sleeping in my bed. But then I shall be sleeping in someone else's bed in Nicosia. They are a Scottish family and they will spend the year in Glasgow, probably in someone else's flat. And the Glasgow family, they'll have to go off and live somewhere, won't they? Isn't it astonishing that we should all be sleeping in one another's beds. A sort of roundabout almost. Whoever you are, if you should happen to be a child (I am nine and a girl) perhaps you would like to write me a letter. I would be delighted to reply. I am exceedingly fond of writing letters but have no connexions at the moment. So please write. Isn't the kitchen a fright! Not like the ones in the films at all.

Your obedient servant,
ANITA DREW SPALDING   9

It took Richard more than a month to write back, although I reminded him once or twice. He hates writing letters, and was busy with other things; I did not press him.

But one dark chilly Sunday afternoon he asked me for some paper, and for an hour he sat at the kitchen table scratching away, asking me once whether there was an "e" in homesick; his or hers, we never knew, for he didn't offer to show us what he'd written. He sealed it shyly, and the next day took it to the post office and sent it on its way to Cyprus.

Anita's reply was almost instantaneous. "It's from her," he explained, showing us the envelope. "From that Cyprus girl." That evening he asked for more paper.

Once a week, sometimes twice, a thick letter with the little grey Cyprus stamp shot through our mail slot. At least as often Richard wrote back, walking to the post office next to MacFisheries at the end of our road in time for the evening pickup.

We never did meet the Spaldings. We left England a month before they returned. We thought Richard would be heartbroken that he would not see Anita, but he seemed not to care much, and I had the idea that the correspondence might drop off when he got home to Canada. But their letters came and went as frequently as ever and seemed to grow even thicker. Postage mounted up, draining off Richard's pocket money, so they switched occasionally to airletters. Always when Richard opens them, he smiles secretly to himself.

"What on earth do you write about?" I asked him.

"Just the same stuff everyone writes in letters," he dodged.

"You mean just news? Like what you've been doing in school?"

"Sort of, yeah. Sometimes she sends cartoons from *Punch*. And I send her the best ones out of your old *New Yorkers*."

I find it curious. I don't write to my own sister in Vancouver more than four times a year. To my mother in Scarborough I write a dutiful weekly letter, but sometimes I have to sit for half an hour thinking up items to fill one page. Martin's parents write weekly from Montreal, his mother using one side of the page, his father the other, but even they haven't the stamina of these two mysterious children. Richard's constancy in this correspondence seems oddly serious and out of proportion to childhood, causing me to wonder sometimes whether this little witch in England hasn't got hold of a corner of his soul and somehow transformed it. He is bewitched. I can see it by the way he is sitting here in the kitchen folding her letter. He has read it twice and now he is folding it. Creasing its edges. With tenderness.

"Well, how is Anita these days?" My light voice again.

"Fine." Noncommittal.

"Has she ever sent a picture of herself?"

"No," he says, and my heart leaps. She is ugly.

"Why not?" I ask foxily. "I thought pen-pals always exchanged pictures."

"We decided not to," he says morosely, wincing, or so I believe, at the word pen-pal. Then he adds, "It was an agreement we made. Not to send pictures."

Of course. Their correspondence, I perceive, is a formalized structure, no snapshots, no gifts at Christmas, no postcards ever. Rules in acid, immovable, a pact bound on two sides, a covenant. I can't resist one more question.

"Does she still sign her letters 'your obedient servant?' "

"No," Richard says, and he sighs. The heaviness of that sound tells me that he sighs with love. My heart twists for him. I know the signs, or at least I used to. Absurd it may be, but I believe it; Richard is as deeply in love at twelve as many people are in a lifetime.

The house we live in—Martin, the children and I—is not really my house. That is, it is not the kind of house I once imagined I might be the mistress of. We live in the suburbs of a small city; our particular division is called Greenhills, and it is neither a town nor a community, not a neighbourhood, not even a postal zone. It is really nothing but the extension of a developer's pencil, the place on the map where he planned to plunk down his clutch of houses and make his million. I suppose he had to call it something, and perhaps he thought Greenhills was catchy and good for sales; or perhaps, who knows, it evoked happy rural images inside his head.

We are reached in the usual way by a main arterial route which we leave and enter by numbered exits and entrances. Greenhills is the seventh exit from the city centre which means we are within a mile or two of open countryside, although it might just as well be ten.

Where we live there are no streets, only crescents, drives, circles and one self-conscious boulevard. It is leafy green and safe for children; our lawns stretch luscious as flesh to the streets; our shrubs and borders are watered.

As soon as the sewers were installed nine years ago, we moved in. The house itself has all the bone-cracking clichés of Sixties domestic architecture: there is a family room, a dining ell, a utility room, a master bedroom with bath *en suite*. A Spanish step-saving kitchen with pass-through, colonial door, attached garage, sliding patio window, split-level grace, spacious garden. The only item we lack is a set of Westminster chimes; the week we moved in, Martin disconnected the mechanism with a screw-driver and installed a doorknocker instead, proving what I have always known, that despite his socialism, he is 90 per cent an aristocrat.

It is a beige and uninteresting house. Curtains join rugs, rugs join furniture; nubby sofa sits between matching lamps on twin tables, direct from Eaton's show room. Utilitarian at the comfort level, there is nothing unexpected. This is a shell to live in without thought.

And in a way it is deliberate, this minimal approach to decorating. My sister Charleen and I, now that we are safely grown up, agree on one thing, and that is that as children we were cruelly overburdened with interior decoration. The house in which we grew up in Scarborough—the old Scarborough that is, before television, before shopping centres, the Scarborough of neat and faintly rural streets—that tiny house was in a constant state of revitalization. All our young lives, or so it seemed, we dodged stepladders, stepped carefully around the wet paint, shared the lunch table with wallpaper samples. Our little living room broke out with staggered garlands one year, with French stripes the next, and our girlish bedroom at the back of the house was gutted almost annually. Shaking his head, our father used to say that the rooms would grow gradually smaller under their layers and layers of paint and paper. We would be pushed out on to the street one day, he predicted. It was his little joke, almost his only joke, but straining to recall his voice, do I now hear or imagine the desperate edge? *Better Homes and Gardens* was centred on our coffee table, cheerful with new storage ideas or instructions for gluing bold

fabric to attic ceilings. The dining table was in the basement being refinished, or the chesterfield was being fitted
for slipcovers. The pictures were changed with the seasons.
"My house is my hobby," Mother used to say to the few
visitors we ever had; and even as she spoke, her eyes turned
inward, tuned to the next colour scheme, to the ultimate
arrangement, just out of reach, beamed in from *House and
Garden*, a world the rest of us never entered. Nor wished to.

Still we have put our mark on this place, Martin and I.
The floor tiles rise periodically, reminding us they are now
nine years old. The utility room is so filled with ski equipment that we call it the ski room. The dining ell has been
partitioned off with a plywood planter which looks tacky
and hellish, though we thought it a good idea at the time.
Hosiery drips from the shower rail in the *en suite* bathroom. In the cool dry basement our first married furniture
glooms around the furnace, its Lurex threads as luminous
and accusing as the day we bought it; Richard's electric
train tunnels between the brass-tipped legs. The spacious
garden is the same flat rectangle it always was except for
a row of tomato plants and a band of marigolds by the
fence.

The house that I once held half-shaped in my head was
old, a nook-and-cranny house with turrets and lovely sensuous lips of gingerbread, a night-before-Christmas house,
bought for a song and priceless on today's market. Hung
with the work of Quebec weavers, an eclectic composition
of Swedish and Canadiana. Tasteful but offhand. A study,
beamed, for Martin and a workroom, sunny, for me. Studi-
ous corners where children might sit and sip their souls in
pools of filtered light. A garden drunk with roses, criss-
crossed with paths, moist, shady, secret.

This place, 62 Beaver Place, is not really me, I used to
say apologetically back in the days when I actually said such
things. "We're just roosting here until something 'us' turns
up."

I never say it now. If we wanted to, Martin and I could

look in his grey file drawer next to his desk in the family room. Between the folders for Tax and Health, we would find House, and from there we could pluck out our offer-to-purchase, the blueprints, the lot survey, the mortgage schedule and, clipped to it, the record of payments along with the annual tax receipts. It's all there. We could calculate, if we chose, the exact dimensions of our delusions. But we never do. We live here, after all.

Up and down the gentle curve of Beaver Place we see cedar-shake siding, colonial pillars, the jutting chins of split-levels, each of them bought in hours of panic, but with each one, some particular fantasy fulfilled. The house they never had as children perhaps. The house that will do for now, before the move to the big one on the river lot. The house where visions of dynasty are glimpsed, a house future generations will visit, spend holidays in and write up in memoirs. Why not?

Something curious. One day last week, having been especially energetic about Susanna Moodie and turning out six pages in one morning, I found myself out of paper. There must be some in the house, I thought and, although I prefer soft, pulpy yellow stuff, anything is useable in a pinch, I searched Meredith's room first, being careful not to disturb her things. Everything there is so carefully arranged; she has all sorts of curios, souvenirs, snapshots, a music award stencilled on felt, animal figurines she collected as a very young child, cosmetics in a pearly pale shade standing at attention on her dresser. Everything but paper.

In Richard's room I found desk drawers filled with Anita Spalding's letters, each one taped shut from prying eyes. Mine perhaps? Safety patrol badges, a map of England with an inked star on Birmingham, a copy of *Playboy*, hockey pictures, but not a single sheet of useable paper.

Martin will have some, I thought. I went downstairs to the family room to look in his desk. Nothing in the top drawer except his Xeroxed paper on *Paradise Regained*, recently rejected by the *Milton Quarterly*. In his second drawer were clipped notes for an article on *Samson Agonistes* and offprints of an article he had had printed in *Renaissance Studies*, the one on Milton's childhood which he had researched in England. The third drawer was full of wool.

I blinked. Unbelievable. The drawer was stuffed to the top with brand new hanks of wool, still with their little circular bands around them. I reached in and touched them. Blue, red, yellow, green; fat four-ounce bundles in all colours. Eight of them. Lying on their sides in Martin's drawer. Wool.

It couldn't be for me. I hate knitting and detest crocheting. For Meredith perhaps? An early Christmas present? But she hadn't knitted anything since Brownies, six years ago, and had never expressed any interest in taking it up again.

Frieda? Frieda who comes to clean out the house on Wednesday? She knits, and it is just possible, I thought, that it was hers. Absurd though. She never goes in Martin's desk, for one thing. And what reason would she have to stash all this lunatic wool in his drawer anyway? Richard? Out of the question. What would he be doing with wool? It must be Martin's. For his mother, maybe; she loves knitting. He might have seen it on sale and bought it for her, although it seemed odd he hadn't mentioned it to me. I'll ask him tonight, I thought.

But that night Martin was at a meeting, and I was asleep when he came home. The next day I forgot. And the next. Whenever it pops into my mind, he isn't around. And when he is, something makes me stumble and hesitate as though I were afraid of the reply. I still haven't asked him, but this morning I looked in the drawer to see if it was still there. It was all in place, all eight bundles; nothing had been touched. I must ask Martin about it.

As Meredith grows up I look at her and think, who does she remind me of? A shaded gesture, a position struck, or something curious she might say will touch off a shock of recognition in me, but I can never think who it is she is like.

I flip through my relatives—like flashcards. My mother. No, no, no. My sister Charleen? No. Charleen, for all her sensitivity, has a core of detachment. Aunt Liddy? Sometimes I am quite sure it is my old aunt. But no. Auntie's fragility is neurotic, not natural like Meredith's. Who else?

She has changed in the last year, is romantic and realistic in violent turns. Now she is reading Furlong Eberhardt's new book about the prairies. While she reads, her hands grip the cover so hard that the bones of her hands stand up, whey-white. Her eyes float in a concerned sweep over the pages, her forehead puzzled. It's painful to watch her; she shouldn't invest so much of herself in anything as ephemeral as a book; it is criminal to care that much.

Like my family she is dark, but unlike us she has a delicious water-colour softness, and if she were braver she would be beautiful. She is as tall as I am but she has been spared the wide country shoulders; there are some blessings.

It is an irony, the sort I relish, that I who am a biographer and delight in sorting out personalities, can't even draw a circle around my own daughter's. Last night at the table, just as she was cutting into a baked potato, she raised her eyes, exceptionally sober even for her, and answered some trivial question Martin had asked her. The space between the movement of her hand and the upward angle of her eyes opened up, and I almost had it.

Then it slipped away.

Last night Martin and I went to a play. It was one of Shaw's early ones, written before he turned drama into social propaganda. The slimmest of drawingroom debacles, it was a zany sandwich of socialism and pie-in-the-eye, daft but with brisk touches of irreverence. And the heroes were real heroes, the way they should be, and the heroines were even better. The whole evening was a confection, a joy.

During the intermission we stood in the foyer chatting with Furlong Eberhardt and his mother, our delight in the play surfacing on our lips like crystals of sugar. Mrs. Eberhardt, as broad-breasted as one of the Shavian heroines, encircled us with her peculiar clove-flavoured embrace. A big woman, she is mauve to the bone; even her skin is faintly lilac, her face a benign fretwork of lines framed with waves of palest violet.

"Judith, you look a picture. How I wish I could wear those pant suits."

"You look lovely as you are, Mother," Furlong said, and she did; if ever a woman deserved a son with a mother fixation, it was Mrs. Eberhardt.

Martin disappeared to get us drinks, and Furlong, by a bit of clever steering, turned our discussion to his new book, *Graven Images*.

"I know I can count on you, Judith, for a candid opinion. The critics, mind you, have been very helpful, and thus far, very kind." He paused.

For a son of the Saskatchewan soil, Furlong is remarkably courtly, and like all the courtly people I know, he inspires in me alleys of unknown coarseness. I want to slap his back, pump his hand, tell him to screw off. But I never do, never, for basically I am too fond of him and even grateful, thankful for his most dazzling talent which is not writing at all, but the ability he has to make the people around him feel alive. There is an exhausted Byzantine quality about him which demands response, and even at that moment, standing in the theatre foyer in my too-tight pantsuit and my hair falling down around my rapidly ageing face, I was swept with vitality, almost drunk with the recognition that all things are possible. Beauty, fame, power; I have not been passed by after all.

But about *Graven Images*, I had to confess ignorance.

"I've been locked up with Susanna for months," I explained. It sounded weak. It *was* weak. But I thought to add kindly, "Meredith is reading it right now. She was about halfway through when we left the house tonight."

At this he beamed. "Then it is to your charming daughter I shall have to speak." Visibly wounded that I hadn't got around to his book, he rallied quickly, drowning his private pain in a flood of diffusion. "Public reaction is really too general to be of any use, as you well know, Judith. It is one's friends one must rely upon." He pronounced the word friends with such a silky sound that, for an instant, I wished he were a different make of man.

"Meredith would love to discuss it with you, Furlong," I told him honestly. "Besides, she's a more sensitive reader of fiction than I am. You, of all people, know fiction isn't my thing."

"Ah yes, Judith," he said. "It's your old Scarborough puritanism, as I've frequently told you. Judith Gill, my girl, basically you believe fiction is wicked and timewasting. The devil's work. A web of lies."

"You just might be right, Furlong."

When Martin came back with our drinks, Furlong issued a general invitation to attend his publication party in November. He beamed at Martin, "You two must plan to come."

"Hmmm," Martin murmured noncommittally. He doesn't really like Furlong; the relationship between them, although they teach in the same department, is one of tolerant scorn.

The lights dipped, and we found our way back to our seats. Back to the lovely arched setting, lit in some magical way to suggest sunrise. Heroines moved across the broad stage like clipper ships, their throats swollen with purpose. The play wound down and so did they in their final speeches. Holy holy, the crash of applause that always brings tears stinging to my eyes.

All night long memories of the play boiled through my

dreams, a plummy jam stewed from those intelligent, cruising, early-century bosoms. Hour after hour I rode on a sea of breasts: the exhausted mounds of Susanna Moodie, touched with lamplight. The orchid hills and valleys of Mrs. Eberhardt, bubbles of yeast. The tender curve of my daughter Meredith. The bratty twelve-year-old tits of Anita Spalding, rising, falling, melting, twisting in and out of the heavy folds of sleep.

I woke to find Martin's arm flung across my chest; the angle of his skin was perceived and recognized, a familiar coastline. The weight was a lever that cut off the electricity of dreams, pushing me down, down through the mattress, down through the floor, down, into the spongy cave of the blackest sleep. Oblivion.

October

The first frost this morning, a landmark. At breakfast Martin talks about snow tires and mentions a sale at Canadian Tire. After school these days Richard plays football with his friends in the shadowy yard, and when they thud to the grass, the ground rings with sound. Watching them, I am reassured.

It is almost dark now when we sit down to dinner. Meredith has found some candles in the cupboard, bent out of shape with the summer heat but still useable, so that now our dinners are washed with candlelight. I make pot roast which they love and mashed potatoes which make me think of Susanna Moodie. In the evening the children have their homework. Martin goes over papers at his desk or reads a book, sitting in the yellow chair, his feet resting on the coffeetable, and he hums. Richard and Meredith bicker lazily. Husband, children, they are not so much witnessed as perceived, flat leaves which grow absently from a stalk in my head, each fitting into the next, all their curving edges perfect. So far, so far. It seems they require someone, me, to watch them; otherwise they would float apart and disintegrate.

I watch them. They are as happy as can be expected. What is the matter with me, I wonder. Why am I always the one who watches?

One day this week I checked into the Civic Hospital for a minor operation, a delicate, feminine, unspeakable, minimal nothing, the sort of irksome repair work which I suppose I must expect now that I am forty.

A minor piece of surgery, but nevertheless requiring a general anaesthetic. Preparation, sleep, recovery, a whole day required, a day fully erased from my life. Martin drove me to the hospital at nine and came to take me home again in the evening. The snipping and sewing were entirely satisfactory, and except for an hour's discomfort, there were no after effects. None. I am in service again. A lost day, but there was one cheering interlude.

Shortly before the administering of the general anaesthetic, I was given a little white pill to make me drowsy. In a languorous trance I was then wheeled on a stretcher to a darkened room and lined up with about twelve other people, male and female, all in the same condition. White-faced nurses tiptoed between our parked rows, whispering. Far below us in another world, cars honked and squeaked.

Lying there semidrugged, I sensed a new identity: I was exactly like a biscuit set out to bake, just waiting my turn in the oven. I moved my head lazily to one side and found myself face to face, not six inches away from a man, another biscuit. His eyes met mine, and I watched him fascinated, a slow-motion film, as he laboured to open his mouth and pronounce with a slur, "Funny feeling, eh?"

"Yes," I said. "As though we were a tray of biscuits."

"That's right," he said crookedly.

Surprised, I asked, "What are you here for?"

"The old water works," he said yawning. "But nothing major."

Kidneys, bladder, urine; a diagram flashed in my brain. "That's good," I mumbled. Always polite. I cannot, even here, escape courtesy.

"What about you?" he mouthed, almost inaudible now.

"One of those female things," I whispered. "Also not major."

"You married?"

"Yes. Are you?" I asked, realizing too late that he had asked because of the nature of my complaint, not because we were comparing our status as we might had we met at a party.

"Yes," he said. "I'm married. But not happily."

"Pardon?" Courtesy again, the scented phrase. Our mother had always insisted we say pardon and, as Charleen says, we are children all our lives, obedient to echoes.

"Not happily," he said again. "Married yes," he made an effort to enunciate, "but not happily married."

A surreal testimony. It must be the anesthetic, I thought, pulling an admission like that from a sheeted stranger. The effect of the pill or perhaps the rarity of the circumstances, the two of us lying here nose to nose, almost naked under our thin sheets, horizontal in midmorning, chemical-smelling limbo, our conversation somehow crisped into truth.

"Too bad," I said with just a shade of sympathy.

"You happily married?" he asked.

"Yes," I murmured, a little ashamed at the affirmative ring in my voice. "I'm one of the lucky ones. Not that I deserve it."

"What do you mean, not that you deserve it?"

"I don't know."

"Well, you said it," he said crossly.

"I just meant that I'm not all that terrific a wife. You know, not self-sacrificial." I groped for an example. "For instance, when Martin asked me to type something for him last week. Just something short."

"Yeah?" His mouth made a circle on the white sheet.

"I said, what's the matter with Nell? That's his secretary."

"He's got a secretary, eh?"

"Yes," I admitted, again stung with guilt. This was beginning to sound like a man who didn't have a secretary. "She's skinny though," I explained. "A real stick. And he shares her with two other professors."

"I see. I see." His voice dropped off, and I thought for a minute that he'd fallen asleep.

Pressing on anyway I repeated loudly, "So I said, what's the matter with Nell?"

"And what did he say to that?" the voice came.

"Martin? Well, he just said, 'Never mind, Judith.' But then I felt so mean that I went ahead and did it anyway."

"The typing you mean?"

"Uh huh."

"So you're not such a rotten wife," he accused me.

"In a way," I said. "I did it, but it doesn't count if you're not willing." Where had I got that? Girl Guides maybe.

"I never ask my wife to type for me."

"Why not?" I asked.

"Typing I don't need."

"Maybe you ask for something else," I suggested, aware that our conversation was slipping over into a new frontier.

"Just to let me alone, to let me goddamned alone. Every night she has to ask me what I did all day. At the plant. She wants to know, she says. I tell her, look, I lived through it once, do I have to live through it twice?"

"I see what you mean," I said, hardly able to remember what we were talking about.

"You do?" Far away in his nest of sheets he registered surprise.

"Yes. I know exactly what you mean. As my mother used to say, 'I don't want to chew my cabbage twice.' "

"You mean you don't ask your husband what he did all day?"

"Well," I said growing weary, "no. I don't think I ever do. Poor Martin."

"Christ," he said as two nurses began rolling him to the doorway. "Christ. I wish I was married to you."

"Thank you," I called faintly. "Thank you, thank you."

Absurdly flattered, I too was wheeled away. Joy closed my eyes, and all I remember seeing after that was a blur of brilliant blue.

"You haven't read it yet, have you?" Meredith accuses me.

"Read what yet?" I am ironing in the kitchen, late on a

Thursday afternoon. Pillowcases, Martin's shirts. I am travelling across the yokes, thinking these shirts I bought on
sale are no good. Just a touch-up they're supposed to need,
but the point of my iron is required on every seam.

"You haven't read Furlong's book?" Meredith says
sharply.

"The new one you mean?"

"*Graven Images.*"

"Well," I say apologetically, letting that little word
"well" unwind slowly, making a wavy line out of it the way
our mother used to do, "well, you know how busy I've
been."

"You read Pearson's book."

"That was different."

Abruptly she lapses into confidence. "It's the best one
he's written. You've just got to read it. That one scene
where Verna dies. You'll love it. She's the sister. Unmarried. But beautiful, spiritual, even though she never had a
chance to go to school. She's blind, but she has these fantastic visions. Honestly, when you stop to think that here
you have a man, a man who is actually writing from inside,
you know, from inside a woman's head. It's unbelievable.
That kind of intuition."

"I'm planning to read it," I assure her earnestly, for I
want to make her happy. "But there's the Susanna thing,
and when I'm not working on that, there's the ironing.
One thing after another."

"You know that's not the reason you haven't read it," she
says, her eyes going icy.

I put down the iron, setting it securely on its heel. "All
right, Meredith. You tell me why."

"You think he's a dumb corny romantic. Flabby.
Feminine."

"Paunchy," I help her out.

"You see," her voice rises.

"Predictable. That's it, if you really want to know,
Meredith."

"I don't know how you can say that."

"Easy." I tell her. "This is his tenth novel, you know, and I've read them all. Every one. So I've a pretty good idea what's in this one. The formula, you might say, is familiar."

"What's it about then?" her voice pleads, and I don't dare look at her.

I shake a blouse vigorously out of the basket. "First there's the waving wheat. He opens, Chapter One, to waving wheat. Admit it, Meredith, Saskatchewan in powder form. Mix with honest rain water for native genre."

"He grew up there."

"I know, Meredith, I know. But he doesn't live there now, does he? He lives here in the east. For twenty years he's lived in the east. And he isn't a farmer. He's a writer. And when he's not being a writer, he's being a professor. Don't forget about that."

"Roots matter to some people," she says in a tone which accuses me of forgetting my own. Nurtured on the jointed avenues of Scarborough, did that count?

"All right," I say. "Then you move into his storm chapter. Rain, snow, hail, locusts maybe. It doesn't matter as long as it's devastating. Echoes of Moses. A punishing storm. To remind them they're reaching too high or sinning too low. A holocaust and, I grant you this, very well done. Furlong is exceptional on storms."

"This book really is different. There's another plot altogether."

I rip into a shirt of Richard's. "Then the characters. Three I can be sure of. The Presbyterian Grandmother. And sometimes Grandfather too, staring out from his little chimney corner, all-knowing, all-seeing, but, alas, unheeded. Right, Meredith?"

Stop, I tell myself. You're enjoying this. You're a cruel, cynical woman piercing the pink valentine heart of your own daughter, shut up, shut up.

She mumbles something I don't catch.

"Then," I say, "we're into the wife. She endures. There's

nothing more to say about her except that she endures. But her husband, rampant with lust, keep your eye on him."

"You haven't even read it."

"Watch the husband, Meredith. Lust will undo him. Furlong will get him for sure with a horde of locusts. Or a limb frozen in the storm and requiring a tense kitchen-table amputation."

"Influenza," Meredith murmurs. "But the rest really is different."

"And we close with more waving wheat. Vibrations from the hearthside saying, if only you'd listened."

"It's not supposed to be real life. It's not biography," she says, giving that last word a nasty snap. "It's sort of a symbol of the country. You have to look at it as a kind of extended image. Like in Shakespeare."

"I'm going to read it," I tell her as I fold the ironing board, contrite now. "I might even settle down with it tonight."

We've had the book since August. Furlong brought me one, right off the press one steaming afternoon. Inscribed "To Martin and Judith Who Care." Beautiful thought, but I cringed reading it, hoping Martin wouldn't notice. Furlong seems unable to resist going the quarter-inch too far.

Furlong's picture on the back of the book is distressingly authorly. One can see evidence of a tally taken, a check list fulfilled. Beard and moustache, of course. White turtleneck exposed at the collar of an overcoat. Tweed and cablestitch juxtaposed, a generation-straddling costume testifying to eclectic respectability.

A pipe angles from the corner of his mouth! It's bowl is missing, the outlines lost in the dark shadow of the over-coat, so that for a moment I thought it was a cigarillo or maybe just a fountain pen he was sucking on. But no, on close examination I could see the shine of the bowl. Every-thing in place.

The picture is two-colour, white and a sort of olive tone,

bleeding off the edges, *Time-Life* style. Behind him a microcosm of Canada—a fretwork of bare branches and a blur of olive snow, man against nature.

His eyes are mere slits. Snow glare? The whole expression is nicely in place, a costly membrane, bemused but kindly, academic but gutsy. The photographer has clearly demanded detachment.

The jacket blurb admits he teaches creative writing in a university, but couched within this apology is the information that he has also swept floors, reported news, herded sheep, a man for all seasons, our friend Furlong.

Those slit eyes stick with me as I put away the ironing; shirts on hangers, handkerchiefs in drawers, pillowcases in the cupboard. They burn twin candles in my brain, and their nonchalance fails to convince me; I feel the muscular twitch of effort, the attempt to hold, to brave it out.

Poor Furlong, christened, legend has it, by the first reviewer of his first book who judged him a furlong ahead of all other current novelists. Before that he was known as Red, but I know the guilty secret of his real name: it is Rudyard. His mother let it slip one night at a department sherry party, then covered herself with a flustered apology. We grappled, she and I, in a polite but clumsy exchange, confused and feverish, but I am not a biographer for nothing; I filed it away; I remember the name Rudyard. Rudyard. Rudyard. I think of it quite often, and in a way I love him, Rudyard Eberhardt. More than I could ever love Furlong.

Meredith slips past me on the stairs. She is on her way to her room and she doesn't speak; she doesn't even look at me. What have I done now?

"Martin."
"Yes."
"What are you doing?"
"Just going over some notes."

"Lecture notes?"

"Yes."

It is midnight, the children are sleeping, and we are in bed. Martin is leaning into the circle of light given off by our tiny and feeble bedside lamp, milkglass, a nobbly imitation with a scorched shade.

"Do you know I've never heard you give a lecture?"

"You hate Milton." He says this gently, absently.

"I know. I know. But I'd like to hear you anyway."

"You'd be bored stiff."

"Probably. But I'd like to see what your style is like."

"Style?"

"You know. Your lecturing style."

"What do you think it's like?" He doesn't raise his eyes from his pile of papers.

But I reply thoughtfully. "Orderly, I'm sure you're orderly. Not too theatrical, but here and there a flourish. An understated flourish though."

"Hummm."

"And I suppose you quote a few lines now and then. Sort of scatter them around."

"Milton is notoriously unquotable, you know." He looks up. I am in my yellow tulip nightgown, a birthday present from my sister Charleen.

I ask, "What do you mean he's unquotable. The greatest master of the English language unquotable?"

"Can you think of anything he ever said?"

"No. I can't. Not a thing. Not at this hour anyway."

"There you are."

"Wasn't there something like tripping the light fantastic?"

"Uh huh."

"It's hard to see why they bother teaching him then. If you can't even remember anything he wrote."

"Memorable phrases aren't everything."

"Maybe Milton should just be phased out."

"Could be." I have lost him again.

"Actually, Martin, I did hear you lecture once."

"You did? When was that?"

"Remember last year. No, the year before last, the year after England. When I was taking Furlong's course in creative writing."

"Oh yes." He is scribbling in the margin.

"Well, on my way to the seminar room one day I was walking past a blank door on the third floor of the Arts Building."

"Yes?"

"Through the door there was a sound coming. A familiar sound, all muffled through the wood. You know how thick those doors are. If it had been anyone else I wouldn't even have heard it."

"And it was me."

"It was you. And it's a funny thing, I couldn't hear a word you were saying. It was all too muffled. Just the rise and fall of your voice. And I suppose some sort of recognizable tonal quality. But it was mainly the rise and fall, the rise and fall. It was *your* voice, Martin. There wasn't a notice on the door saying it was you in there teaching Milton, but I was sure."

"You should have come in."

"I was on my way to Furlong's class. And besides I wouldn't have. I don't know why, but I never would have come in."

"I'd better just check these notes over once more."

"Actually, Martin, it was eerie. Your voice coming through the wood like that, rising and falling, rising and falling."

"My God, Judith, you make me sound like some kind of drone."

"It's something like handwriting." I propped myself up on one elbow. "Did you know that it's almost impossible to fake your handwriting? You can slant it backhand or straight up and down and put in endless curlicues, but the giveaway is the proportion of the tall letters to the size of the small ones. It's individual like fingerprints. Like your voice. The rhythm is personal, rising and falling. It was you."

"Christ, Judith, let me get this done so I can get some sleep."

"The funny thing is, Martin, that even when I was absolutely certain, I had the oddest sensation that I didn't know you at all. As though you were a stranger, someone I'd never met before."

"Really?" He reaches for my breasts under the yellow nylon.

"You were a stranger. Of course, I realized it was just the novelty of the viewpoint. Coming across you unexpectedly. In a different role, really. It was just seeing you from another perspective."

"Why don't we just make love?"

But I am still in a contemplative frame of mind. "Did you ever think of what that expression means? Making love?"

"They also serve who only stand and wait."

"Milton, eh?"

"Uh huh."

"Well, that's quotable."

"Fairly."

"Martin. Before you turn out the light, there's a question I've been wanting to ask you for weeks."

"Yes?"

"I don't want you to think I'm prying or anything."

"Who would ever suspect you of a thing like that?" His tone is only slightly mocking.

"But I notice things and sometimes I wonder."

His hand rests on the lamp switch. "Judith, just shoot."

"I was wondering, I was just wondering if you were really happy teaching Milton year after year?"

The light goes out, and we fall into our familiar private geometry, the friendly grazing of skin, the circling, circling. The walls tilt in; the darkness presses, but far away I am remembering two things. First, that Martin hasn't answered my question. And second—the question I have asked him— it wasn't the question I had meant to ask at all.

I spend one wet fall afternoon at the library researching Susanna Moodie, making notes, filling in the gaps.

This place is a scholarly retreat, high up overlooking the river, and the reading room is large and handsome. Even on a dark day it is fairly bright. There are rows of evenly spaced oak tables, and here and there groupings of leather armchairs where no one ever sits. The people around me are bent over enormous books, books so heavy that a library assistant delivers them on wheeled trolleys. They turn the pages slowly, and sometimes I see their heads bobbing in silent confirmation to the print. Unlike me, they have the appearance of serious scholars; distanced from their crisp stacks of notes, they are purposeful, industrious, admirable.

What I am doing is common, snoopy, vulgar; reading the junky old novelettes and serialized articles of Susanna Moodie; catlike I wait for her to lose her grip. And though she is careful, artfully careful, I am finding gold. The bridal bed she mentions in her story "The Miss Greens," a hint of sexuality, hurray. Her democratic posture slipping in a book review in the *Victoria Magazine*, get it down, get it down. Her fear of ugliness. And today I find something altogether unsavoury—the way in which she dwells on the mutilated body of a young pioneer mother who is killed by a panther. She skirts the dreadful sight, but she is really circling in, moving around and around it, horrified, but hoping for one more view. Yes, Susanna, it must be true, you are crazy, crazy.

Susanna Strickland Moodie 1803–1885. Gentle English upbringing, gracious country house, large and literary family, privately tutored at home, an early scribbler of stories. Later to emerge in a small way in London reform circles, a meeting with a Lieutenant Moodie in a friend's drawingroom, marriage, pregnancy, birth, emigration, all in rapid order. Then more children, poverty, struggle, writing, writing by lamplight, a rag dipped into lard for a wick, writing to pay off debts and buy flour. Then burying her husband and going senile, little wonder, at eighty, and death in Toronto.

It is a real life, a matter of record, sewn together like a leather glove with all the years joining, no worse than some and better than many. A private life, completed, deserving decent burial, deserving the sweet black eclipse, but I am setting out to exhume her, searching, prying into the small seams, counting stitches, adding, subtracting, keeping score, invading an area of existence where I've no real rights. I ask the squares of light that fall on the oak table, doesn't this woman deserve the seal of oblivion? It is, after all, what I would want.

But I keep poking away.

No wonder Richard seals his letter with Scotch tape. No wonder Meredith locks her diary, burns her mail, carries the telephone into her room when she talks. No wonder Martin is driven to subterfuge, not telling me that his latest paper has been turned down by the Renaissance Society. And concealing, for who knows what sinister purposes, his brilliant hanks of wool.

And John Spalding in Birmingham.

Poor John Spalding, how I added him up. Lecturer in English, possessor of a shrewish wife and precocious child, querulous and slightly affected, drinking too much at staff parties and forcing arguments about World Federalism, writing essays for obscure quarterlies; John Spalding, failed novelist, poor John Spalding.

How was he to know when he rented his flat to strangers that he would get me, Judith Gill, incorrigibly curious, for a tenant. Curious is kind; I am an invader, I am an enemy.

And he is a right chump, just handing it over like that, giving me several hundred square feet of new territory to explore. Drawers and cupboards to open. His books left candidly on the shelves where I could analyze the subtlety of his underlining or jeer at his marginal notations.

All that year I filtered him through the wallpaper, the kitchen utensils, the old snapshots, the shaving equipment, distilling him from the ratty blankets and the unpardonable home carpentry, the Marks-and-Spencer lamp shades and the paper bag in the bathroom cupboard where for mysterious reasons he saved burnt-out lightbulbs. Why, why?

The task of the biographer is to enlarge on available data.

The total image would never exist were it not for the careful daily accumulation of details. I had long since memorized the working axioms, the fleshy certitudes. Thus I peered into cupboards thinking, "Tell me what a man eats and I will tell you who he is." While examining the bookshelves, recalled that, "A man's sensitivity is indexed in his library." While looking into the household accounts—"A man's bank balance betrays his character." Into his medicine cabinet—"A man's weakness is outlined by the medicines which enslave him."

And his sex life, his and Isabel's, strewn about the flat like a mouldering marriage map; ancient douche bag under a pile of sheets in the airing cupboard; *The Potent Male* in paperback between the bedsprings; a disintegrating diaphram, dusty with powder in a zippered case; rubber safes sealed in plastic and hastily stuffed behind a crusted vaseline jar; half-squeezed tubes of vaginal jelly, sprays, circular discs emptied of birth control pills—didn't that woman ever throw anything away—stains on the mattress, brown-edged, stiff to the touch, ancient, untended.

Almost against the drift of my will I became an assimilator of details and, out of all the miscellaneous and unsorted debris in the Birmingham flat, John Spalding, wiry (or so I believe him to be), university lecturer, neurotic specialist in Thomas Hardy, a man who suffered insomnia and constipation, who fantasized on a love life beyond Isa-

bel's loathsome douche bag, who was behind on his telephone bill—out of all this, John Spalding achieved, in my
mind at least, something like solid dimensions.

Martin was busy that year. Daily he shut himself inside
the walnut horizons of Trinity Library, having deluded
himself into thinking he was happier in England than he
had ever been before. The children were occupied in their
daily battle with English schooling, and I was alone in the
flat most of the time, restless between biographies, wandering from room to room, pondering on John and Isabel for
want of something better to do.

Gradually they grew inside my head, a shifting composite
leafing out like cauliflower, growing more and more elaborate, branching off like the filaments of a child's daydream.
I could almost touch them through the walls. Almost.

Then I discovered, on the top shelf of John's bookcase,
a row of loose-leaf notebooks.

His manuscripts.

I had noticed them before in their brown-and-buff covers,
but the blank private spines had made me disinclined, until
this particular day, to reach for them.

But taking them down at last, I knew before I had opened
the first one that I was onto the real thing; the total disclosure which is what a biographer prays for, the swift fall
of facts which requires no more laborious jigsaws. That
first notebook weighed heavy in my hands; I knew it must
all be there.

I had already known—someone must have told me—that
John Spalding had written a number of novels, and that
all of them had been rejected by publishers. And here they
were, seven of them.

Since I had no way of recognizing their chronology, I
simply started off, in orderly fashion, with the notebook on
the far left. In a week I had read the whole shelf, the work,
I guessed, of several years. I swallowed them, digested them
whole in the ivory-tinted afternoons to the tune of the ticking clock and the spit of the gas fire.

Before long a pattern emerged from all that print, the rickety frame upon which he hung his rambling stream-of-consciousness plots. Like ugly cousins they resembled each other. Their insights bled geometrically, one to the other.

The machinery consisted of a shy sensitive young man pitted against the incomprehensible world of irritable women, cruel children, sour beer, and leaking roofs. Suddenly this man is given the gift of perfect beauty, and the form of this gift varies slightly from novel to novel. In one case it appears in the shape of a poetry-reciting nymphet; in another case it occurs as a French orphan with large unforgettable eyes. And large unforgettable breasts. A friendship with a black man, struck up one day on a bus, which leads into a damp cave of brothels and spiritualism. Thus stimulated, the frail world of the sensitive young man swirls with sudden meaning, warming his heart, skin, brain, blood, bowels, each in turn. And then a blackout, a plunge as the music fades. The blood cools, and the hand of despair stretches forth. On the journey between wretchedness and joy and back to wretchedness, the young man is tormented by poverty and by the level of his uninformed taste. He is taunted by his mysterious resistance to the materialistic world or his adherence to fatal truths. Thousands and thousands of pages, yards and yards of ascent and descent, all totally and climactically boring.

Although, in fairness, the first book—at least the one on the far left which I judged to be first—had a plot of fairly breathless originality. I pondered a while over the significance of that. Had he lived this plot himself or simply dreamed it up? The rest of the books were so helplessly conventional that it was difficult for me to credit him with creativity at any level. Still, it seemed reasonable, since the least of us are visited occasionally by genius, that this book might have been his one good idea.

Later I was to ask myself what made me pry into another person's private manuscripts, and I liked to think that having discovered the bright break of originality in the first book, I read to the end in the hope of finding more. But it was more likely my unhealthy lust for the lives of other people. I was fascinated watching him play the role of tormented hero, and his wife Isabel too, floating in and out, bloody with temper, recognizable even as she changed from Janet, Ida, Anna, Bella, Anabel, Ada, Irene.

But more was to come. Besides the loose-leaf notebooks there was a slim scribbler which turned out to be a sort of writer's diary. I should have stopped with the novels, for opening and reading such a personal document made me cringe at his candour, my face going hot and cold as his ego stumbled beyond mere boyish postures, falling into what seemed like near madness. The passages were random and undated.

> This constant rejection is finally taking its toll. I honestly believe I am the next Shakespeare, but without some sign of recognition, how can I carry on?

> Constipation. It seems I am meant to suffer. An hour today in the bathroom—the most painful so far. It is easy to blame I. Fried bread every morning. I am sick with grease. I am losing my grip.

> Have not heard from publishers yet and it is now three months. No news is good news, I tell I. She smirks. Bitch, bitch, bitch.

> My hopes are up at last. Surely they must be considering it—they've taken long enough over it. We are ready to go to London or even New York the minute we hear. Must speak to Prof. B. about leave of absence. Should be no trouble as university can only profit by having novelist on staff.

> Have been thinking about movie rights. Must speak to lawyer. Too expensive though. Could corner someone in the law faculty.

I am frightened at what comes out of my head. This long stream of negation. Life with I. and A. has become unreal. I exist somewhere else but where?

Manuscript returned today. Polite. But not very long note. Still, they must think I have some talent as they say they would like to see other manuscripts. I expected more after six months. My first book was my best. A prophet in his own country. . . .

Stale, stale, stale. The year in Nicosia will do me good. Freshen the perceptions. Thank God for Anita, who doesn't know how I suffer. Had another nosebleed last night.

I read the notebook to the end although the terrible open quality of its confessions brought me close to weeping. Silly, silly, silly little man. Paranoiac, inept, ridiculous. But he reached me through those disjointed bleeding notes as he hadn't in all his seven novels.

That shabby flat. I looked around at the border of brown lino and the imitation Indian rug. Fluffy green chunks of it pulled away daily in the vacuum cleaner. Why did he save light bulbs? Did he believe, somewhere in his halo of fantasy, that they might miraculously pull themselves together, suffer a spontaneous healing so that the filaments, reunited, their strength recovered, were once again able to throw out light?

I put the notebook back on the shelf with the sad, unwanted novels. I never told anyone about them, not even Martin, and I never again so much as touched their tense covers. John Spalding and his terrible sorrowing stayed with me all winter, a painful bruising, crippling as the weather, pulling me down. I never really shook it off until I was back aboard the BOAC, strapped in with a dazzling lunch tray on my lap and the wide winking ocean beneath me.

November

Richard's friends are random and seasonal. There are the friends he swims with in the summer and the casual sweatered football friends. There is a nice boy named Gavin Lord whom we often take skiing with us but forget about between seasons. There is a gaggle of deep-voiced brothers who live next door. For Richard they are interchangeable; they come and go; he functions within their offhand comradeship. In their absence he is indifferent. And, of course, he has Anita.

Meredith's best friend is a girl named Gwendolyn Ackerman, an intelligent girl with a curiously dark face and a disposition sour as rhubarb. She is sensitive: hurts cling to her like tiny burrs, and she and Meredith rock back and forth between the rhythm of their misunderstandings; apology and forgiveness are their coinage. It is possible, I think, that they won't always be friends. They are only, it seems, temporarily linked together in their terrible and mutual inadequacy. After school, huddled in Meredith's bedroom, they minutely examine and torment each other with the nuances of their daily happenings, not only what they said and did, but what they nearly said and almost did. They interpret each other until their separate experiences hang in exhausted shreds. They wear each other out; it can't last.

For a quiet man, Martin has many friends. They exist, it seems to me, in separate chambers, and when he sees them he turns his whole self toward them as though each were a privileged satellite. A great many people seem to be extraordinarily attached to him. There are two babies in the world named after him. Old friends from Montreal telephone him and write him chatty letters at Christmas as though he really might care about their new jobs or the cottages they are building. His university friends often drop in on Saturday afternoons and, in addition, he hears regularly from his colleagues in England. He is not an effervescent man, but when he is with his friends he listens to them with a slow and almost innocent smile on his face.

His closest friend at the university is Roger Ramsay who teaches Canadian Literature. Roger has a fat man's face, round and red, with a hedge of fat yellow curls. But his body is long and lean and muscular. He is younger than we are, young enough so he is able to live with someone without marrying her, and he and Ruthie have an apartment at the top of an old Gothic house which is cheap and charming and only a little uncomfortable. Posters instead of wallpaper, ragouts in brown pots instead of roasts, candles instead of trilights, Lightfoot records instead of children. A growing collection of Eskimo carvings and rare Canadian books.

Ruthie St. Pierre is small, dark and brilliant; assistant to the head of the translation department in the Central Library. They both smoke the odd bit of pot or, as Roger puts it, they're into it. We love them, but what we can't understand is why they love us, but they do, especially Martin. In this friendship I am the extra; the clumsy big sister who is only accidentally included.

My closest friend is a woman named Nancy Krantz. She is about my age, mother to six children and wife to a lawyer named Paul Krantz, but that is strictly by the way. Nancy is not really attached to anyone, not even to me, I admit sadly. I am an incidental here as well.

She generally drops in unexpectedly between errands, usually in the morning. She almost, but not quite, keeps the Volkswagen engine running in the driveway while we talk. She is in a rush and she dances back and forth in my kitchen with the car keys still jingling in her fingers. I cannot, in fact, imagine her voice without the accompaniment of ringing car keys. Our friendship is made up of these brief frenzied exchanges, but the quality of our conversation, for all its feverish outpouring, is genuine.

We talk fast, both of us, as though we accelerated each other, and there is a thrilling madness in our morning dialogues. Nancy has always just been somewhere or is on her way to somewhere—to an anti-abortionist meeting, to a consumers' committee, to a curriculum symposium. And into these concerns, which in the abstract interest me very little, she manages to sweep me away. I stand, coffee cup in one hand, wildly gesticulating with the other, suddenly stunningly vocal. The quality of our exchanges is such that she enables me to string together miles of impressive phrases; my extemporaneous self reawakened. I pour more coffee, and still standing we talk on until, with a loud shake of her key ring, Nancy glances at her watch and flies to the door. I am left steaming with exhaustion and happiness.

Today she has come from a committee which is fighting rate increases in the telephone service. It is her special quality to be able to observe these activities as though she were a spectator at a play. She can be wildly humorous. This morning, as a footnote to her recital, she delivers what I think to be a stunning theory of life, for she has discovered the mechanism which monitors her existence.

Every month, she tells me, the water bill arrives in the mail. The Water and Sewerage Office informs her how much money she must pay and, in addition, how many gallons of water her household has consumed during the month. But that isn't all. Underneath that figure is another which is even more fascinating, the number of gallons which she and her family have consumed on the previous billing.

She has noticed something: since she and her husband Paul have been married, the number of gallons has gone up every month. There have been no exceptions over eighteen years, not one in eighteen years, twelve billing each year. By thousands and thousands of gallons she has gone steadily up the scale. It is inexorable. She and the meter are locked in combat. She would like to fool it once, to be very thrifty for a month, use her dishwater over again, make everyone conserve on baths, flush the toilet once a day, just to stop the rolling, rolling of the tide.

It has become a sign to her, a symbol of the gathering complexity of her life. Tearing open her water bill she finds her breath stuck in her chest. Travelling from gallon to gallon she is inching toward something. Is there such a thing as infinity gallons of water, she has wondered.

But recently it has occurred to her that she will never reach infinity. One month—the exact date already exists in the future, predestined—one month there will be a very slight decrease in number of gallons. And the next month there will be a further decrease. Very small, very gradual. It will work its way back, she says. And it will mean something important. Maybe that she is reverting to something simpler, less entangled.

She doesn't know whether it will be a good thing or bad, whether she is frightened or not of the day when the first decrease comes. But she sees her whole life gathered around that watershed. It may even mean the beginning of dying, she confides to the rhythm of her chromium-plated key ring.

Winter is about to fall in on us. Early this morning when I woke up I could almost feel the snow suspended over the backyard. Outside our window there was a dense gathering of white, a blank absence of sun, and through the walls of the house the blue air pinched and gnawed.

Downstairs in the kitchen I made coffee, and I was about to wake Martin and the children when I heard a thin waterfall of sound coming from behind the birch slab door leading to the family room. I opened it and found the television on.

Richard and Meredith were sitting on the sofa watching.

All I could see from the doorway were the backs of their heads, the two of them side by side, Richard leaning slightly forward, his hands on his knees. The sight of them, the roughed fur of their hair and the crush of pajama collars, and especially the utter attentiveness to the screen, made me weak for a moment with love.

"What's going on?" I asked hoarsely.

"Shhh," Richard rasped. "They're getting into the Royal Coach."

"Who?" I asked, and then remembered. It was Princess Anne's wedding day.

"How long have you two been up?" I asked.

"Five o'clock," Meredith said shortly, never for a moment taking her eyes off the picture. "Richard woke me up."

"Five o'clock!" I felt my mouth go soft with disbelief.

"It's direct by satellite," Richard said.

"But it will all be rebroadcast later," I said with sternness, feeling at the same time wondering amazement at their early rising.

"It's not the same though," Meredith said.

"They leave out half the junk," said Richard.

(Would Anita Spalding be watching too? In the Birmingham flat, linked through satellite with Richard? Probably.)

While the coffee breathed and burped in the kitchen, I sat on the arm of the sofa watching the glittering coach drive through London. A camera scanned the crowds, and the announcer reminded us how they had stood all night waiting. The London sky looked tea-toned, foreign, water-thin.

"I thought you didn't like Princess Anne," I challenged Meredith.

"I don't," she told me, "but this is a wedding."

Later, when Martin was up, we ate breakfast, and I told them about Princess Margaret's wedding. There was no satellite in those days, so we didn't have to get up at five o'clock to watch. Instead, a film of the wedding was shot in London and rushed into a waiting transatlantic jet.

We were at home in our first apartment; Martin was writing the final draft of his thesis. It was just after lunch, and Meredith, who was very young, had been put into her crib for a nap. Our television was old, a second-hand set with a permanent crimp in the picture.

The camera was focused on a bit of sky off the coast of Newfoundland and, while Martin and I and millions of others stared at the blank patch, a commentator chattered on desperately about the history of royal weddings.

Finally a tiny speck appeared on the screen. The jet. We watched, breathless, as it landed. A man leaped out with an attaché case in his hand—the precious reels of film. Fresh from London. Rushed to the colonies. I remember my throat going tight. Stupid, but this man was a genuine courier, in a league with Roman runners and, though Martin and I were indifferent even then to royalty, we recognized a hero when we saw one.

We watched him race, satchel in hand, across the landing field and then into a flat terminal building where the projector was oiled and waiting. There was a moment's blackout, and the next thing we saw was the Royal Coach careening around Pall Mall. Miraculous.

While I was telling Meredith and Richard this story over cornflakes and toast, their eyes were fixed on me; they never miss a word. The genes are true; my children are like me in their lust after other people's stories.

Unlike Martin, whose family tree came well stocked with family tales, I am from a bleak non-storytelling family. I can remember my father, a tall, lank man who for forty years worked as inventory clerk in a screw factory, telling only one story, and this he told only two or three times. It was so extraordinary for him to tell a story at all that I remember the details perfectly.

A single incident fetched from his childhood: a girl in his high school tried to commit suicide by leaping into the stairwell. My father happened to be coming down a corridor just as she was sailing through the air. On impact she broke both her ankles and promptly fainted. This brought my father to the point of the story, the point as he conceived it being that the act of fainting was a benefice which spontaneously blocked out pain. He didn't explain to us why the girl was trying to take her life or whether she managed to live it afterwards. He seemed oddly incurious about such a dramatic event, and it must have been his bland acceptance of the facts which restrained us from asking him for details.

It is one of my fantasies that I meet this suicidal girl. She would be about seventy now—my father has been dead for ten years—and I imagine myself meeting her at a friend's. She is someone's aunt or family friend, and I recognize her the moment she touches on her attempted school suicide. I interrupt her and ask if she remembers a young boy, my father, who rushed to her when she fell and into whose arms she fainted. Yes, she would say, it happened just that way, and we would exchange long and meaningful looks, embrace each other, perhaps cry.

From my mother I can recall only two frail anecdotes, and the terrible thin poverty of their details may well account for my girlhood hunger for an expanded existence.

Once—I must have been about four at the time—my mother bought a teapot at Woolworth's, carried it home, and discovered when she opened it on the kitchen table that it was chipped. It was quite a nice brown teapot, she later explained to us, and it might have been bumped on the door coming out of Woolworth's. Or, on the other hand, it might have been chipped when she bought it. Should she return it?

She never slept a wink that night. After a week she had still not made up her mind what to do, and by this time she had broken out in a rash. It attacked the thin pink meat of her thighs and I can recall her, while dressing in the closet one morning, raising the hem of her housedress and showing me the mass of red welts. But I don't remember the teapot. She kept it for a year and used it to water her plants; then somehow it got broken.

Her other story, frequently told, concerned a friend of hers who greatly admired my mother's decorating talents. The friend, a Mrs. Christianson, had written to *Canadian Homes* suggesting they come to photograph our house for a future issue. For a year my mother waited to hear from the magazine, all the while keeping the house perfect, every chair leg free from dust, every corner cheerful with potted plants. No one ever called, and she came to the conclusion in the end that they were just too hoity-toity (a favourite expression of hers) to bother about Scarborough bungalows.

That was all we had: my father's adventure in the stairwell, which never developed beyond the scientific rationale for fainting, my mother's teapot and rash and her near-brush with fame. And a sort of half-story about something sinister that had happened to Aunt Liddy in Jamaica.

My sister Charleen, who is a poet, believes that we two sisters turned to literature out of simple malnutrition. Our own lives just weren't enough, she explains. We were underfed, undernourished; we were desperate. So we dug in. And here we are, all these years later, still digging.

On Tuesday Martin felt a cold coming on. He dosed himself with vitamin C and orange juice and went to bed early. He turned up the electric blanket full blast and shivered. His voice dried to a sandy rasp, but he never complained. It is one of the bargains we have.

Years ago, he claims, I put him under a curse by telling him that I loved him because he was so robust. Can I really have said such a thing? It seems impossible, but he swears it; he can even show me the particular park bench in Toronto where, in our courting days, I paid allegiance to his health. It has, he says, placed him under an obligation for the rest of his life. He is unable to enjoy poor health, he is permanently disbarred from hypochondria, he is obliged to be fit. So he went off to the university, his eyes set with fever and his pockets full of Kleenex.

I know the power of the casual curse. I have only to look at my children to see how they become the shapes we prepare for them. When Meredith was little, for instance, she, like any other child, collected stones, and for some reason we seized on it, calling her our little rock collector, our little geologist. Years later, nearly crowded out of her room by specimens, she confessed with convulsions of guilt that she wasn't interested in rocks any more. In fact, she never really liked them all that much. I saw in an instant that she had been trapped into a box, and I was only too happy to let her out; together we buried the rocks in the back yard. And forgot them.

Another example: Furlong, reviewing my first book for a newspaper, described me, Judith Gill, as a wry observer of human nature. Thus, for him I am always and ever wry. My wryness overcomes even me. I can feel it peeling off my tongue like very thick slices of imported salami, very special, the acidity measured on a meter somewhere in the back of my brain. Furlong has never once suspected that it was he who implanted this wryness in me, a tiny seedling which flourished on inception and which I am able to conceal from almost everyone else. For Furlong, though, I can be deeply, religiously, fanatically wry.

Just as for me Martin is strong and ruddy, quintessentially robust. But by the end of the week he was ready to give in. "Go to bed," I said. "Surrender."

Three days later he was still there, sipping tea, going from aspirin to aspirin.

I brought him the morning mail to cheer him up. "Just look at this," I said, handing him a milky-white square envelope.

I had already read it. It was an invitation to Furlong's lunch party in celebration of his new book. A one-thirty luncheon and a reading at three; an eccentric social arrangement, at least in our part of the world.

I squinted at the date over Martin's shoulder. "It's a Sunday, I think."

"It is," Martin said. "And I think—" his voice gathered in the raw bottom of his throat, "I think it's Grey Cup Day."

"That's impossible."

"I'm sure, Judith. Look at the calendar."

I counted on my fingers. "You're right."

He muttered something inaudible from the tumble of sheets.

"How could he do it?" I said.

"Well he did."

"He can't have done it on purpose. Do you think he just forgot when Grey Cup is?"

"Furlong's not your average football fan, you know."

"Nevertheless," I said, breathless with disbelief, "to give a literary party on Grey Cup."

"For 'one who embodies the national ethos,'" Martin was quoting from a review of *Graven Images*, "he is fairly casual about the folkways of his country."

"What'll we do?" I said. "What can I tell him."

"Just that we're terribly sorry, previous engagement, et cetera."

"But Martin, it's not just us. No one will come. Absolutely no one. Even Roger, worshipper though he be, wouldn't give up the game for Furlong. He'll be left high and dry. And there's his mother to consider."

"It's what they deserve. My God, of all days."

"And he's so vain he'll probably expect us to come anyway."

"Fat chance."

"I'd better phone him right away."

"The sooner the better."

"Right."

"And Judith."

"What?"

"Make it a firm no."

"Right," I said.

But I didn't have to phone Furlong. He phoned me himself late in the afternoon.

"Judith," he said, racing along. "I suppose you got our invitation today. From Mother and me."

"Yes, we did but—"

"Say no more. I understand. It seems I've made a colossal bloop."

"Grey Cup Day."

"Mother says the phone's been ringing all day. And I ran into Roger at the university. Poor lad, almost bent double with apology. Of course, the instant we realized, we decided on postponement."

"That really is the best thing," I said, relieved that I would not have to admit we put football before literature in this house.

"We'll make it December then, I think. Early December,"

"Maybe you should check the bowl games," I suggested wanting to be helpful.

"Of course. Mother and I will put our heads together and come up with another date. Now I mustn't keep you from your work, Judith. How is it coming, by the way?"

"Well. I think I can honestly say it's going well."

"Good. Good. No more novel-writing aspirations?" he asked, and for an instant I thought I heard a jealous edge to his voice.

"No," I said. "You can consider me cured of that bug."

"That's what it is, a wretched virus. I can't tell you how I envy you your immunity."

"It was madness," I said. "Pure madness."

"That was Furlong on the phone," I told Martin when I took up his supper tray. Soup, toast, a piece of cheese. He was sitting up reading the paper and looking better.

"And? What did he have to say for himself?"

"All a mistake. He never thought of Grey Cup. So don't

worry, Martin. It's been postponed. Way off in the future. Sometime in December."

"We might even be snowed in with luck," he said going back to his paper. "Anyway, that's the end of that story."

Story, he had called it. He was right, it was a story, a fragment of one anyway. A human error causing human outcry and subdued by a human retraction. A comedy miniaturized.

It's the arrangement of events which makes the stories. It's throwing away, compressing, underlining. Hindsight can give structure to anything, but you have to be able to see it. Breathing, waking and sleeping; our lives are steamed and shaped into stories. Knowing that is what keeps me from going insane, and though I don't like to admit it, sometimes it's the only thing.

Names are funny things, I tell Richard. We are having lunch one day, and he has asked me how I happened to name him Richard.

"I liked the 'r' sound," I tell him. "It's a sort of repetition of the 'r' in your father's name."

"And Meredith?" he asks. "Where did you get that?"

"I'm not sure," I tell him, for the naming of our babies is a blur to me. Each time I was caught unprepared; each time I felt a compulsion amidst the confusion of birth, to pin a label, any label, on fast before the prize disappeared.

Meredith. It is, of course, an echo of my own name, the same thistle brush of "th" at the end, just as Richard's name is a shadow of Martin's. Unconscious at the time; I have only noticed it since.

"I'm not sure," I tell Richard. "Names are funny things. They don't really mean anything until you enlist them."

Now he confides a rare fact about Anita Spalding, introducing her name with elaborate formality.

"You know Anita Spalding? In Birmingham?"

"Yes," I say, equally formal.

"Do you know what she does? She calls her parents by their first names."

"Really?"

"Like she calls her father John. That's his first name. And she calls her mother Isabel."

"Hmmmm." I am deliberately offhand, anxious to prolong this moment of confidence.

But he breaks off with, "But like you say, names are funny things."

"Richard," I say. "Do you know what Susanna Moodie called her husband?"

There is no need to explain who Susanna Moodie is. After all these months she is one of us, one of the family. Every day someone refers to her. She hovers over the house, a friendly ghost.

"What did she call her husband?" Richard asks.

"Moodie," I tell him.

"What's wrong with that? That was his name wasn't it?"

"His last name. Don't you get it, Richard? It would be like me calling Daddy, Gill. Would you like a cup of tea, Gill? Well, Gill, how's the old flu coming along? Hi ya, Gill."

"Yeah," Richard agrees. "That would be kind of strange."

"Strange is the word."

"Why'd she do it then? Why didn't she call him by his first name?"

"I don't know," I tell him. "It was the custom in certain levels of society in those days. And there's her sister, Catherine Parr Traill. She called her husband Mr. Traill. All his life. Imagine that. Moodie is almost casual when you think of Mr. Traill."

"I guess so," he says doubtfully.

"I like to think of it as a sort of nickname. Like Smitty or Jonesy. Maybe it was like that."

"Maybe," he says. "I suppose it depends on how she said it. Like the expression she used when she said it. Do you know what I mean?"

I did know what he meant, and it was a common problem in biography. Could anyone love a man she called by his surname? Was such a thing possible? I would have to hear whether it was said coldly or with tenderness. One minute of eavesdropping and I could have travelled light-years in understanding her.

It was Leon Edel, who should know about the problems of biography if anyone does, who said that biography is the least exact of the sciences. So much of a man's life is lived inside his own head, that it is impossible to encompass a personality. There is never never enough material. Sometimes I read in the newspaper that some university or library has bought hundreds and hundreds of boxes of letters and papers connected with some famous deceased person, and I know every time that it's never going to be enough. It's hopeless, so why even try?

That was the question I found myself asking during the year we spent in England. My two biographies, although they had been somewhat successful, had left me dissatisfied. In the end, the personalities had eluded me. The expression in the voice, the concern in the eyes, the unspoken anxieties; none of these things could be gleaned from library research, no matter how patient and painstaking. Characters from the past, heroic as they may have been, lie coldly on the page. They are inert, having no details of person to make them fidget or scratch; they are toneless, simplified, stylized, myths distilled from letters; they are bloodless.

There is nothing to do but rely on available data, on diaries, bills, clippings, always something on paper. Even the rare photograph or drawing is single-dimensional and self-conscious.

And if one does enlarge on data, there is the danger of trespassing into that whorish field of biographical fiction, an arena already asplash with the purple blood of the queens of England or the lace-clutched tartish bosoms of French courtesans. Tasteless. Cheap. Tawdry.

That year in England I was restless. I started one or two research projects and abandoned them. I couldn't settle down. Everything was out of phase. My body seemed disproportionately large for the trim English landscape. I sensed that I alarmed people in shops by the wild nasal rock of my voice, and at parties I overheard myself suddenly raucous and bluff. It was better to fade back, hide out for a while. I became a full-time voyeur.

On trains I watched people, lusting to know their destinations, their middle names, their marital status and always and especially whether or not they were happy. I stared to see the titles of the books they were reading or the brand of cigarette they smoked. I strained to hear snatches of conversations and was occasionally rewarded, as when I actually heard an old gentleman alighting from his Rolls Royce saying to someone or other, "Oh yes, yes. I did know Lord MacDonald. We were contemporaries at Cambridge." And a pretty girl on a bus who turned to her friend and said, "So I said to him, all right, but you have to buy the birth control pills." And then, of course, I had the Spalding family artifacts around me twenty-four hours a day, and on that curious family trio I could speculate endlessly.

It occurred to me that famous people may be the real dullards of life. Perhaps shopgirls coming home from work on the buses are the breath and body of literature. Fiction just might be the answer to my restlessness.

"I think I might write a novel," I said to Martin on a grey Birmingham morning as he was about to leave for the library.

"What for?" he asked, genuinely surprised.

"I'm tired of being boxed in by facts all the time," I told him. "Fiction might be an out for me. And it might be entertaining too."

"You're too organized for full-time fantasy." he said, and later I remembered those words and gave him credit for prophecy. Martin is astute, although sometimes, as on this particular morning, he looks overly affable and half-daft.

"You sound like a real academic," I told him. "All footnotes and sources."

"I *know* you, Judith," he said smiling.

"Well, I'm going to start today," I told him. "I've been making a few notes, and today I'm going to sit down and see what I can do."

"Good luck," was all he said, which disappointed me, for he had been interested in my biographies and, in a subdued way, proud of my successes.

Notes for Novel

Tweedy man on bus, no change, leaps off

beautiful girl at concert, husband observes her legs, keeps dropping program

children in park, sailboat, mother yells (warbles) "Damn you David. You're getting your knees dirty."

letter to editor about how to carry cello case in a mini-car. Reply from base player

West Indians queue for mail. Fat white woman (rollers) cigarette in mouth says, "what they need is ticket home."

story in paper about woman who has baby and doesn't know she's preg. Husband comes home from work to find himself a father. Dramatize.

leader of labour party dies tragically, scramble for power. wife publishes memoirs.

hotel bath. each person rationed to one inch of hot water. Hilarious landlady.

Lord renounces title so he can run for House of Commons, boyhood dream and all that.

My random jottings made no sense to me at all. When I wrote them down I must have felt something; I must have thought there was yeast there, but whatever it was that had struck me at the time had faded away. There was no centre, no point to begin from.

I paced up and down in the flat thinking. A theme? A starting point? A central character or situation? I looked around the room and saw John Spalding's notebooks. That was the day I took them down and began to read them; my novel was abandoned.

After that I was too dispirited to do any writing at all. I spent the spring shopping and visiting art galleries and teashops and waiting for the end to come. I counted the days and it finally came. We packed our things, sold the Austin, gave the school uniforms away and, just as summer was getting big as a ball, we returned home.

Martin is better. Still on medication, but looking something like his real self. Today he went back to the university, and the house is quiet. For some reason I open his desk drawer, the one where the wool is.

It's gone. Nothing there but the wood slats of the drawer bottom and a paper clip or two. I look in the other drawers. Nothing.

I hadn't thought much about the wool while it was still there. I'd wondered about it, of course, but it was easy to forget, to push to the back of my thoughts. But now it has gone.

It has come and gone. I have been offered no explanations. Was it real, I wonder.

My hands feel cold and my heart pounds. I am afraid of something and don't know what it is.

December

The first snow has come, lush and feather-falling.

As a child I hated the snow, thinking it was both cruel and everlasting, but that was the hurting enemy snow of Scarborough that got down our necks, soaked through our mittens, fell into our boots and rubbed raw, red rings around our legs. It is one of the good surprises of life to find that snow can be so lovely.

Nancy Krantz and I skied all one day, and afterwards, driving home in her little Volkswagen with our skis forked gaily on its round back, we talked about childhood.

"The worst part for me," Nancy said, "was thinking all the time that I was crazy."

"You? Crazy?"

"It wasn't until I hit university that I heard the expression *déjà vu* for the first time. I had always thought I was the only being in the universe who had experienced anything as eerie as that. Imagine, discovering at twenty that it is a universal phenomenon, all spelled out and recognized. And normal. What a cheat! Why hadn't someone told me about it? Taken me aside and said, look, don't you ever feel all this has happened before?"

"Hadn't you ever mentioned it to anyone?"

"What? And have them know I was crazy. Never."

"You surprise me, Nancy," I said. "I would have thought you were very open as a child."

"Not on your life. I was a regular clam," she said, shifting gears at a hill. "And scared of my own shadow. Especially at night. At one point I actually thought my mother, my dear, gentle, plump, little mother with her fox furs and

59

little felt hats was trying to put poison in my food. Imagine! Well, thank God for second-year psychology, even though it was ten years too late. Because that's normal too, a child's fear that his parents will murder him. And if they didn't, someone else would. Hitler maybe. Or some terrible maniac hiding out in my clothes cupboard. Or lying under my bed with a bayonet. Right through the mattress. Oh God. It was so terrible. And so real. I could almost feel the cold, steely tip coming through the sheet. But I never told anyone. Never."

"I wonder if children are that stoic today? Not to tell anyone their worse fears."

"Mine are pretty brave. I can't tell if they're bluffing or not, though. Weren't you ever afraid like that, Judith?"

"Of course," I said, "I was a real coward. But it's funny looking back. Do you know what it was that frightened me most about childhood?"

"What?"

"That it would never end."

"What do you mean?"

"I was frightened, but it wasn't so much the shadows in the cupboard that scared me. It was the terrible, terrible suffocating sameness of it all. It's true. I remember lying in bed trembling, but what I heard was the awful and relentless monotony. The furnace switching off and on in the basement. Amos and Andy. Or the kettle steaming in the kitchen. Even the sound of my parents turning the pages of the newspaper in the living room while we were supposed to be going to sleep. My mother's little cough, so genteel. The flush of the toilet through the wall before they went to bed. And other things. The way my mother always hung the pillowcases on the clothesline with the open end up, leaving just a little gap so the air could blow inside them. With a clothes peg in her mouth when she did it, always the same. It frightened me."

"I always thought there was something to be said for stability in childhood."

"I suppose there is," I agreed. "But I always hoped, or rather I think I actually knew, that there was another world out there and that someday I would walk away and live in it. But the long, long childhood nearly unhinged me. Take the floor tiles in our kitchen at home. I can tell you exactly the pattern of our floor in Scarborough, and it was a complicated pattern too. Blue squares with a yellow fleck, alternating in diagonal stair-steps with yellow squares with brown flecks. And I can tell you exactly the type of flowers on my bedspread when I was six and exactly what my dotted swiss curtains looked like when I was twelve. And the royal blue velvet tiebacks. It was so vivid, so present. That's what I was afraid of. All those details. And their claim on me."

"And when you finally did get away from it into the other life, Judith—was it all you thought it would be?" She was driving carefully, concentrating on the road which was getting slippery under the new snow.

I tried to shape an answer, a real answer, but I couldn't. "Oh, I don't know," I said with a hint of dismissal. "The trouble is that when you're a child you can sense something beyond the details. Or at least you hope there's something."

"And now?" she prompted me.

"And now," I said, "I hardly ever think about the kind of life I want to live."

"Why not?"

"I suppose I'm just too preoccupied with living it. Much less introspective. And one thing about writing biography is that you tend to focus less on your own life. But I think of Richard and Meredith sometimes, and wonder if they're taking it all in."

"The pattern on the kitchen floor?"

"Yes. All of it. And I wonder if they're waiting for it to be over."

"Maybe it's all a big gyp," Nancy said. "Maybe the whole thing is a big gyp the way Simone de Beauvoir says at the end of her autobiography. Life is a gyp."

I nodded. It was warm in the car and I felt agreeable and

sleepy. My legs and back ached pleasantly, and I thought that the snow blowing across the highway looked lovely in the last of the afternoon light. The motor hummed and the windshield wipers made gay little grabs at the snow.

"It can't all be a gyp," I told her. "It's too big. It can't be."

And we left it at that.

"Judith." Martin called to me one evening after dinner. "Come quick. See who's being interviewed on television."

I dropped the saucepan I was scraping and peeled off my rubber gloves. Probably Eric Kierans, I thought. He is my favourite politician with his sluggish good sense so exquisitely smothered in rare and perfect modesty. Or it might be Malcolm Muggeridge who, nimble-tongued, year after year, poured out a black oil stream of delicious hauteur.

But it was neither; it was Furlong Eberhardt being interviewed about his new book.

I sank down on the sofa between Martin and Meredith and stared at Furlong. We were tuned to a local channel, and this was a relaxed and informal chat. The young woman who was interviewing him was elegantly low-key in a soft shirtdress and possessed of a chuckly throatiness such as I had always desired for myself.

"Mr. Eberhardt—" she began.

"My friends always call me by my first name," he beamed at her, but she scurried past him with her next question.

"Perhaps you could tell our viewers who haven't yet read *Graven Images* a little about how you came upon the idea for it."

Furlong leaned back, his face open with amusement, and spread his arms hopelessly. "You know," he said, "that's a perfectly impossible question to ask a writer. How and where he gets his ideas."

Smiling even harder than before, she refused to be put down. "Of course, I know every writer has his own private source of imagination, but *Graven Images*, of all your

books, tells such an extraordinary story that we thought
you might want to tell us a little about how the idea for the
book came to you."

Furlong laughed. He drew back his head and laughed
aloud, though not without kindness.

The interviewer waited patiently, leaning forward
slightly, her hands in a hard knot.

"All I can tell you," he said, composing himself and
assuming his academic posture, "is that a writer's sources
are never simple. Always composite. The idea for *Graven
Images* came to me in pieces. True, I may have had one
generous burst of inspiration, for which I can only thank
whichever deity it is who presides over creative imagination. But the rest came with less ease, torn daily out of the
flesh as it were."

"I see," the interviewer said somewhat coldly, for plainly
she felt he was toying with her. "But Mr. Eberhardt, this
new novel seems to have an increased vigour. A new im-
mediacy." She had recaptured her lead and was pinning
him down.

Furlong turned directly into the camera and was caught
in a flattering close-up, the model of furrowed thoughtful-
ness. "You may be right," he nodded in response. "You just
may be right. But on the other hand, I wouldn't have
thought I was exactly washed up as a writer before *Graven
Images.*"

"If I may quote one of the critics, Mr. Eberhardt—"

"Furlong. Please," he pleaded.

"Furlong. One of the critics," she rattled through her
notes, cleared her throat and read, "Eberhardt's new book
is brisk and original, as fast moving and exciting as a
movie."

"Ah," he said his hands pulling together beneath his
beard. "You may be interested to know that it is soon to
become a film."

Her eyes widened. "*Graven Images* is to be made into a
film?"

"We have only just signed the contract," he said serenely, "this afternoon."

"Well, I must say, congratulations are in order, Mr. Eberhardt. I suppose this film will be made in Canada?"

"Ah. I regret to say it will not. The offer was made by an American company, and I am afraid I can't release any details at this time. I'm sure your viewers will understand."

Her eyes glittered as she leaned meaningfully into the camera. "Wouldn't you say, Mr. Eberhardt, that it is enormously ironical that you, a Canadian writer who has done so much to bring Canadian literature to the average reader, must turn to an American producer to have your novel filmed?"

He was rattled. "Look here, I didn't go to them. They came. They approached me. And I can only say that of course I would have preferred a Canadian offer but—" an expression of helplessness transformed his face—"what can one do?"

"I'm sure we'll all look forward eagerly to it, Mr. Eberhardt. American or Canadian. And it has been a great pleasure to talk to you tonight."

The camera grazed his face one last time before the fade-out. "An even greater pleasure for me," he said with just a touch too much chivalry.

Meredith sitting beside me looked flushed and excited, and Martin was muttering with unaccustomed malice, "He's got it made now."

"What do you mean?"

"Your friend Furlong has just struck it rich."

I shrugged. "He's never been exactly wanting."

"Ah, Judith, you miss the point. A movie. This is no mere trickle of royalties. This is big rich."

"Well, maybe," I said, not really seeing the point.

"The old bugger," Martin said. "He's going to be really unbearable now."

"Tell me, Martin. Have you read it yet? *Graven Images*?"

"No," he said. "I keep putting it off."

"His party is next week. Sunday."

"I know. I know," he said despairingly.

"It may not be too bad."

"It'll be bad."

"Do you really despise him, Martin?"

"Despise him. God, no. It's just that he's such a perfect asshole. Worse than that, he's a phoney asshole."

"For example?" I asked smiling.

"Well, remember that sign he had in his office a few years ago? On his desk?"

"No. I never saw a sign."

"It was a framed motto. *You Shall Pass Through This Life but Once.*"

"Really? He had one of those? I can't imagine it. It seems so sort of Dale Carnegie for Furlong."

"He had it. I swear."

"And that's why he's an asshole?"

"No. Not that."

"Well, why then?"

"Because, after he got the Canadian Fiction Prize, and that big write-up in *Maclean's* and the New York *Times*, both in the same month—"

"Yes?"

"Well, right after that happened, he took down his sign. Just took it away one day. And it's never been seen since."

"He'd never own up to it now," I said.

"When I think of that sign and the way he stealthily disposed of it, another notch of sophistication—I don't know. That just seems to be Furlong Eberhardt in a nutshell. That one act, as far as I'm concerned, encapsulates his whole personality."

Meredith leapt from the sofa, startling us both. "I think you're both being horrible. Just horrible. So middle-class, so smug. Sitting here. It's character assassination, that's what. And you're enjoying it." She flew from the room with her breath coming out in jagged gasps.

For a moment Martin and I froze. Then he very slowly

picked up the newspaper from the floor, reached for the sports page, and gave me a brief but hurting glance. "I don't understand her sometimes," was all he said.

It was then that I noticed Richard sitting quietly in a corner of the room, unobtrusive in his neat maroon sweater. He was watching us closely.

"What are you doing, Richard?" I asked.

"Nothing," he said.

Frantically, neurotically, harried and beleaguered, I am addressing Christmas cards. Richard, home with a cold, sits at the dining table with me; he is checking addresses, licking stamps, stacking envelopes in their individual white pillars; the overseas stack that will now have to be sent expensively by airmail, the unsealed ones with nothing but a rude "Judith and Martin Gill" scrawled inside them, the letters to old friends where I've crammed a year's outline into two or three inches—"A good year for us, Martin busy teaching, the children are getting ENORMOUS, am working on a new book, not much news, wish you were closer, happy holidays." And Martin's stack, the envelopes which Richard and I will leave unsealed so that tonight, after he gets home from the university, he can sit down and quickly, offhandedly write the funny, intense little messages he is so good at.

The afternoon wears on, and outside the window snow is falling and falling. Since noon we have had the overhead light on. Richard in striped pajamas looks pale.

This is a long, tedious task, and it irritates me to separate and put in order the constellations of our friends and to send them each these feeble scratched messages. But for the sake of the return, for the crash of creamy envelopes blazing with seals that will soon spill down upon us, I push on. For I want to hear from the O'Malleys who lived across the hall from us in our first apartment. I want to know if the Gorkys are still together and where the best man at our wedding,

Kurt Weisman, has moved. Dr. Lawrence who supervised Martin's graduate work and his wife Bettina always write us from Florida and so do the Grahams, the Lords, the Reillys, the Jensens. What matter that they were often dull and that we might have drifted apart eventually? What matter that they were sometimes stingy or overly frank or forgetful? They want to wish us a merry Christmas. They want to wish us all the best in the New Year. I can't help but take the printed card literally; these are our friends; they love us. We love them.

Richard is studying the airmail stamp which goes on the letters to Britain. It is a special issue with a portrait of the Queen, an enormous stamp, the largest we have ever seen. The image is handsome and the background is filled in with pale gold. On the corners of the tiny Rustcraft envelopes, all I could find at this late date, it gleams like a gem.

I write a brief note to the Spaldings, a spray of ritual phrases. "We often remember the wonderful year we spent in Birmingham. The children have such happy memories. Hope your family is well and that you are having a mild winter, best wishes from the Gills."

Richard seals it and affixes the great golden stamp. "He's writing a book," he says.

"Who?" I ask absently.

"Mr. Spalding. He's writing a novel." Richard seldom mentions the Spaldings, but when he does, it is abruptly, as though the words lay perpetually spring-loaded on the tip of his tongue.

"I suppose Anita wrote you about it?" I say inanely.

"Yes."

"And is it going well? The novel?"

"I don't know," he says. "But she says that sometimes he stays up all night typing."

"Well, I wish him luck," I say, thinking of his row of rejected manuscripts.

Richard makes no reply, and after a minute I ask him, "What's it about? The novel Anita's father is writing?"

"How should I know?" he says, suddenly querulous.

I snap back. "I only asked."

But I really would like to know what John Spalding is writing about. Maybe he's incorporating some new material from the year in Cyprus. Or perhaps reworking one of his old plots. He might even have resurrected his one good one.

I think of him typing through the night in the chilly, gas-smelling flat while the frowsy Isabel snores in a distant bedroom. I imagine his small frame, tense, gnatlike, concentrating on the impossible mass of a novel, and for a moment I see him as almost touchingly valiant.

Then guilt attacks me; a pain familiar by now, a spurt of heat between my eyes, damn.

The Magic Rocking Horse was the name of the novel I wrote the year we came back from England. I intended, and for a while even believed, that the title would convey a subtle, layered irony—a childlike innocence underlying a theme of enormous worldliness.

But the novel never materialized on either level. Instead it simply stretched and strained along, scene after scene pitiably stitched together and collapsing in the end for want of flesh. For, unlike biography, where a profusion of material makes it possible and even necessary to be selective, novel writing requires a complex mesh of details which has to be spun out of simple air. No running to the public library for facts, no sleuthing through bibliographies, no borrowing from the neat manila folders at the Archives. That year the most obvious fact about fiction struck me afresh: it all had to be made up.

And where to begin? For two or three months I did nothing at all but think about how to begin. Dialogue or description? Or a cold plunge into action? Once or twice I actually produced a page or two, but later, reading over what I had written, I found the essential silliness of make-believe disturbing, and I began to wonder whether I really wanted to write a novel at all.

I discussed it with everyone I knew and got very little support. Roger and Ruthie told me, flatteringly, that it was a waste of my biographical skills. Nancy Krantz, sipping coffee, pursed her lips and pronounced, in a way which was not exactly condemning but almost, that she seldom read novels. Martin said little, but it was obvious that he viewed the whole project as somewhat dilettantish, and the children thought it might be a good idea if I wrote something along the line of Agatha Christie but transferred to a Canadian setting.

Furlong Eberhardt was the only one who volunteered a halfway friendly ear, and when he suggested one day that I might want to sit in on his creative writing seminar, it seemed like a good idea; a chance to sit down with a circle of other struggling fiction writers, sympathetic listeners upon whom I might test my material and who, in turn, might provide wanted stimulation or, as Furlong put it, might "prime the old pump."

Looking back, I believe the idea of again being a student appealed to me too. I bought a notebook and a clutch of yellow pencils, and each Wednesday afternoon I dressed carefully for the class which met in an airless little room at the top of the Arts Building; my fawn slacks or my bronze corduroy skirt, a turtleneck, something youthful but never going too far, for what was the point of being grotesque for the sake of ten undergraduates ranging from eighteen-year-old Arleen whose black paintbrush hair fell to her hips, all the way to Ludwig, aged about twenty-four, horribly pimpled, who stared at me with hatred because I was married (and to a professor at that), because I lived in a house, because I was a friend of Furlong's, and possibly because my fingernails were clean.

No, I didn't fool myself that I was going to be one of them. And how could I since, despite my urging them to call me Judith, they always referred to me as Mrs. Gill. And when I read my short weekly contributions, always a quarter the length of theirs, they listened politely, even Ludwig, and never ventured any remarks except perhaps, very deferentially, that my sentences were a bit too structured or that my situations seemed a little, well, conventional and contrived.

Somewhat to my surprise I found that Furlong ran his creative writing seminar in a highly organized manner, beginning with what he called warming-up exercises. These were specific weekly assignments in which we were to describe such things as the experience of ecstasy or the effect of ennui, a dialogue between lovers one week and enemies the next.

I sweated through these assignments, typing out the minimum required words and, when my turn came, I read them aloud, feeling like a great overblown girl, red-faced and matronly, who should long since have abandoned such childish games.

The rest of them were not the least reticent; indeed they were positively eager to celebrate their hallucinations aloud. Arleen dragged us paragraph by paragraph through her thoughts on peace and mankind, and a girl named Lucy Rimer was anxious to split her psyche wide open, inviting us to inspect the tortured labyrinth of her awakening sexuality. Joseph, an African student, disgusted and thrilled us with portraits of his Ghanian grandparents. Someone called George Riorden dramatized his feeling on racial equality by having two characters, Whitey (a Negro) and Mr. Black (a white) dialogue over the back fence, reminding us, in case we missed it, of the express irony implied by their names. Ludwig poked with a blunt and dirty finger into the sores of his consciousness, not stopping at his subtle and individual response to orgasm and the nuances of his erect penis. On and on.

They were relentless, compulsive, unsparing, as though they had waited all their lives for these moments of catharsis, these Wednesday afternoon epiphanies. But looking around, when I dared to look around, I watched them wearing down, week by week exhausting themselves, and I wondered how long it could go on.

Eventually Furlong, who until then had merely listened and nodded, nodded and listened, called a halt and announced that it was time to begin the term project. Each of us was to write a short novel, about ten chapters he suggested, a chapter a week, which we were to bring to class to be read aloud and discussed. I breathed with relief. This was what I had hoped for, a general to command me into action and an audience who, by its response, might indicate whether I was going in the right direction.

I began at once on my first chapter, carefully introducing my main characters, providing a generous feeling of setting, and observing all the conventions as I understood them. It was all quite easy, and when my turn came to read, the class listened attentively, and even Furlong beamed approval.

And then I got stuck. Having described the personalities of my characters, detailed where they lived and what they did, I didn't know what to do with them next. The following week when my turn came, I apologized and said I was unprepared.

The others in the class seemed not to suffer from my peculiar malady which was the complete inability to manufacture situations, and I envied the ease with which they drifted off into fantasies, for although they strained my credulity, their inventiveness seemed endless.

A second week went by, leaving me still at the end of Chapter One. A third week. Furlong questioned me kindly after class.

"Are you losing interest, Judith?"

"I think I'm losing my mind," I said. "I just can't seem to get any ideas."

He was understanding, fatherly. "It'll come," he promised. "You'll see."

I waited but it didn't come, and I began to lie awake at

night, frightened by the emptiness in my head. In the small hours of the morning, with Martin asleep beside me, I several times crept out of bed, padded downstairs, made tea, sat at the kitchen table and felt myself overcome by vacancy, barrenness, by failure.

A Wednesday afternoon came when I phoned Furlong before class pleading a violent toothache and a sudden dental appointment. The following Wednesday I went one step further: I absented myself without excuse. I was in descent now, set on a not-too-painful decline. There were days when I seldom thought about the novel at all.

I went skiing. I had my hair restyled at a place called Rico's of Rome and I shopped for new clothes. I painted the upstairs bathroom turquoise and joined a Keep Fit class. I went to the movies with Martin and Roger and Ruthie. I fringed and embroidered Richard's jeans, wrote a long letter to my sister Charleen. Everyone was kind; no one said a word about my novel. No one inquired about the seminar I was attending. No one except Furlong.

He kept phoning me. "You made a brilliant start, Judith. Your first chapter showed real strength. Head and shoulders above the rest of the little brats."

"But I can't seem to expand on that, Furlong. And not for want of trying."

"You say you really have been trying?"

"I have rings under my eyes," I lied.

"How about just letting your mind go free. Conduct a sort of private brainstorming. I sometimes find that helps."

"You mean you've felt like this too? Bereft? Not an idea in your head?"

"If you only knew. The truth is, Judith, I can be sympathetic because I haven't had a good idea in almost two years. And that, my old friend, is strictly entre-nous."

"And you've no solutions? No advice?"

"Try coming back to class. I know you think you can't face it at this point, but steel yourself. Most of what they write is garbage, but it's stimulation of a sort."

I promised, and I did actually go back for one or two sessions. And at home I forced myself to sit down and type out a paragraph every morning, but the effort was akin to suffering.

And then one day, just as Furlong had said, it came. In the middle of a dazzling winter morning, ten o'clock with the sun bold and fringed as a zinnia, it came. I would be able to save myself after all.

I would simply borrow the plot from John Spalding's first abandoned and unpublished novel, the one I had so secretly consumed in Birmingham. Such a simple idea. What did it matter that his writing was banal, boyish, embarrassingly sincere; the plot had been not only clever —it had been astonishingly original. Otherwise I wouldn't have remembered it, for like many rapid readers, I forget what I read the minute I close the covers. But John Spalding's plot line, even after all these months, was surprisingly vivid.

What I couldn't understand was why I hadn't thought of it before now. It was so available; what a waste to leave it stuck in a buff folder on a dusty shelf in an obscure flat in Birmingham, England. A good idea should never be orphaned. Luxuriously, I allowed the details to circulate through my veins, marvelling that the solution to my dilemma had been so obvious, so right, so free for the taking; it had an aura of inevitability about it which made me wonder if it hadn't been incubating in my blood all these months—germination, growth, now the burst of blossom.

I thought of the Renaissance painters, and happily, gleefully, drew parallels; the master painter often doing nothing but tracing in the lines, while his worthy but less gifted artisans filled in the colours. It had been a less arrogant age in which creativity had been shared; surely that was an ennobling precedent. For I didn't intend anything as crude as stealing John Spalding's plot outright. I already had my line-up of characters. My setting had been composed. All I needed to borrow was the underlying plot structure.

I woke the next day feeling spare, nimble, energetic, sinewy with health and muscle, confident, even omnipotent. I felt as though the blood had been drained out of me and replaced with cool-flowing Freon gas. My fingers were lively little machines exciting the keys; my eyes rotated mechanically, left to right, left to right; the carriage rocked with purpose. My brain ticked along, cleanly, accurately, uncluttered. The first day I wrote fifty pages.

I telephoned Furlong, shrilling, "I've finally got started."

"All you needed was an idea," he said. "Didn't I tell you."

The second day I wrote thirty pages. Somewhere I had lost my miraculous clarity; my idea had softened, lost shape; everything was blurring.

The third day I wrote ten pages and, for the first time, sat down to read what I had written.

Appalling, unbelievable, dull, dull. The bones of my stolen plot stuck out everywhere like great evil-gleaming knobs, accusing me, charging me. The action, such as it was, jerked along on dotted lines; there was no tissue to it. It was thin; worse than thin, it was skinny, a starved child.

Always when I had heard of writers destroying their manuscripts or painters shredding their canvases, I had considered it inexcusably theatrical, but now I could understand the desire to obliterate something that was shameful, infantile, degrading.

But I didn't tear it up. Not me, not Judith Gill, not my mother's daughter. I wrote a quick concluding chapter and retyped the whole thing before another Wednesday afternoon passed. I even made a special trip to Coles to buy a sky-blue binder with a special, newly patented steely jaw. And I carried it on the bus with me and delivered it to Furlong's office.

"But I don't want to read it to the class," I told him firmly. "Just do me a favour and read it yourself. And let me know what you think."

He nodded gravely. He consoled me with his tender

smile. He understood. He would take it home with him. I got on the bus and came home and started cooking pork chops for our dinner. And it was then, with hot fat spattering from the pan and the pale meat turning brown that I lurched into truth.

Six-thirty; the hour held me like a hand. Doors slamming, water running, steam rising, the floor tiles under my feet squared off with reality. The clatter of cutlery, a knife pulling down on a wooden board, an onion halved showing rings of pearl; their distinct and separate clarity thrilled me. This was real.

I flew to the phone. My fingers caught in the dial so that twice I made a mistake. *Please be home, please be home!*

He was.

"Furlong. Listen, this is Judith."

"What on earth's the matter?"

"My novel. *The Magic Rocking Horse.*"

"But Judith, I just got home. I've hardly had more than a few minutes to glance at it. But tonight—"

"The point is, Furlong, I've decided not to go ahead with the novel."

"What do you mean—not go ahead? Judith, my girl, you've already done it."

"I mean I want you to dispose of it. Burn it. Tear it up. Now. Immediately."

"You can't be serious. Not after all your work."

"I can. I am." *Christ, he's going to be difficult.*

"Judith, won't you sleep on it. Give it some thought."

"I really mean this, Furlong. Listen to me. I mean it. I'm a grown-up woman and I know what I'm doing."

"Judith."

"Please, Furlong." I was close to tears. "Please."

He agreed.

"But on one condition. That you at least let me finish reading it. You may not have any faith in it, but I think, from the little of it I've seen, that it's not entirely hopeless."

"I don't care, Furlong, just as long as you keep your

promise to get rid of it. And please don't ever discuss it with me. I couldn't bear that."

"Oh, all right. I promise, of course. But what are you going to do, Judith? Try another novel? Take another tack?"

"I'm going to write a biography."

"Who this time?"

"I was thinking of Susanna Moodie."

I had said it almost without thinking, only wanting to reassure Furlong that I wasn't mad. But the moment I uttered the name Susanna Moodie, I knew I was on my way back to sanity, to balance. I was on the way back to being happy.

The very next morning I began.

Sunday afternoon.

We are late, but since it is icy and since Martin is reluctant to go at all, we drive very slowly down the city streets to Furlong's party. I feel under my heavy coat for my wrist watch. We should have been there at one-thirty, and it's almost two now.

I am sitting in the front seat beside Martin, and through my long apricot crepe skirt the vinyl seat covers feel shockingly cold. Because of the snow I have had to wear heavy boots, but my silver sandals are in a zippered bag on the seat.

Meredith is in the back seat and she is leaning forward anxiously, concerned about being late and concerned even more about how she looks. She has been invited at the last minute. Mrs. Eberhardt phoned only this morning to suggest that she come along with us. I had hung about near the telephone listening, knowing for certain that she was being invited to replace some guest who was not able to come, knowing she would be filling in as a fourth at one of the inevitable little tables set up in Furlong's dining room. I had been to Furlong's parties before and knew how carefully the glasses of Beaujolais were counted out, how the seating would have been arranged weeks before and how the petit fours, the exact number, would be waiting in their boxes in the pantry. I would have cheered if Meredith had refused, if she had said she had other plans for this afternoon, but of course she didn't, nor would I have done so in her place.

Under her navy school coat she is wearing a dress of brilliant patchwork, made for her by Martin's mother last Christmas and worn only half a dozen times. She has done something marvellous and unexpected with her hair, lifted it up in the back with a tiny piece of chain, her old charm bracelet perhaps, and her neck rises slenderly, almost elegantly, out of the folds of her coat collar. But her nervousness is extreme.

Martin brakes for a red light and comes slowly, creepingly to a halt. I see his jaw firm, a rib of muscle, he wants only for this afternoon to be ended, to be put behind him.

Now is the moment, I think. Right now in the middle of the city, with apartment buildings all around us. I should ask him now about the eight bundles of wool that had been in his drawer. The fact that Meredith is here with us will only make it seem more normal, just a matter-of-fact question between husband and wife.

"Godamn," he mutters. "We should have bought those snow tires when they were on sale."

I sit tight and don't say a word.

Furlong and his mother live in a handsome 1930s building built of beef-red brick encircling a formal, evergreened courtyard. There is a speaking tube in the walnut foyer, rows of brass mail boxes; and today the inner door is slightly ajar, propped open with a spray of Christmas greenery in a pretty Chinese jardinière. We make our way up a flight of carpeted stairs to the panelled door with the brass parrot-headed knocker. Beyond it we can hear a soft rolling ocean of voices. Meredith and I bend together as though at a signal and exchange our boots for shoes, balancing awkwardly on each foot in turn. Only when we are standing in our fragile sandals does Martin lift the knocker.

It seems miraculous in all that noise that we can be heard, but in a moment Furlong throws open the door and stands before us. He is flushed and excited, and only scolds us briefly for being late. "Of course the roads are deplorable. Meredith, we are delighted, both of us, that you were able to come. You must excuse our phoning you so late, but it just occurred to us that you were a grown-up now and why on earth hadn't we asked you earlier. But give me your coats. I want you to taste my Christmas punch. Martin, you are a man of discernment. Come and see if you can guess what I've concocted this year."

He leads us into a softly lit living room where small circles of women in fluid Christmas dresses, and men, darkly suited and civilized, stand on the dusty-rose carpet. It is a large pale room, faintly period with its satin-covered sofa, its brocaded matching chairs, a cherry secretary, a Chinese table laid out with a punch bowl and a circle of cut-glass cups.

Furlong pours us ruby-pink cups of punch and watches, delighted, as we sip. "Well?" he asks Martin.

"Cranberry juice," Martin says.

"And vodka," I add.

"And something spicy," Martin continues. "Ginger?"

"Eureka!" Furlong says. "You two are the only ones who guessed. Meredith, I'm sure your parents will allow me to give you a little."

"Of course," she and I murmur together.

In a moment Mrs. Eberhardt is upon us, gracious and dramatic in deep purple velvet gathered between her breasts. "We were so afraid you had had an accident. This wretched snow. But I told Furlong not to worry. I knew you wouldn't let us down. Judith, you look delightful." She kisses my cheek. "I can't tell you how grateful we are that you let us have Meredith this afternoon."

Across the room Roger salutes us gaily. I am beginning to make out distinct faces in the early-afternoon light. I recognize Valerie Hyde who writes a quirky bittersweet saga of motherhood for a syndicated column in which she describes the hilarity of babyshit on the walls and the riotous time the cat got into the bouillabaisse just before the guests arrived. Her estranged husband Alfred is on the other side of the room with a hard-faced blonde in a sea-green tube of silk. Ruthie in cherry-coloured pants and a silk shirt is standing alone sipping cranberry-vodka punch and looking drunk and not very happy. I am about to speak to her when I see an immense fat man in a coarse, hand-woven suit. "Who's that?" I ask Mrs. Eberhardt.

She whispers enormously, "That's Hans Kroeger."

"The movie producer?"

"Yes," she says, hugging herself. "Wasn't it lovely he could be here. Furlong is so pleased."

Somewhere a tiny bell is ringing. I look up to see Furlong, silver bell in hand, calling the room to silence. "I know you must be ready for something to eat," he announces with engaging simplicity. "Lunch is ready in the dining room as soon as you are."

It is a large room painted a dull French grey. Half a dozen little tables are draped to the floor in shirred green taffeta—in the centre of each a basket of tiny white flowers.

Close behind me I hear Martin sighing heavily, "Jesus."

"Shut up," I say happily in his ear.

On the buffet table is Sunday lunch. There is a large fresh salmon trimmed with lemon slices and watercress, a pink and beautiful roast of beef being carved by a white-suited man from the caterers; cut-glass bowls of salad, tiny raw vegetables carved into intricate shapes, buttered rolls, crusty to the touch, fine and soft and patrician within; Mrs. Eberhardt's homemade mayonnaise in a silver shell-shaped dish, cheeses, fruit, stacks of Spode luncheon plates.

We serve ourselves and look about for our name cards on the little tables. I am by the window. There is heavy silver cutlery from Mrs. Eberhardt's side of the family, and a thick, luxurious linen napkin at each place. Furlong circulates between tables with red wine, filling each crystal glass a precise two-thirds full.

Everyone is talking. The room is filled with people eating and talking. Talk drifts from table to table, accumulating, rising, until it reaches the ceiling.

Roger is saying: "Of course Canadian culture has to be protected. For God's sake, you're dealing with a sensitive plant, almost a nursery plant. And don't tell me I'm being chauvinistic. I had a year at Harvard, remember. I tell you that if we don't give grants to our writers now and if we don't favour our own publishers now, we're lost, man, we're just lost."

Valerie Hyde is saying: "Of course women have come a long way, but don't think for a minute that one or two women in Parliament are going to change a damn thing. Sex is built-in like bones and teeth, and, remember this, Barney, there's more to sex than cold semen running down your leg."

Alfred Hyde is saying: "Tuesday night we had tickets to *The Messiah*. The tenor was excellent, the baritone was passable, but the contralto was questionable. The staging was commendable, but I seriously question the lighting technique."

Ruthie is saying: "There's just no stability to anything. Did you stop to think of just where this salmon comes from? The fisherman who caught this fish is probably sitting down to pork and beans right now. And what happens when all the salmon is gone? And that just might be tomorrow. What do you say to that? There's just no stability."

Hans Kroeger is saying: "Twenty per cent return on the investment. And that ain't hay. So don't give me any shit about bonds."

A woman across the room is saying: "Take Bath Abbey for instance. Have you been to Bath Abbey? No? Well, take any abbey."

Furlong is saying: "In my day we talked about making a contribution. To the country. But that sounds facile, doing something for one's country. Now don't you agree that one's first concern must be to know oneself? Isn't that what counts?"

Meredith says: "I don't know. I really don't. Like in *Graven Images*, first things come first. I've started in on it for the third time. Empathy. That's what it all comes down to. I mean, doesn't it? Maybe you're right, but making a contribution still counts. I mean, really, in the end, doesn't it? Fulfillment, well, fulfillment is sort of selfish if you know what I mean. I don't know."

The blonde in green is saying, "Anyone from that socio-economic background just never dreams of picking up a book. What I'm saying is this, intelligence is shaped in pre-adolescence. Not the scope of intelligence. Anyone can expand, but the direction. The direction is predetermined."

A man is saying in a very low voice. "Okay, okay, you've had enough booze. Lay off."

Barney Beck is saying: "Class. You're damned right I believe in class. Not because it's good, hell no, but because it's there. Just, for instance, take the way kids cool off in the summer. You've got the little proletarians splashing in the street hydrant, right? And your middle-class brats running through the lawn sprinklers. Because lawns mean middle class, right? Then your nouveaus. The plastic-lined swimming pool. Cabanas, filter systems, et cetera. Then the aristocrats. You don't see them, not actually, because they're at the shore. Wherever the hell the shore is."

Mrs. Eberhardt is saying: "The important thing is to use real lemon and to add the oil one drop at a time, one drop at a time."

And I, Judith Gill, am spinning: I feel my animal spirit unwind, my party self, that progressive personality that goes from social queries about theatre series to compulsive anecdote swapping. I press for equal time. *Stop*, I tell myself. *Let this topic pass without pulling out your hospital story, your vitamin B complex story, your tennis story, your Lester Pearson snippet. Adjust your eyes. Be tranquil. Stop.* I admonish myself, but it's useless. I feel my next story gathering in my throat, the words pulling together, waiting their chance. Here it is. I'm ready to leap in. "Speaking of bananas," I say, and I'm off.

Martin, at the next table, is not talking. What is he doing? He is lifting a forkful of roast beef, and slowly, slowly, he is chewing it. What is he doing now?

He is listening.

January

It was on the first day of the new year that I discovered the reason for Martin's secret cache of wool; the explanation was delivered so offhandedly and with such an aura of innocence that I furiously cursed my suspicions. What on earth had I expected—that Martin had slipped over the edge into lunacy? That, saddened and trapped at forty-one, he might be having a breakdown? Did I think he nursed a secret vice: knitting instead of tippling? Or perhaps that he had acquired a mistress, a great luscious handicraft addict whose fetish it was to crochet while she was being made love to? Crazy, crazy. I was the one who was crazy.

On New Year's Day Martin sat talking to his mother and father who had come from Montreal for the weekend. His father is a professor too, himself the son of a professor; he teaches history at McGill. Gill of McGill, he likes to introduce himself to strangers. He is a spare, speckled man, happiest wearing the loose oatmeal cardigans his wife knits for him and soft old jackets, frayed at the pockets and elbows. His habitual stance is kindly (a Franciscan kindness) and speculative; he is what is known in the world as a good man, possessing all the qualities of a Christian with the exception of faith.

The relationship between Martin and his father is such as might exist between exceedingly fond colleagues. Like brothers they flank Martin's mother, Lala to us, a small woman who except for an unmanageable nest of sparrow-brown, Gibson-girlish hair is attractive and bright, known to her friends in Montreal as a Doer. Her private and particular species of femininity demands gruff male attendance, and she is sitting now in our family room between "her two men," although that is a phrase which she herself would consider too cloying to use.

We have had a late breakfast, coffee and an almond ring brought by Lala from her local ethnic bakery in Montreal. The sun is pouring in through the streaky windows making us all feel drowsy and dull. Richard and Meredith, both of them blotchy with sleep, sprawl in front of the television watching the Rose Bowl Parade. There are newspapers everywhere, on the floor and on the chairs, thick holiday editions. And cups and saucers litter the coffee table. Lala leans back on the sofa, lazily puffing a duMaurier.

Grandpa Gill asks Martin how his course load is going and whether he is doing a paper at the moment. Lala leans bird-like towards them, eager to hear what Martin has to say. I too am roused from torpor. We all wait.

Martin tells his father about the paper that has been turned down. "I'll show it to you if you like," he says. "Apparently it just didn't measure up in terms of originality. One of the referees, anonymous of course, penciled 'derivative' all over it."

"That was bad luck," Grandpa Gill nods.

"What a shame, Martin," Lala adds.

I marvel for the thousandth time at the constancy and perfect accord with which they underscore their son's ability.

"To be honest," Martin continues, "it was pretty dull. But I'm working on something else now which might be a little different."

"Yes?" his mother sings through her smoke.

"Well," Martin says, addressing his father automatically, "I think I can say that I actually got this idea from you."

"Really?" Grandpa Gill smiles.

"Remember that chart you showed me. In your office last fall? A coloured diagram with the structure of world power charted in different colours?"

"Oh, yes. Of course. The Reynolds Diagram. Very useful."

"Well, after I saw that I got to thinking that it might be a good idea to use a diagram approach to themes in epic poetry. To *Paradise Lost* specifically."

"But how would you go about it?" his mother presses him.

"I thought it might be possible to make a graphic of it," Martin says. "Like the Reynolds Diagram, only using wool instead of paint since the themes are so mixed. In places it's necessary to interweave the colours. Sometimes, as you can appreciate, there are as many as four or five themes woven together."

His father nods and asks, "And how have you gone about it?"

"I thought about it for a long time," Martin says.

Where was I while he thought so long and hard?

"Finally I decided on a large rectangle of loose burlap for each of the twelve books. That way the final presentation could be hung together. For comparison purposes."

"I don't get it, Martin," I say, speaking for the first time.

He looks faintly exasperated. "All I did was to take a colour for each theme. For instance, red for God's omnipotence, blue for man's disobedience, green for arrogance, and, let's see, yellow for pride and so on. But you can see," he says, turning again to his father, "that one theme will predominate for a time. And then subside and merge into one of the others."

"And how do you know just where in the text you are?" Grandpa Gill asks.

"I wondered about that," Martin says.

Where was I, his wife, when he wondered about that?

"And I decided to mark off the lines along the side. I've got them printed in heavy ink. The secretary helped ink them in."

She did, did she?

"I think that sounds most innovative," his mother says nodding vigorously and butting out her cigarette.

"Is it nearly finished?" his father asks.

"Almost. I hope to present it in March."

"Present it where?" I ask, trying to control the quaver in my voice.

"The Renaissance Society. It's meeting in Toronto this year. I've already sent in an abstract."

"I'm anxious to see it," Lala says. "Is it here at home?"

"No. I've been putting it together at the university. But next time you come down I'll show it off to you. It should be all done by then."

"But Martin," I say, "you've never mentioned any of this to me."

"Didn't I?" He gazes at me. "I thought I did."

I give him a very long and level look before replying, "You never said a single word about it to me."

"Well, now that I have told you, what do you think?"

"Do you really want to know?"

All three of them turn to me in alarm. "Of course," Martin says.

Wildly I reach out for the right word—"I think it's, well, I think it's absurd."

"Why?" Martin asks.

"Yes, why, Judith?" his father asks.

I am confused. And unwilling to hurt Martin and certainly not wanting to upset his parents whom I like. But the project seems to me to be spun out of lunacy.

I try to explain. "Look," I say, "I can't exactly put it into words, but it sounds a bit desperate. Do you know what I mean?"

"No," Martin says, more shortly than usual.

"What I mean is, literature is literature. Poetry is poetry. It's made out of words. You don't work poems in wool."

"What you're saying is that it's disrespectful to the tradition."

"No, that's not really it. I don't care about the tradition. It's just that you might look foolish, Martin. And desperate. Don't you see, it's gimmicky, and you've never been one for gimmicks."

"For Christ's sake, Judith, don't make too much of it.

It's just a teaching aid."

The children have turned from the television now and are watching us. Grandpa Gill and Lala, almost imperceptibly, shrink away from us.

"Martin, you've always been so sensible. Can't you see that this is just, well, just a little undignified. I mean, I just feel it's beneath you somehow."

"I don't see what's so undignified about trying something new for a change. Christ, Judith. You're the one who thinks the seventeenth century is such a bore. Literature can be damn dull. And especially Milton."

"I agree. I agree."

"What I'm doing is making a pictorial presentation of themes which will give a quick comprehensive vision of the total design. It's quite simple and straightforward."

"Couldn't you just do a paper on it?"

"No. No, I could not."

"Why not?"

"How can you put a design image into prose?"

"What about that paper they turned down. Couldn't you do that one over for them?"

"No."

"So instead you've dreamed up this lunatic scheme."

"Judith, we're talking in circles. I don't think it's all that idiotic. What do you think, Dad?"

Grandpa Gill regards me. Clearly he does not want to join in the foray, but he is being pressed. He speaks cautiously: "I think I partially understand what Judith is worried about. The publish-or-perish syndrome does occasionally have the effect of forcing academics to make asses of themselves. But, on the other hand, cross-disciplinary approaches seem to be well thought of at the moment. A graphic demonstration of a literary work, with the design features stressed, might make quite an interesting presentation if—"

I interrupt, out of exasperation, for I know he can go on in this vein for hours. "Look, Martin there's another thing.

And I hate to say this because it sounds so narrow-minded and conventional, but I, well, the truth is—I can't bear to think of you sitting there in your office weaving away. I mean—do you know what I mean?—do you—don't you think it's just a little bit—you know—?"

"Effeminate?" he supplies the word.

"Eccentric. It's the sort of thing Furlong Eberhardt might dream up."

"And I suppose you think that reference will guarantee instant dismissal of the whole idea."

"Oh, Martin, for heaven's sake, do what you want. I just hate you to look ridiculous."

"To whom? To you?"

"Forget it. I don't even know why we're discussing it." I start picking up newspapers and gathering together the coffee cups. Lala springs to my side, but I tell her not to bother; I can manage.

I feel strange as I carry the cups into the kitchen. A nervy dancing fear is spinning in my stomach, and I lean on the sink for support. A minute ago I had been overjoyed that Martin's wool was to be put to so innocent a purpose. What has happened? What am I afraid of?

Guilt presses; I should have been more consoling when his paper was turned down. I should take greater interest in his work. Year after year he sweats out the required papers and what interest do I show? I proofread them, take out commas, put his footnotes in order. And that's it. No wonder he's developed a soft spot on the brain. To conceive of this bit of madness, actually to carry it through.

And to carry it out furtively, covertly. For I am certain he deliberately withheld the project from me. Perhaps from everyone else as well. He probably even pulls the curtains in his office and locks the door when he weaves. I try to picture it—Martin tugging at the wool, sorting his needles, tightening his frame, and then pluck, pluck, in and out, in and out. My husband, Martin Gill, weaving away his secret afternoons.

It might even be better if he did have a mistress. One could understand that. One could commiserate; one could forgive. But what can be done with a man who makes a fool of himself—what do you do then?

Martin is crazy. He's lost his grip. Or is it me? I try to think logically, but my stomach is seized by pain. I try to construct the past few months, to remember exactly when Martin last mentioned something about his work. I sit down on the kitchen stool and try to concentrate, but my head whirls. When did he last discuss the seventeenth century? *Paradise Lost?* The Milton tradition? Or something temporal such as his lecture schedule. When? I can't remember.

And then I think with a stab of pain, when did we last make love with anything more than cordiality?

My head pounds. I open the cupboard and find a bottle of aspirin. And then, though it is just a little past noon, I creep upstairs and get into bed. The sheets are cool and deliciously flat. Below me in the family room I can hear the Rose Bowl Game beginning.

Hours later I awake in the darkened room. In the upstairs hall the light is burning brutally; long, startling El Greco shadows cut across the bedroom wall. Footsteps, whispers, the rattle of teacups. Someone reaches for my hand, places a cold cloth on my forehead.

"Thank you, thank you," I want to say, but my voice has disappeared, in its place a dry cracked nut of pain. My lips have split; I can taste blood. The inside of my mouth is unfamiliar, a clutch of cottonwool.

"Drink this," someone says.

"No, no," I rasp.

"Please, Judith. Try. It may help."

Lala was sitting on the edge of my bed, a figurine, a blue-tinted shepherdess. She was pressing a teaspoon toward me. I opened my mouth. Aspirin. Aspirin crushed in strawberry jam; its peculiar bitter, slightly citrus flavour reaches me from the forest of childhood (my father crushing aspirin on the breadboard with the back of a teaspoon when my sister and I had measles, yes).

A drink of water, and I lay back exhausted. Again the cool, wet cloth. Again the mellifluous voice. "There, there. Now just sleep. Don't worry. Just rest, dear."

What choice had I but to obey; the lack of choice, the total surrender of will enclosed me like a drug. I slept.

There followed another long blurred space.

Several times I woke up choking on the thick cactus growth in my throat. And to my inexplicable grief, every time I opened my eyes it was still dark. If only it were light, I remember thinking, I could bear it. If only this long night would end, I would be all right.

But when the light finally did come, milky through the frosted-over windows, I couldn't look at it without pain. It battered my stripped nerve ends, pierced me through with its harsh squares. Anguish. To be so helpless. The wet plush tongue of the facecloth descended again. Coolness. It was Meredith.

In all her sixteen years I had never heard such sadness in her voice. It curled in and out of her breath like a ballad.

"Mother. Oh, Mother. Are you any better?"

Was that my voice that squawked "yes"? I said it to comfort her, not because it was true.

"The doctor's coming. Dr. Barraclough is coming. Any minute, Mother. After his hospital rounds. He said as soon after ten as he could make it."

I moaned faintly, involuntarily.

"Is there anything you'd like, Mother? A nice cup of tea?"

In my angle of pain I could only think of what a strange phrase that was for Meredith to use—a nice cup of tea. Did I ever say it? My mother certainly did. Lala did too. Even Martin did. But did I? Out of kindness or ritual or sympathy did I ever in all my life offer anyone such a thing as a "nice cup of tea"? If not, then how did I come to have a daughter who was able to utter, unself-consciously, such a perfect and cottage phrase—*a nice cup of tea*?

Her voice rocked with such mourning that I felt I must accept. From the roof of my mouth a small scream escaped, saying "Yes please."

She fled to the kitchen joyfully, only to be replaced by Martin. "My poor Judith. My poor little Judith."

Again it was the phrase I perceived, not the situation. "My poor little Judith," he had called me. Echoes of courtship, when he had used those exact words often. And I am not little. Tall and lanky then, I am tall and large now, not fat, of course, only what the world calls a fair-sized woman; my size has always defined my sense of myself, made me less serious, freer of vanity, for good or bad.

"My poor little Judith," he had said. I reached out a hand and felt it taken.

"Poor Judith. My poor sick Judith."

So that was it: I was sick.

"Just try to rest, love. You've got some kind of flu. And you've had a bugger of a night."

I strangled with agreement.

"Mother and Dad had to leave. Early this morning. They were awfully worried, especially Mother."

I thought of Lala sitting on the edge of my bed in some half-blocked fantasy. Aspirin and strawberry jam. We had met at that level. I clutched Martin's hand harder. I wanted him to stay and, miraculous, he didn't hurry away.

Richard poked his head around the doorway. I was shocked at his size, for viewed from this unfamiliar angle, he seemed suddenly much taller. A stranger. And miserably shy.

"Meredith says, do you want some toast?"

"No," I croaked. Then I added, "No thank you." Etiquette. My mother's thin etiquette surfacing.

I fell asleep again, woke momentarily to see the tea, cold and untouched in its pottery cup. Sleep, sleep.

The doctor comes. A provincial tennis champion, now barely thirty-five. Too young to wield such power. Permanently suntanned from all those holidays in the Bahamas, hands lean across the backs, a look of cash to his herringbone jacket. Money rolling in, but who cares, who cares?

"Well, well, what have we here?" he whistles good cheer.

Sullenly I refuse to answer or even listen to such heartiness.

He does the old routine, listens to heart—is my nightgown clean?—temperature, pulse, blood pressure. A searing little light with a cold metal tip pokes into throat, nostrils, ears. Eyelids rolled back.

"You're sick," he says leaning back. "A real sick girl."

And you're a fatuous ass, I long to say, but how can I, for he and only he can deliver me from my width of wretchedness. Already he is writing something on a pad of paper. I can—I can be restored.

He speaks to Martin; perhaps he considers that I am too ill to comprehend. "I can only give her something to make her more comfortable. It's a virus, you know, a real tough baby, it looks like, and there's nothing we can give for a virus."

"Nothing?" Martin asks unbelieving.

"Rest, plenty of liquids, that's about it."

"But how about an antibiotic or something?"

"Won't work," he says, brushing Martin off—how dare he!—picking up his overcoat, feeling in his pocket for his car keys.

Meredith sees him to the door, and Martin and I are left in immense quiet. The Baby Ben is ticking on the night table. In spite of my contagious condition, Martin lies down on his side of the rumpled bed. He lies carefully on top of the bedspread and in less than a minute he has fallen asleep. I am obscurely angered that he has violated my bed with his presence. The walls dissolve, the silence is enormous. I think, *I can't bear this.* And then I too fall asleep.

For days the fever laps away at me. My scalp, after a week, feels so tender that I can hardly comb my hair. My arms and legs ache, and my back is so sore that I keep an extra pillow under it.

The efforts of Martin and the children to comfort me are so great and so constant that I wish I could rouse myself to gratitude. But it is too tiring. I can do nothing but lie in bed and accept.

I have never in my adult life been so ill. I can hardly believe I am suffering from something as ubiquitous as flu, and it seems preposterous that I can be this ill and still not require hospitalization. The doctor comes once again, pats me roughly on the back and says, "Well, Judith, I think you're going to surprise us and weather this after all."

My illness shocks me by giving me almost magical powers of perception; the restless, feverish days have sharpened my awareness to the point of pain. Phrases I hear every day acquire new meaning. I find myself analyzing for hours what is casually uttered. The way, for instance, that Dr. Barraclough calls me Judith now that I have become an author. All sorts of people, in fact, whom I know in a remote and professional way began using my first name the moment my first book came out, as though I had somehow come into the inheritance of it, as though I had entered into the public domain, had left behind that dumpy housewife, Mrs. Gill. *Judith.* I became Judith.

And Meredith who has called me Mother for years is suddenly calling me Mommy again. I lie here in bed, a sick doll, my limbs helpless, living on asparagus soup, and am called Mommy by my sixteen-year-old daughter.

Another observation. Richard doesn't call me anything. He pokes his head in, sometimes even sits for a minute on the edge of the bed. "Would you like the newspaper?" he will ask. Or "Do we have any postage stamps? Any air-letters?" But these statements, requests, questions have, I notice, a bald quality. I analyze them. I have time to ana-lyze them. What gives them their flat spare sound is the lack of any salutation. I ponder the reasons. Is he caught in that slot of growth where Mommy is too childish, Mother too severe and foreign? What did he use to call me? When he was little? Now that I think of it, did he ever call me anything? I can't remember. It's curious. And worrying in an obscure way which I am unable, because of my present weakness or because of a prime failing, to understand.

After ten days I began to stay awake longer. The nights lost their nightmare quality, and the joints in my body tormented me less. I was cheered by a letter from my sister and wryly amused by another from my mother. Martin had phoned to tell her I was sick; she was not to worry if she didn't get her weekly letter. Her letter to me was a harping scold from beginning to end. I did too much, she wrote. I wore myself out, wore my fingers to the bone. I should get Martin to take over more of the household chores. Meredith should be washing dishes at her age, and there was no reason she couldn't take over the ironing. Richard could be more helpful too. But basically, I was at fault. I had done too much Christmas entertaining, she accused. Too much shopping, sent too many cards. I shouldn't have invited Martin's parents for New Year's; they had a home of their own, didn't they? And very comfortable too. And why didn't Martin's sister in P.E.I. have them for a change. I should forget about my biographies until the children were older and off my hands.

I read it all, shaking my head. It had always been that way. My sister and I had been scolded for every scraped knee—"I told you you weren't watching." There were no bright badges of mercurochrome for us—"Next time you'll be more careful." For diarrhea we were rewarded with "Play with the Maddeson children and what do you expect?" Even our childhood illnesses were begrudged us. I thought of Lala spooning aspirin into me on New Year's night. And I recalled the first time I had met her. Martin had taken me home for a weekend to Montreal, and he had mentioned to his mother that he had a slight rash on the back of his hands. "Oh dear," she had cried, "what a bother! That can be so irritating. Now let me see. I think I have just the thing. Just squeeze a little of this on, and if that doesn't work we'll just pop you over to the doctor."

I had listened amazed; such acceptance, such outpouring concern. Such willingness to proffer cups of tea, cream soups, poached eggs on toast. Imagine!

And so, although I lie suffering in my arms, legs, stomach, sinus, throat, skin, ears, eyes and kidneys, I am, at least, free of guilt. It is incredible, but no one with the exception of my mother—and she is far away in her multihued bunga-low in Scarborough—no one blames me for being sick. Indeed, they almost seem to believe that I am entitled to an illness; that I have earned the right to take to my bed.

I heard Meredith talking to Gwendolyn on the tele-phone, her voice arched with pride, saying that I had never been sick before. And when Roger dropped in one evening to bring me an armful of magazines, Martin told him in a somewhat self-congratulatory tone, "First time in her life that Judith's been hit like this."

The children went back to school early in January, and Martin too had to go back to the university. But he left me only for his lectures, spending the rest of the time at home. It was curious, the two of us in the house together day after day, reminiscent almost of our early married years when he had been a graduate student and we had lived a close, intimate and untidy apartment life with no special hours for meals or bedtimes; our rituals were in their infancy then.

He works at the little card table in our bedroom where I usually work. Because he is here so much and because my sinuses hurt too much for me to read, I find myself locked into an absorbing meditation with Martin, my husband Martin, at its centre. Endlessly I think about him and the shape his life has taken and about the curious but not disagreeable distance that has grown between us. My days of fever confer on me a ferocious insight, and I find I can observe Martin with a startling new, almost X-ray vision.

Martin. Martin Gill, I try to define you, and since I've no machinery, no statistical tools, I do it the easy way, by vocation—but you know yourself how little vocation defines anyone. I play categories; I take the number of universities in this province—it's about ten, isn't it?—and divide that number into departments, allowing about one-twelfth of any university involved in the teaching of English language and literature. And then I divide that in six, allowing for Am. Lit., Can. Lit., Anglo-Saxon, Elizabethan, Victorian, Mods—better make that about one-seventh in Renaissance, and there—I have you pinned down, Martin. You see, you are statistically definable, but where do we go from here? Isolate the Renaissance group and ask, how many of them are in their early forties, own a house with a still sizable mortgage, are married to largish wives with intellectual (but not really) leanings. And children. Children with the usual irritations but, thank God, cross yourself unbeliever though you be, no mongoloids, no cleft palates, no leaky hearts, leukemia, no fatal automobile accidents, no shotgun weddings, no drug charges, just two normal children, and we do love them, don't we Martin?

Once, about ten years or so ago, I came across a pile of Martin's lecture notes. And scribbled in the margin were clusters of scribbled notations in his handwriting. "Explain in depth." "Draw parallel with Dante." "Explain cosmos—the idea at the time—use diagram." "Joke about Adam's rib—ask, is it relevant?" "Stress!!!" "Question for understanding of original sin." "Don't push this point—alien concept." "What would Freud say about this response?" "Ask for conclusions at this point—sum up."

They were messages. Messages partly cryptic, partly illuminating, the little knobs upon which he hung his communications, notations to himself. *Did I write messages to myself? What were they?* Martin's fringe of marginal notes and messages reminded me—yes, I admitted it—reminded me that he possessed an existence of his own to which I did not belong, which I did not understand and which—be truthful now, Judith—which I did not really want to understand.

On Martin's side of the family, no one has the slightest degree of mechanical ability. His grandfather never even learned to drive a car, and his father cannot do the simplest household repairs; he is even somewhat vain about his lack of dexterity. A handyman, a Mr. Henshawe who is almost a family retainer, comes regularly to change washers, re-hang doors, even to install cuphooks.

It is only natural that Martin has inherited the family ineptness—how could it be otherwise?—but unlike his father, it is not a source of pride with him. Handymen are expensive and unreliable nowadays, and professors do not earn large salaries. I suspect he would like to be able to fix the water heater or put up bookshelves himself. When he looks at Richard he must see that his son will be heir to his inabilities and subject to his niggling expenses. What does he think then?

About three years ago Martin came home with a small flat box from the Hudson's Bay Company. I was making a salad in the kitchen, and I glanced at the box hopefully, thinking that he might have bought me a gift as he sometimes does. "What's that?" I asked, slicing into a tomato.

He folded back a skin of tissue paper and lifted out a small bow tie, a small crimson silky bow-tie, and held it aloft as though it were a model aircraft, rotating it slowly for my inspection.

I was so astonished I could only gasp, "What is it?"

"A tie."

"But who is it for?"

"For me," he said, smiling and holding it under his chin.

"But you've never worn a bow tie."

"That's where you're wrong. I wore one for years. A red one. Just like this. Every Friday night at the school dance."

"But Martin, that was back in the days when people wore bow ties."

"They're making a comeback. The man at the Bay said so."

"I can't see you in it," I said. "I just can't see you actually wearing a thing like that."

And he never did. When I straighten his top drawer I always see that same flat Hudson's Bay box, and inside is the bow tie still in its tissue paper. When I see it I can't help but speculate about the moment that prompted him to buy it, but the impulses of others are seldom understandable; they seem to spring out of irrational material, out of the dark soil of the subconscious. But I have respect for impulses and for the mystery they suggest. Even the madness they hint at. That's why I have never mentioned the tie to Martin again. I just straighten his drawer and put everything back neatly and then shut it again.

Why then can't I shut out the wool?

Martin Gill, B.A., M.A., Ph.D. (with distinction)

Age—forty-one

Appearance—somewhat boyish. Never handsome but has been described as agreeable looking, pleasant; his greatest physical charm springs from a slow-motion smile (complete with good-looking eye crinkles, dimple on left cheek, decent teeth) and accompanied by rough-tumbling tenor laugh.

Profession—Associate Professor of English. Specialty— Milton.

Politics—Leftish, Fabianish, believes socialism is "cry of anguish." Like his father, grandfather, etc. Milton would have been a socialist, he believes, if he were alive now. He has made this remark, at the most, three times. He is not a man who is "given" to certain expressions.

Likes—simple things (one friend calls him Martin the Spartan). Reads newspapers, a few magazines, anything written before 1830 and a selection of contemporary writings. Also likes family, friends, a good meal, a good beer, a good laugh, a well-told story, a touchdown or a completed pass, Scrabble (if he is winning), sex (especially in the morning and with a minimum of acrobatics), children (his own exclusively), a clean bathroom in which to take a vigorous shower with very hot water.

Prospects—getting older. More of same. One or perhaps two more promotions, continued fidelity.

Susanna Moodie always called her husband Moodie. His name was John Wedderburn Dunbar Moodie, but she called him Moodie, and I frequently wonder how a woman could love a man she called Moodie. But she must have loved him, at least at first. I am reminded of a girl I knew at university, a small, rodent-faced girl, excessively intellectual and rather nasty, named Rosemary, who was majoring in modern poetry and who, when I told her I was going to marry Martin Gill, said, "How could anyone fuck a Milton specialist?"

Martin has a touching respect for modern technology, regarding it as a cult practised by priests in another dimension of human intelligence.

Once when our car was still new, we were driving in an ice storm, and he turned on the defrost button. Together we watched a semicircle of glass mysteriously clear itself; soft, moist breath came out of nowhere, ready at the touch of a button to lick through the ice. "Wonderful," he murmured, smiling his slow smile. He shook his head and said it again, "Wonderful."

Another time we phoned to Canada from England. I stood with him in the cramped and freezing corner callbox. The operator said, "Just a minute, love," and somehow the wires obeyed. Voices actually filtered through, recognizable voices from across the ocean. He could hardly believe it. He held the receiver a little away from him and regarded it with wonder. "God," he said to me, "can you believe it?"

And flying home to Canada in the gigantic jet he watched out the window as the wing flaps went through their taking off performance. The wheels rushed under the floor, a stewardess passed out chewing gum; everything seemed wonderfully orchestrated; even the no-smoking signs blinked in time and a quartet of lissome stewardess demonstrated an oxygen mask in the aisle, stylized as a ballet. When we were aloft with the green fields curving beneath us, Martin looked out the window, incredulous, almost mad with joy, gripping my hand. "What do you think of that?" he whispered.

The little battery shaver I gave him for Christmas holds magic for him. He cups it in his hand, loving its compressed and secret energy. The timing mechanism of my oven delights him, and he likes to think of the blue waterfalls performing inside the dishwater. Sometimes I think he has not quite caught up to this age, that he is hanging back a little on purpose out of some mysterious current in his disposition which hungers for miracles.

I am still sick. Not in a state of suffering as I was, but exhausted. The least effort is too much for me. Yesterday I got up to look for a library book, and after a moment's searching I collapsed back into bed. It wasn't worth it; I am too tired to read anyway.

In the mornings I lie in bed listening to the radio. The melange of music, news spots and interviews soothes; it is a monotonous droning, familiar and comforting; it demands nothing of me. I welcome passivity.

One morning Martin climbed back into bed with me. We scanned the newspapers together and then lay back to listen to the radio. We heard some funny tunes from the Forties, an interview with an ecologist whose passion leaked out over the airwaves, a theatre review, another interview, this one quite funny. I noticed that Martin and I, lying on our backs, laughed in exactly the same places. Almost as though we were reading cue cards. We have never done this before, never lain in bed all morning listening to the radio, laughing together. The novelty of it is striking. It comes as a surprise. And it is all the more surprising because I had thought there could be no more surprises.

Martin fell in love with me because of my vivacity, or so he says, which would mean that he at forty-one is sadly swindled. Perhaps he didn't understand that what he took to be vivacity was only a gust of nervous energy which surfaced in my early twenties, a reaction probably to the cartoon tidiness of Scarborough. Whatever it was, it has more or less drained away, appearing only occasionally in lopsided, frenetic moments. But I can still, if I try, conjure it up. I can charm him still, make him look at me with love. But it requires a tremendous effort of the will. Concentration. Energy. And that may eventually go too. People change, and I suppose everyone has to accept that.

I've noticed, for instance, something about my mother, who all her married life busied herself redecorating her six small rooms in Scarborough; plaster, paint, paper, varnish, they were her survival equipment. But when my father died, a quiet death, a heart attack in his sleep, she stopped decorating. The house seemed to fall away from her. She still lives there, of course, but there is no more fresh paint, no newly potted plants; she has not even rearranged the furniture since he died. And though I know this must be significant and that it must in some way say something about their life together, I am reluctant to dwell on the reasons. I want to push it away from me like Martin's plans to reproduce *Paradise Lost* in wool. (He has not mentioned it since New Year's Day; he has, in fact, very carefully avoided it. And so have I.)

I am feeling well enough to have visitors. Nancy Krantz came one day bringing a chicken casserole for the family, and for me, a new Iris Murdoch novel, expensively hard-covered and just exactly what I had yearned for.

Roger Ramsay brought us a bottle of his homemade wine, and he and Martin and I sit one evening in the bed-room sipping it, I in my most attractive dressing gown, propped up by pillows. But to my tender throat the wine is excruciatingly acidic.

Roger is despondent; his blue jean jacket hangs mourn-fully from his shoulders, and his hair falls in his eyes. It seems he and Ruthie have quarreled and that she has left him. Where has she gone? I ask him. He doesn't know. He phones the library where she works every day, but she re-fuses to speak to him. What is the problem? I ask. He shrugs. He isn't sure.

I find I cannot join into his depression. Three weeks in bed have made me incapable of sympathy. Besides I cannot believe Ruthie would leave him for good.

We sip wine and talk; it's only nine-thirty and already I'm wearing down. Martin notices, and I see him signal Roger that it's time to go. He stands up awkwardly, but-tons his denim jacket, kisses my hand with such gentleness that I feel tears standing in my eyes. Poor Roger.

Ruthie doesn't come to see me, but she sends a basket of fruit and a card saying only: "Jude, take care. I love you, Ruthie."

Furlong brings a huge and expensive book of photo-graphs. $21.50. He has neglected to detach the price. *Canada: Its Future and Its Now*, the sort of book I seldom pick up. But it's somehow perfect for convalescence. And his mother sends along a jar of red currant jelly which is the first good thing I've tasted all month. She made it herself and poured it into this graceful pressed-glass jar. Meredith spreads it on toast every day and brings it with a pot of tea before she leaves for school. She brings bread from our favourite Boston Bakery which means she walks an extra two miles. I could weep.

Richard lends me his portable record player and from his allowance he buys me a new LP. Stravinsky. He has grown shy. He doesn't quite look me in the eye, but he talks about "when you get better" as though all things of worth hinge on that condition.

Martin is attentive. Unfailing. Why am I so surprised? Is it because he's not been tested before? He sets up my typewriter on the bed one day when I feel that I've neglected Susanna Moodie long enough.

Susanna. I've reached a place in her life where she makes, with a single imaginative stroke, an attempt to rescue herself, an attempt to alter her life. It is the single anomaly of her life, an enormous biographical hiatus, a time-fold, a geological faultline which remains visible for the rest of her life.

Bizarre though it may seem today, her single decisive act proceeded directly out of the skein of her desperation, and it's possible that her intercession wasn't all that remarkable in the context of her time.

The situation couldn't have been worse. John Moodie, Susanna's husband had botched it as a farmer; not his fault perhaps, for the sort of gentlemanly farming he had envisioned was simply not possible in the Canadian bush. But he had gone down with a deplorable lack of style, and comes across as a limping, whining man, a poor loser, dogged by misfortune, the sort of misfortune which is almost invited. He sold his only possession, a military commission, and squandered the money on worthless steamboat stock. Although Susanna tried gamely to lighten his portrait here and there by referring to his flute playing, his literary discourse, his attempts at writing, he is ever sour and irritable and heavy-footed, not a man to grow old and mellow with.

By 1837 he admitted that he had failed as a backwoodsman; he was in debt; his wife was expecting her fifth child, and winter was coming. Their condition was deteriorating rapidly when they received word that a rebellion had broken out in Toronto. Almost all the ablebodied men in the neighbourhood, including John Moodie, were called away to fight, and the prospect of regular pay was greeted with joy. Moodie sent home some of his money to Susanna who used it to pay off debts. Alone all winter with her children and a hired girl, she had a chance to reflect on the family prospects. She too admitted the farm had been a mistake. Worse still, Moodie wrote that the rebellion was over and the regiment was about to be disbanded; he would soon be without pay again.

Driven nearly to madness, Susanna sat down and wrote a long confessional and impassioned letter to Sir George Arthur who was the Lieutenant-Governor of Upper Canada, outlining the series of disasters that had befallen the family and begging him to keep her husband on in the militia. Her efforts were rewarded, for Moodie was soon made Paymaster to the Militia and later appointed Sheriff of the District of Victoria.

The letter is astonishing enough; but even more extraordinary is the fact that John Moodie never knew about it. He speculated that he was probably awarded the paymaster position because of his exemplary sobriety while in the militia. And the office of sheriff because of his honest performance as paymaster.

It seems almost beyond belief that the story of the letter never leaked out, that Susanna herself never once in all those years let slip to her husband the true cause of his sudden elevation in society. Or was John Moodie bluffing? It is a possibility; to save face he may have neglected to mention the enormous step his wife took to save him. But it is just as possible, even probable, that she kept her secret, kept it all her life, either to spare his pride or to avoid seeming too much the schemer.

They were a married couple, shared a bed, faced each other over a supper table well into old age—all this with a secret between them. Secrets. I never did tell Martin that I had read John Spalding's manuscripts. He would not have liked it; he would have looked at me with less than love; it might even have damaged the balance between us. And he, for perhaps the same reason, put off telling me about the woollen tapestries. He must have guessed how I would react. Secrets are possible. And between people who love each other, maybe even necessary.

One night I woke at one o'clock. I had been asleep for two hours; the house was deathly quiet, and beside me, Martin was breathing deeply. I sat up and wondered what had wakened me so suddenly and so completely. A loud noise? a branch breaking? an icicle falling? a burglar? I listened. There was nothing but a faint gnawing of wind. I got out of bed and went over to the window. There everything was serene; the curving road was touched with ice-blue shadows. The street light poured a steady milk-white light on the snow, beautiful.

Then I realized what it was that had wakened me: I was well. I was restored to health. In the complicated sub-knowledge of my body chemistry, health had been re-announced. A click like an electric switch marked the end of illness. I stretched with health, with a feeling almost of being reborn. Strength, joy.

I had been sick almost a whole month, enclosed in the wide, white parentheses of weakness, part of a tableau of trays and orange juice and aspirin tablets. I had inhabited a loop of time, been assaulted by an uneasy coalition of suffering and perception, and now I was to be released.

Outside the window, possibility sparkled on every bush and tree. My household was asleep; in dark caves my husband and children dreamed. Heat puffed up from the basement furnace and entered every corner of the house. In the kitchen marvellous things lay on shelves, delicate and tempting. The refrigerator held the unspeakable pleasures of bacon and eggs. I was starved.

Downstairs I switched on a light, blinded at first by the brightness. I found a frying pan and butter, lots of butter, and humming I prepared my feast. And ate it all, believing that nothing had ever tasted so good before.

Thoughts stormed through my head, plans, what I would do tomorrow, the next day, the next. I paced. There was no point in going back to bed in this state. I poked in the family room for old magazines, something, anything to read.

Graven Images lay upside down on the arm of the green chair where Meredith had left it. Furlong glinted at me from the back cover. I picked it up thinking, why not see what it's about. This was the perfect time.

I slung myself on the sofa, my feet dragging over one end, my dressing gown pulled around me, for I was beginning to feel chilly. And the greyness of fatigue was making my head ache. But I opened the book and began to read.

I went through the first chapter quickly, irritated by the familiar Eberhardt style. But I went on to the second chapter anyway, proceeding through waves of boredom into shock, incredulity, anger. I finished the last chapter at dawn, at seven o'clock, a thin nervous time, my whole body chilled with disbelief and dull accumulated rage. How could you, Furlong!

My heart was beating wildly; I could feel it through the heavy quilting of my dressing gown. Anger almost choked me, but in spite of it (or maybe even because of it), I fell instantly asleep where I was, cramped on the sofa with *Graven Images* upside down on my chest.

February

"These severe cases of flu are almost always followed by depression," Dr. Barraclough warned me. "Watch out not to get too tired or emotionally overwrought. Just sit back, Judith. No running around. And above all," he warned, "no worrying."

But the minute I was on my feet, the solicitude around me evaporated. Meredith's morning trays came to a halt and Richard took back his record player. Martin woke me at seven-thirty sharp to make breakfast. If it hadn't been for Frieda who came once a week to clean the house, we would have fallen apart completely. For I *was* tired. I *was* depressed; the world did indeed seem full of obscure threatening dangers, treacheries, mean cuts and thrusts, insults briskly traded, conniving jealousies, nursed grudges, selfish hang-ups, greed, opportunism, ego, desperation and stupidity; in addition, I felt too weary to cope with the overpowering, wounding and private betrayal of *Graven Images*.

I dragged through the first week of February alternating between rage and depression, sore to the bone and overwhelmed by exhaustion. Furlong Eberhardt and his casual treason plucked at me hourly. I could not forget it for a minute. I had been used. Used by a friend. Taken advantage of. Furlong who had been trusted (although not always loved) had stolen something from me, and that act made him both thief and enemy.

So simply, so transparently, and so unapologetically had he stolen the plot for *Graven Images*—stolen it from me who had in turn stolen it from John Spalding who—it occurred to me for the first time—might have stolen it from

107

someone else. The chain of indictment might stretch back infinitely, crime within crime within crime.

But the fact remained that it was Furlong who had actually gone through with it. A nefarious, barefaced theft. I had at least resisted temptation; and although it had not been the thought of plagiarism which had deterred me, but rather the inability to reconcile the real with the unreal—"that willing suspension of disbelief" when the moment required—still I had resisted, and that resistance bestowed on me a species of innocence. I was no more than a neutral party, a mere agent of transfer. On the other hand, was corruption transferable by simple infection?

I preferred not to think about it; large abstract problems of sin have never been my specialty. It is the casual treason between individuals, the miniature murders of sensibility which chew away at me, and what Furlong had done was to help himself to something that had been mine. That it hadn't been mine in the first place was immaterial, for as far as he knew the plot had been my idea, my conception, my child.

Would it have mattered, I asked myself, if he had told me, or if he had asked permission; if he had perhaps suggested that, since I wasn't interested in developing the idea myself, would I mind terribly if he more or less appropriated it? Would I have smiled, gracious at such a request? Would I have said, of course, help yourself, someone might as well have the use of it, as though it were a pound of hamburger he was borrowing or the use of my typewriter?

I doubt it. I'm too possessive, and besides I would then have had to confess my theft from John Spalding. And the thought of John Spalding was beginning to weigh on me. Furlong, after all, had done quite well with the sales of *Graven Images*. It was, in fact, selling better than any of his previous books for the simple reason that it was better than any of the others. And there was no doubt about the reason for that: it was the first book he had ever written which contained anything like a structure, a structure which was derived from a plot which he had stolen, which he had acquired (to use horse-breeders' jargon) by me out of John Spalding.

Not only were his royalties promising, but he had sold the film rights for what Martin assured me must be a handsome figure. He was going to benefit enormously, while John Spalding, in contrast, sat tormented and constipated in Birmingham, lusting for recognition and trying to stretch his lecturer's salary, month by meagre month, to cover the cheapest existence he could devise: bacon dripping on his bread, I imagined, and doing his own repairs on the third-hand Morris, tripe and onion instead of Sunday joint, and smoking his Woodbines down to their frazzled ends. It was monumentally unjust.

Of course I realized I would have to confront Furlong; it was unthinkable to let this pass. But for that I needed strength. I would have to wait until I was stronger. The phrase "girding my loins" occurred to me. I would need to arm myself, for I was still weak, hardly able to cook a meal without flopping exhausted back into bed. And for reasons which Dr. Barraclough might recognize, I was continually on the verge of weeping.

Tears stood like pin pricks in the backs of my eyes. I was prepared to cry over anything. Martin called from the university to say he would be staying late to work. He didn't say what he would be working on, but we both knew; and when I thought of him in his cork-walled solitude, selecting and blending his wools, threading his needles and weaving away, woof and warp, in and out, I wanted to sob with anguish.

Meredith encloses herself in her room. She is re-reading all of Furlong's books, and our copy of *Graven Images* has been marked and underlined. Exclamation points stand in the margins, the corners of pages have been turned under to indicate her favourite passages. She listens to music and reads and reads. Her loneliness and the sort of love she is imagining tears at me, but there is nothing I can do but leave her to her disk jockeys and the comfort of printed pages.

And I bleed for Richard. There was no letter for him this week. He could hardly believe it at first. Then we read about the postal strike in Britain, and he breathed with relief. The reason, at least, was known. Circumstances were beyond his immediate control; he would have to wait.

He checks the newspapers daily for news of the strike, mentioning it offhandedly to us so we won't suspect how much he cares or how dependent he has grown on the weekly letters from Anita Spalding. "When the strike ends, there's going to be a real bonanza," he says, picturing the accumulated letters pouring in all at once. The thought sustains him for a while, but then he worries because his letters aren't getting through. Will she understand about the strike? he wonders. Of course, we assure him, how could she not understand? He hears somewhere that top priority mail is trickling through, and he feels obscurely that he deserves to be top priority, that his letters matter.

The strike drags on, and Martin and I suggest things he can do to keep busy. Martin takes him skiing, and in spite of my fatigue I help him with a school project on Tanzania. We trace maps; I type an agricultural output chart for him. He has taken to sighing heavily.

Even Susanna Moodie has let me down. I am writing now about her later life when she has moved with her husband and children to the town of Belleville. No longer destitute, she has grown cranky. She says unkind things about the neighbouring women. She minimizes the efforts of the town builders; she has lost the girlish excitement and breathless gaiety which made life in the bush cabin seem an adventure; the glory of fresh raspberries and the thrill of milking a cow are forgotten pleasures. She is a matron now, and she makes hard, grudging judgments. She has lost her vision. She is condescending. The action goes too fast; she telescopes five years into a maddening paragraph. There are no details anymore.

It would help if it snowed. The ground is covered with old crusted snow and pitted with ice. The roads and sidewalks are rutted and hard to walk on, and driving is dangerous. A layer of grime covers everything. One soft and lovely fall of snow might at least keep me from this overwhelming compulsion to put my head down and cry and cry and cry.

I don't really feel like cooking, but I feel so sorry for Roger that one night we invite him for a family dinner. He hasn't heard from Ruthie. He doesn't know where she's living. He would feel better, he tells me, if he knew where she was staying.

"Are you really that worried about her?" I ask, putting a slice of meatloaf on his plate.

"No. I know she's all right because she's at work."

"What then?"

"I just want to know where she's living."

"You've tried her girl friends?"

"Yes. And they don't know."

"What about her family?" I ask. I know she is from a small town in northern Ontario. "Couldn't you write to them?"

"God, no. They never liked the idea that we were living together. Not married. They're pretty rigid."

"Why don't you follow her home from work?" Richard asks, taking the words out of my mouth.

"Don't be stupid," Meredith says sternly. "This isn't a James Bond movie. That would be just plain sneaky, following her like that."

I say nothing. Roger shakes his head sadly. "I couldn't. Believe me, I've thought about it, but it does seem to be an invasion—and, I don't know—I just couldn't."

Martin interrupts us with, "Look, if she wants it this way, isn't it better to leave her alone. You've got to get your mind on something else, Roger."

"God knows I'm busy enough at work," Roger says. "It seems I've just got the Christmas exams marked, and now we're onto a new set. I don't even have time to do enough reading to keep up."

"What did you think of *Graven Images*?" I ask him suddenly.

"Great." He barks it out. "Absolutely his best."

"Why?" I ask, trying not to sound too sly.

"I don't know, Judith. It's got more—more body to it."

"A better plot?" I suggest.

"That's it. A real brainstorm. No wonder the films snatched it up."

"I just loved it," Meredith murmurs.

Martin says nothing; he still hasn't got around to reading it.

"Tell me, Roger," I ask, "would you say that Furlong is an original writer?"

"Damn right I would."

"How is he original?" I ask. "Tell me, in what way is he original?"

Roger leans back, shaking his thick curls out of his eyes, and for a moment Ruthie is forgotten, for a moment he seems happy. He is recalling phrases from his thesis. "All right, Judith, take his use of the Canadian experience. Now there's a man who actually comprehends the national theme."

"Which is what?" Martin asks.

"Which is shelter. Shelter from the storm of life, to use a corny phrase."

"Corny is right," Richard says.

"Who asked you, Richard?" Meredith tells him.

In the kitchen I serve ice-cream drizzled with maple syrup; I haven't the energy to think of anything else. Meredith carries in the plates for me. Roger is expanding on the theme of shelter.

"I don't, of course, mean just shelter from those natural storms which occur externally. Although he is tremendous on those. That hail sequence in *Graven Images*—now didn't that grab you? Even you'd like it, Martin. It's got a sort of Miltonic splendour. Like the hail is a symbol. He makes it stand for the general battering of everyday life."

"So what about the shelter theme?" Martin is smiling broadly, happy tonight.

"Okay, I'm getting to that. Remember the guy out on the prairie, Judith, just standing there. And the hail starts. Golfballs. His dog is killed. Remember that?"

"Christ," Martin says. "It sounds like *Lassie Come Home*."

"It sounds bad, I'll admit. But that's the beautiful thing about Furlong. He can carry it off when no one else can. What someone else makes into a soap opera, he makes part of the national fabric."

"But Roger," I plead, "getting back to originality for a moment, do you really think he comes up with original plots?"

"Well, we don't use that word plot much anymore. Not in modern criticism. But, yes, sure I think he does. You read *Graven Images*. Wasn't that a real heart-stopper?"

"What about the others though?" I ask. "Where do you think he got the ideas for those early books? Did you go into that when you wrote your thesis?"

"I suppose you want me to admit that his stories are a bit on the formula plan. So, okay, I admit it. But *Graven Images* confirms what I said then—that he's a pretty original guy."

"He really is," Meredith says smiling.

"Hmmmm," Martin says.

I say nothing. I am sitting quiet. Girding my loins. I know that my present weakness is trivial and temporary. Next week, I promise myself, next week I'm going to have it out with Furlong. He's going to have to do some explaining. Or else.

Or else what? Endlessly, silently, I debate the point. What power do I have over Furlong? Who am I, the far from perfect Judith Gill, to judge him, and how do I hope to chastise him for his dishonesty?

I only want him to know that I know what he did.

Why? What's the point? Why not let it pass?

Because what he's done may be too small a crime to punish, but at the same time it's too large to let go unacknowledged. Talk about scot-free.

Is Furlong a bad man then? A criminal?

No, not bad. Just weak. Complex, intelligent, but weak. I've just discovered how weak. But he has a glaze of arrogance, a coloratura confidence that demands that I respond.

In what way is he weak?

Let me explain. When I was about fifteen years old I read a very long and boring novel called *Middlemarch*. By George Eliot yet. I got it from the public library. (All girls like me who were good at school but suffered from miserable girlhoods were sustained for years on end by the resources of the public libraries of this continent.) Not that *Middlemarch* offered me much in the way of escape. It offered little but a rambling plot and quartets of moist, dreary, introspective characters, one of whom was accused by the heroine of having "spots of commonness." I liked that expression, "spots of commonness," and even at fifteen I recognized the symptoms, interpreting them as a familiar social variety of measles.

Furlong suffers more than anyone I know from this exact and debilitating malady. Witness the framed motto he once had in his office, and witness also the abrupt banishment of it. Observe the clichés on his book jacket, remember his cranberry-vodka punch, his petty jealousies of other writers, his dependence on nationality which permits him his big-frog-in-little-pond eminence.

His sophistication is problematically wrought; it's uneven and sometimes, when instinct fails, altogether lacking. He can, for instance, be too kind, too lushly, tropically kind, a kindness too rich and ripe for ordinary friendship. And, in addition, he is uncertain about salad forks, brandy snifters, and how to use the subjunctive; he finds those Steuben glass snails charming and he favours Renoir; he sometimes slips and says supper instead of dinner, and, conversely, in another pose, he slips and says dinner instead of supper; he is spotted, oh, he is uncommonly spotted.

But is he less of a thief for all that?

A thief is a thief is a thief.

Very profound. But don't forget, you stole the plot in the first place.

That was different. I didn't actually go through with it. And I didn't profit from it the way Furlong has profited.

So that's what's bothering you. You're jealous.

No, no, no, no. Not for myself. For Martin maybe. Here is Furlong, enjoying an unearned success. And Martin gets nothing but crazy in the head.

Are there no mitigating circumstances in this theft?

Many. Obviously he was desperate. He admitted that much, letting slip the fact that the well had gone dry. He was on the skids, hadn't had a good idea for two years. Poor man, snagged in literary menopause and sticky with hot flushes. And he *is* nice to his mother. And patient with his students. And always touchingly, tenderly gallant with me, actually thinking of me as a fellow writer, and accepting me, great big-boned Judith Gill, as charming, a really quite attractive woman. And what else? Oh, yes. He has a passionate and pitiable desire to be loved, to be celebrated with expletives and nicknames, to be in the club. And then, an alternating compulsion to draw back, to be insular and exclusive and private. Psychologically he's a mess. I suppose he was driven to theft.

But who does it really harm?

I refuse to answer such an academic question.

Don't you like him at all?

Like him? I do. No, I don't, not now. I suppose I'm fond of him. But no matter how charming he will be in the future, no matter how he disclaims his act of plunder and he will, no matter what amends he may make for it, I will not be moved. I don't know why, but he will never, he will never, he will never be someone I love. Only someone I could have loved.

Nancy Krantz and I went out to lunch one day to celebrate my recovery from the flu. We went to the Prince Lodge where Paul Krantz is a member (and has a charge account) and sat at one of the dark oak tables which are moored like ships on the sea of olive carpet. Around us quiet, dark-suited businessmen in twos and threes talked softly; glasses and silver clinked faintly as though at a great distance.

"Two dry sherries," Nancy told the waiter briskly. I longed to tell her about Furlong's plagiarism, but that was out of the question since it would have necessitated the disclosure of my own theft, not to mention my prying into John Spalding's private manuscripts.

We ordered beef curry, and while we waited we discussed the alternating vibrations which regulate female psychology.

"Up and down," Nancy complained. "A perpetual see-saw ride. Pre-menstrual, post-menstrual. Optimism, pessimism."

I agreed; it did seem that the electricity of life consisted mainly of meaningless fluctuations in mood, so that to enter an era of happiness was to anticipate the next interlude of depression.

"Of course," Nancy said, "there are those occasional little surprises which make it all worthwhile."

"Such as?" I asked.

"The peach," she said. "Did I ever tell you the peach story?"

"No," I said, "never."

So she told me how, last summer, she and Paul and their children, all six of them, had been stalled in heavy traffic. It was a Friday evening and they were working their way out of the city to get to the cottage sixty miles away. The children were quarrelsome and the weather was murderously humid. In another car stalled next to them, a fat man sat alone at the steering wheel, and on the back seat, plainly visible, was a bushel of peaches. He smiled at the children, and they must have smiled back, for he turned suddenly and reached a fat hand into his basket, carefully selected a peach, and handed it out the window to Nancy.

She took it, she said, instinctively, uttering a confused mew of thanks. Ahead of them a traffic light turned green, and the fat man's car moved away, leaving Nancy with the large and beautiful peach in her hand. It was, she said the largest peach she had ever seen, almost the size of a grapefruit, and its skin was perfect seamless velvet without a single blemish. Paul shouted at her over the noise of the traffic to look out for razor blades, so she turned it over carefully, inspecting it. But the skin was unbroken. And the exact shade of ripeness for eating.

"What did you do with it?" I asked.

"We ate it," Nancy said. "We passed it around. Gently. Like a holy object almost, and we each took big bites of it. Until it was gone. One of the children said something about how strange it was for someone to do that, give us a peach through a car window like that, but the rest of us just sat there thinking about it. All the way to the cottage. A strange sort of peace stuck to us. It was so—so completely unasked for. And so undeserved. And the whole thing had been so quick, just a few seconds really. I was—I don't know why—I was thrilled."

I nodded. I was remembering something that had happened to us, an incident I had almost forgotten. It was perhaps a shade less joyous a story than Nancy's, but the element of mystery had, at the time, renewed something in me.

It had happened, I told Nancy, on our first day in England. We had taken a train from London to Birmingham. Everything was very new and crowded and confused; the

train puffing into Birmingham seemed charmingly miniature; the station was glass-roofed and dirty with Victorian
arches and tea trolleys and curious newspapers arrayed in
kiosks; odd looking luggage, belted and roped, even suitcases made of wicker, were stacked on carts. Martin, the
children and I struggled with our own bags, hurrying
down the platform, disoriented by the feel of solid ground
underfoot, bumped and jostled at every step by people
hurrying to board the train we had just left. Passengers
pulled down the train windows, leaned out talking to their
friends while paper cups of tea changed hands and kisses
flew through the air. Children with startling red cheeks,
wearing blue gabardine coats, hung onto their mothers'
hands. A cheerful scruffiness hung over the station like
whisky breath.

And at that moment a short, dark little man stopped
directly in front of me and pushed a small brown paper
parcel at me. I must have shaken my head to indicate that it
wasn't mine, but he pushed it even harder at me, speaking
all the time, very rapidly, in a language I didn't recognize.
Certainly no species of English; nor was it French or German; it might have been Arabic we speculated later.

I pushed the parcel back at him, but he placed it all the
more firmly in my hand, speaking faster and more agitatedly
than before. "Come on, Judith," Martin called to me. So
clutching my suitcase again as well as the parcel, I followed
Martin and the children out into the thin sunshine where
we flagged a taxi and drove the mile or two to the Spaldings'
flat.

The parcel was forgotten for an hour or more; then
someone remembered it. I opened it slowly while the children watched. Inside was a box of stationery. Letter paper.
About twenty sheets of it in a not very fresh shade of pale
green. There was some sort of pinkish flower at the top of
each sheet, and at the bottom of the box there were piles of
slightly faded looking envelopes.

For a day or two we speculated on what it could mean.

We examined every sheet of paper and looked the box over carefully for identifying marks; we tried to recall the man's appearance and the sound of his voice. "He must have thought you'd left it on the seat in the train," Martin said, and in the end we all agreed that that was the most likely answer, the only sensible conclusion really. But it didn't seem quite enough. The little man had been running on the platform. He had searched the crowd, or so I believed, and for some reason he had selected me. And he had run away again in a state of great excitement. We never thought for a moment that the parcel might have been dangerous since this occurred before the invention of letter bombs, but Richard did suggest we run a hot iron over the sheets of paper in the hope of discovering messages written in invisible ink.

Those first few days in England were so filled with novelty, with odd occurrences and curious sights, that this tiny incident, bizarre as it was, seemed no more than a portion of that larger strangeness, and we soon ceased to talk about it. I even used the writing paper for my first letters home, and when it was all gone I forgot about it. Or almost.

For if it seemed a commonplace enough adventure at the time, it grows more strange, more mysterious as time passes. This afternoon, telling Nancy about it, it seemed really quite wonderful in a way, utterly unique in fact, as though we had accidentally brushed with the supernatural.

And the two of us, stirring sugar into our cups of coffee at the Prince Lodge, smiled. It was after three; the businessmen had crept away without our noticing, back to their conference rooms, to their teak desks and in-trays. Here in the restaurant two waiters fluttered darkly by a sideboard, and in all that space I felt myself lifted to a new perspective: far away it seemed, I could see two women at a table; they are neither happy nor unhappy, but are suspended somewhere in between, caught in a thin, clear, expensive jelly, and they are both smiling, smiling across the table, across the room, smiling past the dark stained panelling, out through the tiny-paned window to the parking lot which is slowly, slowly, filling up with snow, changing all the world to a wide, white void.

"It's over. I just heard it on the news," Richard yells. "While I was getting dressed. It's all settled."

"What's settled?" It's early, eight o'clock, and I'm pouring out glasses of orange juice, not quite awake.

"The postal strike."

"The postal strike?"

"You know. In the U.K. Don't you remember?"

"Oh, yes, that's right. Heavens, that's been going on a long time."

"Three weeks."

"Really? Where does the time go?"

He sits down at the table and cuts the top off his boiled egg. Joy makes him violent, and the slice of egg shell skitters to the floor. He leans over to pick it up. "Man, it'll be a real pile-up. Three weeks of mail!"

I pour my coffee and sit beside him. "It'll take a while to sort it all out."

"I know."

"I mean, you mustn't expect any mail for a while."

"I know. I know."

"It may be several days. A week even."

"Is there any honey?"

"In the cupboard."

"Say about six days. Today's Tuesday. I should be getting something by next Monday."

"Hmmmmm."

"What do you think? Tuesday at the latest?"

"Maybe, but don't count on it."

"Don't worry about me."

He managed to get through the week, casting no more than a casual eye at the hall table under the piece of red granite where I keep the mail. Over the weekend we all went skiing, and time passed quickly.

But when he came home from school at noon on **Monday**, I could tell how disappointed he was. He spooned his soup around in circles, and picked at his sandwich, and for the first time I noticed how pale he looked. On Tuesday, because again there was no mail for him, I made him waffles for lunch. But even that failed to cheer him.

"Look, Richard," I told him, "have you looked in the newspapers? Did you see that picture of all the unsorted mail. A mountain of it. It's going to take longer than we thought."

"I guess so."

He kept waiting. Watching him, I observed for the first time the simplicity of his life, the almost utilitarian unrelieved separation of his time: school, home, sleep. Endless repetition. He needed a letter desperately.

On the weekend we skied again, scattering our energies on the snow-covered hills and coming home in the late afternoon. Richard was so weighted with sleep that England must have seemed far away, indistinct and irrelevant, a point on a dream map.

But Monday morning he tells me he feels sick. His throat is sore, he says, and his head aches. I can hear an unfamiliar pitch of pleading in his voice, and know intuitively that he only wants to be here when the mail arrives. Martin is impatient and peers down his throat with a flashlight. "I can't see a thing," he says. "And his temperature is normal."

"He might as well stay home this morning," I say, "just in case he's coming down with something." (How expertly I carry off these small deceptions. And how instinctively I take the part of the deceiver.) Richard, listening to us debate his hypothetical sickness, looks at me gratefully. And humbly crawls back into bed to wait.

The mail comes at half-past ten. There is quite a lot for a Monday. Bills mostly, a letter from Martin's parents, two or three magazines. And a letter from England. A tissue-thin blue air letter. But it is from a friend of Martin's, not from Anita Spalding.

I go up to Richard's room, a tall glass of orange juice in

my hand and an aspirin, for I want to continue the fiction of illness long enough for him to recover with grace." Take this, Rich," I say. "You may even feel up to going to school this afternoon."

"Maybe," he says. "Any mail?"

"Nothing much," I say, duplicating his nonchalance.

"Wonder if the mail's getting through from England," he speculates as though this were no more than an abstract topic.

"I think it is, Richard," I tell him quietly. "Dad got one this morning."

"Oh."

"But I suppose it will just trickle in at first."

"Probably."

"It may take another good week to clear it all."

"Yeah."

"How do you feel?"

"A little better," he says.

"Good," I say. "After lunch, how about if I drive you over to school?"

"Okay," he says.

But there was no mail for him that week or the next. The month was slipping by, and I still had not confronted Furlong. I weighed it in my mind, rehearsed it; I fortified myself, gathered my strength, prepared my grievances. Soon.

But there are other things to think of. Meredith will be seventeen on February twenty-seventh, and Martin suggests we all go to Antonio's for dinner. I fret briefly about the cost, but listening to my own voice and hearing the terse economical echoes of my mother, I stop short.

"A good idea," I say.

The day before her birthday I take the downtown bus and shop for a birthday present. This is a far different quest than shopping for my mother or for Lala; for them we can never think of anything to buy. But for Meredith, for a girl of seventeen, the shops are groaning with wonderful things. Things. It is the age for things, each of which would, I know, bring tears of delight rushing into her eyes. There are Greek bags woven in a shade of blue so subtle it defies description; chunks of stone, looking as though they were plucked from a strange planet, fastened into chains of palest silver; there are sweaters of unfathomable softness, belts in every colour and width, jeans by the hundreds, by the thousands, by the millions. Things are everywhere. All I have to do is choose.

But I can't. Instead I buy too much. I spend far more money than I'd intended; it is irresistible; it is so easy to bring her happiness—it won't always be this easy—so easy to produce the charge plate, to tuck yet another little bag away. But finally the parcels weight me down; my arms are filled, and I think it must be time for me to catch my bus. But first a cup of coffee.

In the corner of Christy's Coffee Shop I sink into a chair. The tables here are small, and the tile floor is awash with tracked-in snow; there is hardly room for me to stow my parcels under the table. At all the other little tables are shoppers, and like me they are weary. The February sales are on, and many of these women are guarding treasures they have spent the day pursuing. Waitresses bring them solace: cups of coffee, green pots of tea, doughnuts or toasted Danish buns, bran muffins with pats of butter. Outside it's already dark. Only four-thirty and the day is ending for these exhausted, sore-footed women. All of them are women, I notice.

Or almost all. There *is* one man at a table in the back of the room. Only one. Oddly enough, he looks familiar; the bulk of his body reminds me of someone I know. I do know him. I recognize the tweed overcoat. Of course. It's Furlong Eberhardt. With a cup of tea raised to his lips.

And who's that with him? Two women. Students? Probably. I peer over the sea of teased hairdos and crushed wool hats. Who is it?

One of them looks like Ruthie. What would Ruthie be doing here with Furlong? Impossible. But it is Ruthie. She is pouring herself a cup of tea, tipping the pot almost upside-down to get the last drop. She is lifting a sliver of lemon and squeezing it in. The small dark face, Latin-looking. It *is* Ruthie.

And who is that other girl? I can't believe it. But the navy blue coat thrown over the back of the chair is familiar. Its plaid lining is conclusive. The slender neck, the lift of dark brown hair. I am certain now. It is—yes—*it's Meredith!*

Every day I work for two or three hours on the Susanna Moodie biography. What I am looking for is the precise event which altered her from a rather priggish, faintly blue-stockinged but ardent young girl into a heavy, conventional, distressed, perpetually disapproving and sorrowing woman. And although I've been over all the resource material thoroughly, I'm unable to find the line of demarcation. It seems to be unrecorded, lodged perhaps in the years between her books, or else—and this seems more likely—wilfully suppressed, deliberately withheld.

There are traumatic events in her life to be sure. Illness. The drowning of a son which she mentions only in passing. Poverty. And the failure of her husband to assume direction. Perhaps that's it—her husband, John W. Dunbar Moodie.

There's a clue in an essay he wrote as an old man. It is a sort of summary of his life in which he lists the primary events as being, one, getting stepped on by an elephant as a young man in South Africa, two, the breaking of a knee in middle life and, three, painful arthritis in old age. He was, it would seem, a man who measured his life by episodes of pain, a negative personality who might easily have extinguished the fire of love in Susanna.

But despite her various calamities she survived, and it seems to have been her sense of irony that kept her afloat when everything else failed. Over the years she had abandoned the sharp divisions between good and evil which had troubled her as a young woman; the two qualities became bridged with a fibrous rib of irony. Sharp on the tongue, it became her trademark.

Irony, it seems to me, is a curious quality, a sour pleasure. Observation which is acid-edged with knowledge. A double vision which allows pain to exist on the reverse side of pleasure. Neither vice nor virtue, it annihilated the dichotomy of her existence. Smoothed out the contradictions. Forstalled ennui and permitted survival. An anesthetic for the frontier, but at the same time a drug to dull exhilaration.

For example, when Susanna was a middle-aged woman and ailing from unmentionable disorders, she took a cruise to see Niagara Falls. It was, she says, what she had dreamed of all her life.

The imagined sight of that mountain of water had sustained her through her tragic years, and now at last the boat carried her closer and closer to the majestic sight.

She can hear the thunder of water before she can see it, and her whole body tenses for pleasure. But when she actually stands in the presence of the torrent, she loses the capacity for rhapsody. She has exhausted it in anticipation.

But irony rescues her from a pitiable vacuum. Turning from the scenery, she observes the human activity around her, and, paragraph by paragraph, she describes the reactions of her fellow tourists. Their multiple presence forms particles through which she can see, as through a prism, the glorious and legendary spectacle of Niagara Falls. Once again she finds her own way out.

I easily recognize the nuances of irony because, lying sleepless in bed on this last night in February, I too am rescued; I too do my balancing act between humour and desperation.

It seems I've always had a knack for it. Perhaps I was born with it; maybe it came sealed in the invisible skin of a chromosome, ready to accompany me for the rest of my life. I can feel it: a tough-as-a-tendon cord which stretches from the top of my head to my toes, a sort of auxiliary brain, ready as a knuckle to carry me through.

All through my endless barren childhood I had my special and privileged observation platform. My parents did not succeed in souring me as they did my sister Charleen who writes and publishes poems of terrifying bitterness. My sad lank father and my sad nervous mother have faded to snapshot proportions. They have not twisted or warped me or shaped me into a mocking image of themselves. There may be warnings in the blood, but, at least, there are no nightmares.

And now, in spite of my insomnia—that too is temporary—I find I'm able to coexist with Richard's agony as, day after day, the mail doesn't come for him. Somewhere in a larger pattern there's an explanation; I am confident of it.

And the complex dark secrecy of the scene in Christy's Coffee Shop—Furlong, Ruthie, Meredith—I can absorb that too, and I can even refrain from quizzing Meredith about it. I can put it aside, tuck it away; I can title it "An Anomaly."

Detached and nerved by irony, I can even look squarely at Furlong's devious theft. And at my own role as an agent of theft. I can live outside it. I can outline it with my magic pencil. Put a ring around it.

Martin's madness is more difficult to assimilate, but my vein, my good steady vein of irony, gives me just enough distance to believe he may be only temporarily deranged. And so, although everything seems to be falling apart and though I'm assailed by an unidentifiable sadness and though it has snowed solidly for eight days—there is one thing I am certain of: that, like Mrs. Moodie of Belleville, I will, in the end, be able to trick myself; I can will myself into happiness. No matter what happens I will be able to get through.

If only I can get through tonight.

March

"You swine, Furlong. You swine."

"Judith! Are you talking to me?"

"You thieving swine!"

"Judith, what is this? Some kind of joke?"

It is not a joke, not even a nightmare; this is real. At last I am confronting Furlong.

"Swine."

"Judith."

This isn't the way I'd planned it. But here we are, the two of us in the hall of Professor Stanley's country house with its pegged oak floors and its original pre-Confederation pine furniture and the acre of land which he and his wife Polly always refer to as "the grounds." We are face to face in front of the cherrywood armoire, and now that I have begun, I can't stop.

"Swine."

"Judith, are you serious? Are you calling me a swine?"

"That's exactly what I said. An evil swine."

"Come on, Judith." He steps back, half-shocked. And then enrages me further by allowing a curl of a smile to appear behind his beard.

Where had I got that word—swine? It is a word I haven't used since—since when? Since 1943 at least, since those fanatical early Forties, the war years, when the villains in our violent-hued comic books were resoundingly labelled swine by the hero, Captain Marvel, Superman, Captain Midnight, whoever it might be.

Swine meant the ultimate in the sinister, a being who was evil, whose skin was tinged with green and whose eyes were slits of gleaming, poisonous, rancid, incomprehensible Nazism. Japanese and Germans were swines (we didn't know how to pluralize it, of course), Hitler being the epitome of swinehood. It was a word we spit out between clenched teeth, saying it with a fiendish east European accent—"You feelthy schwine." When we jumped on tin cans at the school scrap drive we shouted, "Kill the swine."

I remember, years later, taking part in a school play called "The Princess and the Swineherd," and the term swine was explained to me for the first time. How disappointing to find that it meant no more than pig, for though I associated pigs with filth and gluttony, that animal didn't begin to approach the wickedness of swine.

"You heard me, Furlong. I said swine. And I meant swine."

"My dear girl, what on earth is the matter?"

"I am not your dear girl."

We are at a party, an annual get-together for the English Department, traditionally hosted by the department chairman and his wife, Ben and Polly Stanley.

I am fond of them both. Ben is reserved but charming, a specialist in Elizabethan literature, a man who at fifty seems perpetually surprised by his own dimensions. One hand is constantly rummaging through his coarse, silver-grey hair as though it cannot believe that such beautiful hair exists on so common a head. The other hand, nervously, mechanically, pats and circles the sloping paunch which bulges under his suede jacket, as if he is questioning its clandestine and demeaning swell.

His wife Polly is about fifty too, a woman both stout and shy. Sadly she is the victim of academic fiction, for she is never free of her role as faculty wife; she plays bridge with the wives, bowls with them, discusses Great Books with them, laments pollution, listens to string quartets, attends convocations, all with an air of brooding and bewilderment. Despite her girth, her charm is wispy, a fragile growth which advances and contracts in spasms. I would not want to embarrass her.

"I don't care if they hear us," I hiss.

"Well, damn it, I do."

As it happens, no one hears us. Everyone has gone into the wainscotted dining room for a buffet of clam chowder and the Stanley speciality, chunks of beef afloat in red wine, which they will carry on plates into the living room, the den, the solarium, anywhere they can find a perch. We are alone in the hall, Furlong and I, but nevertheless I lower my voice.

"Furlong, I want you to know that I know everything."

"You know everything," he repeats numbly. He is not smiling now.

"Everything."

"Everything," he echoes.

"You might have known I'd find out."

"I didn't. No, I didn't."

"How could you be so devious, Furlong?" I ask. Already I have passed from the peak of rage into vicious scolding.

He has the grace to cover his face with both hands, and I notice with satisfaction that he is swaying slightly.

"How could you be so deceitful?" I say again.

"Ah Judith." His hands extend in a gesture of helplessness. "This is all much more complicated than you seem to think."

"Complicated? Devious is more like it."

"Believe me, Judith, I never meant to hurt anyone."

"All you wanted was to watch out for yourself and your precious reputation."

"You're wrong. There were other considerations. Really Judith, you're being unbelievably narrow-minded. And it's not like you."

"Please, please, please spare me any semblance of flattery, Furlong. I'm not in the mood."

"All I'm saying is, and for God's sake, lower your voice won't you, try to think of this in a broader perspective."

"Deception is deception," I say lamely but loudly.

"Believe me, Judith, I never meant for this to get out of hand."

"You admit then that it did get out of hand?"

"Of course I do. My God, do you think I've got no conscience at all?"

"I wonder about that."

"If you only knew. I've felt the most terrible remorse, believe me. I've been tormented day and night by all this. There were times when I thought I should go on television, on national television, and make a public confession."

"Well? Are you going to?"

He winces. Takes a step backwards. Raises his hand as though to ward me off. Sinks down on one of Polly's ladderback chairs.

"Sit down. Please, Judith, we have got to talk this over sensibly."

I sit facing him. My knees buckle with faintness. "We *are* talking this over, Furlong."

"Now listen closely, Judith. I am not defending what I did."

"I hope not."

"I am not bereft of honour, whatever you may choose to think."

"I wonder if you know what I really do think."

"I can guess. You are utterly disgusted. You trusted me, and now you find out what a sham I really am."

"You're getting close," I say cruelly.

"Do you know something, Judith. I even hate myself. When I look in the mirror I cringe. I actually cringe."

"You'd never guess it from the pitch on your book jackets."

"I don't write those, as you perfectly well know. The publishers look after that."

"I see."

"You don't see. You're being deliberately rigid, Judith, and I'm doing my best to explain to you the full circumstances."

"Go ahead. Try. I want to hear how you're going to explain this away."

"All right then." He takes a deep breath. "It seemed a harmless enough thing to do at the time. That's all. What more can I say. Perhaps I lacked perspective at the time. Yes, I definitely lacked a sense of balance. And then I just got trapped into it. Everything happened too fast. It just got away from me, that's all."

"And that's what you call an explanation?"

"It's not much. It's not much, I'll admit, but it's all I have. My God, Judith, you love to twist the knife when you get hold of it, don't you?"

"Well, I *am* the injured party."

"The injured party?"

"I'm the one you took advantage of."

"Why you?"

"For heaven's sake, Furlong, don't be obtuse. I can't stand that on top of all this rotten deception."

"I'm afraid I must be obtuse. I just fail to see why you are more injured than anyone else."

"You really can't?"

"No. I'm afraid not. I mean, all right, you're a member of the public. Maybe a little more astute than some, but you're just one member of a large public, and I can't see what gives you the right to be personally aggrieved."

I can't believe what I'm hearing. "Think, Furlong," I say, "think hard."

"I am. But I can't for the life of me think why you should feel persecuted."

"I can't stand this."

"You think I'm enjoying it. I came here tonight expecting to enjoy myself, and I hardly get in the door and you leap on me."

"Believe me, I would have leapt a lot sooner than this, but I took a few weeks to cool off."

"And you call this being cool? If you don't mind my saying so, Judith, this really isn't your style, not at all. Pouncing on an old friend in public and yelling 'swine' at him."

"Well, you behaved like a swine, Furlong, and I don't see that you deserve any special consideration now."

"Didn't I tell you I was guilty. Do you want me to go down on my knees. And I really am sorry about it, Judith." His voice cracks, dangerously close to tears. "If you only knew what I go through. Do you know that I have to take sleeping pills almost every night. Not to mention my pre-ulcer condition."

"If that's the case, what in heaven's name made you do it?"

"I told you. I got trapped. It didn't seem so dreadful at the time. But listen, Judith. You're an old friend. I know I acted like a bloody fool and that I've no right to ask this of you, but do you think we could—you know—do you think we could more or less keep this between ourselves? I mean, now that the damage is done, do we have to spread it around?"

"What you're really asking is, can we sweep it neatly under the rug."

"Of course I don't mean that. I just mean, couldn't we confine this thing?"

"I don't know. I'll have to think."

"Judith. Please." His eyes fill with real tears and his nose reddens, making him look piercingly elderly. "Please."

I can't bear it; he is going to cry. "All right," I say grudgingly. "I suppose nothing would be served by a public disclosure."

"Oh, Judith, you are kind." He reaches blindly for my hand. "You've always been so kind, so good."

"But," I say firmly, drawing my hand away, "I do think you owe me, at the very least, an apology."

His face straightens; his eyes cloud with opaque bafflement. "Tell me, why do I owe you a *personal* apology?"

"It was, after all, my plot that you stole."

"Your plot. I stole your plot?"

"For *Graven Images*. As you perfectly well know."

"You think I stole a plot from you for *Graven Images*?"

"You certainly did. From my novel. The one I wrote for your class. And you promised me you'd destroyed it. And then you went and took it. Maybe not incident by incident, but the main idea. You took the main idea. And made a killing."

"Come, come, Judith. Writers don't steal ideas. They abstract them from wherever they can. I never stole your idea."

"You must be joking, Furlong. Do you mean to sit there and tell me your novel bears no resemblance to the one I wrote?"

He answers with an airy wave of his hand, an affectionate pull at his beard. "Possibly, possibly. But, my good Lord, writers can't stake out territories. It's open season. A free range. One uses what one can find. One takes an idea and brings to it his own individual touch. His own quality. Enhances it. Develops it. Do you know there are only seven distinct plots in all of literature?"

"So you told us in creative writing class."

"Well, can't you see?" He is smiling now, suddenly sunny. "This is no more than a variation on one of those great primordial plots."

I am hopelessly confused. It is unbelievable that he should be sitting here beside me smiling. That he has shaken off every particle of guilt like an animal shaking water from his coat. My mouth is open; I am literally gasping for air; I cannot believe this.

"I'm sure you'll understand, Judith, when you take time to think about it."

My hands are shaking, and my mouth has gone slack and shapeless like a flap of canvas! I am unable to speak for a moment. Finally I sputter something, but even to me it is unintelligible.

"Ah, Judith, just think for a minute, where did Shakespeare—not that I am placing myself in that orbit for a second—but where did Shakespeare get his plots? Not from his own experience, you can be sure of that. I mean, who was he but another young lad from the provinces? He stole his plots, you would say, Judith. Borrowed them from the literature of the past, and no one damn well calls it theft. He took those old tried and true stories and hammered them into something that was his own."

"It's not the same," I manage to gasp.

"Judith, Judith, it is. Surely you can see that this is all a terrible misunderstanding."

I am numb. Is it all a misunderstanding? I try to think. But at that moment Polly Stanley, doing her hostess rounds, discovers us. "Oh, dear. I've been neglecting you two," she frets. "Here I am, about to serve dessert, and I don't believe you two have had a thing to eat."

"We were having a chat." Furlong beams. "Judith and I were discussing some old established literary traditions."

"Oh, dear, shop talk." She giggles faintly, but she is clearly annoyed that we have confused the progression of her dinner, and she takes Furlong firmly by the arm and leads him into the dining room. He goes off gratefully, and I follow behind them, mechanically filling a plate with food. The beef is rather cold; there is a dull skin of grease floating on top, but I load my plate anyway. Furlong hurries away to join a cheerful group in the solarium, and I am left.

Something is wrong. There is something I have not quite managed to assimilate. Furlong has declared his innocence. He has refused to accept a grain of guilt. He is emphatic; he is all sweet reason.

But then what in heaven's name have he and I been talking about?

"Judith."

"Yes." I am almost asleep. I had thought that Martin was asleep too.

"Why don't you come with me?"

"To Toronto?" I ask. Martin is leaving on the morning train for the Renaissance Society meeting.

"Why not come, Judith? Meredith could look after things here, and it would do you good to get away."

"I could never never be ready in time."

"We could take a later train."

"I don't know, Martin. Richard is so sort of depressed that I hate to leave him."

"Richard?"

"He still hasn't got a letter from England. What do you suppose has happened?"

"Oh, I wouldn't worry, Judith. Everything comes to an end eventually."

"I suppose so," I say.

I lie very still on my side of the bed. I am waiting for Martin to encourage me, to list the reasons why I should go to Toronto with him, and to brush aside my petty objections. I wait, believing that he will succeed in persuading me. I could wear my green skirt on the train; my long dress is back from the cleaners; I could have my hair done in Toronto; leave the rest of the ham for the children; phone them in the evening.

A street light shines into our bedroom from the place where the curtains don't quite meet, making a white streak down the bed. About two inches wide I estimate. It is very quiet. I can hear the Baby Ben ticking. Martin has set the alarm for six so he can make the early train.

Under the electric blanket I lie at attention. In a moment he will speak again, pressing me to go. But five minutes pass. I check the luminous dial of the clock. Ten minutes. I lift myself on one elbow to look at Martin.

He is very relaxed. His eyes are shut and he is breathing regularly, very deeply with a low diesel hum, and I notice that he is definitely asleep.

"Teen-agers are often sulky, resentful and hostile," writes Dr. Whittier Whitehorn in the second of a series of articles on adolescent behaviour. "And because they revolve so continuously around their own tempestuous emotions, they tend to interpret even the most general remarks as applying to themselves."

I read these newspaper articles less for their factual information than for the comfort of their familiar, kindly rhetoric. I know that Dr. Whitehorn can do no more in the end than counsel patience for "this difficult and trying emotional time," and I skip through the paragraphs to the closing line, noting with cheerful satisfaction that "in the battle to win a teen-ager's confidence, sensitivity and patience are the only weapons a wise parent can wield."

I let the newspaper fall to the floor, switch off the bedside lamp and try to sleep. When Martin is away the bed feels irrationally flat; I kick a leg out sideways, testing the space.

Dr. Whitehorn's advice glows in front of me as I review in my mind the strange, almost surreal discussion I had with Meredith this morning.

She had slept late, and at eight-twenty on a Monday morning she was still tearing through the house looking for her books.

"Do you have your bus tokens?" I asked her.

She answered with a short and heavy, "Yes, Mother."

"Your books?"

"No. I can't find *Graven Images*."

"What do you want with that?"

"I'm doing a report on it. For English."

"A report on *Graven Images*?"

"Why not?" she asked sharply. "Most people consider that it's quite good."

"It's in my room," I confessed.

"Do you mind if I take it?" she asked, elaborately polite now.

I replied with a tart, heavy-on-every-syllable voice, "Not in the least."

She whirled around, studied my face closely, and pronounced, "You really do have something against Furlong."

"I suppose."

"What?"

I shrug. "I just don't trust him."

"Why not?"

"I used to," I said, "but not anymore."

She was plainly alarmed at this. And hastened to his defence. "Look, Mother, I think I know what you're saying. About not trusting him. I mean, I know what you think."

"What?"

"I—I can't say anything. But just take my word for it that it's not true. It may look true at this moment but it isn't."

"What isn't?" I asked.

"That's all I can say. Just that it isn't true." And then with a touch of melodrama she added, "You'll just have to trust me."

"You'll miss your bus, Meredith," I said suddenly.

Why had I said that? Because it was all I could think of to say.

Now, Dr. Whitehorn, what do you make of that? Is that enigmatic enough for you? Perhaps I have remembered the conversation imperfectly. Or perhaps I have missed some of the underlying nuances, failed to exercise that sensitivity you're so big on. But why is my daughter talking in these tense, circular riddles? And why is it that I, her mother, can't understand her?

Nancy Krantz is a practising Roman Catholic, but she is also a believer in signs. Nothing so simple as horoscopes or palm reading; the signs she watches for and obeys are subtle and, to the casual eye, minuscule. She has come to rely on these small portents (a postage stamp upside-down, an icicle falling on the stroke of midnight, a name misspelled in the telephone book) but she is uneasy about admitting her faith in them. "If I confessed to sign-watching," she says, "I would be asked to name a Regulating Agent who sets up the signs and points the way." She prefers to see her omens as part of a system of electrical impulses which relate unlike objects, suggesting mysterious connections in another dimension of time. But admitting to such a belief, she says, leaves her open to charges of superstition or worse, marks her as a follower of the cult of intuition. Yet, she believes in signs and, furthermore, she believes that most other people do too.

Susanna Moodie, in one of her splendidly irrelevant asides, says much the same thing. "All who have ever trodden this earth, possessed of the powers of thought and reflection, have listened to voices of the soul and secretly acknowledged their power; but few, very few, have had the courage boldly to declare their belief in them."

And today I too have received a sign. Nothing flimsy like a dream, or mysterious like the surfacing of a familiar face: just a word, a single word, that started a chain reaction.

It began with a book by Kipling which Richard is reading for school. He hates it; it's dull, and he doesn't like the stylized way in which the characters speak. It is also rather long. Every night he brings it home from school, puts it on the front hall table, and in the morning he carries it back again, unopened. It is an old book from the school library. The binding is an alarming tatter of cloth and glue, and the dull-red cover is frayed around the edges. Its position on our hall table is becoming familiar, part of the landscape now; we expect it to be there. The lettering on the cover is shiny gold, and the title is curved along a golden hoop. Underneath it, curled the other way, is the name Rudyard Kipling.

Rudyard. Poor man to have such a strange name. Cruel Victorians to name their children so badly. I am struck by something half-remembered. Of course! Furlong's real name is Rudyard. His mother let it slip out once by mistake when she was talking to me. He never uses it, of course, and as far as I know no one else knows it. Rudyard. A secret name.

Secret. It hints at other secrets. Why is it I have kept this particular secret to myself? Why not?—it is a trifling fact—but it seems strange I've never mentioned it to Martin or to Roger.

Roger. Does Roger know about the name Rudyard? He did his Ph.D. thesis on Furlong. He is the authority on Furlong Eberhardt in this country; he cornered that little market about six years ago and stuffed it all into a thesis.

Thesis. Where is Roger's thesis? It is, without a doubt, where all doctoral theses are—on microfilm in the university library.

Library. What time does the library close? It's open all evening, of course. Until eleven o'clock. Martin is still in Toronto and I have the car.

The car. It is sitting outside on the snowy drive. The tank is full of gas and the keys are on the hall table. I can go. I can go this very minute.

Roger's thesis proved to be disappointing.

I had no trouble finding it. The librarian was helpful and polite: "Of course, Mrs. Gill. I'm sure we have Dr. Ramsay's thesis here." With her bracelet of keys she opened cupboards and pulled out metal drawers which were solidly filled with rows of neatly boxed microfilm. Hundreds of them. Each loaded with information which had been laboriously accumulated and assembled and then methodically stuffed away in these drawers where they were wonderfully, freely—almost, in fact, recklessly—available.

The films were arranged alphabetically, and it took only a few minutes before I found what I wanted: Ramsay, Roger R.—*Furlong Eberhardt and the Canadian Consciousness.* I yanked it out, electrified with happiness; it was so easy.

It took something like two hours to read it on the microfilm machine, but after the first hour I contented myself with skimming. For there was almost nothing of interest. And it was hard to believe that Roger with his fat yellow curls and Rabelaisian yelp of laughter could have produced this river of creamy musings. He had actually got past the examining committee with these long, elaborate, clustered generalizations, all artificially squeezed between Roman numerals and subdivided and re-subdivided until they reached the tiny fur of footnotes, appendices and, at last, something called the Author's Afterword? Hadn't someone along the line demanded something solid in the way of facts?

And the timidity, the equivocation—the use of hesitant pleading words like conjecture, hypothesis, probability—alternating with the brisk, combative, masculine "however" which introduced every second paragraph, as though Roger had been locked into debate with himself and losing badly.

His design, as outlined in the Preface, was to survey the texts of Furlong's first four novels, collate those themes and images which were specifically related to the national consciousness—which were, in short, definitively Canadian—all this in order to prove that Furlong Eberhardt more or less represented the "most nearly complete flowering of the national ethos in the middle decades of this century."

I had to remind myself that I hadn't come to carp at Roger's prose or even to question his ultimate purpose; I had come to unseal some of the mystery surrounding the person of Furlong Eberhardt. I had come for biographical material, and in that respect Roger's thesis was useless.

The explanation for the omission of personal data came in the Afterword in which Roger explained at length that in his study of Eberhardt he had attempted to follow the dictates of the New Criticism, a critical method which, he explained, eschewed the personality and beliefs of the author and concentrated instead on close textual analysis.

It was a disappointment. And it came as a surprise to me after spending a year and a half painfully abstracting the personality of Susanna Moodie from the rambling, discursive body of her writing, that anyone would deliberately set out to purify prose by obliterating the personality that had shaped it.

A paradox. I saw that I would have to find another way.

Thursday. I wake up early remembering that this is the day Martin is to make his presentation to the Renaissance Society.

When I drove him to the train on Monday I noticed that, in addition to his battered canvas weekender, he was carrying a heavy cardboard carton to which he had attached a rough rope handle. His woven tapestries must be packed inside, although he didn't mention them to me. Were they finished, I wondered. How had they turned out? How would he display them? But because they seemed to represent something obscurely humiliating, I kept silent. The subject of the *Paradise Lost* weavings had been so assiduously avoided by both of us, that I felt a last-minute plea on my part to abandon the presentation would be ridiculous.

So I said nothing; only kissed him and told him I would meet his train on Friday night, and watched him walk toward the train in a wet sludgy snow, carrying the shameful suitcase, a ludicrous umbrella from Birmingham days, and the damning cardboard box that banged against his leg as he climbed aboard, set on his lunatic journey. Oh, Martin!

This morning at ten o'clock he is scheduled to give his talk and presentation. I have seen the conference program which says "Dr. Martin Gill—*Paradise Lost* in a Pictorial Presentation." I will have to keep busy; I will have to make this day disappear.

It strikes me that I might as well continue my pursuit of information regarding Furlong. So after lunch I go to the big downtown library.

Granite pillars, crouched lions, the majestic stone entrance stairs covered with sisal matting and boards for five months of the year (what a strange country we live in!), a foyer imperial with vaulting, echoes, brass plaques, oil portraits, uniformed guards, a ponderous check-out desk and on it, purring and whirring, the latest in photostatic machines. Two librarians, tightly permed, one fat, one thin, stand behind the desk. The card catalogue snakes back and forth in a room of its own; surely I will find something here.

I carry books to a table, check indexes, cross-check references, try various biographical dictionaries and local histories, and conclude after several hours that Furlong had done a remarkable job of obscuring his past. He seems hardly to have existed before 1952 when his first book was published. I do find two passing references to a Rudyard Eberhart in the forties; the surname is misspelled and the geographical location is wrong; they are cryptic notations which I don't really understand but which I nevertheless make note of. I will have to go to the Archives if I am to discover anything more. Another day.

This is the library where Ruthie St. Pierre works, and as I put on my coat and scarf, I think that it would be nice to stop and have a chat with her.

Her office is on the top floor, a tiny glassed-in cubicle in the Translation Department. I climb the stairs and go past a maze of other tiny offices.

And then I glimpse her through the wall of glass. She is bending over a filing cabinet in the corner and she is wearing a pantsuit of daffodil yellow and platform shoes of prodigious thickness. She finds what she wants, straightens up and turns back to her desk.

And I would have knocked on the glass, I would have gone in and embraced her and told her how much I had missed her all winter (for I *had* missed her) and told her how morose and sullen and seedy Roger is looking and how he doesn't even know where she is living or how she is getting along—but I don't go in because I can see plainly that she is in the seventh, perhaps eighth, and who knows—she is such a tiny girl—maybe even the ninth month of blooming, swelling, flowering pregnancy.

I watch her for a moment to be sure, to be absolutely certain, and then, quickly and quietly, I make my retreat.

Afterwards, driving home, I can't understand why I had left her like that. It was a shock, of course, and then too I hadn't wanted to create what for Ruthie might be a painful and embarrassing meeting. Certainly she had gone out of her way to avoid friends all winter.

When I was sick with the flu she had sent a basket of fruit —not ordinary apples and oranges, but wonderful and exotic mangoes, kiwifruit, red bananas, passion fruit, figs and pomegranates, and I had written her a thank-you note, mailing it to the library where she works. Once in the following weeks she had phoned to see if I was better. "I'm fine now, Ruthie," I had said, "but how are you?"

"Fine, Jude, fine." (She is the only person in the world who consistently calls me Jude.) "I guess you know that Roger and I have called it quits."

"Well," I said uneasily, "yes, and I'm sorry."

"It's all for the best. Roger's not one for settling down, you know. Look, Jude, I've got to go. The big boss is prowling today. Bye for now. Keep the faith."

"You too," I said, not knowing which faith she referred to, but sensing that she had meant: respect my privacy, leave me alone for a while, ask me no questions, hold off, give me time, keep faith in me.

So I hadn't phoned her again, and today I hadn't rushed into the little office. But later I wished I had. She had looked both brave and fragile in her yellow suit, and I had been moved by the gallantry with which she concentrated on her filing cabinet, pencil in hand, and that enormous abdomen bunching up in front of her.

I am late getting home from the library. It is dinner time, and Richard suggests we send out for a pizza.

When it arrives Meredith and Richard and I eat it in the family room, along with glasses of ginger ale. The curtains

are pulled and the television is on. It gets late and I should
send the children to bed; I should remind them that this is
a school night, but I am reluctant to break up our warm,
shared drowsiness. Ruthie is far away now, as far away as a
character in a story—did I really see her? Furlong Eberhardt
seems foreign and trifling—what matters is our essential
clutter of warmth and food and noise.

Eleven o'clock. The news comes on. More Watergate,
more Belfast, another provincial land scandal, and then, to
wind up the news, a lighter item. Dr. Martin Gill is introduced. Unbelievably his face spreads across the screen.

There is not a sound from us. The three of us, Meredith
and Richard and I, do not speak; we do not even move; we
are frozen into place.

The interviewer explains that Dr. Gill has startled both
the art and the literary world by creating—he consults his
notes—a graphic presentation of *Paradise Lost* (a famous
seventeenth century poem, he explains to all of us out in
TV land). Presented today at a national symposium on literature, it was a tremendous sensation. Two art galleries
have already made impressive bids for the tapestries. "Is
that true, Professor Gill?" the interviewer asks.

The camera goes back to Martin. "Yes, it does appear to
be true," he says with engaging modesty.

The interviewer continues with a long information-
packed question, "In that case, it would seem that this work
of yours, quite apart from the interest in connection with
the poem, has an intrinsic, that is, a beauty of its own."

"I am really quite overwhelmed by the response," Martin
says, his slow, slow smile beaming out across the country.
Beautiful. It is a highly individual smile, both provocative
and sensual—I've never noticed that before.

The two faces fade, giving way to sports and weather,
and the children and I slowly turn to look at each other.
Richard and Meredith are staring at me and their mouths
hang open with awe. And so, I perceive, does mine.

And then we leap and dance around the room; singing,

shouting, laughing, hugging each other. We order another pizza, a large special combination. Friends phone to ask if we've seen Martin, and we phone Martin several times at his hotel and finally, at two o'clock in the morning, we reach him and talk and talk and then dizzy, crazy, mad with happiness we go stunned to bed.

In the morning there are three things for me to read. First the Toronto newspaper—a write-up on Martin and a picture of him posing in front of the weavings. I peer intently at the tapestry but, as in most newsphotos, it is smeary and porous and not very effective. Martin though, with his nice white teeth open in a smile, comes out very well.

PROFESSOR WEDS ART TO LITERATURE

English professor Martin Gill delighted his colleagues at the Renaissance Society yesterday with a change from the usual staid academic papers. His presentation was a pictorial representation of *Paradise Lost*, Milton's famous epic masterpiece. Using the techniques of tapestry making, Dr. Gill, a distinguished scholar, used different colours to represent the themes in the poem, and produced not only a visual commentary on the piece, but a stunning work of abstract art. Three art galleries, including the National Gallery, have placed bids for the work.

The idea was intended as a teaching aid, Dr. Gill explained. "The poem is so complex and so enormous that often the student of Literature loses the total Miltonic pattern."

Dr. Gill is the son of Professor Enos Gill of McGill University, author of *Two Times a Nation*. His wife is Judith Gill, the biographer. About the future Dr. Gill denies that he will divorce literature for art. "It's only been a temporary romance," he said to reporters with a chuckle. "I wouldn't trust my luck twice."

Next I read a note from Furlong. I had been expecting this, knowing that once he realized he had tipped his hand, he would make haste to smooth over the traces.

> My dear Judith,
>
> I'm sure you regret as much as I our little mis-understanding the other night. I must say I was more than usually rattled by your startling lunge at my throat, and I'm afraid I lost what the youth of today would call my cool. No doubt I babbled like a complete looney. As soon as I realized what it was that concerned you—I refer to your mistaken impression that I had appropriated your plot for *Graven Images*—I came to my senses, and can only hope that you came to yours as well. Judith, my pet, we have been good friends for too long to allow this misunderstanding to come between us. The truth is, I value your friendship and, yes, I admit it, perhaps I did get a new slant from your aborted novel, but as I explained to you, writers are no more than scavengers and assemblers of lies. You have done me a good turn; perhaps I may be able to do the same for you one day."
>
> Fondly,
>
> FURLONG

Last of all I read an airletter from England. At first, see-ing the bright blue paper and feeling the familiar feather-weight paper, I thought that Anita Spalding had finally come through. But no, it is addressed to us, to Dr. and Mrs. Martin Gill.

> Dear Dr. and Mrs. Gill,
>
> First of all let me thank you for your very kind Christmas card. I apologize for the silence from

this end. I will be passing quite near you in a month's time, and if it is not too terribly inconvenient, might I call on you? I will be in New York for a few days conferring with my publisher (I am about to have a novel published) and there is an item of some urgency which I am anxious to discuss with you. In addition, I am most desirous of making your acquaintance. Please do not go to any trouble for me. I shall be in the city only two nights (I have already secured hotel accommodation) and I should be distraught if my sudden appearance were in any way to inconvenience you.

I remain,

Your obedient servant,

JOHN SPALDING

P.S. We have had a nasty winter compounded by strikes and fuel shortages, not to mention my own distressing personal affairs. I trust all is well with you and your family.

JS

April

I wake early one morning. Something is amiss. A wet smell. What is it? I sniff, and instead of the usual hot metal smell of the furnace, I smell something different.

And I hear something. Water running. Someone has left a tap on all night. "Martin," I say. "Are you awake?"

"No," he says crossly. "It's only six-thirty."

"What's that sound, Martin?"

"I can't hear anything."

"Listen. It's water dripping. Can you hear it?"

He listens for a minute. "I think it's just the snow melting," he says. "It's the snow on the roof."

I listen again. It *is* the snow; it's running off the roof in rivulets. It's pouring through the downspout.

And that explains the funny smell. It's the grey-scented, rare and delicate-as-a-thread smell of the melt. Spring.

At last.

Hurriedly I write a letter to John Spalding.

> Dear John, (*I use his first name, availing myself of the North American right to be familiar.*)
> We were delighted to get your letter and look forward to seeing you at the end of the month. Are you sure you wouldn't like to change your plans and stay with us? We have plenty of room and would enjoy having you. Martin and I are anxious to know if you are bringing your wife and daughter. All of us, and especially Richard, of course, would love to meet them. If this note reaches you before you leave England, do drop us a line and let us know.

Our congratulations to you on the publication of your novel. We look forward to hearing more about it.

Sincerely,

JUDITH GILL

(*And then because no letter to or from Britain seems complete without a reference to the weather, I add—*) P. S. We have had a long winter and lots of snow, but spring is on the way now, and by the time you arrive the last of the snow will be gone.

JUDITH

In a week I had a reply.

Dear Judith, (*Aha, familiarity is contagious.*)
Thank you for your kind offer of a bed which I accept with gratitude. As for my wife, she and I have recently separated. Isabel has returned to Cyprus and has taken Anita with her. I supposed —wrongly I see—that Anita had written to your son about the chain of events. But then she has not even written to me very regularly. All this is rather upsetting to her, no doubt. Her mother has attached herself to a rogue of a gigolo, a cretinous beach ornament, and Anita has no doubt seen more of the unsavoury world in the last month than is good for her. The whole subject is exceedingly painful to me at the moment; thus, perhaps it is for the best that you know before I come.
There are daffodils blooming all over Birmingham. Truly glorious.

Best wishes,

JOHN SPALDING

Isabel Spalding gone off with gigolo! I picture him, heavy with grease, cunningly light-fingered and handsome. And her, pale and sluttish in a bikini. Poor Anita.

I hasten to tell Richard about what has happened in far-off Cyprus. For although the correspondence may be ended, it is better for him to know that there is, at least, an explanation; he has not been rejected; he has not accidentally written something offensive, he has not been the victim of a love that was unrequited.

I explained to him how traumatic a sudden shift in geography can be to a child, not to mention the catastrophic splintering of a family. He nods; he can understand that. Later she may feel like writing, I tell him. Yes, he says, perhaps. I gaze at him, trying to think of something further to comfort him, but he dashes away saying, it doesn't matter, it doesn't matter. Does he mean it? He has survived this long.

BUFFET SUPPER
WHERE—*62 Beaver Place*
WHEN—*April 30th, 8:00*
Judith and Martin Gill

We are going to have a party. Or, as my mother would say, we are going to entertain. Not that entertaining was something she ever did. Only something she would like to have done. She would love to entertain, she always said, if only the slipcovers were finished, if only the lampshade was replaced, if only Bert—our father and her husband—would fix the cracked piece of tiling in the bathroom. She would entertain if she had more room, if the children were older and off her hands, if chicken weren't so expensive, if her nerves didn't act up when she got over-tired.

But she never did. Only her sister and a few close relatives and neighbours ever sipped coffee at our kitchen table. Mrs. Christianson, Loretta Bruce who lived across the street in a bungalow identical to ours, which my mother always

said needed some imagination as well as some spit and
polish, a Mrs. McAbee; timid women, all of them, who
flattered our mother on her "taste," who asked, when they
had finished their Nescafé, well, what have you been doing
to the house lately? Then she would lead them into the
living room, or bedroom or whatever, and point out the
new needlepoint cushion or the magazine rack with its felt
appliqué, and they would chorus again how clever she was.
Poor swindled souls, believing that women expressed their
personalities through their houses. A waste. But maybe they
really thought differently.

The buffet supper was Martin's idea. "We have to do
something with him," he said when he read John Spalding's
letter. "Besides we haven't had a party since December."

I make up a list of people. About thirty seems right.
Nancy and Paul Krantz, the Parks and the Beerbalms from
the neighbourhood. And some university people. Furlong?
I can't decide what to do with him, first thinking that nothing could persuade me to have him, the traitor, the thief,
the liar. But it is unthinkable, on the other hand, to exclude
him. Besides, I might have a chance to ask him a few searching questions. But then, I argue, why should I invite him,
especially after that self-serving note he sent me in which
he cast me in the role of a crazy woman who lunged and
who took easy neurotic offence, and himself as the worldly
artist, just self-depreciating enough to admit to minor dis-
honesties. Swine. But I had to invite him. For one thing,
Mrs. Eberhardt must be invited, for I could depend on her
to draw out John Spalding, should he turn out to be someone who needed drawing out.

And what about Ruthie? Should I invite her? She would
probably refuse, but just what if she didn't? I decided to
consult Roger, so I phoned him at his office.

"Roger," I said, "we're having a party. Martin and I. In
a couple of weeks."

"Terrific."

"John Spalding is coming from England. Remember
hearing about him?"

"Sure. Your old landlord."

"Right. Well, I'm writing invitations and I wonder if—well—I'd like to invite Ruthie, of course, but I don't want to put either of you on the spot."

"Ruthie," he mused.

"Just tell me what you think, Roger. Shall I ask her or not?"

A pause. And then he said, "Sure. I suppose we can't avoid each other forever. Not in a city this size."

"Okay then," I said. "Ruthie's on the list. I'll have to send this to her at the library I suppose. Or have you discovered where she's living?"

Another pause. Longer this time. "Well, yes. I guess I do know where she's living."

"Really? Where?"

"This may sound odd, Judith, but it seems she is staying at the Eberhardts' apartment."

I am surprised. Very surprised. "At Furlong's? Ruthie is staying at Furlong's?"

"Yeah."

"Are you sure?"

"Sure I'm sure."

"How'd you find out?"

"Well," he paused again, "the truth is—I guess I should come right out with it—the truth is I followed her home one night. From the library."

"And she went to Furlong's?"

"Yes. Amazing isn't it. I couldn't believe it at first, so the next night I followed her again. Same time. Same place."

Cunningly I asked, "How did she look, Roger? I mean—is she okay?"

"Fine, as far as I could tell, fine. It was fairly dark, of course. I'd love to say she was thin and pinched and lonely looking, but actually she looked quite okay. I think she's even put on some weight."

"Really?"

"Yes. And, of course, when I thought it over, it isn't all that extraordinary you know. Her staying there. They were always good to both of us, both Furlong and his mother. Sort of adopted us. And God knows she's safe enough with Furlong. As you well know."

"Roger. This is sort of a personal question and you don't have to answer if you don't want to."

"What is it, Judith?"

"Why is it you and Ruthie never got married?"

"I had a feeling you were going to ask that. Well, the answer is that Ruthie never wanted to get tied down."

"That's funny."

"Why?"

"Because she once said the same thing about you. That you didn't want to get tied down."

"I suppose we both spouted a lot of nonsense."

"Do you suppose things would have worked out if you had been married?"

"I suppose. I mean, it makes it a little more difficult to split if you've got all that legal mess."

"Is it really over then, Roger? With you and Ruthie? Not that it's any of my business."

"I'd hate to think so. I think she just needs time on her own. To sort things out. Get her head together."

I had been sympathetic to this point, but suddenly I was enraged. "Damn it, Roger. Damn it, damn it."

He sounded alarmed. "Judith, what have I said?"

"All that blather about getting heads together."

"It's just an expression. It means—"

"I know what it means. But it's so—so impossibly puerile. Do you think anyone ever gets it all sorted out? Gets it all tidied up, purged out, all the odds and ends stowed away on the right shelves? Do you really believe that, Roger?"

"Sometimes you need time. How can you think in a thicket?"

"That thicket happens to be a form of protection. It's thinking in a vacuum that's unreal."

"Judith, I just don't know," he sighed. "I just don't know anymore."

"Look, Roger, I think I'll just send this invitation to

Ruthie's office. I don't want her to know that I know where she's staying if it's such a big mystery."

"Good idea."

"She probably won't come anyway."

"Probably not," he said dolefully.

I am putting the finishing touches on Susanna Moodie. In the mornings I go over the chapters one by one, trying to look at her objectively. Does she live, breathe, take definite shape? Is the vein of personality strong enough to bridge the episodes? The disturbing change in personality: it bothers me. Dare I suggest hormone imbalance? Psychological scarring? It's unwise to do more than suggest. I'm not a psychologist or a doctor, as the critics will be quick to point out. But I do have a feeling about her. I wonder though, have I conveyed that feeling?

Aside from her two books about life in Canada, Susanna Moodie wrote a string of trashy novels, potboilers really, limp-wristed romances containing such melodramatics as last minute rescues at the gallows and death-bed conversions and always, unfailingly, oceans and oceans of tears. She was desperate for money, of course, so she wrote quickly and she wrote for a popular audience, the Harlequin nurse stories of her day.

But one of the books she wrote has been invaluable to me. It is a novel entitled *Flora Lindsay* or *Episodes in an Eventful Life*. Astonishingly, it is Susanna's own story, or at least an idealized picture of it, an autobiography in fictional form. The heroine, Flora, is like Susanna married to a veteran of the Napoleonic Wars. Like Susanna, Flora and her husband (also named John) emigrate to Canada. Even the ship they sail on bears the same name, the *Anne*. Like Susanna, Flora has a baby daughter and, like her again, she has employed an unwed mother as a nurse for her child.

Thus, by watching Flora, I am able to see Susanna as a young woman. But, of course, it isn't really Susanna; it's only a projection, a view of herself. Flora is refined, virtuous, bright, lively, humorous; her only fault is an occasional pout when her husband places some sort of restraint on her. Did Susanna really see herself that way?

How do I view myself?—large, loose, baroque. Compulsively garrulous, hugely tactless, given to blurts, heavy foot in heavy mouth. Fearsome with energy, Brobdingnagian voice, everything of such vastness that my photographs always surprise me by their relatively normal proportions—ah, but that's only my public self. And Martin, does he view himself—now flushed with victory from the Renaissance Society—as a cocky counterculture academic? Does he carry a newsreel in his head with himself as maverick star, a composed and witty generalist who nimbly leaps from discipline to discipline, who proved his wife wrong about the whole concept of poetry portrayed in wool, but resists saying I told you so? Just smiles at her his slow and knowing smile and thinks his secret thoughts, maybe wondering how he would look with long hair and that ultimate obscenity on middle-aged men, beads?

Susanna wrote *Flora Lindsay* when she was a middle-aged woman, and she had by that time suffered repeated trials, many births, several deaths, unbearable homesickness and alienation, not to mention a searing lack of intellectual nourishment. Looking back, she may have viewed that early life, that time of high expectations and simple married love as a period of comfort and happiness, seeing herself as the nimble and graceful heroine, not the prudish, rather shallow and condescending woman she more than likely was. She was so shrewd about her fellow Canadians that she enraged them, but nevertheless seemed to have had little real understanding of herself. Is it any wonder then, I ask myself as I send the manuscript off to a typist—is it any wonder that I don't understand her?

"Why hello, Mrs. Gill."

"Judith! Long time no see."

"What can we do for you today, Mrs. Gill?"

They know me at the Public Archives. I've spent hours and hours in these shiny corridors working on my biographical research, exploring filing cabinets, pulling out envelopes, and going through the contents, sometimes finding what I need, but just as often not. And always I am astonished at the sheer volume of trivia which is being watched over.

The librarians guard their treasures diligently, and they are unfailingly kind in their willingness to spend an hour, sometimes two or three, finding the origin of a single fact. But today I don't need any help. I am quite sure I can find what I want.

Name and year: Furlong Eberhardt (possibly Rudyard Eberhart). As for dates, I work backwards from the present.

It takes longer than I think. A clue, tantalizing, leads nowhere, and I spend an hour in a cul-de-sac; just when I think I'm finding my way out, the reference turns out to apply to someone else. I press my hands to my head. Exhaustion. What am I doing here?

In the cafeteria I have a bowl of soup and a sandwich, and later in the afternoon I get lucky. One reference leads to another; I skip from drawer to drawer, putting the pieces together. And they fit, they fit! I have it. Or almost. I'll have to check at the Immigration Department, but I know what they'll say. I am already positive.

It's this: Furlong Eberhardt, Canadian prairie novelist, the man who is said to embody the ethos of the nation, is an American!

I want to hug the fact, to chew on it, to pull it out when I choose so I can admire its shiny ironic contours and ponder the wonderful, dark, moist, hilarious secrecy of it.

Rudyard Eberhart, born Maple Bluffs, Iowa, only son of Elizabeth Eberhart, widow.

Eligible for draft in 1949 (Korean War), left
Maple Bluffs the day notice was delivered.

Landed immigrant status (with mother) in Saskatchewan.

Attended U. of Sask., was once written up in local
paper as grand loser (shortest fish) in a fishing
competition.

Began writing short stories under the name of
Red Eberhart. Gradual shift to Eberhardt spelling, finalized with publication of first novel,
1952.

Christened Furlong by a kindly critic, after which
he travelled from strength to strength until
arrival at present eminence.

Ah, Furlong, you crafty devil.

I could not remember being so wonderfully amused by
anything in all my life. My throat pricked continuously
with wanting to laugh, and for the first few days it was all I
could do to keep the corners of my mouth from turning up
at inappropriate moments, so amused was I by the spectacle of Furlong Eberhardt who, with scarcely a break in
stride, traded Maple Bluffs for the Maple Leaf; marvellous!

But in my delight I recognized something which was
faintly hysterical, something suspiciously akin to relief.
What had I expected to find? That Furlong had his novels
written for him by a West Coast syndicate? That he might
be guilty of a crime more heinous (murder? blackmail?)
than mere trifling with the facts of his private life? That
something unbearably sordid had poisoned his previous
existence? Yes, I had been badly frightened; I admitted it
to myself.

Poor Furlong. I could see it all: how he had—I recalled
his own words—got into it innocently enough and then was
unable to extricate himself, taking a free ride on the band
wagon of nationalism and unable to jump off. Well, don't
worry, Furlong, I won't betray you now.

Poor Furlong, so eager to be accepted, to be loved.

Poor Furlong, suffering in miserable and ageing secrecy.
Poor Furlong. Dear Furlong.

"Martin," I whisper after the lights are out, "what do
you think of John Spalding?"

Pause. "He seems okay," Martin says. "Not quite the nut
I expected."

"Me either. Where did I get the idea he was going to be
short?"

"And fat! Christ, he's actually obese. Cheerful guy
though."

"Shhhhh. He's only one thin wall away."

"Never mind. He should be dead to the world after those
three brandies he tucked away."

"Did you ask him about his wife? While I was making
coffee?"

"Good God, no. What would you have me say, Judith?
'Sorry to hear you've been made a cuckold, old man.' "

"Did you at least mention that we were having a party
tomorrow night?"

"Yes."

"What did he say?"

"Just sort of rumbled on about how he hoped we weren't
going to any trouble for him."

"He certainly is different than what I expected. It's a
good thing we had him paged at the airport or we'd never
have found him."

"Funny, but he said the same thing about us."

"What?"

"That he wouldn't have recognized us in a thousand
years. He had us pictured differently."

"Really? I wonder what he thought we were like."

"I didn't ask him."

"I would have."

"You would have, Judith, yes."

"It might have been interesting. Don't you ever wonder,

Martin, how you look to other people? The general impression, I mean."

"No," he said. "To be truthful, I don't think I ever do."

"That's abnormal."

"Are you sure?"

"No. Maybe it's abnormal the other way. But still I would have asked him."

I turn to look at Martin. The street light shining into our room and neatly bisecting our bed, permits me to study him. He is lying on his back, relaxed with his hands locked behind his head. And on his face I see a lazy, enigmatic smile. I peer at him intently.

"Why are you smiling, Martin?"

"Me? Am I smiling?"

"You know you are."

"I suppose I was just thinking foul and filthy midnight thoughts."

"About?"

He runs a hand under my nightgown. Stops in the slope between my thighs.

"Sshhhhhh," I say. "He'll hear us."

"Fuck him."

"Well, that's a switch."

"Shhhhhhhh."

Nancy Krantz came a little early to give me a hand with the party.

Martin and Paul Krantz and John Spalding drank gin tonics in the living room, and she and I flicked dust bits out of wine glasses with paper towels, heated pots of lasagna and cut up onions for the salad. My party menus (like my décor, my hair style, my legally married status) are ten years out of date; I know that elsewhere women, prettier than I and wearing gowns of enormous haute daring, are serving tiny Viennese pancakes stuffed with herring, or scampi à la Shanghai, but I willingly, wilfully, shut my eyes to all of that.

Nancy, larky and ironic, takes note of our female busy work; contrasts us to the booze swillers in the next room, lolling in chairs, dense in discussion. She is in violent good cheer, dextrous with the stacks of plates and cutlery, ingenious with the table napkins, setting out candles in startling asymmetrical arrangements, never for an instant leaving off her social commentary. "Parties are irrational but necessary. Where are the extra ashtrays, Judith? If you set aside those parties which are merely chic, which exist just for the sake of existence, then there is something biblical and compelling about raining down a lot of food and drink on a lot of people gathered under a single roof at an appointed hour. Almost the fulfilment of a rite. And it brings on a sort of catharsis if it really works. And why not? You've got an artificial selection of people. The personalities and the conditions are imposed. A sort of pre-ordered confrontation. I thought you had one of those hot tray things, Judith."

"I do. Now where did I put it last time I used it?"

She finds it on the top shelf above the refrigerator, polishes it briefly, plugs it in. Ready to go.

Roger is the first to arrive. "I know I'm early," he apologizes, "but I wonder if—you know—is Ruthie coming? Or not?"

"Not," I tell him. "She phoned to say she'd like to come but couldn't make it."

"Why not?" he says, flinching visibly.

"She didn't say."

"Oh, Jesus," he says. " I knew it."

"Come on, Roger. I want you to meet John Spalding. He's in the living room."

"Oh yeah," he says. And whispers, "What's he like?"

"I don't know. I've hardly seen him. He slept until noon and had an appointment this afternoon. We haven't had too much time to talk to him."

"Nice guy?"

"Nice enough," I say. "But I'd stay off the topic of faith-less women. He's in the midst, so to speak."

"Righto," he says, disappearing into the living room.

After that things get busy. The doorbell rings continu-ously it seems, and since it is raining heavily outside, I am occupied with finding places for boots while Richard ferries dripping umbrellas to the basement and Meredith hangs raincoats upstairs on the shower rail.

From the living room, the family room and even the kitchen there is a rising tide of noise, stemming at first from polite muted corners, erupting then into explosive con-tagious laughter, passing through furniture, through walls, melding with the mingled reverberations of wood, china, cutlery, a woman's shrill scream of surprise.

Bodies are everywhere, slung on couches, chair arms, kitchen counters; I have to move two people aside to find room to set the casseroles down.

Our parties are always like this, a blur from the first door-bell to the last nightcap—fetching, carrying, greeting, serv-ing, clearing, scraping, rinsing, smiling hard through it all, wondering why I ever thought it was going to be a good idea, and yet exhilarated to fever pitch and this on barely half a glass of wine.

I am at the centre of a hurricane, the eye of calm in the middle of ferocious whirling circles. Between the kitchen and hall I pause, trying to sense the pattern. What has be-come of John Spalding, guest of honour whom I have intro-duced to absolutely no one? Ah, but Martin has looked after him. There he is in the exact centre of the beige sofa, plumply settled with a brimming glass, a woman on either side of him and Polly Stanley, awkward but surprisingly girlish, on the floor at his feet. All are laughing; I can't actually hear them laughing, not over all this noise, but they are locked into laughing position, heads back, teeth bared.

Mrs. Eberhardt is sitting in our most comfortable chair

doing what she was invited to do, drawing out quieter guests and being charming and kindly and solid; she is the oldest person in the room. By far the oldest. Does she mind? Does she even notice?

Ben Stanley and Roger have their heads very close together near the fireplace; they look vaguely theatrical as though they had selected this location to accent the seriousness of their discussion. I can tell from the confidential tilt of their heads that they are on the subject of departmental politics. Roger is mainly listening and nodding as befits his junior status. Beside he is apolitical; power doesn't interest him yet.

From far away I hear the telephone briefly pierce the hubbub. Two rings and someone answers it. Someone's baby sitter probably. No, it's for Furlong. Meredith goes to find him. She discovers him refilling a plate with salad, and she whispers lengthily into his ear. I can see them talking. Meredith is distraught; her hands are waving a little wildly. Furlong puts down his plate and hurries off to the phone where he talks for some time, cupping his hand to shut out the noise. After that I am too busy to watch.

Someone knocks over a glass of wine. I wipe it up. I set out cream and sugar on the table. Check the coffee. Someone arrives late and I find him some scrapings of lasagna and a heap of wilted salad. But later, serving plates of chocolate torte, I see that Meredith and Furlong are again conferring earnestly in a corner. After a moment they motion to Roger to join them, and the three of them huddle together. Furlong is explaining something to Roger who is leaning backwards, stunned, shaking his head, I don't believe it, I don't believe it.

"How about some dessert?" I break in on them.

There is a sudden catch of silence. Embarrassment. Uncertainty. A fraction of a second only. Then Furlong takes my hand gently, "Judith, you must forgive me, but I'm afraid I'll have to leave early. Something unexpected has come up."

"Nothing serious?" I ask, for I'm suddenly alarmed by their shared gravity.

"No. Not exactly."

"You'd better tell her," Meredith directs.

"Perhaps I'd better."

"I wish to Jesus someone had told me," Roger says, half-sullen, half-violent.

"What's happened?" I demand.

"It's Ruthie." Furlong says her name with surprising tenderness.

"Ruthie?"

"I don't suppose you know, but she is—well—expecting a baby."

"Yes, I did know, as a matter of fact."

"I *knew* you suspected something," Meredith says ringingly.

"Why didn't you tell me, Judith?" Roger charges. "You never said a word to me about it."

"I've only known for a few weeks. I saw her. At the library. She didn't see me, but I saw her. I haven't told anyone. Except Martin, of course."

"You could have phoned me. One lousy phone call."

"Look, Roger," Furlong says, "Ruthie didn't want you to know. That was the point."

"I have a right to know. Who has a better right?"

"Well now you know."

"How did *you* find out, Meredith?" I ask.

"I met her one day. A couple months ago. Downtown after school. Furlong had just taken her to the doctor. They sort of had to tell me. I mean, it was pretty obvious.

"Anyway, Judith," Furlong breaks in, "that was Ruthie on the phone a few minutes ago."

"Don't tell me—"

"Yes. At least she thinks so. She's had a few twinges."

"But it's not supposed to be for another two weeks," Meredith says.

"What kind of twinges?" I ask Furlong.

"I don't know. That is, I didn't ask her what sort. Baby twinges, I presume."

"How far apart?"

"I didn't ask her that either."

"I'm surprised," I can't resist chiding him. "All those women in your books who die of childbirth. I would think you'd at least ask how far apart the pains are."

"Twenty minutes," Meredith interrupts. "I asked her."

"Christ. Twenty minutes." Roger moans.

"I think I'd better be going," Furlong says. "She's all by herself. She's been staying with Mother and me for the last little while."

"Yes. I think you'd better go too," I say. "And you'd better hurry. It could be quick."

"Jesus." Roger yells.

"Why don't you go too, Roger?" I say.

Furlong nods. "Maybe he should."

"What about me?" Meredith pleads. "Can't I come too?"

Furlong glances at me. I nod.

"The three of us then," Furlong says. "Mother can get a taxi later. I'll just have a word with her on the way out."

In a moment they are gone, and no one has even noticed their leaving. The wall of noise encloses me again; the volume after midnight doubles, trebles. In the living room I hear singing: "There's a bright golden haze on the meadow." Someone is rolling up the rug; someone else has found Meredith's rock records.

Unexpectedly I come across Richard who is carrying towers of coffee cups into the kitchen. As he passes I reach out automatically to pat the top of his head. The springy spaniel hair is familiar enough, but there is something different. My hand angles oddly; can it be that he's grown this much?

He shouts something into my ear. What is it? "Great party, Mother," he seems to be saying. Or something like that.

Finally they go home, the last guest disappears into the rain-creased darkness, the last car swerves around the corner of Beaver Place where all the other houses are dark. It's after three.

Martin carries a pot of tea into the wreckage of the living room, three cups on a tray, milk and sugar, a fan of spoons. "Sit down, Judith," he commands.

John Spalding, boulder-like, is still occupying the middle of the sofa. Has he moved all evening, I wonder?

At this hour we abandon the last remnant of formality. I kick off my silver shoes, note where the straps have bitten into the instep, and put my stockinged feet on the coffee table. Martin pours tea and hands me a cup.

"John," he says, "surely you'd like some too."

"Please," he booms from the cushions.

We sip in silence, letting the quiet wash over us.

Martin inquires about John's plane. It leaves at ten-thirty, a mere seven hours away. Martin has an early appointment, so it is decided that I will drive John to the airport.

"I hope the noise wasn't too much for you tonight," I say.

"Not in the least. I enjoyed it all. My first gimpse of North American informality. Spontaneous and delightful."

"I'm sorry your visit has been so short," I tell him. "We've hardly had a chance to get acquainted." He waves aside my remarks with a plump hand. "I feel I've got to know you well just by staying with you."

"Perhaps you'll be back this way before long," Martin says politely. "Seeing publishers and so forth."

"When exactly is your novel coming out?" I ask.

"In about a month's time," he says. "And that reminds me, there was a little something I wanted to mention to you both." He looks around the room, glances at his watch and says, "That is, if it's not too late for you?"

"Oh, no," I say. "It's not too late for us. Is it, Martin?"

"No, of course not," Martin says wearily.

"Well, the fact is," John Spalding says, making an effort to sit up straight, "the fact is that this isn't the first novel I've written."

"Really?" I say brightly. Too brightly?

"The truth is I've written several. But none of them was ever published. I never seemed to hit on an idea worth developing. Until a year or so ago."

"Yes?" Martin and I chorus.

"Finally I struck on something workable. And I owe the idea for my novel to you. To your family that is."

"To us."

"You see, I have, in a matter of speaking, borrowed the situation of your family. A Canadian family who spend a year in England."

"Your novel is about us?" Martin asks incredulously.

"Oh, no no no no. Not really about you, not exactly about you. Just the situation. A professor on sabbatical leave comes to an English university in an English city."

"Birmingham?"

"Well, yes. But I'm calling it Flyxton-on-Stoke. They have two children—"

"A boy and a girl?"

"Right. You've got the picture."

"But," Martin says, setting down his cup, "I suppose the resemblance ends there."

"Almost," John Spalding says, smiling a little nervously. "You may find a few other trifling similarities. That was why I wanted to mention this to you. So that when you read it, if you read it, you won't think I've—well—plagiarized from real life. If such a thing is possible."

"But how did you know anything about us?" I ask.

He laces his fingers across his broad stomach and, settling back, says, "Firstly, one can tell something about people simply by the fact that they have occupied the same quarters."

I nod, thinking of the bag of lightbulbs in the Birmingham bathroom, the sex manual under the mattress. Not to mention the shelf of manuscripts.

"Then there were the letters," he continues.

"But we never wrote you any," Martin says. "The university arranged the letting of the flat."

"No no no no no. I mean Anita's letters. The letters

which your son Richard, a fine boy by the way, wrote to our daughter."

"You read the letters?"

"Good Lord yes. We all quite looked forward to them. Anita used to read them aloud to us after tea. Ah, those were happier days. He writes a fine letter, your lad."

Martin and I exchange looks of amazement. "And your novel is based on Richard's letters?"

"Oh, no no no no." Again he fills the air with a spray of little no's like the exhaust from a car. "I didn't exactly *base* the novel on it. Just got a general idea of the sort of people you were, how you responded to things. That sort of thing."

"And you just took off from there?"

He beamed. "Exactly, exactly. But I did want you to know. I mean, in case you had any objections."

"It seems it's too late for objections even if we did have some," Martin says dryly.

"Well, yes, that is more or less the case. But you see, a writer must—"

"Get his material where he can find it," I finish for him.

"Quite. Quite. Exactly. And, of course, I have changed all the names entirely."

"What are we called?" I ask eagerly.

"You, I have called Gillian. Martin is simply inverted to Gilbert Martin."

"Very clever," Martin says, tight-lipped.

"We'll look forward to reading it," I say. "Will you send us a copy?"

"You may be sure of that. And I'm more than pleased that you seem to understand the situation."

"What I can't understand," Martin says, "is how you could find material for a novel out of our rather ordinary domestic situation. I mean, what in Christ did Richard write you about?"

"Yes what?" I ask.

John Spalding opens his mouth to speak, but we are interrupted by someone banging on the back door.

Martin rises muttering, "Who on earth?"

"Oh," I suddenly remember. "It's Meredith. I completely forgot about her."

"Meredith! I thought she was in bed hours ago. What's she doing out at three in the morning?"

She's standing before us, a raincoat over her long patchwork dress, her hair clinging siren-like to her slender neck. Her face is shiny with rain, but more than that, it is irridescent with happiness, and she says over and over again as though she can't quite believe it, "It's a boy. It's a boy, seven pounds, ten ounces, a beautiful, beautiful baby boy."

May

It is the morning after our party, the first morning in May.

"I know what you think," Meredith charges, "and it isn't true."

"What isn't true?" I ask. I am cleaning up after the party, putting away glasses, trays, and casseroles that won't be needed again. Until the next time.

"About Ruthie's baby."

"What about Ruthie's baby?"

"I'm just saying that I know it looks suspicious. With Ruthie living at the Eberhardts' and all that. But it really isn't the way it looks."

"Meredith!" I face her. "You've got to make yourself clear. What is the awful thing that you suspect me of suspecting?"

"I know you've had doubts. I can tell by the way you talked about Furlong."

"And how exactly did I talk about Furlong?"

"You said you didn't trust him. Remember? You didn't trust him anymore."

"Well, that may be true."

"But if you'd only listen to me for a minute, I'm trying to tell you that it wasn't Furlong at all."

"What wasn't Furlong?"

Meredith sighs and with enormous deliberation pronounces, "Furlong is not the father of Ruthie's baby."

"But, Meredith, I never thought he was."

"You didn't?" she says, her voice draining away.

"No, not for a minute.'

"But—"

"Whatever gave you that idea?"

She flounders. "I just thought—well here was Ruthie, big as a barn—and living with Furlong—what else could you possibly think?"

"Well, I never once thought of Furlong. You can be sure of that."

"But why not?"

Can it be that she doesn't realize about Furlong? Must I tell her? "Meredith," I say, "don't you know that Furlong—well—surely you must have noticed—I mean, I just wouldn't ever suspect Furlong of anything like that. It's just not the sort of thing he would do. At all."

For some reason she has started to cry a little, and, sniffing, she says, "I thought for sure you thought it was Furlong."

"No, Meredith, no," I tell her. "Never for a moment. Truly."

She reaches blindly for a Kleenex, blows her nose and looks at me wetly, smiling somewhat foolishly, and I am struck, not for the first time, by her unique blend of innocence and knowledge; a curious imbalance which may never be perfectly corrected; out of stubborn perversity she wills it not to be, conjuring a guilelessness which is deliberate and which perhaps propitiates life's darker offerings. Always at such moments she reminds me of someone, someone half-recalled but never quite brought into focus. I can never think who it is. But today I see for the first time who it is she reminds me of: it's me.

Now that the warmer weather is here to stay, Richard and his friends are outside most of the time. Baseball has taken possession of him, but not only baseball. His disappearances are often long and unexplained, and his comings and goings marked only by the banging of the back door.

Lately the phone rings for him often, school friends, kids in the neighbourhood, and one day there is someone who sounds almost girl-like.

It is a girl. His startled blush confirms it. She begins to phone fairly often—her name is Maureen—and sometimes he talks to her for an hour or more. About what? I don't know because he speaks in his brand-new low-register voice and cups his hand carefully over the receiver. And says nothing to us.

But he is suddenly happy again. I knew, of course, that it would come, knew that he was too young and resilient to be slain by the death of a single love. Martin told me he would get over it. And I knew all along that he would.

But I never dreamed it would be this; something so simple, something so natural.

And so soon.

"Living meanly is the greatest sin," Nancy Krantz tells me. "Needless economy. It thins the blood. Cuts out the heart."

It is so warm this morning that we have carried our coffee cups out on the back porch. "What about thrift?" I ask her.

"A vice," she says, "but an okay vice. Thrift, after all, implies its own raison d'être. But cheapness for its own sake is destructive."

We swap frugality stories.

She tells me about a man, a lawyer, well-to-do, with a beautiful house in Montreal, a summer place in the Rideau, annual excursions to London, the whole picture. And whenever he wanted to buy any new clothes, where do you think he went? You'll never guess. Down to the Salvation Army outlet. He'd pick through piles of old clothes until he'd find a forty-four medium. And that's what he wore. Pinstripe suits with shiny elbows. Navy blue blazers faded across the shoulders. Pants that bagged at the knees. Fuzzy along the pockets. He just didn't care. He'd take them home with him in a shopping bag and then he'd put them on and look at himself in the mirror. And he'd say, "Well, I'm no fashion plate but it only cost me three and a half bucks."

"Terrible, terrible," I breathe.

172

And I tell her about a widow, not wealthy, not even well-to-do, but not poverty-stricken either. She owns her own house, has an adequate pension and so on. But she had to have a breast removed, a terrible operation, she suffered terribly, cancer, and after she was discharged from the hospital she took the subway home. The subway! With a great white bandage where her left breast had been. On the subway.

"That's awful," Nancy says in a shocked whisper.

"But," I tell her, "that's not the worst part."

"What could be worse than that?" she asks.

I hesitate. For Nancy who is my good, my best friend, has never been an intimate. But I tell her anyway. The really awful thing was that the woman with the sheared-off breast riding home on the subway was my own mother.

"Oh, Judith, oh, Judith," she says. "Why didn't I tell you?"

"Tell me what?"

She gives a short harsh laugh. "That the man with the second-hand suits—was my father."

After that we sit quietly, finishing our coffee not talking much.

What have we said? Nothing much. But we have, for a minute, transcended abstractions. Have made a sort of pledge, a grim refusal to be stunned by the accidents of genes or the stopped-up world of others. We can outdistance any sorrow; what is it anyway but another abstraction, a stirring of air.

Although Ruthie no longer believes in the Catholic Church, or in marriage for that matter, she and Roger have asked a priest to officiate at their wedding. Not a priestly priest, Roger tells us. Father Claude is young and liberal-leaning, attached in some nebulous way to the university; his theology is aligned with scholarship rather than myth; he is a good guy.

Both Roger and Ruthie want to have the ceremony out-of-doors, but this proves difficult to arrange. A hitherto un-known bylaw prohibits weddings in city parks. And going outside the city involves a procession of cars, which is aesthetically unacceptable to them. And, besides, what if it rains?

They ask us if they can have the wedding in our back yard. At first I protest that our yard is too ordinary for a wedding, having nothing to offer but a stretch of brownish grass, a strip of tulips by the garage, a few bushes, and a fence.

"Please," they say, "it will be fine."

And it is fine. The sunshine is a little thin, but there's no wind to speak of; for the middle of May it's a chilly but reasonable afternoon. The boys next door agree to carry on their ball game at the far end of the street, so it's fairly quiet except for an occasional thrust of birdsong. Best of all, the shrubs are in their first, pale-green budding.

Ruthie wears a long, wide-yoked dress printed with a million yellow flowers, and Roger arrives in that comic costume of formality, a borrowed navy blue suit.

There are no more than fifteen guests, a few friends of Ruthie's from the library, Furlong and his mother (in purple crimplene and mink stole), a friend of Roger's who makes guitars, a gentle couple (he batiks, she crochets) who live in the flat beneath them. Ruthie has not invited her parents; they would not feel comfortable at this type of wedding, she thinks.

She and Roger and Father Claude stand near the for-sythia, and the rest of us wait, shivering slightly, in a circle around them. Ruthie, who has been taking a night course in jewelry making, has made the rings herself out of twisted strands of silver. Roger has written the wedding service which, surprisingly, is composed in blank verse. "For you, Martin," he says. "I want you to be able to speak your part to a familiar rhythm."

We all have parts which we read from the Xeroxed

scripts Roger has prepared; even Richard and Meredith have a few lines. I read:

> *Let peace descend upon this happy day*
> *That Man and Woman may with conscience clear*
> *Respect each other yet remain themselves*
> *Their first commitment to the inner voice.*

(A dog barks somewhere, a delivery van whines around the bend in the road; a few neighbourhood children peer hypnotized through the fence.)

After the exchange of rings, Meredith fetches the baby from the pram (our wedding gift) which has been parked in a spray of sun near the garage. Bundled in a blanket, he is brought forward and christened Roger St. Pierre Martin Ramsay, a name lushly weighted with establishment echoes. Roger loves it: "Listen to that roll of r's," he says. "Pure poetry."

A friend of Ruthie's sits cross-legged on the grass and plays something mournful on an alto recorder, and then we go into the house to drink Roger's homemade wine and eat the plates of exotic fruit which Ruthie has brought. And a surprise: Meredith has made a beautiful multi-layered cake topped with flowers, beads and sea shells. Why sea shells? "For fertility," she deadpans.

The afternoon drains away, leaving us steeped in a pale, translucent peace, relaxed, very much at our ease, talking quietly, content, but it occurs to me finally that there is a distinct lack of festivity. Something is missing from this gathering. It's joyous enough, but it's contained and diminished in some way. At first—out there in the garden—I had felt something more, something trying to come into being. Perhaps it was those heavy iambic lines we uttered or the sombreness of the recorder music, but there is no fine edge of nerve in this marriage rite, no undercurrent, no sense of beginning or expectation. Why?

I look at the bridal pair. Ruthie rocks little Roger St.

Pierre while big Roger leans over them, bottle in hand, anxiously testing it against his wrist. Ruthie looks up at him, and what passes between them is a look of resignation, a little tired already, an arc of strain so subtle I think afterwards that I may have imagined it.

At five the baby begins to cry, and Roger and Ruthie go home. Everything has been fine, just as they said it would be. Just fine. I want to rush after them and tell them: everything will be just fine.

Near the end of the term the English Department has a dinner. As always it is held at the Faculty Club, and as always we eat thinly sliced roast beef, mashed potatoes, peas, and, for dessert, molded ice cream.

Whoever arranges these things, Polly Stanley probably, has placed me next to Furlong. (I have only this morning received a communication from the Citizenship Branch informing me that one Rudyard Eberhart was made a Canadian citizen in a private ceremony two years ago.)

"Well, well, Judith," he says. "How is Susanna Moodie these days?"

"About to go to the publishers," I tell him. "The typist has it now."

"And did you do it this time, Judith? Did you really wrap it up?"

I sense his genuine interest. And am oddly grateful for it. "No, not really," I admit. "I have a few hunches. About the real Susanna. But I can't quite pin it all down."

"You mean she never came right out and admitted much that was personal?"

"Hardly ever. I had to look at her through layers and layers of affectation."

"Such as?"

"Oh, the gentle lady pose. The Wordsworthian nature lover. And the good Christian mother. She's in there somewhere, lost under all the gauze."

"Perhaps," he suggests, "all those layers act as a magnifying glass."

"How do you mean, Furlong?"

"Simply that instead of obscuring her personality, they may pinpoint her true self. Those particles of light which are allowed to escape, and I assume she occasionally emitted a few, can be interpreted in a wider sense. In a way it's easier than sorting through buckets and buckets of personal revelations."

"If I'd only been allowed five minutes with her," I tell him. "Five minutes, and I could have wrapped it up."

"I don't know, Judith. Perhaps you're expecting too much. People must be preserved with their mysteries intact. Otherwise, it's not real."

"Do you really believe that?"

"From my soul."

"Can I take that as a particle of light?"

"You may."

"Well, next time I'm going to write about someone still living. So I can get those five minutes."

"Who is it to be?"

"I'm not sure," I tell him. Then I smile and say, "Maybe I'll do you, Furlong."

I have startled him; he isn't sure whether or not I'm serious. "Surely you're joking?" he asks.

"Why not, Furlong? You're an established writer. Your life story might make fascinating reading."

"It wouldn't, it wouldn't, I assure you. And besides I'm not nearly old enough to have a biography written about me."

"Lots of younger people have been done. We could title it *A Biography Thus Far*. That sort of thing."

"Judith, you're not serious about this?" He is genuinely alarmed now.

"Wouldn't you like it?" I ask teasingly.

"Absolutely not. I prohibit it. I'm sure I have that right. I refuse permission, Judith."

"But I never asked."

"Judith, you know perfectly well you can't write about a living subject if he objects."

"But you're famous. You're in the public domain."

"It doesn't matter. Now Judith, tell me you're not serious."

I tell him. "I'm not serious, Furlong. I was only joking."

"Fine, fine." He relaxes, goes back to his ice cream. "And now let's talk about something interesting. Tell me what Martin has up his sleeve for the next Renaissance Society meeting. Tell me what you're planning for the summer. Tell me about the children. That's a lovely dress you're wearing. And isn't your hair different? Tell me, Judith. Tell me anything."

Any day now John Spalding's book will be out. *Alien Interlude* it's called, and when I think about it, my breath hardens in my chest. We are about to be revealed to ourselves. It's a little frightening.

Martin and I have decided not to tell Richard about the book and the fact that he was unwittingly the provider of material. For one thing it would make a mockery of his own jealous secrecy, and he might, with reason, look upon it as an act of treachery.

Martin and I, a little nervously, await our promised autographed copy. "Chances are," Martin tells me, "we won't even recognize ourselves. Remember what he told me when we met him at the airport? That we didn't remotely fulfil his image of us."

"And he didn't look the way we had pictured him either," I add. "Which proves something."

"Besides, writers use material selectively."

"Right."

"And another thing, Judith, I have a feeling that John Spalding is given to wild hyperbole."

"What do you mean?"

"Remember the famous Cyprus beachboy who carried his Jezebel-Isabel away?"

"Yes?"

"Just before the party, when he and I and Paul were talking about Cyprus, he happened to mention that when they were there his wife had been rushed into hospital one night for an emergency appendectomy. And while she was there she fell in love with her doctor. It turns out the gigolo he wrote us about, is also chief surgeon in a Nicosia hospital."

"I see," I say slowly.

"Not quite the penniless, suntanned seducer we were led to believe."

"Interesting," I say.

And though I don't tell Martin, I too have reasons to believe we may not recognize ourselves in *Alien Interlude*. I have seen how facts are transmuted as they travel through a series of hands; our family situation seen through the eyes of pre-adolescent Richard and translated into his awkward letter-writing prose, then crossing cultures and read by a child we have never seen, to a family we have never met, then mixed with the neurotic creative juices of John Spalding and filtered through a publisher—surely by the time it reaches print, the least dram of truth will be drained away.

And there is something more. When I drove John Spalding to the airport, I brought up the subject of Furlong Eberhardt and his book *Graven Images*. "Have you read it, by any chance?" I asked him.

"Curiously enough," he answered, "I did read it. Stuffy prose. But a ripping good yarn I thought."

Astonishing. He hadn't recognized his own plot which had passed first through my hands and then into Furlong's. More fuel for the comforting fire.

Martin says we'll probably get a good laugh out of the whole thing. Maybe. Maybe not.

Anyway, we're waiting.

With true capitalistic finesse, Martin has sold his tapestries of *Paradise Lost* to the highest bidder, an anonymous private collector; for us it is a sizable sum.

And with true middle-class flair, we have used the sum to lighten our mortgage, a fact that depresses us somewhat. Have we no imagination?

"Let's at least go out to a good dinner," Martin says. "Let's go to the revolving restaurant."

It has another name—something French and chic, but in this city it is always known as the revolving restaurant. We've not been there before, although it was constructed more than two years ago. It is expensive, we've been told, and quiet with subdued lighting and intimate tables; the food is rumoured to be good but routinely international, running from shrimp Newburg to steak Diane. Nothing unexpected. Just a nice evening out.

When we arrive at eight o'clock for dinner, having carefully made reservations, the restaurant is almost deserted. "That seems odd," I say to Martin. "Hardly anyone here."

"It's Monday night," he reminds me. "Probably pretty slow early in the week."

"Why are we whispering?" I say over the tiny table.

"I don't know," he whispers back.

There is another whispering couple next to us, and a short distance away is a party of eight. But, strangely enough, they aren't talking at all. I don't understand it.

But when the waiter comes to light our little claret-tinted hurricane lamp and my eyes become focused, I see what it is that is so puzzling about the group of eight: they are a party of deaf-mutes.

Their hands wave madly in the half-dark, making shadows on the walls, and their heads bob and dip over their shrimp cocktails.

The unreality of the scene enthralls me. I order mechanically—mushrooms à la grecque and pepper steak. Salad? Yes, Thousand Island please. Martin orders a bottle of wine, but I hardly notice what he's asked for. I am watching the delicate opening and closing of those sixteen hands.

Their animation is apparent, and that is what is so startling, for it is an animation which is associated with voices, with sounds, with noise. And from this circle of people, this circle of delicately gesturing hands, fringed and anxious as the petals of an exotic flower, comes a cloud of perfect, shapely silence.

They are eating their salad now. They indicate to the waiter the type of dressing they prefer, and something amuses them. Their faces break, not into laughter, but into the positions of laughter, the shapes, curves and angles of mirth. It is not quite real.

One of them has chosen filet of sole which the waiter expertly bones at a side table. This leads to a mad flurry of wrists and flying fingers, takes the shapes of birds, flowers, butterflies, the rapid opening and closing of space, shaping a private alphabet of air.

They are drinking wine, several bottles and, though it does not loosen their tongues, they grow garrulous; their hands fly so fast that they have hardly a moment to take up their knives and forks and, by the time they eat their desert, Martin and I have caught up with them.

There are three women and five men, all about the same age, in their late thirties probably. It must be a club, and this, perhaps, is their end-of-season wind-up.

What does the waiter think as he hands them their Black Forest cake and fresh strawberries? Will he knock off work tonight happier than usual? Sail home in the knowledge that he has shared in a unique festival of silence? Will he climb into bed with his wife and tell her how they pointed out their choices on the menu, how they were never still for a moment, how they, with consummate skill and, yes, grace, communicated even over the final coffee and liqueurs?

Martin watches them too. But for him it is no more than picturesque. A charming scene. He will remember it, but not for long.

For me it's different. I am expanded by the surreal and passionate language of their speechlessness. Their gathered presence enlarges me; we revolve together through the lit-up night. I can imagine them parting from each other after this evening is over, boarding their buses or taxis and branching out to their separate destinations, trailing their silence behind them like caterpillar silk. I can see them producing keys from pockets, opening doors, and entering the larger stories of their separate lives.

I am watching. My own life will never be enough for me. It is a congenital condition, my only, only disease in an otherwise lucky life. I am a watcher, an outsider whether I like it or not, and I'm stuck with the dangers that go along with it. And the rewards.

They are rising from the table now. Shaking hands. Exchanging through their fluttering fingers a few final remarks. A benediction. I am watching them, and out of the corner of my eye I see Martin watching—not them—but me. He has no need of the bizarre. What he needs is something infinitely more complex: what he needs is my possession of that need. I am translator to him, reporter of visions he can't see for himself.

Though I can't be sure even of that. Furlong may be right about embracing others along with their mysteries. Distance. Otherness. Martin's wrist on the table: it hums with a separate and private energy.

But I note, at least, the certainties, the framework, the fact that he will shortly add up the bill, overtip about 5 per cent, smile at me from across the table and say, "Ready, Judith?"

And I, of course, will smile back and say: "Yes."

the box garden

For my son John

Chapter 1

What was it that Brother Adam wrote me last week? That there are no certainties in life. That we change hourly or even from one minute to the next, our entire cycle of being altered, our whole selves shaken with the violence of change.

Ah, but Brother Adam has never actually laid eyes on me. And could never guess at the single certainty which swamps my life and which can be summed up in the simplest of phrases: I will never be brave. Never. I don't know what it was—something in my childhood probably—but I was robbed of my courage.

Even dealing with the post-adolescent teller in my branch bank is too much for me some days. She punches in my credits, my tiny salary from the *Journal*, the monthly child support money (I receive no alimony), and the occasional small, miniscule really, cheque from some magazine or other which has agreed to publish one of my poems.

And the debits. I see her faint frown; a hundred and fifty for rent. Perhaps she thinks that's too much for a woman in my circumstances. So do I, but I do have a child and can't, for his sake, live in a slum. Though the street is beginning to look like one. Almost every house on the block is subdivided now, cut up into two or three apartments; sometimes even a half-finished basement room with plywood walls and a concrete floor rented out for an extra sixty-five a month.

Oh, yes, and a cheque for thirty dollars written out to Woodwards. A new dress for me. On sale. I have to have something to wear on the train. If I turn up in Toronto in one of my old falling-apart skirts, my sister Judith will shrink away in pity, try to press money into my hands, force me with terrible, strenuous gaiety on a girlish shopping trip insisting she missed my birthday last year. Or the year before that.

Food. I am frugal. Seth at fifteen undoubtedly knows about the other families, those laughing, coke-swilling, boat-tripping families in bright sports clothes who buy large pieces of beef which they grill to pink tenderness on flagged patios, always plenty for everyone. Second helpings, third helpings. We have day-old bread some-times. Bruised peaches, dented cans on special. Only the two of us, but food still costs. It's a good thing Watson in-sisted we have only one child.

And what's this? A cheque made out to the Book Nook. I had forgotten that. A hardcover book, bought on impulse, a rare layout. Snapped up in a moment of over-whelming self-pity. *I'm thirty-eight, don't I have the right to a little luxury now and then? They never have anything new at the library—you have to sign up for re-quests and then wait half the year to get your hands on it and this way it comes all swaddled in plastic, you just can't get into a library book the same way, why is that?* Eight dollars and ninety-five cents. I'll have to be more careful. But I'll have it to read on the train.

It's not only bank tellers. Landladies wither me with snappish requests for references.

"And why did you move from the west side, Mrs. For-rest? You say you're divorced; well, just so you pay regu-lar."

And I do. I am my mother's daughter; cash on the line and cash on time. Her saying. She had hundreds like it, and although it's been twenty years since I left home, her sayings form a perpetual long-playing record on my inner-ear turntable.

The squeaky wheel gets the grease. No need to chew your cabbage twice. A penny saved—this last saying never fully quoted, merely suggested. A penny saved: we knew what that meant.

By luck Watson came from a family with a similar respect for cash; thus he has never once defaulted on the small allowance for Seth. The cheque is mailed from The Whole World Retreat in Weedham, Ontario where he lives now. On the fifteenth of every month; no note, nothing to indicate that we once were husband and wife, just the cheque for one hundred and fifty dollars made out to me, Charleen Forrest.

My name, the name Forrest, is the best thing Watson ever gave me. After being Charleen McNinn for eighteen years it seemed a near miracle to be attached to such a name. Forrest. Woodsy, dark, secret, green with pine needles, exotic, far removed from the grim square blocks of Scarborough, the weedy shrubs and the tough brick bungalows. Forrest. After the divorce friends here in Vancouver suggested that I announce my singlehood by reverting to my old name. Give up Forrest? Never. It's mine now. And Seth's of course. I may not be brave but I recognize luck when I see it, and I will not return to the clan McNinn.

McNinn: the first syllable sour, familial; the second half a diminishing clout, a bundle of negative echoes—minimum, minimal, nincompoop, ninny, nothing, nonentity, nobody. Charleen McNinn. No, no, bury her. Deliver her from family, banktellers, exhusbands, landladies, from bus drivers who tell her to move along, men on the make who want her to lie back and accept (this is what you need, baby), friends who feel sorry for her. Deliver me, deliver me from whatever it was that did this thing to me, robbed me of my courage and brought me here to this point of time, this mark on a nowhere map, this narrow bed.

You made your bed, you can lie in it, my mother always said.

*

"You really ought to get into meditation," the Savages urge me as we wait for the waiter to bring us our food.

"Why?" I ask.

They exchange quick, practiced looks of communion. Doug receives from Greta the miniature nod to proceed.

"For true peace of mind, Char," he says. "For release."

"Look," I say in what I think of as my Tillie the Toiler voice, flip bravery mingled with touchiness, "who says I need peace of mind? Or release. I'm not ready to die yet."

"We're talking about serenity," Greta leans over the hurricane lamp so that her tiny, earnest creases are transformed by shadow into grey, lapped folds; a seared, oddly attractive gargoyle of a face. Her pouched eyes plead with me.

"It's really far more than serenity," she urges softly. "It's an answer, a partial answer anyway, to—you know—fragmentation. Isn't it, Doug? I mean, it gives you a sense of your own personhood."

"What Greta means is that it frees you from trivia," Doug explains. "And who, I ask you, needs trivia? You want to trim it off. Like fat off a chop. Cut it out." He sits back, pleased with himself.

Doug and Greta Savage are in their mid-forties. Where do butterflies go when it rains? Where do hippies go when they get old? They get frowsier, coarser, more earnest or more ridiculous like the Savages; they look fun-

nier in their beads and long hair, they becon
ately reverent about their causes, they becor
stridently tolerant and fair-minded, but they d(
become more well-meaning. And more possessive of
friends.

The Savages, of course, were never more than weekend hippies. Doug is a scientist, a botanist; in fact, he is a
scientist with an enviable reputation, employed by a rep-
utable university. They live comfortably, if a trifle uncon-
ventionally, on two acres of woodland at the edge of the
city. Their kindness is exquisite, a work of art.

In fact, they fuss in an almost parental way about their
younger friends, of whom I am one. Childless (who
would bring children into a world like this?) they adopt
their friends. I am perhaps their favourite child. They
take me out to the Swiss Chalet for dinner—very campy,
Doug says, but at least it's pure camp—and they invite
me around to their house on Friday nights for red wine
and crêpes; they confer enthusiastically about my mental outlook, and lately they have been hinting hugely that
Eugene is not nearly good enough for me.

They have even offered to look after Seth while I am in
Toronto next week. They are unbelievably fond of him
and worry about the lack of a male influence in his life.
(Eugene doesn't count; they see him as a negative influence.) Greta is concerned about Seth's natural ease with
people and his ability to form indiscriminate friendships,
and even Doug maintains that there's such a thing as
being too well-adjusted.

"You don't want him falling into the middle-class-
mentality trap with nothing but straight teeth to recommend him. Some of these high school teachers have
never been out of British Columbia and the only reason
they're teaching school anyway is for the tenure."

"Well, you have tenure too," I remind him cheerfully.

"Ah, but university tenure has a place," he cries. "It exists for a reason."

"That's right," Greta says.

"Why is it different?" I ask. They are buying me this meal, this succulent chicken. They are paying for the bottle of good French wine. I shouldn't argue with them, but watching Doug squirm out of his bourgeois lapses is one of the few entertainments I can afford. "What's different about university tenure?"

"Simply that at university level it's necessary to project views which are independent, which are not a part of the university philosophy, the provincial philosophy, or any other damn philosophy. Tenure guarantees livelihood while permitting positive deviation in thought."

"Hear, hear," Greta says, and Doug scowls in her direction. (What would Brother Adam think of that speech? What would he think of that scowl?)

Slyly I ask, "Don't school teachers need protection too?"

Doug spreads his hands. Charmingly. Paternally. "Perhaps," he admits. "In the abstract. But look at the reality. All they really want is money enough to hustle themselves into split levels with their bowling, curling wives and Pablum-dribbling babies. . . ."

"Pablum," Greta murmurs. "What was that we were reading about Pablum, Doug? Just the other day? In Adelle Davis." Greta tends to forget exact references. Information sleeps beneath her pores, for she is an intelligent woman, but it is always disjointed, disassociated; she's never been the same since she underwent shock therapy. "Remember, Doug, Pablum is a really remarkable food. Or something like that."

"Vitamin B," he pronounces, nodding in her direction. "But getting back to meditation, Char; it's not a gim-

mick. It's a positive power. By forcing the brain to concentrate on an absurdity . . ."

Greta's tiny mouth puffs into a circle of protest, but he
hurries on.

". . . by forcing the brain to concentrate on an absurdity, you let the mind go free."

"What exactly do you mean by 'free'?" I ask. My question is not frivolous, nor am I stalling for time. Free
might apply, for instance, to any of Greta's passions over
the years—free love, free bird houses to the citizens of
New Westminster, free thought, free food stamps, free
university, free rest cures for the mothers of battered
babies, free toilets in airports (she picketed outside one
for two weeks in support of that cause), free lunch-time
concerts for office workers, free tickets home for runaway teenagers. The word "free" ranges wildly and gid-
dily in Greta's consciousness, and often—a special
irony—it means something like its opposite since she
will go to extraordinary lengths to enforce her concept of
freedom.

"Into peace," Greta says, leaning toward me again.
"Into a larger peace than I ever knew. And I should
know—if anyone does." She is referring, Doug and I
know, to the breakdown she suffered in her middle thirties and which she mentions at least once on every occasion we are together.

"But you've only been in the meditation thing for a
month," I remind her, playing my role of visiting skep-
tic.

"You're right," she whispers, and the bones of her
small face gleam with alabaster zeal through her unbelievably fragile skin. Such a tiny woman, she is far too
small to hold all that latent forcefulness. But her voice is
full, chalky with mysticism, rich with caring. "I thought

I knew myself before, but I was wrong. I didn't know what real peace was."

"Really?" I ask.

"Charleen, Charleen," Doug says fondly but disapprovingly. "You are the ultimate disbeliever."

"Me? A disbeliever?"

"You. Don't you believe in anything?"

I chew my chicken and think hard. They watch me and wait patiently for an answer. Their concern touches me; I want to please them.

"Friends," I say. "People. I believe in people."

They relax. Smile. Sit back. We sip the last of the wine slowly and fold our red linen napkins with bemused inattention. Doug pays the bill and we rise together.

Arms linked, the three of us stroll down Granby. I walk in the middle as befits my position of erstwhile child. The street is full of people leaving restaurants, buying newspapers, walking dogs. Drunks and lovers lounge in the greyed shadows of buildings, and, though it is eleven o'clock at night, there is a Chinese family, a father, mother and a string of smiling children strolling along ahead of us. We are all melting together in this soft and buzzing electric blaze.

Greta and Doug walk me all the way home. I know they would like me to invite them up for coffee. They are pleased with me tonight, cheered by my declaration of faith and by the warmth of our friendship. They don't want to let me go. I sense their yearning for my straw-matted living room and my blue and white striped coffee mugs, my steaming Nescafé. Their faces turn to me.

But I shake my head. Hold out my hand. "Thank you both for a good evening," I stretch out that little word *good* to make it mean more than it does "I'll see you when I get back from Toronto."

Doug embraces me; Greta kisses my cheek, a crepe

paper grazing. I get out my key and don't turn around again.

❧

My apartment consists of three rooms on the second floor of a narrow, old house. I don't count the kitchen which is no more than a strip of cupboards and a miniature stove in a shuttered off end of the green and white living room. The living room has a serenity which does not in any way reflect my personality; perhaps I am attempting, with these white walls and this cheap, chaste furniture, to impose order and bravery on my life; it takes courage to live with wicker; it takes purity, a false purity in my case, to resist posters, beaded curtains and one more piece of handthrown pottery. There is a small, blue Indian rug on the wall which Watson and I bought for our first apartment. There is a painted plywood cube for a coffee table; Seth made it in grade eight woodworking class. A few books, some greenery on the window sill, a glowing jewel of a cushion which Greta Savage made for me years ago. My friends believe this to be a totally unremarkable room. This is not a room for a poet, they perhaps think, for it lacks even a suggestion of eccentricity or excitement; instead of verve there is a deep-breathing dreaminess, especially in the evening when the one good lamp throws soft-edged shadows halfway up the wall.

There are two bedrooms, a room for Seth and a room for me. That's all we need. His door is closed, but I push it open and in the rippled dark see his humped form under a light blanket. I listen, just as I listened when he was a baby, for the sound of his breathing. He has probably been asleep for hours. His tuba sits on the floor on the tiny hooked rug I made for him years ago. (A blue swan swimming on a pale yellow sea.) I move the tuba beside his dresser, tiptoeing, but there is no need to worry about waking him up. He sleeps deeply, easily,

and his ability to sleep is one more point of separation between us, another notch for evolutionary progress. I almost always sleep poorly, jerkily, my nights filled either
with hollowed-out insomnia or strings of short, ragged
kite-tail dreams that flap and jump in the dark and leave
me sad-eyed in the morning, like the worndown women
in coffee commercials. Seth's nervous system seems to
have been put together by agents other than Watson or
me; Watson with his combination of creative energy and
lack of talent was predestined to fall apart. And I, suffering from a lack of bravery, must expend all my energies
preparing for the next test. And the next. And the next.

Seth. I adore his blunt normalcy and good health. His
unspectacular brain. His average height and weight. His
willingness to please. His ability to go along with things,
not objecting for instance, to staying with Greta and
Doug for a week, even though he knows they will stuff
him with peanut and raisin casseroles and counsel him
endlessly on attaining personal peace. He just smiled
when I told him. Smiled and nodded. Sure, sure, he said.
And when I told him that Eugene might be going along
with me to Toronto, all he said was, great, great. Ah
Seth, I do love you. Sleeping there, breathing. Keep puffing your tuba, keep smiling, keep on, and, who knows,
you might get out of this unscathed.

There's a whole list of things to be done before I leave
for Toronto. First, I must pick up my pay cheque at the
university, and this means seeing Doug Savage again
after having bid him a final goodbye in front of my apartment last night. Something inside me cringes at the
carelessness of this oversight; it is the sort of messy mis-
arrangement I create instinctively. Tag-ends. Clutter. A
lack of cleanliness. An inability to end things neatly.
What Brother Adam would classify as non-discipline.
But there is no question of my not going to pick up the
cheque; I need the money.

Why in the seven years on the *Journal* have I never thought of having the cheque mailed to me at home or, better yet, sent directly to the bank? Other people make such easy and sensible arrangements without thinking. But from my first month on the *Journal*, Doug has handed me my cheque personally, more often than not with his inked signature still wet on the paper. He pushes it my way off-handedly, avoiding my eyes; sometimes it comes floating loosely on top of a pile of proofs. It is as though a more formal payment might rupture our relationship, might make of my job on the *Journal* something serious and official instead of a part-time piece of noblesse oblige, a pittance for an abandoned woman, a soupçon for the bereft wife of his former friend. Nevertheless the cheque is never late, an acknowledgement that though my position might be undefined, my need for cash is absolute and recurring.

Not that I don't work hard. The *National Botanical Journal* comes out quarterly, and except for selecting the articles which are to appear, I do everything. The *Journal* is a generally dull and uninspired affair with its buff-and-brown cover and the names of the main articles listed on the front. Our next issue is devoted almost entirely to new disease-proof grains with a short piece on "Unusual Alberta Wildflowers" tacked on as a sort of dessert. It is a periodical (it would be too much to call it a magazine) by academics and for academics.

Doug is the nominal editor and I am the only employee. First I edit the manuscripts which is a long, picky, and sensitive tightrope of a job; it is essential not to under-edit since clarity and a moderate level of elegance are desirable, but I must not over-edit and thereby obliterate personal style and perhaps injure the feelings of the submitting authors. (Will he object if I pencil out his "however"? Will he fly into a tantrum when I chop his sentences in two or sometimes three or even four?

Will he mind if I switch the spellings to Canadian standard or rearrange the tangle of his footnotes?) Sometimes I consult Doug.

"You worry too much, Char," is what he usually says, or "Screw the bastard, he's lucky we're going to run his lousy article at all." Doug inherited the editorship of the *Journal* from Watson who abandoned it along with his other responsibilities, and not surprisingly he regards it as a time-consuming stepchild. He is entirely unwilling to worry about the theoretical sensitivities of contributing botanists. But I do; I rarely make a change in an article without anticipating a blast of indignation. In actuality it hardly ever happens, because, for some reason, these unseen scientists are astonishingly submissive to the slash of my red pencil; they quite willingly accept mutilations to their work, the dictates of Charleen Forrest, a thirty-eight-year-old divorcée who knows nothing about botany and who has no training beyond high school unless you count a six-week typing course. Amazing.

After the galley proofs and the layout dummy come the vandykes, these blueprints of the final round, and then another issue is on its way. Time to begin the next. It is relentless but sustaining. Maybe rhythm is all I need to keep me going.

I only work in the mornings since there isn't enough money to pay a full-time employee, and theoretically my afternoons are saved for the writing of poetry, what Doug Savage calls the practice of my craft. Craft. As though one put poetry together from a boxed kit. Not that it matters much what you call it, for it is a fact that in the last two years I've hardly written a line. What once consumed the best of my energies now seems a dull indulgence.

My afternoons just melt away. Sometimes I meet Eugene if he isn't too busy at the office. I shop for groceries, read, worry. I write letters to anyone I can think of, for chief among my diseases is an unwillingness to let friendships die a natural death. I cling, pursuing old friends, dredging up school mates from Scarborough like Sally Cork and Mary Lou Lester. I write to Mary Lou's mother, too, and to her sister in Winnipeg whom I scarcely know. I badger the friends Watson and I once had with my insistent, pressing six pages of hectic persevering scrawl. I even write regularly to a woman named Fay Cousins in northern California who once shared a hundred-mile bus ride with me. And for the last fifteen months I've been writing to Brother Adam, the only correspondent I've ever had who approaches me in scope and endurance.

I cannot let go. It is a kind of game I play in which I pretend, to myself at least, that I, with my paper and envelopes, my pen and my stamps, that I am one of those nice people who care about people. A lovely person. A loving person, a giving person. I dream for myself visions of generosity and kindness. I *care* about Fay Cousin's drinking problem, about Mrs. Lester's ulcerated colon, about Sally's home freezing and Mary Lou's fat braggart of a husband. I *care* about them. At least I want to care.

To my mother I write once a month. And that's hard enough. To my sister Judith perhaps three or four times a year; I would write to Judith more often if I were not so baffled by her lack of neuroses; we had the same childhood, but she somehow survived, and the margin of her survival widens every year so that, though I can talk easily enough to her when I see her, I cannot bear the thought of her reading my letters in the incandescent light of her balanced serenity. Does she understand? Probably not.

And Watson. I never write to Watson. Nor does he

write to me; no one hears from him anymore except Greta who, by trading on a belief that she and Watson are partners in emotional calamity, manages to elicit an occasional note from him. Watson is not cruel; it is only that he is missing one or two of the vital components which happy and normal people possess. Nevertheless, I ache to write to him; just thinking about it makes my fingers want to curl around the words, to smooth the paper. I *long* to write to him. He lives in a commune in Weedham, Ontario, with God only knows who, and all he sends me is child support money. Every month when it comes I examine the handwriting on the cheque, hoping it will contain some kind of declaration, but it is always the same; one hundred and fifty dollars and no cents. Signed, Watson Forrest. That's all.

Sometimes I go for walks in the afternoons and quite often I go all the way to Walkley Street, past the house where Watson and I used to live. We paid exactly $17,900 for that house, and all but one thousand dollars was mortgaged. It is in much better condition than it used to be. The hedges are shaped into startled spheres, and pink and white petunias tumble out of nicely-painted window boxes. There is a new stone patio by the roses, my roses, where I used to park Seth's pram. The curtains are generally drawn in the afternoons as though the owners, an English couple in their fifties I'm told, are anxious about their polished antiques and Chinese carpets. A ginger dachshund yelps from a split cedar pen. An electric lawnmower gleams by the garage. I am unfailingly reassured by these improvements—I rejoice in them, in fact—for I can foresee a time when this house will pass out of our possession altogether, piece by piece replaced so that nothing of the original is left.

❦

At the university, which I reach by a twenty-minute

bus ride, I work in a cubicle of the Natural Science Building. On my door there is a sign which says: 304 Botanical Journal. I have one desk equipped with a manual typewriter, a gunmetal table and matching wastebasket, a peach-coloured filing cabinet with three drawers, two molded plastic chairs and one comfortable, worn, plushy typing chair in bitter green. There are Swedish-type curtains in a subtle bone stripe, by far the best feature of the room, and the walls are painted a glossy café au lait. From the ceiling a fluorescent tube pours faltering institutional light onto my desk. Oddly enough there is no lock on my door. All the other offices on the third floor have locks, but not mine; the lack of a lock and key seems to underscore the valuelessness of what I do. This might be a broom cupboard. Nothing worth guarding here.

This morning when I arrive, Doug is already in the office, bending over the pile of manuscripts on my desk. "Hiya, Char," he says, not bothering to turn around. "I'm just seeing what we should stick in the fall issue."

Though it is only May, we are already beginning to think about the autumn number; we are perpetually leaping across the calendar in six-month strides, so that this job, besides paying only enough to keep me from starving, simultaneously deprives me of a sense of accomplishment. Completion, realization, fulfillment are always half a year away, a point in time which, when finally reached, melts into so much vapour. Now the fall issue is being conceived before the summer has taken shape and before the spring is even back from the printers.

Clearly Doug has been expecting me. Without taking his eyes off the pile of manuscripts, he slides my pay cheque across the desk. I accept it wordlessly, fold it in two lengthwise (I can never remember if it is all right to fold a cheque) and put it in my wallet. The awkward moment passes, and now Doug turns and smiles at me. "Well, are you all set for tomorrow?"

"Almost," I tell him. "Just a few odds and ends to clear up."

"Greta and I thought we'd pick up Seth right from school tomorrow. That okay with you?"

"Oh, no, Doug. Really, that's not necessary at all. He can get a bus."

"No trouble, Char. We'd like to."

"No, that's just too much bother. It's enough that you've offered to have him." I'm playing my game again, protesting, modest, conciliatory, anxious to please.

"For Christ's sake, Charleen, the poor kid will have his suitcase and tuba and everything. We'll pick him up."

"But he's already planned to come out to your place by bus. He mentioned it this morning."

"Look, Char," he sighs, "Greta wants it this way. She wants to pick him up. You know how she gets. I promised her we could do it this way."

I nod. When Doug and I are alone together without Greta, our relationship undergoes a radical reshaping. We drop all pretense of Greta's being our friend and equal; instead we conspire to protect her, to smooth her path, to bolster her up, knowing full well that her present tranquility is a fragile growth. If she has made up her mind to pick up Seth from school, it must be done.

"Sure," I tell Doug, "I'll tell him. I'll make sure he understands that you'll be along."

"Ah, Char," he says fondly, "you're an angel."

Endearments. That's another of the ways in which we change when we're alone. Doug calls me angel, sweetheart, love, baby—words he would never use if Greta were with us, words which are really quite meaningless but which allow him to toy with certain possibilities of freedom. For he is just slightly in love with me, so slightly that I would never have recognized it, were it not that I find myself responding with sprightly manifestations of girlishness. I grin at him wickedly across the desk. I say "shit" when the printer is late with the proofs. Sometimes I poke a pencil in my hair, give a little cat-stretch at eleven-thirty, put my stockinged feet on the chair, call him "Bossman" in a throaty, southland drawl, and grumble about the work he loads on me.

"I need a week away from here," I tell him. "I've had it with tubers and pollen. And mangled prose structure."

"I hope you get a chance to relax when you're away, Char," he says searchingly. "You need a chance to get away from here and think."

"Now what exactly do you mean by that?" I demand.

"Nothing, nothing. Just that we all need a break now and then."

"Now don't go backing down, Doug. I want to know why you think I need to get away and think. Just exactly what do you believe I should be thinking about?"

"Well," he hesitates a small, slightly theatrical instant, "to be honest, you might think about where you're headed. Greta and I have been wondering if you weren't, you know, on the wrong track as it were."

"I suppose you must be talking about Eugene?"

"Not just about Eugene, not only that. But, well, what he represents. The whole bag you might say."

"You've only met him once," I say waspishly. "And that was just for a few minutes."

"Now, now, Char, don't go getting defensive."

"What am I supposed to do? I happen to be very fond of Eugene. *Very* fond."

He waves aside my words. "I can tell you aren't all that sure of yourself about where you're going with Eugene."

"How can you be so sure?"

"Do you really want to know?"

"I asked you."

"Because you never talk about his job."

"Aha," I say triumphantly, "I knew that's what was bothering you."

"Be honest, Charleen baby. Doesn't it bother you a bit?"

"It's an honest profession," I declare piously. "My mother, for one, would think it was the height of success."

"But what do you think?"

"What's wrong with it?"

"An orthodontist. Think about it! A guy who stands around all day putting little wires on little kids' teeth. . ."

"Somebody has to do it," I say. My head aches and I feel a desire to squeeze my eyes shut and weep, but I can't betray Eugene so easily. "It's a service," I sum up.

"Some service. Milking the middle class. God! Dispensing ersatz happiness through the pursuit of perfect middle-class teeth."

"Well, he did a good job on Seth."

"Seth! The poor kid. Thrown to the vanity peddlers before he's old enough to protest."

"Look, Doug," I say, shaping the words into hard little rectangles, "it was the bite. Get it? It wasn't to make him beautiful, it was to correct his bite."

"And on your salary?" Doug mutters softly in his puzzled surrogate-father voice. "How any guy could take fifty bucks a month out of your salary and not be second cousin to a crook—"

Should I tell him that Eugene would not take any money after the first twenty-five dollar consultation?

That he steadfastly refused, once even tearing my cheque into little pieces? Better not risk the suggestion that I was a woman willing to sell her body for dental care, that a pathetically self-sacrificing compulsion had driven me to an absurd martyrdom; it wouldn't take Doug more than a minute to reach that kind of interpretation. "Let's just drop the whole subject of Eugene," I say.

"All I'm saying is that it's probably a good thing you're getting away with him for a few days. To sort of see things *in context*." His voice softens. "I'm only thinking of what's best for you, Char."

"Okay, okay," I say, stuffing the manuscripts in a drawer and slamming it shut.

Why is it I inspire such storms of preaching? It's not only Doug Savage; my most casual acquaintances press me with advice. Doug, though, has become a full-time catechizer; great gushes of his energy are channeled into the sorting out of my life. In an obscure way he seems to feel responsible for Watson's defection, as do all the friends Watson and I once had, as if they shared a guilty belief that their presence in our lives may have proved the fatal splinter. Which is nonsense, of course. But Doug seems to feel he must look after me. He invented this job for me as a therapeutic and practical rescue mission, and at the time I was grateful. I still am. But isn't it time he got back to his plants, I want to tell him. Or concentrated a little more on Greta who rocks continuously between birdlike vagary and thorny obsession, between her wish to reconcile and her appetite for separation. Does Doug realize that Greta, after all these years, still smothers Watson with letters? That she is perhaps outdoing herself as Seth's fairy godmother, wishing him well but not knowing how to make an ac-

ceptable present of her particular caring magic? She is—
why doesn't Doug see it?—she is possibly slipping into
darker and wilder delusions than he realizes.

But since kindness is a sort of hobby with me, a skill
which I feel compelled to perfect, I try to look at Doug
kindly. It is not really his fault, I tell myself, that Doug
judges Eugene harshly. It is part of his generation, this
bias, my generation too, to see people in terms of their
professions. It is, after all, a logical outgrowth of the
work ethic; vocation forms the spiritual skin by which
we are recognized and rewarded. Doug Savage is a botanist, a specialist in certain forms of short ferns. He is defined by his speciality just as his ferns are defined by
their physical properties. His wife Greta is saved from
genuine ordinariness by the fact that she is a professional weaver. Doug's curriculum vitae for her would
run: Greta Savage, weaver, wife. Her actual weaving is
immaterial; it is *being* a weaver which endows her with
worth. In the same way he thinks of me pre-eminently as
a poet, a kindly classification, since I am more clerk than
poet these days. He is able to ignore the lapse of my talent just as he has been able to ignore the presence of Eugene Redding for the last two years.

The Savages' objection to Eugene is, I sometimes suspect, rather lumpily conceived and certainly it is seldom
mentioned: silence says it all. For the most part they
have chosen to ignore Eugene just as they have ignored
my other, briefer liaisons: with Bob the insurance adjuster, with Maynard the dry-cleaning executive,
Thomas Brown-Davis the tax lawyer (lawyers are okay
but only if they practice labour law or take on prickly
civil liberties cases—even then their value may be
marked down by a hyphenated name or a preference for
handmade shirts.)

At parties Doug Savage always introduces me by saying, this is Charleen Forrest, you know, the poet. Then he disappears leaving me to explain with enormous awkwardness that my last book came out more than three years ago and that, though I still dabble a little, poetry is part of my past now. What I don't bother to explain is that having written away the well of myself, there is nowhere to go. The only other alternative would be to join that corps of half-poets, those woozy would-bes who burble away in private obscurities, the band of poets I've come to think of, in my private lexicon, as "the pome people." They are the ones for whom no experience is too small: brushing their teeth in the morning brings them frothing to epiphany. Sex is their private invention, and they fornicate with a purity which cries out for crystallization. They can be charming; they can be seductive, but long ago I decided to stop writing if I found myself becoming one of them.

Both Doug and Greta fear for the future of Seth, that his straight, white teeth and middle-class amiability may propel him toward the untouchable ranks: public relations, stock brokerage, advertising, or even, given the situation, orthodontics.

And if Doug Savage had been acquainted with Eugene for twenty-five years instead of twenty-five minutes, he would still think of him as Eugene the Orthodontist. Pseudo-scientific, or so Doug believes, cosmetic-oriented, a man who tinkers with the design of nature. A shill for pearly teeth. A charlatan with carpeted waiting room, expensive machinery and golf-club manners. Doug sees the already-suspect profession of orthodontia as being coupled with a lack of creativity or discovery; if only he were a real dentist who dealt with the reality of pain and suffering. Eugene, sadly, is in one of the repair professions, a fact which for Doug places the seal on his insignificance. And worse, as far as the Sav-

ages are concerned, Eugene is abundantly rewarded for
what he does.

I sigh heavily, suddenly weary, and Doug says, "Don't
give a thought to the manuscripts, Char." He nods in the
direction of my desk. "They can wait."

"Fine, fine," I say absently. I am thinking of all the
things I have to do before leaving. Laundry, packing,
phone Eugene, make sure Seth has bus fare for school.
And there must be something else. Something I've forgotten. Laundry, packing, phone, bus fare? Something
is missing.

The wedding present!

"I never bought a wedding present," I cry out. "I completely forgot about it."

Doug says nothing.

"How could I forget!" I marvel. And then I add, "Do
you think there's something Freudian about that? Forgetting to buy my own mother a wedding present?"

He shrugs. Drums his fingers on my desk. He is determinedly nonchalant about my oversight, but I can see by
the faint, grey frown on his face that he has stored it
carefully away. Something Freudian. Hmmm. Yes.

❧

When my mother wrote from Toronto early in April to
tell me that she was planning to remarry, the first thing I
thought of was her left breast. No, not her left breast but
the place where her left breast had been before the
cancer.

What I pictured was a petal of torn flesh, something
unimaginably vulnerable like the unspeakable place behind a glass eye or the acutely sensitive and secret skin
beneath a fingernail. A pin-point of concentrated shrinking pain. A wound almost metaphysical, pink edged, so
tender that a breath or even a thought could break it
open.

I haven't seen her since her operation which was two years ago. In fact, I have not seen her for five years. She lives alone in the Scarborough bungalow where my sister and I grew up. What fills her life I cannot imagine; I have never been able to imagine. Plants. Pots of tea. Her pension cheque. The daily paper with the advertised specials. Taking the subway to Eaton's. Her appliquéd shopping bag, maroon and moss green, the wooden handles faintly soiled. Her housecoat (a floral cotton, washable), her reading glasses, and toast cut into triangles. Her kitchen curtains, her waxed linoleum. The decaffeinated coffee which she drinks from thick, chipped cups—the rows and rows of bone china cups and saucers, stamped with violets and bordered with gilt, are preserved in the glass-fronted china cabinet for the by-now entirely hypothetical day when guests of inexpressible elegance arrive unexpectedly to sip coffee and sit in judgement on my mother.

My mother is getting married. I have known for a month now—since her short, awkwardly-phrased letter with its curiously bald declaration, *Mr. Berceau has asked me to marry him*—but the thought still sucks the breath from the floor of my chest. I cannot believe it. I cannot believe it.

And why not? Why this perplexity? Certainly there is nothing improper about it; she has, after all, been a widow for eleven years, since our father, to whom she was married for thirty years, died in his sleep, a heart attack in his sixtieth year. A massive heart attack, the doctor had called it. Massive. I pictured a tidal wave of pressure, a blind wall—darkness crushing him as he lay sleeping beside my mother in the walnut veneer bed. He never woke up. My mother, always a light nervous sleeper, heard only a small sound like someone suppressing a cough and that was all. By the time she had switched on the pink glass bedside lamp with its pleated paper shade, he was gone.

And next week she is getting married again. To some-one called Louis Berceau, someone I have never seen or even heard of. On a Friday afternoon at the end of May, she is getting married. And why shouldn't she, a healthy woman of seventy? Why not? Only someone bitterly per-verse would object to what the whole world celebrates as a joyous event. But easy abstractions are one thing. It is something else to absorb an event like this into the hurt-ing holes and sockets of real life. I should rejoice. In-stead a sucking swamp tugs at me, a hint of Greek trag-edy, dark-blooded and massive like the violent seizure of my father's heart. My timid, nervous, implacable mother with her left breast sheared off and her terrible indif-ference intact, is getting married. It can't be happening, it can't be coming true.

When I leave the office I run for the bus, waving like a crazy woman at the driver, "Wait, wait!" The sun is blinding and I stumble aboard fumbling for a dollar bill and handing it to him.

"That all you got? Nothing smaller?"

"No," breathlessly, "I'm just going to the bank now." *Never apologize, never explain*, Brother Adam wrote.

"Okay, okay."

I sink into a seat only to be struck anew by panic: did I drop my pay cheque in my frantic search for change? I grope; there it is, folded in my wallet.

I am perspiring heavily. The weather is more like mid-summer than spring, and the air is weighed down with dampness. My blouse clings to me across the back. It is an old blouse, six years old at least, with a collar that sags. There is too much material under the arms sug-gesting rolls of mottled matronly flesh; I should have thrown it out long ago.

What I should do, I think, is go and get my hair cut. But that would cost at least fifteen dollars, even if I could get an appointment and there isn't much hope of that. Like my sister Judith I have heavy, wiry, wavy hair. Crow black hair. Irish hair, my mother always called it with a hint of contempt. Wild. I've never been able to formulate a plan for it. I'm tall, too, like Judith, but rangier, craggier, more angled than contoured; she is older by three years and beginning to widen slightly. I probably will too.

Yes, I decide, I must get my hair cut. Definitely. Right after I finish at the bank. I pat my purse with the cheque folded inside.

In addition to the cheque I have something else in my purse; a three-by-five card with Brother Adam's address written on it. It is really less a piece of information than a personal note to myself, for Brother Adam's address is firmly engraved on my brain: The Priory, 615 Beachwood, Toronto. Nevertheless, leaving the office, I scribbled it down on impulse and tucked it in the zippered middle section of my purse. Impulse? Of course not, I admit to the leafing-out trees; and hedges outside the bus window. I shake my head, a smile fanning out across my face; I have planned this from the very day I decided to go to Toronto for my mother's wedding. Not actually planned it; no, nothing so definite as that. The idea formed itself like a clot in the back of my head, gradually knitting itself into a possibility: I could, if I had time, that is, visit Brother Adam.

Perhaps not an actual visit. Just a phone call, just to say hello. This is Charleen Forrest. Remember? From the *Botany Journal.* Yes, it *is* a surprise, well, I just happened to be in Toronto for a few days, sort of a family reunion, and well, I just couldn't come this close and not give you a call when your letters have meant such a lot to me and, and, then what?

Maybe I could drop in. Why not? That would be better, nothing like a direct face-to-face after all. Then I could see just what sort of place the Priory is. I'd wear something decorous, my new dress probably, pants wouldn't do, and I could wear a little kerchief on my head; no, that would be ridiculous. I would ring the bell. Or lift the knocker. A heavy old knocker, probably wrought iron, rusted slightly, ornately carved with religious symbols. A tiny, frocked figure would eventually appear at the door, and I would state my purpose. My name is Charleen Forrest and I am anxious to see Brother Adam for a few minutes. If he can be spared, that is. No, I'm not actually a friend of his, but we correspond. Through letters, you know. For over a year now. And I thought since I was in Toronto anyway on family business that . . . .

Perhaps I should send a little note first. Plain white note paper. Nice small envelope, very maidenly, expressly plain. If I mailed it today it would be there in a day or two. Then I wouldn't have to worry about taking him by surprise. Really much more polite and, well, thoughtful. The sort of thing that lovely, caring people do, the sort of thing *he* might do: Dear Brother Adam, I know how busy you are with your grass research and spiritual studies and so on, but I wondered if you could spare a few minutes to see me. I'm going to be in Toronto for a few days visiting my family, and there are so many things I'd like to talk to you about, and some things are hard for me to write about. Your letters have meant so much to me—much more than I can tell you—as I have no one I can really talk to, Brother Adam, no one in the world.

❧

At Mr. Mario's Beauty Box the eyes of the receptionist transfix me. Green-hooded, beetle bright, too close together, riding above a sharp little nose like glued-on ornaments from a souvenir shop.

"I don't know if we can fit you in today," her voice clinks away uncaringly. "What about tomorrow at three?"

"I have to go out of town," I stutter. Am I pleading? Am I giving way to my tendency to be obsequious? I firm up my voice, "It has to be today."

"Well," she says tapping a pencil on the appointment book—and already I can see she is going to work me in—"Mr. Mario himself is free in twenty minutes. If you only need a cut, that is,"

"That's all I need," I chant gratefully, "just a cut, just a simple cut."

She stands up suddenly, reaches across the kidney-shaped desk and tugs a hank of my hair. "About three inches?" she demands.

Three inches off? Three inches left on? What?

"Three inches?" she asks again, more sharply this time.

"Yes, yes, three inches, that would be fine."

I have never been to Mr. Mario's before. In fact, I avoid beauty salons almost entirely except for the occasional cut and one or two disastrous hair-straightening sessions in the days when Watson was trying to transform me into a flower child. Mr. Mario's place shimmers with pinkish light. Light spills in through the shirred Austrian curtains and twinkles off the plastic chandeliers. Little bulbs blaze around the mirrors reminding me of movie stars' dressing rooms. Pink hair dryers buzz and the air conditioners churn. The wet, white sunlight of the street is miles away. I wait for Mr. Mario in a slippery vinyl chair, suddenly struck with the fear that this rosy elegance might hint at undreamt of prices. Much more than fifteen dollars, maybe even eighteen. Or as much as twenty. Twenty dollars for a hair cut, am I crazy? I turn to the kidney desk in panic, but the receptionist eyes me coldly, leanly. "Now," she says.

Mr. Mario marches me to a basin, thoroughly, roughly, drenches my hair and neck, and then he seats me in front of his mirror. For a moment I am reassured by his relative maturity; he has a mid-life shadow of fat under his chin, and his fingers are competently plump and strong. Taking hold of my hair at both sides he pulls it straight out and regards my image in the mirror. Together we stare in disbelief: such Irish coarseness, such obscene length, such unspeakable heaviness.

"What did you have in mind?" he inquires sleepily.

"I don't know," I gasp. "Something different. Just go ahead and cut."

"Okay," he yawns and stepping back he examines me from another angle. "Okay."

The sight of the razor raises new fears—where did I hear that razor cuts are more haute than scissor cuts? This might even cost—I feel faint at the thought—as much as twenty-three dollars. And then I'll have to tip him. Another dollar. God, god.

My hair begins to fall to the floor, and without a hint of delicacy he kicks it to one side where it is almost immediately swept up by a girl in a green uniform. Too late now.

He combs, sections, and clips silently and steadily, his lips curled inward with concentration. "Coarse," he says finally, breaking the silence.

"Yes," I confess, "it runs in the family."

"Italian?" he asks with a flicker of interest.

"No. Half Irish, half Scottish."

"Yeah?" His interest evaporates.

To my right a small shrunken woman of enormous old age sits swathed in a plastic cape; her wisps of hair are briskly sectioned for a permanent, and the pink scalp shows through like intersecting streets. One by one I watch the tight plastic rollers being wound and pinned to the bony scalp. I imagine the ammonia burning through her thin, pink skin, aching. Why does she do this to herself? Her chin wobbles like a walnut as though a scream is gathering there. Her lips move, but she says nothing.

On the other side of me a vigorous woman of about fifty bends forward and lights a cigarette while her rollers are removed by the slimmest of boys in striped purple jeans. "Yesterday," she says, blowing out puffed clouds of smoke, "I went all the way to the fish market for some red snapper."

"For what?" the boy asks, leaning toward her.

"Red snapper. It's a fish. And ex-pen-sive! But I was in the mood for a splurge. Well, I cooked it in a little butter. Then you cover it, you know, and leave it just on simmer. Not too long, say about ten minutes."

"Ten minutes," he murmurs back-combing her gun-metal shrub.

"Ten minutes. Then just a little lemon, you know, cut in a wedge to squeeze. And my husband said to me, you know, you could serve this to the P.M. if he happened to drop by."

"He liked it, eh?"

"So he said, so he said, and he's a hard man to please. Tonight I'm going to do lamb chops. You like lamb?"

"Not too much."

"It's all in how you do it. Most people don't get all the fat out, and with lamb you've got to get all the fat out. But do you know what really makes it?"

"What?" he listens. I listen. Even Mr. Mario seems to listen.

"After you brown it really well, you add just a sniff of white wine."

"White wine?" The striped-pants boy seems a little disappointed.

"You don't have to use the expensive stuff. Why waste good booze in cooking. Just the ordinary poison will do you."

"Do you want to have a little hairspray?"

"Just a little. My husband says it's bad for the lungs. Did you know that?"

"Maybe."

"No, it's true. The whole atmosphere's being destroyed by spray cans. But just a little. It's awfully humid out. And I've got to pick up the lamb chops. That husband of mine.

Husband. Strange word. Medieval. Husbandry, husband your flocks; keep, guard, preserve, watch over.

"Bitch," Mr. Mario whispers lazily in my ear as she leaves.

I say nothing, only smile, obscurely gratified that I have somehow gained his favour. He cups my head with his hands, turning it slightly, then begins cutting again, slowly, slowly, alternating between razor, scissors, clippers; razor, scissors, clippers. Cautious as a surgeon.

"Hold still now," he hisses. "The back of the neck is the most important."

I begin to feel sick. Could this possibly cost as much as twenty-five dollars? In New York hair cuts cost up to forty dollars—where did I read that? Mr. Kenneth or something. But this is Vancouver. Still with inflation and everything, twenty-five dollars is not impossible. Twenty-five dollars! Stop cutting, I want to cry out. That's enough. Stop.

Then he is going all over my head with an electric blower and a little round brush, catching my hair from underneath and drawing it out into rounds of dark fur. Turning, rolling, curving. Stop, stop.

At last. Flick, flick with the brush. Off with the towel.

A puff of spray. I stagger to the kidney desk.

He follows me, drowsy-eyed.

Now.

"How much?" my mouth moves.

"Fifteen dollars," he drawls.

I pull out the bills. Blindly stuff an extra dollar in the pocket of his smock. Run for the door. And in the dancing, white heat I see myself blurred across the window. Or is it me?

Oh, Mr. Mario, Mr. Mario. Always, always, always I've wanted to look like this. Soft, shaped, feathered into a new existence. Me.

My lips perform the smallest of smiles. My neck turns a fraction of an inch. My legs stretch long and cool and slow. What's the hurry. Slowly, slowly, I walk home.

❧

Greta telephones to say good-bye. "Is it true," she asks, "is it true what Doug says? That Eugene What's-his-name is going with you?"

I picture her holding the phone in an attitude of anxious, frowning disbelief, her crow's-feet deepening. (Greta's crow's-feet reach all the way to her soul.)

"Yes," I tell her briskly. "Yes, Eugene happened to have a convention in Toronto at the same time. Wasn't that lucky?"

"A dentists' convention," Greta says sadly, dully.

I want to comfort her. Poor Greta with her Gestalt therapy, her psychodrama, her awareness clinic, her encounter group, her trauma team, her megavitamin treatment and now her obsession with meditation. All she needs is just enough psychic epoxy to keep her from slipping apart. Can't I summon a few words to reassure her? Is my heart so hard that I can't give her those few words?

"Look Greta," I say, "thanks for phoning, but I've got to run. Seth just got in from band practice and I've got a million things to do."

"Seth," I turn to him.

"Yes."

"You have the phone number in Toronto? If anything goes wrong?"

"It's on top of the list you gave me."

"Well, look, Seth, if you lose it, just on the wild chance that you might lose it, you can ask the Savages. I gave it to Doug too. You never know."

"Okay."

"And you've got enough money?"

"Sure."

"Positive?"

"All I need is busfare and milk money."

"You might have an emergency."

"I've got plenty."

"Just to make sure, you'd better take this extra five."

"You keep it, you'll need it."

"I've got lots. Your father's cheque came yesterday. And I got paid today. I'm rich for once. You take it."

He pokes it in his back pocket. "I'll take it but I won't need it."

"I wish you were coming. I hate leaving you here like this."

"It's okay," he smiles across at me. "Anyway, there's band practice every day this week."

"At least we'll be back for the concert. Did you get the tickets?"

"Yeah."

"For Eugene too? And his kids?"

"Yeah. In my wallet. Want me to hang on to them 'til Saturday night?"

"Maybe you'd better, the way I lose things. Anyway, I hope everything goes O.K. here."

"Why wouldn't it?"

"It's just that Doug and Greta can be a little . . . well . . . you know."

"Uhuh."

"A little too much."

"I know."

"Just tune them out, Seth. If they start getting to you."

"Okay."

"You'll be ready after school? When they pick you up?"

"I'll be ready."

"And you won't forget your suitcase?"

"No."

"There are clean socks for every day. And I put in your Lions T-shirt in case it stays hot like this."

"Thanks."

"And your retainer is in a plastic bag under your pajamas."

"Okay."

"Your toothbrush. What about your toothbrush?"

"I'll put it in tomorrow morning."

"Don't forget."

"I won't."

"I sound like a clucking hen. I know I sound like an old hen."

"No, you don't."

"It's just that I'm sort of nervous, I guess. All the rushing around and the whole idea of Grandma,"—I say the word Grandma with a sliding self-consciousness since Seth cannot even remember seeing his grandmother—"getting married and everything. It's just got me a little more rattled than usual."

"That's okay."

"That's why I'm clucking away at you like this."

"I don't mind," he says smiling.

"You've got a nice smile, you know that?"

"I ought to for eight hundred bucks."

"I don't mean your teeth. I mean you *have* really got a nice smile."

"Thanks. So do you."

"Really?"

"Yeah, sort of."

"I wish you were coming."

"I'll be okay," he says. And then he adds, "And you'll be okay too."

Chapter 2

"There's nothing about myself that I like," I say to Eugene as we lie side by side in our lower berth. Contentment, momentary contentment, has lulled me into confession. "The bottoms of my feet are scaly," I tell him, "and have you ever noticed what big ugly feet I've got? Slabs. And two huge corns. One on each foot. I've had those same corns since I was thirteen."

"Luckily no one dies of corns."

"My big toes are crooked," I continue. "I'd go to see a chiropodist if I weren't so ashamed of my feet. And they're the kind of feet that are always clammy, summer and winter. At least in the winter I can cover them up with shoes. But then as soon as it's warm enough for sandals, hot like it was today, that's when I remember how much I hate my feet."

"Try to sleep, Charleen."

"It's too lurchy on this train to sleep."

There is a pause, and for a moment or two I think Eugene may remind me that it had been my idea to take the train. But he doesn't. His divorce has made him cautious, fearful of anything resembling marital bickering. Instinctively he shuns that almost unconscious coinage which passes between husbands and wives: *I told you it wouldn't work. Remember, this was your big idea. What will you think of next? Didn't I tell you? Not again! Are you going to start in on that? Don't you ever listen when I'm talking to you? Don't you care anymore? Don't you love me?*

"Try to sleep anyway," Eugene says gently.

"I keep meaning to buy a pumice stone for my feet," I tell him. "Do you know something, Eugene—I've been meaning to buy a pumice stone since I was fifteen and read in *Seventeen* that there was such a thing. And now, here I am, thirty-eight. What's the matter with me, I can't even organize my life enough to buy a pumice stone."

"We'll buy you one in Toronto." He is only faintly mocking.

"I would love to have beautiful feet."

"Great."

"It would be a start."

Eugene says nothing but yawns hugely.

"It would be a start," I say again, drifting off. I am wearying of my self-hatred. It's only a tactical diversion anyway, a pale cousin to the ferocious self-inquiry which ransacks me on nights less peaceful than this. This is more reflex than ritual, stuffing for my poor brain, packing for the wound I prefer not to leave open.

But it opens anyway, freshly perceived, when I'm wakened at three A.M. by the long, pliant, complaining train whistle. Somewhere in all that darkness we are bending around an unseen curve. It's cold in the Pullman, and my nightgown is wound across my stomach. Reaching over Eugene and jerking the blind up an inch or two, I admit a bar of blue light into our dim shelf. Moonlight.

Sharp as biblical revelation it informs me of the total unreality of this instant: that I am lying in bed with a man who is not my husband, rolling through mountains of darkness to my mother's marriage. This is not melodrama (though the vocabulary it requires is); this is madness, lunacy, calling into doubt all the surfaces and shadows of my thirty-eight years.

Berth. Birth. My yearning to see things in symbolic form is powerful; it always has been; it is the affliction of the hopelessly, cheerlessly optimistic, this pinning together of facts to find patterns. And it is a compulsion I resist, having long ago discovered it to be a grandiose cheat. The rhythms of life are random and irreducible.

Suddenly I am shivering from head to foot. I would like to wake Eugene for the warmth of his body, but at this moment I can't bear to include him. And besides, his green-pajamaed back slopes away from me at an angle which suggests an exhaustion even greater than my fear.

❦

Both of us, Eugene and I, are secondary victims of separate modern diseases, mid-century maladies hatched by the heartless new social order: Eugene because his wife abandoned him for the Womens' Movement and I, because I married a man who couldn't bear to leave his youth behind.

We are the losers. (Misery loves company, my mother always said.) The hapless rejectees, the jilted partners of people stronger than ourselves. Social residue. Silt. Whatever exists between Eugene and me—and Doug Savage is at least partly accurate when he accuses me of bewilderment—is diminished by the fact that each of us has been cast aside, tossed out like some curious archeological implement whose usefulness is no longer understood. Even our lovemaking is lit with doubt: are we anything more than two cripples holding each other up? Can our passion be more than second-rate? Can anything come from nothing?

"She was always something of a bitch," Eugene said about his wife, Jeri, shortly after I met him, "but at least in the early days she confined her bitchiness to outsiders. Like waiters in restaurants. The first time I took her out to dinner—I'd only known her a week or so then and I wanted to take her somewhere, you know, impressive. To show her that country boys don't necessarily dribble soup out of the corners of their mouths. We went to the Top of the Captain and she sent the rolls back because they were cold."

"No!" I gasped delightedly. "Really?"

"Really. She said that she thought more people should take that kind of responsibility when the service wasn't up to standard. Sort of a battlecry with her."

"And you married her after that! Oh, Eugene, how could you?"

"There's one born every minute, you know."

"What else did she do?" I asked greedily.

"Well, then she got into the consumer thing. That must have started after we'd been married a year or so. She started out by returning groceries."

"Like what?"

"You name it. Once she had a jar of apricot jam with a wasp in it. That was the worst, I guess. She mailed that to Ottawa."

"And what happened?"

"All she got, I think, was a form letter. It was being looked into or something. She took back all kinds of things to the store. Lettuce that was brown in the middle. Coffee if it tasted a bit off. Fungussy oranges from the bottom of the bag. Smashed eggs, bony meat. Once, as a joke, I accused her of deliberately buying rotten stuff so she'd have something to return."

"And . . .?"

"Jeri never did have much sense of humour."

"Why did she do it anyway? Did she really care all that much?"

Eugene shrugged. "I could never figure it out. I mean, even then we weren't all that hard up for cash. She always said it was the principle of the thing. She seemed to be mad at the whole world. And consumerism kind of opened a somewhat legitimate channel to her. God, she could work up a rage. Nothing timid and retiring about Jeri. Funny, at first she had seemed, I don't know, just discerning. Knowledgeable. Discriminating. How the hell was I supposed to know if rolls should be served warm. I'd never even thought about it. We never had rolls at home. Bread maybe, or biscuits, but never rolls. And here was this dish with long, blonde hair knowing all about rolls."

"You're too trusting, Eugene."

"Later it got so every supermarket manager in the greater Vancouver area knew her. Once she tried to get me to return something for her. A box of broken cookies. Gingersnaps. It was raining like a bastard and she was about eight months pregnant with Donny and she wanted me to get the car out of the garage and go give the store manager hell."

"And did you?"

"No. Absolutely not. I told her I just couldn't get that worked up about a few broken cookies. I've never seen anyone cry the way she did that Saturday afternoon. She cried so hard she was sick. And she couldn't stop being sick. She was kind of half kneeling on the bathroom floor with her head on the edge of the toilet. I finally phoned a drugstore for a tranquilizer, and when she heard about that she started all over again. Hadn't I ever heard of thalidomide? Was I trying to mutilate the baby and maybe kill her?"

"Maybe she really was crazy."

He paused, thinking. "Sometimes I used to think so. Now I think she was just plain angry. An angry, angry woman. And probably still is. The only decent thing she's ever done is let me have the two boys for weekends.

How they've survived I don't know. You know, sometimes when she was at her worst I would lie awake for hours and make up dialogue. Daydreams, only mine were at night. Just lay there and dreamed up things for her to say, the things I wanted her to say. I'd invent whole scenes just like movies. I'd have her running in the front door all smiling and her hair falling all around her and she would be saying something like, 'look at these beautiful apples,' and then she'd bite into one of them. Or she might be bending over me in bed, smiling and telling me how she was the most—" he stopped, smiling, "the most *satisfied* woman on the Pacific coast and that for once she was contented."

"She must have been satisfied once in a while," I said knowingly to Eugene.

"I don't know. I can't ever remember her looking really happy until she joined the West Van Consumer Action Group. The night she got elected secretary-treasurer was the horniest night we ever had in eight years of marriage. Of course I was more or less incidental to the whole scene." He drew a breath. "God, I still think of that night with a kind of glow."

"Why did you have to say that?"

"What? About feeling a glow?"

"Yes," I said, for I liked to think Eugene had nothing but the most wretched memories of Jeri. Eugene is the same: he prefers to think of Watson as a pure, black-hearted villain.

"Actually Watson was a psychic disaster," I volunteered helpfully.

"Like Jeri," Eugene said. "Selfish, immature."

"Never should have married anyone."

"She couldn't see past her own dumb self-satisfaction."

"He could be utterly, utterly unfeeling."

"Blind. And biting. Even with the kids."

Thus we reassure ourselves, Eugene and I, by contesting the unworthiness of our former partners. Sometimes we grow shrill in our denunciations; they were shallow, insensitive, childish, pathetic. I match Eugene, horror story for horror story, as we conspire to reduce our two partners to ranting maniacs; if they hadn't walked out on us when they did, they would most assuredly have been committed to an institution, no doubt about it.

In this way we contrive our innocence. We reshape our histories; we have not been abandoned, only misled, and we insist that we now are liberated from the impossible, the unbearable, that we are free. I am happy now, I tell Eugene. He is happy too, he says, happier than he ever was with Jeri.

We cling together. Legs entwined, playing at love, we wake early in the morning (who could sleep with all this racket?) and we lie in our lower berth clinging together like children.

❧

In the dining car we are served breakfast by a serious young man with a raw, new haircut and a glistening red neck. A university student, probably, hired for the summer. Under the eyes of anxious authority his hands tremble slightly as he puts down our glasses of chilled grapefruit juice. His eyes never leave the rims of the glasses and his mouth sags open slightly in concentration. It's only May; by August he'll be performing with the gliding familiar detachment of a professional.

Who dreams up breakfast menus on trains? Someone splendidly elevated and detached from the rushed, sour determinate of instant coffee sloshed onto saucers, the whole crumbly-cupboard, soggy cornflake world. Here fresh haddock is offered, haddock in cream, imagine. With a tiny branch of parsley. Poached eggs exquisitely shivering on circles of toast. Or a bacon omelet. Nested in homefries. Marvellous. Served with a broiled tomato half. The pictorial effect alone is dazzling. English muffins on warmed plates. Yes, please. Honey or raspberry jam? Ahh, both please. Butter, carved into chilly balls on a green glass dish. Coffee brewed to dense perfection and poured from a graceful silvery pot. Well, just one more cup. Eugene smiles across at me.

A tenderness seizes us for a middle-aged man sitting all alone at the next table and, half turning, Eugene and I exchange pleasantries with him. Over third and fourth cups of coffee he talks about how he found happiness by selling his car.

"Suddenly it came to me," he tells us. "I had an ulcer. You know? I'm a worrier, and you know what they say. Finally I said to myself, look, what are you always worrying about? And do you know what it was?"

"What?" I ask. I am always polite, and besides it is part of the burden of my life to pretend that I am a benevolent and caring person. "What were you worrying about?"

"Well," he continues, "I didn't realize it then—it was like a kind of subconscious thing with me—but what I was always thinking about was my car. Like any minute the brake linings were going to need replacing. So I'd be driving along and all the time I'd be listening to some little noise in the engine. My wife used to say I'd get a crick in my neck from bending over listening like that. Every time I heard any knocking in there I'd always automatically think the worst. Like the motor was stripped for sure. Or the carburetor was giving out. I used to have nightmares, honest to God nightmares, about needing four new tires all at once."

"And did it ever happen?" I ask.

"No. That's the thing, it never happened like that. Maybe there would be a dirty sparkplug or some two-bit wiring job, and when they told me at the garage that was all it was, I'd break into a sweat. A cold sweat. Well, finally I couldn't take it anymore. Landed in hospital and I was only forty-three years old. An ulcer. I bled twenty-four hours, they couldn't stop it. I'm telling you, that makes you think, when something like that happens."

"I'll bet," I agree emphatically.

"So to hell with this, I said. I want to live my life, not worry it away."

"So you sold your car?"

"That's exactly what I did. Just called over a second-hand dealer and said, 'Take it away, I never want to set eyes on it again.' And the day I sold it was like a stone was rolled off my shoulders. You know what?" He paused. "I was happier that day than the day when I got my first car."

"And you're really happier now?" I ask earnestly. I'm not feigning kindness anymore, for I collect, among other things, recipes for happiness. "You really are?"

"You're darned right," he said, draining his coffee cup and setting it thoughtfully on the saucer. "So I spend a buck or two on a taxi now and then. And train fares and all the rest. But I've got my health, and what's more important than that? I'm telling you, I didn't know what happiness was."

A prescription for contentment. I think of Greta Savage in Vancouver who, for the moment at least, has found a quiet place to store all her missionary longings. And Brother Adam—what did he write me? The only way to be happy is to have no expectations. How fortunate they are to have found their perfect, definable, tailored-to-fit solutions.

And my mother. My mother who achieved, if not happiness, at least a sort of jealous, truncated satisfaction in perpetually revising and reordering her immediate surroundings. All the time my sister and I were growing up, for at least twenty-five years, the main focus of her life was an eccentric passion for home decoration, an enslavement all the more bizarre because of the humbleness of our suburban bungalow, a brick box on a narrow, sandy lot with a concrete stoop, a green awning, and a clothes line at the back.

Always one of the six small rooms was in the process of being 'done over', so that we never at any one time in all those years lived in a state of completion. Decorating magazines formed almost the only reading matter in our house, and from those pages, which my mother turned with anxious, hungering fingers, she fanned her fanatical energy. She could do anything. Velvet curtains, swagged and bordered by hand for the living room, were cut up a year later to make throw cushions. She was nothing if not resourceful, for the throw cushions were later picked apart and upholstered onto the dining room chairs. End tables were cut down and patiently refinished. Often wallpaper samples were propped up along the mantle of the imitation fireplace for months at a time before a decision was reached. Her options were limited, of course, by our father's modest income (he was a clerk in a screw factory). She saved quarters in a pickle jar for two years in order to buy a fake-crystal ceiling fixture for the hall.

She learned to make the most complicated and sheerest of curtains complete with miles of ruffling. She learned to paint, solder, wallpaper, stain and upholster. Several times she rewebbed and covered the armchairs in the livingroom. Mother. A tall woman with a caved-in, shallow chest; she went about the house wearing an old shirt of my father's over her print house dresses and on her feet, socks and running shoes; her legs, I remember, were a mottled white with clustered purplish, grape-jelly veins at the backs of the knees. Sometimes we would wake up in the morning to find that she was already at work, the dining-room floor covered with drop-cloths, the step ladder set up, and there she tottered, her bush of hair snugged in an "invisible" net, her Scottish jaw set, painting a stenciled cornice around the ceiling. A sea-shell motif in antique ivory.

Her decorating effects were invariably too heavily ba-roque. Not that I realized this at the time; what I felt in that house was a curious choking pressure as though the walls were being slowly strangled; we were all smother-ing in layers and layers of airless drapery and plaster. Over the years she showed a tendency toward progressi-vely darker, richer textures. The pine buffet was trans-formed to walnut, an effect laboriously achieved with the aid of stain and graining tools. In the tiny front hall under the chandelier hung a great, gilded imitation-Ita-lian mirror bought at an auction. Under it was a 'gossip bench' painted gold. She ran to luxurious ornamental fabrics, velvets and brocades bought as remnants, and the sumptious effects of tassles and draping. "You don't need money," she used to say, "if you have taste."

Taste. Taste was what the neighbours didn't have. Taste and imagination. All they ever did, she scoffed, was open the Eaton's catalogue and order rooms full of mail-order furniture. And if they were short of cash they put up with faded curtains when all they had to do was buy a packet of dye from the chain store. (She herself frequently went on the rampage with dying. Perhaps my great insecurity springs from nothing more serious than the fear that my pink cotton scatter rug might be snatched from me at any minute to reappear later in vivid, startling, foreign purple.) The neighbours didn't know what taste meant, she said, or were too lazy to make any improvements. All they needed was to get

busy and roll up their shirt sleeves. "Just look," she often
sighed, "look what I've managed to make of this
house."

Our bedroom, Judith's and mine, was a vision of con-
torted femininity. For us she favoured shirred taffeta or
dotted swiss, pale chintz or nylon net. I remember one
summer morning, perspiration streaming down her face,
dark circles staining the arms of her housedress as she
knelt on the floor of our stifling bedroom off the kitchen,
her lips grim with zeal and full of pins, attaching an in-
tricately ruffled skirt to our dressing table. Once, for wall
hangings, she framed squares of black velvet to which
she appliquéd (the discovery of appliqué opened a whole
new chapter in her life) stylized ballet figures. A
McCall's pattern, twenty-five cents plus postage. She
made us a bedroom lamp from an old, pink perfume bottle from Woolworth's and covered the shade with white
tulle; this was one of her least successful ideas, for the
tulle began to smoke one evening while Judith was
studying, and our father had to carry it outside to the
backyard and spray it with the garden hose. Our mother
watched its destruction with a minimum of sorrow, for
any sign of wear or tear or obsolescence immediately
opened a hole in the house which her furious energies
conspired to fill.

Our father: what did he think of it all? He was so silent
and laconic a man, so shy, so nervously inarticulate that
it was impossible to tell, but he seemed to sense that the
compulsive forces of her personality were cosmic manifestations which must not be interfered with; to stop her
was to invite danger or disaster. All I can remember is
his occasional resigned sigh: "You know your mother
and her house," as once again we were plunged into
chaos.

While she was working on a room she was in a state of

violent unrest, plagued by insomnia and shocking fits of indigestion. She planned her rooms as carefully as any set designer, bringing into life whole new environments. Finally, as the metamorphosis was nearing completion, she would become almost electrically excited, impatiently dabbing on the last bit of paint, taking the last stitch, and, with breath suspended, unveiling her creation.

Later she would suffer agonies of doubt. Was it in good taste or was there something maybe just a little bit tacky or gawdy about it? That pink vase, was it a little too much accent? Too bright? Too garish a shade? Maybe if she spray-painted it dusty rose, yes. Yes.

No one except a few out-of-town relatives and the occasional neighbour ever witnessed her decorating marvels although she always talked of having something, a tea perhaps—the exact type of entertainment was never decided upon—when she got the whole house organized. Organized! And the telephone on the gilded gossip bench seldom rang; she never used it herself except to phone our father at the screw company to ask him to bring home another half quart of enamel for the kitchen cupboards or to tell him she had a headache from the varnish fumes and could he come straight home after work and get the girls some scrambled eggs for supper, she would just slip off to bed if he didn't mind.

I never doubted that she loved the house more than she loved us. Our father and Judith and I only impeded her progress as she plunged from one room to the next. Our very presence made the rooms untidy; sitting on the new chintz slipcover we pulled the pattern off-centre, and our school books on the sideboard disturbed the balance of her ornaments. Once I chipped the Chinese blue kitchen cupboards with the broom handle, thus necessitating a frantic search through all the hardware stores in

Scarborough for patch-up paint, a search she suddenly abandoned when it was decided that the cupboards should be painted a pale pumpkin to match the striped cafe curtains which she planned to "run up" as soon as she finished gluing on the moulding in the front bedroom.

Suddenly it stopped. Overnight her obsession became a memory, the way she was before she got old. Judith says it was about the time our father died. I think it was a little earlier. It's been years now since she has made even the slightest alteration to the house. All the upholstery is faded, slightly soiled on the arms, and when I was last there five years ago I actually saw a patch of the old Chinese blue paint in the kitchen showing through the pumpkin. And under that? A scratch of pink? Perhaps.

I don't know why she stopped. I must ask her when I see her. Casually mention something like, "Remember how interested you used to be in decorating—why is it you don't do it anymore?"

But of course I won't actually say anything of the kind. These offhand conversations which I always rehearse in my mind before seeing my mother never materialize because, once in her presence, I freeze back to sullen childhood when all such phenomena were accepted without comment. To question would be to injure the delicate springs of impulse and emotion. For an obsession such as the one which ruled my mother's life could only have existed to fill a terrible hurting void; it is the void we must not mention, for, who knows, it may still exist just below the uneasy quaking surface. Quicksand. So easy to get sucked under. Better to walk carefully, to say nothing.

She may have lost her nerve and become, in the end, finally doubtful about what she had once taken to be taste. Perhaps she simply became exhausted. Or the cost of paint and paper may have strained her small pension. It may be that she suddenly realized one day that all her energy was being poured into an unworthy vessel. Or perhaps she was struck with the heart-racking futility of altering mere surfaces and never reaching the heart: her world was immutable, she may have decided. What was the point of trying to change it?

❧

Because the Vistadome is packed with people, Eugene and I sit side by side in the day coach, I by the window and he in the aisle seat. We are leaving the mountains behind and for an hour we've watched their angles collapse; they are softening and melting into green, elongated hills which, with their hint of cultivation, are mannerly and almost English. Eugene tells me he has never crossed the Rockies by train before.

"Why not?" I ask.

He shrugs; he is a man much given to shrugging, resignation being the principal inheritance of his forty years. "I don't really know."

"How did you get out of Estevan in the first place?" I demand.

"Bus," he says. "I left on a Thursday afternoon and got into Vancouver late on a Friday night. September. It was the first Friday in September, I remember exactly. I'd just turned eighteen."

"Why didn't you take the train?" I ask, wanting details.

"The bus was cheaper," he explains carefully as though I were exceedingly simple. "Probably only a buck or two, but to my folks—" he stops, shrugging again.

"How did you get home for holidays," I ask, "when you were at university?" These questions are necessary, for though Eugene and I have known each other for two

years now, there are miles of unknown territory to recover. Thirty-eight years of his life, thirty-six of mine.

"Hitchhiked," he says. "Then in my third year I
bought that old, tan Chevvy. I told you about that."

I nod. Eugene's life is chronicled by the different cars
he has owned, separated into periods as distinct as the
phases of civilization; his stone-age, bronze-age, iron-
age. First the Chevvy, a fourth-hand, first love which he
restored to humming perfection on lonely, broke,
womanless weekends on the street outside his boarding
house on west 19th. Then the Volkswagen beetle with
only one previous owner; by graduation he had discovered the benefits of good mileage and reliable repair service. With the navy blue Ford Jeri entered his life. The
Rambler: Sandy was born and Donnie on the way and
what with diaper bags, carbeds, safety seats and economy . . . the Plymouth wagon, good for groceries. Then
the Chrysler; orthodontics was beginning to be rewarding, and though Jeri didn't believe in luxury transport
(she had a small Sunbeam of her own anyway), the
dealer had offered a package Eugene couldn't turn
down. "We used it on weekends," he says, "but I never
really knew it inside out. Not like with the Chevvy." The
Chevvy. He speaks of it tenderly. "She took me back and
forth from Estevan to university three times a year and
never once let me down." He smiles, stretched with nostalgia. "She was a good girl. A great old girl."

"And you never once flew."

"Christ, no. It was all I could do to buy gas. I never
even set foot in a plane until I was twenty-six and Jeri
wanted to go to Hawaii for our honeymoon."

Now, years later, he flies routinely as though no other
form of transportation exists. When he decided to come
with me to Toronto he tried for days to persuade me that
we should fly. "It would save time," he pressed, "and

you'd have longer with your mother and sister." (An argument which demonstrates how shallowly he knows me after two years, for what matters to me is to shorten the time in Toronto, not lengthen it.) Besides I went by train the other three times—when I brought Seth as a baby to show him off to his grandparents, then when my father died, and five years ago, when I came home to tell my mother, very belatedly, about my divorce. I had always taken the train; the pattern had been set; and besides, I told Eugene, the train was cheaper.

At the mention of expense, Eugene hesitated, and I knew what he was thinking: that he could easily afford the plane fares for both of us, and since he was planning to attend a dental convention in Toronto, he could write off the whole thing as a business expense. How simple life is for those with professions, savings accounts and good tax lawyers. It was, in fact, this very simplicity that I refused; I'm not ready yet to lay myself open to such soft and easy alternatives.

For days we discussed the matter of plane-versus-train, trading small gently reasoned arguments, each of us having lost the taste for full-scale battle, and, at last, Eugene relented, "But," he said, "if we go by train let's at least come home by air. And let's get ourselves a compartment."

"I sat up the other three times," I said, "and it was fine." Actually it hadn't been fine, but I had, on those three previous trips, accepted discomfort as a kind of welcome detached suffering.

"A roomette?" he bargained. "At least a roomette."

In the end we found we had left it too late; by the time we came to an agreement on the roomette, there was nothing left but one Pullman and at that we were lucky to get a lower. I wanted to pay for half the Pullman but backed down when Eugene began to show signs of genuine impatience. But if he had been even a trifle reasonable I would have preferred to pay my way. Just as I'm not ready for comfort (since I've done nothing to deserve it), neither am I ready to give up what remains of my shattered independence. First it was dinners Eugene paid for; then Seth's dental care; last spring a holiday for the two of us in San Francisco; now my Pullman. And when I went shopping for a new dress for Toronto, he had wanted to pay for that too.

I look down at the dress which is really quite comfortable for the train, but like most of my purchases it is proving to be something of a disappointment; a shirtdress in tangerine knit which, even though it is supposed to be permapress, creases across the lap. It is slightly baggy in the hips and a little snug across the top so that the spaces between the shiny white buttons gap slightly like little orange mouths. And beneath my soft, glossy new hair style of forty-eight hours ago the natural, black, Irish-witch contours are beginning to reassert themselves.

Still the two of us sitting here could pass for any happily married couple. Eugene, prosperous and healthy in his chocolate, doubleknit sixty dollar pants and lightweight, brown, ribbed pullover, and I, his wife ('the little wife' you could almost say if I weren't so tall) going along for the ride, a little shopping, a little holiday from the kids. That is to say, there is nothing grotesque about us. We are not perhaps a stunning couple; Eugene has a loose fabric-like face and thin, beige, wooly hair cut too short. Without being actually overweight, there is a somewhat loose look around his stomach and hips. And I have my usual rangy, unconfined awkwardness. Nevertheless we are not in any way identifiable as the victims of failed marriages. Nothing gives us away, a fact which seems remarkable to me. Nothing betrays us, nothing sets us apart. And because I never let go of anything if I can help it, I am still wearing the wedding ring, a band of Mexican worked silver, which Watson gave me when I was eighteen.

Eugene, I'm a little relieved to see, seems to be enjoying the train trip after all. Soon we'll be getting into the prairies, Saskatchewan, the real prairies where he grew up, and he's looking exceptionally thoughtful. It may be that he's thinking about his father again.

By habit he sees almost everything he does through the double lens of his dead father's limitations, and these reflections are necessarily rimmed with regret, for his father, a hard-working farmer on a piece of worthless land, lived a life of unrelieved narrowness. "My father never slept in a Pullman," Eugene may be thinking. "He never made love behind a hairy green curtain going seventy miles an hour through the mountains." "My father never slept in a tent," he had thought when he went camping for the first time at the age of twenty-five. "My father never rode in a Citroen, never had a glass of wine with his dinner, never went to a concert, never rode in a subway, never ate a black olive, never skied down a hill, never read Hemingway. My father never had a hundred dollar bill in his pocket. He never wore a ring on his finger in all his life. He never sat in a sauna and watched the steam rising off his chest. He never tipped a bellhop or smoked a cigar. Or watched a tennis match or slept in a waterbed in a fifty-dollar a day room with colour television. For that matter, he died while people were still wondering if there would ever be such a thing as colour television."

I am right; Eugene *is* thinking about his father. After a minute he begins to tell me how his father introduced him to the mystery of sex. Of course, Eugene explains, it was already too late. He was a boy of thirteen at the time, and on a farm there are no such mysteries. "But someone must have told my father that he owed me something more. It might even have been my mother. No, on second thought, I don't think so. I think he just made up his mind that he should explain everything about sex to his only son."

"So he had a long chat with you out in the barn?" I suggest.

"Oh, no. Better than that. Or worse than that, it depends on how you look at it. I mean, he was a man who didn't really know how to have a long talk. They didn't talk much at home, neither of them, and I was the only kid and fairly quiet too. But he must have figured out in his head that the time had come for sex. It was when we were at the fair. The same fair we had every year in town. More of a carnival really, pretty junky, but there were some farm animals and home preserving and all that too. We always went, it was the big deal, the three of us. There wasn't all that much else to do."

"Go on about the sex."

"Well, this particular day when we were standing in the fairgrounds, he turned to my mother and said that he was going off with me for a while and we would meet her later by the cattle judging yard. So off we went."

"Where?"

"To a girlie show."

"No! Really?"

"Really. It was in one of the tents way, way at the end of the grounds. There was a big sign—'See The Prairie Lovelies—Only Twenty-five Cents.' "

"The Prairie Lovelies?"

"And under that was another sign. 'Twenty-five cents extra for the Whole Show'. Only there was a circle around the W. The Hole Show."

"And did you know what that meant?"

"Christ, yes, I was thirteen. But I didn't want to go in, at least not with my old man. And I don't think he really wanted to either. He just wasn't that kind of guy. I think he figured he owed it to me or something. God only knows."

"And how were the Prairie Lovelies?"

"Well, we went in and stood around this platform and out came these three girls in kind of Arabian Nights costumes. And they started dancing around. Over at one side some guy was playing the accordian."

"Were they any good?"

"Terrible. Not that I'd ever seen any dancing girls before, but even I could tell they were no good. The audience, of course, was all men, farmers mostly, standing around in their overalls. One of the girls was so fat we could hear her huffing and puffing the whole time she was dancing."

"Wasn't it erotic at all?"

"I suppose, in a way, it was. First the veils came off. Then whatever they were wearing on top. Only this was a few years back and they had flower petals on their nipples. And G-strings under their skirts."

"What about the Hole Show?"

"That came after. That was when the accordian player stopped and announced that we'd have to pay an extra quarter for the Hole Show. The Hole Show. I can remember how he smacked his lips when he said it. He passed a plate around, and I guess pretty well everyone stayed for that."

"And . . .?"

"Then two of the girls kind of faded away, and the other one, the fat one, started in with the bumps and grinds and the accordion going faster and faster all the time while she untied the sides of her G-string. It seemed like forever before she got it off. It was so hot in there you wouldn't believe it, and my father and I standing right in the front. Finally, there she was, peeled right down and sort of squatting and turning so everyone could have a chance to see. There sure wasn't much to see, just a blur really. Then she started dancing again, grinding away, and suddenly she leaned over and grabbed my father's hat off his head."

"His hat?"

"A work hat. A blue cloth hat he had with a peak in front. He never went anywhere without that hat, not that I can remember anyway. You just didn't see farmers bareheaded in those days."

"And what did she do with it?"

"First she sort of bent over and started rubbing it up and down her thighs, wiggling away all the while. Everyone was clapping and yelling like mad by then and banging my father on the back. And then she got wilder and wilder and starting rubbing the hat up against her crotch."

"No!"

"Then everyone went crazy and so did she, just rubbing it and rubbing it."

"What did your father do?"

"Just stood there. Paralyzed. Stunned. Remember he was over fifty then. He just stood there with his mouth open. And his hands reaching out for his hat. Finally she took it and kind of swept it under his nose—that was the worst part—and then she banged it on top of his head."

"Oh, Eugene."

"He grabbed hold of it and ripped it off his head. And threw it on the ground and stomped on it. Then he took hold of my arm, hard, and pushed me on out through the whole damned bunch of them. Right out the doorway. Past the next bunch of suckers lining up outside for the next show. God."

"And what did he say? Afterwards?"

"Nothing. Not one damn thing. I didn't either. We just walked fast all the way to the other end of the fairground where my mother was waiting. He walked so fast I had to run to keep up. I wanted to say something, to tell him it was okay, that I didn't mind all that much about the hat thing, but we never said anything, either of us. Not then or ever."

"Ah, Eugene. And that was your sex education."

"I'm almost sure that's what he intended it to be. Because he sure as hell would never have blown two bits just for the fun of it. He never wasted money. There was never any to waste. I think it was all for me. And she blew it for him, the poor old guy, by grabbing his hat. And so did I by not saying anything."

Eugene shakes his head and, looking out the window, remarks flatly, "It seems a long time ago."

We sit quietly. When Eugene talks about his life, it is always with a sorrowing regretful futility as though the thin distances of his childhood could produce nothing better. But for me there is something compelling about his family, a sort of decency which surfaces unconsciously. I see them in prairie gothic terms, stern but devoted, humble but softened by an unquestioned tradition of love. Nevertheless, at the same time, I find myself listening for something more robust and redeeming, a note of valour perhaps; in Eugene's stories he seems deliberately to choose for himself a lesser role. I yearn for him to demonstrate an aptitude for heroism, and I don't know why. I must ask Brother Adam about that—why do I require bravery from Eugene when I don't possess it myself?

I rest my hand in his lap. We are racing past tiny towns raised to significance by brightly painted grain elevators. Beyond them, fields, a sullen sky, a pulsing lip of brightness behind the clouds. Our train, shooting through air, is the slenderest of arrows, a hairline, a jet trail; it cares nothing for the space it splits apart and nothing for us; all we are required to do is sit still and watch it happen.

🌺

From Winnipeg I phone Seth. There is only twenty minutes, but luckily the call goes right through. And it's a good connection.

"Hello. Is that you, Doug?"

"Yes. Charleen! Where are you?"

"Winnipeg. We've just got a few minutes, but I thought I'd phone and see how everything was."

"Everything's fine here. We're all getting along fine."

"Is Seth there?" I ask, and suddenly realize that it is two hours earlier on the coast; Seth might be asleep.

But surprisingly Doug says, "Sure he's here. Hang on a minute, Char, and I'll get him."

I hang on for more than a minute, two minutes, unbelievable! Here I am calling long distance. Long distance—I remember how my mother used to say those two words, her voice stricken, worried and worshipful at the same time.

"Hello."

"Seth," I say, "where were you just now?"

"I was just here," he says maddeningly.

"Well, how are you getting along?"

"Fine."

"How come you're up so early on a Saturday?"

"I just woke up now."

"And you're getting along fine?" I ask again.

"Yeah, just fine."

"You sound all out of breath."

"Oh? I guess I'm just surprised to hear from you."

"I had a few minutes in Winnipeg and I thought I'd just make sure everything was okay."

"How are you?"

"Oh, fine. We get in tomorrow night. Aunt Judith will already be there. She'll probably meet us. At least I think so."

Silence from Vancouver.

"Hello, Seth. Can you hear me? Are you there?"

"I'm still here. I can hear fine."

"Good. Well, I'd better go. Just phone me if you need anything, okay?"

"Okay."

"You've got the number?"

"Yeah."

"Well, I guess I'd better say good-bye."

"Good-bye."

Two years ago when Seth started the orthodonture treatment he was advised to give up his tuba temporarily; for the year and a half while the bands were on his teeth he played the double bass. He was good at it; everyone remarked about how quickly he picked it up.

We bought the double bass third-hand through the want ads; we got it cheap because there was no case. It's a big, waxy, humming buzzard of an instrument, and because its bulk so nearly approximates that of a human being, I soon began to think of it as a sort of half-person, a rather chuckly, middle-aged woman, rather like me in fact.

One day Seth forgot to take it to school and he phoned me between classes asking if I could drop it off. I took it on the bus, feeling enormously proud of her polished, nut-brown hippiness, her deep-throated good nature, the way the sun struck off gleaming streaks on her lovely sides. Seth waited for me on the steps outside the school, frowning and a little anxious that I might be late. When he saw me getting off the bus he jumped up and ran to meet me, taking the instrument out of my arms, whirling about with it and kissing the air about its bridge. I can never get that picture out of my mind, how extraordinarily and purely happy he looked at that instant.

But the minute he had the bands off his teeth he went back to playing the tuba. I can't understand it. A tuba is such an awkward machine with its valves and convolutions; it's such an ugly brassy armload, and I don't understand what Seth likes in the choking, grunting noise that comes out of it.

There seems something rather perverse about his preference. He explains that he likes the tuba better because it's his voice that makes the sounds; the double bass has a voice of its own—it's just a question of letting it out, something anyone can do. I don't think he's touched the bass since. It stands, serene as ever, in a corner of his bedroom. He keeps a beach towel draped over it to keep off the dust, but no one loves it anymore.

Sometimes I think there's something symbolic about it, but symbolism is such an impertinence, the sort of thing the "pome people" might contrive.' (God knows how easily it's manufactured by those who turn themselves into continuously operating sensitivity machines.) Of course, symbols have their uses. But something—my cramped Scarborough girlhood no doubt—ties me to the heaviness of facts. Tubas and double basses are not symbols but facts, facts which can be—which must be—assimilated like any of the other mysterious facts of existence.

❧

As the train moves closer to Toronto I decide I must warn Eugene a little about my mother. "She's always been a difficult person," I say.

"How do you mean, difficult?"

"Well, to begin with—you'll notice this right away—she's never been what you'd call demonstrative."

"But she must have loved you. You and your sister?"

"It's hard to explain," I say. Hard because she *had* loved us but with an angry, depriving love which, even after all these years, I don't understand. The lye-bite of her private rancour, her bitter shrivelling scoldings. When she scrubbed our faces it was with a single, hurting swipe. When we fell down and scraped our knees and elbows she said, "that will teach you to watch where you're going." Her love, if that's what you call it, was primitive, scalding, shorn of kindness. I can't explain it to Eugene; instead, I give him an example.

"When she brushed our hair in the morning, Judith's and mine, when she brushed our hair . . ."

"Yes?"

"She yanked it. Hard. It really hurt. She'd catch us in our bedroom, just before we left for school. She'd be holding the brush in her hand. When I think about it I can still feel her yanking my head back."

Eugene listens without comment.

I shrug, afraid I've betrayed a streak of self-pity. "That's just the way she is, and don't ask me why. I don't understand it. So how could you."

❧

I had forgotten about the thousand miles of bush between Winnipeg and Toronto. But here it is. Eugene and I are sitting high up in the Vistadome with nothing but curved glass separating us from turquoise lakes, whorled trees, the torn, reddened sky and, here and there, clumps of Indian cabins. We're sitting close to the front and so high up that we can overlook our whole train from end to end. We seem to vibrate to a different rhythm up here; the side-to-side swaying is gone; from this position we glide on cables of pure ozone. And music pours sweetly out of the chromium walls: Some Enchanted Evening. The hills are alive with the Sound of Music.

Dancing in the Dark. Temptation—a tango—*You came, I was alone, I should have known you were temptation.* Eugene reaches over and takes my hand.

We met two years ago through mutual friends, the Freehorns, at a small dinner party in late May. It had been an utterly respectable occasion, in every way the reverse of my meeting with Watson which had occurred in a run-down neighbourhood drugstore, a meeting which was described in those days as a pick-up. *Watson was someone who picked up people. I was someone who had allowed myself to be picked up; was that what doomed us?*

But the meeting between Eugene and me was impeccably prearranged, although Bea Freehorn assured me before the party that even though she was inviting a single man, I was not to suspect her of matchmaking. "There's nothing that burns me up more than being accused of fixing someone up," she told me over the phone. "But Eugene's a pet, you'll like him. Merv thinks he's terrific."

Merv and Bea are old friends, so old that they date from the days when I was still married to Watson; the four of us, in times which now seem impossibly idyllic, used to take Sunday picnics up to the mountain; I would bring potato salad and a cake and Bea always brought salami and corned beef and sometimes cold chicken. Now they give dinner parties; I've tried to fix the year when they stopped inviting me to dinner and started inviting me to dinner parties. Sometime when Merv was between assistant and associate in the Law School. Or maybe after they moved into the new house, yes, I think that was it. They have a patio overlooking the ocean where Bea likes to serve dinner on tiny lantern-lit tables. She is an accomplished cook, and I would never turn down one of her dinner invitations with or without a suspicion of matchmaking.

"Actually," Bea had confided, "you and Eugene have something in common."

"What?" I asked cautiously.

"You were both married for exactly eight years."

It's hard sometimes to tell when Bea is being serious. I waited for the rough curl of her laughter but heard only earnest confidence. "He's really had a rough time of it. His wife got screwed up with Womens' Lib and just took the two kids one day and moved out. He has the boys on weekends, nice kids, but she won't take a penny from him, so in a way he's lucky. Anyway, he's a nice guy."

Nice. Yes, I could see that right away when I met him. Nice, meaning polite, presentable, moderate, inquiring and almost sloshily good-natured. He arrived a little late with his right hand freshly bandaged and was apologetically unable to shake hands with the Freehorns, the Stevens, the Folkstones, or with me.

"I was cutting off a piece of beef at noon today," he told us sadly. "The whole plate slipped suddenly and there I was with a bloody gash."

"Oh, Eugene," Bea crooned kindly, "did you need stitches?"

"A few," he said bravely. "The whole thing's been so damned stupid."

I was prepared to dislike him. First for so perfectly fulfilling the role of the inept and picturesque bachelor who couldn't make a sandwich without sawing through his hand. And second for being a self-pitying poseur, and now monopolizing the conversation with his idiotic stitches.

"How are you going to be able to work?" Merv asked him conversationally, and, turning to me, he explained that Eugene was an orthodontist and thus required the use of his hands.

Eugene shrugged and smiled somewhat goofily, "I'll take a week off. There's nothing else to do really."

"What about all your appointments?" Gordon Stevens asked.

"I'll have to get Mrs. Ingalls to cancel everything Monday morning."

"What a shame," Bea mourned, "what a rotten shame. But look, Eugene, let Merv get you something to drink. That hand must be painful."

"It *is* a bit," he admitted.

Did I detect a hint of a whine? Was this ridiculous tooth straightener trying to solicit sympathy? If so, I was not prepared to give it. No wonder his wife ditched him, the big baby. I sipped my gin and tonic sullenly.

"Merv says you're a poet," he said to me later, sitting beside me at one of the little tables along with Gord Stevens and Clara Folkstone. I gave him a long look; with enormous difficulty he was eating his stuffed artichoke with his left hand.

"Yes," I said knowing that he was about to tell me he never read poetry.

"I can't pretend to know much about poetry," he said. "Except the usual stuff we had at school."

"That's all right," I said socially. "It's a sort of minority interest. Like lacrosse."

I had dressed for this evening with deliberate declassé nonchalance, aware that Bea expects me to contribute a faint whiff of bohemia to her parties; I wore a badly-cut gypsy skirt and black satin peasant blouse, both bought at an Anglican Church rummage sale. Fortunately Bea's expectations conform to what I can afford. I had also brought my special party personality, the rough-ribbed humorous persona which I had devised for myself after Watson left me. I earn my invitations and even for an old friend like Bea Freehorn I knew better than to sulk all evening. So I smiled hard at Eugene as Bea brought round the veal fillets.

Encouraged he asked, "What sort of poet are you? I mean, what kind of things do you write about?"

"About the minutiae of existence," I said with mock solemnity.

He looked baffled and, putting down his fork, he leaned over to whisper in my ear. Now, I thought, now he is going to ask me why poetry doesn't rhyme anymore.

But I was wrong; in a very low murmur, so low that I could hardly hear him, he asked if I would mind cutting up his meat for him.

I almost laughed aloud. But something stopped me; perhaps it was the extraordinary humility of the request or the reserve with which he made it. I leaned over, my elbows grazing his chest and, picking up his knife and fork, I began sawing through the pale, pink veal. My arm sliding back and forth touched the top of his wrist. Clara and Gordon smiled and watched at what seemed a great distance. Three, four, five pieces. I kept cutting, my eyes on Eugene's plate, until I had finished. Then I sat back breathless.

For while I was cutting Eugene's meat, a sudden blood-rush of tenderness had swept over me. A maternal echo? I had once cut Seth's meat in just this way. Perhaps someone had once cut up mine—I half remembered. Eugene's helpless right hand wound in beautiful gauze lay on the edge of the table, and it was all I could do to keep from seizing it and holding it to my lips. I wanted to put my arms around him, to cover him with kisses. The brutal knife, the surgical stitches, the vicious wife who had left him and exposed him to all the hurts of the world—I wanted to stroke them away; I wanted to comfort, to sooth, to minister. I wanted—was I crazy?—I wanted to love him.

We're not far from Toronto now. Another hour and we'll be there. It's getting darker; the towns are closer together now and the farmland is falling into round derby-shaped hills. Eugene is holding my hand and with his middle finger he is tracing slow circles on the palm of my hand. Around and around. The Vistadome where we sit is a tube of darkness. Now he is moving his thumb back and forth across the inside of my wrist. Slowly, slowly. I relax, put back my head, half-shut my eyes. The soundtrack of *Zorba the Greek* is washing over us. Lighted towns, squared and tidy, flash by. Eugene has slipped a finger between the buttons of my dress and I can feel it sliding on my nylon slip. Then it retreats; he is carefully, quietly undoing one of the buttons. Now his hand is inside. It is spelling out something on my stomach, a sort of code. I smile to myself.

We flash by Weedham, Ontario. Watson. I had forgotten he was so close to Toronto. No more than thirty miles. Not much of a place; the train doesn't even stop.

Eugene's hand is slowly, slowly inching up my slip, gathering the folds of material. It slides easily. There. He's reached the lace hem. Now I can feel his hand on my bare thighs, the inside of my thighs. The music swamps us. I want to say something but nothing comes; my lips move in miniature as though they were preparing tiny, perfect chapel prayers.

He has reached the edge of my nylon elastic and for an instant we seem balanced on the brink—I think for sure he is stopped. We sit so still.

Then I feel his fingers slip quickly under the elastic and move toward darkness, moisture, secrecy. We are covered with darkness, but on the horizon the sky is soft with reflections. I sit still, half-drowning in a stirring helium happiness. The music rises like moisture and presses on the dark windows, and in this way we ride into the city.

Chapter 3

"Well," I whisper to Judith when we are finally alone.

"Well," she answers back, smiling.

It's midnight and we're standing in our slips in our mother's bedroom at the front of the old house in Scarborough. White nylon slips; Judith's is whiter than mine and fits better. Is there something symbolic about that? No, I reject the possibility.

I love Judith. I had forgotten how much I loved her until I saw her standing with her husband Martin and our mother behind the chaste iron gate at Union Station. She and Martin had come from Kingston on the morning train; we would have a few days together before the wedding.

Judith looked larger than I had remembered, or perhaps it was the colour and cut of her floppy, red denim dress. She has even less fashion sense than I, but unlike me she's able to translate her nonchalance into a well-meaning, soft-edged eccentricity which is curiously touching and even rather charming. She's aged a little. I haven't seen her since she and Martin were in Vancouver for a conference three years ago, and since then she's had her fortieth birthday. And her forty-first. Her daughter is eighteen now and her son is almost as old as Seth. I find myself involuntarily listing the areas of erosion: a small but generalized collapse of skin between her nose and mouth, the forked lines like fingers of an upturned hand between her eyes which make her look not querulous, but worried and kindly, a detached dry point madonna. Her eyes are dreamier than I remembered. Our mother used to fret that Judith would ruin her eyes from so much reading as a girl, swallowing Lawrence and Conrad and Dreiser on summer afternoons stretched on a bath towel in our tiny back yard. Her eyes were sharper then, darting and energetic, the sort of eyes you would expect to harden with age, but they now show such softness. Of course, Judith's life has been embalmed in a stately, enviable, suburban calm. She has a husband who loves her, healthy children, a large, airy house in Kingston, not to mention a respectable reputation as a biographer. And most important, she has a seeming immunity to the shared, sour river of our girlhood.

The house is quiet. Our mother with a long, shrunken, remembered sigh has surrendered to us her bedroom. Green moire curtains discoloured in the folds, a fortywatt bulb in the ceiling fixture. And on the walnut veneer bed, a candlewick bedspread, here and there missing some of its fringe. There is a waterfall bureau, circa 1928, on which rests a precisely-angled amber brush and mirror set which has never, as far as I know, been used. This was our father's bedroom too; how completely we have put away that silent, hard-working husband and father. His wages met the payments on this bungalow; his bony frame rested for thirty years on half of this bed, and yet it seems he never existed.

Since there are only three bedrooms in the house, there was really no other way to arrange the sleeping. No one, of course, had counted on Eugene, least of all Eugene himself who would have preferred a downtown hotel room. It is at my perverse last minute insistence that he is staying here in Scarborough.

Why do I need him here? Perhaps because playing the role of pathetic younger-sister-from-the-west places too

great a strain on me. Maybe I am anxious to make a final
defiant gesture and give rein to my self-destructive urge
which relishes awkward situations—such as how to introduce Eugene to my mother. "This is a friend of mine.
Eugene Redding."

Friend? But in my mother's narrow lexicon women
don't have male friends. They have fathers, husbands
and brothers. Her face, meeting Eugene at the station,
had dissolved into a splash of open pain. Had I intended
to cause such pain? Why hadn't I written ahead to explain about Eugene? But no one voiced these questions.
Nevertheless she shook Eugene's hand slowly as if trying to extract some sort of explanation through his finger
tips.

"I really don't want to put you out, Mrs. McNinn," Eugene had insisted. "I told Charleen I would be perfectly
happy in a hotel."

There followed a small silence which could be measured not by seconds or minutes but by the cold, linear
dimension of my mother's hurt feelings.

"I'm sure we can find room for everyone," she said at
last, sounding half paralyzed, like someone who had recently suffered a stroke. "Of course," she trailed off de-
fensively, "it's only a small house."

There was, naturally, no possibility of Eugene and me
sharing a room. Anxious to please, I suggested sleeping
with my mother and putting Eugene in the spare room,
but she shuddered visibly at this idea. "I'd never sleep a
wink," she said, plainly vexed. "I'm used to sleeping
alone."

Another silence as we absorbed the irony of this statement; in less than a week she would be sleeping with a
stranger called Louis Berceau.

Finally it was agreed that Martin and Eugene should
take the twin beds in our old bedroom off the kitchen.

Judith and I would occupy our mother's double bed, and our mother, perhaps for the first time in her life, would sleep in the old three-quarters bed in the spare room.

"Couldn't I sleep on the chesterfield?" Eugene suggested desperately.

We waited, breathless, for what seemed like the perfect solution. "No," our mother said with finality. "No one on the chesterfield. That won't be necessary."

What Eugene didn't know, what he couldn't possibly guess, was that no one had ever slept on our chesterfield. Never. Years ago our father, exhausted after a day at work, would occasionally stretch out for a minute and close his eyes. She would poke him, gently but relentlessly. "Not here, Bert. Not on the chesterfield." It was as though she saw something threatening in the way he spread himself, something disturbing and vulgar about the posture of ordinary relaxation.

"Not on the chesterfield," she had said, giving us her final terms, and, like children, we accepted her decree. But inwardly I bled for Martin and Eugene in their forced awkward fraternity. I could imagine their inevitable stiff conversation—*All right with you to open the window? Whichever you prefer. Maybe you'd rather have the bed by the closet? You don't mind if I read for a while? Not at all, not at all.*—Strangers, two men in their early forties, shut up from their women in a tiny back bedroom with no more than a foot or two between their beds, and nothing in common in all this world but a bizarre attachment to the McNinn sisters, Charleen and Judith; they might, for that matter and with good reason, be silently questioning that attachment at this very moment. Martin, an easy man, though somewhat remote, would accept the situation, but he could not help minding the separation from Judith. He had even pleaded for the spare room himself. He and Judith wouldn't object to the three-quarters bed, he had said. But our mother, who seemed to feel that her hospitality was being challenged, had insisted on taking the spare room herself.

"Well?" Judith says again from across the room.

"How do you think she looks?" I ask.

That is always our first question when we're together, how is she, how does she look. Our voices dip and swim with the novel rhythm of concern, childrens' concern for a parent.

"Better than I expected," Judith says.

"When did you see her last?"

"A couple of months ago. I came down on the train with the kids for the weekend."

"She's still getting treatment?"

"She goes every month now. But next year it will probably be less. Down to every three months."

"You talked to the doctor?"

"Yes. A couple of times. He thinks she's made a fantastic recovery."

"What about a recurrence?"

"It could happen. That's why they want her to keep coming to the clinic."

"She looks so thin."

"She was always thin, Charleen. You've forgotten."

"Well, then, she looks old."

"She is old. She's seventy."

"She's so pale though."

"Not compared to what she was after the operation."

"How soon after did you see her?"

"A month. She never told me she was even having an operation. Which was odd when you think how she always used to complain about her aches and pains. She never told anyone. She just went."

"I didn't know until you wrote."

"When I heard—the doctor finally phoned and told

me—I came down and spent a week with her. She was feeling fairly strong by then and there was a nurse who came round every day to check up. She never talked about *it*. It. The breast. Just about the hospital and how rude the nurses had been and how thin the blankets were and how they hadn't given her tea with her breakfast. You know how she goes on. But the breast—she never mentioned it."

"Does it hurt do you think?"

"I don't know. She never says."

"What does she wear? I mean, does she have one of those false things?"

"It looks like it to me. What do you think?"

"She looks just the same there. With her dress on anyway."

"Did you ever see her breasts, Charleen? I mean when we were little."

"Never. You remember how she used to dress in the closet all the time. That was why it was so odd when you wrote me about the operation."

"How do you mean, odd?"

"That she had a breast removed. It never seemed real to me. I just never thought of her as someone who had breasts."

"What did she call them?"

"Breasts? I don't know. She must have called them something."

"Not that I can remember."

We sit on the bed thinking. The house is still and through the window screen we can hear a warm wind lapping at the edge of the awning.

"Developed," Judith says at last, "I think she just used the verb form. Like how so-and-so was developing. Or someone else was very, very developed or maybe not developed."

Remembering, I smile. "She always thought Aunt Liddy was too developed. Poor Liddy, she used to say, she's too developed to buy ready-made."

Judith and I laugh together, quietly so no one will hear. This is the way it used to be. Lying in bed at night, laughing.

"Can't you just hear her telling the doctor that she has a lump in one of her developments," I say.

"And he says, sorry to hear that, Mrs. McNinn, but we'll just have to remove half your development."

We laugh again, harder this time, so hard that the bed rocks. Crazy Judith. I put my hand over my mouth but Judith lets out a yelp of the old girlish cackle. Now we are both shaking with laughter, but there is something manic about all this mirth; it occurs to me that we are perilously close to weeping, and for that reason I reach over and switch off the light.

In the dark Judith asks, "Were you absolutely stunned to hear about Louis?"

"Stunned!" I say. "I'm still trying to get used to it. Is that the way you pronounce his name? Looey?"

"Yes. Like Louis the fourteenth, fifteenth, and sixteenth."

"Have you met him?"

"Last time I was down. But just for a minute. He's coming over tomorrow though. To get acquainted with all of us."

"Where on earth did she meet him? I mean, she never goes anywhere."

"At the cancer clinic," Judith says.

"Really?"

"Yes."

"You mean . . ."

"Yes."

"What exactly?"

"You mean what kind of cancer?"

"Yes."

"I'm not sure. That is, she didn't go into details. But he's had three operations."

"Three operations?"

"Amazing, isn't it?"

"Judith. Do you realize—that means he's missing three parts."

"Possibly."

"What," I speak slowly, "do you think they could be?"

"I don't know. But he doesn't look all that sick. At least not the quick look I had at him."

"What *does* he look like, Judith?"

"Thin. Naturally. And I'm not sure but I think he may be a couple of inches shorter than she is."

"Three operations! I can't get over it. What I mean is . . . don't you think . . . I mean, imagine embarking on marriage when you're in that state."

"Maybe they were only minor operations."

"Is he the same age she is?"

"Two years older. He's seventy-two."

"But he was married before. She wrote that—that he had been married before."

"Yes, but I don't know anything about his first wife, when she died or what."

"Where does he live?"

"He has a furnished room. Not so far from here, just a few minutes. But he's giving it up and moving in here. After the wedding."

"After the wedding," I repeat the words.

"Doesn't it sound crazy? *The Wedding*."

"And he's retired. What did he do before he was retired?" I reflect suddenly that I'm not so different after all from Doug Savage; what did he do—that was what I had to find out.

"He taught manual training. In a junior high school."

"Manual training?"

"You know, like woodworking. And metalwork. Like when the girls went for cooking and sewing. Remember?"

"And that was his job? That's what he did?"

"Apparently."

"And he lived in Toronto?"

"I think so. He doesn't speak a word of French, in spite of the French name; I asked him. But he used to be a Catholic."

"A Catholic?"

"Uhuh."

"How do you know?"

"She told me. When she told me about the manual training and all that."

"She would never have told me that. She never tells me anything."

"She doesn't tell me much, either," Judith says. "She writes every week, but it's always about the same old thing: the weather and her aches and pains or how much everything costs these days. I had to pump her about Louis."

"I don't think she's ever forgiven me for running away with Watson."

"Oh, Charleen, that was ages ago. I'm sure she never thinks about it anymore."

"The scandal of it all," I say bitterly. "Having all the neighbours think I might be pregnant."

"Charleen, you exaggerate."

"Well, she never tells me anything."

"Actually, there's something she hasn't told me. And I'm dying to know."

I can't see Judith's face in the dark. "What?" I ask.

"If she loves him. If he loves her."

"I suppose they must. At least a little." But I say this doubtfully.

"I'd give anything to know."

"It's your biographical urge coming through."

"It could be. What I want to know is, do they say romantic things like . . . well, like, 'I love you' and all that."

"I can't imagine *her* saying it."

"I can't either. But maybe he does. Anyway, I wish I knew."

"I don't suppose you could ask her?"

"God, no!" Judith says. "She'd have a fit."

"What I'd like to know is *why*."

"Why what?"

"Why she's getting married. It just doesn't make sense. She's comfortable enough. Why on earth does she want to go and get married?"

There is a long pause. Perhaps Judith has fallen asleep, I think. Then I hear her short sigh, and what she says is: "Well, why does anyone get married?"

❧

"What I'd really like," I say into the darkness, "is some coffee."

"So would I," Judith says. "I wonder if she's got any. She mostly drinks tea now."

"Let's look," I say, slipping out of bed.

"We'll wake everyone up."

"Not if we're quiet."

We move down the darkened hall. Judith walks ahead of me in an exaggerated clownish prowl, her knees pulling up through her yellow cotton nightgown in a burlesque mime of caution. The door to the kitchen is shut; she turns the knob slowly so that there is no sound, and we close it behind us with the smallest of clicks, snap on the overhead light and breathe with relief. Judith faces me, her upper teeth pulled down over her lower lip, girl-ish and conspiratorial.

Here in the kitchen there is a faint smell of roasted meat. Lamb? A fresh breeze blows through the window screen and the mixed scent of dampness and scouring powder rises from the sink. A newspaper, yesterday's, is folded neatly under the step-on garbage can beside the back door so that there will be no rust marks left on the squared linoleum; it has always been like this.

Our room, the bedroom which Judith and I shared as girls, leads off the kitchen; it is the sort of back bedroom which was commonplace in depression bungalows. Eu-gene and Martin—it excites me a little to think of it—are sleeping there now. Their door, which stands between the refrigerator (a model from the early fifties) and the old cupboard, is shut; Judith and I freeze for a moment in front of it, listening, straining to hear their fused breathing, but all we hear is the stirring of the wind out-side the kitchen window. The trees in the back yard are swaying hugely, and I picture their new green buds, not yet fully opened, turning hard and black in the darkness. "It looks like rain," Judith remarks.

I find the jar of instant coffee at once; without think-ing my hand finds the right shelf, reaches for the place beside the tea canister where I know it must be. A very small jar, the lid screwed tightly on. Judith boils water in the green enamel kettle and finds the everyday cups, and then we sit facing each other across the little brown formica table.

Suddenly there is nothing to say. We are uneasy; we are guilty invaders in our mother's clean-mopped kitchen; we have disturbed the symmetry of her lightly stocked shelves, have helped ourselves to sugar from her blue earthenware sugar bowl with its two flat-ear han-dles and its little flowered lid. "Never leave a sugar bowl uncovered," she always said. "You never know when a fly might get in." It is as though she is sitting here with us now, measuring, observing, censoring, as though she is holding us forcibly inside the sudden, unwilled silence we seem to have entered. I try to drink my coffee, but it's too hot.

Judith says at last, a little warily, "Eugene seems nice." It is not a statement; Judith would never make a statement as banal as that; it is a question.

And I answer conversationally. "I wrote you about him, didn't I?"

As always there is a kind of ritual to our dialogue, for of course I know that I have written to Judith about Eugene and she knows it too. I wrote to her long ago telling her I had met Eugene, that he was working on Seth's teeth, that we had taken a holiday together in San Francisco. I can even recall some of the careful phrases I used in my letters to her. She has not suddenly forgotten, not Judith. It is only that she and I see each other so rarely that we are afraid we might misjudge the permitted area of intimacy. It is necessary to prepare the ground a little before we can speak. There is on Judith's side a wish not to weigh too heavily what I might have written off-handedly and perhaps now regret. On my side there is a wish to project nonchalance and laxity, to preserve at least a shadow of that fiction she half-believes me to be, a runaway younger sister, a casual libertine who has the edge on her, but only superficially, as far as worldliness goes. West-coast divorcée, free-wheeling poet, and now a sort of semi-mistress. We talk in careful, mutually drawn circles.

"When exactly did you meet him, Charleen?"

"Two years ago," I tell her, "two years now."

"And?" Judith asks.

"Just that. Two years."

"What about marriage?" she asks suddenly, recklessly, apparently tiring of fencing with me.

"I don't know," I tell her.

"He's divorced too?"

"Yes."

"It's all final and everything?"

"Yes. It's not that. Actually he'd like to get married again. I like his two boys and they like me. There's nothing to stop us really."

"But you're not quite sure of him? Is that it?"

"I just can't seem to think straight these days."

"What about Seth? What does he think of Eugene?"

"That's no problem. He likes Eugene. And he gets on great with the two kids. Seth likes everyone."

It's so quiet in the kitchen. The red and white wall clock over the stove says five minutes past two. The refrigerator whines from its muffled electric heart and a very fine rain blows against the screen over the sink. Judith gets up and shuts the window.

"Seth likes everyone," I say again. To understate is to risk banality, and these words echoing in the silent kitchen sound both trite and untrue. But they are true; he *does* like everyone, a fact which makes me feel—and not for the first time—a little frightened at my own child's open, unquestioning acceptance. Is it natural? Is it perhaps dangerous?

Judith doesn't notice. "That's good," she says. And waits for me to go on.

"I'm just waiting until I'm sure," I tell her. "I'm not rushing this time. I'm going to wait."

How can I tell her what it is I'm waiting for; I hardly know myself. But I feel with the force of absolute, brimming certainty that there is something bulky and positive in the future for me, a thing, an event perhaps, which is connected with me in some way, with me,

Charleen Forrest. If I were superstitious I might say it was written in the stars, and if I were half as bitter as Judith believes me to be, I might say it is because I deserve something at last. I know it's there. The numbers tell me: I lived in this brick bungalow for eighteen years. Then I was married to Watson Forrest for eight years. Now I have been divorced for twelve. The shapes, the pattern, the order of those random numbers spell out a kind of logic in my brain; they suggest the approach of another era, another way of being. I'm not a mystic but I know it's there, whatever it is.

❧

I tell Judith about Brother Adam.

She is, as I might have expected, skeptical. Though she prizes her tolerance, in actual fact the edges of her life are sealed to exclude the sort of human flotsam which I have always been able to embrace. The title Brother is not definitive enough for Judith; it is loosely and embarrassingly sentimental, hinting at imposed familiarity and chummy handshakes.

"What's it supposed to mean exactly?" she questions. "Is he a priest? Or what?"

"I think so. I'm not sure."

"You mean in all these letters you've written, you've never asked him?"

I pause; it's hard to explain; some things do not yield to simplicity. "That's the sort of question he might consider trivial. Too particularized, if you see what I mean."

"But you think he *might* be a priest?"

"Well, he lives in a place called the Priory."

"Which priory."

"Just 'The Priory'."

"And it's in Toronto?"

"Yes. In the Beaches area."

"Are you going to see him?"

Another pause. "Maybe," I mumble this 'maybe', chewing the side of my cup, trying to conceal the leap of sensation this 'maybe' excites in me.

"But he *is* a botanist?" Judith asks.

"Yes. In a way. Actually, it's hard to tell."

"What do you mean?"

"He seems to know all about plants. And he sent an article to the *Journal*. I more or less assumed that only a botanist would submit an article to a botanical journal."

"What was it about?"

"Grass."

"Grass? Was it any good?"

"Yes. And no. I liked it. But Doug—you remember Doug Savage, you met him in Vancouver when you were there—he thought it was hilarious."

"You mean actually funny?"

"It wasn't funny. He wasn't trying to be funny at all. It was a serious article, passionately serious, in fact. And scientific in a way. It was a sort of sociology of grass, you might say. He has this theory about the importance of grass to human happiness."

"Maybe he's talking about marijuana."

"No. Just ordinary grass. Garden grass. He's trying to prove that where people don't have any grass, just concrete and asphalt and so on, then the whole human condition begins to deteriorate."

"It sounds a little fanciful," Judith's old skepticism again.

"In a way. I don't understand it all, to tell you the truth. But he writes with the most pressing sort of intensity, something much larger than mere eloquence. Anguished. But reflective too. Not like a scientist at all. More like a poet. Or like a philosopher."

"But nevertheless the *Journal* turned it down?"

"Naturally. Doug thought it was just plain crazy."

"And he gave you the job of returning it."

"Yes. I send back all manuscripts we can't use. And usually I do it fairly heartlessly. But with Brother Adam it was different. I couldn't bear to have him think we utterly rejected what he'd written, that we sneered at what he believed in. I mean, that would be like saying no to something that was beautiful. And humiliating someone who was, well, beautiful too. Don't look so exasperated, Judith. I know I sound fatuous."

"Go on. You sent the manuscript back to the Priory?"

"Yes. But instead of the usual rejection card, I enclosed a little note."

"Saying . . .?"

"Oh, just that I'd enjoyed reading the article, at least the parts I understood. I thought I'd better be honest about it. And I said I thought it was a shame we couldn't use an article like that now and then to break the monotony. Everything we print is so detached. You wouldn't believe it, Judith. I should send you an issue. It's inhuman. The prose style sounds factory-made, all glued together with qualifying phrases. And here at last was an article spurting with passion. From someone who really loved grass. To lie on, to walk on, to sit on. Or to smell. Just to touch grass, he feels, has restorative powers."

"Why grass? I mean, why not flowers or fruit or something? Or trees, even? Isn't grass just a little, you know, ordinary? After all, there's a lot of it around. Even these days."

"That's partly why he loves it, I think. The fact that grass is so humble. And no one's ever celebrated grass before."

"Walt Whitman?"

"That was different. That was more of a symbolic passion."

"What happened after you wrote to him?"

"Nothing at first. A month at least, maybe even longer. Then I got a parcel. Delivered to the *Journal* office."

"From Brother Adam."

"Yes. But you'd never guess what was in it."

"Grass."

"Yes."

We both laugh. "It wasn't really grass, of course." I explain. "It was only the stuff to grow it with. There was a sprouting tray. And some earth in a little cloth bag. Lovely earth really, very fine, a kind of sandy-brown colour. It was clean, clean earth. As though he'd dug it up especially and sieved it and prayed over it. And then there was the packet of seeds. Not the commercial kind. His own. He does his own seed culture."

"And a letter?"

"No. No letter. Not even instructions for planting the seeds. Just the return address. Brother Adam, The Priory, 256 Beachview, Toronto."

"How odd not to send a note."

"That's what made it perfect. A gift without words. As though the grass *was* the letter. As though it had a power purer than words."

Judith laughs. "You always were a bit of a mystic, Charleen."

"But what really touched me, I think, was the parcel itself. The way it was wrapped."

"How was it wrapped?"

"Beautifully. I don't mean aesthetically. After all, there's a limit to the power of brown paper and string. But it was so neatly, so handsomely done up." *With such touching precision. The paper, two layers, that crisp, waxy paper, every corner perfect, and the knots were tight and trimmed and symmetrical like the knots in diagrams. And the address was printed in black ink in lovely blocky letters.* "I hated to open it, in a way," I risk telling her.

Opening it I had had the sensation of being touched by another human being; I had felt the impulse behind the wrapping—and the strength of his wish, his inexplicable wish to please me. Me!

Judith smiles and says nothing, but from her amused gaze I see she thinks I am absurd. Nevertheless she's waiting to hear more. My account of Brother Adam cannot really interest her much—though she is currently writing a biography of a nineteenth-century naturalist and is somewhat curious about the scientific impulse— but she listens to me with the alert probing attention which she has perfected.

"At first I thought of planting the grass at the office, but I was worried it would go dry over the weekend. Besides I didn't want to answer any questions about it. Doug Savage has a way of taking things over." *And besides it would have given his imagination something to feed on; he and Greta cherish my eccentricities as though they were rare collectables.*

"Go on."

"So I took the whole thing home on the bus. Seth thought it was a wonderful present, not at all peculiar, just wonderful. And we put in the seeds that same day. There's quite a lot of sun in the living room. At least for Vancouver. Anyway you don't need strong sunlight for grass. One of the things Brother Adam likes about grass is the way it adapts to any condition. It has an almost human resilience. He hates anything rigid and temperamental like those awful rubber plants everyone sticks in corners these days."

"I like rubber plants."

"Anyway grass can put up with almost anything. I have it in a box by the window and it does well there."

I have to hold my tongue to keep from telling Judith

more: the way, for instance, I felt about those first little seeds. That they might be supernatural, seeds sprouted from a fairy tale, empowered with magical properties, that they might produce overnight or even within an hour a species of life-giving, life-preserving grass. How that night I fell asleep thinking of the tiny, brown seeds lying sideways against the clean, pressing earth, swelling from the force of moisture, obeying the intricate commands of their locked-in chromosomes. Better not tell Judith too much; she might, and with reason, accuse me of overreacting to a trifling gift. She, who has never doubted herself, couldn't possibly understand how I could attach such importance to a gift of grass seed or the fact that it placed a burden on me, a responsibility to make the seeds sprout; their failure to germinate would spell betrayal or, worse, it would summarize my fatal inability to sustain any sort of action.

"Was it any good?" Judith asks. "The grass seed, I mean?"

"Within three days," I tell her, making an effort to speak with detachment, "the first, pale green, threadlike points of grass had appeared. I watered them with a sprinkling bottle, the kind Mother used to dampen clothes on the kitchen table. Every morning and again at night. Sometimes Seth took a turn too."

"And then you wrote to thank Brother Adam for the grass and that was the start of your friendship?"

"Actually I made myself wait two weeks before I wrote. I wanted to make sure the grass was going to survive. By the time I wrote, all of it was up. Some of it was over an inch high. And I cut two or three shoots with my manicure scissors and Scotch-taped them to the letter."

Judith smiles dreamily; I have managed, I can see, to delight her. "But what," she asks, "does one do with a box of grass?"

"It's strange, but I've become very fond of it. It's

divinely soft, like human hair almost. And brilliant green from all that water. I have to trim it about once a week with sewing shears. Sometimes I sprinkle on a little fertilizer although Brother Adam says it's not really necessary." *I also like to run my hand over its springy tightly-shaved surface, loving its tufted healthy carpet-thick threads, the way it struggles against the sides of the box, the industry with which it mends itself.*

"And you've been writing to each other ever since?"

"Yes, more or less."

"Often?"

"Every three or four weeks. I'd write more often but I don't want to wear him down." There is also of course, the fact that an instant reply would place Brother Adam in the position of a debtor—and to be in debt to a correspondent is to hold power over a creditor, a power I sensed he would not welcome.

"What do you write about, Charleen?"

I have to think. "It's funny, but we don't write much about ourselves. He's never asked me anything about myself—I like that. And I don't pester him either. He usually writes about what he's feeling at the moment or what he's seeing. Like once he saw a terrible traffic accident from his window. Once he wrote a whole letter about a wren sitting outside on his fire escape."

"A whole letter about a wren on a fire escape!"

"Well, yes, it was more on the metaphysical side."

"And you do the same?"

"Sort of. I don't so much write as compose. It takes me days. I've hardly written any poetry lately. All of it seems to go into those letters, all that old energy. Writing to him is—I don't know how to explain it—but writing those letters has become a new way of seeing."

"Therapeutic," Judith comments shortly, almost dismissively.

"I suppose you could call it that."

"I wish you wrote to me more often."

"I wish you wrote to me too."

"We always say this, don't we?"

"Yes."

"Charleen?"

"What?"

"What does Eugene think of your . . . your relationship with Brother Adam?"

Judith has always been clever. A bright girl in school, a prizewinner at university; now she is referred to in book reviews as a clever writer. But her real cleverness lies not in her insights, but in her uncanny ability to see the missing links, the ellipses, the silences. Like the perfect interviewer she asks the perfect question. "What does Eugene think?" she asks.

Eugene doesn't know, I tell her. He doesn't know Brother Adam even exists.

After a while Judith asks me if I'm feeling hungry. "We could make some toast," she suggests.

I nod, although I'm not so much hungry as emptied out; a late night hollowness gnaws at me, the grey, uneasy anxiety I always feel in this house. The rain is coming down hard now, leaving angry little check marks on the black window, and the house has grown chilly.

In the breadbox we find exactly one-third of a loaf of white, sliced bread. The top of the bag has been folded down carefully in little pleats to preserve freshness. "A penny saved . . ." our mother had always said. Meagreness.

A memory springs into focus: how I once asked for a piece of bread to put out for the birds. "They can look after their own the same as we have to," she replied. Ours, then, had been a house without a birdfeeder, a house where saucers of milk were not provided for stray cats. This was a house where implements were neither loaned nor borrowed, where the man who came to clean the furnace was not offered a cheering cup of coffee, where the postman was not presented with a box of fudge at Christmas. (Such generosities belonged only to fairy tales or soap operas.) In this house there was no contribution to the Red Cross nor (what irony) to the Cancer Fund. Meagreness. I had almost forgotten until I saw the bread in the breadbox.

"Maybe we'd better not have any toast after all," Judith says, tightlipped. "She'll be short for breakfast."

Instead we make more coffee, stirring in extra milk and sugar. I turn to Judith and ask if she has bought a wedding gift for our mother.

"Not yet," she says clutching her hair in a gesture of frenzy. "And it isn't because I haven't thought and thought about it."

"I haven't bought anything either," I admit. "Not yet anyway."

"Do you have any idea what she'd like?"

"Not one."

"Why is it," Judith demands, "that it's so hard to buy our own mother a present? It isn't just this damned wedding present either. Every Christmas and birthday I go through the same thing. Ask Martin. Why is it?"

I'm ready with an answer, for this is something about which I've thought long and hard. "Because no matter what we give her, it will be wrong. No matter how much we spend it will be either too much or too little."

"You're right," Judith muses. (I marvel at her serene musing, at her willingness to accept the way our mother is.)

"She's never satisfied," I storm. "Remember when we

were in high school and put our money together one Christmas and bought her that manicure kit. In the pink leather case? It cost six dollars."

"Vaguely," Judith nods. (Fortunate, fortunate Judith; her memories are soft-edged and have no power over her.)

"I'll never, never forget it," I tell her. "We thought it was beautiful with the little orange stick and the little wool buffer and scissors and everything all fitted in. It was lovely. And she was furious with us."

"Why was that?" Judith wonders.

"Don't you remember? She thought we were criticizing her, that we were hinting she needed a manicure. She told us that if we worked as hard as she did we would have ragged fingernails too."

"Really? I'd forgotten that."

"And the things we made at school. For Mother's Day. I made a woven bookmark once. She said it was nice but the colours clashed. It was yellow and purple."

"Well," Judith shrugs, "gratitude was never one of her talents."

"Eugene suggested I give her an Eaton's gift certificate. But you know just what she'd say—people who give money can't be bothered to put any *thought* into a gift."

"That's right," Judith nods. "Remember how Aunt Liddy used to send us a dollar bill for our birthdays, and Mother always said, 'Wouldn't you think with all the time Liddy has that she could go out and buy a proper birthday present.'"

"Poor Aunt Liddy."

"I thought of a new bedspread," Judith says, "but she might think I was hinting that her old one is looking pretty beat up. Which it is."

"And *I* thought of ordering a flowering shrub for the yard, but she would be sure to say that was too impersonal."

"On the other hand," Judith says, "if we were to get her a new dressing gown that would be *too* personal."

"There's no pleasing her."

"Why do we even try?" Judith asks lightly, philosophically. "Why in heaven's name don't we give up trying to please her?"

This is a question for which I have no answer, and so I say nothing. I drink my coffee which is already cold. We're on a psychic treadmill, Judith and I; we can't stop trying to please her. There's no logic to it, only compulsion; even knowing it's impossible to please her, we can't stop ourselves from trying.

❧

I hadn't intended to talk about Watson; my divorce is a subject I've never really discussed with Judith. It should be easy these free-wheeling days to discuss ex-husbands, but it is never easy for me. In spite of the statistics, in spite of the social tolerance, there is nothing in the world so heavy, so leaden, so painfully pressing as love that has failed. I rarely talk about it—I make a point not to talk about it—but somehow Judith and I have got onto the subject.

We've crept back into bed, and shivering under a light blanket, I ask Judith if she minded turning forty.

"Yes," she answers thoughtfully, "but only a little."

"You didn't feel threatened or anything?"

"Not really. Of course, it helps that Martin gets to all the terrible birthdays first."

"But what about Martin? Didn't he mind?"

"I don't know," Judith says, sounding surprised. And then she adds, "But he doesn't *seem* to mind."

"Eugene is forty," I burst out.

There is a pause; Judith doesn't know what to do with this information.

"Is he?" she says politely.

"And he doesn't mind a bit. He insisted we go out and celebrate it. Cake, candles, the works."

"Well, why not?"

"He likes being forty. I think he'd even like to be older. Forty-five, fifty maybe."

"That's nice for him," Judith comments.

"It's a little worrying, don't you think, rushing into old age like that?"

"Maybe his youth wasn't all that marvellous," she suggests.

I think of Jeri and agree.

"Anyway," Judith says, "the saving grace of reaching forty is that most of your friends get there about the same time."

"I suppose that's a comfort."

"It helps."

"Watson is forty-two," I say. "Imagine!"

"That's right," Judith says, "he was about the same age as me."

"It must have killed him turning forty."

"Why do you say that?"

"Remember how he went berserk at thirty? Forty must have been a funeral for him."

"Of course," Judith says slowly, "I never knew Watson very well, but it's hard to believe that a mere birthday could hit anyone so violently."

"It did though. I saw it coming, of course. Even when he was twenty-seven he was starting to get a bit shaky. Once I even heard him lie about his age. He told some people we met, for no reason at all, that he was only twenty-five."

"Strange."

"He seemed to take it into his head that he could go backwards in time if he put enough energy into it. And that was the same year he started hanging around with his students all the time, especially the undergraduates. And talking about the university as 'they.' He even had me go and get my hair straightened so I'd look like one of his students."

"Poor Char," Judith says softly.

Her sympathy is all I need. Now I can't stop myself. "Then he really began to get desperate. The first time I saw him wearing a head band I was actually sick. Literally. I went into the bathroom and was sick. I wouldn't have minded if someone had given him the head band, one of his students maybe, but what killed me was the deliberation of it all, that he woke up one day and decided to go to a store—it was Woolworth's—and buy himself an Indian head band. And then picking it out and paying for it and then slipping it on his head. And looking at himself in the mirror. That's the moment I couldn't live with, the moment he looked in the mirror at his new head band."

Judith sounds puzzled. "Lots of people wore head bands at one time."

"But don't you see, other people sort of drift into it. They don't suddenly make a conscious decision to hold on to their youth by running out and buying some costume accessories."

"And then what happened?" She is right when she says she scarcely knew Watson. She met him only twice and all she knows about the divorce is that Watson suffered a breakdown. A breakdown?

Perhaps not really a breakdown, although that was the term we used at the time, since it was, at least, medically definable. It was Watson's breakdown which made him a saint to Greta Savage: she saw it as a powerful link between them, as though their mutual lapse from the coherent world spelled mystical union, impenetrable by those of us coarsened by robust mental health.

But what Watson suffered was something infinitely more shattering than poor Greta: more of a break-up than a break down. He broke apart. At the age of thirty he fell apart. Watson broke into a thousand pieces, and not one of those pieces had any connection with past or future.

"When he was twenty-nine," I tell Judith, "he decided we should sell the house so he and Seth and I could walk across Europe."

"*Walk* across Europe."

"With backpacks and sandals, a sort of gypsy thing. He had this crazy idea that he could earn enough money by playing the recorder, you know, in the streets of Europe."

"Did Watson play the recorder? I didn't realize he was musical."

"He wasn't. It was another of his delusions. Oh, he could play all right, about three tunes, and one of them was 'Merrily We Roll Along.' It was awful. I don't know where Seth got his musical ability but it wasn't from Watson."

"How odd."

"Doug Savage says he became totally detached from reality. In fact everyone we knew told him he was crazy, but he wouldn't listen. He actually had this image of himself tootling away in cute Greek villages with all the fat, red-faced fishermen loving him. I was supposed to write poems, Joan Baez style, and he would set them to music. And if this scheme fell through, he wasn't worried. He was into brotherly love—remember love-ins?—

and he was convinced that love was a commodity, like cash, that could take us anywhere. All we had to do was project it."

"What do you suppose would have happened if you'd actually gone?" Judith asks.

"I've asked myself that a hundred times. What if I'd said okay, I'll come. What if I'd taken him at his word, bought myself an Indian skirt and a guitar and followed him. At one point, you know, I had almost decided to go."

"Why didn't you then?"

"Two reasons. First, he stopped wanting me to come. By that time he'd already quit the university. Just walked in one day and told Doug Savage he was finished with Establishment values. He used the word 'establishment' all the time as if it was a hairy, yellow dog nipping at his heels. And then, overnight, it seemed I was part of the Establishment too. Wife. Kid. House. We were all part of it. He stopped talking about walking across Europe with us. We just weren't in the picture any longer. For that last year, in fact, I was his wife on sufferance."

"So he left alone?"

"The day after his thirtieth birthday. Which we did not celebrate, needless to say. He must have got up at dawn. Later I reconstructed the whole thing—I used to torture myself with it. He probably wanted to see the sun rise on the first day of his new life. He was like that you know, very big on symbols. I could just picture how he must have stood in the doorway of our house, very theatrical, with the sun coming up over the hedge. And the note he left! It was like the head band, very studied, very deliberate. A big, fat gesture. I tore it up. Oh, Judith, it was so terribly dumb. I've never told anyone about the note. It was just page after page of youth cult hash. Abstractions like freedom and selfhood, you know the thing. I've never had any stomach for words like 'challenge' and 'fulfillment' anyway, but from Watson . . . I could have died. I was so embarrassed for him."

"Oh, Char."

"I tore it up. And I wanted to burn it but of course we didn't have a fireplace in that house. And bonfires are illegal in Vancouver, so I burned all the little pieces in the habachi out in the yard. And all the time I was burning them I thought how he would have relished the symbolism. He hated barbecues. He always thought they were the altars of North America where people gathered to worship big pieces of meat. He was already into vegetarianism, of course. In fact—and that was what I hated most—he was into everything. Name any branch of the counter-culture and Watson had swallowed it whole. Oh, it was all so desperate. And so badly done. Do you know what I mean? If only he had done it . . . gracefully."

For a minute Judith says nothing. Then she says, "You said there were two reasons."

"What do you mean?"

"You said there were two reasons you didn't go with him to Europe. What was the other one?"

"Because," I say with a short, harsh laugh, "because I was afraid of what Mother might think."

"What about Seth?" Judith asks after a long pause.

"What about him?"

"I don't suppose he remembers Watson. He was only three, wasn't he?"

"No, he doesn't remember anything. Not even the house we lived in."

"He must be curious about him. His own father. You'd think he'd want to meet him."

"No, it's funny but he's never mentioned wanting to meet him. But once he told me he was going to write him a letter. He was about ten then, I think, and it was just after the monthly cheque came. Just before he went to sleep he told me he had decided to write a letter."

"And did he?"

"Yes, he did, and he spent a long time on it. I helped him a little. And it really was a nice kid-like letter all about school and sports and hobbies and his favourite TV programs, sort of a pen pal thing."

"And did Watson ever write back?"

"No. Months and months went by and I kept thinking any day it'll come. I figured Watson couldn't be so cruel as not to write to his own son—after all, he *does* drop Greta a line now and then. Finally I said to Seth how strange it was his father hadn't answered his letter. And do you know what he said?"

"What?"

"He just laughed and said, 'I never mailed that letter.' "

"Why not?"

"I asked him why. I asked him two or three times why he hadn't mailed it. But he would never tell me."

❧

Three-fifteen. The luminous dial of Judith's travel clock announces the hour. She is asleep, lying on her side facing the wall with one arm slung awkwardly, almost grotesquely, over her shoulder. I'm jealous of her ability to sleep, but I am also irrationally pained that she has been able to fall asleep just minutes after I have recounted the miserable story of Watson's breakdown.

My breakdown too; that's the part I didn't confess, the part I conceal even from myself except when I am absolutely alone in the middle of the night as I am now. The day Watson left, everything more or less fell apart for me too. The world, which I was just beginning to perceive, was spoiled. Everything ruined, everything scattered.

Scattered like me, the way I'm scattered through this house: in the spare room where my aggrieved mother sleeps her thin, complaining sleep. And here where Judith lies drugged on my wretchedness. And in the silent back bedroom where Eugene dreams of us riding into Toronto on the Vistadome. In Weedham, Ontario, where Watson Forrest lies amidst the welter of his strange compulsions. And in Vancouver where my son Seth—think of it—I have a fifteen year old son who is sleeping safely in a strange glass and cedar bedroom in the corner of the Savages' house.

But it is not three-fifteen in Vancouver. A rib of joy nudges me. No, it is not three-fifteen. In Vancouver it is late evening. There is probably a soft, grey rain falling. It is not even midnight yet. The TV stations are going strong; the late show hasn't even begun. Doug and Greta almost certainly are still awake; they never go to bed until one or two in the morning. Greta likes to read in bed—she is addicted to crime thrillers—and Doug likes to smoke his pipe and listen to Bartok on the record player. True, Seth may be asleep; he is usually in bed fairly early, but it isn't as though this were the middle of the night.

I'll telephone. I can dial direct; I know the number by heart. It's long distance, but I can keep track of the time and leave money to cover the call. My mother will object—the thought of the charge on her monthly bill will be grievous to her—but it will be too late then. I should have thought of phoning earlier, but there's no harm in calling now, not if I go about it quietly. In fact, this is a good time to phone because the Savages are sure to be at home.

The telephone is in the hallway, a black model sitting on my mother's gossip bench, a spindly piece of furniture from the twenties, half way to being a real antique. I need only the light of the tiny table lamp, and I dial as quietly as I can, marvelling at the technology which permits me, by dialing only eleven numbers, to sift through the millions of darkened households across the country and reach, through tiny electronic connections, the only person in the world who is really and truly connected with me.

But in Vancouver no one answers. I hang up, wait five minutes and try again. The phone rings and rings. I can picture it, a bright red wall model in the Savages' birch and copper kitchen. It rings twelve times, twenty times. No one is home. Can they possibly sleep through all this wild ringing? Impossible. No one is home.

Why can't I sleep? Why can't I be calm like Judith, why can't I learn to be brave? Why is my heart thudding like this, why can't I sleep?

Chapter 4

In the morning my mother's bedroom is filled with sunlight. Someone has opened the curtains, and high above
the asphalt-shingled roof of the house next door floats an
amiable, blue, suburban sky terraced with flat-bottomed
clouds, lovely. Shutting my eyes again I tense, waiting
for fear to reassume its grip on me, but it doesn't come.

The sun has brought with it a calm perspective, and
suddenly I can think of dozens of reasons why Doug and
Greta might not have been at home last night. They
might, for instance, have had concert tickets; Doug is a
music lover and never, if he can help it, misses the symphony. They might have gone to an exhibition at the university and taken Seth along; hadn't I seen a notice
about the opening of a pottery show or something like
that in the Fine Arts Building? Or they might have gone
out for a late dinner. (Greta frequently has days when,
maddened by the world's unhappiness, she cannot summon the strength to cook a meal.) Or taken in a movie.
Or gone for a stroll on the beach. There were countless
possibilities, none of which had occurred to me the night
before.

And this morning, waking up, I yawn, stretch, smile to
myself. Nine o'clock. There is no reason to hurry. This
evening I can phone Vancouver again; if I phone about
ten o'clock I will be sure to catch them at home.

I dress lazily, savouring the rumpled feel of the un-
made bed, the open suitcases on the floor, the faintly

stale bedroomy air. Through the shut door a burr of lowered voices reaches me, my mother's, Martin's, and whose is that other voice? Of course, Eugene's.

A determined indifference is the perfect cure for anxiety. That's what Brother Adam wrote me. I take my time. I unpack and hang up my clothes in my mother's closet, arranging them next to her half dozen dresses—such dresses: limp, round-shouldered, jersey-knit prints, all of them, in off-colours like maroon and avocado, grey and taupe. They give off a sweetish-sourish smell, very faint, a little musty. Beside them my new orange dress appears sharply synthetic and aggressively youthful. I am sorry now I bought it. For today, I decide, I will put on my old beige skirt instead. And a blouse, a dotted brown cotton which is only slightly creased across the yoke.

In the living room I find Martin, hunched on the slip-covered chesterfield with several sections of the Globe and Mail scattered around him. After all these years I scarcely know him. He is an English professor, Renaissance, and as is the case with a good many academics, his essential kindness is somewhat damaged by wit. And a finished reserve. As though he had spent years and years simmering to his present rich sanity, his pot-au-feu pungency. He is a little uneasy with me—I am so brash, so non-Judith—but his uneasiness has never worried me; our present non-relationship has a temporary, transitional quality; at any moment, it seems to me, we will find our way to being friends. For Martin is a man with a talent for friendship, and in this respect I once believed that Watson resembled him, Watson who knew hundreds and hundreds of people, whole colonies of them secreted away in the cities and towns between Toronto and Vancouver. The difference, I later observed, was that for Watson friendship was not a pleasing dispensation of existence but a means, the only means he knew, by which he could be certain of his existence.

"Well," Martin greets me, "I hear you and Judith made a night of it last night."

"We had a lot of catching up to do," I say. "I hope I didn't wear out her ear drums." I add this apologetically, feeling that Martin might begrudge me a night of Judith's companionship while he himself has been relegated to the back bedroom.

But he smiles quite warmly and says, "Why don't you come and spend a week with us after the wedding and really get caught up?"

"I wish I could," I tell him, "but Seth's staying with friends. And there's my job."

"Surely you could take a few days?" he urges.

Does Martin think I have no responsibilities, nothing to nail me down? No life of my own? And what about Eugene? But I sense that his invitation is no more than a rhetorical exercise; cordial, yes, but mechanically issued. Martin grew up in a hospitable, generous Montreal household where the giving and receiving of invitations was routine, as simple as eating, as simple as breathing.

"Where's Judith now?" I ask, looking around.

"She went out for a few groceries."

I nod, remembering the few slices of bread and the half quart of milk in the refrigerator. "Has everyone had breakfast?"

"Everyone but you. Judith thought you'd prefer to get some sleep. Afraid we didn't leave you anything though. She's gone for some more coffee and bread," he looks at his watch, "but she should be back in a few minutes."

In the kitchen my mother stands washing dishes in the sink; Eugene in a well-pressed spring suit stands next to her, drying teacups and valiantly trying to make conversation. Seeing me in the doorway he almost gasps with relief. "Charleen!"

"Well, you had yourself a good sleep," my mother says, not turning around. (Couldn't she even turn around? Does Eugene notice this greeting, this lack of greeting?)

"Yes," I say, determined to remain unruffled. "I thought I'd be lazy today."

She turns around then, carefully assessing me from top to toe, hair, blouse (creased), skirt, stockings, shoes, and says tartly, "Mr. Berceau—Louis I should say—is dropping by this morning to meet you."

"Good," I answer, rather too lightly, "I'm looking forward to meeting him."

"In that case it's too bad you picked this morning to sleep in. Because you haven't had your breakfast and he's coming at ten o'clock. He's always right on time, right on the dot. We all had breakfast at eight o'clock. Toast and coffee. I told Dr. Redding," she nods sharply at Eugene, "that I hoped he wasn't expecting a big breakfast. We never were a bacon and egg house here. I can't eat all that fried food for breakfast anyway. We just have toast and coffee and always have, guests or no guests. But there's no toast for you. We just completely ran out of bread. That's something I never do normally, run out of things. I plan carefully. You remember, Charleen, how I always planned carefully. There's no excuse for waste, I always say. Of course, I didn't know Dr. Redding would be here, you didn't write about him staying here, or I would have bought an extra loaf. Martin always eats at least three pieces of toast. Not that he needs it. I told Judith this morning he should watch his starches. I never have more than one. I've never been a heavy eater, and a good thing with the price of food. Well, we're right out of bread. Martin even ate the heel, not that there's anything wrong with that. Waste not. Then Judith said, never mind, she'd go down to the Red and White. You'd never know the Red and White now. The floor, it's filthy, just filthy, they used to keep it so clean in there; you remember, Charleen, it used to be spotless when the old man was alive. Spotless. And they let people bring their dogs in, and I don't know what. I thought Judith would be back by the time you woke up but she isn't. I don't know what in the world's keeping her. She always was a dawdler, it's only a block away and it shouldn't be crowded at this time of the morning. And here you are up already. Judith thought you'd sleep in until she got back and here you are and there's nothing for breakfast. You should have got up with the rest of us. And here's Dr. Redding wiping dishes, he insisted, and he's in a rush to get downtown. But Judith said the two of you were up half the night talking away. I thought I heard someone up banging around in the kitchen. You and Judith need your sleep, you don't need me to remind you about that, and here you are up to all hours. How do you expect to get your rest when you sit up all night? You've got all day to talk away. The rest of us need our sleep too."

Eugene, rose-stamped teacup in hand, listens stunned. I have to remember that he has come unprepared, that he has never met anyone like my mother, that she has always been like this. Nevertheless I feel an uncontrollable tremour of pity seeing her this morning in her exhausted, chenille dressing gown, white-faced, despairing and horribly aged, her wrists angry red under the lacy suds.

I watch Eugene standing by the sink, slightly stooped, tea towel in hand, looking at once humble and affluent with his well-trimmed, wooly hair and faintly anxious and uncomfortable expression. It isn't difficult for me to imagine the questions taking shape in Eugene's head, questions he would never voice or perhaps even acknowledge as his own. Questions like: Why is Mrs. McNinn angry with Charleen? What has Charleen done? Why don't these two women, mother and daughter, embrace? Why don't they smile at each other? Why doesn't Charleen ask her mother how she's feeling? Why doesn't Mrs. McNinn ask if Charleen slept well?

As I imagine the questions, the answers too spring into being, the answers which Eugene would almost certainly formulate: Mrs. McNinn is angry because she is not in good health; she is possessed of a rather nervous disposition; it is probable that she slept poorly last night. She is, in addition, confused about who I, Eugene Redding, am, and she is somewhat bothered by the fact that she hadn't been expecting an extra guest. She is unused to house guests and is now embarrassed because she has run short of food. But it is nothing serious; it will pass.

I am able to frame these answers because I know Eugene and trust him to find, as he always does, the most charitable explanation, the most kindly interpretation. Kindness, after all, comes to him naturally; he was hatched in its lucky genre and embraces its attributes effortlessly. Gentleness, generosity and compromise are not for him learned skills; they have always been with him, wound up with the invisible genes which determine the wooliness of his hair and the slightly vacant look in his grey eyes. It may, for all I know, have existed in his family for generations. He is not at the frontier as I am.

For me kindness is an alien quality; and like a difficult French verb I must learn it slowly, painfully, and probably imperfectly. It does *not* swim freely in my bloodstream—I have to inject it artificially at the risk of all sorts of unknown factors. It does *not* wake with me in the mornings; every day I have to coax it anew into existence, breathe on it to keep it alive, practice it to keep it in good working order. And most difficult of all, I have to exercise it in such a way that it looks spontaneous and genuine; I have to see that it flows without hesitation as it does from its true practitioners, its lucky heirs who acquire it without laborious seeking, the lucky ones like Eugene.

❧

Louis Berceau arrives precisely at ten o'clock in a small, dark-green Fiat which he parks at the curb in front of the house. When he knocks at the back door, Judith is making fresh coffee, and Eugene has just left by taxi for the dental convention downtown, an extravagance which both shocked and impressed my mother. ("Doesn't he know we have a subway? Well, I know it's pokey, but it's good enough for most people.")

Judith has been mistaken about Louis's height; he is considerably shorter than our mother, perhaps as much as six inches. And he is thin—certainly I had not expected that he would be robust—with enormously wrinkled, whitish-yellow skin; his gnarled peanut face—how humble he looks!—and his thickish, wall-like eyelids make him look like a dwarfed, jaundiced Jesus. This man has had three operations, I chant to myself. Three operations.

Judith puts down the coffee pot, and he takes both her hands in his and presses her warmly, a warmth which takes Judith by surprise; they have met only once before. Then he turns to me and I see him hesitate an instant before speaking. He has a choked and gummy voice—did tumors nest in that plugged up throat?—but friendliness leaks through. "So this is Charleen."

For a man, he has a tiny hand, harshly-formed, dry and papery as though the flesh were about to fall away from the gathered bones. His clothes, too, seem curiously dry, an old, blue suit, far too hot for today, with faintly dusty seams and buttonholes.

Martin comes into the kitchen to be introduced, and with his hearty "How do you do, Mr. Berceau," we all breathe more easily. My mother, like a minor character in a play, has frozen during these introductions, literally flattening herself against the refrigerator door, nervously observing Louis's presentation of himself to the "family."

"I've just made some coffee," Judith announces.

"Exactly what I need," Louis replies from the top of his strangled, phleghm-plugged throat. "I've been up for hours." And with a rattling sigh he sinks down at the kitchen table.

"We could go into the living room," my mother says with the pinched voice she uses when she wants to be genteel.

"The kitchen is fine, Florence," Louis says, breathing rapidly. Florence! Well, what had I expected?

We sit down at the table while my mother finds cups and saucers in the cupboard. There is a moment's silence which I rush to fill; it seems so extraordinarily painful for Louis Berceau to speak that all I can think of is the necessity of sparing him the effort.

"I'm really very happy to meet you," I rattle away inanely. "At first I thought I wasn't going to be able to come. But I managed to get a week off work, and some friends offered to keep an eye on Seth—my son—and I thought, why not?"

Louis stirs his coffee and lifts his eyes in a disarming, skin-pleated smile. Gasping between spaced phrases he manages, "We are so grateful—both of us—your mother and I—that you could come all these—thousands of miles—to be with us—on Friday. We are—we are—" he searches for a word, then with a final burst says, "we are honoured."

Honoured! Honoured? I glance at my mother, take in her tightly shut lips, and look away. Louis is honoured—how touching—but only Louis.

"It was Mr. Berceau's idea," my mother explains sharply, "to have a proper wedding. And invite," she pauses, "the family."

"Well, you see," Louis chokes, "I never . . . never had a family."

"Well, now you do," Judith says with firm cheerfulness. (How easily I can picture her performing at faculty receptions.) "The children, my two kids that is, have exams this week, but they'll be coming on the train Friday in time for the wedding."

"I hope," Louis says, his thick lips cracking puckishly, "that I'll get to know them well in time."

He drinks his coffee with a long, pleasurable slurp, leans back in his chair—such tiny shoulders—quite amazingly relaxed. Again he strains to speak, and we lean forward, Martin, Judith and I, to catch what he says. "Do you mind . . ." he whispers raspily, "if I smoke?"

He puffs contentedly on a Capstan, using, to my astonishment and horror, the rim of my mother's saucer for an ashtray. The smoke curling from his lips and rather oily nostrils makes him look exceptionally ugly. He has always—I feel certain of this—been ugly; he wears his ugliness with such becoming ease, as though it were a creased oilskin, utilitarian and not at all despised. And as he smokes, he talks, a light and general conversation, faintly paternal with a scattering of questions, the sort of conversation which has rarely filled these rooms. I feel myself grow tense at the obvious exertion of his voice, its separate sounds eased out of the creaking wooden machinery of his throat, dry, high-pitched, harshly monotone, a voice pitted with gasped air as though his windpipe is in some dreadful way shredded and out of his control.

Judith and Martin and I attend scrupulously to his questions, making our replies as lengthy as possible in order to relieve him of the torment of speaking. Turning deferentially to Martin, he inquires about his position at the university, and Martin, not quite blushing but almost, tells Louis that he has recently been appointed chairman of his department.

I am startled. Judith has never mentioned Martin's promotion to me; indeed, at that moment, listening to her husband describe the duties of his new office, Judith fidgets, rises, reheats the coffee, even yawns behind a politely raised hand. She has never pretended to be a standard, right-hand wife, but her nonchalance about Martin's success seems excessive, almost indifferent.

Is Martin himself pleased about his promotion? I wonder. It is difficult to tell because, with his academic compulsion toward truth, he outlines for Louis the enormous liabilities of the position, the toll it takes in terms of time, patience and friendship. Never have I heard Martin so expansive, never so carefully expository, and it occurs to me that he is deliberately prolonging his explanation out of an inclination to break through the aura of surrealism which possesses us, to flatten with his burly, workaday facts the sheer unreality of our being gathered here around this particular kitchen table on this particular late May morning.

Louis turns next to Judith—I am becoming accustomed to his dry-roofed rasp—and asks her whether she has read the biography of Lawrence Welk, a question which disappoints me somewhat by its banality. (Already I am investing Louis with wizened, cerebral kindliness.)

No, Judith answers, she hasn't read it but she respects those who discover ways, whatever they may be, of uncovering currents of the extraordinary in even the most ordinary personalities. Actually, Judith protests, she doesn't believe there is such a thing as an ordinary person, at least not when examined from the privileged perspective of the biographer. What consumes her now, she tells Louis, is her investigation into the scientific impulse—no, not impulse, she corrects herself; in the case of scientists, impulse becomes compulsion. Louis nods; his twisted muzzle face registers agreement. Judith continues: science, she says, often drowns men with its overwhelming abstractions, snuffing out human variability and hatching the partly true myth of the cold, clinical man of science. Human whim, human dream if you like, become obscured, and for the biographer, Judith admits, not unhappily, the scientific life is the most complex of all to write about.

Louis questions me next—I wonder if he has rehearsed the pattern of our discussion—asking me if dreams inspire the poems I write. (It is a morning for speeches, each of us taking a turn, except, that is, our mother who sits in one corner of the table, peevishly sipping her coffee and filling the dips and hollows of our phrases with nervous, trailing "yes's" and "well's"). No, I tell Louis, I never write poems inspired by dreams.

"Why not?" he creaks.

I shrug, thinking of the Pome People who treasure their dreams as though they were rare oriental currency blazoned with symbolic stamping. For me dreams are no more than rag-ends caught in a sort of human lint-trap, psychic fluff, the negligible dust of that more precious material, thought. To value one's dreams is to encourage the most debilitating of diseases, subjectivity. (Watson nearly died of that disease; our marriage almost certainly did.) To pretend that dreams are generated whole out of

some vast, informing unconsciousness is to imagine a
comic-strip beast (alligator, dragon?) slumbering in
one's blood. The inner life? I shrug again. The poet has
to report on surfaces, on the flower in the crannied wall,
on coffee spoons and peaches, a rusted key discovered in
the grass. Dreams are like—I think a moment—dreams
are like mashed potatoes.

Martin awards me a yelp of laughter. Louis smiles a
yellow, fish-gleam smile, and Judith, smiling approval,
refills my cup. She is flushed with her own impromptu
eloquence and proud of mine. And puzzled too. Is it
Louis's questions that have stirred us? Or our desire to
make him understand exactly how far we have travelled
from this cramped kitchen?

After this it is Louis's turn to speak.

"With your permission," he begins hoarsely, "I would
like to invite each of you—you, Judith and you, Charleen—to have lunch with me." He stops; a coughing fit
seizes him, shaking his thin shoulders with wrenching
violence. We watch helplessly, tensely, listening to the
dry, squeezed convulsions of his heaving chest.

"It's just the asthma," our mother tells us calmly, almost flatly, sipping again at her coffee. "It happens all
the time."

Three operations *and* asthma!

At last Louis's coughing stops and he pulls out a handkerchief and blows his nose noisily. Half choking, he
begins again, explaining how he hopes to get better acquainted with us by taking us in turn, Judith today and
me tomorrow, out for a nice, long lunch. (The order, I
can only think, is dictated by our relative ages; Judith
being older has priority, and I cannot help smiling at the
thoroughness of his planning.) When he has finished his
arduous invitation, he sits back again, smashes his cigarette in my mother's saucer, and asks "Well?"

Judith—brave, kind, curious Judith—leaning over the
table and placing her hand on Louis's amber-stained fingertips, repeats the word Louis used earlier, a word
which has never before, as far as I know, been used in
this house and which is now being spoken for the second
time in a single morning. "I would be honoured," she
pronounces.

"In that case," Louis says rising, "I think we should be
on our way."

"You mean right now?" Judith stammers.

"I know a nice quiet place," he rasps, "in the country.
It'll be after twelve o'clock before we get there."

Turning to me he says, "Tomorrow then, Charleen?
We can . . ." he coughs his parched, tenor cough, "we
can talk some more about poetry."

Judith, a little bewildered, picks up a sweater and her
handbag and they leave by the back door, walking together around the lilac tree at the side of the house. My
mother rises at once to place the cups in the sink. Martin
returns to his newspaper and I, following him into the
living room, watch the two of them move toward the car;
Judith is a full head taller than Louis; she seems to lope
by his side.

It is very strange watching Louis walk to his car.
Louis, sitting in the kitchen and puffing his cigarette,
seemed dwarfed and bleached and freakish, like an
aged, yellowed monkey, but Louis walking to the car is
close to nimbleness; with his lightsome step, his short,
little arms swinging cheerfully, and his head tossing as
though he were searching out the best possible breath of
air, he appears, from the back and from a distance, like a
man in his prime.

We have scrambled eggs on toast for lunch, Martin,
my mother and I.

In this household, guests have never been frequent: occasionally when we were children my Aunt Liddy, my mother's older sister who lived in the country, would come to spend a day with us. And there was a second cousin of our father, Cousin Hugo, who owned a hardware store, a large, fat man with wiry black hair and curving crusts of dirt beneath his fingernails. And once a neighbour whose wife was in the hospital with pneumonia had been invited for Sunday lunch, an extraordinary gesture which remained for years in my mother's mind as the "time we put ourselves out to help Mr. Eggleston." Always on these occasions when guests were present she would serve scrambled eggs on toast.

Doubtless she considered it a dish both light and elegant. She may have read somewhere that it was the Queen Mother's favourite luncheon dish (she is always reading about the Royal Family). Certainly she is convinced of the superiority of her own scrambled eggs and the manner in which she arranges the triangles of toast (side by side like the sails of a tiny boat), for she always compares, at length, the correctness of her method with the slipshod scrambled eggs she has encountered elsewhere.

"Liddy doesn't put enough milk in hers and I always tell her that makes them rubbery. If you want nice, soft scrambled eggs you have to add a tablespoon of milk for every egg, just a tablespoon, no more, no less. And use an egg beater, not a fork the way most people do. Most people just don't want to bother getting out an egg beater, they're too lazy to wash something extra. They think, who'll notice anyway, what's the difference, but an egg beater makes all the difference, all the difference in the world. Otherwise the yolk and white don't mix the way they should. Liddy always leaves big hunks of white in her scrambled eggs. And she doesn't cut the crusts off her toast. She thinks it's hoity-toity and a waste of bread, but I always save the crusts and dry them in the oven to make bread crumbs out of them afterwards so there's no waste, not a bit; you know I never waste good food; you'll have to admit I never waste anything. Most people won't bother, they won't go to the trouble; they're too lazy; they don't know any better. And I always add the salt before cooking, that makes them hold their shape, not get hard like Liddy's but just, you know, firm. But not pepper, never pepper, never add pepper when you're cooking, let people add their own pepper at the table if that's what they want. Me, I never liked spicy food like what the Italians and French like. And Greeks. Garlic and onions and grease, and I don't know what, just reeking of it on the subway these days, reeking of it; I don't dare turn my head sideways when I go downtown. Toronto isn't the same; not the way it used to be, not the way it was way back."

We eat lunch in the kitchen. Martin is quiet. So am I. Our forks clicking on the plates chill me into a further silence.

"Hmm, delicious," Martin says politely.

"Yes." I agree, forcing my voice into short plumes of enthusiasm, "Really good. So tender."

Afterwards she washes the dishes and I dry. *Always take a clean tea towel for each meal. It may be a little bit extra in the wash but when you think of the filthy tea towels some people use . . . .*

I yearn desperately to talk to her; to say that, despite my foreboding, I have been rather taken with Louis Berceau, that I am immeasurably pleased that he and she have found each other and she will no longer have to endure the loneliness of the ticking clock, the sound of the furnace switching on and off, the daily paper thudding against the door, the calendar weeks wasting, the reminders of time slipping by which must be unbearable for those who are alone. But the words dry in my throat; if only I knew how to begin, if only I could speak to her without shyness, without fear of hurting her. Instead I poke with my tea towel into the spokes of the egg beater.

"Don't bother drying that," she turns to me, taking it out of my hands. "Here," she says, "I always put it in the oven for a little, the pilot light dries it out; the gears are so old, I've had it since just after the war, it was hard to get egg beaters then. Cousin Hugo got it for me from the store. I don't want the gears to rust, they would if I didn't get it good and dry. I've had it so long and it will have to last me until—"

Until what? Until death? Until the end? That is what she means; the words she couldn't say but which she must have recognized or why did she stop so suddenly? I have never thought of the way in which my mother thinks of her own death. No doubt, though, she has a plan; she will do it more neatly, more thoroughly than her sister Liddy, better than the neighbours, more genteely than Cousin Hugo, more timely than our father; no one will laugh at her, no one will look down on her.

Still, it may be that she is a little uncertain: the way she plunges into vigorous silence beside the scoured sink hints at uneasiness, an acknowledgement at least of life's thinned reversal, of the finite nature of husbands and egg beaters and even of one's self.

After lunch Martin carries a kitchen chair out into the backyard (my mother has never owned a piece of lawn furniture) and there in the sunshine he reads a book of critical essays, a recent paperback edition which he opens with a sigh. He is, I suspect, a somewhat reluctant academic, preferring perhaps to while away his time with the small change of newspapers and magazines.

Nevertheless he enjoys the warmth and the serious Sisley sky, finely marbled, gilt-veined, surprisingly large even when viewed from the postage stamp of our tiny, fenced yard.

One-thirty. My mother goes about the house closing the curtains, first the living room and then the three bedrooms. (Much of her life has gone into a struggle against the fading of furniture and curtains and rugs.) Then she goes into the spare bedroom where she slept last night and closes the door. She is going to lie down, she is going to have her rest. She has always, since Judith and I were babies, had a "rest" after lunch. Never a nap, never a sleep, never, oh never, a doze, but a rest. She will remove her laced shoes and her dress, she will button a loosely knit grey and blue cardigan over her slip and she will turn back the bedspread into a neat fan; then she will get into bed, and there she will remain for between an hour and an hour and a half. Sometimes she falls asleep, sometimes she just "rests." "A rest is as good as a sleep," she has said at least a hundred times. A thousand times?

Quietly I carry the *Metropolitan Toronto and Vicinity* telephone book from the hall into the kitchen and settle myself down at the table. I turn to the P's, running my finger down a column, looking for The Priory, Priory, the. For some reason my heart is beating wildly. But there is nothing listed. I look under the The's where I find quite a few listings: The Boutique, The Factory, The Place, The Shop, The Wiggery. But not The Priory. I even look under the B's for Brother Adam. There is no Brother Adam, (nor any other Brothers) then I try Adam, Brother. Nothing.

Perhaps the Priory is listed under Religious Houses or under Churches, but my mother has no Yellow Pages. I decide to phone Information.

It is necessary to whisper into the phone because my mother is resting a few yards away behind a closed door; she may even be sleeping. The operator is enraged by my muffled voice and my lack of specificity—"Did you say it was a church?"

"No."

"Well, is it or isn't it?"

"I'm not sure. I think it is but I'm not—"

"Is Adam the first name or last name?"

"His first. I think."

"I have to have a last name."

"I've got the address. It's on Beachview."

"Sorry. I need the last name."

"But I don't have it."

Actually, I reflect hanging up, it was absurd of me to think that a contemplative man like Brother Adam would have a telephone. Hadn't he implied in his many letters his ascetic obsession, his distrust of cramped, urban industrial society? A man like Brother Adam would never put himself in bondage to Bell Telephone; a man like Brother Adam would no sooner have a telephone than he would own a car. (He does, however, have a typewriter— all his letters were typewritten—but it is undoubtedly a manual model.)

I carry the phone book back to its place. I am not going to be able to phone Brother Adam after all. And it's too late now to drop him a note. I should have written from Vancouver as I had planned. What's the matter with me that I can't even make the simplest of social arrangements? I'll have to go to The Priory, there's no other solution. If I want to see him at all I will have to turn up at his door unannounced.

But I can't go today; my mother wouldn't like it if I disappeared on an unexplained errand, and besides Eugene is going to phone me from downtown at three o'clock. And tomorrow? Wednesday? Tomorrow is my day to have lunch with Louis Berceau. Friday?—the wedding is on Friday, and Friday night we're flying back to Vancouver.

Thursday—if I go at all I'll have to go on Thursday. Yes, I will definitely go to see Brother Adam on Thursday. He is in the city, he is within a few miles of me, looking out of his window perhaps, sitting in the sun on his fire escape perhaps, and who knows, maybe he is writing a letter, perhaps even a letter to me, a letter beginning Dear Charleen, the sky is benignly blue today, the sun falls like a blessing across this page . . .

❦

Martin is restless. He has brought his chair inside; the sky has clouded over with alarming suddenness, and a few drops of heavy rain have already fallen onto the pages of his book. He is brooding mysteriously by the living room window.

I can never quite believe in the otherness of people's lives. That is, I cannot conceive of their functioning out of my sight. A psychologist friend once told me this attitude was symptomatic of a raging ego, but perhaps it is only a perceptual failure. My mother: every day she lives in this house; it is not all magically whisked away when I leave; the walls and furniture persist and so do the hours which she somehow fills. When Seth was five and started school I came home the first day after taking him and grieved, not out of nostalgia for his infancy or anxiety for his future, but for the newly revealed fact that he had entered into that otherness, that unseeable space which he must occupy forever and where not even my imagination could follow. It is the same with Martin who, year after unseen year, pursues objectives, lives through unaccountable weeks and months. Martin by the window, shut up in his thoughts, might be standing on the tip of the moon.

When my mother wakes up she goes into the kitchen

and begins browning a small pot roast on the back of the stove. "Nothing fancy," she explains. "I'm not going to fuss even for company, not at today's prices, not that there's anything wrong with a good honest pot roast and they don't give those away nowadays. Maybe it takes a few hours, you have to brown it really well, each side and the ends too, most people don't want to bother, they'd just as soon take a steak out of the freezer, never mind the cost, and call that a meal."

Because I make my mother nervous in the kitchen I go into the living room and stand beside Martin. He glances at his watch and says, "They should be home soon."

Is it a question or a statement? "You mean Judith?" I ask.

He nods.

"It's quite a distance," I remind him. "Remember? Out in the country somewhere."

"He's over seventy," Martin says grimly.

"Seventy-two," I nod.

"These old coots really shouldn't be on the road," Martin says with surprising ferocity.

The word "coots" shocks me; it seems a remarkably uncivilized word for Martin to use. What is the matter with him?

I spring to Louis's defence. "He seems alert enough for a man of his age. I'm sure he wouldn't drive if he felt he wasn't capable."

Martin looks again at his watch, and I can see by the involuntary snap of his wrist that he's seriously worried.

"I'm sure he's a careful driver," I insist again.

"But how do you *know*?"

I shrug. "He certainly didn't strike me as the reckless type."

"Didn't strike you," he says sourly, mockingly. But

then he asks seriously, "How *did* he strike you, Char-leen?"

"Why are you so worried, Martin?"

"Because," Martin says, "have you considered that we don't know a damn thing about this man? Absolutely nothing."

"He used to be a Catholic," I say, as though that fact were exceptionally revealing, "and he used to teach carpentry or something like that. In a junior high. In the east end I think."

"Yes, yes," Martin says wearily, "but what do we *really* know about him?"

"His health, you mean?"

He sighs, faintly exasperated. "No, not his health. What I mean is, we don't know anything. Christ, maybe he's queer. Or maybe he molests children. Or sets fire to buildings or passes bum cheques. How would we know?"

I feel my mouth pulling into the shape of protest.

Martin continues, "He's an odd enough looking bird, you can see that. For your mother's sake we should have looked into him a bit more. And now here he goes off with Judith to God only knows where. We never even asked exactly where they were headed. And now a storm's coming up." He sighs again. "I don't know."

How odd Martin is becoming. I point out to him the obvious facts: that it is not even quite three o'clock yet, that it was after eleven when Judith and Louis left the house; that Louis distinctly said it was an hour's drive. True, we know next to nothing about him, but we couldn't very well call in a detective three days before the wedding; we would have to go by instinct, and my instinct—but would Martin believe it?—my instinct is to trust him. An odd-looking man, yes, and a strange marriage, perhaps—I nod in the direction of the kitchen—

but I feel certain, a certainty which I can in no way justify, that there is nothing to be afraid of.

Martin shakes his head, not entirely convinced but obviously wishing to be. He regards the empty street and the pulsing sky; the rain is holding back, squeezing laboured tears out of the scrambled grey clouds. Clearly Martin will not be happy until Judith is safely home; his devotion touches me, especially when I think of Judith's careless departure, how she went off without a thought about how Martin would pass the day, making a swift grab for her bag, yanking a cardigan over her shoulders; she took Louis's arm with huge, loping cheerfulness and sailed past the lilac tree; she drove away in his little Fiat without so much as a good-bye wave. And what else? Oh, yes, she hadn't told me about Martin's promotion; she hadn't, in fact, mentioned Martin at all; it is rather as though he were no more than a distant acquaintance.

I want to reassure Martin about Louis's reliability. "I don't know how to explain it," I tell him, "but I know Louis's okay. And I'm usually right about things like this." (Am I?)

He smiles a twisted, academic smile. "Intuition, I suppose."

I smile back. We will be friends. "Look," I say, "it's a rather odd marriage, but they may surprise us by being happy."

"Happy?" He looks amused at the idea.

"Well, a kind of happiness."

Happiness. Such a word, such a crude balloon of a word, such a flapping, stretched, unsightly female bladder of a word, how worn, how slack, how almost empty.

"Happiness," Martin repeats dully.

And before I can say anything more, the telephone rings. It's Eugene.

"Charleen."

"Yes. Eugene? How's it going? The conference?"

"Not bad. A bit draggy." (I rejoice at his detachment. If he had greeted me with ecstasy my heart would have sickened; I am queasy about misplaced enthusiasm.)

"What time are you coming?" I ask him.

"That's why I'm phoning. What I'd really like is if you could come downtown."

"Tonight?"

"We could have dinner." His voice slants with pleading. "Just the two of us."

"I don't know, Eugene. My mother. She's already making dinner. I don't know what she'd say."

"Couldn't you say I had to stay downtown later than I'd thought? Because of the conference?"

"I don't know, Eugene," I say doubtfully, thinking, poor Eugene, this morning must have been too much for him, and last night too, stuck in the back bedroom. Then I think of the pot roast my mother is cooking, reflecting that it is really rather small to feed all of us; wouldn't it, in fact, be a kindness to go out for dinner?

"Okay, Eugene. What time?"

"Any time. We're through for the day."

"I don't think I can make it before five," I tell him.

"Five then. Get a taxi and I'll wait for you at Bloor and Avenue Road."

"I'll come by subway. No need to take a taxi all the way from here."

"Charleen. Please."

"Eugene. I can't," I hiss into the phone. "My mother."

"It'll take you hours."

"No, it won't. Remember, I used to live here. I know the subway."

"You're crazy, you know. I'll be waiting. Bloor and Avenue Road, all right? By the museum."

"Okay," I promise. I think of my mother fretfully turning her pot roast in the kitchen, of Martin sighing by the window; suddenly I can't wait to get out of this house. "See you soon," I tell Eugene.

Of course my mother minds. Or, perhaps more accurately, she goes through the motions of minding; the pot roast has shrunk alarmingly.

"You might have said something about it this morning," she says with a short, injured sniff. "I could have done chops if I'd known there would be only three of us. I'm surprised your Dr. Redding, him a doctor and all, didn't have the courtesy to tell me this morning. It isn't like this was a hotel, whatever you may think. But go ahead, go ahead if you've made up your mind. All I say is it's a waste of money eating in fancy restaurants and you never know what you're getting, food poisoning, germs and I don't know what. I'd just as soon have a good honest pot roast if you asked me, not all that foreign food. You don't know what it is. I wouldn't have gone to the trouble of a pot roast if I thought you were going to take it into your head to go eat in a restaurant. I suppose you won't be too late?"

I listen; I bear with it; in a few minutes, I tell myself, she will have exhausted herself and I will be free to go. No, I tell her, we won't be too late. I speak calmly, lightly, remembering to be kind, reminding myself that her nerves are poor, that her health is shaky, that she has never, no never, eaten in a downtown restaurant, that she has been little rewarded in her life for her efforts: her scrambled eggs and careful housekeeping have not won her the regard she might have liked. I remind myself, above all, that she is weak.

And from her weakness flows not gentleness but a tidal wave of judgment. No wonder she has no friends. Over the years those few people who have approached her in friendship have been swept aside as prying and nosey, their gestures of help construed as malicious arrogance. Underpinning all her beliefs is the idea that people "should keep to themselves." They should stand on their own feet, they should mind their own business, they should look after their own, they should steer their own ship, they should tend their own gardens. Judgment colours her every encounter: "Mrs. Mallory said she admired my new slipcovers. Imagine that, she *admired* them. She couldn't just say she *liked* them, no, she *admired* them. I don't know what gives her the right to be so high and mighty. I've seen *her* slipcovers."

The world which she has constructed for herself is fiercely, cruelly, minutely competitive, a world in which each minimal victory requires careful registration. "Well," she would say, "I had my washing out first again today; first in the neighbourhood." Or, "At least we don't eat our dinner at five o'clock like the Hannas, only country people eat at five o'clock. I told Mrs. Hanna how we always sat down at six o'clock when my husband got home from the office, from the office I said, and that ended that."

My poor, self-tormented mother with her meaningless rage, her hollow vindictiveness, her shrinking fear—how had it happened? Heredity suggested a partial answer. My mother's mother, Elsie Gordon, had been one of two sisters born in a village in the Scottish lowlands; she had married a farmer named Angus Dunn, and the two of them had immigrated to Ontario where they rented and finally bought a thirty-acre farm and produced two daughters, Liddy (poor witless Aunt Liddy) and, three years later, Florence, our mother. And Florence, as though responding to a cry for symmetry, had also produced two daughters, Judith and me. So here we are, three generations of paired sisters; had we been shaped by a tradition of kindness and had our sensibility been monitored by learning, we might even have resembled Jane Austen's loving, clinging, nuance-addicted chains of sisters with their epistles and their fainting spells and their nervous agitation and their endless, garrulous, wonderful concern for one another. As it was, we were stamped out of rougher materials: dullness and drudgery, ignorance and self-preservation. Our father too had been a man without ancestors: to go back three generations was to find nothing but darkness; as the "Pome People" might say, our family tree was no more than a blackened stump. I don't even know the name of the Scottish village my grandparents came from. There have been no pilgrimages, there are no family legends, no family Bible with records of births and deaths, no brown-edged letters, no pressed flowers, few photographs and even those few stiffly obligatory; there are no family heirlooms and, of course, no family pride. Each generation has, it seems, effectively sealed itself off from its lowly forebears. My mother had not wanted to remember the muddy thirty acres where she grew up, the roofless barn, the doorless outhouse, the greasy kitchen table where the family took meals, the chickens which wandered in and out the back door, the thick-ankled mother who could neither read nor write and who had little capacity for affection or cleanliness. Hadn't my mother, in spite of all this, finished grade nine and hadn't she gone to Toronto to work in a hat factory? (Ah, but that was another sealed-off area.) Hadn't she married a city boy, someone who worked in an office, and hadn't they, after a few years, bought a house of their own, paid for it too, a real house in Scarborough with a back yard and plumbing, hadn't she kept it spotless and proved to everyone that she was just as good as the next person, hadn't she shown them? Yes.

Yes, yes, I understand it; why can't I put that understanding into motion? Why am I running down the sidewalk like this? The rain is pouring in sheets off the sides of my borrowed umbrella. My feet in my only good shoes are soaked already.

I'm on my way downtown, running to the subway station. How unfair to blame my mother for the fact that I am taking the subway—I clutch my scratched vinyl purse and admit the truth—I am the one who lacks the largesse to phone a taxi. Meagreness. I am Florence McNinn's daughter, the genes are there, nothing I've done has scratched them out.

My ankles are wet and rimmed with mud. Oh, God, one more block and at least I'll be out of the rain.

As I run splashing along, a sort of song thrums in my crazy head: Seth, Seth, where are you? Oh, Watson, why did you leave me? Brother Adam, why can't you save me? Eugene, Eugene, Eugene.

❧

Actually I love the subway. Not its denatured surfaces, not its weatherless tunnels, but its mad, anonymous, hyperactive, scrambling and sorting: the doors sliding open in the station, the rush of people, their faces declaring serious and purposeful journeys they are undertaking. Then another stop—they push their way out and are instantly replaced with equally serious, equally intent others. Their namelessness pleases me, their contained and dignified singularity comforts me. And it amazes me to think of the intricate, possibly secret connections between them, perhaps even connections of love. I like to think that at the end of each of these rushed, wordless, singular journeys, there is someone waiting, someone who is loved. How extraordinary—of course there are all sorts of chemical explanations—but still, how extraordinary is the chancy cement of love; a special dispensation which no one ever really deserves but which almost everyone gets a little of. Even my unloving mother has found someone finally to love. Even Louis Berceau with his scraped-out lungs and his screwed-up, druid face has found someone to love.

Joy seizes me fiercely, sweetly. I am one of the lucky ones after all with my hard-as-a-kernel nut of indestructibility. My hereditary disease, the McNinn syndrome, has riddled me with cowardice, no question about it, but happiness will always return from time to time—as on this train blindly tunnelling beneath Bay and Bloor.

At the end of the trip, above ground, Eugene is waiting, his gull-grey raincoat flapping in the wind and his face fixed with its own peculiar flat uncertainty. I am ridiculously happy to see him.

Eugene steers me into a taxi and down the street toward a big, new hotel; through the chrome-framed doors into a warm, bronze-sheeted lobby, strenuously contemporary with revolving lucite chandeliers and motorized waterfalls. The elevator is a cube of perfect creature comfort: softly lit and carpeted, ventilated, soundless and swift.

In a darkened cocktail lounge high over the city, Eugene and I sit on strangely shaped, grotesquely padded chairs and sip long, cold drinks and nibble on tiny smoked, salty, crackling things. And we talk in the strange, curiously-shy fashion of reunited lovers. I tell Eugene about Louis Berceau, and he tells me about an old dental school friend he ran into today who asked him how "his charming wife was." When Eugene told him he was now divorced, the friend backed off and, in a blind flurry of honesty, said, "Actually I never could stand Jeri." Or was it honesty, Eugene wonders now, drumming his fingers on the table. Maybe the friend was, belatedly and pointlessly, scrambling for sides.

Maybe he was trying in an unfocussed way to comfort
Eugene or to congratulate him for having rid himself of
an unpleasant wife. "Strange," Eugene murmurs, looking into his gin and tonic. "Strange how people react to
divorce. Not knowing whether sympathy is in order or
not."

I agree with him. Death is so much simpler; the rituals
are firmer, shapelier; social custom will never be able to
alter or diminish the effect of death; one need never be
confused about the proper response.

Later, in the restaurant, we eat marvellous little things
from a wagon of hors d'oeuvres. Tiny fishes, oily and
frilled with lemon; sculptured vegetables lapped with
mayonnaise, glazed and healthy under parsley coverlets,
sharp little sausages and miniature onions, gherkins and
lovely, lovely olives, black, green, some of them an astonishing pink. After that we have tornedos in cream (the
speciality of the house, the beaming, gleaming waiter
tells us.) I eat less guiltily knowing Eugene will be able
to write off almost every penny this meal is costing; at
the same time I feel our feast is meanly diminished by
that very fact. A paradox. Eugene says he feels the same
way. Why?

He says it is a question of puritan ethic: you can only
enjoy what you have laboriously worked for. Pleasure
must be paid for by sacrifice, at least for those like us. It
must not come too easily or too soon. He shakes his head
sadly over the fact, but accepts it, admitting that most
middle class rewards will no doubt continue to elude
him.

"It might be better for the kids though," he says,
speaking of his two boys, Sandy and Donny, who live
with Jeri and stay with him in his apartment most weekends. He is always impressed with their unalloyed enjoy-
ment of the presents he gives them. "They don't think

they have to do a damn thing in return," he says. "I mean, God, they're little primitives. They just open their arms to whatever rains down on them. Damned ungrateful too, but maybe that's better than being screwed up with the debt-to-the-devil complex."

"Maybe," I say. And yet I'm glad Eugene is not entirely guilt-free about tax deductions; I'm grateful for his company here on the ethical edge, in the no-man's-land between youth and age, between puritan guilt and affluent hedonism; what a pair we are, half-educated, half-old, half-married, half-happy. I should marry him and relieve a little of the guilt he suffers. He would like that: living alone in an apartment is frightening for a man like Eugene; he feels his ordinariness more than ever. Maybe I will marry him. What a nice man he is. I don't even mind his being an orthodontist. What if his proportions are less than heroic? Isn't goodwill a kind of prehensile heroism in this century? Does it really matter that Doug Savage thinks he is miserably average, even slightly substandard, and that Greta fears his mediocrity will place a ruinous stain on Seth's character? I cannot, after all, choose a husband just to please my friends.

Nothing is simple. After dinner we take a taxi back to Scarborough, sitting in the back seat with our arms around each other. The sky has cleared; there's a rounded, whited, theatrical moon cleanly cruising along behind us. Eugene's raincoat is still damp and rather cold against my thighs but I like the feel of his lips on my face, unhurried, soft.

❧

Coming into my mother's dimly lit living room with its flickering television screen and its cleanly shabby furniture, my senses play a perceptual trick on me: I see, it seems, not those who are actually there—my mother with her mending, Judith with her book, and Martin with his newspaper—but the ghostly shadowed presence of those who are missing. My father—shy, secretive, stoic, perpetually embarrassed—reading his paper much as Martin does, with hunched concentration as though he were perched temporarily in a doctor's waiting room. And Judith's children, Richard and Meredith: their absence is marked by her weary inattentiveness to the novel she's reading, the way she jerks the pages over; her real life belongs to another place now. And Seth, the grandson my mother has not even inquired about, the grandson for whom she does not knit mittens or mufflers and whose birthdays she does not remember (he is, after all, the extension of a daughter who has twice disgraced her family, first by running away and then by getting divorced); Seth who is the most important person in my world is suddenly briefly visible, filling this little room with his absence.

"Seth!" I suddenly exclaim.

"What's the matter?" Judith says, looking up.

"I've forgotten to phone Seth."

"It's not too late, is it?" Eugene asks, hanging up his raincoat.

"Do you mean long distance?" my mother asks.

"I just want to see if he's all right."

"But it's long distance."

"It's after eleven," Judith says helpfully. "Don't the rates go down after eleven?"

"After twelve, I think," Martin says.

"It's all right," I tell my mother. "I'll leave the money for the call."

"A waste of money," she shrugs. "And when you've been out to a restaurant and everything."

"I really must see how he is."

"But you're going home Friday night. Why would you want to go and run up the phone bill for nothing?"

"But I have to. I really must," I insist, knowing I sound unreasonable and shrill. "I simply couldn't sleep a wink tonight unless I know everything is all right."

"But what could go wrong?" my mother says giving one last dying protest.

"There's the phone ringing *now*," Eugene says. "Maybe it's Seth calling *you*."

But it isn't Seth. It's Doug Savage and he's phoning from Calgary.

"Hiya, Char," he says as breezily as though he were phoning from next door.

"Doug!" I stumble, a little confused. "Well, hello."

There is a short pause—perhaps we have a poor connection—and then I hear Doug saying, "Just wanted to tell you not to worry."

"Worry?"

"Just wanted to let you know everything's fine."

"But . . . but what are you doing in Calgary?"

"Oh, you know me, just a little trip. Always here, there, or somewhere."

"And Greta?"

Another pause. "Has Greta phoned you at all?"

"No. Was she going to?"

He hesitates. "Just thought she might give you a buzz."

"Well, no she hasn't, but as a matter of fact I thought I'd phone her tonight. Have a word or two with Seth."

"Oh, God, Char, save your shekels. As a matter of fact, I don't think they're home tonight anyway."

"Are you sure?"

"Yes. Yes, I'm sure. Something about the band. A rehearsal, I think."

"Oh," I say, feeling suddenly let down and disappointed. "I forgot about that."

"Well, don't let it worry you. Everything's fine. Fine." His voice trails off.

"Maybe I'll try tomorrow night."

"Great idea. You do that. Having a good time?"

"What? Oh, yes, uhuh, a good time."

"Take care then. Bye for now."

"Bye, Doug. And Doug . . .?"

"Yeah?"

"Thanks for calling. That was really nice of you to think of phoning. But why . . . I mean why exactly *did* you phone me?"

"Didn't want you worrying, that's all. Just thought I'd let you know everything's fine. Good night then, baby."

"Good night," I say. And stupidly, cheerfully, add, "Sleep tight."

Chapter 5

"She never talks to me anymore," Judith is saying of her daughter Meredith. "Not the way she used to when she was a little girl."

Children. Judith and I lie in bed listening to our mother in the kitchen making breakfast and we talk about our children.

"I'm always reading those articles about how parents are supposed to keep the lines of communication open," Judith says. "And now and then out of duty I make a stab at it."

"And what happens?"

"Nothing. Absolutely nothing. She—Meredith—just smiles. Mona Lisa. At least *sometimes* she smiles. Other times she cringes. As though the thought that we might have something in common was unspeakable. Everyone's always telling me how charming she is, and it's true she's got this non-McNinn effervescence. And a kind of wild originality too, but to me she doesn't say one word."

"You don't sound as though you mind all that much," I say.

"Mind? Oh, I suppose I should. After all, I'm her mother, she's my only daughter, why shouldn't she be able to pour out her heart now and then. But the truth is, Charleen, I couldn't bear it if she did. All that anguish."

"You must be curious though."

"In a way. I'm always wondering what she's thinking

about. Or what she does when she's not home. After all, she's eighteen. But eighteen is such a . . . well . . . such a suffering age. Remember? Sometimes I feel I've only just recovered from it myself. To listen to her ups and downs would kill me, and I think she knows it too. She senses it. She's got a kind of rare psychic radar—she always had but now and then she looks so bedeviled that I'm afraid she's going to break down and take me into her confidence. She's come close a couple of times. But then she stops herself. I can almost see her mumbling her vows of silence. And, strangely enough, I'm rather proud of her for it, for going it alone. I admire her for it. And I'm grateful, even though I know I'm failing her somehow, I'm grateful to be left alone."

"What about Richard?" I ask her.

"Richard," she shrugs. "He's always kept things to himself. Of course he's a boy. They're always more secretive. I suppose that's what you call a sexist judgment. Does Seth confide in you?"

I pause for a moment, not really wanting to admit that he doesn't. "No," I say slowly, "but I don't think it means anything."

It's true that most of the time these days Seth and I speak to each other in monosyllables—sure, yeah, okay—but these words are our accepted coinage of familiarity, the sort of shorthand which forms unconsciously between people who are naturally in harmony. It has never occurred to me to think that his lack of explicit communication might be an attempt to hide something from me; his nature has always been exceedingly open, and, if anything, it is this openness that worries me, openness with a suggestion of vacuum, a curious, perhaps dangerous acquiescence.

"I used to think it was strange," Judith is saying, "that we never told Mother anything when we were girls. All my friends used to rush home and tell their mothers everything. But we never did. At least I never did."

"Neither did I," I say firmly. "Never once."

"You know," Judith says thoughtfully, "looking back, I don't think it's all that strange. I think she must have sent out a kind of warning signal, a thought wave, saying 'Don't tell me anything because I've got enough to cope with as it is.' "

"Perhaps," I nod.

"Anyway," Judith continues, "I've come to the place now where I know she and I will never be able to talk. I'm absolutely sure of it."

Her certainty surprises me; it seems rather shocking to be so final, and I am forced to admit to myself that I have by no means surrendered. Somehow—it is only a question of finding the point of entry—I will break through our terrible familial silence. I came close, very close, yesterday drying the eggbeater.

Judith springs out of bed and begins to get dressed, but I lie under the blanket a few minutes longer; I am still sleepy, my mind begins to wander, but I am not thinking about Meredith or Judith or about my mother or even about the girl I once was. For some reason I am thinking about Seth. And the small string of worry that plucks away at me.

❦

After breakfast—toast and coffee in the kitchen—we take up yesterday's small routines. Eugene goes downtown for his conference, and Martin carries his newspaper into the back yard. It is rather cool outside; a wooly sun struggling through massed clouds, the grass still wet from yesterday's rain. My mother sets up the ironing board in the kitchen (the smell and sight of its scorched cover pierces me with nostalgia) and she presses, through a clean, damp tea towel, the dress she will wear for her wedding. Cocoa-brown crimpeline with raised ribs, a row of dull, wood-looking buttons down the front, long sleeves and no collar.

"It came with a scarf," she says, frowning narrowly, "as if a scarf made up for no collar." Her lips turn inward thinly, visible, measurable emblem of her complaint. "But I'm certainly not going to wear it, all those bright colours, cheap, of course it was in the March sales; nothing is well made anymore, imagine not even a collar. But it will have to do, that's all there is to it."

I am thinking: the wedding is Friday, tomorrow is Thursday and with luck I'll be seeing Brother Adam at last. Today is Wednesday; today I am having lunch with Louis. He is coming for me at eleven. When I asked Judith if she enjoyed her lunch yesterday, she smiled somewhat mysteriously. "It was interesting," she said.

"Did you find out anything about Louis?" I asked.

"A little," she smiled, "and so will you."

For a moment I pondered this, and then I asked, "Where did you go?"

"A little place in the country."

"Where exactly?" I pressed her.

"West of Toronto. Weedham. Just a little spot."

"Weedham? Weedham, Ontario? Are you sure?"

"Yes," she had answered, puzzled. "Weedham. Spelled WEEDHAM. Being literal-minded, I naturally expected it to be full of weeds but it turned out to be a pretty little place. You'll like it."

Weedham. Weedham, Ontario. Watson. I am going to Weedham, Ontario. I am going there today. An arc of anticipation, not unlike sexual desire, brightens inside me. I look at the kitchen clock. Nine-thirty. In an hour and a half I will be sitting in Louis Berceau's little green Fiat bouncing along the road to Weedham, Ontario.

❦

I am sick, oh, I am sick with shame, I am in hell. I

want to die of it, oh God, such pain, such humiliation, to be so humiliated. Stupid, stupid, I am sick with shame, it won't go away, it's done, nothing will take it away, dear God.

I am lying on my mother's bed in the middle of the morning, I am rocking from side to side, my fists in my eyes. I want to moan out loud, I want to weep, but no one must hear me, no one must know, oh, the shame of it.

Martin. Martin knows. Will he tell Judith? I cannot bear the thought of Judith knowing. She would think it was—what?—she would think it was *amusing,* too amusing for words. It would be awful to hear her laughing over it; I couldn't stand that.

Yet, isn't it her fault, isn't she the cause of it's happening? If I hadn't been thinking about her and her peculiar baffling indifference to Martin, it would never have happened.

She had been so busily occupied after breakfast. She had settled down at the dining room table with her portable typewriter and her reference books and her lovely calf-hide attaché case which she snapped open on her lap; inside were bundles of five-by-seven cards, each bundle bound with a rubber band; I thought of the way Mafia men carry their wads of money. Her notes, she explained, and with an air of enormous concentration she had selected one bundle, had whipped off the rubber band with a clean snap, and, one by one, she arranged the cards around her in a large semi-circle, a zombie playing at solitaire. I watched admiringly, such concentration, such independence. Judith explained that she had set herself a deadline for her next book. "It's odd," she said to me, "I seem to be getting compulsive in my old age. Writing used to be just a kind of hobby. Now if a single day goes by without working, I feel as though the day's been lost."

Martin, on his way in from the back yard to get his book, had paused and regarded her affectionately. Judith gave him a level look over her circle of cards; she looked at him, but I could tell she didn't really see him; what she gave him was a wide spatial stare, an empty optic greeting as though he were a smallish portion of the wallpaper; then she broke her gaze abruptly, scratched her head with vigour and, slowly, thoughtfully, inserted a sheet of paper into her typewriter.

Martin picked up his book and went outside, and out of a kind of pity—I think that's what it was—I followed him.

For a few minutes we sat together on the back steps, letting the frail, glassy sunlight fall on our backs. The little lawn looked exceptionally fine. Louis had put some fertilizer on it, my mother had explained with her mixture of shyness and sarcasm, and two pounds of grass seed. Martin seemed rather lonely, rather bored, a little restless, he seemed glad enough of my company. I even dared to tease him a little about how he'd worried about Judith's outing with Louis; he had laughed at himself in an altogether pleasant way, and then we talked for a few minutes about modern criticism. Yes, we were starting to be friends. We were comfortable sitting there together; the sun was growing stronger; it might be a nice day after all, and I was just about to say so when Martin leaned over and whispered into my ear.

"Look, Charleen, just between us, what do you think of the archaic sleeping arrangements here?"

"Pardon?" I said. Our mother had always taught us to say pardon.

"The sleeping arrangements," he repeated. "You know, the boys' dorm and the girls' dorm."

"Well—" I started to say.

He leaned closer, he put his arm around my shoulder,

he whispered in my ear, "How about switching around tonight?"

"Martin!" I breathed, completely shaken.

"We could switch back later," he leered. "No one would ever know."

"Martin," I said again in a dazed whisper, "I couldn't. I couldn't possibly."

There was a short chilly silence. A dead hole of a silence.

Then Martin asked, "Why not?"

I stood up abruptly, choking back rage, "Because Judith happens to be my sister. My own sister. What kind of person do you think I am?"

"My good Christ, Charleen, don't go all moral on me."

"And what makes you think I would want to sleep with you anyway?"

Then, then Martin's expression underwent a profound shocking, nightmarish change. Then suddenly he began to laugh, very softly so that my mother, still ironing in the kitchen, wouldn't hear. Manic tears squeezed out of the corners of his eyes, he rocked back and forth on the step hugging himself, "Oh, Charleen, oh, my God, I can't stand it, it's so funny. I didn't mean you and me. Oh, God." He broke into another obscene spasm of laughter.

I stared. What was he laughing about? Had he gone crazy?

Then quite suddenly I understood. Then I knew.

"I meant you and Eugene," Martin gasped. "And Judith and me. After all," he continued, making an effort at control, "we are joined in holy wedlock and all that."

I hardly heard him. I dashed away, up the steps and through the back door. I ran past my mother and here I am in the bedroom, rocking and moaning in a suffering parody of Martin rocking and moaning on the back

steps. How he laughed. I could die, I could die, I wish I
could die.

❧

Louis will be here any minute. I roll over in bed and
look at the clock. I must get changed. I must try to look
cheerful and eager and grateful to be taken on an outing.

I put on my stockings and slip into my new orange
dress. Then I brush my hair, trying to turn it under
smoothly the way Mr. Mario had done. It doesn't look too
bad. And the dress looks surprisingly becoming. I even
hum to myself a jerky little comforting tune while I clean
my shoes with a Kleenex. They're still a little damp from
yesterday.

Too bad about Martin, I say to myself in mock dismissal, peering into the mirror. Just when we were starting to be friends. If only I'd laughed I might have carried
it off. Ah well, with my typical faulty reflex I blow it every
time, a fatal quarter-step behind the rest of the world.
Martin, without a doubt, will have been repelled by my
embarrassment; not only that, but I with my gross misinterpretation have left myself vulnerable to a host of
other questions: exactly what kind of a woman was I
anyway? Just answer that.

Then I hear the little car pulling up in front, I hear
Louis and Martin in the back yard talking about lawn
care. One last reassuring grimace in the mirror and I
emerge.

Louis does not embrace me, but he gives me a smile
and a cherishing handshake over the kitchen table. My
mother, sighing as she puts away the ironing board, says
sharply, "Don't be too late. I'm making my tunafish bake
for supper."

We walk to the car; Louis is cheerful and nimble and I
shorten my steps to match his. The sun is blazing mer-

rily overhead, and Martin and Judith walk with us to the street; Judith's writing is going well this morning and she seems immoderately happy. "Have a good afternoon," she sings.

I don't dare look at Martin. But after Louis has turned the ignition and we start to slide away from the curb, I turn back and find my eyes looking directly into his. His eyes look funny as though he is squinting into the sun. No, he isn't, no he isn't. He is—yes—he is winking at me.

Without thinking, without reflecting, I wink back, and then we move down the street, Louis and I, slowly, almost elegantly.

❧

Louis's car is a Fiat 600, a 1968 model, recently repainted, the interior worn but exceedingly clean. This is the car that takes my mother back and forth to the cancer clinic, this is the car that carries her out for Sunday drives, this is the car which in two days will become their car, used for their minor errands, for their weekly trips to the Dominion Store, for their little jaunts into the country.

Louis, as I had predicted, is a cautious driver. He sits tightly in the driver's seat, moving the steering wheel and gearshift with intense little jerks, with careful, choppy, concentrated deliberation. The car moves down the suburban streets, delicately shuddering, and Louis, leaning forward, appears rather gnomelike with his wreaths of wrinkles, his puckered, colourless mouth, his contained and benign ugliness. Taking the 401 he heads west across the city.

On the way to Weedham Louis talks about the wedding. And I think how strange that it is so easy for people to talk in cars. It must have something to do with the enforced temporary proximity or with the proportion of space or perhaps the sealed, cushioned interior silence which must resemble, in some way, the insulated room where Greta Savage meets each week with her encounter group. It is as though the automobile were a specially designed glass talking-machine engineered for human intimacy. Furthermore, in a car the need to watch the road diverts and relieves the passengers, giving to their conversation an unexpected flowing disinterestedness.

Louis clears his throat and explains that both he and my mother were anxious to avoid fuss and expense; that was why they decided to be married in my mother's living room in the middle of the afternoon. Afterwards there would be tea in the dining room. And a small cake which Louis has ordered from a bakery; a United Church minister, a local man, has been asked to perform the ceremony.

This last piece of information surprises me. The McNinns have always been vaguely Protestant; at least Protestant is the word Judith and I supplied when we were asked our religious denomination. But we had never been a church-going family. The reason: I am not entirely sure, but it stemmed, I think, from my mother's belief that people only go to church in order to show off their hats and fur coats and to sneer at those less elegantly dressed. Certainly it had nothing to do with those larger issues such as the existence of God or the requirement of worship.

"Is anyone else going to be at the wedding?" I ask Louis. No, he answers, only the family. He himself has no family, none at all anymore.

The neighbours. I wonder if the neighbours have any inkling that my mother is to be remarried on Friday. Has she told anyone or has she kept her secret? The leitmotif of her anxiety, for as long as I can remember, has been her fear of being judged by the neighbours; what would the neighbours think? When twenty years ago I ran away with Watson to Vancouver, she had been struck almost incoherent with shame: what would the neighbours think? All the other girls in the neighbourhood were going on to secretarial school or studying to be hairdressers, but her daughter—the shame of it—had eloped with a student, had left a note on her pillow and ridden off to Vancouver on the back of a motorcycle.

Later I learned from Judith exactly how shattered she had been, how for months she'd hardly left the house, how for years she'd been unable to look the neighbours in the face. The fact that I had not been pregnant as she had supposed, the fact that Watson and I had been quite legally if rather sloppily married before we set off for the west, and the fact that Watson, three years later, received his Ph.D. (with honours)—none of these things seemed to ease the terrible shame of my extraordinary departure. And then the divorce, the embarrassing blow of the divorce which for years I tried to conceal from her. No one else in the neighbourhood had a daughter who was divorced. The neighbours had daughters who were buying property in Don Mills and producing families of children who came visiting on Sundays. Our mother alone had been cursed by strange daughters: Judith with her boisterous disturbing honesty, bookish and careless, and I with my now fatherless child, my unprecedented divorce, my books of poetry. The neighbours' children hadn't dismayed and defeated and failed their mothers.

And now my mother is getting married and she doesn't, it seems, worry at all about what the neighbours will think. She doesn't care a fig; she doesn't care a straw. For after all these years she has, in a sense, triumphed over the neighbours. Or, more accurately, the neighbours no longer exist. Both Mr. and Mrs. Maddison with their wailing cats and shredded curtains have died. The MacArthurs—lazy Mrs. MacArthur, always hanging out the clothes in her dressing gown, and Mr. MacArthur with his gravel truck sitting by the side of the house—have moved to a duplex in Riverdale to be near their married daughter. The Whiteheads—he drank, she used filthy language—have gone to California. Mrs. Lilly and her crippled sister, so sinfully proud of their dahlias, have disappeared without a trace, and the Jacksons, whom my mother believed to be very common, have become rich and live in south Rosedale. All the houses in our neighbourhood are filled with Jamaicans now, with Pakistanis, with multi-generation, unidentifiable southern Europeans who grow cabbages and kohlrabi in their backyards and rent out their basements. My mother is not in the least afraid of their judgment on her. She has, after all, lived for forty years in her little house, she has lived on the block longer than anyone else, she is widowed old Mrs. McNinn, the woman who keeps a clean house, the woman who minds her own business; she is respectable old Mrs. McNinn.

❧

"We're almost there," Louis says, steering carefully. "Another mile or so."

"What a pretty little town," I exclaim. For Weedham, Ontario, in the blond, spring sunlight has a tidy green rural face. A sign announces its population: 2,500. Another sign welcomes visiting Rotarians. Still another, a billboard of restrained proportions, urges visitors to stop at the Wayfarers' Inn.

"That's where we're going," Louis says.

The Wayfarers' Inn at the edge of town is relatively new, built in the last thirty years or so, but in the style of more ancient inns it has a stone courtyard, a raftered ceiling, here and there curls of wrought iron, and rows of polished wooden tables ranged round the walls. Light filters glowingly through stained glass windows which, Louis explains, are the real thing; they were taken from an old house in the area which was being demolished.

"It's charming," I say politely.

Shyly he tells me, "I brought your mother here for lunch. When I asked her to marry me."

I am taken by surprise. In fact, I am dumbfounded, for I cannot imagine my mother submitting to the luxury of lunch at the Wayfarers' Inn. And it is even more difficult to imagine her absorbing—in this room at one of these little tables peopled with local businessmen and white-gloved club women—a declaration of love.

"Was it . . . sudden?" I dare to ask.

His face crinkles over his mushroom soup, engulfed in pleasant nostalgia. "Yes," he nods, choking a little. "Only three months after we'd met at the clinic."

His openness touches me, but at the same time I am unbelievably embarrassed. Much as I would like to pursue it, to ask him, "and do you really love each other?" I cannot; Judith might have, in fact she probably did. I am certain he told her too, just as I am certain he would tell me if I asked; why else has he brought me out for lunch if not to make me feel easy about him. But I draw back, I can't ask, not now at least. To pursue the subject beyond Louis's first eager revelation might diminish it, might bury it. Why shouldn't he love my mother? If there *is* such a thing as justice, then surely even the unloving deserve love. She's like everyone else, I suddenly see; inside her head are the same turning, gathering spindles of necessity; why shouldn't he love her?

Louis smiles at me with almost boyish gaiety, his teeth, dark ivory with flashes of gold at the sides, his wrinkles breaking like waves around the hub of his happiness—a happiness so accidental, so improbable and so finely suspended—hadn't Brother Adam written that happiness arrives when least expected and that it tends to dissolve under scrutiny. Better to change the subject.

I glance around the room, taking in the polished wood and coloured glass; a square of ruby-red light falls on Louis's soft old hair. "How did you find this place?" I ask him. "Had you been here before . . . before the day . . . you brought her out here?"

"Oh, yes, yes, yes," he is pleased with my question. "When I was teaching school—I used to be the wood-work teacher, your mother must have told you. Always was good with my hands." He spreads them for my inspection.

"Simple carpentry, nothing complicated, knife racks and wall shelves mostly. At the end of the school year, round about the middle of June, I'd say, we used to come out here, all the teachers, and have lunch." He coughs, a sudden attacking hack of a cough. "Sort of, you know, a celebration."

"Which school was it?" I ask politely.

"St. Vincent." He chokes again. "Not so far from where you went to school."

"St. Vincent," I say, remembering. "That's a Catholic school, isn't it?"

He nods, watching me closely.

"Some of the kids in our neighbourhood used to go there," I tell Louis. "The MacArthurs. Billy MacArthur? Red hair, fat, always in trouble?"

"I don't think I remember him," Louis says regretfully.

"Judith and I always kind of envied the Catholic kids. It seemed—I don't know—sort of exotic going to a school like that. Like a pageant. First communion and all those white dresses. And veils even. And catechism. And always calling their teachers Sister this and Father that."

Louis nods and smiles.

"But," I say thoughtfully, "I always thought that the teachers in those days had to be nuns and priests."

Louis nods again.

"But you . . ."

"Yes," Louis says.

Silence. "A priest?" I whisper.

"Yes," he says in a level voice, "a priest."

"I can't believe it."

"I wanted you to know."

"Does Judith . . ."

"I told her yesterday."

"And my mother. Of course she . . ."

"Of course."

"But—" I try to gather in my words, I struggle for the right words but there don't seem to be any for this moment, "but weren't you . . . I thought . . . weren't you married before?"

"Only to the Church," he says with a faint, modest rhetorical edge.

"But now . . ."

"I made the decision to leave," he says, "three years ago."

My mother is marrying a sick, seventy-two-year-old ex-priest, I can hardly breath, I cannot believe this.

"But Louis," I stumble on, "why did you . . . I mean, it's none of my business . . . but why did you leave?"

He is ready to tell me; he has, I can see, brought me here to make me understand. "It was when I first started to . . . get sick. I know it seems strange. You'd think sickness would make me cling to my vocation. But it wasn't like that."

"What was it like then?"

"I started to feel afraid."

"Of death?"

"I could never be frightened of death. I'm still a Catholic."

"What were you afraid of then?" I ask, but already I know. Oh, Louis, I know what it is to be afraid.

"I wasn't sure. I'm still not sure now. But I think I was afraid I'd missed half my life."

For a sickening half-instant I think he is referring to celibacy, surely he doesn't mean that.

"I'd never lived alone," Louis explains carefully. "I'd never had the strength. But then, when I got sick, it seemed possible. Anything seemed possible. It doesn't make sense, I know."

But to me it does make sense, for why had I married Watson? Because his sudden arrival into my life had said one thing: anything was possible. Possibility rimmed those first days like a purplish light; love was possible; flight was possible; my whole life was going to be possible.

"So you decided to leave?" I say to Louis.

He nods. His face has become alarmingly flushed. How difficult this must be for him. I want to reach out and pat his arm, but I'm too awestruck to move.

"I've been quite happy," he says, "surprisingly so. Of course, being alone has its problems too."

I know. I know.

"Then I met your mother."

I smile uncertainly.

He makes a little laced basket of his hands and says, "I hope you don't think . . . you don't think we're just old and foolish."

"Of course not," I gasp truthfully.

"Because we don't have . . ." he pauses, "surely you

realize ... we don't have all that ... much time." He says this lightly, he even gives a faint, ghoulish, baffling sort of chuckle which I find both shocking and admirable.

Now I *do* reach out and pat his hand, his chamois-coloured, brown-spotted, hairless little hand. We sit in the red and yellow and blue pooled light without saying a word. A young waitress takes our plates away and brings us ice cream in tiny imitation pewter bowls.

Louis sighs at last and says thickly, "It would have been nice ... nice ... to have a priest at the wedding, that's all. It doesn't matter though. Not really."

"You mean to perform the ceremony?" I ask him.

"Oh no. That would be a little ... uncomfortable for your mother, I think. But it would have been nice to have a priest, just to, you know, be there."

"Couldn't you invite one?" I ask him earnestly.

"It's awkward," he says. "I'm a little ... out of touch."

I tease the bitter chocolate ice cream with the tip of my spoon. I can't stop myself: I say, "Look, Louis, I know a priest. As a matter of fact I'm going to see him tomorrow. Why don't I ask him to come? I don't have to tell him anything about your being a priest. I could just invite him—you know—to my mother's wedding."

He tips his head to one side and smiles a startled amber-toothed asymmetrical smile; pleasure drains into his grouted eyes and, nodding his head, he surprises me by saying, "Why, that would be very kind of you."

❧

Louis's confession has refreshed him; he looks rather tired but he orders coffee with the happy air of a man who has discharged his purpose.

For me the revelation is not so speedily digested; it hangs overhead like a bank of fresh steam, and my imagination struggles to picture Louis of the clerical collar;

Louis of the ivory Sunday vestments, wafer in mouth, cup upraised; Louis as devout young novice; Louis as frightened lonely child—somewhere under the old, soft, yellowed skin that boy must still exist. It is too much for me—the idea of Louis as priest resists belief, but it must, it will be, assimilated.

And what, I ask myself, is so strange about my mother meeting a defrocked priest—an ex-priest, I should say, it is somehow kinder to think of him that way—certainly a lot of them are floating around these days. And how did I imagine they would look if not like Louis? Did I expect them to be exhausted and spiritual, hollow-eyed, pitted with recognizable piety, baroque in manner, fatherly and frightened with damaged holiness sewn into their fingertips? They were men, only men, assorted, various and unmarked. Was Eugene with his moist normalcy and gentle hands identifiable as an orthodontist? And Martin: to see him turning over the pages of the *Globe and Mail* in my mother's back yard, who would suspect the Miltonic peaks and canyons that furnished his intelligence: the very idea was ridiculous.

Meeting Watson Forrest when I was eighteen—there he was drinking orange soda in a run-down, soon-to-be-bankrupt drugstore—a short, frowsy boy of twenty-two with wrinkled corduroy pants, acne scars and tufted crown of reddish hair—I had not believed him at first when he told me he had graduated in botany from the University of Toronto, that he had already written his Master's thesis (what was a Master's thesis? I had asked) on rare Ontario orchids. Later, made restless by the romance of the North, Watson had turned to Arctic lichens; later still, drawn into the back-to-nature movement, he had focussed on the common pigweed and had theorized, often tiresomely, on the pigweed's ability to draw nutrients to the surface of the earth. Orchids to pigweed: Watson had continually evolved toward the more popular, more democratic, more ubiquitous forms of a plant life. Specialty was for those who were content to stand still. Watson had resisted, more than most, the stamp of profession.

And as for me, Charleen Forrest, who, seeing me buying oranges in the Safeway or mailing letters on rainy Vancouver corners, who would guess that I am a poet? My bone structure is wrong; all those elongations; all those undisciplined edges, the ridged thighs, the wirebrush hair, the corns on my feet, the impurities in my heart—how could I possibly be a poet, how could I, as some might say, sing in a finer key?

The truth is, I am a sort of phony poet; poetry was grafted artificially onto my lazy unconnectedness, and it was Watson—yes, Watson—who did the grafting. Watson made me a poet—at least he pushed me in that direction—by his frenzied, almost hysterical efforts to educate me. What a shock it must have been, when he recovered from the first sexual ecstasies, to find himself married to an eighteen-year-old girl of crushing ignorance. Our first apartment in Vancouver was crammed with the books he brought me from the library, books I read doggedly, despairingly, in an attempt to conceal from him the shallowness of my learning. I seemed always to be working against time; the bright lights of possibility he had lighted in my head were already flickering out one by one.

I took a short typing course in Vancouver and for three years I supported both of us by typing term papers for graduate students in the cluttered, dusty nest of our one-room apartment. And in between, in order to forestall Watson's ultimate disenchantment, I sweated through books of history, biography, science; in fact, whatever Watson selected for me. How he had loved the role of tutor, one of his many incarnations: he became a kind of magician and I the raw material to be transformed. His devotion to my education was, to be sure, less than altruistic: his first appointment was in sight; another incarnation, another role—that of brilliant young lecturer—awaited him, and he became, not without reason, worried about the handicap of a stupid wife.

Somewhere along the line my self-education ceased to be a wifely duty. Watson began edging into student politics and laying the groundwork for the *Journal*, and for me, sitting alone in the apartment, literature became a friend and ally. Surrounded by frayed basket chairs, brick-and-board book shelves, a card table desk, studio couch and bamboo blinds—the furniture, in fact, of the newly married—literature became the real world. And poetry, modern poetry, unlocked in me not so much a talent, but a strange narrow aptitude, a knack, at first, and nothing more.

My first poems were experiments; I built them on borrowed rhythms; I was a dedicated tinkerer, putting together the shapes and ideas which I shoplifted. And images. Like people who excel at crossword puzzles, I found that I could, with a little jiggling, produce images of quite startling vividness. My first poems (pomes) were lit with a whistling blue clarity (emptiness) and they were accepted by the first magazine I sent them to. Only I knew what paste-up jobs they were, only I silently acknowledged my debt to a good thesaurus, a stimulating dictionary and a daily injection, administered like Vitamin B, of early Eliot. I, who manufactured the giddy dark-edged metaphors, knew the facile secret of their creation. Like piecework I rolled them off. Never, never, never did I soar on the wings of inspiration; the lines I wrote, hunched over the card table in that grubby, poorly ventilated apartment, were painstakingly assembled, an artificial montage of poetic parts. I was a literary con-man, a quack, and the size of my early success was amazing, thrilling and frightening.

But after Watson left us, after he walked out on Seth and me, poetry became the means by which I saved my life. I stopped assembling; I discovered that I could bury in my writing the greater part of my pain and humiliation. The usefulness of poetry was revealed to me; all those poets had been telling the truth after all; anguish could be scooped up and dealt with. My loneliness could, by my secret gift of alchemy, be shaped into a less frightening form. I was going to survive—I soon saw that—and my survival was hooked into my quirky, accidental ability to put words into agreeable arrangements. I could even remake my childhood, that great void in which nothing had happened but years and years of shrivelling dependence. I wrote constantly and I wrote, as one critic said, "from the floor of a bitter heart."

And the irony, the treachery really, was that those who wrote critical articles on my books of poetry never—not one of them—distinguished between those poems I had written earlier and those that came later. (What grist for the Philistines who scoff at literary criticism.) To these critics my work was one arresting—"the arresting Charleen Forrest"—seamless whole. Which goes to show . . . .

Louis Berceau takes an enormous amount of sugar in his coffee. Four heaped teaspoons. I watch him—his hands are remarkably steady for a man of his age—dipping into the sugarbowl. The smiling girl of a waitress refills our cups several times, and Louis almost succeeds in emptying the bowl of sugar.

The mind is easily persuaded, a fact which Brother Adam mentioned in a recent letter, and Louis suddenly appears to me to be an altogether holy man sitting here stirring his sticky coffee. A monk. He inspires, in fact, a torrent of confession. In half an hour I have told him rather a lot about my marriage with Watson. He is an excellent listener, something I noticed yesterday in my mother's kitchen; he simply nods from time to time and fixes me with his opaque gaze. And out it all spills.

Watson, I tell him, was a man without a centre; he took on the colour of whichever landscape he happened to stumble across. Watson was a man who went to a Cary Grant movie and for a week after spoke in a light, slight, cocky English accent. He also did a weary, sneery Richard Widmark and—his favourite—a lean, mean, sinewy Dane Clark. Watson was a bit like a snake—the comparison is not really a good one for it suggests malice—but he was like a snake in his ability to continually shed his skin. Louis nods, and I hesitate, remembering that Louis too is a man who has shed his skin.

No, not like a snake, I correct myself, but like an actor who plays a number of roles one after the other, roles which he takes up energetically but later, with a kind of willful amnesia, shakes off and denies. Louis looks puzzled, and I try to explain. Watson's first incarnation I can only theorize about: he must have been a sort of child prodigy hatched into an otherwise undistinguished Scarborough family, bringing home to his bus-driver father and seamstress mother miraculous report cards and brimming with a kind of juicy, pedantic, junior-sized zeal. But by the time I met him, he had left that scrubbed good-son image behind and transformed himself into a studied, lazy dreamer of a student, tenderly anarchic, determinedly bumbling and odd. Oh, very, very odd. A structured oddity, though, which both thrilled and terrified him; he needed someone, me, to bring reality to the role. Later, as a married graduate student in Vancouver he had stunned me with a whole new set of mannerisms and attitudes; he literally fought his way into all-roundedness—he boxed, he ran for elections, he wrote articles on alfalfa, he signed petitions, he played softball, he even forced himself to attend chamber music recitals and read up on the history of ballet. And I had adored his earnestness, his determination, his rabid certainty which completed, it had seemed to me, some need of my own. I had not quite loved his Young Professor Self, his two year retreat—it seemed longer—into piped and bearded tolerant middle-class academe, his almost British equanimity, the completely unforeseen manner in which he began to utter whole networks of archaisms, words like vouchsafe and gainsay, words strung together with a troubling catgut of hitherto's, wheretofor's and whilst's; once, completely unabashed, he began a sentence with a burbling I daresay. It had been during that period that we actually bought a house with a garden. And actually conceived, with brooding deliberation, a child. House, wife, child, all he needed was the ivy. But already he was on his way to his next creation: rebellious young intellectual. For a while he did a balancing act between the two roles: one Sunday afternoon, sulky and depressed, the three of us had taken a walk around the neighbourhood. Seth, who must have been two years old at the time, walked between us, holding on to our hands. He was a little slow and unsteady, and Watson yanked him now and then angrily. But then we happened to pass by a house where an elderly couple were taking the afternoon sun. Seeing them, Watson had smiled gaily; he had swung Seth merrily to his shoulders in gruff fatherly fashion, crooning nonsense into his startled ears; this extraordinary display of affection had lasted until we were out of sight of the couple. Watching him, I had been sickened; that was when I knew he was a man without a centre.

As he careened toward thirty, he seemed to dissolve and reform with greater frequency, and each reincarnation introduced a new, more difficult strain of madness. Watson seemed unable, psychologically unable, physiologically unable, to resist any new current of thought. He was the consummate bandwagon man. Yet, I had loved him through most of his phases. Riding off to Vancouver on the back of his motorcycle, my face pressed for thousands of jolting miles into the icy smooth leather of his shoulders, hadn't I thought that I would be safe forever? And for most of the eight years we were together I tried to be tolerant, sometimes even enthusiastic. But what I could never accept was the way in which he coldly shut the door on his past lives. The fact that he so seldom wrote to his parents was a troubling warning; I could sympathize, but still it seemed heartless not to acknowledge the birthday gifts of knitted gloves and homemade fruitcake. Friends, abandoned along the way, wrote imploring letters—what is the matter with Watson, why doesn't he write or phone? The *Journal* which he founded in a burst of professional ardour became another dead end. He and Doug Savage quarrelled irrevocably over the definition and degree of scientific responsibility. And he refused to have anything to do with the Freehorns after they once teased him about his intermittent vegetarianism. Seth he regarded as a kind of recrimination, a remnant of a former, now shameful, life which he wanted to forget. Of course I saw that eventually I too would have to go.

"So it wasn't such a shock," Louis says, "when he . . . when you separated."

"It was still a shock," I tell him. "I knew it was coming, but I couldn't believe it when it actually happened."

When I look at snapshots of myself taken during that period I am amazed that I am not deformed by unhappiness, that I am not visibly disfigured, bent over and shredded with grief. In fact, except for my bitter, lime-section mouth, I look astonishingly healthy. In the first months I was so weighted with sorrow and relief that I slept twelve hours every night. I was so emptied out that I ate greedily and constantly, buying for myself baskets of fruit as though I were an invalid. My eyes in those photographs gleam like radium; perhaps I was crazed by the cessation of love, still disbelieving, always certain that Watson would return in another guise.

And in an entirely hopeless way I know I am still half-expecting him to turn up, remorseful, shriven, re-deemed. Why else am I keeping Eugene waiting if not for my poor bone of expectation? Waiting has become my daily religion. Tomorrow I must remember to ask Brother Adam why, after all these years, I am still wear-ing my four-dollar wedding band.

When Louis speaks again, he asks with phlegm-plugged caution the perfect question. "Where is your Watson Forrest living now?"

One lives for moments like this. "Here," I pronounce solemnly, feeling my tongue cooling in delicious irony. "Watson lives right here. Isn't that amazing, Louis? Can you believe it? He lives here in this very town."

Louis shows perhaps a lesser degree of astonishment than I would like, but nevertheless he shakes his head in slow, grinning wonder.

And both of us, sitting in silence over our coffee cups are stewing in the rarified, blood-racing excitement of knowing exactly what will happen next.

❧

The Whole World Retreat is two and a half miles south-east of Weedham, reached by a neglected section of secondary road. The young-brown-eyed waitress at the Wayfarers' Inn is pleased to give us directions. "We buy all our lettuce and onions from them," she dimples, "and I don't care what anyone says about them, they make the best whole-wheat bread you ever tasted. Sort of nutty like, you know what I mean. Crunchy. All our customers ask where we get it."

We take the road slowly, swerving here and there to avoid potholes still glittering with yesterday's downpour. The countryside is green and rolling like calendar country; and the farms, though small, seem prosperous with good straight fences, herds of healthy cows and cheerful country mail boxes: The Mertins, Russell K. Anderson and Son, Bill and Hazel Rodman, Dwayne Harshberger, and, at last, a mail box that announces in blocky, green letters, The Whole World Retreat. Louis pulls the car to a stop on the shoulder of the road.

Back at the restaurant we agreed that we would simply drive past the place. It would be fun—I had emphasized the word *fun*, while despising the sound of it—it would be fun, out of curiosity, to drive by and see what the place looked like. I had proposed this to Louis in my lightest, most floating accents, as though this were no more than a crazy whim, a mad impulse, as though I were one of those programmed eccentrics who love to do mad, mad, mad things on the spur of the moment. Like Greta Savage who spends her life crouched on the contrived lip of unreason with her: *who else does crazy things like eat sardines for breakfast, who else is mad enough to take a holiday in Repulse Bay, who else is demented enough to tune in everyday to the Archers.* I have long suspected that her insanity is partly an affectation; now I adopt her shrill cry—"I know it sounds silly, Louis, but let's, just for the fun of it, drive by."

An act of adolescence, for don't high school girls in love with their math teachers furtively seek out their houses so they can cycle by, half-drowning in the illicit thrill of proximity. I hate Louis to see this undeveloped, irrational side of my personality which hungers for cheap drama, but not enough to pass up the opportunity of seeing the Whole World Retreat. And besides, hasn't something more than chance brought me this close? Isn't there at least a suggestion of predestination in this afternoon's events, and hasn't Louis with his surprise revelation introduced a note of compelling, almost mystical significance? This day clearly has not been designed for rationality. Even though it is almost four o'clock, it does not seem right to turn back toward Scarborough where the tunafish casserole awaits, no doubt about it, already browning in my mother's oven, and where my mother herself waits with her contained, wordless questioning. Something entirely unforeseen has been set into action; I can feel the piping tattoo of my pulse in my throat, and, looking sideways at Louis's suddenly brightened eyes, I can see that he shares at least a measure of my excitement.

Beside the mail box a sign in heavy lettering announces: Green onions, Rhubarb, Homemade Bread, Fresh Eggs, Nursery Plants. And at the bottom in larger letters: Absolutely No Chemical Fertilizers. Louis and I sit, thoughtful for a moment, reading the sign and thinking our thoughts.

The house itself is set well back from the road. It is a top-heavy house, late Victorian in old-girlish brick, and its porch skirt of turned, white spindles gives it a blithe knees-up-Mother-Brown gaiety. Red and yellow tulips, not quite open, stand cheerful in a curved bed. The sloping front lawn is exceptionally beautiful with its twilled, gabardine richness and its fine finish of new growth.

There is no one in sight.

"They sell nursery plants," I remark to Louis.

"Yes," he says, "they do."

"I wonder what kind of things they have at this time of year."

"Hmmm."

"Actually," I take a deep breath, "actually I'd thought of buying some nursery plants."

No response from Louis.

I try again. "For you, Louis, the two of you. Something for the backyard. I thought it might make a good wedding gift."

More silence, and then Louis says cheerfully, "The perfect thing."

"We could just see what they have in stock."

"Are you . . . that is . . . are you sure?"

I pause. Then lunge. "Yes. I'm sure."

We leave the car—Louis checks both doors to make sure they are locked—and walks up the loose-gravelled drive toward the house. He stumbles slightly, then catches himself, but I don't even turn my head. I can feel excitement leaking in through my skin and for an instant I feel I might faint.

Up close the house looks slightly less picturesque. There is an old wringer washing machine on the porch, a pair of men's work gloves hanging on a nail (Watson's gloves?), two rain-sodden cartons of empty pop bottles. The screen door, rather rusty, has been inexpertly patched.

I knock.

"Hang on a minute," a woman's low voice calls from the shadows behind the screen, "I'm coming."

From inside the house we hear a young baby wailing. Baby! It takes my brain an instant to decode the message: a baby, oh God. Then plunging grief—Watson's baby. And in another instant I will be seeing Watson. He will come striding through that screen door and see me standing here with my old, grotesque vulnerability hanging around me like a hand-me-down raincoat. What am I doing here?

A young woman, plumply tranquil, wearing granny

glasses, pushes open the door. She wears a dirty, pink shirt over her jeans and on her hip rides a screaming, naked baby of about fifteen months. "Sorry to keep you waiting," she says in a flat but friendly southern Ontario voice. "I had the baby on the pot."

"That's all right," Louis says wheezing.

"What a lovely baby," I half moan . "Is it—" I peer closely, "Oh, it's a little girl."

"Faith," the woman says.

"Pardon?"

"Faith. That's her name."

Louis receives this information silently. He is searching his pockets for a handkerchief. Automatically, never missing a beat, my kindness act uncoils itself. "What an interesting name."

"My husband calls her Mustard Seed."

"Oh!" The word husband pierces me. "Oh?"

"Just a joke. Faith of a mustard seed. From the Bible."

"Oh, yes," my head bobs.

"Well," she says smiling and shifting the still wailing baby to her other hip, "is there anything I can help you with?"

"We saw your sign," Louis says indistinctly. His asthma is threatening; he is alarmingly tired. I should never have dragged him here; we should never have come.

"Nursery plants," I say, clearing my throat. "We were interested in nursery plants."

"Terrific," the young mother beams. (Young! she can't be older than twenty-five. I am shaken by a shower of dizzy shame for Watson, this is too much.)

"I wanted to buy something for a wedding gift," I say. "A shrub, I thought, something like that."

"Just a sec," the woman says. She peers over her

shoulder into the kitchen. "My husband can show you what we've got. Of course, it's early, there's not much, but he can at least show you what we've got."

"Look," I say, taking a step backwards, "we'll come back another time. When you've got more in."

She won't stop smiling at me; her yeasty good cheer glints off her glasses, making creamy Orphan Annie coins of her eyes. "You might as well have a look," she says. "He's right here. He'll be glad to show you what we've got."

Footsteps across the kitchen floor, a man's footsteps, a man's muffled pleasant voice saying, "I'm coming." *Watson.*

But the face which appears in the doorway isn't Watson; it is younger, leaner; it has blue eyes. And this man is taller. Not only that but he has straight, straw-coloured hair hanging to his shoulders and a muscular chest moving under his T-shirt. "How do you do," he says, stepping onto the porch.

"How do you do," Louis and I chorus. Louis gives me a quick, quizzing look, and I manage to flash him the smallest of smiles.

"Hey," the young man says, squinting at me, "hey, aren't you Charleen Forrest?"

Run, I cry, *bolt. Now. Make for the road. Leap in the car, run.* "Yes," I say, "I am."

"Well, for Pete's sake," the smiling girl says, showing a place in her lower jaw where a tooth is missing.

"Can you beat that," her husband mutters with awesome gentleness. The baby stops whimpering and holds herself suddenly rigid. Then she wets herself; a surprisingly wide stream of pale baby pee creams off her mother's hip and splashes to the porch floor.

"Oh hell," the girl says with equanimity, stepping sideways out of the puddle.

"Charleen Forrest," her husband murmurs again. He sends me a warm, slow smile.

"How do you know who I am?" I ask, thinking: Watson, he must keep a picture of me, imagine that, who would have thought it of Watson?

"I've got all your books," he says. "And your picture's on the back. I would have recognized you anywhere."

"Oh," I say, disappointed.

"And then, of course, knowing Watson—" he shrugs and smiles, "not that that matters. We really dig your stuff. Cheryl and I."

"That's for sure," Cheryl says.

"Thank you," I say absurdly. Sweetly?

"Don't suppose you've seen Watson lately?" he asks me.

I stare.

"We sure miss him," Cheryl says in tones soft with regret. "It's just not the same here without Watson. Is it, Rob?"

"He was a beautiful guy," Rob says mournfully. "One real beautiful guy, that's all I can say."

"But look," I say to the two of them in a sharply raised voice, "he still lives here? Doesn't he?"

"Gosh, no," the gap-toothed Cheryl says. "Gee, it's been—what Rob?—two years now?"

"Yeah. More than two years. He split—let's see—it was round the end of March, wasn't it, Cheryl? Two years ago March. We haven't had a postcard from him even."

"But that's impossible," I tell them firmly. "It can't be true."

A look of concern passes between them, a look which firmly shuts me out, and I feel a nudge of suspicion. Are they trying to protect Watson, pretending he isn't here, trying to fool me like this?

"You see," Rob says, taking the baby from his wife, "Watson sort of, well, I guess you could say he got disenchanted. You know, with the whole scene, the whole group thing, what we were trying to do here."

"And the others," Cheryl prompts him.

He nods. "That was part of it too, I guess. There were about eight of us, Cheryl and me and the others. All of them younger than Watson. Mostly kids who'd dropped out of the whole city thing. Younger kids. Watson kept saying they were getting younger and younger all the time. He finally got to thinking, I guess, that it was time to move on to another scene."

"He was forty," I tell them abruptly. "Two years ago he had his fortieth birthday. In March."

"Gee," Cheryl says, "Forty!"

"But he must be here," I insist, "because every month he sends me a cheque from here. The child support money. For our son. He sends it every month. Always right on the fifteenth and it comes from here. Weedham. I know because I always check the postmark."

They laugh softly as if I'd said something outlandishly amusing. "That's Rob," Cheryl explains grinning. "Rob's the one who sends off the cheque."

"You mail me the cheque?" I ask dazed.

"It was the one thing Watson wanted me to do. He left, Christ, I don't know how many postdated cheques. Enough 'til the boy's eighteen, I think, isn't it Cheryl?"

"And enough money in the bank to cover them. That's what's important, I guess, eh?"

Rob continues, "He wrote a note, left it on the backdoor, this door here. All about the cheques, like where to send them and all. And I haven't forgotten one, not so far anyways."

"That's very kind of you," I say, feeling my mouth freeze with etiquette and sorrow.

"But you know," Rob rambles on, "I might forget sometime. Memory's not my strong point, ask Cheryl here. What I should do, since you're standing right here, is just give you the whole bunch of cheques. Right now. That way you'd have them right with you and you could just cash them as the dates roll round."

Cheryl nods enthusiastically at this piece of logic, and I feel suddenly flattened by confusion. Something inside me twists, something sour, something sharp, but I manage to smile and say, "Sure. Why not? While I'm here I might as well take them with me."

Cheryl goes into the house and comes back in a minute with a large brown envelope. "They're in here. You can count them if you want."

"That's okay," I say. "I don't have to count them. And thank you."

"No need to thank us," Rob says. And then he adds wistfully, "We sure miss Watson. It's not the same."

Should I ask them? I have to. "Where's Watson living now?"

"East," Rob says. "He went east."

"You mean the Maritimes?"

He laughs again. "No, not geographical east. Philosophical east. He was into the mysticism thing. Hindu mainly.

"Buddha too," Cheryl offers.

"You don't know where he went?" I can hear a shameful pleat in my voice. "Geographically, I mean?"

"No. Like I said, we haven't heard anything from Watson. Not in two years. Just that note stuck on the door. He didn't say where he was going, just that he was going East. With a capital E. East."

"And that's all?"

"That's all. The others, they kind of drifted off one by one too. After the baby was born. Some of them couldn't really ride with the baby thing. So now there's just Cheryl and me. And Mustard Seed here." He blows a noisy kiss into the baby's fat neck. "We're just kind of a family now, you might say. We still do some farming but not like when Watson was here. But our bread baking operation is going along pretty well."

"And the nursery plants," Cheryl adds.

"Oh, yeah, the nursery plants. That's what you folks were looking for, wasn't it?"

Behind the greenhouse in the spilled, late afternoon sunlight, Louis and I pick out some good healthy shrubs: six mock orange with their roots bound in sacking. And a flat of petunias, white and pink mixed. I pay Rob with a twenty-dollar bill, and he helps Louis put them in the trunk of the car. Then we shake hands all around and head for home.

I sit beside Louis with the brown envelope on my lap and it occurs to me that I will never again receive a message from Watson, Watson my lapsed-bastard, first-love, phantom husband. The last link—a smudged, treasonous postmark— has just been taken away from me. It wasn't much, but it was better than nothing. The arrival of Watson's cheques—the regularity, the suppressed silence—offered me something: not hope, certainly not hope, I am not such a fool as that, but a pencil line of connecting sense in the poor tatter I'd made of my life. A portion of renewal. And a means by which the worth of other things might be tested. Damn you, Watson.

"There, there," Louis is saying. "There, there now." The curving kindness of his voice—what a good man he is—makes me conscious of the tears falling out of my eyes.

Chapter 6

It takes us a long time to get back to Scarborough. For twenty minutes we're stalled in traffic. An accident maybe; it could be anything. So many people in this city. Louis's cautious driving style, so reassuring earlier in the day, is an irritant now that it's five-thirty, five-forty-five, six o'clock. A heavy rug of sky pushes down on the streaked sunlight; my head aches. At exactly six-thirty my mother will be placing her Pyrex casserole on the blue, crocheted hotpad in the middle of the kitchen table. I twitch with nerves. Doesn't Louis know how punctual my mother is about meals? Well, he'll soon learn.

Louis tries to cheer me up by talking about his favourite poet, Robert Service. I wish he wouldn't. *Please, Louis, don't.* His voice cracks with strain and it's disappointing to hear he hasn't read Hopkins. But his lips smack with pleasure over a stanza of "The Shooting of Dan McGrew," and I chide myself for expecting more than I deserve.

At last Scarborough, the shopping centre, the school where I went to kindergarten (I was the one whose socks were always sliding down), the grid of streets so minutely familiar but whose separate names now seem cunningly elusive. At seven o'clock Louis pulls up in front of the house, and from the living room window a face (whose?) registers our return.

"Aren't you coming in, Louis?" I ask. "Aren't you staying for supper?"

"I'm a little tired," he says weakly. "This chest of mine."

"Are you sure you won't come in? Just for a minute?"

"I think I'll have an early night," he says. "You'll explain to your mother, won't you?"

"Sure."

"I'll bring over the shrubs in the morning. Put them in first thing in the morning."

"Fine. And Louis . . . thanks for everything." I emphasize the word everything; suddenly I'm tired, too.

"Good night."

"Good night."

I'm late. Will my mother dare to scold me. Yes, she won't be able to help herself. This in itself is alarming enough, but something else is even more frightening, something unnatural about the crouched, waiting house, or is it that strange car parked in front? Or perhaps there are such things as psychic waves, perhaps Greta Savage is right after all about telepathic electricity, perhaps tense, waving vibrations actually penetrate my skin as I walk around to the back door. I don't know. But coming into this house alone at this hour makes me suddenly and ridiculously weak with fear.

The first thing I see in the kitchen is my mother's tuna fish casserole. Its tender breadcrumb crust is unbroken. A serving spoon lies tentatively by its side, but the table hasn't been set. How odd.

Eugene. What is he doing here? He is supposed to be at the Orthodontists' banquet eating warmed-up roast beef and hard little scoops of mashed potato. He crosses the kitchen and presses me in his arms. Eugene, not here, really, can't you see my mother's standing right here?

354

My mother is standing by the stove. Her hands can't seem to find a resting place. They're not clutched behind her back, they're not clenched at her hips, not folded across her chest, not nervously laced beneath her chin; they are floating freely in a frightening pantomime of helplessness.

Martin and Judith. They are standing in the doorway. How curious, they aren't actually touching each other, so why do they seem to swim before me in blurry tandem unison like synchronized dancers. Married people grow to look alike—it must be true—just look at those two twin jaws slung in the same attitude of guarded concern. Concern? What is the matter with them?

And then there are the two policemen. Why do policemen wear that dispirited shade of blue, snow-shovel blue, looseleaf notebook blue? Two policemen sitting at the kitchen table. Sitting there. But when I come in the door, they shuffle politely to their feet. A dream, of course.

"Charleen," Eugene holds me close.

"Thank heavens you're home," Judith's mordant contralto escapes in a gasp.

"Now don't get excited, Judith," Martin says. "Give her a minute, everyone."

"Are you Mrs. Forrest?" one of the policemen demands.

"Wouldn't you like to go into the living room?" my mother frets.

"You must be calm," Eugene says into my shoulder. "You must try to remain calm."

"And your regular domicile is Vancouver?"

"Just take it easy, take it easy now."

"Keep things in proportion . . ."

"You'll find the living room more comfortable."

"We have one or two questions for you, Mrs. Forrest."

"Here, Charleen, sit down. Martin, get her to sit down."

"You'd better sit down; you must sit down."

"There, that's better isn't it?"

"And when was your departure from Vancouver, Mrs. Forrest?"

"Leave her alone for Christ's sake, can't you see she's confused."

"Take it easy, Char, take it easy—"

" . . . if you'll just answer a few questions . . ."

"The living room is cooler and you could . . ."

"Keep your balance, that's the important . . ."

"Your exact arrival in Toronto was . . .?"

"Hey, give her a chance . . ."

"You tell her."

"I'm only trying to help."

"I think Eugene should be the one. He's . . ."

"We understand this is upsetting, Mrs. Forrest . . ."

"The living room . . ."

" . . . unfortunately they expect a complete report at headquarters."

"Charleen, listen to me. Are you listening?"

"Yes." Was that my voice? Was it?

Eugene is sitting next to me with both my hands in his and he is saying the most preposterous things. Incredible things. How melodramatic—I wouldn't have thought it of Eugene. Seth has disappeared, Eugene is saying that Seth has disappeared. What a joke. Is it a joke? It can't be because these policemen are writing things down and besides my mother doesn't like jokes. And neither, I realize for the first time in my life, neither do I.

Seth has been taken somewhere by Greta Savage. Taken away. Several days ago. No one knows for sure when. Or how. But they have both been missing for several days. Now don't get excited. No one knows where they are at this precise moment, but in all probability they are safe. Greta Savage has disappeared with my son and Doug Savage has called in the police, that is what has happened, Charleen.

"Say something, Charleen," Eugene commands.

"Is she going to faint?" Judith's arm is on my shoulder.

"It looks like it. Someone get some water."

"Are you going to faint, Charleen?"

"Darling."

"No," I say distinctly. "No, I'm not going to faint."

All I have to do is hold on to consciousness. Nothing is more important than that, for the moment nothing more is required of me. But if I shut my eyes for even a second I will never see Seth again. I must sit still, I must pretend I am composed of dry, unjointed wood, if I move one inch from this table there will be an explosion.

I must try to understand. Slowly, perfectly like a child memorizing the Twenty-third Psalm, *He restoreth my soul for his something-or-other sake.* Certain facts must be absorbed.

Doug Savage has been trying to reach me all day. The last call came from Parry Sound. He phoned at least four times today. Finally he agreed to talk to Judith. Judith phoned downtown immediately and had Eugene paged at the conference. Eugene came home at once and since then he has been trying unsuccessfully to reach Doug Savage. But Doug Savage promised Judith he would phone back at eight o'clock. That's less than an hour, Judith says, only fifty minutes now, and until then there is nothing anyone can do.

Seth and Greta have been missing all week. While I was eating English muffins on the train, while I was kissing Eugene in the back of a taxi and, Oh God, while I was chasing around the countryside with Louis Berceau on a foolish, pointless, private, childish quest Greta and Seth disappeared; they took the Savages' car in the middle of the night—there is some confusion about which night it was, Sunday? Monday? The Vancouver police think—there is reason to believe—that Greta may have given Seth some sleeping pills. Sleeping pills!

For the first two days Doug thought he could avoid calling in the police. He had a hunch that Greta might have taken Seth to a cottage they own in the mountains in Alberta. He borrowed a car and drove all night, but when he got there, he found only rumpled beds and tire tracks. They must have spent the first night there. After that, he thought they might have gone to Winnipeg where Greta has old friends, but when he got there, twenty-four hours later, he couldn't find any trace of her. So he phoned here last night— Can that possibly have been only last night?—hoping Greta had made some kind of contact; after that he phoned the police. There had been no alternative.

The police: they are looking right across the country, but they have to move cautiously (are they dealing with a mad woman?). They don't know. I don't know. The situation has been judged too risky for public appeals, but they are making all sorts of inquiries. It seems Greta is driving mostly at night. A gas station attendant just outside Thunder Bay is almost certain they stopped there: a woman and boy resembling the police description stopped for gas and a hamburger. Did the woman appear dangerous? No. Had the boy appeared intimidated or drugged? No one had noticed. Which way were they headed? The attendant wasn't sure. All he could remember was that they were in a hurry.

❧

There is nothing to do but wait until Doug calls again.

The two police officers wait courteously in the living room. My mother frets about whether or not to offer them coffee. Eventually she decides against it. She is more confused than alarmed; her six-thirty supper has been disrupted and in some indefinable way the untouched casserole precludes the making of coffee. As always she is just outside of events, hovering—ghostlike but demanding—at the perimeter. "How could you leave him with people like that?" she scolds me sharply. "What kind of friends are they?"

Judith tries to soothe her, but Martin flushes with anger. Martin is convinced that what I need is a stiff drink, but of course there is nothing, not in this house. "I've got some Scotch in my suitcase," he says, suddenly assertive. He brings it out, and my mother, her hands still flapping wildy, finds a juice glass. But my stomach leaps and dissolves; I can't even look at it; Martin picks up the glass, regards it mildly, and then drinks it off neat.

Judith's voice floats over my head in a sort of chanting reassuring descant. "Look at it like this, Charleen, they've both been seen alive and well. Yesterday. So they're okay. Maybe she's a bit on the crazy side, but she isn't dangerous, that's what Doug Savage said on the phone. He said try not to get Charleen upset because Greta wouldn't hurt a fly, it's just a matter of hours before they find him."

Martin pats me awkwardly on the crown of my head. "Look here now, Charleen, she's a little unbalanced maybe, but, God, who isn't, and you've known her for years. You know she wouldn't do anything to hurt him, nothing *really* crazy. You've got to keep thinking what she's really like."

Eugene sits wordless beside me. He's not a wordy man, he never was a wordy man. He's still holding on to my hands, and I'm grateful to him. There's nothing to say. And nothing we can do.

I think of the huge distance between Toronto and Vancouver, the blending agricultural regions, the mountain ranges, river systems, squares of acreage, contours, city limits, county lines, townships and backyards with chickens and shrubs and children. I try to hold that whole terrain in my head; it is a numbing exercise, though it shouldn't be all that difficult, for haven't I just crossed that country myself? Haven't I touched every inch of it? I think of all the people strung out over that distance, imbedded in their separate time zones. Seven-thirty: they're washing dishes. I can hear cutlery right across the country dropping into drawers. They're bathing children, playing bridge, reading newspapers, all of them magically sealed in their preserving spheres of activity. Out there in all that darkness is Greta's car, a blue Volvo—it has to be there—cruising past apartment houses and suburbs and farms; and these people, shutting their windows, watering their lawns, walking their dogs, they just *allow* her to go by. Maybe they even wave to her. Maybe she waves back, she has always been so friendly, so pathetically friendly. She would do anything to help a friend; she is so kind, she wouldn't hurt a fly. Remember that, above all remember that; she wouldn't hurt a fly.

❦

Eight o'clock. We wait in the kitchen. The silence is minutely detailed like a blueprint for a piece of immensely complicated machinery. The minutes are sharply cornered and pressing, and each one hangs rigidly separate.

Eight-fifteen. Why doesn't Doug call? Something has happened. One of the policemen asks if he might phone in a report.

"No," I gasp.

Eugene shakes his head, "Better not tie up the phone here." The policeman nods politely and asks if he might use the next-door neighbour's phone.

At this my mother looks up, horribly alarmed, and I see her mouth twist into its tight diminishing shape. I know that shape, its denials, negations, interdictions, the way it closes to inquiries, the way it forbids, the way it ultimately blames and refuses. Now. She is going to do it now, going to give one of her terrible, unforgiving no's.

But she doesn't. Bewilderment—or is it fatigue?— makes her thin lips collapse. She nods a shaky assent. Then she rises and puts the kettle on.

In a moment the policeman returns; there are no further developments, he tells us. We will have to wait a little longer, that's all.

My mother is moving around the kitchen putting her trembling hands to work. (What have I done to her, what have I done to her this time?) Now she is making tea, now she is arranging jittery cups on a tray. Judith gets up to help her and together they begin to make sandwiches. How extraordinary, my mother actually has a package of boiled ham in the refrigerator. And cheese. Sandwiches are disaster fare; who would have thought my mother had a sense of occasion. She and Judith stand with their backs to us buttering bread. They are exactly the same height; I never noticed that. Their elbows move together, marionettes on a single lateral string. Abstract kinship suddenly made substantial. But why am I thinking about ham and cheese and kinship? Why am I not thinking about the centre of this disaster; why am I not thinking about Seth?

Because I can't bear to.

Seth dead. No, that's not possible. It's not possible because my life isn't possible without him; it's not possible when I'm sitting here, wired with reality. Pulse, heartbeat, nerves, breath, sudden sweating, hurting consciousness, all the signs of life failing me now by *not* failing. In this kitchen every small sound is magnified; my mother's half-invalid, half-despairing shuffle, the policemen laughing in the living room (laughing!), Martin crashing into his ham sandwich, the sugar spoon which strikes with dead neutrality on the formica table. And my eyes: suddenly I can see with wolfish clarity. I can see the neat hem on my mother's sheer kitchen curtains, her tiny over and under and over stitches, and through the curtains a glittering, mocking, glassware moon is coming into view. Evening. Nine o'clock. Doug Savage, why doesn't he phone? Seth dead. No, it's not possible.

Sleeping pills. Greta stuffing Seth with sleeping pills; she is so small, such a weak, wiry woman, something dark about her face, always a sense of shadow. But Seth is quite strong for his age, well developed, remarkably healthy. His health is startling; something godlike nourishes him despite his inheritance; I've never been able to understand it. I picture his strength against Greta's weakness, and a tiny flashbulb of hope goes off under my skin; she can't possibly harm him.

Then I remember how clever she is, how she is veined with a wily unaccountability. Her secrecy about Watson's letters; she hints she has heard from him but says nothing more. And her sudden, piercing, illogical bursts of purity. Madness? Not really madness. How did Doug once put it to me? "Greta is rational enough, it's just that her rationality is not as evenly distributed as it is in more balanced people." Certainly she is not a fanatic, not in the accepted sense of that word, but she suffers from blinding pinpricks of virtue. The way, for instance, she once burned Doug's thesis on the diseases of short ferns because she believed it had been conceived to fill an artificial academic requirement. (Only by good fortune had she overlooked the carbon.)

Her weaving too is girded by purity; the way she refuses to touch synthetics and swears to give up weaving altogether if she is forced to work with wool which is chemically dyed and treated. Then there is her violent anti-smoking stance. And her contempt for Eugene and what she considers his crass profession. Her leaps into various systems of the human potential movement. Her bright, birdlike fixations: the insistence (I suddenly remember) with which she had determined to pick up Seth at school last week. Then there is her refusal to have children; here perhaps her fanaticism is grounded on objectivity, for she would have made a shocking mother for all her devotion to Seth. But most painful to me has always been her clinging admiration for Watson; she once confided in an orgy of tactlessness that she "reverenced" Watson's decision to alter his life. She keeps track of him with passionate persistence, long after everyone else has given up, smothering him with letters, forcing him to acknowledge her existence, coercing him by her indefatigable energy to keep her supplied with news of his latest incarnations. Ah, Greta, poor Greta, poor, twisted, buggered-up Greta, where are you? It's nine-thirty and I'm going crazy, where are you?

❧

In the living room the policemen have turned on the television. Hawaii Five-O. Screams, sirens, the sound of bullets, throaty accusations, weeping, all so bearably unreal. What a poor tissue fiction is, how naively selective and compressed and organized, justice redressed in exactly sixty calculated minutes, the violence always just marginally tolerable, the pressure just within the bounds of human acceptance, tragedy in an airtight marketable tin.

Martin paces. My mother and Judith wash plates and cups, and Eugene goes next door to phone a car rental firm. He has decided that the minute Seth is located we must have a car to get to him.

I think bitterly of Watson. Wherever he is, he is being spared this hour. Of everything he has left undone as a father this seems the worst.

Even Louis—I think of him with a flash of envy—even Louis in his furnished room, so wonderfully protected from all this. So innocently unaware. What peace not to know.

And Brother Adam, you with your abstract wisdom, your fire-escape view, you know nothing of what I'm suffering, you are a dream, you don't even exist for me now.

And Seth, what are you thinking, wherever you are? Are you safe?

❧

Judith, always compulsive, is tidying the kitchen. She covers the tunafish casserole with a dinner plate and puts it in the refrigerator. Then she swirls a wet cloth over the table, picking up my purse and putting it on top of the cupboard.

"What's this?" she asks, picking up an envelope.

I am slow to react; am I losing consciousness after all? Then I say, "Oh. That's mine."

It is the envelope containing the child support cheques, my last connection with Watson. A business envelope, eight-by-eleven in business-coloured brown. Closed with a huge paperclip.

I open it idly, and the cheques slide out on my lap. What a lot of cheques, twelve for each year, and yes—I count them—enough to last until Seth's eighteenth birthday. And a stack of addressed envelopes with a rubber band around them. There's even a sheet of postage stamps. How wonderfully organized of Watson, beneath his many layers he must still be in touch with that boy prodigy of his youth and with his dull parents who always paid their bills, in touch too with his unknown, sober ancestors who never ran away from their debts.

There is something different about the final cheque: it is dated for Seth's eighteenth birthday, May 21, and it is made out for five thousand dollars. Five thousand dollars! I feel my breath harden; how had Watson managed to save five thousand dollars? He must have been exceedingly careful over the years to save that much money. But how pointless, how useless, a piece of paper for a son who is missing. A son who can't be found.

I can't help it. I'm starting to cry. I can't help it. This piece of paper, this five thousand dollars—it isn't enough. It's so futile, it's just like Watson to make a gesture like this, so stagey, so impressive and so utterly, utterly useless.

But there's something else in the envelope. Still crying I pull it out. It's another piece of paper, a page raggedly torn from a notebook. But the message on it is carefully typed.

I have to read it twice before I realize what it is. It is Watson's farewell note, the one he must have stuck on the screen door before he left the Whole World Retreat. Rob and Cheryl, those two good children, had been more than worthy of the trust he placed in them, guarding not only the cheques but his final words of good-bye. How absurd, though, to write a farewell note on a typewriter, how somehow incongruous, how like Watson. The note he once left me, the one I burned in the barbeque, that note had been typed too. I had forgotten Watson could type; I had forgotten a lot about Watson. But I had not forgotten his embarrassing penchant for prophecy; reading his words of good-bye, it all seems suddenly very familiar.

Dear Brothers and Sisters,
These words are written in love and sadness.
The life of the spirit is love
but it is also containment and peace.

It is time for me to leave you.
Time to go East.
You will understand.
Understanding is all.

Two things I ask of you.
First, care for the land which
We have made green.
It will feed you purely.
But the grass will give you
Peace and delight.
Care for the grass before the grain.

Secondly, I leave an envelope of envelopes.
Please mail one each month for me.
I put my faith in all of you.

Remember
There will be other lives
Other Worlds.
                Watson Forrest

At last the telephone is ringing. Eugene leads me to the hallway, holding my arm as though I were a thousand years old. Everyone—Martin, my mother, the two policemen—gather around me.

"Hello."

"Charleen."

"Doug."

"Are you all right?"

"What's happened? Have you found them?"

"No, but I think we're onto something now."

"Where are you?"

"I'm out at Weedham, Ontario with the cops. At the Whole World place."

"Yes?" I breathe.

"They said you were here—"

"Yes, but—"

"They're not here. But we haven't given up."

"Tell me," my voice bends with pleading. "do you think they're . . . all right?"

"Oh, God, Charleen, if you knew how terrible I feel about all this. You and Seth and . . . if you only knew. But I think it's going to be all right, I think we're going to find them."

"What happened? Do you know what happened?"

"I just don't know. I thought Greta was okay on Sunday. A little edgy, but no worse than usual anyway. But as near as we can figure out, she overdid the meditation thing. She rounded. That's what we think. She just rounded."

"Rounded?"

"Went over . . . you know, over the top. It happens sometimes. She lost touch with the real world, what they call rounding. But I know she'll come around. You know Greta, she wouldn't hurt a—"

"But why did she take Seth?" I am crying into the phone. "Why did she have to take Seth?"

"We're not sure. That is, the police can't figure it out unless she was just crazy to have a kid of her own. But I tried to tell them I don't think that's it. I've got a crazy hunch—this sounds really crazy—but I think maybe she's trying to take Seth to Watson."

"Watson?"

"I know it sounds insane, but you know Greta. She might take it into her head that Seth would be better off with Watson. You know how she idolized the guy, always has. And she was, well, a little uneasy in her mind about Eugene and all that, you know how she is sometimes . . ."

"You really think . . ."

"It's just a guess, that's all. That's why I came out here, out to Weedham. But the kids here haven't laid eyes on him for a couple of years."

"Greta is taking Seth to Watson?" I repeat this numbly.

"That's all I can think of. I'm going crazy trying to think. That's why I'm two hours late calling you. I turned my watch back instead of forward when the time zone changed, I just found out, that's how mixed up I am. I've just been looking and looking all week and I'm just about out of my mind."

"We'll find them," I say falteringly, unbelievingly.

"Look, I'm sure Greta knows where Watson's living. I mean, I know she writes to him now and then."

"Yes. I know."

"Look, Char, I don't suppose you've got any idea yourself where Watson might be."

I think for a quarter of a minute and then I say, "Yes."

I give Doug the address very slowly so he will be able to write it down.

Standing in my mother's crowded little hall, we make hurried plans. Eugene and I and one of the policemen will go to the meeting point and wait for Doug Savage.

The police will send reinforcements immediately.

The other officer will stay here with the family. He has just received a message, he tells us a motel operator near Parry Sound reported renting a room last night to a middle-aged woman who was driving a dark coloured Volvo with B.C. plates. Was she alone? The report is not entirely clear, the officer explains. It was late at night, very dark, and no one is sure whether she was alone or not.

"We can take my car," Eugene says.

"Your car?" Martin asks.

"A rental," Eugene explains shortly. "They've just brought it over."

"God," Martin says, "that was quick." He says this with mingled surprise and admiration, and for a moment all of us turn and regard Eugene who is checking his wallet for his license. Such a simple thing, renting a car; Eugene would never be able to understand why my family stands in awe of such simple acts. I pick up my purse in the kitchen, and Eugene and I follow the policeman out the back door.

It is a big car, hugely clean, and the three of us fit in the front seat easily, Eugene driving, I in the middle, the policeman enthusiastically giving directions from the right. Eugene turns the car south toward the lake.

For me every passing car takes on extraordinary significance; each one must be checked off against Greta's blue Volvo. *She is sure to be in the city now.* I strain in the dark to see.

Vancouver, Calgary, Thunder Bay, Parry Sound, what could it signify? Perhaps a straight meaningless sweep across the whole country. What if they kept going, across Quebec, across the Maritimes, what if they dropped senseless into the sea like lemmings?

Then suddenly I am overcome with flooding despair. A moment ago, hearing the gassy zoom of the rented car I had felt temporarily buoyant. Now, from nowhere, comes the knowledge that Seth is dead. The certainty arrives in the middle of a breath. I had inhaled with hope and by the time my breath left me I was certain he was lost forever. This dark road, this silence.

It was a night like this when Seth was born. A spring night, the streets dry and dark with only a cold knot of a moon in the sky. Watson was out at a peace rally and I, drinking coffee in the apartment and feeling the first kick of pain, had been shocked and frightened and then, suddenly, for no reason, I had become serenely confident, packing quickly and neatly, phoning the doctor, locking the windows, calling the taxi, and then riding down the tree-arched Vancouver streets, sucking in the cool, friendly darkness as though it were somehow edible, exaltation knocking inside my heart. This was it, this was the beginning of my life, the only life that was going to matter.

"You want to take a left here," the officer advises Eugene after a mere ten minutes. "This is a one-way."

"Okay."

"Now, you want to jog right at the stop sign. I know this neighbourhood pretty well."

"Parking?"

"Anywhere now."

Eugene slows the car. "Maybe we'd better not park right in front of the building," he suggests.

"Squeeze in there by the hydrant, what the hell. Anyway there it is, that's the house. That big bugger on the left."

This is a certain type of Toronto street—narrow and, despite the streetlights, deeply shadowed. Cars park all along one side. The houses are tall and narrow and old; wooden porches hang on to their blackened brick fronts. It's a warm night, and here and there people are sitting out on their front steps; I can see the glowing red tips of their cigarettes. The front yards are small and, though I can't see in the dark, I know they are made up of packed earth and clumps of weeds; this is the kind of neighbourhood where there are always too many children and where it is shady even on the brightest days.

The blue flicker of television sets fills most of the front windows. Eugene turns off the ignition and says, "Let's go."

The policeman stands outside for a moment checking the other cars on the block. "That's one of ours," he says pointing to an unmarked Ford. "And those two guys are ours too."

"Let's go in," Eugene presses.

"But Doug Savage isn't here," I say, suddenly confused.

"They'll be a few minutes yet," the policeman says, checking his watch, "all the way from Weedham. Even in good traffic that's a fair run."

"No sign of a Volvo," I hear Eugene saying.

"She could've ditched it anywhere."

"I'll go in," I tell them.

"I wouldn't advise that," the policeman says, "you never know about these characters."

"I'm going in," I tell him again.

"I'll come with you," Eugene says.

"I think it would be better if I went alone, Eugene."

"We could back you up," the policeman says, thinking hard.

"If I could just talk to him alone. For a few minutes."

The policeman ponders a moment and then asks, "Is he, well you know him, he was your husband. What I mean, is he a dangerous guy?"

"Is he, Charleen?" Eugene turns to me.

"No," I almost smile. "He's not dangerous at all. He's like a . . . like . . . like a baby."

❧

The policeman checks with his friends in the parked car. When he comes back he nods at us and says, "Okay. We'll have a go."

It's a large house, one of the largest on the street, a three storey with jutting bays and ugly round-topped windows. Even in the dark I can see that it's in shocking condition. A few of the windows are broken, and most of them, except for two or three at the top, are dark. The front steps are shaky. The open porch is garishly lit by a naked bulb and it's filled with dirty plastic toys, a wicker chair with a rotted cushion, a dead plant in a pot. I'm frightened now, reluctant; perhaps I've made a crucial error in coming here.

The three of us stand on the porch for a moment, and for some reason the policeman is telling us about himself. His name is Bill Miller, he says, and he doesn't usually come out on jobs like this. He's filling in, he tells us, because this is a special case. Of course, he says shrugging, every case is special if you think about it. "We'll back you up," he says again in what sounds to me like Dragnet dialogue. "If your boy's up there, we'll get him out."

There are six doorbells stacked in a wiggly line on the door frame, but the name we want isn't there. A man appears in the doorway, a short, scrawny man, neither young nor old, with a rabbitty neck and a small, sharp nose. He is so drunk he has to lean on the door jamb to keep from falling down.

"Yeah?" he challenges us.

I explain whom we want to see.

"Sure, sure, he's up there," he tells us. "Lives at the

top. I told him I'd put up a lousy doorbell for him, but what the fuck for, no one ever comes to see him."

"Is there anyone up there with him now?" Eugene asks.

"Naw. 'Less they come up the fire escape. I been here all night."

Bill Miller says, "Look, mister, what we want to know is, did a woman come in here tonight?"

"Woman, eh?" he winks obscenely. "I always tell him that's what he needs, a good roll in the hay to straighten him out. He's a real nut."

"A woman with a boy?" Eugene asks carefully.

"Search me," he shrugs. "Why don't ya go up and have a look for yerself. Third floor. Name's on the door, ya can't miss."

Eugene and Bill Miller position themselves on the dark second floor landing. The stairway to the third floor is narrower and there is no railing, but a dim lightbulb shows the way.

I am at the top of the house standing in a tiny hall; there is only one door and it is clearly marked in blocky, hand-painted letters, The Priory, Bro. Adam. (The diminutive "Bro." is a warning.) Silence. Then the sound of my own breathing rushing out into the silence. I knock smartly on the door. Twice. Three times.

No answer, but through the old cracked wood I can hear something stirring. Like cloth being moved. Like someone sighing. Someone moaning.

I knock once more and wait. And then I turn the knob. It opens easily, a wide swinging, and I call out, "I'm coming in."

Afterwards I could hardly believe that I spent less than five minutes in that room. A small square room under the eaves, and yet my first impression was one of blinding, dazzling space. It was the mirrors, of course, huge mirrors mounted on two facing walls and lining the sloping ceiling, so that the small space seemed endless and unbelievably complex, like the sudden special openings that sometimes occur in dreams.

It was like stepping into the warm, glowing, artificial interior of a greenhouse with its combination of plant life, glinting glass and stillness. The air, after the reeking hallway, was deliciously fresh and smelled of earth and new growth. A narrow window let in the fragrant early spring air and on the other side a door stood open to an iron fire escape.

The room was alive with tiny lights. They were strung on wires and they beamed like miniature suns on the wooden flats of grass. The whole room, except for a neatly made-up army cot, was carpeted with grass. In the rebounding arrangements of mirrors and lights, the grass stretched endlessly, acres of it, miles of it; it was like coming upon a secret Alpine meadow, like a pocket of perfect and perpetual springtime where there was no night, no thought of cold or death. Even time seemed to fall away from me, as though the endless grass lived in another dimension altogether where growth and fertility took the place of hours and days.

Watson sat on the bed in a lotus position; I was conscious first of his gleaming skull and then of a certain bodily heaviness under his robe of dull red cloth. A book lay open on his lap. "I was afraid you might try to come," he said after a moment.

My throat closed soundless over his name: Watson, Watson, Watson. Still there, still there, that tender—no, no, more than tender—sliver of pain and youthful love lodged in the centre of my body. A twisting breathlessness like a rising funnel-shaped cloud of anguish pressed on my lungs, robbing me of speech and, for a moment, of coherence. What was I doing here leaning on this doorway, gasping for breath and for that portion of love that had surely died?

"Why are you here?" he asked again.

Then, like a stone sinking, I regained the powers of speech and thought.

"Brother Adam." I pronounced the words with finality, as though they were a summation. He gazed at me with detached calm.

"Brother Adam," I said again, deriving a curious energy from the flat sound of those two words. I couldn't summon surprise. I couldn't pretend surprise even to myself; nor could I distinguish the moment in time when I'd begun to know who Brother Adam might be. It seemed to me at that moment, standing in that incredible room, that I must always have known.

"You shouldn't have come," he said. (No, I shouldn't have. I had wanted a holy man with a bright prophetic eye and a tongue threaded with psalms, not this squatting, middle-aged would-be-sage grunting his way into being.) Of course Watson's vision of himself had never been less than apocalyptic. It occurred to me that the name Adam was just slightly substandard in its patent simplicity. A swindle really. Adam, king of his rooming-house Eden.

"There's something I have to ask you," I said firmly.

"I'm leaving tomorrow."

"Where?"

"East. I'm going East."

I came close to smiling, for there was a central, unnourished innocence in the way Watson pronounced the word East, and I saw that I would have to be careful or run the risk of destroying him entirely.

"Tell me exactly where you're going," I persisted.

"India, Japan," he waved vaguely.

"Alone?"

"Of course!"

"You're not taking anyone with you?"

"No one."

"Something's happened, Watson. Something you should know about."

"Is it really so important? I'm sure you can look after whatever it is."

"Seth is missing."

I watched his eyes; they blinked once, that was all. I remembered once years ago when Watson had seen a dwarf tapping his crutch by a bus stop; he had come close to weeping; something should be done, he had said. But the compulsion to relieve suffering was an abstraction for him, a folk belief in husk form. (Later I realized that outrage was only another form of innocence.) For a missing son he could only blink.

"I said Seth is missing."

"Missing?"

"Have you seen him, Brother Adam? Just tell me if you've seen him."

"No. Why would I see him?"

"Greta Savage has taken him. Taken him away."

"Greta Savage."

"We think . . . the police think . . . she's going to bring him here."

"Why would she do that?"

"Are you sure they didn't come here?"

"They wouldn't come here."

My throat closed with helplessness. Why did he have to speak in these dead, ritualized negatives? This convoluted room with its lights and mirrors and riotous grass was just another dead-end. I bent down for a moment and touched the tops of the grass. "You're leaving all this behind?" I asked.

"I'll take seed," he said, pointing to a suitcase beside the bed.

I stood up abruptly, and at that instant Watson's face

took on a startled expression. For the first time I became aware of a commotion down below on the street, a screeching of brakes, car doors slamming, people running on the road, some of them shouting. We heard too the sound of footsteps on the stairs of the house. Brother Adam rose with haste; the folds of his robe sighed around him.

Then, quite clearly, I heard Eugene's voice calling me. It seemed to come from the street. Or was it echoing up the stairwell? He was shouting something. It sounded like, "We've got Seth, Charleen, we've got him. We've got Seth and he's okay." I stood completely still. I had never, it seemed, listened before with this degree of intensity. There were more voices. And again there was the sound of running on the stairs.

Brother Adam picked up his suitcase, and with a sweep of his robe, he moved toward the fire escape. But he stopped there, staring at me for a moment as though waiting to be released.

"Charleen," was all he said. A question or a cry? Even afterwards I couldn't decide. Who was it who said that the sounds of our own names are the only recompense we have for the difficulties of living? I am certain, however, of one thing: that Watson didn't actually step out onto the fire escape until I nodded across at him. Then without a sound he dropped into darkness. I never even wished him good luck.

The next face I saw was Seth's. He burst into the room with Eugene behind him, absurdly off-hand in his tan windbreaker. My arms around him, his tumbled hair smelling of potato chips, his familiar face laughing at me above the brilliant jungle of living grass.

❧

Late Wednesday night. Some days are too long; it seems too much to ask of mere human beings that we live through them. What we need, what *I* need, is release from today. I need sleep, darkness.

But I can't sleep. Consciousness is flaking away, but I'm still absorbing the various levels of unreality which have suddenly invaded my mother's Scarborough bungalow; I'm breathing them in, examining them, puzzling over their intricate folds and, like a classic insomniac, reliving all of it.

The policemen—they've all gone home now. How do policemen manage to get to sleep after a night like tonight? Of course, it's probably nothing to them; line of duty and all that; a ho-hum affair really; wouldn't even make the papers, one of them had told us.

Doug and Greta. It has been so simple in the end, so completely unspectacular. (Greta had simply driven up to the house and opened the car door. She never even suspected she was being followed.) How tender Doug had been with her. In the middle of the street with the searchlights and the beginning of a curious crowd, how gently he had held her, crooning into her hair, "It's okay now, baby, I'll take care of you, there now, don't cry like that." But she had cried. A small, animal weeping perforating the quiet neighbourhood, her thin shoulders shaking, "I don't know what I was doing. He was going to India. I wanted Seth to see him. I didn't know what to do. All I want to do is go to sleep."

"I know, I know," Doug had said. "You need to sleep. I'll take care of you now. You don't have to worry about anything."

Watson. No one had seen him come down the fire escape. No one knew where he went. "Too much confusion," one of the officers had said, rather embarrassed. "Anyway, it looks as though he wasn't involved."

"He was moving out anyway," the scrawny man told us. "Paid up his rent yesterday, but the bugger left all his goddamn garbage behind. Lived there two years and you oughta see the goddamn junk he's got. A real nut, one of yer hopheads, oughta be in jail."

Watson living alone for two years! Watson, a crouching ascetic! How extraordinary really, considering his terrible need for an audience. (Then I remember the mirrors.)

Louis Berceau, another solitary—but his time is coming. What a lot he's giving up, the enormity of the sacrifice! Why? Why? His blissful detachment is ending; now he will be assaulted by all sorts of troubling concerns; his life will begin to overlap with others in ways which are not casual but responsible and which may throw into jeopardy his springy step and his childish good faith. Ah, Louis, sleep well tonight.

My mother who will be married the day after tomorrow: she has taken a sleeping pill. As soon as we came home with Seth, she announced that she was going to take a sleeping pill and go to bed. She explained that she does not normally indulge in such drugs. The doctor had given her these, but she takes them very sparingly. Only for pain and anxiety, she explained. Pain and anxiety: she pronounced these two words absently as though they amounted to nothing more than a case of indigestion, a stomach cramp, a twinge of heartburn. Judith and I exchanged wry looks. Only pain and anxiety? Was that all?

Judith and Martin. They are sleeping together in the back bedroom off the kitchen. Judith has been offhand but tactful. "Look, Char, it's not that I don't love you and all that, but as long as Mother's dead to the world—if you don't mind—the fact is, I just can't sleep soundly unless Martin and I are . . . you know . . . you get used to the feel of someone, and Eugene probably—"

Eugene, yes. Lying in my mother's veneer bed, his

arms around me—he is sound asleep now, but he has thought of everything: he has set his travel alarm for six-thirty so we can be sure to switch back before morning. He has also driven Greta to a hospital, found Doug a hotel room nearby, bought Bill Miller a bottle of rye. And checked Seth over for damages: "Of course I'm not a doctor, but there's nothing wrong with him that a good night's sleep won't fix."

And Seth is here in this house. Still a little baffled, a little confused—"I know it sounds crazy but she said you and Dad were getting back together again and she was supposed to take me to Toronto and I was too mixed up and half asleep. I guess I even believed her for the first day or two. It sounded like a dream, you know . . . like a wish come true."

"A wish? You mean you wished—?"

"Well, not exactly a wish—" He stopped, smiling suddenly, a self-mocking grin, but I could tell he was smiling at something else too, smiling at that swelling intangible that the "pome people" refer to as fate and others simply call life. It was a dazzling smile.

He was glad to see Eugene. Eugene is going to get him a plane ticket so we can fly back together Friday night after the wedding. The concert is Saturday; with luck they'll let him play even if he did miss a few rehearsals. He's in good spirits and went to sleep almost immediately.

And that's the most extraordinary thing of all: Seth is asleep in this house and he's sleeping where no one else has ever slept before, not my father, not Cousin Hugo, not Aunt Liddy, not Eugene, not anyone. Wound in a sheet and topped with a single blanket—for it is surprisingly warm tonight—he is sound asleep in the living room on my mother's sacred chesterfield.

The whole house, in fact, is asleep.

Chapter 7

Friday. My mother's wedding day. I wake up early and something whispers to me: get this right. Remember every detail. Be accurate, be objective, be thorough. Make a Chronicle of this, make a Wedding Album, get it Right. Begin with the cloud-crammed dawn, the sky oily-blue and unsettled. A heavy dew, a choking, webby haze. Around noon the sun nuzzles its way through, making the day exceptionally humid. A little cooler late in the afternoon. At six there is a brief downpour, at eight a swollen, streaky-eyed sunset, but by that time Eugene and Seth and I are on our way back to Vancouver and it's all over.

❦

We start the day by eating breakfast together, my mother and I, Eugene and Seth, Martin and Judith. Since there are only four kitchen chairs, Eugene carries in two from the dining room. It occurs to me that this is perhaps the largest number ever to gather in this room for breakfast.

We drink coffee—my mother allows for exactly two cups each—and eat buttered toast. "Margarine is cheaper," she reminds us, "but the day hasn't come when I can't afford a bit of butter in the morning."

There is a great deal of conversation around the table; the six of us are surprisingly comfortable together.

Eugene, laughing, tips his chair back slightly and fails to respond to my mother's sharp, disapproving glance.

My mother speaks to Seth—this grandson she scarcely knows, this grandson whose arrival has occasioned embarrassment and chaos but whose presence has somehow enlivened and restored the household—"I suppose you'd like some corn flakes for breakfast?"

"Yes," he answers, "if you have any."

"Well, I don't," she returns. "I refuse to spend good money on rubbish like that."

At this Seth laughs uproariously, as though his grandmother has said something exceptionally witty.

"What *you* need is a good haircut, that's what you need," she continues.

Seth claps his hands over his ears in mock horror. Or is it mock horror? I refuse to meet his eyes.

"Maybe you're right, Grandma," he says amiably, demonstrating his instinct for the inevitability of things. "I'll give it some thought."

"If I were you I'd give it more than thought," she retorts with spirit.

"I think there are some hedge clippers in the basement," Martin says.

We linger over our coffee with the languor of passengers on a steamship, the last leg of the journey in sight. The wedding looms ahead—three-thirty in my mother's living room—but even that event is overshadowed by the liberating awareness of our separate departures, the return to our other lives which, like real sea voyagers, we view with a mixture of reluctance and anticipation.

"Martin," Judith says after breakfast as she tidies my mother's kitchen, "did you see that thing in *The Globe and Mail* about the judge?"

"No," Martin answers, "what judge?"

"You know, that Supreme Court judge, old what's-his-name. Seventy-six years old and getting married."

"Oh yes," Martin says, "I think I *did* see the headline."

"And he's marrying a woman about the same age. Second marriage for both of them."

"Hmmm," Martin comments.

"So it's not so odd really, people getting married in their seventies."

"Who ever said it was odd?"

"Maybe it's the coming thing."

"Maybe."

"It's logical, when you think of it," she says thoughtfully. "There's a nice—you know—economy to the whole thing. In fact, it sort of fits in with the recycling philosophy."

"Oh?"

"After all, here's Mother getting an escort and chauffeur. And Louis is getting a cook and housekeeper."

"Is that all?" Martin looks up amused.

Judith scours the sink with energy.

"Is that all?" Martin asks again. Then he starts to laugh.

"What's so funny?" Judith asks turning around.

But Martin is laughing too hard to answer.

❧

My mother spent almost all morning at the hairdresser's.

It had been Judith's idea: "Look," she had reasoned with her, "you don't even have a hair dryer. And it's so damp this morning your hair will never dry. It would be a whole lot easier if you just went down to that little beauty place next to the Red and White. Eugene could drive you over, couldn't you Eugene? And you can have it washed and set and be back by noon."

"It's such a waste . . ."

"I'll phone right now and see if they can work you in. I'll explain . . ."

"There's so much to do here . . ."

"Charleen and I can tidy up the house. You have a nice restful morning under the dryer. I'll phone . . ."

"I don't know . . ."

"I'll ask if they can take you at ten-fifteen."

She had gone. Judith had won. It was in every way a sensible plan, but I had been appalled by my mother's quick surrender, her willingness to be led. This weakness is something new; she *is* getting old.

"She's getting old," I say later to Judith.

"Yes," Judith nods briskly. She is plugging in the old vacuum cleaner, and I watch as she attacks the living room rug. How realistic Judith is, how offhandedly she deals with the externals of life. She knows how to manage our mother, how to persuade her against her will, and she accepts her victories with stunning ease.

The vacuum cleaner is thirty years old, an upright Hoover with a monstrous black bag, and the sound of its roaring motor fills the house.

I picture my mother in the hands of a bullying shampoo girl in platform shoes, I think of the painful plastic rollers and the chemical sting, the scorching heat of the hairdryer, the futile aggression of *Harper's Bazaar,* and suddenly I am swept with a desire to rush out and find her and protect her. That is when it strikes me that I must . . . love . . . her in a way which Judith would never comprehend.

"It'll do her good to get out of the house," Judith yells over the roar of the vacuum cleaner.

❦

Yesterday morning Louis came to put in the shrubs I had bought. He worked slowly but with pleasure.

"Good healthy roots on this one," he said, patting the soil around a mock orange.

"I don't know why you thought I needed more bushes," my mother called to me crossly from the back door. "There are already more than I can look after."

"I like the smell of a mock orange," Louis said to me. "When it's in bloom it's the most wonderful perfume in the world."

After my mother went back into the house, Louis whispered to me, "Remember what we were talking about yesterday?"

"Yesterday?" I blinked.

"About that friend of yours. The priest."

I stared.

"You were going to ask him to come to the wedding."

"Oh," I breathed, "oh, yes, I remember."

"I've been thinking it over. And on second thought maybe it wouldn't be such a good idea after all."

"Oh?" I said.

"I appreciate it, I really do, but you know, a stranger and all," he paused and nodded almost imperceptibly toward the house, "maybe it wouldn't be such a good idea."

Later, when he had finished the planting, he went inside the house. He and my mother sat at the kitchen table talking a little and drinking coffee, Louis stirring in sugar, and my mother primly, awkwardly, perseveringly sipping. Seeing them sitting there like that I had a sudden glimpse of what their life together would be like. It would be exactly like this; there would be nothing mystical about it; it would be made up of scenes like this.

Not that I understand the complex equation they teeter upon, or the force that brought them together in the first place. It occurs to me that there are some happenings for which the proper response is not comprehension at all, but amazement and acceptance.

❧

Eugene drove my mother to the hairdresser's, and Seth, feeling restless, went along for the ride. While they are gone Judith and I vacuum and scrub, dust and polish. Martin, whistling, helps us wash the windows with vinegar and old newspapers. Then we stand back and regard the living room with its old, slipcovered chesterfield, its bulky armchairs, dark tables, heavy curtains and the rounded archway into the even gloomier dining room. It is scrupulously clean, but for all the crowding of furniture it looks barren, pinched and depressing.

"We'll put the lace table cloth on," Judith decides. "That should help a little."

Martin takes the tablecloth down from the top of my mother's linen cupboard, and throwing it over his arm, begins to tap out a soft cha-cha-cha. "Ta ta tatata, ta ta tatata," he sings as he whirls and swoops in the narrow space between the china cupboard and the dining room table. The tablecloth swirls and circles, cascading to the floor as he steps deftly and lightly around the chairs. "Down, down, down South America way," he hums to the lacy folds.

Judith smiles at him lazily. "You'll tear it, Martin, and then you'll catch it."

"Then I'll catch, catch, catch, catch it," Martin sings, dipping gracefully past us.

Judith takes the cloth from him and opens it on the table. "Well," she eyes the yellowed edges, "you can't say it looks exactly festive."

But then Eugene comes in the front door carrying armloads of spring flowers.

"Flowers!" I exclaim.

"I never thought of flowers," Judith marvels.

"Voila!" Martin cries, and, slowing to a cool elbow-spinning, shoulder-dipping softshoe, he shuffles into the kitchen to look for vases. For an instant—it couldn't have been more than a second really—I wish, feverishly wish, that I could dance away after him. I wish Judith would stop frowning and tugging at the edge of the tablecloth, and most of all I wish Eugene would stop standing there in the doorway, heavy and perplexed, with the tulips slipping sideways out of his arms.

Then Judith cries, "You're a genius, Eugene, I love you."

Then something happens: I look at Eugene in a frenzy of tenderness and begin to be happy.

❧

Yesterday afternoon Louis offered to cut the grass.

"It's too much work," my mother told him, "especially after putting in all those useless bushes."

"I'll cut the grass," Seth volunteered.

My mother considered, "Might as well keep busy," she said. "Idle hands . . ."

Seth laughed; he seems to find his grandmother's sayings shrewd and amusing. He carried the old hand mower up from the basement, oiled it carefully and began cutting back and forth across the tiny back lawn.

Watching him, I suddenly remembered the box of grass I had left behind in Vancouver, Brother Adam's grass. I had left it on the window sill, abandoned it without a thought, when I might easily have arranged for a neighbour to come in and water it. By the time I get home it will probably have turned brown; in all this heat it might even have died. How, I demanded of myself, had I been so neglectful?

The idea came to me that there may have been something willful in my oversight, that I may unconsciously have conceived a deathwish for my lovely grass, hating it while I pretended to love it. (The mind is given to such meaningless mirror tricks.) Had I subconsciously recognized Watson in those lengthy, grassy letters, had something about them touched a vein of familiarity, a flag of memory. Toying with these thoughts, I couldn't decide, but my aptitude for self-deception pressed me closer and closer toward belief. Poor Brother Adam, his love of grass which I had believed was prompted by an Emersonian vision of oneness, was only one more easy commitment, an allegiance to a non-human form, a blind and speechless deity. And poor Watson, his life hacked to pieces by his endless self-regarding; every decade a ritual pore cleansing, a radical, life-diminishing letting of blood. (After he had disappeared down the fire escape, after the excitement of seeing Seth had died down, I had picked up the book he had been reading; it was titled *The Next Life*.)

❦

It is a good thing Eugene kept the rented car because it turns out to be quite useful. At noon he picks up my mother from the hairdresser's and brings her home. Seth arrives a few minutes later by foot; he has had his hair trimmed and, smiling sheepishly, he allows us to admire him.

We eat sandwiches standing up in the kitchen, and then Eugene drives Martin and Judith to Union Station to meet their children who arrive on the one o'clock train.

I hardly know Meredith and Richard, and Seth has never seen them. Richard is shy, somewhat sulky, and, after three hours on the train, wild with hunger. Meredith at eighteen is beautiful. Judith has told me that her daughter's beauty has made her own aging bearable. "It's an odd consolation, isn't it?" she said. "You'd think I'd be jealous, but I revel in it."

Meredith kisses her grandmother with surprising force. "Well, how does it feel to be a bride again?" she bursts out.

"I was just going to lie down for my rest," my mother says in a wavy-toned way she has.

"Right now?" Meredith's eyes open wide.

"Just for an hour. I always have a rest after lunch, you know that."

"Hold it for five minutes, Grandma. I've got a surprise for you."

"A surprise?"

"You wait here. I'll set it up in the kitchen."

Meredith, shopping bag in hand, races into the kitchen opens her blue umbrella on the kitchen table, balancing it carefully on two spokes. Underneath it she arranges a dozen small parcels wrapped in silver paper and tied with pale pink ribbon.

"Okay now, Grandma. You can come in."

"What in the world . . ."

"It's a shower, Grandma, a kitchen shower."

"But I've got everything I need . . ."

"I know, Grandma," Meredith dances around the table, "but you're a bride, you've got to feel like a bride."

There is a new set of measuring cups in copper-tinted aluminum.

"But I have some measuring cups . . ."

"But they're all dented and ancient. I noticed last time we were here."

There is a new ironing-board cover.

"Now you can throw that old rag away." Meredith chortles.

There is a little needle-like device to prick the bottoms of eggs with.

"So they won't break when you boil them," Meredith explains.

"But all you have to do is add some salt . . ."

There is a wooden spoon. A new spatula. A twisted spring for taking lumps out of gravy. Two tiny soufflé dishes in white china.

"For you and Mr. Berceau," Meredith tells her joyfully, "and you can put them right in the oven."

There is a miniature ladle for melted butter. A painted recipe box made in Finland. And a beautiful, new streamlined egg beater with a turquoise plastic handle and whirling, purring, silvery gears.

"Lovely," everyone agrees.

"Just what you needed."

"Merangues, cakes . . ."

"—a beauty—"

"But I have an egg beater . . ."

"Grandma, smile. This is your wedding day, you're a bride."

While my mother rests we set up the presents on the buffet. There aren't many. Judith and Martin are giving bedspreads.

"Two bedspreads?" I ask.

"Well . . . yes. One seemed sort of, you know, suggestive. I mean, that's the way she might see it. Two sort of cancels out the whole thing. One for the guest room and one for her room, more like a general refurbishing. God, I hate all this delicacy, but you know how she is, and the fact is, we couldn't think of anything else."

Eugene has bought them a kitchen radio which we think was rather an inspiration, a trim little model in white plastic with excellent tone and a year's guarantee. And since my shrubs hadn't been very successful, I decided yesterday to buy something else, something small but personal: I decided to give them my complete works, my four books of poetry.

Curiously enough my mother has never read anything I've written. She has, in fact, never expressed the slightest desire to do so, and a species of shyness has prevented me from ever sending her a copy. Furthermore, though she is not an astute reader, it has always worried me that she might comprehend something of the darkness in my poetry. It might wound her; it might remind her of something she would rather forget.

But now seemed like a good time to make a presentation. Like Judith, I had begun to know that I might never be able to talk to her. Who knows? Perhaps this was a way.

I had to buy the books retail by going to a bookstore and paying the regular price instead of getting them directly from the publisher as I normally do in Vancouver. Eugene and I went downtown yesterday to a very large bookstore, and there, in the poetry section, I found all four of my books. (They have recently been re-issued as a rather attractive set.) My picture in rainbow hues smiled happily at me from the back covers.

It was an altogether surreal experience to be buying my own books; I felt as though I were participating in a piece of cinema vérité. I felt, in fact, extraordinarily foolish placing those books in the hands of the cashier at the front of the store.

She checked the titles and then she turned the books over to check the price. Now, I thought, now she's going to suffer a brief instant of confusion; then her mouth will fall open in astonished recognition.

But none of this happened. Instead she took my twenty dollar bill, slapped it down on the cash register, sighed sharply, and snapped at me, "I suppose this is the smallest you've got."

"Yes," I said weakly, faintly, "I'm afraid that's all I have."

❧

Meredith and Judith and I make three bouquets, one

for the dining-room table, one for the mantle of the artificial fireplace and a tiny one to set on the telephone table by the front door.

"Shouldn't we save some for Grandma's bouquet?" Meredith asks. "Or is Mr. Berceau bringing that?"

Judith and I stare at each other; neither of us had thought of a bridal bouquet. "Damn it," Judith bursts out, "I should have ordered something."

"Maybe Louis *will* bring one," I say, not very convincingly.

"Hmmmm," Judith says, "I doubt it."

"I don't suppose she could carry some of these tulips?" Meredith asks.

"Not really," Judith says, "tulips aren't quite the thing for a bridal bouquet."

"Maybe if we phoned a florist right away . . ." I begin.

"Lilacs!" Meredith says. "They'd be perfect."

"I don't know," Judith says doubtfully.

"They'd make a perfect bouquet," Meredith assures us, "and there are tons of them in the backyard. And they're at their best right now."

"Well," I say, "why not?"

"The only thing is," Judith hesitates, "well, you know how Mother always was about lilacs. They're just weeds, she used to tell us. Remember that, Charleen?"

"No," I reply, "I don't remember her ever saying that."

"We were always wanting to take a bunch to school— you know—flowers-for-the-teacher sort of thing. And she'd never let us because she said they were just weeds."

"I don't remember that," I say again, and saying it I am conscious of a curious lightening of heart. It is somehow wonderful and important to know that at least part of the burden of memory has been spared me.

"But lilacs are beautiful," Meredith protests, "they're heavenly flowers; I can't think of more gorgeous flowers. I'll make a bouquet for Grandma, just leave it to me," she says.

❧

Eugene, who is not normally introspective about his profession, just as he is not particularly critical or adulatory about it, once told me that he occasionally has moments when he is visited by a sharp sense of unreality. It happens most frequently when he is delivering to his young patients lectures on the importance of brushing their teeth. For a moment or two he feels himself undergoing a dizzying separation: suddenly he is the farmboy from Estevan eavesdropping on a solemn, middle-aged professional in a white jacket who is piously pressing for dental hygiene as though it were a system of morality. He is invariably self-amused when this occurs and at the same time awed by the transcendental experience of seeming to overhear himself.

I had something of the same feeling myself yesterday talking to my mother about Greta Savage; I had replied to her questioning with a calm I hadn't known I possessed, and hearing myself I had felt very close to being the person I would like to be.

"What are you going to do about that woman?" she asked.

"What woman?"

"That crazy woman. That kidnapper."

Without really intending to, I heard myself defending Greta, explaining to my mother that Greta had taken Seth as an act of love. She loves Seth, and, in a neurotic, labyrinthian way, she loves me too.

My defense of Greta was all the more surprising because I defended her instinctively. Like the kind people of the world—like Eugene-the-orthodontist—I had judged with instant charity; like the good folk in fairy tales I had performed magic, spinning gold from straw, transforming apples to golden guineas. Kindness, kindness—a skill which I have nourished and rehearsed and worried into being—had jumped out and taken me by surprise. Without thinking, without laborious reflection I had fallen into its easy litany.

Even more surprising, it had given me a temporary ascendancy; my mother had been silenced; perhaps kindness and bravery have a common root.

"Greta acted out of love," I told my mother again, and, overhearing myself, I knew it was true.

❧

"Here comes Louis Cradle," Martin calls from the front window.

"Louis who?" I ask.

"Louis Cradle. And he's all zooted up."

Judith, setting out teacups, explains, "Berceau is French for cradle."

"Oh," I say, for an instant stung by my ignorance— how spotty my education was—was I going to spend a lifetime meeting such voids?

Louis Cradle, Mr. and Mrs. Cradle. Mentally I thrust about for the symbolism, cradle of a new life, no, too pat, the sort of pearl the "pome people" dived after—the "pome people" could never leave a paradox unturned, seeing life as a film strip jerking along from insight to insight, a fresh truth revealed every three and a half minutes—better forget about symbolism; yes.

Louis coming into the house looks no more dressed up than he was when he took me for lunch; indeed he wears the same old navy blue suit which does, however, look as though it has been brushed and perhaps even pressed.

But he is wearing a hat, a soft cloth cap in a fine wool,

rather a strange choice for so warm a day. Yet, the effect seems not unsuitable. I've often noticed that men who cover their heads, sweetly and solemnly concealing the tops of their heads with turbans, hoods, fezzes and skull caps, seem to be putting on a spiritual covering which announces piety and humility and which, in the short-hand of costume, declares that life is perishable, vulner-able and worthy.

At half past two my mother has her bath; then she re-tires to her room again in order to get dressed. The house is ready. Martin and Eugene have even managed to pry open one of the living room windows, long ago painted shut, and a breeze drifts in. The cake has been delivered, and there is a box of tiny, paper-thin cookies too. Judith and I arrange them on a tray; we put out milk and sugar, and I even set out a circle of lemon slices on a glass plate.

The only thing missing is a scene which I half-imag-ine might take place, the scene where my mother takes Judith and me aside and asks us if we object to the fact that she is remarrying, if we have any sensitivities about our father being more or less supplanted. Some faint, quivering, awkwardly-delivered apology, a seeking of ap-proval or even permission, at the very least a fumbling for consensus or a simple explanation: she is lonely, she needs someone to look after the furnace, see to the insur-ance, someone to talk to. But now it's almost time for the wedding. The missing scene is clearly not going to take place; thank God, thank God.

"Where's Grandma?" Meredith asks us.

"Getting dressed," I say nodding at the closed door.

The minister has arrived, a young man, no more than twenty-five, with a prominent bridge of bone above his eyes; his face gleams with sweat. "Hot day for May," he announces nervously.

"Wonderful, isn't it?" Judith says a little defiantly. She has changed to a striking sleeveless dress in rough, lemon-coloured cloth.

"Perhaps you'd be more comfortable if you took off your jacket," suggests Martin, who does not intend to wear a jacket.

"My mother will be out in a minute," Judith says. "She's just getting dressed."

"This really is a happy occasion," the young man remarks.

Louis, supremely relaxed and almost dapper, invites him to sit down by the window. "It was very good of you to agree to come."

"Do you think I should see if Grandma needs a hand?" Meredith whispers to me.

"No. She'll be out in a minute," I answer.

"It's half past three."

"Really?"

"On the dot."

"Not like her to be late."

"Especially for her own wedding."

" . . . really should check, don't you think?"

"Give her a minute or two."

"You're sure she's all right?"

"Maybe we should . . ."

"Ah, there she is now."

"Mother."

"Mrs. McNinn?"

"Oh, Grandma!"

"My dear."

❧

The ceremony, a shortened version of the traditional marriage service, is performed in front of the artificial fireplace (symbolism?) and, since it is short, we all remain standing. Judith and Martin stand in the archway to the dining room, Eugene and I by the window, and the three children beside the television set.

My mother's voice repeating the vows is exceptionally matter of fact. She might be reading a recipe for roast beef hash, and curiously enough, I find her lack of dramatic emphasis reassuring and even admirable. Louis, on the other hand, seems quite overcome. He chokes on the words and once or twice he dabs at his eyes, though this may be the result of asthma rather than emotion.

From where I stand I can see only their backs; my mother leans slightly to the left; perhaps her operation has unbalanced her. And Louis stoops forward as though anticipating an attack of coughing. They look rather fragile as people always do from the rear; it is after all the classic posture of retreat. Retreat from what? Age, illness, loneliness? Louis slips a ring on my mother's hand and they stand for a moment with hands joined. Two is a good number, I think, and like a chant it blocks out the remainder of the service for me. Two is better than ten; two is better than a hundred; two is better than six; when all is said, two is better than one; when all's said, two is a good number.

❧

"That's a lovely bouquet you're carrying, Mrs. McNinn. Oh, I'm so sorry, I should have said Mrs. Berceau."

"Well, lilacs aren't my favourite, but my granddaughter here . . ."

"Won't you have some tea, Louis?"

"Yes, please, Judith, that's just what I need."

"And a piece of cake?"

"A nice cake, isn't it?"

"You weren't a bit nervous, were you, Louis?"

"Well, to tell you the truth—"

"Welcome to the fold, Louis."

"Well, well, thank you, Martin, very kind of you."

"Great institution, marriage."

"Do you think she's holding up okay, Char?"

"She looks a little tired. But not bad."

"Considering . . ."

"Nice you could come east with Aunt Charleen, Eugene."

"I wouldn't have missed it, Meredith."

"You're just being polite."

"No, really."

"What do you think, Judith, should I bring out the champagne?"

"I don't know, Martin. You know Mother. What do you think?"

"I don't know. Oh, hell, why not?"

"And that woman over there? Mrs. Forrest? She's your aunt, is that right?"

"Yes, she's a poet. Most people think we look alike."

"And the man with her? Dr. Redding? In the grey suit?"

"That's Eugene. Her lover."

"Lover?"

"You look so shocked. Are you really shocked?"

"Of course I'm not shocked. Why should I be shocked?"

"You must have been scared getting kidnapped like that."

"Scared?"

"I mean, did you think she was going to try for ransom or something like that?"

"Naw, it wasn't like that. It was—I don't know—it was kind of fun, the whole thing."

"You look beautiful, carrying that bouquet."

"Have some more cake, someone has to eat all this cake."

"It's good cake."

"A little dry, if you ask me."

"May I propose a toast . . ."

"Good idea."

"I've never had champagne before."

"Neither have I."

"Really?"

"Delicious."

"Like ginger ale, only sour."

"Ah, look at the bubbles rising."

"You're supposed to *sip* it, Richard."

"Here, have another glass, Judith."

"If you're sure there's enough . . ."

"Lovely."

"Tea is plenty good enough for me."

"Here's to marriage."

"Here's to the bride and groom."

"Here's to the future."

"Happy days."

❧

"I love you, Eugene."

"Charleen, Charleen."

Nothing is what it seems. Our plane flying west is defying a basic natural law which says that on any given day the sun sets only once; but here it is setting over

Lake Superior, again over Winnipeg, over the prairies, over the mountains. We're diving into its fiery, streaming trail, we're chasing it down to its final, almost comic, drowning. *Don't tell me about the curve of the earth.*

Eugene, peering down through grey mist, says, "What we should do is buy a farm. A few acres. For weekends, you know. Maybe grow some vegetables, have a horse for the kids. Might even be a tax advantage there . . ."

My childhood is over, but at the same time—and this seems even more true—it will never be over. Say it fast enough and it sounds like a scuttling metaphysic of survival. *Who ever said you can't live without logic.*

"Ladies and gentlemen," a voice says, "this is your captain speaking." *But how do we know it is our captain?*

"We've just been told there's a light rain over Vancouver—" *A light rain, a light rain, the beginning of a poem, a light rain.*

"But visibility is excellent—" *Watch out for symbolism now.*

"We hope you have enjoyed your flight. This is your captain wishing you a good evening." *Good evening, good evening.*

swann

Almost every novelist writes one book that is inexplicably rewarding. Usually it is a book that has given special pleasure in the making and about which one continues to feel a warm affection. For this reason I am delighted to see my favourite offspring, SWANN, reprinted in this new edition. It was written during a period of my life when I was feeling particularly brave — though I've no idea why — and when I was beginning to understand just how capacious and flexible a form the novel is. In it I tried to bring together two mysteries: the enigma of Mary Swann's disappearing manuscripts, and that larger conundrum of art — who makes it and how? What transformative power allows an ordinary person like Mary Swann to achieve extraordinary results, and can we ever really know that person?

CAROL SHIELDS
Winnipeg, December 1995

For Sara Ellisyn Shields

SWANN

ℒ❧

The rivers of this country
Shrink and crack and kill
And the waters of my body
Grow invisible.

Mary Swann

SARAH MALONEY

1

As recently as two years ago, when I was twenty-six, I dressed in ratty jeans and a sweatshirt with lettering across the chest. That's where I was. Now I own six pairs of beautiful shoes, which I keep, when I'm not wearing them, swathed in tissue paper in their original boxes. Not one of these pairs of shoes costs less than a hundred dollars.

Hanging in my closet are three dresses (dry clean only), two expensive suits and eight silk blouses in such colours as hyacinth and brandy. Not a large wardrobe, perhaps, but richly satisfying. I've read my Thoreau, I know real wealth lies in the realm of the spirit, but still I'm a person who can, in the midst of depression, be roused by the rub of a cashmere scarf in my fingers.

My name is Sarah Maloney and I live alone. Professionally — this is something people like to know these days — I'm a feminist writer and teacher who's having second thoughts about the direction of feminist writing in America. For twenty-five years we've been crying: *My life is my own*. A moving cry, a resounding cry, but what does it *mean*? (Once I knew exactly what freedom meant and now I have no idea. Naturally I resent this loss of knowledge.)

Last night Brownie, who was sharing my bed as he does most Tuesday nights, accused me of having a classic case of burn-out, an accusation I resist. Oh, I can be restless and difficult! Some days Virginia Woolf is the only person in the universe I want to talk to; but she's dead, of course, and wouldn't like me anyway. Too flip. And Mary Swann. Also dead. Exceedingly dead.

These moods come and go. Mostly Ms. Maloney is a cheerful woman, ah indeed, indeed! And very busy. Up at seven, a three-kilometre run in Washington Park — see her yupping along in even metric strides — then home to wheat toast and pure orange juice. Next a shower, and then she gets dressed in her beautiful, shameful clothes.

I check myself in the mirror: *Hello there*, waving long, clean, unpolished nails. I'll never require make-up. At least not for another ten years. Then I pick up my purse-cum-briefcase, Italian, $300, and sally forth. *Sally forth*, the phrase fills up my mouth like a bubble of foam. I'm attentive to such phrases. Needful of them, I should say.

I don't have a car. Off I go on foot, out into a slice of thick, golden October haze, down Sixty-second to Cottage Grove, along Cottage Grove, swinging my bag from my shoulder to give myself courage. Daylight muggings are common in my neighborhood, and I make it a point to carry only five dollars, a fake watch, and a dummy set of keys. As I walk along, I keep my Walkman turned up high. No Mozart now, just a little cushion of soft rock to help launch the day with hope and maybe protect me from evil. I wear a miraculous broad-brimmed hat. The silky hem of my excellent English raincoat hisses just at knee length. I have wonderful stockings and have learned to match them with whatever I'm wearing.

"Good morning, Dr. Maloney," cries the department

secretary when I arrive at the university. "Good morning, Ms. Lundigan," I sing back. This formal greeting is a ritual only. The rest of the time I call her Lois, or Lo, and she calls me Sarah or Sare. She's the age of my mother and has blood-red nails and hair so twirled and compact it looks straight from the wig factory. Her typing is nothing less than magnificent. Clean, sharp, uniform, with margins that *zing*. She hands me the mail and a copy of my revised lecture notes.

Today, in ten minutes, Lord help me, I'll be addressing one hundred students, ninety of them women, on the subject of "Amy Lowell: An American Enigma." At two o'clock, after a quick cheese on pita, I'll conduct my weekly seminar on "Women in Midwestern Fiction." Around me at the table will be seven bright postgraduate faces, each of them throwing off kilowatts of womanly brilliance, so that the whole room becomes charged and expectant and nippy with intelligence.

Usually, afterwards, the whole bunch of us goes off for a beer. In the taproom on Sixty-second we create a painterly scene, an oil portrait — women sitting in a circle, dark coats thrown over the backs of chairs, earrings swinging, elbows and shoulders keeping the composition lively, glasses held thoughtfully to thoughtful lips, rolling eyes, bawdiness, erudition.

They forget what time it is. They forget where they are — that they're sitting in a taproom on Sixty-second in the city of Chicago in the fall of the year in the twentieth century. They're too busy talking, thinking, defining terms, revising history, plotting their term papers, their theses, and their lives so that no matter what happens they'll keep barrelling along that lucent dotted line they've decided must lead to the future.

2

Last night my good friend Brownie — Sam Brown, actually — aged thirty, earning his living as a dealer in rare books, living in an Old Town apartment decorated in mission-revival fashion, son of a State of Maine farm labourer, dropped in to chat about the theme of castration in women's books. While I was demurring a little about the way in which he arrives at his critical judgments — like a noisy carpet-sweeper darting under obscure chairs and tables — he dropped the golden name of Mary Swann. "Your Mary," he announced, "is a prime example of the female castrator."

That surprised me, though I knew Brownie had been reading Mary Swann's book, since I had lent him my only copy; and I demanded proof for his conclusion. He was prepared for this — he knows me well, too well after all these months — and he pulled from his jacket pocket a piece of folded paper. Clearing his throat and holding his head to one side, he read:

> A simple tree may tell
> The truth — but
> Not until
> Its root is cut.
>
> The bitter leaf
> Attacks the stem,
> Demands a brief
> Delirium.

"Preposterous," I said. "She's talking about societal and family connections and you're thinking about crude anatomy. Roots! Stems!"

He smiled, refolded his piece of paper, and invited me for a walk in the park. We set off into the cold, I in my winter things — knitted scarf, woolly hat — and with my collar turned up to my ears. I slipped my arm through Brownie's. Cordially. Affectionately.

I am fond of him, *too* fond, too fond by far, and he may well love me, but with an ardour sunk under a drift of vagueness, as though he's playing through that crinkled head of his scenes of former conversations and encounters. He's too lazy, too preoccupied, too much a man who dallies and dreams and too given to humming under his breath that insouciant little tune that declares that nothing really *matters*. That is why I'm drawn to him, of course, seeing him as an antidote to my own passionate seizures. For Brownie, today's castration theory will be tomorrow's soap bubbles. His mind, like a little wooden shuttle, is forever thinking up theories to keep himself amused. Being amused is his chief ambition. And getting rich. Dear Brownie.

We walked along in silence for a few minutes, watchful for muggers, kicking the piles of fallen leaves. The cold was intense for so early in October. Brownie gave me a quick hug and, putting on his fake cockney accent, said, "I thought you'd be chuffed that I gave your bird a turn."

I am, *I am,* I told him. I'd been urging him for two years to read Mary Swann, ever since I wandered into his store on Madison Street, The Brown Study, and found no more than half a shelf of poetry. Inferior poetry. We had an argument that first day. Real money, he told me, big money, was in vintage comic books. He was depending on his Plastic Man collection to keep him in his old age. Poetry gave him pyloric spasms, economically speaking, and he only carried the biggies, Carl Sandburg and Robert Frost and that ilk. Volumes of poetry didn't sell, didn't move. Whereas a first

edition of *The Sun Also Rises*. . . . And Updike. And lately,
Ivy Compton-Burnett. I like to argue with Brownie about
such things. He shouts. I shout back. An extra piquancy
settles on us, a round little umbrella of heat. Still, one can't
count on Brownie.

I like to think that my view of him is detached.

This man has serious limitations, I tell myself. I
should overlook the cynical addiction to comic books. I
should discount that smile, which flashes too readily, too
indiscriminately. What is the value of a smile anyway?

Still he has a certain erudition, an appealing, splintery
intelligence that, like the holes in his sweaters, conceals
a painstaking grasp on the business of reality. Yes, but he
is a lightweight; though he denies it, he thinks of a book as
a commodity. Yet, a lightweight can be good company
at times, especially when that lightweightedness is so
arduously cultivated and so obviously a defence. Or is it?
That shunting breath and laughter of his ripples with
energy. But can he be trusted, a man whose brain dances and
performs and hoists itself on market trends and whimsical
twenty-four-hour theories? No. Yes. Possibly.

I keep my objectivity about Brownie polished and
at the ready, yet again and again it yields to wild unaccountable happiness when in his company. Yes, but he is indolent.
Ah, but under the indolence he has ambition. That may be,
but it's a scheming ambition. Remember what he once said,
that he'd cheat his own granny to make a buck. He cares for
nothing. But why should he? Why should anyone? I don't
altogether understand him, but what does understanding
between people really mean — only that we like them or
don't like them. I adore Brownie. But with reservations.
Last night I was close to loving him, even though he
dumped my Mary Swann into the same bathtub with

Sigmund Freud. He didn't mean a word of it though; I could almost bet on it.

3

For a number of years, for a number of reasons, I had a good many friends I didn't really like. One of them was a fellow graduate student, a downy-cheeked boy-man called Olaf Thorkelson who kept hounding me to marry him. He was young, wise, opinionated, good, and joyful, but weak at the centre. What I wanted was a man of oak. My mother had one, my grandmother had one, but at that time I had only Olaf.

I told him that I was afraid of marriage, that it could only lead to a house in Oak Park and the tennis club and twin beds and growing deaf. He said he could see my point, but that at least we could live as lovers. No, I said, that wouldn't be fair to him. He said he didn't care a fuck for fairness. I said that fairness was the rule I lived by. (A fugitive conscience is better than no conscience at all.) This went on all one spring and left me so exhausted that by June I had to go to bed for a week. Oh yes, the indomitable Sarah, slain by indecision.

The sight of me spread weakly in bed moved Olaf at last to guilt, and he urged me to go away for a bit and "think things through." His sister had a friend who owned a cottage on a lake in Wisconsin, and since it was empty for the summer he would get me the key and put me on a Greyhound bus.

Two days later I was there, walking on a pebbly strip of beach and admiring the cleanliness of cirrus clouds and bright air. The cabin was a flimsy, friendly affair with wood

floors that sloped and creaked and a fireplace so smoky and
foul that on chilly nights I lit the cookstove instead for
warmth.

I particularly loved that cookstove, the prepossessing
way it stood away from the wall, all bulging girth and
black radiance. The wondrous word *negritude* formed on
my tongue as I opened its door and poked in newspaper
and kindling and lit a match. At the top of its heat it
shuddered and hissed like a human presence, and I thought
how fortunate a woman I was to have such a good, natural,
uncritical companion at this time in my life. All month
I amused myself by making sweet soufflés — rum and
apricot and lemon — and in that black hole of an oven they
rose to perfection.

When I wasn't making soufflés I plunged into the
singular pleasure of cottage housekeeping. There are
rewards in cleaning things — everyone should know this —
the corners of rooms, dresser drawers, and such. I concocted
a primitive twig broom and bashed joyfully at cobwebs and
dustballs. A clothesline that I found stretched between two
trees seemed to say to me: *Isn't life simple when pared down to
its purities?* In the cabin, resting on an open shelf, were an
eggbeater, a wooden spoon, an iron frying pan, four bowls,
four cups, and a plastic dishpan, which I emptied out the
door on to a patch of weeds. Swish, and it was gone.

The cabin had a screened porch where I took to sitting
in the hottest part of the afternoon, attentive to the quality
of filtered light and to the precarious new anchoring of
my life plan. Serenity descended as the days wore on. I
absorbed the sunny, freckled world around me. Olaf could
be dealt with. His supple sexual bulk faded, giving way to a
simple checklist. My thesis revision could also be managed,
and so could the next two years of my life; that was as wide

a span of time as I cared to think about. In the distance was the heaving, spewing lake, broad as a small sea and impossible to see across. The long afternoons dipped and shimmered. Flies grazed stupidly against the screen. "Hello, fellow creatures," I said, suspecting I was going blobby in the head but welcoming the sensation.

Seated in a wicker chair on that dim porch I seemed to inhabit an earlier, pre-grad-school, pre-Olaf self. My thesis, *The Female Prism,* and the chapter that had to be rewritten were forgotten, swirled away like the dishwater. Instead there were trashy old magazines to read, piles of them in a mildewed wicker basket, and a shelf full of cottage novels with greenish, fly-spotted pages. I read my way through most of them, feeling winsomely trivial, feeling redemptively ordinary, and, toward the end of the month, at the end of the shelf, I discovered an odd little book of poems written by a woman named Mary Swann. The title of the book was *Swann's Songs.*

4

At that time Mary Swann had been dead for more than fifteen years. Her only book was this stapled pamphlet printed in Kingston, Ontario, in 1966.

There are exactly one hundred pages in the book and the pages contain one hundred and twenty-five poems. The cover design is a single musical note stamped on rather cheap grey paper. Only about twenty copies of *Swann's Songs* are known to have survived out of the original printing of two hundred and fifty — a sad commentary on literary values, Brownie says, but not surprising in the case of an unknown poet. How Mary Swann's book found its way

down from Canada to a cottage on a lonely Wisconsin lake
was a mystery, *is* a mystery. A case of obscurity seeking
obscurity.

Even today Swann's work is known only to a handful
of scholars, some of whom dismiss her as a *poète naïve*.
Her rhythms are awkward. Clunky rhymes, even her
half-rhymes, tie her lines to the commonplace, and her
water poems, which are considered to be her best work,
have a prickly roughness that exposes the ordinariness of the
woman behind them, a woman people claim had difficulty
with actual speech. She was a farmer's wife, uneducated. It's
said in the Nadeau area of Ontario that she spoke haltingly,
shyly, and about such trivial matters as the weather, laying
hens, and recipes for jams and jellies. She also crocheted
doilies. I want to weep when I think of those hundreds of
circular yellowing doilies Mary Swann made over the years,
the pathetic gentility they represented and the desperation
they hint at.

Her context, a word Willard Lang adores, was narrowly
rural. A few of her poems, in fact, were originally published
in the back pages of local newspapers: "A Line a Day,"
"Rimes for Our Times," and so on. It was only after she was
killed that someone, an oddball newspaper editor named
Frederic Cruzzi, put together and printed her little book,
Swann's Songs.

Poor Mary Swann. That's how I think of her, *poor*
Mary Swann, with her mystical ear for the tune of words,
cheated of life, cheated of recognition. In spite of the fact
that there's growing interest in her work — already thirty
applications are in for the symposium in January — she's
still relatively unknown.

Willard Lang, the swine, believes absolutely that
Swann will never be classed as a major poet. He made this

pronouncement at the MLA meeting last spring, speaking with a little ping of sorrow and a sideways tug at his ear. Rusticity, he claimed, kept a poet minor and, sadly, there seemed to be no exceptions to this rule, Burns being a different breed of dog. My Mary's unearthly insights and spare musicality appear to certain swinish critics (Willard is not the only one) to be accidental and, therefore, no more than quaint. And no modern academic knows what to do with her rhymes, her awful moon/June/September/ remember. It gives them a headache, makes them snort through their noses. What can be done, they say, with this rustic milkmaid in her Victorian velours!

I tend to get unruly and defensive when it comes to those bloody rhymes. Except for the worst clinkers (giver/liver) they seem to me no more obtrusive than a foot tapped to music or a bell ringing in the distance. Besides, the lines trot along too fast to allow weight or breath to adhere to their endings. There's a busy breedingness about them. "A Swannian urgency" was how I put it in my first article on Mary.

Pompous phrase! I could kick myself when I think about it.

5

I live in someone else's whimsy, a Hansel and Gretel house on a seventeen-foot lot on the south side of Chicago. Little paned casement windows, a fairy-tale door, a sweet round chimney and, on the roof, cedar shakes pretending to be thatch. It's a wonderful roof, a roof that gladdens the eye, peaky and steep and coming down in soft waves over the windows with fake Anne Hathaway fullness. The house

was built in 1930 by an eccentric professor of Elizabethan
literature, a bachelor with severe scoliosis and a club foot,
and after his death it was, briefly, a restaurant and then a
Democratic precinct office. Now it's back to being a house.
At the rear is an iron balcony (loosely attached, but I intend
to have it seen to) where I stand on fine days and gaze out
over a small salvage yard crowded with scrap iron and a
massive public housing project full of brawling families and
broken glass.

I bought my freak of a house when the first royalties started coming in for *The Female Prism*. I had to live
somewhere, and my lawyer, a truly brilliant woman named
Virginia Goodchild, said it could only happen to a person
once, turning a Ph.D. thesis into a bestseller, and that I'd
better sink my cash fast into a chunk of real estate.
She'd found me just the place, she said, the cutest house in
all Chicagoland.

This house has been sweet to me, and in return I've kept
it chaste; that is, I haven't punished it with gaiety. No posters
or prayer rugs or art deco glass here, and no humanoid
shapes draped in Indonesian cotton. I've got tables; I've got
a more than decent Oriental rug; I've got lamps. (Lord,
make me Spartan, but not yet.) In my kitchen cupboards
I've got plates and cups that *match*. In the dining-room,
admittedly only nine feet by nine feet, I've got — now this is
possibly a *little* outré — a piano that used to sit in a bar at the
Drake Hotel, and after I finish my paper on Swann for the
symposium in January, I intend to take a few piano lessons.
Brownie says playing the piano is as calming as meditation
and less damaging to the brain cells.

I hope so, because I've never been able to see the point of
emptying one's mind of thought. Our thoughts are all we
have. I love my thoughts, even when they take me up and

down sour-smelling byways where I'd rather not venture. Whatever flickers on in my head is mine and I want it, all the blinking impulses and inclinations and connections and weirdness, and especially those bright purple flares that come streaming out of nowhere, announcing that you're at some mystic juncture or turning point and that you'd better pay attention.

Luckily for me, there have been several such indelible moments, moments that have pressed hard on that quirky narrative I like to think of as the story of my life. For example: at age eight, reading *The Wind in the Willows*. Then saying goodbye to my blameless father (bone cancer). At age fourteen, reading Charlotte Brontë — Charlotte, not Emily. Then saying goodbye, but only tentatively as it turned out, to my mother, a woman called Gladys Shockley Maloney. Next, reading Germaine Greer. Then saying goodbye to my virginity. (Goodbye and goodbye and goodbye.) Then reading Mary Swann and discovering how a human life can be silently snuffed out. Next saying goodbye to Olaf and Oak Park and three months of marriage, and then buying my queer toy house downtown, which I fully intended to sell when the market turned. But unsignalled, along came one of those brilliant purple turning points.

It came because of my fame. My mother has never understood the fame that overtook me in my early twenties. She never believed it was really me, that mouth on the book jacket, yammering away. Neither, for that matter, did I. It was like going through an epidemic of measles, except that I was the only one who got sick.

Six months after *The Female Prism* appeared in the bookstores someone decided I should go on a book-promotion tour — as though a book that was number six on the nonfiction bestseller list needed further pumping up. I started out in Boston, then went to New York, Philadelphia, Pittsburgh, and Cleveland, then hopped to Louisville, skipped to Denver and Houston, and ended up one overcast afternoon on a TV talk show in L.A. The woman who interviewed me was lanky and menacing, wore a fur vest and was dangerously framed by lengths of iodine-glazed hair. To quell her I talked about the surrealism of scholarship. The pretensions. The false systems. The arcane lingo. The macho domination. The garrison mentality. The inbred arrogance.

She leaned across and patted me on the knee and said, "You're not coming from arrogance, sweetie; you're coming from naked need."

Ping! My brain shuddered purple. I was revealed, uncloaked, and as soon as possible I crept back to Chicago, back to my ginger-cookie house on the south side, and made up my mind about one thing: that as long as I lived I would stay in this house. (At least for the next five years.) I felt like kissing the walls and throwing my arms around the punky little newel post and burying my face in its vulva-like carving. This was home. And it seemed I was someone who needed a home. I could go into my little house, my awful neediness and I, and close the doors and shut the curtains and stare at my enduring clutter and be absolutely *still*. Like the theoreticians who currently give me a bad case of frenzies, I'd made a discovery: my life was my own, but I needed a place where I could get away from it.

6

God is dead, peace is dead, the sixties are dead, John Lennon and Simone de Beauvoir are dead, the women's movement is dozing — checking its inventory, let's say — so what's left?

The quotidian is what's left. Mary Swann understood that, if nothing else.

A morning and an afternoon and
Night's queer knuckled hand
Hold me separate and whole
Stitching tight my daily soul.

She spelled it out. The mythic heavings of the universe, so baffling, so incomprehensible, but when squeezed into digestible day-shaped bytes, made swimmingly transparent. Dailiness. The diurnal unit, cloudless and soluble. No wonder the first people on earth worshipped heavenly bodies; between the rising and the setting of the sun their little lives sprouted all manner of shadows and possibilities. Whenever I meet anyone new, I don't say, "Tell me about your belief system." I say, "Tell me about your average day."

Dailiness to be sure has its hard deposits of ennui, but it is also, as Mary Swann suggests, redemptive. I busy my brain with examples.

Every day of his short life, for instance, my father pulled on a pair of cotton socks, and almost every day he turned to my mother and said, "Cotton lets the skin breathe." He also made daily pronouncements on meat that had been frozen: "Breaks down the cell structure," he liked to say. "Destroys the nutrients." In the same way he objected to butter, white bread, sugar — "attacks the blood cells" — garlic (same reason), and anything that had green pepper in it.

He was otherwise a mild man, a math teacher in a west-side high school. His pale red hair, the drift of it over his small ears, his freckled neck and the greenish suits he wore in the classroom — all these things kept him humble. His small recurring judgements on garlic and green pepper were, I've come to see, a kind of vanity for him, an appetite that had to be satisfied, but especially the innocent means by which he was able to root himself in the largeness of time. Always begin a newspaper on the editorial page, he said. Never trust a man who wears sandals or diamond jewellery. These small choices and strictures kept him occupied and anchored while the cancer inched its way along his skeleton.

My mother, too, sighing over her morning cup of coffee and lighting a cigarette, is simply digging in for the short run. And so is my sister, Lena, with her iron pills and coke and nightly shot of Brahms; and Olaf with his shaving ritual, and Brownie with his daily ingestion of flattery and cash. Who can blame them? Who wants to? Habit is the flywheel of society, conserving and preserving and dishing up tidy, edible slices of the cosmos. And there's much to be said for a steady diet. Those newspaper advice-givers who urge you to put a little vinegar in your life are toying, believe me, with your sanity.

Every day, for instance, I eat a cheese on pita for lunch, then an apple. I see no reason to apologize for this habit. Around two-thirty in the afternoon Lois Lundigan and I share a pot of tea, alternating Prince of Wales, Queen Mary, and Earl Grey. She pours. I wash the cups. Sisterhood. Between three and five, unless it's my seminar day, I sit in my office at my desk and work on articles or plan my lectures. At five-thirty I stretch, pack up my beautiful brief-case, say good night to Lois and hit the pavement. The sun's still keyed up, hot and yellow. Every day I walk along the same route, past grimy shrubs and run-down stores and apartment buildings and trees that become leafier as I approach Fifty-seventh Street. About this time I start to feel a small but measurable buzzing in the brain that makes my legs move along in double time. There I am, a determined piece of human matter, but adrift on a busy street that has

suddenly become a conduit — a pipeline possessing the
power of suction. Something, a force more than weariness, is
drawing me home.

There's no mystery about this; I know precisely what
pulls me along. Not food or sex or rest or succour but the
thought of the heap of mail that's waiting for me just inside
my front door.

Among my friends I'm known as the Queen of Correspondence, maintaining, in this day of long-distance phone
calls and even longer silences, what is considered to be a
vast network. This is my corner on quaintness. My crochet
work. My apple sauce. Mail comes pouring in, national and
international, postcards and air letters and queer stamps
crowded together in the corners of bulging envelopes.
Letters from old school friends await me or letters from
sisters in the movement. Perhaps a scrawl from my six-year-
old nephew, Franklin, and my real sister, Lena, in London.
My editor in New York is forever showering me with witty,
beseeching notes. Virginia Goodchild, my former lawyer,
writes frequently from New Orleans where she now has her
practice. Olaf, in Tübingen, keeps in touch. So do last year's
batch of graduate students and the year before's, a sinuous
trail of faces and words. There are always, always, letters
waiting. A nineteenth-century plenitude. I tear them open,
I burn and freeze, I consume them with heathenish joy,
smiling as I read, tapping my foot, and planning what I'll
write back, what epics out of my ongoing life I'll select,
touch up, and entrust to the international mails.

Mailless weekends are hell, but Monday's bounty
partially compensates. Every evening I write a letter, sometimes two, while the rest of the world plays Scrabble or
watches TV or files its nails or whatever the rest of the
world does. I write letters that are graceful and agreeable,

far more graceful and agreeable than I am in my face-to-face encounters. My concern, my well-governed wit, my closet kindness all crowd to the fore, revealing that rouged, wrinkled, Russian-like persona that I like to think is my true self. (Pick up a pen and a second self squirms out.) The maintenance of my persona and the whole getting and sending of letters provide necessary traction to my quotidian existence, give me a kick, a lift, a jolt, a fix, a high, a way of seizing time and keeping it in order.

Today there's a thick letter from Morton Jimroy in California. A four-pager or I'm an elephant's eyebrow. I can't get it open fast enough. There I stand, reading it, still in my coat and hat with my beautiful briefcase thrown down on the floor along with the mutilated envelope.

I read it once, twice, then put it aside. While eating dinner — a boned chicken breast steamed in grapefruit juice and a branch of broccoli *al dente* — I read it a third time. I've been writing to Morton Jimroy for almost a year now and find him a teasing correspondent.

Today's letter is particularly problematic, containing as it does one of Jimroy's ambushing suggestions. I'll wait exactly one week before I reply and then — now I'm eating dessert, which is a slice of hazelnut torte from the local bakery — I'll send him one of my two-draft specials.

It's a guilty secret of mine that I write two kinds of letters, one-drafters and two-drafters. For old friends I bang out exuberant single-spaced typewritten letters, all the grammar jangled loose with dashes and exclamation points and reckless transitions. Naturally, I trust these old friends to read my letters charitably and overlook the awful girlish breathlessness and say to themselves, "Well, Sarah leads such a busy life, we're lucky to get *any* kind of letter out of her."

But in my two-draft letters I mind my manners, sometimes even forsaking my word-processor for the pen. Only
yesterday I wrote a double-drafter to Syd Buswell in
Ottawa. "Dear Professor Buswell," I wrote. "On behalf of
the Steering Committee of the Swann Symposium, may I
say how much we regret that you will not be presenting your
paper in January. Nevertheless, we hope you will attend and
participate in discussions." I keep myself humble, am mind-
ful of paragraph coherence, and try for a tincture of charm.

For Morton Jimroy, *the* Morton Jimroy, biographer of
Ezra Pound, John Starman, and now Mary Swann, I get out
my best paper and linger over my longhand, my lovely
springy I's and e's, aglide on their invisible blue wires. And I
always do a second draft.

Once again — now I'm having coffee, feet up on the
coffee table — I read Jimroy's letter. Though his home is
in Winnipeg, Canada, this letter is from California where
he's spending a year putting together his notes on Mary
Swann. Today's letter, like his others, is imbued with a sense
of pleading, but for what? — who can tell? His are letters
from which the voice has been drained off, and instead
there's a strenuous concentration, each casual phrase
propped up by rhetoric and positioned so as to signal
candour — but a candour undercut by the pain of deliberate
placement. Ring around the rosy. How am I supposed to
interpret all this? Painstaking letters are born of pain; I must
be generous, I must overlook transparent strategy, stop
sniffing for a covert agenda. But there's something unset-
tling in the way he's always wringing a response from me. I
am summoned, commanded to comment and comfort and
offer gifts of flattery.

He has one rare quality that I suspect is genuine: an urge
for confession, or at least intimacy. We've never met and

have no claims on each other, and there's no real reason for
him to tell me about the depression he suffered after his
book on Starman was published, a long painful depression,
which — he told me all this in a previous letter — neither
medication nor analysis was able to heal.

My dear Sarah,

    I am someone who can understand how Flaubert
must have felt when seized with doubt about the validity
of art, his terrifying perception — false, thank God —
that art was nothing but a foolish and childish plaything.
This was exactly the state of my mind when Oxford Press
sent me my advance copy of the Starman biography some
years back. It arrived, I remember, at breakfast time —
forgive me if I've written this before — swathed in a
padded envelope. I opened it at once, regarded its gleaming cover and experienced — nothing. The granola and
milk in my bowl had more reality than this pound and a
half of text with its appendices, its execrable, sprawling
annotation, and, worst of all, its footnotes. These footnotes, I realized at that moment, were footnotes on
Starman's footnotes. And I could imagine what would
occur in the future, as surely as day must follow night: a
graduate student would one day construct footnotes on
my footnotes to *Starman's* footnotes. The thought brought
a physical sense of shame. I felt not only self-disgust but
the fierce sadness of a wasted life, the conviction that I had
done nothing but dally with the dallyings of other human
beings. Such a feeling of depression — perhaps you know,
though I hope you don't — can be swift and overwhelming. It seemed to me at that moment that not a single man
on earth had ever spoken the truth. We were all, every last
one of us, liars and poseurs.

Ah, but on that same morning, in the same lot of mail, came the latest issue of *PMLA* (a periodical, by the way, that I often feel contributes to the gastritis of the lit business). On this particular morning I opened the journal to your article on Swann. Who is this Mary Swann? I wondered. And who is this Sarah Maloney? I read quickly through your introduction to *our* poet. And then came to those eight quoted lines from "March Morning." (By coincidence, it *was* a March morning, a murky, tenebrous Winnipeg morning.) Reading, I felt a oneness with this Mary Swann. (I never think of her by her Christian name alone, do you?) I felt that same "Iron flower of my hand/ Cheated by captured ice and/Earth and sand." (I have little patience with those who consider Swann a primitive because she didn't use four-syllable words. She was — is — a poet of great sophistication of mind.) But it was the vigour of the lines that struck me at first, the way they shifted and worked together, cross-bonded like plywood sheets. (You see how she infects me with her colloquial images.) My only disappointment was in finding she had written so little, though one is grateful for what does exist, and there are the love poems to come — *if* they come, I've never trusted Lang — and, of course, the notebook.

About Swann's notebook, I am wondering once again if I can persuade you to change your mind about sharing its contents, at least partially. My research here has gone extremely well, but I've been frustrated by having to rely on secondary and tertiary sources almost exclusively. (Swann's daughter, whom I've been interviewing, is a woman of opaque memory and curious insensitivity — she has, for instance, saved only the most cursory notes from her mother, not the confiding letters that I am sure must have existed.) It seems to me that a page or two from

the notebook — I would of course pay for photocopying
and so on — would bring our graceful Swann out of the
jungle of conjecture and, as she herself would say —

> Into the carpeted clearing
> Into the curtained light
> Behind the sun's loud staring
> Away from the sky's hard bite.

Do, Sarah, let me know if this request from a
fellow scholar is impertinent. I feel, and I am sure you will
agree with me, that Mary Swann belongs to all of us, to
the world, that is — her poems, her scraps and ciphers,
her poor paltry remains.

It now looks as though I will be able to come to the
symposium after all, and I will be happy to deliver a few
remarks, as you suggest, on the progress of the Life. I am
sorry to hear that Buswell has cancelled, though it seems a
trifle paranoid of him to think his notes were stolen.
Mislaid, perhaps; but — stolen!

I so look forward to meeting you in person, though I
know you already as a dear friend. Such is the power and
warmth of your letters.

                                    With affection,
                                    Morton Jimroy

He's ingenious, Morton Jimroy. But worrying. Every
sentence, the way it shapes itself around a tiny, tucked
grimace — I feel the weight of it all. (Lifting the paper to
my face I inhale the faint smell of cigarettes.) I will have to
write him a careful letter. (Now I'm dressed in the old
sweatshirt I wear to bed, part of my dark ritual. I've already
phoned Brownie to whisper good night, and I've propped
myself up in bed with my reading light shining over my

shoulder.) I will have to tell the good persevering Morton Jimroy how pleased I was to hear from him, how warmed I was to hear him assert, once again, that it was I who introduced him to the work of Mary Swann. All of this is true. It will flow out of my pen untroubled.

But I will have to say *no* to him about the notebook. Politely. Correctly. But conceding nothing. *No*, Morton. I cannot. I am sorry, Morton. I regret. I wish. I understand your position. But no, no, no, no, no. I am not yet ready to publish the contents of Mary Swann's notebook.

Dear Morton. (I'm sliding into sleep, adrift between layers of consciousness.) Dear Morton. Soon the prima facie evidence will be in the public domain, available to all, et cetera, et cetera, but now, for a few months longer, until January, please forgive me (yawn), Mary Swann's notebook is mine.

7

Happiness is not my greatest need. My greatest need is to feel that every part of me is fully in use, or *engagé* as people used to say a mere ten years ago, and that all my sensory equipment is stretched as nervously as possible between a state of apprehension and a posture of pounce. I want my brain to be all sinew and thrum, chime and clerestory, crouch and attack.

Which more or less describes my condition on Saturday, a gilded October afternoon, when I attended a new exhibition of pencil drawings executed by my extraordinary friend and sometime mentor, Peggy O'Reggis.

I had spent a frivolous morning in bed with Virginia Woolf, lunched on herrings in sour cream, and then taken

the bus down to the Dearborn Gallery. By the time I got
there the room was filled with a zesty mix of friends and
strangers, mostly between the ages of twenty and forty, all of
them chatting, nodding their heads, embracing, drinking
wine and peering with squinty eyes into Peggy's tiny
crowded drawings, which always remind me of snapshots of
the brain's prescient vibrations. The colours she favours
include a lollipop pink and a rich oily green, and what she
draws are ideas. With resolute angular turnings, each pencil
line duplicates the way that precious commodity *thought* is
launched and transformed. Here there was a calculated
mimetic thrust, there a microscopic explosion of reason, here
an intellectual equation of great tenderness and, next to it, a
begging void exerting its airy magnetism.

As in her previous exhibitions, the drawings were all
titled — for which, being part of the word culture, I
thanked God. Images can speak, yes, but some of us need
to be directed toward the port of entry. Yet there's never
anything authoritarian about Peggy's titles, just a nudging,
helpful "Untroubled Night" or "Open Heart" or, the one I
most admired yesterday, "Vision Intercepted."

Standing before "Vision Intercepted" with my glass of
red wine in hand, I experienced that sharp electrical fusing
that sometimes occurs when art meets the mind head-on.
Beside me, sharing my brief flight of transcendence, were a
yellow-haired woman in a rawhide jacket and my old friend
Stephen Stanhope, the juggler. We didn't speak, not even to
exchange greetings, but instead continued to gaze. The
moment stretched and stretched, the kind of phenomenon
that happens so rarely that the experience of it must be cherished in silence and persuaded to linger as long as possible.

And so, riding home on the bus, I gave myself over
to the closed eye's bright penetration, trying to call back

the image of Peggy O'Reggis's circling, colliding lines and colours. A pattern or perhaps a sensual vibration began to dance across my retina and grope toward form. I summoned it, let it emerge, luxuriously let it have its way. But something kept spoiling my satisfaction, some nagging thought or worrying speck at the periphery of vision. I opened my eyes. The sun poured in the dirty windows, warming my arm. A woman with a blanket-wrapped baby on her lap sat across from me, a slender, long-necked black woman with amber eyes, clearly infatuated with her child's beauty. With a free hand she stroked its knitted blanket. The baby made cooing sounds like a little fish and stared dreamily up into an advertisement for men's jockey shorts. In the ad, a man with a bulging crotch was leaping over a bonfire, an expression of rapture on his daft face. He and the small baby and the baby's mother and I seemed suddenly to form one of those random, hastily assembled families that are hatched in the small spaces of large cities and come riding atop a compendium of small pleasures. But today's pleasures, pungent though they were, made me less willing than usual to surrender my earlier perception.

What was it that was getting in the way? I poked part way into my subconscious, imagining a pencil in my hand. There was my usual catalogue of shame. Wasted time? Careless work? Had I forgotten to phone my mother? — no. Shopping to be done? Someone's feelings hurt?

Guilt has the power to extract merciless sacrifices, but it was not guilt that was interfering with my attempt to bring back the voluptuous sensation that briefly enclosed me in the Dearborn Gallery. It was something smaller and less formed, an act of neglect or loss that scuttled like an insect across my consciousness and that, because of the wine or the wooziness of the sunshine, I was unable to remember.

Later it came to me. It was midnight of the same day. I
was ready to go to bed, but first I was locking the doors,
checking the windows, turning out the lights, listening to
the silence and darkness that blew through the house. My
thoughts were of Mary Swann, how she must also have
performed night rituals, though not the same ones as mine.
I tried to imagine what these rituals might be. Might she
have looked out the kitchen window into the windy, starry
night, trying to guess at the next day's weather? Would she
hook a screen door or perhaps set a kettle of soup or oats on
the back of the woodstove? Perhaps there was a cat or dog
that had to be let out, though she had never in her poems or
in her notebook mentioned such a cat or dog.

And then I remembered — Lord! — what had been
begging all day to be remembered. It was Mary Swann's
notebook, which I keep on a bookshelf over my bed. I had
not seen it there for several days.

8

In a sense I invented Mary Swann and am responsible
for her.

No, too literary that. Better just say I discovered Mary
Swann. Even Willard Lang admits (officially, too) that
I am more or less — he is endlessly equivocal in the best
scholarly tradition — *more or less* the discoverer of Swann's
work. He has even committed this fact to print in a short
footnote on page six of his 1983 paper "Swann's Synthesis,"
naming me, Sarah Maloney of Chicago, the one "most
responsible for bringing the poet Mary Swann to public
attention." This mention on Willard's part is an academic
courtesy and no more.

Ah, but Willard's kind of courtesy amounts to a professional sawing off, a token coin dropped in a bank to permit future withdrawals. Willard Lang's nod in my direction — "S. Maloney must be cited as the one who" — is a simple declaration of frontier between authority and discovery, Willard being the authority, while S. Maloney (me) is given the smaller, slightly less distinguished role of discoverer.

In truth, no one really discovers anyone; it's the stickiest kind of arrogance even to think in such terms. Mary Swann discovered herself, and therein, suspended on tissues of implausibility, like a hammock without strings, hangs the central mystery: how did she do it? Where in those bleak Ontario acres, that littered farmyard, did she find the sparks that converted emblematic substance into rolling poetry? Chickens, outhouses, wash-day, woodpiles, porch, husband, work-boots, overalls, bedstead, filth. That's the stuff this woman had to work with.

On the other hand, it's a legacy from the patriarchy, a concomitant of conquest, the belief that poets shape their art from materials that are mysterious and inaccessible. Women have been knitting socks for centuries, and probably they've been constructing, in their heads, lines of poetry that never got written down. Mary Swann happened to have a pen, a Parker 51 as a matter of fact, as well as an eye for the surface of things. Plus the kind of heart-cracking persistence that made her sit down at the end of a tired day and box up her thoughts into quirky parcels of rhymed verse.

It was an incredible thing for a woman in her circumstances to do, and in the face of so much implausibility I sometimes chant to myself the simple list that braces and contains her. Girlhood in Belleville, Ontario; schooling limited; nothing known about mother; or father; worked for a year in a local bakery; married a farmer and moved to the

Nadeau district, where she bore a daughter, wrote poems, and got herself killed at the age of fifty. That's all. How Jimroy intends to boil up a book out of this thin stuff is a mystery.

My own responsibility toward Mary Swann, as I see it, is custodial. If Olaf Thorkelson hadn't badgered me into near breakdown and driven me into the refuge of northern Wisconsin where Mary Swann's neglected book of poems fell like a bouquet into my hands, I would never have become Swann's watchwoman, her literary executor, her defender and loving caretaker. But, like it or not, that's what I am. Let others promote her and do their social and psychoanalytical sugarjobs on her; but does anyone else — besides me that is — detect the little smiles breaking around her most dolorous lines? Willard Lang, swine incarnate, is capable of violating her for his own gain, and so is the absent-minded, paranoid, and feckless Buswell in Ottawa. Morton Jimroy means well, poor sap, but he'll try to catch her out or bend her into God's messenger or the hand-maiden of Emily Dickinson; or else he'll stick her into a three-cornered constellation along with poor impotent Pound and that prating, penis-dragging Starman. Someone has to make sure she's looked after. Because her day is coming. Never mind what Willard Lang thinks. Mary Swann is going to be big, big, big. She's the right person at the right time for one thing: a woman, a survivor, self-created. A man like Morton Jimroy wouldn't be bothering with her if he didn't think she was going to take off. Willard wouldn't be wasting his time organizing a symposium if he didn't believe her reputation was ripe for the picking. These guys are greedy. They would eat her up, inch by inch. Scavengers. Brutes. This is a wicked world, and the innocent need protection.

Which is why I find it impossible to forgive myself for losing her notebook.

9

It's been lost for several days. Since Monday probably, maybe Tuesday.

I'm not willing yet to admit that it is *irretrievably* lost; it is just — what? — misplaced. Any day now, tomorrow maybe, I'll find it under a pile of letters in my desk drawer. It might have got slipped into a bookcase, it's so small, one of those little spiral notebooks the colour of cheap chocolate. It's just waiting, perversely, to surprise me one day when I least expect it. It might be under a corner of a rug. Or right out in plain sight somewhere, only my eyes are too frantic to focus on the spot.

I'm not a careless person, though I remind myself a dozen times a day, as a kind of palliating commentary, that this is not the first thing I've lost. Once, when I was married to Olaf, I lost my wedding ring. I was devastated, almost sick, and hadn't been able to tell Olaf about it because I knew he would see it as a portent; and there it was, two weeks later, in a little ceramic dish where I kept my paper-clips. Another time I lost my first-edition copy of *The Second Sex,* which I'd bought at Stanton's for ten bucks back in the good old days. For months I'd wandered around like a mad woman, wrenching cushions off chairs and wailing to the walls, "Books don't just get up and walk away." In the spring a dear friend, Lorenzo Drouin, the medievalist, found it wedged behind a radiator in my living-room.

About the lost notebook my mother is sympathetic but vague. She asks if I've checked the pockets of my

raincoat or lent it to a friend or thrown it out with the
newspapers — preposterous suggestions all, the utterance of
which points to her essential helplessness and to how little
she understands my life. "It'll turn up," she murmurs and
murmurs, my comforting plump spaniel of a mother. But
helpless, helpless.

I visit my mother every Sunday. On Sunday morning
in the city of Chicago other people wake up thinking:
How will this day be spent? What surprises will it bring?
Sunday is a day with a certain lustre on it, a certain hum.
The unscheduled hours seduce or threaten, depending on
circumstances, on money or friends or on health or weather;
but there is always, I'm convinced, an anticipatory rustle, a
curtain sliding open onto possibility.

Not for me, though. You might say I'm a professional
daughter, or at least a serious hobbyist. On Sundays I get on
the L and go to see my mother, who lives in a third-floor
apartment on the west side. She expects me at 1:00 P.M. give
or take five minutes. She watches from the window as I
come trotting down the tree-lined street, slips the brass
chain off the lock, and enfolds me in her heated feathery
arms, saying, "Hi there, sweetie pie."

Immediately the two of us sit down in the dinette to a
full dinner, roast chicken or ham with mashed potatoes,
frozen peas or string beans, and for dessert ice cream in a
cereal bowl. My mother and I talk and talk, and if I stop
now to think of those scattered others outside in the streets
or parks of Chicago who are freely disposing of the day,
it's with scornful pity. The beckoning Sunday spaces are
revealed in all their dinginess. Whatever possibilities had
winked and chittered in the morning have by this time dried
up, and here sit I, the luckiest of women, brimming with
home-cooked food and my mother's steady, unfocused love.

Nevertheless, I'm full of jumps and twitches today.

"Something's bothering you," she divines.

"That idiotic notebook," I rage. "I still can't find the damn thing."

"Oh, dear." The mildest profanity confuses her. "Let me give you some more coffee. It'll calm you down."

My mother's the only person I know who believes coffee possesses tranquilizing properties. She lifts the coffee pot, holds on to the lid, and pours. Light filters through the Venetian blind. Above her head, on a small shelf, is her row of Hummel figurines and Delft plates. Also a small Virgin Mary, rather crowded to one side, which she was given as a young girl. (I'd be a better woman if I didn't notice such things.) My mother's dressed today in a pantsuit, her new coral double-knit, which is generously cut and comfortable around the hips. She never wore pants until she was in her late fifties; then her legs lost their shapeliness, overnight becoming straight and thick as water pipes. Her grey hair is always combed and pinned in place to form a roll at the back of her head; if this roll of hair were pinned a mere eighth of an inch higher, it would be stylish instead of matronly. Still, she takes pains with her appearance. Even when she's home alone in her apartment, she wears lipstick, a bright pink shade, and a touch of blue eye shadow. She also wears large button earrings; she likes silver; not real silver, of course — she's never been able to see the sense of expensive jewellery. She owns about twenty pairs of these large round earrings, which she keeps on a clear plastic earring rack on her bureau.

All that stands between my mother and me are trivial preferences of diet and reading matter and decor. I don't own an earring rack like the one on her bureau, and she has never heard of Muriel Rukeyser. And what else? Not much.

A scholarship, a few exams, some letters after my name instead of before. *(Mrs. — she would like me to be a Mrs.)*

"How's that pain in your side?" I ask, to change the subject. "What did LeBlanc have to say about that?"

"Dr. LeBlanc?" Her sly courtesy. "He just said we'd have to keep an eye on it." She shakes her head, trying hard to look merry. "But you know, I think it's going away, the pain."

"That's good."

"Yes, I've got a feeling — "

"It's not keeping you awake then?"

"Heavens no, you know me, I sleep like a log."

"Last Sunday you said — "

"Nothing wrong with my sleep. I've always been a good sleeper."

"Hmmmm," I say, knowing my mother's habits, how she stays up until two every morning watching TV talk shows, and then is wide awake by six-thirty, sitting at the table, her heavy shoulders erect over a bowl of All-Bran, a cup of coffee before her, alert for the seven o'clock news coming out of her kitchen radio, ready to reach for her first cigarette of the day.

My mother has weathered life reasonably well, upheld, my sister and I believe, by her natural inclination toward sadness and turned by it into a kind of postulant, fumbling her way through small, meaningless acts of contrition. She always seems fresh from the country of tears, though I haven't seen her cry openly since Olaf and I announced our divorce. The divorce cast her down, perhaps because she perceived some motive unconfessed. My sister's divorce caused similar alarm and confusion but, except for my father's death and the two divorces, her sadness seems starved of particulars. Like a spider who eats her mate, she has absorbed the sadness of the world into her heavy bones and bloodstream. It's always there, like a low-grade fever.

I'm amazed by how, despite it, she manages. She reads the newspapers, goes to mass, plays canasta. Today she's leaning on the table and talking calmly about the price of baby-beef liver. After that she tells me about an article in the back of the leisure section of the newspaper: how to remove thrips from gladiolus bulbs.

I know what she suffers from: she suffers from "it." The nameless disease. An autumnal temperament. Constitutional melancholy. *Ennui. Angst* is close, the word I'd use if it weren't such a cheap scrubbing-brush of a word. I once tried to explain *Angst* to my mother, who said she found the idea of it incomprehensible. But existential anxiety is what she has, a bad case, a suspicion — she would never acknowledge it — of emptiness at the heart of life.

I imagine that my father watched with bewilderment the spectre of this large, perpetually grieving woman. My coked-up sister, Lena, has been driven by it to fits of self-indulgence, new cities, new lovers, and a series of bizarre jobs. And I've been forced into a kind of reckless ebullience; my mother's malaise, or whatever it is, has declared that the regions of despair must be forever closed to me, and that the old Sarah Maloney, dimly remembered even by me, is far behind — that mild Catholic daughter, that reader of Thomas Hardy, with shoulder-length hair and wide pleated skirts. Another Sarah has taken over, twenty-eight, sanguine, expectant, jaunty, bluffing her way. Her awful sprightly irrepressible self appals me.

How does it happen that this giddy girl and tenacious scholar inhabit the same small swervy body? A good question. A *meaty* question. Unanswerable.

I kiss my mother goodbye energetically, praise her

cooking, tell her to look after herself, remind her of her doctor's appointment, and then go swinging off down the street. The light, so lurid and promising earlier in the day, is feeble now, and the trees look misshapen, as though they've been recycled from dead brush. Autumn. This is a time of day I particularly like and feel attuned to. A narrow passageway, dilated just for me. The word *crepuscular* pops into my head, then disintegrates, too queenly a word for a patchy night like this. And here comes a gust of wind, knocking the leaves off the branches and leading me back to reality.

Ah, but what is reality? In a fit of self-mockery, thinking of Brownie, I ask myself this question, and an answer comes dancing in front of my lips. Reality is no more than a word that begins with *r* and ends with *y*.

Exactly. Oh, Lord!

10

Most of the men I know are defective. Most of them are vain. My good friend and mentor Peggy O'Reggis lives in a universe in which men are only marginally visible. Ditto my lawyer, Virginia Goodchild, a committed citizen of Lesbos. At least half of my graduate students are determined to carry their own tent pegs, to hell with the male power structure and to hell with penetration as sexual expression. They've bailed out. All these women send me invitations, literal and subliminal, but something in me resists.

Genes probably, or maybe conditioning. At least once a month, ever since my divorce, my mother inquires, shyly, stumblingly, fingering her St. Agatha's medal, whether I've "found someone." A man, she means. She looks at me sideways, her large round earrings at attention. Am I still seeing that nice . . . Stephen Stanhope? Only occasionally, I tell her, not having the heart to explain that Stephen and I ended our love affair months ago. I'm not sure what happened. Maybe just that his identity was threatened because I wouldn't move in with him — as though anyone in her right mind would abandon the uniqueness of a fantasy house on the south side for a brick duplex out in Maywood. He also accused me, gently, of being ashamed of his profession, which is juggling, an accusation with not a shred of truth to it. Didn't I once live (briefly) with a tree surgeon? Didn't I make a trip to the Everglades with a man who repaired pianos?

I don't like to raise my mother's hopes, and so it wasn't until last week that I admitted to her that I was "seeing" a man called Brownie.

The minute I made this statement, over roasted turkey breast and mashed turnips, it all seemed ludicrously untrue, a story I'd invented in order to please her.

It happens fairly often, this sensation of being a captive of fiction, a sheepish player in my own *roman-à-clef*. My dwarfish house is the setting. The stacked events of the day form the plot, and Brownie and I are the chief characters, sometimes larger than life, but just as often smaller. Tonight, Tuesday, we are shrunken and stagey, a pair of fretting silhouettes lolling on a sofa in front of my fireplace.

The first time I saw this fireplace I thought it was hideous, a wavy opening in the wall, framed all around by shiny, ginger-coloured tile that in the daylight always looks faintly dusty. It has turned out to be surprisingly efficient, as fireplaces go, deep and with a strong draft. Once lit, the fire burns cleanly. A wide brush of calm, bright, yellow-centred flames that are reflected all around the

tile edges and transformed into something cool and marble-
toned. I burn good, dry, sweet-smelling logs, which cost me
exactly one buck apiece, but I save on kindling, making do
with my students' old term papers and exam booklets.

"Try to be calm," Brownie, just back from California,
is saying about Mary Swann's lost notebook. "You're overreacting. You're — "

"If you're going to suggest I'm ovulating you can go
straight to hell." I say this nicely.

"When did you last see it, the notebook? Try to
reconstruct."

This is the problem. I don't know. A week ago, maybe
two weeks ago. It was on my bookshelf. It's been on my
bookshelf for several years now, part of the decor, resting on
a copy of V.S. Pritchett's autobiography, casually abandoned
as if it were worthless, under-appreciated — only now that
it's lost, it suddenly vibrates with uniqueness and value. I
should have kept it in a safe-deposit box — which is what
Brownie does with his *Plastic Man* collection — or at least in
a locked desk drawer.

"What about your office?" Brownie suggests. (I can tell
he's bored with the topic, his tongue on his teeth like that.)
"Or in your briefcase?"

"I never take it to the office."

"Maybe you wanted to show it to someone." The contours of his face are unreadable, and make me feel like a
child, on my honour to behave.

"No, I don't think so." Wavering now.

"Your mother's place? On Sunday?"

"Of course not," I snap. This is getting us nowhere.

"It'll turn up," Brownie croons.

His face rearranges itself, shifting from pinkness
to something more determined. His arm is around me, his

fingers dancing on my bare arm, and for some reason I am unsettled by his phrase, *it'll turn up*. Perhaps because it's the same phrase my mother used. A placebo, a mindless tablet of optimism, *it'll turn up*. Did they think it was going to leap out of the walls?

Brownie rubs my back and tells me how, when he was twelve, he lost an envelope of stamps an uncle had sent him from Mexico. The loss was so grievous to him — not because he collected stamps or even liked stamps, but because he felt stupid and careless and unworthy — that he had actually wept, privately of course, with his head in his pillow. Later the stamps were found pressed inside his school dictionary where he must have placed them for safekeeping. (Ah, Brownie; I imagine a slim boy with brown wooly hair cut short over sunburned ears, sitting alone in a small room, opening a book with a blue cloth cover and lifting from its pages a small glassine packet.)

"It's bound to turn up," he says again. "And besides" — his words form a calm electric buzzing at the nape of my neck — "besides, it's been photocopied."

Yes, of course, I admit it; the *contents* have been photocopied, but *it* is lost.

"You can't say it's really lost," Brownie says, giving me a fine ironic smile. "Not if there's a copy in the archives."

"A copy's not the same thing. As you know perfectly well." And I yawn to show him I'm sleepy and ready to climb into bed, ready to bury all this fuss in the creases of his body. A muscle inside me unclasps itself.

"You're tired," Brownie says. "I'd better not stay tonight." And he grabs for his coat. Quickly.

There's no talking him out of going, not without pleading. So I get into bed alone and toss for several hours. My trick of timing my breath to match a line of iambic

pentameter fails and so does my other trick of reciting the
ingredients for blanquette de veau, one large onion, one
carrot quartered, two celery stalks. Two o'clock comes and
goes, then three o'clock. I entertain myself with miniature
horror stories. Could the notebook have got mixed up with
that bundle of newspapers, those same bundled papers I
used to start a fire in the fireplace last week, the night when
frost was predicted and Brownie came through the door
with a nimbus of cold around his hair and — or maybe I
picked it up with the offprints on Sara Teasdale and took
it to the office and maybe Lois Lundigan, thinking it was
scrap paper — no, ridiculous. But not impossible. Four
o'clock, four-thirty. I go over and over the possibilities until
they strum a rusty plinked tune in my head, one of those old
half-lisped songs from the sixties that are all refrain and
three-quarters nonsense. Lost, lost, lost, gone.

11

It's possible to be brilliant without being profound — or, in
Mary Swann's case, profound without being brilliant.

Think of brilliance as sunlight sparking off salty little
waves, as particles of glare or shine that tease the eye. Then
think of the underwater muscle of a very large ocean or the
machinery of the earth's shifting plates.

Reading Mary Swann's poetry for the first time
(Wisconsin, that screened porch, flies buzzing) I found
myself suddenly grabbed by an elemental seizure of the
first order. I was instantly alert, attenuated, running my
fingers under the words, writing furiously in the margin
(and recognizing at the same time the half-melancholy truth
that this was what I would always, somewhere or other,

be doing.) I *read Swann's Songs* at one sitting. Then I sat perfectly still for a few minutes, and then I read it again. A note on the back of the book said only that Mary Swann, 1915-1965, had lived in Nadeau, Ontario.

A week later I was back in Chicago packing my bags. I rented a car and drove up through the state of Michigan and after that across the little humped hills of western Ontario. In twenty-four hours I was standing in front of the town hall of the village of Nadeau, population 1,750, a village with a cheese factory and a knitting mill and a dozen or so quiet green streets shaded by maples and poplars and elms.

The first person I saw — this was very early on a Sunday morning in the month of August — was a balding old guy in a wrinkled cotton suit, Mr. Homer Hart (as I later found out), retired school principal, recovering (though I didn't know it then) from a nervous breakdown, his third. He was walking a large golden retriever, and he and the dog, Spanish Jim, had paused beneath a half-dead elm, the dog to raise his leg and Mr. Hart to peer up sorrowfully into the lattice of drooping branches. We froze, the three of us, as though we'd taken our assigned places on a small grassy stage. All around us I could hear the twittering of bird-song and feel the cool stirring of morning air. Then Spanish Jim opened his mouth, yipped excitedly, danced over to where I was standing and began sniffing at my jeans, pulling back a meaty lip and huffing hard so that I felt his breath through the cloth. "He won't hurt you," Mr. Hart called in a tissuey voice, his hands flapping in his pockets. "That's his way of saying good morning to you."

I explained — while Mr. Hart nodded and nodded — who I was and why I'd driven all the way from Chicago up to Nadeau, Ontario. "What I'd really like," I said, "is to talk to someone who actually knew Mary Swann."

"The person you want to talk to," Homer Hart said, composing himself, "is the one and only Rose Hindmarch."

"Rose Hindmarch?" I bared my teeth, a sort of smile, but not too eager, I hoped. Spanish Jim had left off licking my shoes and was chasing squirrels across the broad lawn. "Is Rose Hindmarch a relative?"

"Oh, dear, no, there aren't any relatives, afraid not. You see, Mary Swann's people came from over Belleville way. Oh, there's a daughter, but she's out in California, on the coast, married, never comes back here, not since her mother passed on."

"Rose Hindmarch, you said?" Where was my tape recorder when I needed it?

"Well," he said, "Rose was a friend, you might say, of Mary Swann. Rose's our librarian, you see, also our township clerk, and she knew Mary Swann pretty well. Well, now, let me qualify that last statement of mine. Let's say that Rose knew her as well as anyone did. Mrs. Swann wasn't what you'd call a mixer. She more or less kept to herself, a farm woman, only came into town every couple of weeks."

"Every couple of weeks?" I squeaked, wondering if I could remember all this to write down later.

"Did her shopping and then went over to the library to borrow herself a couple of books to read. She was a reader, Mrs. Swann, a real reader, as well as quite the celebrated poetess. Had a real way with words. Could spin off a poem on any subject you could mention. Snow storms, the lake when the ice was going. A really nice one she did about an apple tree, I believe. Wish I could remember just how it went. 'De dum, de dum the apple tree.' Something like that. You read that poem and all of a sudden you can see that tree in your own imagination, the blossoms coming out, a picture made out of words. It was extraordinary what that woman could do with hardly any schooling. Well, as I say, Rose Hindmarch is our librarian. We have a dandy library for a place this size, and if anyone can tell you about Mrs. Swann, it's Rose."

Rose Hindmarch turned out to be a little turtle of a woman with a hair on her chin like a hieroglyph, quintessentially virginal, mid-forties, twinkly eyed, suppliant, excitable. We spent all of Sunday afternoon together, sitting in the sweltering living-room of her apartment — her suite as she called it — which was the second floor of an old frame Nadeau house. I marvelled that Mary Swann's only friend should be a librarian with a little escutcheon face and a nervous laugh. I could see right away that I frightened her.

I often frighten people. I frighten myself, as a matter of fact, my undeflectable energy probably. I did what I could to put Rose at her ease, praising the ferns in her window, the lamp on top of her colour TV, the afghan on her sofa, the crocheted runner on her oak table, her method of brewing tea, her enthusiasm for spy stories, and for local history, and, especially — I approached the subject delicately — especially her interest in the poet Mary Swann.

In an hour she was won over, so quickly won over that I winced with shame. Rose seemed a woman inseparable from the smell of face powder and breath mints, and on that powdery, breathy face was the dumb shine of stunted experience. But she was, and there is no other word for it, a good woman. A true sense of humility, the sort I would like to claim for myself, made her open and truthful. I knew I could trust her. As she talked, I took notes, feeling like a thief but not missing a word.

It came out slowly at first. Yes, she had known Mary Swann. Their mutual love of books had brought them together; she actually uttered that face-powdery phrase,

looking straight into my eyes: *our mutual love of books*.
I pressed for details. How well had she known her? Well,
she said, better than most folks. Most folks only saw Mary
Swann from a distance, a farm woman buying groceries,
wearing a man's old coat and an awful pair of canvas shoes.
But Mary Swann liked to linger at the desk in the library
when she could and talk about her favorite writer who
was Bess Streeter Aldrich. Oh, and Edna Ferber, she was a
true-blue Edna Ferber fan.

Later in the afternoon Rose offered me a drink of
rye whisky and ginger-ale in a juice glass. She went into a
hostessy flutter, bringing out a bowl of potato chips, and also
a bowl of sour-cream dip. Her tongue loosened and she told
me about Mary Swann's husband, who was a dirt-poor
farmer, an ignorant man given to rages. He begrudged his
wife's visits to the village library, that much was clear.
He told anybody who'd listen that women had better things
to do than gobble up time reading story books. He waited
outside for her in his truck, giving her only a few minutes to
get her books, honking the horn when he got impatient, and
letting her check out just two books at a time. That was his
limit. He had a beaky red face and button eyes. No one
could figure out why she stayed with him. He didn't have so
much as a single friend. People shied away from him. Their
daughter, though, a smart girl, did well in her schooling,
her mother's influence likely, and won herself a scholarship.
She got away, but not Mary. Some people in the district
said Angus Swann beat his wife up regularly. Once she
appeared in town with a black eye and a sprained arm. It
was also said he burned some of her poems in the cookstove
and so she took to hiding them under the kitchen linoleum.
A regular scoundrel, a monster. "And of course you know
what happened in the end," Rose Hindmarch said.

"What?" I asked.

"You mean to say you really don't know?"

"No."

Rose's eyes glistened. Then she said, "Why that man put a bullet right through her head and chopped her up into little pieces."

12

I stayed in Nadeau for two days, getting myself a room at the Nadeau Hotel over the beer parlour. Rose Hindmarch, along with Homer Hart and his wife, Daisy, accompanied me out to the cemetery to see where Mary Swann was buried. There was a pretty piece of sloping land with a neat stone, a modest block of granite, and the words "Mary Swann, 1915–1965, Dear Mother of Frances." (Angus Swann was cremated and his ashes went unclaimed, so Daisy Hart righteously informed me.)

The four of us, chatting away like old friends on a holiday, next drove over to the Swann farm, which was deserted. A tattered For Sale sign stood in front of the house. It had been there for close to ten years, Rose Hindmarch told me, and it looked like the place would never sell. We waded through overgrown grass. The house and barn were of unpainted grey wood, their roofs sagging. The porches, back and front, were shaky and the windows were boarded up. Towering above the bleak outbuildings was the silo where Angus Swann had dumped the dismembered body of his wife — head, trunk, and severed legs — before shooting himself in the mouth as he sat at the kitchen table.

No one knows for sure what happened between them. There was no explanation, no note or sign, but one

of Swann's last poems points to her growing sense of claus-
trophobia and helplessness. The final stanza goes:

> Minutes hide their tiny tears
> And Days weep into Aprons.
> A stifled sobbing from the years
> And Silence from the eons.

Rose Hindmarch — by now she was my devoted
guide — offered to get the key from the real-estate agent
so I could see the inside of the house, but for once I
demurred. This surprised me, since demurral is not my
usual stance, far from it. But standing on that front porch,
watching the wind whip across the overgrown yard, I felt
the queasy guilt of the trespasser. The fact that art could
be created in such a void was, for some reason, deeply
disturbing. And what right did I have to dig up buried
shame, furtive struggle? Besides, I'd seen enough; though
later, hearing about the poems Willard Lang discovered
under the linoleum, I had regrets.

Whatever had swamped Mary Swann in her last
days — suffocation, exhaustion — now engulfed me, and I
think the others felt it too. Homer Hart leaned heavily
on the fragile railing, panting, his face white, and Rose's
hand was travelling back and forth across her chin as it had
done when we first met. Even the ebullient Daisy Hart, a
broad-busted woman in her bristly mid-fifties, snugged into
a seersucker suit — she would have called it a two-piece —
was reduced to a respectful, repetitious murmur — *that poor
woman, her head cut off even*. We got back into the rental car
and drove to Nadeau in silence. I yearned, all at once, to get
back to Chicago, and decided I would forget about meeting
Mary Swann's publisher, Frederic Cruzzi, in Kingston. I
would leave as soon as I got my gear together.

As a parting gift, to say thank you, I gave Rose a small bottle of French perfume. (It was unopened, still in its box, a gift from Olaf that I fortunately had brought along in my suitcase.) She held out her hand, then hesitated. Her eyes watered with sentimental tears. It was too much, she said. She couldn't imagine wearing such extravagant perfume. She'd seen the adverts in *Woman's Day*. But if I insisted . . . . I *did* insist. I was firm. I pressed it into her hand. Well, then, she would treasure it, save it for special occasions, for her bridge nights, or her trips to Kingston. She shook her head, promising me that every single time she dabbed a little behind her ears she would think of me and remember my visit.

Effusiveness embarrasses me, especially when it's sincere. The gift of perfume was little thanks for the help and insight Rose had been able to give me, but it was hard to convince her that this was true. Her mouth worked; the little hair on her chin vibrated in the breeze. We stood beside the rental car, which I had parked in front of her house, and I wondered if we would presently shake hands or embrace. A good woman. A courageous woman.

"Wait a minute," she said suddenly. "I'll be right back." She dashed into the house and returned a minute later with two objects, which she insisted I take with me. Both had belonged to Mary Swann and had been given to Rose, along with two overdue library books, by the real-estate agent for the Swann farm.

The first was a small spiral notebook, the kind sometimes described as a pocket scribbler. I opened it and saw its little ruled pages covered with dated headings and markings in blue ink. "A diary!" I breathed, unable to believe this piece of luck.

"Just jottings," Rose Hindmarch said. "Odds and ends.

I couldn't make heads or tails of it myself, it was such a mishmash. But *here's* something you'll find really interesting."

She held out a cheap paperback book, a rhyming dictionary. It was titled, if I remember, *Spratt's New Improved Rhyming Dictionary for Practising Poets.* Rose's face glowed as she handed it over, suffused with her own sense of generosity. "Here you are. It would only be wasted on me. What does someone like me know about real poetry?"

I think I thanked her. I *hope* I thanked her. We collided stiffly, I remember. A tentative self-protective hug. The top of her head struck hard on the side of my jaw. My shoulder bag banged on her hip. After that I got into the car and drove slowly away. I drove out of town under a cool lace of leaves with the dictionary and notebook beside me on the seat. Soon I was on the open highway heading west.

A lake flashed by with one or two outboards on its calm surface. Then there were fenced pastures, barns, and long sloping groves of birch. I thought of Sylvia Plath, how someone had told me she used a thesaurus when writing her poems. I was surprised I even remembered this. And sorry to be thinking of Sylvia Plath's thesaurus on such a fine day.

Mary Swann's rhyming dictionary and notebook rested on the seat. I could reach and touch them as I drove along. My thoughts were riveted on the notebook and what its contents would soon reveal to me, but the dictionary kept drawing my eye, distracting me with its overly bright cover. It began after a few miles to seem ominous and to lend a certain unreality to the notebook beside it.

I stopped at the first roadside litter box and dropped it in. Then I headed straight for the border.

13

Standing up in a lurching subway car, clutching a plastic loop and looking healthy, young, amiable, and strong is Stephen Stanhope, my former lover. His shoulder bag is full of Indian clubs, rubber rings, lacrosse balls and other paraphernalia of the professional juggler. He's on his way to a juggling gig, he tells me, a Lions benefit in Evanston. "Why don't you come along and keep me company?" he says, and I say, "Why not?"

It's Saturday. I'm on my way home from a morning of marketing, my shopping bag bulging with sensuous squashes and gourds. The old restlessness has come back, my spiritual eczema as Brownie calls it. (Brownie is out of town, as usual on weekends, scouting the countryside for Plastic Man comics and for first editions of Hemingway or Fitzgerald — or second editions or third — which are becoming harder and harder to find.)

At the Lions benefit I sit on the sidelines and watch Stephen perform. A big man, six-foot-four, he wears loose cotton clothes and, on his feet, white sneakers. Soundlessly, with wonderful agility, he moves about on large white feet, elegant and clownish. He has the gift of enchantment, my Stephen, the ability to cast a spell over the children, some of whom are in wheelchairs, and to put the awkward, hovering parents at their ease. He fine tunes them to laughter. "If you watch very, very carefully," he tells the audience with lowered voice, "you might see me drop this club on my toe." An instant later he deliberately drops one and hops up and down in voiceless agony while the children howl and applaud. Then he executes a quick recovery and goes into his five-ball shower, followed by his reverse cascade, and finishing with the famous triple-torch fire feat. I've seen it

before, but today he performs with special artistry. He's a
master of his comic trade, this thirty-five-year-old son of a
billionaire grain investor.

Clever men create themselves, but clever women, it
seems to me, are created by their mothers. Women can never
quite escape their mothers' cosmic pull, not their lip-biting
expectations or their faulty love. We want to please our
mothers, emulate them, disgrace them, oblige them, outrage
them, and bury ourselves in the mysteries and consolations of
their presence. When my mother and I are in the same room
we work magic on each other: I grow impossibly cheerful
and am guilty of reimagined naiveté and other indulgent
stunts, and my mother's sad, helpless dithering becomes a
song of succour. Within minutes, we're peddling away, the
two of us, a genetic sewing machine that runs on limitless
love. It's my belief that between mothers and daughters there
is a kind of blood-hyphen that is, finally, indissoluble. (All
this, of course, is explored in Chapter Three of my book
The Female Prism, with examples from nineteenth-and
twentieth-century literature liberally supplied.)

The experience of men is somehow different. I look
at Stephen and at Brownie and all the other men I know
and marvel at the distance they manage to put between
themselves and their fathers. Stephen's father, whom I met
only once, presides in a boardroom so high up in the Corn
Exchange that he might be on a mountain top, while
Stephen, his only son, this big, soft-footed boy, blithely
plucks wooden clubs out of the air, rides the subway, and
lives in a rented dump in Maywood, unwilling, it would
seem, to enjoy the material plenty showered on him. And
Brownie, his wonderful little scowl, his scowling eyes
and scowly concentration — I'm sure these are his own
inventions and not an inheritance from his poor but smiley

father (as I imagine him) tramping around up there in his loamy fields. Brownie's life, like Stephen's, seems designed to avoid his father's destiny, while mine is drawn with the same broad pencil as my mother's.

Stephen asks me how my mother is. This is later, over toasted sandwiches and beer in a downtown bar. I explain about the lump in her side, how it sometimes keeps her awake at night, but at least it doesn't seem to be growing, and how next week she'll check into the hospital for a day of tests. There's a possibility of surgery, but in all probability the lump is benign.

"I've missed you," Stephen says, folding and unfolding his hands. "I've missed the amazing times we used to have."

"So have I," I say, a little surprised, and then, spontaneously, invite him to spend the night.

What I've missed is his face, the composure of it, its unique imperviousness, the fact that it's a face for which no spare parts seem possible and beneath which nothing is hidden. It's a face, too, that has profited from the shedding of youth. "An open face," my mother said the first time she met him. "The kind of face that gets better and better with time."

I remember just how she said this. Generally I remember everything she says. The connective twine between us is taut with details. I have all her little judgements filed away, word perfect. There's scarcely a thought in my head, in fact, that isn't amplified or underlined by some comment of my mother's. This reinforces one of my life theories: that women carry with them the full freight of their mothers' words. It's the one part of us that can never be erased or revised.

* * *

14

A graduate student called Betsy Gore-Heppel in my seminar on Women in Midwestern Fiction had a baby today, a
seven-pound daughter. We've all chipped in to buy her a
contrivance of straps and slings called a Ma-Terna-Pak so
that Betsy, after a week or two, will be able to attend class
with her child strapped to her chest. The decision about
the gift, the signing of the card, and a celebratory drink
afterward with the members of the seminar made me two
hours late getting home. Supper, therefore, was a cup of
tomato soup, which I sipped while reading my latest letter
from Morton Jimroy.

As in his other letters, he is all caution and conciliation.
He "understands perfectly," he says, about my reluctance
to "share" the contents of Swann's notebook. He begs me
once again to forgive him if his request appeared "impertinent," and hopes that I understand that his wish to have
"just a peek" proceeded from his compulsion to *document,
document, document!*

On and on he goes in this vein, his only vein I suspect,
ending with a rather endearing piece of professional exposi-
tion: "The oxygen of the biographer is not, as some would
think, speculation; it is the small careful proofs that he pins
down and sits hard upon."

I ask myself: is this statement the open hand of apology
or a finger of blame? I have denied him one of the "small
careful proofs" he requires if his biography is to have substance. Should I, therefore, feel that I've interfered with
the orderly flow of scholarship by asking him to wait
a few additional months before seeing it? Yes. No. Well,
maybe. Even if I were willing to set aside my own interests,
it's hard to see what difference it would make. He's going

to see Mary's notebook eventually, at least a photocopy of it, and what he's sure to feel when he examines its pages is a profound sense of disappointment.

Profound disappointment is what I felt when opening that notebook for the first time. What I wanted was elucidation and grace and a glimpse of the woman Mary Swann as she drifted in and out of her poems. What I got was "Creek down today," or "Green beans up," or "cash low," or "wind rising." This "journal" was no more than the ups-and-downs accounting of a farmer's wife, of *any* farmer's wife, and all of it in appalling handwriting, I puzzled for days over one scribbled passage, hoping for a spill of light, but decided finally that the pen scratches must read "Door latch broken."

Mary Swann's notebook — Lord knows what it was *for* — covered a period of three months, the summer of 1950, and what it documents is a trail of trifling accidents ("cut hand on pump") or articles in need of repair (a kettle, a shoe) or sometimes just small groupings of words (can opener, wax paper, sugar), which, I decided, after some thought, could only be shopping lists. Even her chance observations of the natural world are primitive, to say the least: "branches down," "radishes poor," "sun scorching."

This from the woman whose whole aesthetic was a piece of grief! The woman who had become for me a model of endurance and survival. I felt let down, even betrayed, but reluctant to admit it. In the weeks after I acquired the notebook from Rose Hindmarch I turned over its pages again and again, imagining that one day they would yield up a key that would turn the dull little entries into pellucid messages. Perhaps I hoped for the same dislocation of phrase that frequently occurs in the poems, a skewed reference that is really a shrewd misguiding of those who read it. Her apple tree poem, for instance, which is actually a limpid expression of female sensuality, and her water poems that trace, though some scholars disagree, the clear contours of birth and regeneration. She is the mistress of the inverted image. Take "Lilacs," her first published poem. It pretends to be an idle, passive description of a tree in blossom, but is really a piercing statement of a woman severed from her roots, one of the most affecting I've ever read.

Naturally I opened her notebook hoping for the same underwatery text, and the reason I've refused to share it casually with Morton Jimroy, or anyone else for that matter, is that I still hope, foolishly perhaps, to wring some meaningful juice out of those blunt weather bulletins and shopping lists.

I haven't yet decided how I'll present the journal at the symposium, whether to cite it as a simple country diary ("Swann had one foot firmly in the workaday world and the other . . . ") or to offer it up as a cryptogram penned by a woman who was terrified by the realization that she was an artist. Nothing in her life had prepared her for the clarity of vision visited on her in mid life or for what *things* she was about to make with the aid of a Parker 51 and a rhyming dictionary. (I won't, of course, mention the dictionary, long since returned to dust and, I hope, forgotten.)

But no matter how I present the notebook, the response will be one of disappointment, particularly for Morton Jimroy with his holy attitude toward prime materials. He will be disappointed — I picture his collapsed face, its pursed mouth and shrunken eyes — disappointed by the notebook itself, disappointed by Mary Swann, and also, I have no doubt, by me.

But haven't I been disappointed in turn by him and his biographical diggings? As yet he hasn't turned up a single thing about Mary Swann's mother, not even her maiden name, and he shows not the slightest interest in pursuing her. Doesn't he understand anything about mothers? "Childhood," he wrote in his second to last letter to me, "has been greatly overestimated by biographers in the past, as have family influences."

It's hard to know if this is a tough new biographical tack or if Jimroy is papering over a paucity of material. But one thing I'm sure of: Mary's poems are filled with concealed references to her mother and to the strength and violence of family bonds. One poem in particular turns on the inescapable perseverance of blood ties, particularly those between mothers and daughters. It's a poem that follows me around, chanting loudly inside my head and drumming on the centre of my heart.

> Blood pronounces my name
> Blisters the day with shame
> Spends what little I own,
> Robbing the hour, rubbing the bone.

15

What I need is an image to organize my life. A flower would be nice, an iris, a tender, floppy head of petals and a stem like a long green river. I could watch it sway, emblem of myself, in the least breeze, and admire its aloof purply state. The frilled mouth, never drooping lower than a few permitted degrees — it would put to shame my present state of despondency.

Just why am I sad tonight? I address this question to the Moroccan cushion on the end of my sofa, a tender triangle of soft white leather. (Come on, lady, stop being precious; and what have you got to be sad about anyway?)

Because it rained all day today, because I'm jealous of Betsy Gore-Heppel, because I'm worried about my mother's health, because I still haven't found Mary Swann's notebook, because I had "words" this morning with dear old Professor Gliden about the intertexuality of Edith Wharton's novels, because my only mail today was an oil bill, because Stephen Stanhope sent me flowers, because of Nicaragua, because the Pope made a speech on television reminding me of my lost faith, because I'm sick of my beautiful clothes (those shoulder pads, those trips to the dry cleaners), because the rain continues and continues — because of all this I broke down tonight and phoned Brownie, who hasn't phoned me for two weeks.

He's been incredibly busy, he explains. (All my senses gather to a fine point of attention.) He has had to hire three new assistants at the Brown Study and a full-time accountant. He has just spent two days in Peoria going through a lady-and-gentleman library (his phrase) that was up for auction. After that he made a dash for St. Louis to look at some Wonder Woman comics, which were in lousy condition, though he *did* pick up an excellent signed first edition of Disraeli's *Sybil* for which he has a buyer already committed. Next week he has an appointment in Montreal to look over some sizzling love letters written more than a hundred and fifty years ago.

Being eclectic keeps him hopping. He's busy, *too* busy, he says. He's exhausted. Depleted. A wreck.

Why then this frisson of exaltation running beneath his complaints? I can hear it in every word, even in the little spaces between words, his busy air of enterprise or cunning. "Why don't you come over?" I suggest. "I'll make a fire. We could talk."

The pleading in my voice dismays me. Oh, Lord, why do I love Brownie?

A good question. His crinkly hair, ending in snaky ringlets. The crinkly way he talks and thinks at the same time. His wrists. His wristwatch and the way he's always checking the time as if comparing it to that other clock inside his brain that runs to a different, probably threatening, rhythm. His cool impartial stare. His little shoulders, the Einsteinián hunch of them. His sweaters with their tender broken elbows. His helpless need for money and his belief that he'll never get enough of it salted away for his old age — which he doubts he'll reach. His fingertips on my shoulder, tapping out messages, subliminal. The strength and shortness of his legs, so short that when we walk along in the park together I can hear the rush-rushing of his feet on the gravel. His collection of costumes, Victorian capes, military jackets and the like. The shrewd way he handles his thready old books, his willingness to sock them away for ten years, twenty years, until their value multiplies and zooms. *Treasure, treasure,* his ridgy brow seems to say, meaning by treasure something very different than I would ever mean. The way his mouth goes into a circle, ready to admit but never promise the possibility of love. That almost kills me, his blindness to love.

"Next week for sure," he promises.

After Montreal he goes back to California to have a look at the Stromberg collection of Plastic Man comics, the only cache he knows that rivals his own. There's a rumour out that Stromberg's ready to deal. "I'm getting a cash package together just in case," Brownie tells me. "But after this is over, I'm definitely going to slow down."

Brownie told me once about an economist who cornered the world market on Mexican jumping beans. That impressed him. Now *he's* out for control of *Plastic Man,* every last copy, but after that he's going to relax, he says. He's planning to take it easy, maybe read some of the books in his store. He hasn't read a book in ten years, he tells me. Another reason I love him.

There must be something perverse about me. *You are perverse,* I tell myself; and fill up my head with Brownie, the way he winks when he makes a deal, licks his lips, rolls his eyes like a con man, fooling.

The thought is cheering, and so, buoyed up, I make myself a cup of ginger tea and wander off to bed. It looks like the rain's going to keep on like this all night. I lie on my back and imagine myself applying aggressive kisses to Brownie's warm mouth. The rain continues, sweet, sweet music on my roof.

16

Enough of this shilly-shallying, it's time for me to get my paper for the Swann Symposium knocked together and into the mail. Willard Lang in Toronto has been breathing down my neck; a letter last week, a phone call yesterday afternoon, pipping away in his so awfully polite mid-Atlantic squeal, reminding me of what I already know perfectly well, that he's extended the deadline twice (and only because I'm a member of the Steering Committee) and that November 15 is absolutely (eb-sew-lutley) the cut-off date if l want my paper included in the printed proceedings.

The title I've decided on is "Mary Swann and the Template of the Imagination," not the blazing feminist banner I'd planned on, but a vague post-modern salute, demonstrating that I can post-mod along with the best of them. Begin, begin! I take a deep breath, then punch my title into the word processor.

I bought this word processor from a friend, Larry Fine, the behaviouralist, who was trading up. He had a pet name for it — Gertrude. I paid over my fifteen hundred bucks, cash, always cash, cleaner that way, and promptly dechristened it, not being one to stick funny names on inanimate objects. Larry came over one evening and helped me install it in a corner of the kitchen, which is the room where I work best — a dark, fruity confession, but there it is.

So! The counters are wiped clean. It's Saturday, exceedingly frosty outside. The yellow tea-kettle, a gift from sister Lena, gleams on the stove. Only a sister gives you a kettle. Only an older sister. Get going, I instruct myself, you're such a hot-shot scholar, what're you waiting for?

It would be a big help if I had my copy of *Swann's Songs* on the table beside me, but Brownie hasn't returned it yet. He tells me he's "quite enjoying it." *Enjoying!* Probably he's taken it west with him. Lord, he'd better not leave it behind in a hotel room or on the plane — but he wouldn't do that, not a book. Books he holds very sacred. If only —

Never mind, I don't need the book. I can close my eyes and see each poem as it looks on the page. For the last few years, haven't I lived chiefly inside the interiors of these poems? — absorbed their bumpy rhythms and taken on their shapes? They're my toys, if you like, little wooden beads I can manipulate on a cord.

Unworthy that. Settle down. Enough. write!

I've already made up my mind to skirt the topic of the Swann notebook. A gradual discounting is what I have in mind. Perhaps I'll just note —"allow me to note in passing"— that Swann's journal-keeping prefigured her poetry only in that it linked object with word, experience with language. A bit loose that, but I can come back to it. Put in a paragraph about "rough apprenticeship" or something gooky like that.

I drum on the table. Pine. It might be a good idea to use that queer little poem on radishes as an example, not her best poem, not one that's usually cited, definitely minor, twelve lines of impacted insight of the sort that scholars frequently overlook. I'll do a close textual analysis, showing how Mary, using the common task of thinning a row of radishes — the most grinding toil I can imagine — was able to distil those two magnificent, and thus far neglected, final lines, which became almost a credo for her life as a survivor. "Her credo," I toss into the word processor, "found its form in the . . . "

Noon already. I'm due at an anti-apartheid rally in four hours. Hurry.

I try again. (Oh, that miraculous little green clearing key!) "Thinning radishes was for Swann an emblem for . . . "

Wait a minute, hold on there. There's a gap that needs explaining, a synapse too quickly assumed. What kind of express train am I driving anyway? Radishes to ultimate truth? — that's the leap of a refined aesthete. How did Mary Swann, untaught country woman, know how to make that kind of murky metaphorical connection. Who taught her what was possible?

"Mary Swann was deeply influenced by . . . "

Back to the same old problem: Mary Swann hadn't read any modern poetry. She didn't *have* any influences.

Thinking of Swann makes me think, with the kind of double-storied memory that comes out of family annals, of my grandfather, my father's father, a machinist by trade, a man who worked with his hands, long dead by the time I was born. He was a quiet contemplative man from all reports, who ran his small business out of a shed behind his house in what is now Evergreen Park. Over the years, cutting and shaping sheets of metal, he noticed that there existed peculiar but constant relationships between the different sides of triangles. He kept a record of this odd information, and after a time he was able to discern measurable patterns. Keeping the discovery to himself, he spent several years working up an elaborate table of numerical relationships that was, in essence, an ordinary logarithm chart. He had reinvented trigonometry, or so my father used to say, and when, years later, he found out that it had already been done, he just laughed and threw his charts away. An amazing man. A genius.

In somewhat the same manner, I like to think, Mary Swann invented modern poetry. Her utterances, the shape of them, are spun from their own logic. Without knowing the poetry of Pound or Eliot, without even knowing their names, she set to work. Her lines have all the peculiar rough thrusts and the newly made syntactical abrasions that are the mark of the prototype. You can't read her poems without being aware that a form is in the process of being created.

"Poetry at the forge level," I hurl into the word processor, and then I'm off, shimmying with concentration, tap-tapping my way down the rosy road toward synthesis.

17

The first words my mother utters when she comes out of the anaesthetic are: "Your face is dirty, dear."

My hand flies to my cheek.

It's a bruise actually, the result of a scuffle at the rally, a brief, confused scuffle now that I stop and think about it, a case of my own steaming exuberance, then turning my head

at the wrong instant and meeting an elbow intended
for someone else. Not that my mother needs to know any of
this. Anyway, she's drifting back to sleep now with her large,
soft, dolorous hand tucked in mine. With my free hand I
fish in my bag for the chocolates I intend to leave on her
bedside table.

She's in a room with four other patients, but I passionately resist the notion that she has anything to do with this
moaning team of invalids. I've already spoken with Dr.
LeBlanc and with the surgeon. They were smiling, the two
of them, leaning against a hospital wall, freshly barbered as
doctors always seem to be, their thumbs hooked in the pockets of their greenies. The news they imparted was good,
wholly positive, in fact: the lump removed from my
mother's side this morning was not, as they had feared, the
pulpy sponge of cancer but a compacted little bundle of bone
and hair, which, they told me, was a fossilized fetus, my
mother's twin sibling who somehow, in the months before
her own birth, became absorbed into her body. A genuine
medical curiosity, one of the devilish pranks the human
body plays on itself from time to time.

She's carried her lump all these years, unknowing, a
brother or sister, shrunk down to walnut size and keeping
itself quiet. Now it has been removed, and my mother's
unsuspecting skin sewn neatly back in place. A pathologist
will perform some tests and in a week the results will be
confirmed, but there's no real doubt about what it actually *is*.

It doesn't seem possible, I said at least three times. Dr.
LeBlanc, however, assured me that though unusual, the
phenomenon is not at all rare.

I still can't believe it: my own mother spread out here
on her hospital bed, as calm and white as a cloud, my own
mother the unwitting host to a little carved monkey of

human matter, her lifelong mate. This fleshy mystery drives all other thoughts from my head.

Nelson Mandela is forgotten, the chanting demonstrators with their banners in the air, and an unknown elbow catching me under the eye — it no longer aches, by the way. Also forgotten is my completed paper on Mary Swann, now winging its way to Toronto, sadly late and less definitive than I would have wished. Template of the Imagination! — precious, precious. And Mary's lost notebook, still resolutely lost, no longer gnaws at me — yes, the gnawing has definitely eased — nor does Brownie's silence reach me, though I'm sure he must be back in Chicago by now.

All these recent events, these *things,* seem suddenly trivial and rawly hatched in the light of what has happened: my mother's strange deliverance.

Soon she'll be waking up again. In her sleep her lips move, mouthing a porous message. I watch her eyelids, the way they flutter on top of what must be a swirl of rolling dreams, drug-provoked dreams, and in the middle of that swirl must be imbedded, already, the knowledge of separation and loss. Or is it?

There's no telling how my mother will react.

I regard her large, trunky, sleeping body and think how little I know it, how impossible it is to gauge her response when told about her "lump."

She may shudder with disgust, squeeze her eyes shut and shake her head from side to side, *not me, not me.* She has always been a fastidious woman, not much at peace with the body's various fluids and forces. I can imagine her clearing her throat, ashamed and apologetic.

Or she may surprise me by laughing. I remind myself that she has sometimes demonstrated signs of unpredictable humour — witness her chesty retelling of family stories or the cartoons she occasionally clips from the newspaper and pins up in the kitchen. She may bestow on her little nugget a pet name, Bertie or Sweet Pea, and make a fully rounded story out of it, her very own medical adventure, suitable for the ears of her canasta cronies, more interesting, more *dramatic* than a gall bladder or thyroid condition and a lot more cheerful now that it's out and sitting in a jar of formaldehyde. Would she ask for such a jar? Keep it up on the shelf next to her Hummel figurines? There sits my little Bertie. Or Sweet Pea. Laughing.

Or she may grieve. Lord, *I* would grieve. I *am* grieving. Just thinking of this colouress little bean of human matter sharing my mother's blood and warmth all those years brings a patch of tears into my throat. My mother was the only child of elderly parents. She had a gawky girlhood, married, bore two children, was widowed, grew heavy, grew old; and all the time she was harbouring this human husk under the folds of her skin. It wasn't my father, it wasn't my sister or me, but this compacted little *thing* who followed her through her most secret rituals, bonded to her plunging moods and brief respites, a loyal *other,* given a free ride and now routed out.

Under the hospital sheets her body already looks lighter, making my body — hovering over her, adjusting her pillow, checking the i.v. needle in her arm — correspondingly heavy.

I'm tempted to grope under the band of my skirt, grab hold of my flesh and see what it is that's weighing me down — whether it's Mary Swann who has taken up residence there or the cool spectre of loneliness that stretches ahead for me. Because it does, *it does.*

My mother, still sleeping, breathes unsteadily, grabbing little, light girlish puffs of air. For the first time in my life I envy her, wanting a portion of her new lightness. Probably she'll sleep like this for another hour. Relief begins to settle around me. The bruise on my check resumes its faint throbbing. When she wakes up we'll talk for a bit, and after that I'll slip off to the telephone to call Stephen as I promised.

18

Letters; I've fallen behind in my letter writing, but nevertheless they arrive at the door in bales.

Willard Lang has written me a brisk, cosy little note saying my paper has arrived and been reviewed by the program committee and deemed very suitable *indeed*. A place on the agenda has been given to me, one hour for my lecture and twenty minutes for questions from the floor, should there be any. (He warns me not to go beyond the time limit since a buffet lunch is planned for 12:30, after which there will be a varied program of workshops.) I am to speak at the opening session immediately after the coffee break that follows Dr. Morton Jimroy's keynote address. There is an implication of honour in this.

Morton Jimroy has written a long, disjointed, and somewhat paranoid letter from Palo Alto. He distrusts Lang and dreads the unveiling of the four love poems, fearing they will spawn absurd theories. His own work is going well, despite the fact that Mary Swann's daughter, Frances, has become inexplicably hostile. He despairs of getting anything more from her. Furthermore, the continual California sunshine is oppressive, and there are roses blooming all around his rented house, he says, too many roses, which give the effect of vulgar profusion and untimeliness. He would like to lop off their heads with a pair of shears, but is afraid this might violate the terms of tenancy. Three times he tells me he is looking forward to meeting me: in the first paragraph, again in a middle paragraph, and once more in the closing paragraph. "We will have so much to say to each other," he suggests, declares, promises.

Frederic Cruzzi writes, agreeing, reluctantly, to attend the symposium. A stilted letter and faintly arrogant, but he praises my handwriting.

Rose Hindmarch from Nadeau, Ontario, has sent me a note on the back of a Christmas card, though it is only the first week in December, the Holy Family bathed in spears of blue light. "If my health permits," she writes, "I will be going to the symposium in January. Hope you'll be there so we can have a good gab." This letter stirs in me separate wavelets of emotion: pleasure that she's been invited; guilt (the free-floating variety) at the mention of her poor health; concern, in case she remembers Mary Swann's rhyming dictionary and mentions it to someone; and anticipation at the warm mention of a "gab," my needy self being fed by all manifestations of sisterhood.

A woman in Amsterdam (signature illegible) writes to say she has just finished reading the Dutch edition of *The Female Prism* and that it has changed her life. (Immediately after my book was published I received about two hundred such letters, mostly from women, though three were from men, crediting me with changing their lives, liberating them from their biological braces and so on. Nowadays, I sometimes see my book for sale in second-hand bookstores, and I'm always surprised at how little pain this gives me.)

A letter comes from Larry Fine who has gone out west to interview witnesses of the Mt. St. Helens eruption. "Temporary danger breeds permanent fears," he informs me, "but surprisingly few people can recall the exact date of the disaster."

My sister, Lena, writes from London — at the bottom is a string of pencilled kisses from my adored little Franklin, aged six — begging me to keep close watch over our post-operative mother, which she herself would do if she weren't so far away and hadn't just changed jobs again, abandoning the handcrafted bird-cage business for the more people-oriented field of therapy massage, chiefly whacking the daylights out of forty-year-old Englishmen, nostalgic for their boarding schools.

Olaf writes, reporting on his happiness/unhappiness quotient, describing a decided list toward gloom and outlining three positive steps planned to correct it; for a start he has regrown his beard. "And how are you getting on?" he asks in a postscript.

"How are you?" asks Stephen Stanhope on a little post-card from San Diego (windsurfers on a blue sea) where he's performing for a horticultural convention. No "wish you were here." No jokes. Just: "Hope to see you Thursday night."

"A little token," says a note from Brownie, a note tucked inside a lovely old book of essays by Anna Jameson. It arrives in a padded envelope. A second edition, 1880. Cover: a soft shade of brown with gold thingamajigs on the corners. Title: *Characteristics of Women*. "Sorry I couldn't make it last week," says Brownie in his artful printing. "Up to my neck with the book fair."

"A thousand thanks," says a note from Betsy Gore-Heppel. "Emma loves her little sling and is slowly adapting to life outside the womb. If my mental health holds up I should be back in class some time after Christmas."

A mimeo letter, folded and stapled: "The Free Nelson

Mandela Action Committee will hold its next meeting at 6:30 in the back room at Arnies. WE need YOU."

"You rat," writes my friend-and-sometime-mentor, Peggy O'Reggis, who has gone to Mexico City to teach printmaking. "You promised to write and . . . "

"Just a scrawl to inquire whether you've broken your right wrist," writes Lorenzo Drouin, the medievalist, on sabbatical in Provence.

"Finally tracked down that quotation," says a note from dear old Professor Gliden, "which I think may shed some light on the point I was trying to make . . . "

Another postcard from San Diego (seals sporting in emerald water). "Rained out in Calif. Coming home Weds instead of Thurs."

"Dear Dr. Maloney," says a typewritten letter from Dora Movius at the university archives. "We're experiencing some difficulty tracking down the material you requested. Will you please phone me at the above number between the hours of . . . "

"I haven't heard from you in some time," writes Morton Jimroy, charmingly, the second letter in ten days. "I expect I've offended you by being overly familiar. I've always been such a terrible dolt."

Finally: "Please copy this letter three times and send to above address. In one week you will receive six (6) single earrings of good quality. To break this chain is to invite disaster."

19

Dora Movius who looks after the literary records on the third floor of the archives is an immensely cross woman with solid pads of fat under her eyes. Her heavy lower jaw juts forward as though guarding a mouthful of bitter minerals. Over the years I've run into her a number of times, particularly during the period when I was working on my thesis, and I've never been able to understand how I came to offend her so deeply. A sister in the struggle, I say to myself, blinking and denying.

People who work in libraries, like those in bakeshops, ought to be made peaceful and happy by their surroundings, but they almost never are. Today Mrs. Movius looks preoccupied and impervious in a black gabardine jacket, one hard fabric scouring another. Because she has bad news for me — I sense it already — she produces a small ghost of a smile, or at least the muscles around her mouth move in an outward direction.

"I've looked everywhere for the copy you requested," she says. (A perfumed, high-pitched voice, tense with vibrato.) "*We've* looked everywhere," she adds, as though to dilute blame.

A feeble dignity keeps me from replying at once. Then I tell her in my most reasonable tone, "But I'm sure it's here, Mrs. Movius. I brought it in myself for safe keeping. If you'll remember, it was not to be circulated but — "

"I'm afraid we've been unable to locate it. We've spent most of an afternoon, my assistant and I, looking — " The perfume falls out of the air.

"Maybe I could look — ?"

"I'm afraid that's not possible. I'm sure you understand, Dr. Maloney, that we can't let people just walk in off the street and — "

"But it has to be somewhere," I insist.

"Undoubtedly." Arms locked across a hard front. Always ready with admonishment.

Shove and push, push and shove. I try again. "I don't want to appear melodramatic, Mrs. Movius, but I really do need that copy for a paper I'm presenting next month. I mean, people are counting on me. The Swann symposium, maybe you know, is meeting in Toronto and I'm scheduled — "

She waves her hands to shut me up.

"I can only suggest you use your original. We could photocopy it again for you if necessary, but we cannot — "

"But you see," I take a mouthful of air, humbled, a fourteen-year-old girl again, whimpering with guilt, my iris-in-a-glass-vase nowhere to be seen. "The problem is that the original's been lost."

"Lost?"

"Lost."

"You don't mean you—?"

"Yes."

She pauses at this, a deadly ten seconds, and then righteousness transforms the hard putty of her face. "Well" — shrugging — "that's always the risk we run."

"I know but — "

"As you know, Dr. Maloney, we strongly suggest that the originals be filed with us and the copies be retained by — "

"I know, I know. But surely it's with . . . isn't it filed . . . filed with the rest of the Swann material?"

"That's the problem, I'm afraid." The top half of Mrs. Movius' face gives a little reflective twitch and then softens. For a moment I think she is going to pat me on the shoulder. "We can't imagine how it happened, but *all* the Swann material seems to have disappeared. It's simply" — her voice drops angrily; she looks ready to strike me — "it's simply *lost*."

20

There are times when the stately iris fails, when it's neces-
sary to take a hot curling iron to life's random offerings.
Either that or switch off your brain waves and fade away, as
Mary Swann suggests doing in the first of her water poems.

> The rivers in this country
> Shrink and crack and kill
> And the waters of my body
> Grow invisible.

Tonight, on Christmas Eve, a night of wet snow and
dangerous streets, Stephen Stanhope and I were married.
The wedding was at five-thirty, in the living-room of my
house. We had a roaring fire going, and it got so hot that
Stephen and his father and Gifford ("Whistling Giff")
Gerrard, the judge who performed the ceremony, had to
remove their jackets the minute the ceremony was over.

Stephen's father's new wife, who is the same age as I,
wore pink silk overalls and a pale grey blouse. My mother,
looking tired and ill at ease, wore her best blue crepe dress
and, notwithstanding the heat, a cream stole stretched over
her shoulders. Lois Lundigan wore paisley, and Virginia
Goodchild, who came all the way from New Orleans on
three days' notice, wore a kind of suede tuxedo cinched by a
braided sash. I wore a white challis smock and wonderful
white lacy stockings.

Stephen's father came in a suit of boardroom blue,
"Whistling Giff" in courtroom black, and Stephen in a borrowed blazer of a colour I cannot now remember. Professor
Gliden (in grey knitted vest and maroon tie) proposed the
toast to the bride ("our very own irrepressible Sarah") and
read aloud the pile of telegrams: from Lena wishing me

happiness and from Olaf wishing me contentment and from the women in my Wednesday seminar wishing me success. We all ate and drank a good deal, and Stephen and I sat in the middle of the floor and opened gifts, the largest being a self-assemble perspex table from Lois Lundigan and the oddest being a champagne bottle from Larry Fine filled with Mt. St. Helens ash. Brownie sent us a wooden bowl covered with strange tear-shaped gouges, beautiful, and a printed note that said, "Happiness and prosperity." My mother presented a set of Fieldcrest sheets, and Stephen's father, executing a kind of tribal pounce, gave us a stock certificate worth several times my annual salary.

At midnight, after much embracing, everyone went home in taxis, and Stephen and I took off our clothes and dove into bed.

"Well," said Stephen. His large soft-footed voice.

"Well," said I.

Well, well, here we lie, side by side, two exhausted twentieth-century primates, bare skin against bare skin. What in God's name have we done?

For a fraction of a second, Doubt, that strolling player in my life, stares down from the ceiling, a flicker of menace. I give it a complicit wink, then wonder if this is the same shadow that foreclosed on Mary Swann. But no, the steady unalarming breathing beside me convinces me otherwise. Strange how the whole of this man's body seems to breathe, as though equipped with gills. *Reprise, reprise*; that lovely word mixes with the shadows. A number of thoughts come toward me at full sail, an armada of the night, blown by happiness.

A week ago Morton Jimroy wrote a letter in which he said: "We live in a confessional age."

But he's wrong. This is a secretive age. Our secrets are our weapons. Think of South Africa, those clandestine meetings. Think of the covertness of families. Think of love. How else can we express mutiny but by the burial of our unspoken thoughts. "I love you," says Stephen with his uncomplicated breath. "I love you too," say I, biting into silence as though it were a morsel of blowfish and keeping my fingers crossed.

"As long as it's what you really want," Brownie said politely when I phoned to tell him I was marrying Stephen Stanhope. "I need to have a few things settled in my life," I told him, refusing to take on the tones of a penitent. "And maybe have a baby."

Recently, during these rainy dark fall days, I've grown a little frightened of "the irrepressible Sarah." Her awful energy seems to require too much of me, and I wonder: Where is her core? Does she even have a core?

I want to live for a time without irony, without rhetoric, in a cool, solid metaphor. A conch shell, that would be nice. Or a deep pink ledge of granite. I've tried diligence, done what I could; I've applied myself, and now I want my sweetness back, my girlhood sugar. Not forever, but for a while. I'd like to fix my blinking eye on a busy city street and take in the flow of people walking along hypnotically and bravely, bravely and hypnotically . . .

At last, at last, I feel my limbs begin to relax. The world is both precious and precarious. All I need do is time my breath to match Stephen's. How easily he sleeps, entertaining, no doubt, long chains of dreams in his brain and the mumbled charms of Indian clubs and tennis balls. Clearly he's not given to nightmares. What a miracle that he utterly trusts this sloping roof. There's no real reason why he should. Safe as houses. That odd expression. Where in God's name did it come from? Middle English from the sound of it. Tomorrow I'll look it up. Tomorrow.

I turn on my side, intoxicated now by the gathering weight of my body as it pushes the old worrying world away, my breath adding its substance to the heaviness and safety of the house. Almost there, my lungs tell me; a gateway glimpsed; a dream boiling on a slow burner.

And then, through the thin clay walls of a dream, I hear the telephone beside the bed ringing. Once, twice. On the third ring I catch it and hold it to my ear.

"Hello," I say, stiffening, knowing I am about to be stricken with unbearable news. My mother. The icy streets. Brownie. "Hello," I say again.

But there's no sound at all from the telephone, only the flatness of my own voice striking the painted walls. "Who is this?" I ask. "Who is this please?"

The bedroom is freezing. I am sitting on the edge of the bed, and the cold has invaded my back and shoulders and is causing my hand to shake. "Hello," I say into the silence, and then hear, distinctly, a soft click at the other end.

"Hello, hello, hello," I sing into the wailing dial tone.

First to come is a sense of reprieve, which yields an instant later to panic. I am shivering all over, my eyes wide open.

MORTON JIMROY

Jimroy was feeling lonely his first month in California and decided to go one evening to a student production of *The Imaginary Invalid*. Why he should do this was puzzling; Molière's plays had always seemed to him a waste of time. But his spirits had taken a sudden dip, and he reasoned that an evening out would do him good.

It was not unusual for him to take his pleasures in this way, as though they were doses of medicine. Bookishness had kept him narrow, or so his ex-wife had complained. "You look like a bloody monk," she accused him once, putting her long, purplish neck around the door of his study — she never did learn to knock. "You ought to get out now and then," she scolded. "Mix a little. Have more fun. It'd cure what ails you."

Dear old Aud. Well meaning, sensible, but a woman whose intuitive thrusts had invariably reminded Jimroy of metal shelving screwed to a wall. It was like her always to think she knew what ailed him. He smiled at the thought. Audrey with her frizz of red hair, her narrow shoulders and flat front. And her elbows, the way they went scaly in winter so that she had to rub them with Jergens before she went to bed, his dear, greasy Aud. He thought of her often,

especially in the early evenings, especially in the fall of
the year, and yet it was an indulgence thinking about her,
one that brought him sharp little arrows of pain. But yes,
he admitted it. He missed the cups of strong tea she used
to bring him after dinner, and even the way she set them
down — hard — on his desk.

Well, time dulled petty irritations. Time had even
brought a perverse rosy appreciation for those acts of
Audrey's that he'd found most annoying, so that now it was
with autumnal nostalgia — certainly not love — that he
recalled her voice, clamorous and hoarse from too much
smoking, and the white tea mug grasped in her chapped
hand.

There was no autumn in California, which Jimroy
found disorienting. Here it was, the third week in
September, and all around him trees and shrubs were keeping their shrill green. Numbers of dripping eucalyptus
gave a blue roundness to the air, a roundness cut by the
ubiquitous highways with their terrifying loops and ramps.
Stanford bloomed. Everywhere along the campus walls and
walkways flowers swayed; and what flowers! — like open
mouths with little tongues dragging out. Oppressive, Jimroy
thought, but was careful not to say so aloud.

He reminded himself that there would be no winter to
cope with; he wouldn't miss that, not for a minute. Back
home in Manitoba it made his head ache to hear his acquaintances exclaim year after year about the beauty of trees in
their winter dress or the music of snow crunching underfoot. This year he had escaped all that, as well as the kitsch
outpourings it seemed to inspire. A snowless year. His *annus
mirabilis*. He would be able to sleep all year round with the
windows wide open. For this coup he congratulated himself,
thinking happily of his heavy, hairy coat and gloves and

overshoes left back in Winnipeg in a bedroom closet, locked away from the young tenant who had rented his house. Let him freeze.

This year, his fifty-first, he would be spared the drift of snow around his windows and that confusing ritual with the antifreeze that he had never felt easy with. Californians were spoiled and fortunate, and this green place was clearly paradise, and yet, and yet. . . . When he looked around him at the people he had met in the last few weeks, he could not imagine how they regulated their lives or what it was that kept them buoyant.

The Molière play at the Stanford Student Center began at nine o'clock. This would not have been the case in Winnipeg, where things got under way at eight-thirty. And there were other differences. Here people drifted in, a surprising number of them alone, wearing soft clothes and looking sleepy-eyed and dreamy as though they had just risen from their beds. The girl who showed him to his seat wore old faded jeans and a navy cardigan with the buttons mismatched. This seemed to Jimroy a fey affectation, and so did the high sweet western voice. "There," she crooned to Jimroy, as though he were a person of no consequence. "There at the end."

He was handed a program printed on what looked like a section of newsprint, an immense limp sheet too big to be held on the lap. The ink rubbed off on his fingers, and after the house lights dimmed he let it slide to the floor.

Molière had no heart. Even the French, he was told, admitted that Shakespeare outdid Molière in largeness of heart. There was no worthwhile philosophy, either, and no real intelligence. Surfaces and madcap mischief, coincidence and silliness, hiding in armoires or scrambling under beds; that was the sum of it. Still, once or twice toward the end of

the first act he caught himself smiling, and he welcomed his
own smile with a sense of reprieve, thinking in Audrey's
insipid phrase that this might, after all, be good for what
ailed him.

During the intermission Jimroy remained in his seat
and studied, from the corner of his eye, a man who had
come in late and was sitting to his left. He was a man in
his late twenties, perhaps a little older, with curly brown
hair brushed back from a pale forehead. There was an
expression about the eyes that was close-hauled and secretive — probably he'd been drinking. The nose was beaky;
no, the whole face was beaky. On his chin was a brown
mole, which protruded slightly, though it wasn't large
enough to be disfiguring. But the surprising thing about this
man was that he was wearing a full Scottish kilt. Jimroy
took in the soft reds and greens of the tartan and reflected
that the cloth looked both old and authentic, and there was
one of those little leather purses hanging from his belt.
(There was a name for them. What was it, now?)

Jimroy pondered the significance of this Scottish costume. Probably there was none. Half the people in Palo Alto
seemed to drift about dressed as characters out of a play.
Yesterday, crossing the campus, he'd seen a bare-chested
youth in satin track pants coming toward him on a unicycle,
balancing an armload of books and flashing the tense
nervous smile of an actor. The Creative Sandwich Shop
where he'd eaten lunch today had been filled with long-
skirted gipsy-like girls, and one of them, barely out of
puberty, had worn what looked like a width of carpeting
belted around her hips. Another girl behind the counter,
scooping out avocado flesh and smashing it onto slices of
bread, was dressed in blue bib overalls covered with tiny
embroidered flowers and the stitched message over one

breast, "Taste Me." (Jimroy had stared boldly at this message, wanting to show that he did not find it in the least shocking — which indeed he did not.)

"Pardon me." It was the man in the kilt.

"Are you speaking to me?" Jimroy heard his own voice, priggish and full of Canadian vowel sounds.

"You've dropped your program." Then, "At least I believe it's yours."

"Thank you, very kind." His snorty laugh, never intended, but always ready to betray him.

"Interesting production, wouldn't you say?" The man in the kilt said this in a bright, liturgical, surprised-sounding voice. A Scottish accent, Jimroy noted, though certainly muted, perhaps even counterfeit.

"Quite good," Jimroy said, feeling friendly because of the ambiguity of the accent. "Especially the notary."

"Ah, yes, the notary. Wonderful. Great sense of maturity. And the maid, what do you think of the maid, little Toinette? Now that's a role to conjure with."

"Very demanding, yes," Jimroy said, and rested his gaze on the Scotsman's knees, which were clutched tightly together. Nervous type. Perhaps the kilt eased his limbs and that was the reason he wore it.

He considered his own clothes, the light green cotton pants and the checked shirt, not at all what he might have worn for an evening out at the Manitoba Theatre Centre. They were emergency clothes, bought three weeks ago when the airline admitted, finally, that both of his suitcases seemed to be temporarily lost. (Temporarily — what a joke.) They had gone astray somewhere between Manitoba and California. No one was able to account for it. He phoned the airline office every day or two, but nothing had turned up yet, and meanwhile he alternated between two sets of clothes he'd purchased in a men's store in the Stanford Shopping Mall. The clothes were cheap, but the colours pleased him, these minty green pants and a second pair in a sort of salmon. He had also bought himself a minimal supply of underwear, some white socks — when had he last worn white socks? — and a pair of pyjamas made in Taiwan.

With this limited wardrobe he had managed well enough and, in fact, rather liked the clean feeling of owning so spare a closet of clothes. But soon he would need a suit and a dress shirt or two. More alarming was the loss of some papers he needed for his work and, of course, the photograph of Mary Swann. He would give the airline another week and then begin to press them harder. Luggage didn't disappear into thin air. It had to be somewhere. He realized now that he should have made more of a fuss in the first place.

At the end of the play, after applause faded, the man in the kilt turned abruptly to Jimroy and said, "I wonder if I could persuade you to join me for a drink."

Jimroy hesitated a second, caught off guard, confused by the Scottish accent, which seemed not quite as Scottish as before, and the man quickly amended, "Or a cup of coffee perhaps. They make a very good espresso at a place not far from here."

He had feared something like this. The moment his neighbour had uttered the word "little Toinette," he had been alerted. Certain kinds of people were inevitably attracted to him; he possessed a lean body, neat shoulders, hips that were unusually small; it was probably not a good idea under the circumstances to go in for green pants. "I'm awfully sorry — "

"I just thought. Since you seemed to be alone."

"Very kind of you." Jimroy rose hurriedly, at the same

time mumbling a brief apology, which was courteous, defer-
ential and, in its way, he supposed, convincing: the lateness
of the hour; an early morning appointment; and a delicate
suggestion that he was expected elsewhere, that someone
awaited his arrival.

No one awaited his arrival. He was living alone in a house
he had rented from a famous physicist, a Nobel Prize winner, who had left, months earlier, for a year in Stuttgart. The
house was small, just two bedrooms, a single-story
California-style house with white siding and redwood trim.
The rent was entirely reasonable considering how close it
was to the university, so close he was able to manage without
a car. The famous physicist's wife, Marjorie Flanner, had
been anxious to join her husband in Germany and was
happy to find a tenant like Jimroy who was mature and
responsible.

She showed him the large tiled bathroom and the stacks
of folded sheets in the linen cupboard. In the bedroom she
pressed down on the mattress with the heel of her hand to
demonstrate its firmness and told him who he might phone
if there were problems with the air conditioning. The only
thing she really cared about, she said, was the garden.
Things needed pruning. Occasionally, depending on the
weather, it was necessary to water certain of the plants or
spray for spiders. The gate at the back of the garden had to
be kept latched so the children in the neighbourhood would
stay out of the roses. "I hope you like roses." She smiled at
Jimroy. Her middle-aged face was soft and puffed, rather
like a rose itself.

He knew nothing about roses. He knew none of the
names for any of the flowers in the garden or even the name
of the bent little tree that stood protected by its own low wall

of pink brick. The yard in Winnipeg, his and Audrey's, had contained nothing but a patch of grass, a pair of lilac bushes and what Audrey liked to call her veg patch, her rows of onions and radishes and runner beans. "I hope you like roses." Mrs. Flanner turned her pink face in his direction.

Reluctant to crush her open look of hopefulness, he exclaimed in his awful voice, "I adore roses," and heard himself continue, "Roses, as a matter of fact, happen to be my favourite type of bloom."

Already he was imagining himself carrying his morning coffee into the Flanners' garden, along with his books and papers. There were several garden chairs grouped on the flagged patio. And the little brick wall would serve nicely as a kind of desk. He felt certain that the sun — a whole year of sun — would do him good. As for the Flanners' roses, he would put up a notice somewhere, perhaps run an advert in the local paper. There must be thousands of gardeners in this part of the world.

Marjorie Flanner did *not* treat him as though he were a person of no consequence. She made him a gin and tonic, stirred it carefully, and decorated it with a frilled lemon slice, and they sat for an hour on the wrought-iron garden chairs discussing details about the house. The neighbours were "tremendous," she said, all of them Stanford people; he would be besieged with dinner invitations. Hmmmmm, said Jimroy, who intended to ignore the neighbours. About the rent, she said, would he mind very much giving her postdated cheques. Not at all, Jimroy said, and immediately pulled out his chequebook, asking in a polite, faintly stagy voice, if she would like a bank reference.

At this she almost, but not quite, giggled. "Heavens, no. I mean, in a way I *do* know you. That is," she adjusted her pretty legs, "that is, my discussion group's just done your book on Starman. Someone in the group suggested, way back last year I think it was, that we try one of Morton Jimroy's books."

He fixed his eyes on the brick wall and tried not to look pleased.

"So you're hardly a stranger, Professor Jimroy. But I'm afraid I haven't read your other book, the one on Pound."

"Don't apologize please — " Jimroy began, conscious of a small pink wound opening in the vicinity of his heart, a phenomenon that occurred always when such blithe confessions were brought forth. Irrational. Paranoid.

"But then — " Marjorie Flanner gave a small laugh — "I haven't really read Ezra Pound either. I mean, not really."

"Pound can be difficult," he said kindly. Even more kindly he added, "And he can be an awful old bore too."

Then they both laughed. He imagined their laughter and the blended tinkling of their ice cubes floating through the lathe fence and reaching the ears of the friendly neighbours, the ones who soon would be pressing dinner invitations on him. He dared another look at Marjorie Flanner's warm brown legs and wondered if he should suggest dinner some place. No.

She was back on the subject of roses. Five years ago she and Josh had brought in a load of special soil. Roses like a sandy loam with just the right balance of minerals. Whenever Josh came home from one of his trips he always brought back a new rose cutting. It was illegal, of course, bringing rose cuttings into the country, and so he had become adept at smuggling. There was this little loose piece of lining in his suitcase, and it was under this flap that he hid his contraband.

Josh the Nobel Prize winner, a smuggler of rose cuttings. Jimroy found the fact discreditable but humanizing.

(Later, after he moved in, he would wander about the little house thinking: a Nobel Prize winner sat in this armchair, lay on that pillow, occupied this toilet seat, adjusted this shower head.)

Mrs. Flanner, her face flushed — clearly she liked her drinks — poured him a second gin and tonic and asked what it was that had brought him to California for a year. "Are you working on a new biography?"

"I'm afraid so," he said. Eyes downcast, expression modest. Ever the man possessed, the body snatcher.

"And is it to be another poet?" She asked this in her merry voice.

"I'm afraid so," he said again.

"I don't suppose I really should ask who — "

"I doubt very much if you've heard of her," he began.

"Ah!" she said, and clapped her hands together. Brown hands with rather short fingers and an old-fashioned wedding ring in reddish gold. "A her! A woman! How wonderful. I mean, my group will be thrilled that — "

"As I say, though, she is not well known. Hardly in the same class as Starman or Pound. Still she was quite a remarkable poet in her way — " He wished to appear forthright, honest, but out came the old sly evasions.

"I wonder if I might know her," Marjorie Flanner said. "I used to read a lot of poetry when I was younger. Josh and I — "

"Mary Swann."

"Pardon?"

"Her name. Mary Swann. The poet I'm working on at the moment."

"Aahhh!" A look of mild incomprehension. She took a rather large gulp of gin and then asked politely, "And did she have a fascinating life?"

"I'm afraid not," Jimroy said, feeling a quickening of his body. "I think you would have to say she had one of the dullest lives ever lived."

She looked at him with new interest. "And yet she was a remarkable poet."

"That *is* the paradox," he said, giving a laugh that came out a bark. "That was, I suppose, the thing I could not resist."

"I can imagine," Marjorie Flanner said. She smiled. Her teeth flashed, and Jimroy could see the grindings of an old eagerness. "Well, that's quite a challenge, Professor Jimroy."

Quite a challenge. Jimroy wondered in an idle way if Marjorie Flanner had ever uttered those words *it's quite a challenge* to Joshua Flanner as he sat contemplating the mysteries of mass and energy that glued the universe together. Probably she had. Probably Joshua Flanner, humanist and smuggler of rose cuttings, had not found the phrase objectionable. Why should he? Who but a throttled misanthrope would object to such a trifling remark?

Later, at the motel where he was staying temporarily, falling asleep in his buttoned, made-in-Taiwan pyjamas, Jimroy remembered the brief bright expansion of Mrs. Flanner's face as she handed him the house keys. It had seemed artificially lit, a social expression only, as though she were concealing some minor disappointment she felt toward him. Perhaps she *had* expected him to invite her to dinner, or even to stay the night. It was a failing of Jimroy's, not knowing what other people expected.

Like many an introvert, Jimroy distrusts the queasy interior world of the psyche, but has enormous faith in the mechanics of the exterior world of governments and machinery and architecture and science — all these he sees as being presided over by anonymous but certified authorities who are reliable and enduring and who, most importantly, are possessed of good intentions. He is able to step back from the threat of acid rain, for instance — every softy in Canada is babbling about acid rain — certain that ecologists will arrive any day now at a comprehensive solution. He *trusts* them to find an answer; they will find it chiefly because the burden of their care demands it. AIDS will be conquered too, Jimroy has no doubt about it, what with the piles of research money and all those serious ready faces turned together in consultation.

And on a more self-interested level, he reasons that someone or other will always come forward, ready to defend *his* civil liberties, and someone else will keep him relatively safe on the highways and even flying through the air. A race of incomprehensible (to him) men and women have assumed responsibility for *his* safety, have been willing to make regulations, set standards, and bring into being an entire system of checks and counter checks. When he flicks the switch on the Flanners' microwave oven to warm up his taco dinner he takes it for granted that the tiny crinkled rays will permeate the food and not him, and that the tacos themselves, though tasteless, will be free of botulism. Thus, when he thinks about his lost luggage, he is no more than marginally worried.

His two large vinyl suitcases, one black, one tan, are not, after all, metaphysical constructs, but physical objects occupying definable space. The number of places where these suitcases might reasonably be is finite. It is only a matter of time before they are discovered and identified and shipped to him in Palo Alto, accompanied by official apologies and an entirely plausible explanation, which he will, of course, believe and accept with grace; this is not a perfect world — how well he knows that — but a world, at least, turned in the general direction of improvement.

Besides, he sees now that his Manitoba clothes would be out of place here. Those suits of his, those heavy laced shoes; it would be an act of brutality to bring such dark colours and such thick materials into the delicate latticed light of California. He wears open-weave shirts now, pure cotton preferably, and finds he can get along perfectly well without a tie, even when invited out to dinner. The sandals he bought for $4.95 are about to fall apart after one month — it seems they are stapled rather than sewn — but he is prepared to buy another pair, and another — they are surprisingly comfortable, too, especially when worn over a pair of heavy cotton socks.

It's true he's been inconvenienced by the loss of some of his papers, but it was an easy matter to telephone Mrs. Lynch in Winnipeg and have her send photocopies. His first-draft documents are safely locked away in a desk drawer in his study at home, which is a relief. He does, though, suffer intermittent worry over the photograph of Mary Swann. It had not been a good idea to bring it. It cannot be replaced and is one of only two known photographs of her in existence. (The other, much the inferior, is still in the Nadeau Museum, a blurred snapshot of Mrs. Swann standing in front of her house with her eyes sealed shut by sunlight.) The loss of the photograph would be serious, tragic in a sense, if indeed it is lost, but Jimroy persists, even after days and weeks have gone by, in thinking that his luggage will reappear at any moment.

This occasional nagging worry about the photograph is, in any case, tempered by the relief he feels that at least he has the letters from Sarah Maloney safely in his possession. What amazing luck! He can't help wondering what bolt of

good fortune made him decide at the last minute, packing
his things in Winnipeg, to put Sarah's letters in his briefcase
rather than with his other papers in his luggage. When he
thinks of it, he shakes his head and feels blessed.

He needs the letters more than ever now that he has been
uprooted; they stabilize him, keeping away that drifting
sadness that comes upon him late in the evening, eleven,
eleven-thirty, when the density of the earth seems to empty out.
It's then that he likes to reread her letters, letters that pulse and
promise, that make his throat swell with the thought of sex. He
props himself on the headboard of the Flanners' outsize bed,
cleansed from his shower, toenails pared, a cup of hot milk at
his elbow. (Half his stomach was removed the winter Audrey
left, and he admits to anyone kind enough to inquire that the
hot milk and the early nights are needed now, besides he likes
to think of his homely habits as a precaution against hubris.)

"Dear Morton Jimroy," runs her first letter, sent to him
more than a year ago in Winnipeg. "Will you allow me to
introduce myself? My name is Sarah Maloney, and a mutual
friend, Willard Lang, has told me that you too are interested
in the work of Mary Swann. I am writing to ask you . . . "

"Dear Mr. Jimroy," the second letter reads — Jimroy
keeps the letters in chronological order, each one in its original envelope with its U.S. stamp and the Chicago postmark.
"I am amazed and delighted to have a letter back from you
so quickly, amazed in fact that you replied at all after my
cheeky intrusion — "

"Dear Morton," reads letter three. "Your cheerful letter arrived on a day when I particularly required a cheerful
letter — "

He is glad she waits a decent interval before answering
his letters. The silence torments him, but endows her with
substance.

Ah, Sarah, Sarah. He sings her name aloud, so round a
sound, so annulated — to the walls, the ceiling, the open
window. The smell of flowers floats in from the garden, and
he wonders if it could possibly be jasmine at this time of
year. (The neighbours have mentioned jasmine; he himself
wouldn't recognize a jasmine bloom if it were right before
his eyes, another admission. The neighbours have also cau-
tioned him about leaving the windows wide open. Hasn't he
ever heard of burglars?)

From nowhere comes an overpowering wish to share
the fragrant air with Sarah Maloney of Chicago. He inhales
deeply — the stillness of uncommunicated rapture! —
releases his breath in a long sighing moan, like a man
gasping out of the richness of his cravings, and then picks up
Sarah's letters again. They bring him — what ? — solace.
And connection with the world, a world redolent with
intimate pleasures, sight, sound, touch, especially touch. His
tongue tests the sharpness of his teeth. He imagines Sarah
Maloney's soft lips, and how they must enclose small, white,
perfect teeth, opening and speaking, her teasing voice. *Take
off that ridiculous shirt, she says, and helps him with the buttons.
Hurry, she commands, now those silly green pants, let me do the
zipper for you. There. That's better. Ah, how soft. How adorable.
Like a little bird, all fluttery. Let me put my mouth there for a
minute. Please. See, I told you I'd be gentle.*

It is not quite sane, Jimroy knows, these images, this
caressing of a strange woman's words, but the warmth they
carry has become a necessary illusion, what he appears to
need if he is going to continue his life.

In October Jimroy was asked to address a group of graduate
students and staff.

As a Distinguished Visitor, his official title for the year, he knew he would be required from time to time to "share" his experience as a writer of literary biography. The word *share* is an irritant, nevertheless, for what would these hundred or so naked faces in the audience share with *him*? Their gaping incredulity? Their eagerness for "advice"? What?

Back in Winnipeg he had demanded a year's leave of absence, hoping his life might hold one more surprise. Leave had been granted without a murmur, one of the rewards of fame, and Stanford, also without a murmur, had given him the Distinguished Visitor title, plus office space — if that little cinderblock cube with cracked floor tile could be called an office — and provided him with the services of a typist, as though he would for a minute let anyone, anyone but Mrs. Lynch, handle his personal correspondence. He had, moreover, been "welcomed to the Stanford community of scholars," as Dean Evans put it in his introduction to Jimroy's afternoon talk.

Welcomed? A nebulous word. An ingratiating word. An oily, blackened coin. Community of scholars? Equally cut-rate, and ludicrous, too, since they all looked like tennis players arrayed before him. A ripple of faces, eye slits and dark combed hair, a collage of open-necked T-shirts, muscular forearms, healthy hands gripping biceps, and the conditioned eagerness of beagles, the fools, the idiots.

Stop, Jimroy hissed to himself, in God's name, desist.

He longed for Sarah in Chicago, serene and responsive and saying the right thing, the only thing; he longed for autumn, for the indulgent sadness that autumn brings. He longed for Manitoba and his bumbling starch-fed students who conceived of literature as a comical family product to be gnawed upon between real meals, Shakespeare's Richard, a nutty Oh Henry bar for a vacant Saturday afternoon. And why not?

Didn't these monied Stanford sharpies realize that literature was only a way for the helpless to cope. Get back to
your tennis courts, he wanted to shout. Out into the sunshine. Live! Universities are nothing but humming myth
factories. Dear God. How we love to systemize and classify
what is rich and random in life. How our fingers itch to
separate the tangled threads of theme and anti-theme, moral
vision and moral blindness, God and godlessness, joy and
despair, as though all creativity sat like a head of cabbage on
a wooden chopping block, ready to be hacked apart, first the
leaves, then the hot, white heart. Scholarship was bunk — if
they only, only knew. It was just a matter of time before the
theoreticians got to Mary Swann and tore her limb from
limb in a grotesque parody of her bodily death. But he could
not think about that now; now was not the time.

His talk, entitled "The Curve of Life: Poetry and
Principle," went well. The applause was prolonged and
vigorous, even from the back of the lecture hall, where a
number of people had been forced to stand throughout the
hour. When Dean Evans called for questions from the floor,
Jimroy was flattered to see so many hands in the air. Such
strong brown arms, flailing the air, beseeching. Rather
touching in a way.

"Can you tell us if you think a biographer has a moral
obligation to his or her subject?" This from the slenderest of
young women, lovely, lovely, those frail shoulders. Crushable.
And such hair. A voice clear as bouillon. Pour forth, my beauty.

"What kind of moral obligation are you thinking of?"
Jimroy asked her in his most tender, questioning manner.

She hesitated, raised her lovely shoulders an eighth of an
inch. "I just mean, well, if you're looking at someone's life,
say, and you feel that there's something, like, well, private,
would you — "

"Respect it." Jimroy supplied. Gentlemanly. A thin smile playing on his lips, but nothing committal. He liked to think he had eyes that expressed irony.

"Exactly. Yes. Well, sort of, yeah."

"I think that that would depend on whether the subject was still living. One certainly must respect the living, that goes without saying. And perhaps this will explain why my work, so far anyway, has focused on deceased poets."

Laughter. Right on cue. Discouraging.

"But," cried a young man, excitedly leaping to his feet, "What if the body of work is still alive and breathing? Don't you feel that the work *is* the poet? Take Sylvia Plath — "

"Rexroth says — " came a carroty-textured voice from the front row.

"I believe," said Jimroy, squelching the untimely intrusion, "that you must be alluding to the central mystery of art. Which is — " he paused and sent his long visionary look out over the heads of the audience, "which is, that from common clay, works of genius evolve. That is to say, the work often possesses a greater degree of dignity than the hand that made it."

"But isn't — ?"

Jimroy cut him off. Crapshooter! Dunce! "Of course a biographer of a writer must pay as much attention to the work as to the life. But the life is more than gossip and disclosure. It is what the work feeds on. One's own experience, before it is tainted by art."

"Tainted?" A challenge like gunfire.

He was being doubted; that same shouting voice. "Yes, in a sense." (Give the lad his orotund best.) "The highest work, the most original work, comes, I believe, out of an innocent, ignorant groping in the dark."

The young challenger was on his feet, but now he was

seeking reconciliation. "Would you say, sir, that Pound had a sense of innocence?"

Sir? That was better. But Jimroy paused, always defensive about Pound, always sensitive to the sin of apostasy. "In the beginning, yes. Later on, quite definitely no." The old equivocation, the old yes-and-no trick. Dear Christ, it shamed him to think he could still get away with it.

"But Dr. Jimroy — "

"It's plain mister, I'm afraid — ." He gave the audience his expansive look, hands held out to his sides, palms up, fingers crabbed, as though caught on invisible wires.

"Mr. Jimroy, then. In your book on Starman, you said something or other about his ability to sustain the elegiac by — "

"Up to a certain point."

The afternoon was a success, yes, definitely. Jimroy spoke for some minutes about the mystique of elegy, leaving behind a cloud of allusions for the astute to sniff out, and a final silver *aperçu* that never failed, an after-dinner mint, sinuously phrased, to hold in their mouths while their hands applauded. Dean Evans, summing up ("our speaker is far too modest...") was kind enough to mention Jimroy's three honorary degrees, one of them from Princeton.

Coffee was served, also chocolate doughnuts — an odd choice, Jimroy thought, but enthusiastically consumed. Californians! The young woman — concupiscence — with the blade-carved shoulders came up to him and took his hand and said, "You must feel so close to Pound and Starman. Writing on them like that. You must feel, really, you know, in sync with them. As real people, I mean."

Jimroy detests the popular fallacy that biographers fall in love with their subjects. Such cosy presumption; its very attractiveness makes it anathema to him. So easy, so coy; this romance between writer and subject, so cheerful, so *dear*, such a convenience, such an invitation to sentimentality. And it is, in a sense, brother to that other misconception people hold about the writing of books: that after a certain point a book acquires a life of its own and begins, as they love to say, *to write itself*.

Why in the name of God, Jimroy asks himself, does the world seek so anxiously to lighten the writer's burden by pretending that writing is the product of a grand passion, that it is the effluent of love and ease? That it is *fun*?

Writing biography, as Jimroy perfectly well knows, is the hardest work in the world and it can, just as easily as not, be an act of contempt. Think of the Sartre writing on Flaubert. Ah, God. And — closer to home — who could *love* Ezra Pound? Certainly not he, not Morton Jimroy, moralist *manqué*.

The longer he spent closeted with the Pound papers — and his book on Pound took the better part of five years *(oh waste)* — the more he desired to hold the man up to ridicule. Those long months sitting at his oak table in his study in south Winnipeg, crowded by books, crowded almost to the point of suffocation, he had felt himself being slowly crushed to death by Poundian horrors. And as the horrors accumulated he became convinced that lovers of Pound's poetry should not be spared the truth about their poet. Far from buttering over Pound's nasty little racial theories, Jimroy found himself going out of his way to expose them. This was easy enough; all that was required was that he pile massive incriminating quotations onto the page, worrying not a whit that they might be out of context. What was the point of context anyway? Wasn't Pound, he said to himself, wasn't the flatulent flabby Ezra Pound always and fatally out of context himself? Yes, oh yes! And poor Dorothy, did anyone ever spare a thought for Dorothy?

From time to time, exhausted and appalled by some fresh revelation, Jimroy stopped and demanded of himself why he had ever decided to write about Pound in the first place. Apotheosis? Never! There must have been some initial tinkling attraction — but what? He was unable to remember. But he was certain that he had never had any desire to be Pound's apologist. Meticulously, then, patiently, and with a minimum of annotation, he set out Pound's specious social prescriptions so that they sat on the crisp typescript in all their deadpan execrable naivety for all the world to see. When a line of Pound's poetry failed to yield to analysis, he left it for the stubborn little nut of pomposity it was. Let Pound be his own hangman, Jimroy decided early on, and the correspondence alone was enough to hang him — the pettiness, the fatuous self-stroking, the hideous glimpses into a mind swollen with ghastly ambitions and believing in his tissues that he was a genius. Yes, Pound wrote to one friend, he would remain in Italy until the United States of America established a Department of Beaux Arts and "called him home" to be its director. Dear God. Elephantiasis of the ego, the horror of it.

How is a biographer to respond to delusions of this scale, to this ninny who insisted on performing cartwheels on the tremulous and silly edge of vainglory? "Make it new," the old goat exhorted young poets, tricking them into acts of foolishness. Why should a biographer be expected to explain, justify, interpret or even judge? These are acts one commits out of love, or so Jimroy has always believed.

Nevertheless the willingness, the *glee* with which he offered Pound up to ridicule frightened him slightly and forced him to modify his disgust into a mild and sour sense of distaste. (Miss Lynch, his typist, usually reticent, encouraged these modifications.)

Flinching only slightly, Jimroy observed the disgust he felt, and indeed he recognized a moral ungainliness in himself that vibrated with a near-Poundian rhythm. His original attraction to the old fart, he supposed, must lie in this perverse brotherly recognition. Like persons who in secret sniff the foul odours of their bodies, he had been mesmerized by Pound's sheer awfulness, by his *own* sheer awfulness.

He had had to rethink the book's structure. Certain vivid anecdotes had to be withdrawn or consigned to small temperate type or worked into the inky compression of footnotes where they would scream less shrilly for attention. The rewriting of the book — the neutralizing of the book was how he thought of it — required an additional six months, but the result was a biography that had been regarded, and was still regarded, as being balanced, dispassionate, scholarly, humane. The reviewer in the *New York Times*, describing it as *Ellmanesque*, cited its "marriage of decency and distance" — delicious phrase. Jimroy likes to chant it to himself as a kind of mantra on sleepless nights. Decency and distance, decency and distance.

After a three-month vacation (during which he took Audrey back to Birmingham for a visit; and what a disaster *that* was), he began his book on John Starman who, in the beginning, had seemed less detestable. The poetry, at least, with its intricacies and gymnastic daring, appealed to him as Pound's never had; but there was no avoiding the man's greedy seeking after fame or the slurpy lushness of his *pensées*. Even his suicide note had a hectoring wonderful-me, beautiful-me clamour. There was no way, either, to overlook Starman's childish misogyny (poor Barbara) since the clod insisted on wearing it as openly as a pair of overalls. That line in his love series about keeping his genitalia in a vasculum for all the world to gaze upon and admire! Dear Christ. And finally, at Starman's centre, there was nothing but shallow and injured feelings, a gaping self-absorption that rivalled Pound's. Though Jimroy diligently chronicled the famed acts of generosity and the long lists of kindnesses to friends and fellow poets, the hollowness rang loud. And it rang with a double echo for Jimroy, announcing not only deadness at the centre of life, but a disenchantment with surfaces. The discovery of emptiness affected him like the beginning of a long illness. Once again he seemed to be looking in a mirror. (It was during this time that Audrey finally lost all patience with him.)

Three long years. Despite the fact that the Starman book was highly thought of, almost up to the Pound some said, it seemed to Jimroy that the writing of it had drained away too much of his energy. Three years with the exasperating, unhappy, unswervingly self-regarding John Starman; a thousand days of hanging each morning over his oak table, long hours of shifting notes, idly, despondently, feeling sick, feeling the gnawing of an incipient ulcer, and losing weight he could not afford to lose, and reflecting that this was a man he would not have wanted to spend so much as an hour with.

He told himself that perhaps it was just poets he was weary of, poets from mean northern states, Minnesota, Idaho. Working on the Starman proofs (while the situation with Audrey deteriorated even further), he asked himself whether it was poetry itself he had come to despise. Certainly he was suspicious of it, its scantiness and shorthand. It was so easy for a poem to be fraudulent, for what was the difference, really, between an ellipsis and a vacuum?

What indeed? Even when the words of a poem fell together
in rough, rumbling, delectable rhythms, there might be
nothing beneath them that spoke of thought and feeling.
For this reason he had always distrusted the flashy line and
kept a chilly eye on pyrotechnics, on the hollow stem of the
dead narcissus. Speak to *me*, he wanted to say to poets. To
poetry.

It had always seemed something of a miracle to him
that poetry *did* occasionally speak. Even when it didn't
he felt himself grow reverent before the quaint, queer
magnitude of the poet's intent. When he thought of the
revolution of planets, the emergence of species, the balance
of mathematics, he could not see that any of these was more
amazing than the impertinent human wish to reach into the
sea of common language and extract from it the rich dark
beautiful words that could be arranged in such a way that
the unsayable might be said. Poetry was the prism that
refracted all of life. It was Jimroy's belief that the best and
worst of human experiences were frozen inside these
wondrous little toys called poems. He had been in love with
them all his life, and when he looked back on his childhood,
something he seldom did, he saw that his early years, those
passed before the discovery of poetry, had drifted by empty
of meaning.

Even the failures strike him as touchingly valiant. *That*,
if the truth were known, is what seduces him, the poet's
naive courage. Keats, visiting the rough cottage where
Robert Burns had lived, had wept to think a man had lived
in such a place and tried to be a poet. (When Jimroy tells
this Keats story to students, he comes close to weeping himself.) Which is why, despite everything, he is always moved
when his thoughts settle on the riddlesome nature of his two
large, imperfect men, Pound and Starman, thick-fingered,

crippled by provincialism, morally clumsy — but made graceful, finally, by their extraordinary reach.

And so it was natural (inevitable, he told himself that when he came to write a third biography, he should choose as his subject another poet: not a muling modernist with Left Bank pretensions this time, but a woman named Mary Swann, a woman who had lived all her lean, cold, and unrewarding years in rural Ontario, a place more northerly and restrictive than the most northern state. The decision to write about Mary Swann had been made sitting in his Winnipeg study. (Audrey had departed.) He had felt a momentary sense of elation, the by-now-familiar nascent ritual. A new beginning. Rebirth. The egg, the genes, the reaching out.

Marvellous Swann, paradoxical Swann. He would take revenge for her. Make the world stand up and applaud. It would happen.

Jimroy's nose feels tweaked by tears when he thinks of Mary Swann's reddened hands grasping the stub of a pencil and putting together the first extraordinary stanza of "Lilacs." (But he romances; it is believed that even her early poems were written with a fountain pen — and how can he assume the fact of those reddened hands?)

The discovery of her poems a few years ago had rescued him from emotional bankruptcy, and at first he *had* loved her. Here was Mother Soul. Here was intelligence masked by colloquial roughness. Her modesty was genuinely endearing and came as a relief after two monomaniacs. He treasures, for instance, her little note written to the Nadeau *News* in 1955, "Dear Mr. Editor," she began in that tiny, flat, unmistakable hand of hers. "I've just opened that letter you sent about printing my poem and can't believe my eyes. What a thrill to have something in print. As for the dollar bill, I'm going to frame it and hang it up for inspiration."

Naive, pathetic, obsequious, but certainly sincere. Jimroy has no reason to doubt the letter's sincerity. Mary Swann was forty when "Lilacs" was published. Probably she thought life had passed her by, though her despair was sharp rather than heavy and, oddly, she seemed always to be keeping back little smiles. She may have been menopausal. Even as recently as thirty years ago, women reached menopause earlier, or so Jimroy has read, especially country women. Something to do with diet. He supposes he will have to deal with the biological considerations in his book, though the thought makes him tired and reawakens his ulcer. And he will have to deal also with the peculiar ordinariness of Mary Swann's letters and even the subjects of those letters. Pleading letters to Eaton's returning mail-order underwear. Letters to her daughter, Frances, in California, letters full of bitter complaint about the everlasting Ontario winter — these from the woman who wrote "September Night" and "Apple Tree after the Snow." What can be done with such unevenness? Nothing. (Though Jimroy had decided to withhold the underwear letter from his book, and he had "misplaced" another, which referred to a "nigger family" the astonished Mary Swann saw in Elgin one summer.)

The fact is — and why deny it — Jimroy has come to distrust Mary Swann slightly. In recent weeks he has felt his distrust turn to dislike. Here was an impenetrable solipsism. One was always straining to catch her tone. Furthermore, she was unreliable about dates, contradictory about events, occasionally untruthful. A Poundish falsity was creeping into her life, drowning her, obliterating her. Starmanesque delusion was gaining on her, dear Christ. She was about to become famous at last, a woman who a few years ago, balanced on a thimbleful of praise. And when she was killed in the winter of 1965, there was hardly a person in the world who recognized her for the rarity she was.

Jimroy's days have fallen into a pleasing rhythm.

Disjointed by nature but orderly by choice, he spends his mornings as he had orginally hoped, in the Flanners' garden. Around him are clustered flowers, their colours so brightly pink, so lightly blue and yellow, so moist and silken that they seem to be telling him something. He holds a pencil in one hand; a cigarette burns in the other. How joyous it is to be working again, to set his thoughts adrift on the scholarly sea. How puny they are, these thoughts, but how precious, tossing like flecks of foam, his little loves, his little discovered truths.

The sun falling on his head and arms convinces him that he is entering a period of good health, although instead of the chestnut tan he hoped for he has acquired an oily shine to his face and dry colonies of freckles on his forearm. He has never had freckles before. Well, he is fifty-one, he reminds himself, and changes in the pigmentation of the skin are to be expected. *C'est la vie*. Et cetera.

He wonders at times, and worries, how his fifties and sixties will go, admitting he has no talent for the avuncular and that he feels uneasy in the role of wizened philosopher or generous mentor. A fatigued and coarsened cynic? He hopes not. Love is the word he whispers to his listening self, *love*. He is aware, he alone probably in all the world, of the membrane of sweetness that encases his heart. Well, sweetness perhaps is putting it too strongly. But there is — he is sure of it — a scrap of psychic tissue that he guards and knows to be hopelessly malleable. Audrey once or twice jabbed her careless fingers into its softness, dear old Aud. If he'd tried harder to hang on to her, she might be here now, puttering in the trim little California kitchen, coming out the back door with her shears in hand, eager to prune the flowers and hedges and perhaps start a row of radishes by the lathe fence. Unthinkable, yet he thinks it.

Jimroy can scarcely believe how quickly the garden has gone out of control, and he has given up his search for a gardener. There wasn't so much as a single reply to the ad he placed in the local rag. The neighbours tell him, with puzzled kindness and a hint of amusement, that the people who used to do garden work are now pulling down fat wages in the computer plants. This is Silicon Valley. Who would want to potter away in someone else's weedy yard? These same neighbours insist, with a chauvinism Jimroy finds irritating but charming, that West Coast gardens more or less look after themselves.

Maybe. But the hedge has become grossly misshapen, sending green spiky shoots over the top of the fence. In the cracks between the patio stones, weeds have sprouted. Jimroy nudges at them with the toe of his new plastic sandals and finds them toughly attached. Marjorie Flanner's roses bloom brilliantly; he watches the buds open. The flowers last a few days, then darken. With a flick of his fingers he sends the petals flying to the ground. He likes their perfume, but otherwise ignores them. He hopes the neighbours aren't writing letters to the Flanners in Germany telling them their garden is in ruins.

Normally he works at his improvised desk in the garden from nine each morning until one o'clock, and then he walks a distance of four blocks to Lester's Steak House. The curving domestic green of the street gives way brutally to traffic and a busy shopping centre where Lester's is located. There, every day, he eats a hamburger and drinks a glass of cold beer. A sign on the restaurant door says "Members and

Non-members Only." Another sign inside says "Under
Three Million Burgers Sold," and Jimroy thinks how these
signs — open, disrespectful, collegiate — typify California
humour. Sitting at a booth with his hand closing on the
cold glass, he feels transported back to Manitoba. He rejoices
in his homesickness, always happy to find something in
himself to like. (He had forgotten whether he suffered
homesickness in Rapallo.) Here at Lester's there are no avo-
cados or sesame seeds. The walls are damp, greasy, knotty
pine, dark and smelling like someone's basement rumpus
room. When a door is opened to the outside, the sunlight
cuts across the floor bright as a knife.

Each Wednesday after lunch he walks to the house
where Mary Swann's daughter lives. It is a mile away, and
he stumbles along blindly, not because of the beer but
because of the shock of bright sunlight after the dark hour
inside. He is forced to walk along the side of an extremely
busy thoroughfare since, for some reason, there is a shortage
of sidewalks in California, an unwillingness to serve those
who must go about on foot. Jimroy feels rebuffed by
the passing cars that come perilously close to him, sending
up choking clouds of dust and carbon monoxide. He thinks
as he walks along how pridefully Californians parade
their barbarisms; every day he sees a small chapel, lit up
even in the daytime, with a sign on its roof that says "The
God Shop." And almost every day he is overtaken by a
horde of perspiring runners, young men stripped to the
waist and wearing sweat bands around their heads. (It was
several weeks before he realized it was the same group every
day.) They pass him on both sides, never breaking stride,
calling back and forth to each other between breaths
(". . . theory of applied mechanics" . . . "monitoring the
fucking test results . . . "). Gradually he is beginning to

recognize individual faces as they surge grunting past him, and he nods to them now in a friendly way, breathing in the smell of human sweat that briefly pierces the automobile fumes.

Mary Swann's daughter lives on a street called Largo Lane in a house that is one of the most beautiful Jimroy has ever seen. Well, he asks himself roughly, what had he expected?

He'd expected something hideous. A bleak sitting-room with sagging furniture. Cheap siding damaged by sun. A picnic table in the front yard. Weeds. He'd expected a stubborn fecklessness and a narrowness to correspond with the narrowness of that farmhouse outside Nadeau, Ontario, where Frances Swann Moore (1935 –) grew up. He had not allowed for upward mobility and the miracle of the one-generation leap. He had not expected this, this lovely house, these green moist grounds. Where was the river of loud traffic now; where the exhaust fumes and the sweaty joggers? Even the gravel of the Moores' driveway looked freshly washed. Large palms framed the wide front door, a dark luminous slab of wood without ornamentation of any kind; it had been a challenge, on Jimroy's first visit, to find the doorbell; ah, but there it was, cunningly concealed in the bronze moulding.

When he asked Mrs. Moore ("Please call me Frances") about the style of the house, she told him it was a blend of Japanese and West Coast. "The architect was — " and she said a name that meant nothing to Jimroy but that seemed to carry the heft of international reputation. Low spans of laminated wood rested on rough stone and supported the large coolness of tinted glass. And inside, such calm; the polished oak floors islanded by Navaho rugs or by the small perfect orientals that Frances Moore and her husband collected. Is it, Jimroy asks himself, true connoisseurship, a knowing eye that gluts on carved shapes and intricate shadow? Or is it only Californian acquisitiveness gone mannerly? The Moores also collect antique cars — there are three in the garage — Peruvian baskets, which are displayed on the dining-room wall, and Egyptian pottery, which is arranged on shelves at one end of the wide foyer. The pottery is the first thing Jimroy sees when Frances opens the door to him on Wednesday afternoons.

He cannot understand her availability, why she is always at home, always serenely ready when he arrives, spotless in her pressed blouses and well-fitting golf skirts. An attractive, smooth-faced woman, still slender. Her coil of dark hair contains quite a lot of grey, and Jimroy remembers that Mary Swann is reported to have gone grey before she reached her forties — was it Rose Hindmarch who told him that? Yes, probably; who else would have known? Frances, Mary Swann's daughter, is a woman in her early fifties. Her fingernails are pink and polished and cut short. Her eyes hold the blue of Nordic summers, although Jimroy is impervious to such eyes, and to such metaphors. When she smiles, wrinkles fly into her face. His questions take a long time to reach her. She reflects, touches her earlobes with those pink fingers of hers, then speaks slowly.

She is always alone. Her only son is away at Princeton; her husband, an economist at Stanford, travels a great deal giving lectures and consulting for the government. ("You must meet him," Frances Moore has said, but this meeting has not yet occurred, and Jimroy senses that it never will.)

She leads him to a low, rough-textured sofa and settles beside him, crossing her legs at the knee, a swift elegant series of motions. They sit before a coffee table on which rest a stack of magazines (*The Smithsonian* on top, *The Atlantic* peeking out below), a small stone carving (Tibet, Frances tells him), a lovely, locally made ceramic ash tray (Jimroy has not dared drop an ash in it, nor even light a cigarette) and a pot of freshly brewed green tea.

"And now," she says in that melodious voice that holds only a faint echo of rural Ontario, "now, where did I leave off last week? Oh, yes, I remember. You asked about Ma's relationship with the neighbours. I've been trying to recall. We didn't have a telephone, of course, and it wasn't until 1949 that we had a car. Well, a truck, really. But you know that already. So there wasn't a great deal of neighbouring. We were twelve miles out of Elgin and two out of Nadeau and ten from Westport — which is just a kink in the road, as you know. Mostly my mother didn't bother with neighbours. I believe she went to a wedding shower once. She grew up in Belleville — you've got all that — and in those days that was like coming from the other side of the moon. You've been to Belleville, Mr. Jimroy? Well, then, you know. Are you ready for some tea?"

Dazed he holds out his cup and wonders why he is afraid of so charming a woman. Frances Moore's voice, rhythmic, smoothly modulated, possesses a tonal slant that makes him want to close his eyes, but he doesn't dare for fear of being dismissed. Only the strange disruptive word *ma* ties this exquisitely relaxed woman to Mary Swann; not mother, not mama, but *ma*, a word that breaks from her lips like a barnyard squawk. He gulps his tea and says, "Neighbours?" to prompt her.

"There were the Hannas, of course. I think Ma rather liked Mrs. Hanna, though she wasn't very bright. I don't think she could read or write. I remember once, coming in from school, that she, Mrs. Hanna, was sitting in our kitchen, and Ma was reading her something out of one of her library books. I think I told you, Mr. Jimroy, that there was a library in Nadeau."

"Oh, yes, in fact I've visited — "

"This was the old library, of course. Just two hundred books or so, no more than that. On a shelf in the post office. Ma used to get those books when she went to town, just two each time. You were allowed more, but she only took two."

"I wonder why?" Jimroy feels the need to question her minutely, to pin her down, if only to assure himself that he is really sitting in this room. He is not at ease as an interlocutor; he remembers with impatience his difficulties with Starman's widow. Then, too, he has had litt' to do with women like Frances Moore.

"Heaven only knows. She's dead now, Mrs. Hanna. I don't know what book it was Ma was reading to her. *Gone With the Wind*, perhaps. Or Edna Ferber. She liked Edna Ferber."

Jimroy makes a noise that signifies regret and writes this down in his notebook. Of course he is disappointed. Has he foolishly hoped for Jane Austen? Yes, though he knows better. "And you don't remember that she ever read poetry?" He has asked this question before.

"Not that I can remember. Unless you count Mother Goose as poetry. She certainly knew all those nursery rhymes. Her favourite was 'A Man in the moon/ Came down too soon/ And asked his way to Norwich.' Remember? 'He went by the south/ And burnt his mouth/ From eating'—what was it?—'Cold pease porridge.'"

"I remember," Jimroy says, and makes another note.

"She read to me, too, now and then. In the evenings."

"Ah." His pencil is at attention, his voice affects insouciance. "Can you possibly remember the titles of any of the books she read to you?"

"*Five Little Peppers*. I loved that. And the Bobbsey
Twins books. Not what you'd call great literature. I never
heard of *Winnie the Pooh* and the *Wind in the Willows* until I
had a child of my own. But there we'd sit in the evenings, on
the couch in the kitchen, the two of us. We never used the
living-room, or the front room as we called it, in the winter.
It was just too cold. In the kitchen there was the woodstove,
which we kept going all the time. I suppose it sounds rather
idyllic, the cosy little family gathered in the kitchen. The
wind would be howling outside. We had a couple of those
gas lamps. Ma used to get quite carried away with some of
the Bobbsey Twins' adventures. She'd put this ferocious
expression in her voice. Very dramatic. There was little
Flossie, forever getting lost in the woods. I think Ma enjoyed
it all as much as I did."

"And your father?"

"I think we went through the whole series. Awful stuff,
I don't know why the library carried them — "

"Was your father there, too? In the kitchen, I mean?"

"If you don't mind, Mr. Jimroy — "

"I'm terribly sorry. I just — "

"I think . . . I'm sure I made it clear when you first
wrote to me about these interviews that I was not willing to
discuss — "

"Please forgive me. The scene was so vivid and I . . . I'm
afraid I forgot — " A shamed stutter.

"Under any circumstances."

"I understand. I do understand." He held his lips
together.

"More tea?"

"I would, yes, please, I'm becoming quite addicted to
green tea. I never — " He hears his voice foolish and passionate, his ninny laugh.

"The neighbours. Now, let me see. Mrs. Hanna I've already done. There was one other family. The Enrights. They had a bigger farm, not far from us. A modern barn."

Jimroy, worshipper of images from a disjointed world, is writing as rapidly as he can: "The Enrights. Large farm, modern barn."

He found the evenings difficult at first; what was he to do with these long soft evenings?

In the Flanners' microwave oven he warmed himself meals. He switched on the news as he ate; Californians seemed mired in their own crises, their mudslides and earthquakes and city politics and major art robberies. After dark he went for long walks and felt his lungs expand in the moist evening air, pure oxygen topped with the scent of petroleum. Pollution's cordial edge. The moon, rising, seemed rimmed with Vaseline. What a puzzle California was, even Palo Alto. There was no easy way to understand it. He felt reassured, though, by the lights going on in neighbouring houses. The domesticity of others sometimes made him envious but, as he zipped up his new light windbreaker, he told himself that he had come to feel at home inside his loneliness. In truth he half believed this, and the thought kept Audrey at bay.

After a few weeks he was invited next door to a buffet supper. There the Lees introduced him to the Krauses, who lived on the other side of him. "Meet Morton Jimroy, he's in the Flanners' house." He met at least a dozen other people too. "So you're in the Flanners' house, we've been wondering. So you're the biographer. Well, how're you adapting to the coast?"

They were hospitable people, and soon he was being made welcome in their houses too. He was grateful for these low-key social evenings, even though he sensed he would never have been asked had he not possessed at least a degree of celebrity with which to advertise himself. These people were accustomed to success. Dr. Lee next door (Ian) was forever being driven to the airport by his wife, Elizabeth (a strenuous, combative woman possessing a large elastic mouth, but very kind), so that he could fly half way around the world to lecture on arcane branches of mathematics. And Dr. Krause was a world-class philologist (the expression *world-class* was sprinkled like cayenne on the Stanford community). Krause's heavy body seemed to Jimroy barely able to move beneath its weight of knowledge. His wife, Monique, a psychologist, was an expert on cheesecake and national parks hiking trails. These kind people accepted Jimroy, inviting him in for platefuls of roast beef and baked ham, teasing out of him opinions and anecdotes and asking for his comments on the methodology of biography. Ian Lee pressed him about how a biographer knew when he had at last reached the essence of personality — "Does a light go on or what?" he asked Jimroy, snapping his fingers. August Krause pursued him about the gap between the private and public person. "Ah, but what *is* a public person?" Monique Krause cried, clapping her little hands together. "Only a nude body wearing slightly better clothes."

What good people they were: middle-aged, civilized, tolerant, travelled and tanned and united, all of them, in their contempt for Ronald Reagan. They offered Jimroy, without a thought of return, their delicious food, their good-to-excellent wine, their recorded music, and their conversation, and they sent him home well before midnight.

Jimroy, thankful, could only think: thank God for their honest cuts of beef and the little pings of laughter that leapt from their mouths when he produced his "first impressions" of California. He was less lonely than he had been in aa _

Winnipeg, although he knew similar couples there, the Swensens, the Zieglers, the Mullocks. He marvelled at the steadiness of love that seemed to flow between these husbands and wives. Most of them had been married for well over twenty-five years, and still they maintained toward each other an attitude of courtesy and tenderness. He tried to imagine them coupling in their beds — Ian's plump penis stuck up there between Elizabeth's legs — and couldn't; but that scarcely seemed to matter. Love was what mattered, that enduring, mysterious refuge. Returning home alone to the flatness of the Flanners' bed, he carried some of their circumambient warmth with him.

He reflects on one such night that it has been some weeks since he's surrendered to that hideous weakness of his, which is to make anonymous phone calls to Audrey in Florida. Perhaps he's getting over the need to hear her croaking voice erupting from sleep "Hullo?" she yawks into the phone, like someone testing the depth of a cave. He shuts his eyes and tries to imagine the trailer she's living in, what her bed is like, if she requires a blanket in that ridiculous climate, how she looks sitting on the edge of the bed with the receiver in her hand.

"Hullo, I said. Who is this?"

He never speaks back; just holds the receiver, listening.

"Who is this anyway?" she demands roughly. That Midlands snarl.

More silence. He is careful not to breathe. He would never stoop to being a breather. And he doesn't really want to frighten her. Dear old Aud.

"Who is this, for the love of God?"

A long pause, and Jimroy waits for the voice that will surely come and fill it. Instead she often bangs the phone down hard.

Once she shouted, "You can't fool me. I know who it is, you bugger."

His hands had trembled, but he managed to hang on to the receiver. His lips brushed against the mouthpiece, fear and love entwined. He thought of her large mouth, not an attractive woman, not at all.

It's been several weeks since he's phoned Audrey in the middle of the night. A good sign. He should celebrate, like an alcoholic after a dry month.

If only he could expunge — ah, but he can't. He promises himself, a solemn pledge, that he will make no more phone calls to Sarasota. His work on Mary Swann is coming along; every week he mails a sheaf of papers off to Mrs. Lynch for typing. Fragrant air drifts in through the open window. He's sleeping well. He has just returned from a charming evening with cheerful, intelligent friends who regard him, he knows, as a minion from the North, a role he fancies. And, after all, he doesn't love Audrey any more. That was over years ago.

But he is, he admits to himself, deeply in love. He is sodden with love, foolish with love. And the woman he loves is Sarah Maloney of Chicago whom he has never met.

October 24

Dear Morton,

I knew you'd relent! So! We'll meet at last — I'm delighted. You should be getting your tentative program in a few days, hot off the press. What would our Mary have thought of all this? I'm afraid that when I try to imagine her sitting in the audience listening to someone discussing her use of the çaesura, it all seems suddenly laughable. You may not agree. Do you? Or not?

Toronto in January — it sounds like a piece of misery.

I do agree with you, yes, that it would have been more appropriate to hold the thing in Nadeau, and the Steering Committee did look into it. (Isn't Steering Committee, a curious expression? Fascist almost; invented no doubt to give us false notions of power.) The problem with Nadeau was hotel space — none. Unless you count the six rooms over the beer parlour. And, yes, Elgin was a possibility, though the hotel is one of those drafty old country places, as you must know. And the highway between there and Toronto is sometimes closed in January because of storms. It was agreed that Toronto would have to do if we wanted to attract people. And, astonishingly, it looks as though there will be sixty of us, and maybe more. Who would have believed it? Herb Block is coming from Harvard. When I heard that, little silver bells rang in my head. Herb Block! I suppose you know we invited Frances Moore. "Not quite my thing," she replied. A cool one.

And now, Morton, I want you to know that I was deeply touched by what you said in your last letter, how important it was to you to receive personal mail. Yes, I know about what you call the "loneliness of the half famous" — not, by the way, a category I would place you in. I think a lot about loneliness, surely the most wide-spread of modern diseases — don't I know! As a matter of fact, it was the spectre of loneliness that first attracted me to Mary Swann's work, that she and I shared the same bad cold. Of all her poems, the one that speaks to the very centre of my heart is "Alone in the House."

Especially those lines —

Pity my blood hidden and locked
Pity my mouth shut tight.
Pity my passing unlocked
Hours, pity my unwatched night.

Not her best stanza, but when you think of the anguish behind it! How that poor woman needed some-one to "watch" her. How we all do! I don't, by the way, think she's being self-pitying here as Professor Croft sug-gests in her *PMLA* article. (By the way, Croft is coming to the symposium, a sure sign that our Mary has arrived.)

I'm so glad you weren't miffed by my reluctance to let go of the Swann notebook at this time. If I thought there was material in it that you could use for your book, of course I'd send you a copy. But mostly it's just notes, ideas for poems, lots of scribbles — of which I'll be talking about in my presentation. I feet rotten about this, damn it. But then you know about the selfishness of scholars. What a lousy bunch we are.

                                        All good wishes,
                                        Sarah

Most of the letters that arrive for Jimroy are business letters from his publishers in New York or from his col-leagues in Manitoba. These typed communications, though welcome, hurt his eyes. Too casual, this plinking of print, too easily accomplished. The battering of mechanical keys seems to convince most people that they are witty, when, in fact, they are only verbose. The result, Jimroy finds, is exasperating prolixity and an excess of little dots between sentences, or else that gassy kind of nervousness that came blithering off Ezra Pound's typed notes to his friends — Jimroy always imagines that these letters of Pound's, even the gayest of them, were written with his teeth tightly clenched. Sarah Maloney's envelopes bear jaunty angled stamps and are, Jimroy dares to hope, lovingly licked. The letters themselves are handwritten. Her crisp — but not too crisp — off-white paper suggests harmony and resilience.

The ink is deep blue and flows from a medium-tipped pen, what to Jimroy looks like a nylon nib. He loves the calm way Sarah Maloney writes *honor* and *center* — these words, with their plain American spellings, seem to grow rounded and luminous. Her wide-open a's and o's enchant him. Her capital w's are innocent well-fed young birds, ready to try their wings. She is twenty-eight years old; he knows because the date of her birth was included in the biographical data that accompanied her first published article, but in any case he would have guessed from her handwriting that she was still in her twenties, the lucky age, the emanicipated age. One has only to look at Mary Swann's cramped hand or at his own squashed loops. Her tone is murmurous, womanly.

He distrusts the photo on her book jacket, long hair falling over a long face. A talky mouth and libidinous eyes. A neat little chin, though, redeems her. She might, he thinks, be the kind of woman who hangs prisms or pieces of coloured glass wistfully in her windows. He imagines that she shuns crimson nail polish. A certain bodily stockiness? He fervently hopes not. (At least Audrey had not been stocky.) He knows that Virginia Woolf is Sarah's favourite novelist — as a rule he distrusts a Woolfian bias in women — and that V.S. Pritchett is her favourite essayist. The books of these two authors, he imagines, are placed side by side on a little painted shelf close to the desk where she works, the place where she sits (in a pool of sun?) writing her lovely handwritten letters, licking with her soft tongue, honey at its core, the gummed envelopes and stamps — ah, Sarah. *The soft tongue, pink, travels across his body. For heaven's sake, take off your pyjamas, Sarah whispers, foolish buttons, hurry. Oh, how sweet, let me lick, lick, lick. There now, isn't that what you needed? What you wanted? Yes, of course it is.*

He is sure she has mellowed, changed utterly in fact,
since the publication of her big, beefy, angry book, *The
Female Prism*. Her letters are all soft edges and crisp corners.
Her refusal, for instance, to part with Mary Swann's notebook was tenderly phrased, so that the sting of denial was
scarcely felt. Well, only a flick. And only for an instant.

Her most recent letter is the tenth one she has written
him. Jimroy places it at the bottom of the pile under the
others and replaces the rubber band with a glad snap.
Tonight, since the Lees' party ended even earlier than usual,
he will get into bed, pull up the light cotton blanket, and
treat himself to the whole oeuvre.

He admits that her style leaves something to be desired;
only occasionally does it tilt toward the kind of persiflage he
admires. He wishes she wouldn't use that phrase *deeply
touched*; he imagines reddened nostrils, dampness, appalling
sincerity. The word *lousy* offends him slightly. She seems
unable to produce the long, many-branched sentences he
most admires, but he hasn't the heart to cavil at something
she can't help. And her phrases *do* have a certain sonority,
a stubbornness, her own kind of reckless heat. More than
that, the words seem to be shaped for him and for him only.
He imagines that the letters she writes to others — Herb
Block, that lightweight fake — are thinner and deficient
in vitality.

When he writes to Sarah Maloney he is careful not to
smoke. He doesn't want her to open his envelopes and
inhale staleness. Another thing: he makes a point of insert-
ing one, and only one, personal message that he knows
will elicit a personal response. He tries for something
self-deprecating, the admission of some minor failing or
misadventure, for he knows he is most likeable when he
is being second rate. He rations himself, anxious that this

relationship not turn soppy. He wants hardness, sharpness, *net*, with just the occasional soft spot, rapidly opened and just as rapidly closed. In a recent letter he told her about the guilt (a mild exaggeration, but no matter) he suffers over the Flanners' roses, how he sits among them but ignores their beauty, how they bloom without his appreciation.

"They don't need appreciation," Sarah wrote back, absolving him — and, furthermore, she wrote, "nature wor-shippers are vastly overrated as human beings, particularly in their own estimation."

It was what he needed to hear. Sweet impunity. Everything Sarah (Sarah! Sarah!) writes is what he needs to hear.

Of course he knows this can be explained as a trick of love, that every word spoken by a lover becomes radiantly relevant and overlaid with gold.

Sporran.

Jimroy is awakened in the middle of the night by this word, which appears suddenly spelled out in his dream.

The rest of the dream fades quickly — he has never been able to retain his dreams — leaving only this single word: *sporran*. The letters dance with a garish blue light behind his closed eyelids. There is a background of dull grey and a sensation of shrill music being played off stage.

The image is surprisingly persistent, and in order to make it disappear Jimroy is forced to reach over and turn on the bedside lamp. The alarm clock on the table says 3:00 A.M.

Sporran. Of course. It is the word he was trying to remember, the name of the little purse that Highlanders wear in front of their kilts. He saw one not long ago on that odd young duck of a Scotsman sitting next to him at the University Theater.

This is something that has happened to him fairly frequently. A word or phrase or piece of trivia will completely slip out of his mind, only to reappear later when the need of it has passed. Objects mislaid, an appointment overlooked. It happens to everyone, of course — he knows that — and gets worse with age. From time to time, especially in the middle of a lecture, it has caused Jimroy a flutter of embarrassment. The phenomenon had to do with the breakdown of the oxygen supply to the brain cells. Somewhere he has read an article about it. Was it *Scientific American*? No, must have been *Harpers*. Or else he's seen a television program about it. He hopes he won't become the kind of doddering old fool who forgets to zip up his pants or has to have his phone number pinned inside his shirt.

Probably it's a good sign that the forgotten word or phrase always does come back to him eventually, usually when he's relaxed or even, as tonight, in the middle of sleep. What a curious thing the brain is really, with its intricate circuits and cross channels, all embedded in inches of damp, unpretentious, democratic tissue. Sometimes Jimroy thinks of his brain as a rather thick child, wilful and mischievous and dully unaccountable, that he must carry atop an awkward body. But tonight he is grateful for the sudden flashpoint of memory.

Wide awake now, he tries to recall something that has happened during the day to produce this sudden revelation, this illuminated word *sporran*. There is nothing. And it's been weeks since his encounter with the Scotsman, weeks since he's asked himself what the term was for the little pouch the man wore around his waist. Of course, it's not a particularly common word. One could go years and years without hearing it. But still he should not have forgotten.

It isn't as though this word was something he was trying

to suppress, not like the time he was filling out the divorce papers and quite suddenly couldn't remember Audrey's middle name. In a case like that he was willing to admit there might be an element of unconscious blocking.

Audrey Joan Beamish Jimroy. The name *Joan* came to him the day after he mailed in the papers to the lawyers, when he was sitting in a tub of hot water. He immediately got out, dried himself off and phoned the lawyer, saying that he "might possibly have neglected to include my estranged wife's middle name."

Then he got back into the tub, telling himself, making light of it, that he was thankful his parents had chosen not to give him a middle name or he might very likely have forgotten that, too. After his bath he sat down in a chair by a window and made himself recite some of the Cantos; on one line only, but a line that had once been a favourite, he faltered. He would have to watch himself. In his métier a good memory was essential. Vitamin E was helpful, so some people believed. It was something to look into. If a man was going around forgetting his wife's middle name . . .

Sporran, sporran. He turns out the light and tries to go back to sleep, but the word beeps in his head. He wonders what its origin is. Irish, probably. It has that sound. Nothing to do with spores certainly, though it is hung on the body in a conspicuously spore-related place.

Audrey Joan Beamish. He clearly remembers the first time he saw her name, a signature at the bottom of an application letter. All spring he had been looking for a research assistant, and Audrey, who didn't know research from beans, had applied. Typical of Aud to think she could master anything she put her mind to. At least she could type a little, that was something. And her Birmingham accent had an invigorating effect on him. Her boniness, her rawness —

she had the kind of reddened nose that was always pressed in a wad of damp tissue — invited his tenderness. He wanted to protect her from herself. Poor old Audrey.

Often, even here in California, homeland of long-legged American beauties, he sees extraordinarily unattractive women — sallow or bent or overweight or in some way deformed — riding on buses or dragging through department stores. Their shopping bags and the children they tug along confirm without doubt that these women are married. Who would marry such women? Jimroy has asked himself. Then he remembers: *he* married Audrey. He was even drawn to her because of her long horse's face, her knobbed wrist bones gleaming like pickled onions above her hands.

Even her ignorance gave him pleasure in the early days, telling him he was not alone in his failings. He had amused himself by mumbling inanities to her: Isn't this the most celestial sky, isn't this the most urban city, isn't so-and-so forever putting his foot in his Achilles' heel, wasn't somebody-or-other always looking back in retrospect. Then he would watch her face in canny delight as these remarks bounced off her like rubber bullets. She would frowningly turn her eyes upward in thought or else give her sideways nod; one shoulder would go up. Yes, yes, she would say, riding roughshod over his *jeu d'esprit*, his prickliness, blind to it, oblivious as only Audrey could be oblivious.

What he loved her for, if love in its defective mode can still be called love, was her stubborn though unspoken belief that there existed an order to the universe and that she was part of the human army who propped it up. *Soldiering on* was the phrase Audrey lived by, soldiering on blindly, bravely, doing those thousands of things she deemed worth doing. With a wild flailing of arms, with an inexhaustible noisy flow of energy, she had wallpapered the hall of the

ugly old house Jimroy owned in Winnipeg, scraped paint
from the woodwork, planted her "veg patch" in the scrubby
backyard. He admitted that she was simple-minded — but
there was such *kindness* in the way she misread him. To her
he was not a crippled cynic with a talent for misanthropy; to
Aud he was no more than a poor sap who needed cheering
up. A coarse, awkward woman, but something in her nature
appealed, even her sense of righteousness. He once in conversation used the word *poleaxed*, and she took him to task
for being derogatory about the Polish people.

When he married Audrey Beamish he had been prepared for pity from his acquaintances. He braced himself for
their questioning faces. Why in his fortieth year had he sad-
dled himself with a wife, particularly a wife like Audrey?

Instead of pity there was rejoicing. She was just what he
needed, people said, this noisy good sport of a woman with
a heart the size of a watermelon. (Someone or other had
used those exact words.)

Moments of lamentations. Everyone has them, Jimroy
supposes. His are conducted late at night. *My wound is that
I have no wound.* This is just one of those things Jimroy
chants to himself, not sure how fitting it is — introspection
distorts even the sharpest mind and extremely doubtful
about its originality. (The phrase, the rhythm of it, sounds
suspiciously like something someone else said, someone
starkly confessional and melodramatic — Rupert Brooke,
someone of that ilk.) Nevertheless Jimroy proceeds: *My
wound is that . . .*

His wound, or woundlessness as it were, is a small
organism curled inside him, patient, docile, like a sleeping
spaniel, a dwarf spaniel. It refuses to identify itself, and the
only reason Jimroy knows of its existence is that he sometimes, though rarely, encounters it elsewhere, curled inside

another human body where it is, to his surprise, instantly recognizable. That student he once had at the university, Ely Salterton, fresh off a wheat farm; from Ely Salterton he had kept his distance. And "more recently" that queer fellow in the kilt — well, *he* was not a clear case. But Audrey; in Audrey he had seen it at once, only instead of being repelled by it, he had reached out, a man who at forty was in danger of drowning.

"Never mind, love," Audrey said after his first (and last) sexual attempt. "It doesn't matter in the least, love."

Amazingly, it hadn't.

A miracle. He had been free to withdraw his hand from the damp coarseness of Audrey's pubic curls, from the folded old-man confusion of her wet labia — at least he supposed those spongy tissues were labia.

The relief was awesome. Even more awesome was his conviction that Audrey felt the same exalted sense of relief. The failing between them was recognized at once and surrendered to. Afterwards they lay quietly in the dark, their arms around each other, the happiest hour Jimroy has ever known. Plenitude. A rich verdure, richer than he had ever imagined from his reading of love poetry. And where did it come from? From Audrey. Dumb Audrey with her grating voice. Audrey who thought Shakespeare was "snooty," Audrey who had never even heard of the poet John Starman, Audrey who pronounced Camus so that it sounded like Cam-muss; at that moment, at that level, hidden away in a dark Fort Garry bedroom, they met. Their silence settled on the hairs of his released hand and on Audrey's sadly smiling mouth. Dear Christ, what happiness.

After the divorce a surprising number of their friends sided with Audrey. (There were those who cruelly joked that she was the first of their acquaintance to divorce a man for sarcasm.) Of course she felt rejected, people said this with small lip pursings and an upward glance. They could understand exactly how it must be from her point of view. Even now Jimroy knows that these old friends receive postcards from Sarasota from time to time. Good old Audrey reporting in.

And what does he get? Nothing.

Eastern Airlines was unable to trace Jimroy's lost luggage. They were sorry. They gave him a number of new forms to fill out and told him not to abandon hope entirely. There were hundreds of wild stories about baggage turning up in out-of-the-way places. Of course he would receive a cheque for the replacement value of the contents and for the two pieces of luggage themselves. Was Jimroy absolutely sure that the luggage had been weighed in at the Winnipeg airport? (He had to say no to this, remembering that Mrs. Lynch had looked after the luggage.) Had he, when arriving in the San Francisco airport, gone directly to the luggage pickup or had he stopped somewhere, at the men's room perhaps, or at a coffee machine? (Jimroy could not be sure of this, not after all this time.) Luggage, he was told, was rarely stolen, but on occasion. . . well it was certainly not unknown. Mrs. Myrtle, the adjuster, was sorry about the lost papers, which she realized were extremely valuable as well as being irreplaceable, but with luck, these might still surface. There was a woman just last year who lost her vanity case on a flight between Santa Barbara and L.A., and six months later, after an unexplainable detour to Hong Kong, the case was returned to her. Anything could happen. It could turn up at any moment.

And on November 10 — there was a fall of rain, which prevented Jimroy from working out of doors — it did turn up, though no one was able to say exactly how it had happened. Mrs. Myrtle from the airline phoned Jimroy and informed him in a rocking jubilant contralto that his baggage appeared to have been found. Would he come out to the airport to identify it?

An hour later he was there, inspecting his suitcases. Inside were his clothes, his folded suits and shirts, his shoes still wrapped loosely in the newspaper he had put around them two months earlier. He looked inside his toilet case and saw that his toothbrush had gone green with mould, but that everything else was in order. His neckties were still rolled neatly around his black nylon socks. There was his battery shaver — a gift from Audrey; one of her good ideas — and the striped swimming trunks he had put in at the last minute. A set of towels and face cloths, a knitted vest for chilly days. He reached a hand under the vest, searching for his papers and for the photograph of Mary Swann. His fingers struck glass, then the hard metal frame. "Everything's here," he told Mrs. Myrtle, a heavy black woman with large swinging earrings. "The photograph too."

"Photograph?"

"Of a woman." How silky he sounded saying this: *Of a woman*. "Who unfortunately is no longer alive." Her blue-black forehead became a sheet of crinkles. "Yeah?"

"A wonderful woman." His happiness had made him silly.

"Can I see?"

He held up the picture for her inspection. "The love of my life", he said recklessly.

He observed that her eyes rolled back slightly and that she blew softly through her teeth. "Far out," she said, a phrase that injured Jimroy with its aroma of doubt.

"This is an extremely rare photograph." He heard himself turn weak with pleading. "The only copy in existence."

"Hey." She sounded soft, smoky. He could swear she was laughing at him. "Didn't I tell you we'd find your stuff, Mr. Jimroy?"

When he reached home he unpacked his suitcase and hung his clothes carefully in the closet. He set the photograph on the bureau and then sat down on the bed, his hands icy despite the heat. A moan bubbled its way through his closed lips. She had changed. Her face was hard, unreasonable, closed, and invoked in him a fever of shame. I am a relatively famous man, he said to himself, seeking comfort. My name is well known, and I have no reason to be ashamed.

The sense of shame was surprisingly poignant, and the fact that it was genuine gave Jimroy a perverted stab of pleasure and bestowed on him an odd little capelet of authenticity. But what he could not set aside was the fear that drilled through his shame, for it occurred to him that the photograph had altered and that Mary Swann had, unaccountably, become his enemy.

The thought, irrational and paranoid — he admitted the paranoia, at least — frightened him. He became jumpy, he spilled coffee in his saucer and down the front of his pants, he avoided thinking about it as much as possible. He tried instead to think of South Africa, Nicaragua, the Middle East. His little twisted wordy world; what did it amount to?

Nevertheless his fear persisted. After a week he decided to put the photograph away in a safe place, and then he buried himself in his work as he always did when his life was going badly.

During the past two years Jimroy had conducted extensive interviews with the following people:

Willard Lang, professor and critic (Toronto). Jimroy detests Lang, who has a benighted concept of *art naïf* and who has so far refused to publish the four poems, love poems he claims he found under Mary Swann's kitchen linoleum. A lumpish man. A man whose thought waves come in unindented paragraphs. And vain. Would like to be thought mercurial. But never will.

Frederic Cruzzi, retired editor of the *Kingston Banner* (small-town paper) and the Peregrine Press. Pompous old boy, fond of the sound of his own voice. Fund of wisdom, etc.

George Hanna, nephew of Elizabeth Hanna, neighbour of Mary Swann (Nadeau). Cretin.

William and Alma Lardner, neighbours of Mary Swann (Nadeau). Unreliable. Possibly insane.

Rose Helen Hindmarch, librarian (Nadeau). Lachrymose woman, tears in her eyes saying goodbye. Helpful, of course, more helpful than anyone else, but three days of that whinnying voice. An unpretty woman. Bent on imparting to him her feeble meditations and moony recollections. Small mouth gobbling air. Greedy. No, too harsh. Needy. Awful in a woman, being needy.

The Rev. W.A. Polson, retired (Nadeau). Nothing came of that.

Homer Hart, school principal, retired (Nadeau). Confused. Unreliable.

Grace Saltman, retired teacher (Belleville, now of Victoria, British Columbia). Bulbous nose.

Richard Eckhardt, town clerk (Belleville). Memory intractable.

Susan Hansen Kurtz, niece of Mary Swann (Belleville). Seemed to be retarded. Or senile.

Rupert "Torchy" Torchinski, baker, retired (Belleville). Hopeless.

Frances Swann Moore, daughter of the poet (Palo Heights, California).

In addition to these interviews, all patiently typed out like plays by the faithful Mrs. Lynch, there have been long, reasonably profitable days in the public archives in Toronto gathering background material. He has also spent a few intensely lonely and wasted days in the National Archives in Ottawa gathering nothing at all but a severe headache and an infection in his upper intestine. In the end he abandoned background research — it seemed to have little to do with Mary Swann. The problem was not to reconcile Swann with her background, but to separate her from it, as the poetry had done.

He wills himself not to think about Swann's notebook, which is in the keeping of his beloved Sarah. Not that he has much faith in it. He has seen diaries before and knows how little light they shed, but still there may be some subterranean detail that will throw light on . . . but why think of that now? He can feel the stitch of his old ulcer picking away.

He had read and reread her only book of poems, *Swann's Songs*, published by the Peregrine Press in 1966. (Idiotic title.) He knows these poems so well that he could, if he were called upon, recite most of them by heart. Some of Mary Swann's lines rise spontaneously in his thoughts while he shaves his chin in the morning or tramps along the gravel-edged roadway to Frances Moore's splendid house.

A green light drops from a blue sky
And waits like winter in its jar of glass
Tells a weather-rotted lie
Or stories of damage and loss.

Jimroy murmured these lines one afternoon to Frances
Moore who looked at him blankly and moved her teacup,
swiftly, to her lips.

The fact is, the poems and the life of Mary Swann do not
meld, and Jimroy, one morning, working in the garden,
spreads his handwritten notes in the December sunshine
and begins to despair. The sky today is bordered at the top
with streaks of weak-looking blue. He is not such a fool, he
tells himself, as to believe that poets and artists and musi-
cians possess an integrity of spirit greater than other people.
No, of course he has never gone in for that kind of nonsense.
What an absurdity is that critical term *unity of vision*, for
instance — as though anyone in this universe ever possessed
such a thing, or would want to.

And yet — he shifts his papers, which are weighted
down this cool and breezy morning by small pebbles dug
out of the flower border — how is he to connect Mary
Swann's biographical greyness with the achieved splendour
of *Swann's Songs*? He has gone over and over the chronological events of her life. He has even made a detailed chart,
hoping his inked boxes and arrows and dotted lines may
yield the one important insight, the moment in which she
broke her way through to life. He does not, of course, really
believe in the institution of childhood, and this, he knows,
is a somewhat daring reversal of prevailing biographical
theory. Freudians! But what precisely is the value of childhood? he asks himself. It is a puzzle not worth solving, a
primitive time predating literacy, a dulled period presided
over by dull parents. Nevertheless, he flips through his
index cards once more.

Birth of Mary Moffat Swann: at home, near Belleville, on a
    hundred-acre farm. Parentage unremarkable. (As he

knew it would be; genius owes no debts to parents; one has only to look at his own sad set, their memory not so much suppressed as simply not thought of, and his lack of eccentric aunts and funny uncles. A Sahara.)

Childhood: narrow, poor, uneventful; at least nothing recorded to the contrary.

Schooling: minimal, a meagre, one-room-schoolhouse education; one surviving report card indicating Mary Moffat had not excelled even in that limited environment.

Work: one year selling bread in the Belleville Golden Sheaf Bakery, defunct since 1943.

Marriage: to a farmer, Angus Swann, a Saturday-afternoon service in the Belleville United Church, no existing photographs, but an eyewitness (the dim niece) recalls that the bride wore a blue gabardine dress, buttoned down the back. (How had she met this farmer? No one knows, but the notebook may reveal — when Sarah deigns to release it.)

Later life: Moved to an unproductive farm near Nadeau, Ontario; gave birth to one child, Frances. Never ventured farther than Kingston, and there only occasionally.

Died: violently, at the age of fifty. A cynic might call her death the only dramatic episode in a life that was a long surrender to the severity of seasons.

Buried: outside Nadeau. In the Protestant cemetery.

Even with the background material and critical commentary, this will be a thin book. A defeat. Jimroy is now thinking in terms of a long article.

In desperation he rummages about one chilly day for the photograph of Mary Swann, hoping it will impart the little jolt of insight he requires. He looks first on the closet shelf, then in his bureau drawers, then, a little frantically, in the linen cupboard, under the Flanners' stacked sheets and blankets. He remembers that he put it in a safe place, a particular place, a place where he was unlikely to come across her slyly withholding eyes. But where? It must be somewhere. This is a small house, smooth-surfaced and without secrets. Where? He spends all of one afternoon looking, wearing himself out, wasting his valuable time.

He accuses himself of senility. He accuses himself of hubris, of burying Swann's grainy likeness, keeping her out of sight and shutting her up, a miniature act of murder.

And now that he needs her again, she's bent on punishment. She is a sly one, a wily one. Women, women. Endlessly elusive and intent on victory.

He admits it: for the moment at least, Mary Swann has defeated him.

It is the fact of *seasons*, Jimroy finally decides, their immensity and extremes, that blocks out Swann's personal history. Each year of her life seems a paroxysm of renewed anonymity, for although he is a careful interviewer, his proddings and probings have not yielded much that is specific about her. Recollections of those who knew her — except for Rose Hindmarch, thank God for the moist, repulsive Rose — are maddeningly general and adhere always to the annual cycle, those *seasons*. "In the spring Mary Swann always . . . " or "Usually round about late fall Ma busied herself with . . . " or "In the summers there was the garden to dig and weed and then the canning . . . " The power of these recurring seasons overwhelms the fragile scurryings of that obscure farm wife, Mary Swann, and what is left is a record of dullness and drudgery. And a heartbreaking absence of celebration, a life lived, as the saying goes, in the avoidance of biography.

Of course he can surmise certain things, influences for instance. He is almost sure she came in contact with the work of Emily Dickinson, regardless of what Frances Moore says. He intends to mention, to comment extensively in fact, on the Dickinsonian influence, and sees no point, really, in taking up the Edna Ferber influence: it is too ludicrous.

At times he aches for the notebook, which on good days he imagines to be filled with airy reaches of thought. He's tired of pretending that his partial vision carries a superior and intuited truth. And it pains him, too, to think of the lost love poems in the hands of the lightweight, egregious Willard Lang, who strikes him as a man sweaty with ambition. The bushel of peaches, or was it half a bushel (he has forgotten and anyway he despises involutions), but it was peaches Lang gave the real-estate agent, a bribe, in exchange for vital documentation that by rights belongs to the biographer. To him.

But what Jimroy yearns for even more than the notebook and the love poems is to be told the one central cathartic event in Mary Swann's life. It must exist. It is what a good biography demands, what a human life demands. But now, December, he had begun to lose faith in his old belief that the past is retrievable. He would give a good deal even for a simple direct quotation from Mary Swann, but even Rose Hindmarch, the only real friend she ever had, is halting about direct quotations, and Mary's own daughter, Frances, is unable to recall with accuracy anything her mother ever said. "Oh, she used to get after me about mud on my boots and doing my homework, but Ma wasn't a great one to talk, you know."

Jimroy curses Mary Swann's silences and admits to himself, finally, that he's disappointed in her. Some of this disappointment he shifts to her daughter, Frances; he has, after all, come to California hoping that their conversations might spring open an unconscious revelation, something that will expose the key to Swann's genius. It hasn't happened, he might as well admit it. Frances's revelations, though she furrows her brow convincingly and bites her lower lip in concentration, are too detached for revelation. Her memory is opaque and lacks detail, and Jimroy can't make up his mind about this; is it a personality defect, this bent for invisibility, or a daughterly reflection of the larger opaqueness that was Mary Swann's life? She refuses to talk of her mother's death, and Jimroy knows that it will be impossible to enter that life without understanding its final moment. Reticulated detail is what he needs, and that is being systematically denied. A single glimpse, and the poems would open out and become clear.

On the other hand, he feels a perverse admiration for Frances, especially for the distance she has placed between the harsh, limited scene of her girlhood and her glowing sun-streaked California living-room. She has an aptitude for distance. She remains distant from Jimroy, too, after all these months still cool, still polite, never for a moment presuming friendship, closed in that patrician way Audrey could never master. The hand she holds out to be shaken, though its dryness is oddly intimate, is as exquisitely bent as for a royal handshake.

And then, unexpectedly, one afternoon a week before Christmas, settled on the sofa in the dancing light, she violated this distance for the first time by saying, "You know, Mr. Jimroy, I'm a little surprised you've chosen a woman for a subject."

"Why is that?" he asked her. "We are living in the age of women."

"Well, it's only — " she stopped, gave an awkward flick of her hand.

"Only?" He fixed his glance on hers, waiting for a response, preparing himself for injury.

"Well, only that you seem to be a man who isn't, well—"

"Yes?" He held his breath.

"Well, a man who's not . . . overly fond of women."

Jimroy's eyes flew to the small curled fingers of a terra-cotta figure on the coffee table. Neither he nor Frances Moore spoke for a moment, and the silence grew so heavy it seemed to him to be turning into water. He felt a distinct sensation of drowning. His nose and throat and lungs were filling with water. He was afraid to open his mouth for fear of it spilling out.

"I think — " he began.

"I'm sorry. I've spoken out of turn," Frances Moore said quickly. "It's a bad habit of mine, spouting nonsense — "

"If I've given you the impression — " He felt himself groping for balance. "If I've said anything that gave you the idea that — "

"No, of course not. It's nothing you said. Or did. It's nothing at all. I was just being — well, frivolous. Please, forgive me."

"There's nothing at all to forgive. It's just that — " and to his horror he gave out a sort of snuffling laugh.

"Can I warm up this tea, Mr. Jimroy? It's gone stone cold."

"I — "

"Surely you'd like a little more. I know *I* would. It'll just take me half a minute to boil some more water."

"Well, yes." He coughed hideously. Something seemed

to have entered his throat and lodged there, an avocado pit, oily and dense. Indignation seized him, but indignation at whom? — at this graceful, smooth-haired California matron rising and lifting a pretty teapot from the table? Or with himself, his awful quagmire heart, his flapping hands.

In a few minutes she was back with the teapot, and she had something else in her other hand, a little narrow jeweller's box covered with blue velvet. "I thought you might want to see this," she said.

She opened the box. "It's Ma's Parker 51."

Jimroy made a suitable sound and asked if he might examine it.

"It was sent to me after she died. I don't know why, but the house agent thought I might want it, At any rate, when Ma was given this pen, it was quite something. What I mean is, in our part of the country it was unusual to own a pen like this. It was a gift, a birthday gift, just after the war, I think. Fountain pens were expected to last a lifetime in those days as you must know, and Ma always kept it in this box when she wasn't using it."

"Was it from — ?" He stopped himself in time. The biographer's shameless silky greed.

"She'd write her poems out in pencil and then copy them over in ink. Then she'd burn the pencil copies in the woodstove."

"Such a loss!" Jimroy had already heard this story of the burnt poems, but couldn't stop himself from murmuring, "They would have been of great interest to scholars today — "

"Well yes, but — "

"First drafts are highly prized, almost — "

"Yes, well — "

He went on, relentlessly. "How wonderful it would be if one or two had survived."

"They didn't, though." She said this firmly and snapped the case shut. "I think that tea should be steeped now. You will have a little?"

"Please."

"I'll just get you a clean cup — "

"Please don't bother."

"It's no bother," she said, and excused herself.

What he did next simply happened. He found his hand on the rounded velvet top of the box. Then he lifted the lid, marvelling at the strength of the spring. After all these years, to open so stiffly! It twinkled against the satin lining, a dark blue pen with a fine marbled finish. Then it was in his hand, then in the inside pocket of his new denim sports jacket. He closed the box and positioned it on the table between the bowl of wet flowers and the stack of magazines.

Thief. Robber. He knew he was taking a shocking risk. Frances Moore would suspect him at once. Even if several weeks went by before she reopened the box, she would remember that he had been the last person to see it.

But she would never believe him capable of common thievery, not Morton Jimroy, biographer, Distinguished Visitor. She had given him hours of hospitality, hours of her shared recollections. She had trusted him, and why not? A man of his reputation. He would never bring himself to abuse such a trust!

She would search for the pen under the woven sofa cushions, run her hand across the patterned rug. She would ask herself if there had been a newspaper on the table and if she might have placed the pen on top of the paper and, later, tidying the room, thrown it out? In the end she might decide that that was what had happened, the only explanation.

She would blame herself for her carelessness, berate
herself — a thought that made Jimroy shiver a little with
perverse pleasure. She would remember that she had been
flustered; and now Jimroy was grateful for their awkward
scene. Still, she might decide to question him directly. He
would have to be prepared for that. Did he remember that
afternoon she had shown him the Parker 51? Yes? Did he
remember her replacing the pen in the case afterward? It
seems to be lost, she would say mournfully, and he would
exclaim, "What a pity!" Had she looked under the sofa,
under the rug? Perhaps when she was tidying the table . . .

He relaxed against the soft cushions and awaited his cup
of tea. A sharp sigh, almost a whistle, escaped his lips, and
his hand reached inside his jacket and touched the fountain
pen. The pen of Mary Swann. The pen that had written:

> Ice is the final thief
> First cousin to larger grief.

He would probably not be seeing Frances Moore again.
There was nothing more she could tell him, she said, and
she would be occupied in the days ahead with Christmas
preparations, the return of her son from Princeton, the
return of her husband from a lengthy lecture tour. And
he himself would soon be off to Toronto for the Swann
symposium.

At the door they shook hands gravely. A tinted mirror
on the foyer wall sent back a reflection of cordiality.

"Merry Christmas, Mr. Jimroy," Frances said, her composure restored, her strong, finely veined hand extended.

"Merry Christmas," he returned, once again his extravagantly amiable self, and hurried down the flower-lined
driveway, almost running. He imagined the wind rubbing
the hair on his head and exposing spots of pinkness, a soft

baby's scalp. The smell of eucalyptus was in the air. Green, green, everywhere he looked it was green. He gave a queer little leap into the air as he rushed along his way.

How extremely kind of Ian Lee and his wife, Elizabeth, to include him in their Christmas Eve festivities next door. A last-minute invitation to be sure, but his unpressed pants gave off, he hoped, a creditable air of self-forgetfulness, of social ease. We adore having you, Elizabeth Lee said, and planted a holiday kiss on his cheek. Would he mind helping mix the punch? Would he take the cheese tray around for her? Isn't the tree a dream! Visitors from other parts of the country are always surprised that Californians have Christmas trees, aren't they? Of course they cost the earth. Had he met the Gordens, the Kapletters? Yes, that was real holly, not the imitation stuff. Was he sure he wouldn't like a little more to eat himself, one more plateful? Surely another glass of wine, Ian's special wine, the one he only drags out for Christmas; it goes down like velvet. She was stunned by the news from Africa. This was a violent world. It seemed only yesterday that she and Ian had lighted a Christmas candle for Poland, though they'd both thought it a Reaganesque gesture, empty and theatrical; but, well, why not? Christmas was the time to be aware of others less fortunate, the time to be at peace. No one should be alone on Christmas Eve, didn't he agree? Ah, yes, he did agree; emphatically. (The irony bit, but not deeply.) Yes, yes — his uxorious voice, coming on like corn syrup.

And then he was home again. It was midnight, and he was heating himself some warm milk, hoping he would be able to sleep. There was such a weight of silence in the little house, such chilly stillness. He had slipped his old knitted vest on over his pyjamas (blessings on Mrs. Lynch) and happened to catch a glimpse of himself in the bedroom mirror. How shockingly like an old man he looked tonight. He was white-faced and thin, the wormy, rheumy, pink-eyed old gent of his nightmares, mouth dragging down, cheap pyjamas crushed around the collar and not very clean. He was only fifty-one, he reminded himself. Almost fifty-two actually. He looked again in the mirror. It must be a trick of the hour or perhaps the season. "Old," he said noisily. "Old, old." In the frame of the mirror he had stuck the Christmas cards he had received, six in number. One was from the moony, cheese-faced Rose Hindmarch in Nadeau, Ontario. A snow scene, hills, a barn, and a little boy pulling a sled.

Old, old. He had drunk too much of Ian and Elizabeth's wine. Well, why not, it was Christmas after all — as Elizabeth had remarked at least three times in that rather tedious hostessy voice of hers. (There it was, surfacing again, his caustic self, that sour maliciousness rearing up even on this night. Yes, but it was a *regulated* malice; he *did* practise abstentions, did hold back, aware, even if nobody else was, of that pool of unformed goodness at the bottom of his being. And poetry, thank the gods of poetry, without poetry what kind of monster would he have been?)

Down, down his throat went the warm milk. Ah, better, much better. What was it Dr. Johnson had said about the power of warmed liquids? — something or other. He felt a surge of strength akin to munificence. Merry Christmas, cheery Christmas, glad tidings, the time when no one should be alone. His hand was already on the telephone, already dialling the magic digits that connected with Audrey's mobile home (*quel euphémisme!*) in Sarasota. How amazing that he should know her number by heart. In the back of his brain he offered up congratulations. Not bad, Jimroy, a man of your years. You may lose valuable possessions and forget names, but the real juice is still running.

Audrey's telephone rang and rang. He checked the clock and calculated the time difference. She was probably too lost in sleep to hear the ringing of the phone, though he remembered that she had always been a light sleeper. Even the clicking of the electric blanket used to disturb her sleep). Audrey, Audrey, Audrey, dear Audrey. If he had been a little more patient, if his nature had been inclined toward . . . what? . . . instead of always belittling, accusing, haranguing, those thunderous verbs of incompatibility. If he had waited, been kinder, Audrey might be here now.

He dialled her number again, and once more the phone rang and rang. He felt the old anger returning, damn her, but then the thought of her fuzzy corona of hair, her large kind hands. He would never be able to sleep now. He would be awake all night, shivering and staring into the mirror and listening to the sound of his own breath.

And then, from nowhere, came the thought of Sarah Maloney, asleep in Chicago. He could get her number from the long-distance operator. Why not? It suddenly seemed the most important thing in the world to know what Sarah Maloney's voice sounded like. He loved her, he loved her. He had every right to the sound of her voice. He was a lover, a fifty-one-year-old man, slightly drunk, with a slightly drunken heart that was reduced, through no fault of his own, to a shuddering valentine. Darling Sarah, beloved.

No, it was a despicable thing to do, especially at this hour. It was worse than that: it was perverse. He went to the mirror again, peered at himself and said without mercy, "This is unspeakable." He noted with interest that the colour had come back into his face. A sense of disgust refreshes the spirit, a fact that always inspires chills of uneasiness in Jimroy. That trembling of his hand, was that lasciviousness or was he only nervous? Nerves, he decided, congratulating himself yet again. How troublesome but indispensable the body is.

On his first attempt the lines to Chicago were busy. Of course, it was Christmas; of course the lines would be busy on this night of all nights. Families and friends calling each other from every part of the country; lovers, husbands, wives, children, even the most wayward of them reaching out for affection. He could picture them all in their millions, standing in shadowy hallways, dialling into the darkness with faces that were composed and hopeful. What a wonder it was, the bond that joined human beings. An act of faith, really, faith over reason. Over bodily substance.

The second time he dialled, the call went straight through. On the third ring he heard the phone being lifted. A woman's voice — it could have come from the next room — was saying, "Hello? Hello? Who is this please? Hello."

Enough. Quietly, happily, he replaced the receiver.

Unspeakable. Unpardonable.

And yet, in the fresh morning sunlight it seems to Jimroy entirely harmless. What damage has he actually done, and whom has he hurt? He has never understood the science of casuistry, its fierce labours and silly conclusions.

There he is, sitting in the Flanners' backyard feeling ruddy and healthy. He has risen early, a smallish act of atonement, then eaten a bowl of instant oatmeal and drunk a mug of hot coffee, and now, with one of his Winnipeg cardigans buttoned up to his chin and a pair of warm socks inside his sandals, he is working on his book in the quiet of the garden. Christmas morning. *I saw three ships* . . .

He breathes deeply, offers up an earnest prayer to the blue sky. Astonishing, that blueness. The flowers and weeds around him have coarsened with new growth, and the trees have a fresh lettucey look — how absurd, how delightful that growth should continue even in the month of December.

He is going over some notes covering Mary Swann's middle period (1940 – 1955) and making a few additions and notations with a freshly sharpened pencil. *It is highly probable that Swann read Jane Austen during this period because . . .*

The sun climbs gradually and warms the backs of his shoulders. By noon he is able to unbutton his cardigan and fold it over the back of his chair.

He hears a sharp rapping and looks up. It's Elizabeth Lee next door, waving at him from an upstairs window. A moment later Ian appears, a muzzy bulk behind her, and they both wave. It seems to Jimroy that they are mouthing something at him. Merry Christmas? Yes.

He knows what they're thinking. There sits Jimroy. Alone. Working, and on Christmas Day. Actually working. Sad. Pathetic. That life should come to this. Later they will embrace — already Ian's hand is on Elizabeth's breast, or so it appears from this distance. They have each other, their erotic transports, but poor Jimroy loves no one and must do without the solace of Christmas Day sex and domesticity — poor sad Jimroy.

Ah, but how mistaken they are. How he would like to tell them of his happiness. But the condition embarrasses him; he would never be able to describe it. Even if he could they would never believe him, thinking instead: Jimroy's being brave, one of your hard-bitten Canadian stoics.

This is happiness, he wants to tell them, these scrawled notes, these delicate tangled footnotes, which, with a little more work, a few more weeks, will evolve into numbered poems of logic and order and illumination. The disjointed paragraphs he is writing are pushing toward that epic wholeness that is a human life, gold socketed into gold. True, it will never be perfect. There are gaps, as in every life, accidents of silence and misinterpretation and the frantic scrollwork of artifice, but also a seductive randomness that confers truth. And mystery, too, of course. Impenetrable, ineffable mystery.

Jimroy believes, or is beginning to believe, that the intervening mysteries compensate for the long haul between birth and death, bringing into balance early deprivation and enhancing the dullness of stretched-out days and nights. Always authenticity is registered by the inexplicable. He thinks gratefully of the kilted stranger with his — what was it? — his *sporran*, who sat by his side and reached, albeit feebly, for his friendship. He thinks, warmly now, of the return of his luggage by the airline. Of the lost photograph he will surely stumble upon tomorrow or the next day. Of these fragrant West Coast roses, budding, blooming, replacing themselves without complaint. Of the healing perplexity and substance of Sarah Maloney's voice. Of the small solid fact of the fountain pen that Mary Swann, poet extraordinary, once held in her human hand, and that now rests uniquely beneath his cotton socks in a bureau drawer in the state of California, amazing, amazing; he is skewered with joy.

The Lees, his neighbours, these fine people, his generous friends, are waving to him across the tops of the rose bushes and the tall weeds, and he longs to shout out to them that he is in the embrace of happiness. The proof of it is flowing out of the graphite of his pencil, out of his moving hand.

They won't believe it; not they with their stubborn contentment. Impossible. Nevertheless he lifts an arm in salutation, shouting, in his cheery broken tenor, "Merry Christmas," and smiling broadly at the same time to show them that his life may be foolish, it may be misguided and strange and bent in its yearnings, but it's all he has and all he's likely to get.

ROSE HINDMARCH

Rose's Hats

Rose Helen Hindmarch wears a number of hats. "I wear too many hats for my own good," she has been heard to say.

For instance, if you want to check on surveying details of a piece of farmland in Nadeau township, or if you want to know when your next tax instalment is due, all you have to do is go to the township office on the first floor of the old school any weekday morning between ten and twelve o'clock, and Rose Hindmarch, the town clerk, will be glad to interrupt her typing or bookkeeping, or whatever, to help you. One of her hats.

In the afternoon she moves across the hall to the library. (She takes a packed lunch to work, a sandwich of tuna fish or egg salad, which she eats at the library desk, and afterwards she makes herself a pot of tea, boiling the water on the little hotplate in the storeroom at the back. It is almost, one might say, ordained for women of Rose's age and occupation to huddle over hotplates in ill-ventilated storerooms.) Some winter days it's so quiet in the library she has to keep drinking tea all afternoon in order to stay awake. The sunlight coming through the windows, the dry air, the sulphuric sting of the printed bookcards mailed from a supply centre in Ottawa — all these things tend to induce sleepiness, but luckily business gets brisker after two o'clock when the younger married women, looking fat in their parkas and stretch jeans, drop in with their babies in tow. Quite a number of them — Cathy Frondice, for instance, jigglingly obese but with a clear pink face — are addicted to light romance. Cathy always stops at the desk to ask Rose Hindmarch what she recommends, and it's a rare day when Rose hasn't got a suggestion at the ready.

Later in the afternoon, between four and five o'clock, numerous school children stop by, and Rose helps them look up things in the *Encyclopaedia Britannica* and tries to locate pamphlets for them in her famous pamphlet file. This can be a hectic time of day. She has to keep after the children, the boys in particular, so they don't tramp into the library with their wet boots on, trailing in mud and soaked yellow leaves; and she has to keep a sharp lookout so they don't walk off with books without checking them out first, and all of these things have to be done in the firm, friendly placid manner that people have come to expect of her.

Then there is her role as curator of the Nadeau Local History Museum. The museum has no set hours; if visitors come, Rose simply leaves her desk in the town office or her post in the library and escorts them upstairs to the second floor, first asking them to sign the guest book in the foyer. She is also responsible for classifying donations to the museum — such things as old kerosene lamps and unusual plates and glass sealers — and arranging for insurance and for the small operating grant from the federal government. When the flurry of interest in Mary Swann began five years ago, it was Rose Hindmarch who conceived the idea of the Mary Swann Memorial Room, and it was Rose who spent her spare time scouting around for the articles on display there. Another hat.

And as if this weren't enough, every Wednesday evening at eight sharp she must appear in the Sunday-school room at the Nadeau United Church in the guise of church elder. She and Mrs. Homer Hart (Daisy) are the only women on the board, and Rose takes her position seriously. On the subject of replacing the communion trays or changing alter clothes, she is hearkened to as few others are, though she has to watch her step so as never to betray for a minute the fact that she is no longer a believer in the sacrament of communion, or even, for that matter, in the existence of a heavenly host. It has been some years since Rose's conversion to atheism was accomplished. She had been sitting at home one night, still a relatively young woman, listening to a philosophical debate on the radio, when she suddenly heard one of the debaters say, "Who can really believe there's a God up there sitting at a giant switchboard listening to everyone's prayers?" Rose had laughed aloud at this, and her loss of faith occurred at that moment, causing her not an ounce of pain and scarcely, for that matter, a trace of nostalgia. Only the nuisance of remembering to keep it to herself.

Her changing of hats gets even more confusing on the fourth Monday of every month when she returns to the town clerk's office, having had a light supper of soup and toast, to take her place as a village councillor. She is one of seven and has held the post for fifteen years. Her position is a complicated one, for she must report to herself in a sense; first the library report, then the report of town clerk, then the museum report. For the last twelve years she has also served the council as recording secretary, and this places her in the ludicrous position of writing up minutes in which she herself is one of the starring actors. She writes: "The minutes were read by Rose Hindmarch, and then Rose Hindmarch presented the interim library report," just as though Rose Hindmarch were a separate person with a different face and possessed of different tints of feeling. The Rose she writes about is braver than she knows herself to be. "Stout of heart" is how she thinks of her, an active woman in the middle of her life. (This much is true; Rose at fifty *is* in the middle of her life; her grandmother lived to be a hundred and her mother eighty-five. Those are her other hats, you might say, daughter, granddaughter, though she no longer is obliged to wear them.)

For a brief time after she finished high school Rose worked as the local telephone operator, sitting at the same kind of switchboard over which the nonexistent Ontario God is believed by good-hearted people to preside. To her surprise she found that working for the telephone company was arduous and, contrary to popular belief, she was not privy to tantalizing circuits of gossip. Mostly she heard nothing but farmers ordering machine parts and housewives exchanging recipes for jellied salads. Still in her twenties, she started to grow old, sitting on the uncushioned stool in her telephone office, pulling out plugs, then stabbing them in again. She began to notice, during this period, that she was lonesome all the time.

The town clerk's job fell vacant and she applied. It provides her with respectability. Even the men in Nadeau respect her calm rows of figures and her grasp of recent by-laws. Her post as librarian has given her something else: an unearned reputation for being a scholar, for it is assumed by people in Nadeau that Rose must read the books that fill her library shelves, so easily is she able to locate these books for other people, so adroitly does she thumb the index, so assuredly does she say, her forehead working into a frown, "Here it is, just what you're looking for."

But if you were to ask Rose which of her hats means the

most to her, she would say her role as museum curator. It has, in fact, rescued her from the inexplicable nights of despair she once suffered. This is especially true in recent years, ever since she's taken an interest in the life of Mary Swann. Curiously enough, this new historical interest has not so much opened the past to Rose as it has opened the future. Her life has changed. She has connections in the outside world now, the academic world. Quite a number of scholars and historians have come to Nadeau to call on her.

What a dirty shame she never married: this is what Nadeau people occasionally say, but Rose has never inspired hard pity. Some delicacy of hers, some fineness of bodily tissue or sensibility, the way she moves her hands down an open page or pronounces certain words — with an intake of breath like a person caught by surprise — make it appear that she has *chosen* to remain unmarried.

A woman of many hats, then, which she feels herself fortunate to own and which she wears proudly, almost vaingloriously, though there are moments when she experiences an appalling sensation of loss, the nagging suspicion that beneath the hats is nothing but chilly space or the small scratching sounds of someone who wants only to please others.

When she walks home from work, down Broadway as far as Second, down Second to the corner of Euclid, she moves with an air of purpose and amiability, stepping through the dry leaves like a woman accustomed to making choices. Today something twinkles at her feet: a penny, a lucky penny. She stoops to retrieve it, then continues on her way. Her cinnamon suede coat and smart new boots (bought last year in Toronto) ask you to guess at an inner extravagance, but not one that inspires either envy or pity. Other Nadeau women, looking out their front windows and seeing her pass, think affectionately, "There goes Rose. It must be five-thirty, time to put the potatoes on."

Some Words of Orientation

People are often surprised to find that the geographical centre of the North American continent lies not in Kansas or Minnesota or Indiana, as they've always thought, but farther north — across the 49th parallel, in fact, well within the boundaries of Canada.

If you were to place your finger on the map of Canada where this geological centre is located, and then move it an inch or two to the right (and one-quarter of an inch downwards) you would discover yourself touching the dot that represents the small Ontario town known as Nadeau (pronounced naa-dough, the two syllables equally accented).

Nadeau, with a population of 1,750, has only two main streets, that is to say, streets that comprise the business section of town. Broadway Avenue takes you past the cheese co-op and into town, and then there is Kellog Street (on which is located the feed mill and knitting factory), named for the Kellog family, who were the original settlers in the area, not the Nadeau family as it is often thought. (This is a place whose social strata creak with confusion, but a confusion balanced by tolerance, by habit, by a certain innocence it might be said.)

At the crossing of Broadway and Kellog you will find, on the north-east corner, the Esso garage, closed a year ago but soon to be reopened as a Burger King franchise, and on the second corner, the lovely, slender, grey and white stone tower of the United Church. There are weeds standing knee high in the front yard at the moment, a disgrace, but these will be taken care of presently. On the third (south-west) corner is the Red and White, which sells groceries and a complete line of hardware, plus men's work clothes, caps, and so forth. And on the fourth corner, facing onto Broadway but set back on a wide stretch of lawn, is the old two-story red-brick building that for many years served the community as a high school. This was before the new consolidated school was built out on Highway 17.

The old school in Nadeau — and there *are* still those in town who refer to it as the old school — dates from 1885 and is constructed in a style sometimes known as lean-to Gothic or box-and-beam village Victorian. Distinguishing characteristics include a dressed limestone foundation, which reaches to the first-floor windows and joins, at the front of the building, a handsome set of exterior steps leading up to the main entrance.

The double front doors deserve particular attention, being of heavy oak framing and fitted with long panes of bevelled glass on which are etched charming oval designs of dogwood interwoven with trillium. The hinges on the left-hand door have seized up — this was years ago — but the right-hand door opens easily enough, as you will discover when you turn the door handle.

Notice that the first floor of the old school is divided into two areas, one (on the left) for the Office of the Town Clerk and one (to your right) for the Public Library. The library — open Monday through Friday, 1:00 to 5:00 — is surprisingly comprehensive for a small village, but it is not the library that has brought you here and certainly not the town clerk's office.

Turn to your right and ascend the broad set of old wooden stairs that lead to the second floor. You'll find that these stairs yield a little under foot, pretty much what you would expect of an old school stairway when you stop to think of all the young feet that have pounded these boards smooth. The steps, for all their elegance, look faintly dusty, but in truth they're not; it's only the *smell* of dust that somehow lingers in the old, hollow-sounding stairwell. Be sure to stop at the landing and read the plaque that records the fact that in the year 1967 the Nadeau High School (as such) ceased to exist. The same plaque tells you of the simultaneous coming-into-being of the new Nadeau Local History Museum.

This museum, taking up all of the second floor of the old school, is small by anyone's standards, though it manages to attract more than five hundred visitors annually. The two rooms on the right are lined with glass-fronted display cases inviting you to examine some of the astonishing old arrowheads, fossils, and coins unearthed in the region. You can also look at such curiosities as a spinning wheel, a set of cards for combing wool, and a collection of crockery, some of it locally made (at the end of the last century). Be sure to see the interesting old washing machine, *circa* 1913, and to take in the various articles of clothing that include a christening gown from the "nineties" and a woman's grey wool walking costume, piped in red (1902). You will want to spend at least half an hour looking at these interesting exhibits and also at the framed maps and land certificates in the hall, not to mention an outstanding group of old photographs, one of them labelled "Sunday School Picnic, 1914," illustrating the simple recreational pastimes of bygone days.

On the left of the hallway are the two remaining rooms (the former classrooms for grades 11 and 12). One of these rooms has a small placard over the doorway (the door itself has been taken off the hinges and carted away) that reads: The Mary Swann Memorial Room.

Who on earth, people ask, is Mary Swann?

The answer to their question can be found on a neatly typed sheet of white paper tacked to the doorframe. The late Mary Swann 1915–1965, was a local poet who spent most of her life, at least her married life, on a quarter section of land two miles from Nadeau. Well-known in the area for her verse, some of it originally published in the now defunct *Nadeau News*, she has lately been recognized as a distinguished, though minor, contributor to the body of Canadian literature, and there are those who have gone so far as to call her the Emily Dickinson of Upper Canada. The Mary Swann Memorial Room, established only two or so years ago, contains a number of mementoes of Mrs. Swann's life — a kitchen table and chairs, a golden oak sideboard, an iron bed, handmade quilts, and many household articles (notice particularly the well-worn wooden turnip masher), In addition, there are some examples of her handiwork (chiefly crochet) and a photograph (blurred unfortunately) of the poet herself standing on her front porch, her arms folded on her chest, facing into the sun. If you have time you may want to linger and read a few examples of Mrs. Swann's verse, which are framed and mounted on the wall. Especially recommended is the prophetic poem entitled "The Silo," which was originally printed in the *Athens Record*, June 4, 1958, just seven years before the poet's untimely demise.

Next to the Mary Swann Memorial Room is the room that has proved to be the most popular with the public. Visitors can stand in the roped-off doorway and admire what is, in fact, a re-creation of a turn-of-the-century Ontario bedroom. Of interest is the floral wallpaper, an exact duplicate of an authentic Canadian wallpaper of the period. There is a length of stove pipe running across the room near the

ceiling, carrying heat from the woodstove that can be imagined to exist in an adjoining room. The pine washstand in
the corner is typical of the period (note the towel rack at the
side) and so is the wooden blanket box at the foot of the bed.
The bed itself is unusual, an Ontario spool bed, handmade it
would appear, in a wood that is almost certainly butternut.
There is, of course, the inevitable chamber pot peeping out
from beneath. The mattress on the bed would have been
stuffed with goose feathers — or so a notice on the wall tells
you — or perhaps straw.

The extremely attractive quilt on the bed was made by
the Nadeau United Church Women in 1967 as a Centennial
project. It is composed of squares, as you can see, and each
square is beautifully embroidered and signed by one of the
women of the congregation. From the doorway you can
admire the individual embroidered designs (mostly flowers
and birds) and you will be able to make out some of the
signatures, which are done in a simple chain stitch. Mrs.
Henry Cleary, Mrs. Al Lindquist, Mrs. Percy Flemming,
Mrs. Clarence Andrews, Mrs. Thomas Clyde, Mrs. R. Jack
Rittenhouse, Mrs. Floyd Sears, Mrs. Frank Sears, Mrs.
Homer Hart, Mrs. Joseph H. Fletcher, and so on. Seeing
those names, you may smile to yourself, depending of course
on your age and situation. You might think: didn't these
women have first names of their own? Hadn't women's lib-
eration touched this small Ontario town by the year 1967?
You may even form a kind of mental image of what these
women must look like: lumpy, leaden, securely wedded,
sharp of needle and tongue, but lacking faces of their own
and bereft of their Christian names. Sad, you may decide.
Tragic even.

But wait. There's one square near the centre of the quilt,
just an inch or so to the right — yes, there! — that contains

a single embroidered butterfly in blue thread. And beneath it is the stitched signature: Rose Hindmarch.

Here Comes Rose Now

Here comes Rose now, a shortish woman with round shoulders and the small swelling roundness of a potbelly, which she is planning to work on this fall.

Never mind the leather coat and boots and gloves, there's something vellum and summery in Rose's appearance, and she almost sings out the words, "Good evening." As you stand talking on the corner you see, behind her softly permed head, a fine autumn sunset dismantled in minutes by pillars of deep blue cloud. "Such gorgeous weather," she cries, stretching an arm upward and compelling you to agree.

She asks about your bronchitis and whether you've been into Kingston lately to see the new shopping centre; she comments on how lovely your house looks now that the porch and framework have been painted that nice soft shade of grey, how riotously the geese have been flying over town this past week, how the lake is higher than in recent years, how the Red and White is once again offering discounts on quarters of beef — not that she needs a quarter of beef, not her for heaven's sake, she's just about turned into a vegetarian!

Generalities and pleasantness, the small self-effacements and half apologies and scattered diversions that fit so perfectly the looped contours of Rose's middle life. She does not tell you anything about herself, not about how she will be spending her evening tonight — a Friday evening — or about the recent cessation of her menstrual periods or the lucky penny in her pocket or the square beige envelope she is carrying home in her purse, an envelope containing, if you only knew, an invitation to a symposium (yes, a symposium) on the works of the poet Mary Swann to be held in Toronto during the first week of the new year.

And why doesn't Rose confide any of this to you? You've known her for years, all your life in fact.

Perhaps she detects a lack of interest on your part, sensing that you are already wearying of this casual, peripheral chitchat, that you're shifting from foot to foot, anxious to be on your way, into your own house where a familial disarray awaits and affirms you, where you can sink on to a kitchen chair with your sack of groceries and say. "Oh, for heaven's sake, Rose Hindmarch *does* go on and on, and she never says *anything*."

Or does Rose, so open, so helpful, so stretched by smiles, protect her secrets like a canny nun? For in a sense you might say that her Friday nights *are* a kind of secret, though an innocent one, and that her menopause, except for the headaches, has brought her a flush of covert pleasure, a deserved but shameful serenity, almost dispensation; at last she's released to live freely in the kind of asexual twilight that most flatters her. As for the printed invitation in the silky inner lining of Rose's purse, it glows like a reddened coal, precious, known only — as yet — to her.

Just fifteen minutes ago, on her way home from the library, she stopped to collect her mail from the post office. There were three items for her today — not unusual, not at all. There was her telephone bill; there was a postcard, close to indecipherable, from her friend Daisy Hart who is visiting her sister on the gulf coast of Florida; and there, puzzlingly, was the large square beige envelope (quality paper) addressed simply: Rose Hindmarch, Nadeau,

Ontario. No box number, not that that mattered. No Miss or Ms., just Rose Hindmarch, the sturdy wily Rose, the energetic leading lady of the Nadeau township monthly minutes.

She opened it on the spot — never mind what Johnny Sears thought — but taking care not to destroy the creamy wholeness of the envelope. A symposium? On Mary Swann. January. Toronto. She was invited to attend a four-day symposium. (That must be a meeting or a convention, something along those lines, she will look it up in Funk and Wagnall's when she gets home.) Also included was a small, rather cunning-looking reply envelope, the kind that comes with wedding invitations, already stamped, too, a thoughtful gesture given the current postage rates.

Rose calculated quickly. September to January, four months away. A long time. Hallowe'en, Thanksgiving, Christmas; a very long time. Her excitement dwindled to dullness and she felt a pressure like tears rushing behind her eyes. But no, on second thought, four months would give her time to lose ten pounds — all she'd been waiting for was a good excuse. Five pounds off each hip and a little off the stomach. And time to make a shopping trip into Kingston to find something appropriate to wear, a suit maybe, something in that burgundy colour everyone is so crazy about these days, though Rose can't see why. Turquoise, her old standby, is hardly to be found.

The Harbourview Hotel. Toronto. January. That nice Sarah Maloney might come from Chicago. It wouldn't be any trip at all for her, not the way she travels about. And Professor Lang. Certainly he'll be there, no doubt of that. And maybe, but it would be silly to count her chicks, and so on, but maybe Mr. Jimroy would be there. Morton; he had, on that very first morning they met, asked her to call him

Morton. "All my good friends call me Morton," he'd said.

His good friends. That is what Rose Hindmarch is: one of Morton Jimroy's good friends.

Where Rose Lives

Here we are, coming to where Rose Hindmarch lives. This is her suite, her apartment, 16½ Euclid Ave. Not, probably, the kind of place that comes to mind when people think of the word *apartment*; that is to say, there aren't any concrete towers or elevators or underground parking facilities here. This is a three-room suite (living-room, bedroom, kitchen) on the second floor of an eighty-year-old frame house on the corner of Euclid Avenue, a house owned by a young couple, Howie and Jean Elton (originally from Cornwall), who both happen to teach out at the new township school on Highway 17. (Howard teaches science; Jean, Phys. Ed.) Eventually the Eltons are planning to put in a separate outside entrance for Rose, but for the time being she goes in through their dark narrow front hall. "Hi ya, Rose," Jean calls from the kitchen, where she's usually throwing together something for supper; that's the expression she uses, *throwing something together*. "How are ya, Rose?" Howie will yell. He might be helping Jean make hamburgers in the kitchen or else sitting in the living-room having a beer and watching something on television. "Hi," Rose says in her merry voice, and hurries up the stairway.

She's glad there's a proper door at the top of the stairs, even though there's no lock. She likes Howie well enough and loves Jean, but privacy is important. She senses that they feel this way too.

And now what? She hangs up her coat on its special

wooden hanger, glancing at the elbows for signs of wear. Owning a suede coat is a responsibility. Then quickly, in one long unbroken gesture, she puts on the teakettle and turns on the little kitchen radio, just in time to catch the six o'clock news. About once a week, usually on a Friday — and today *is* Friday — Rose will treat herself to a small rye and ginger-ale, which she sips while stirring up an omelette; two eggs, one green onion minced, a quick splash of milk. And just one slice of toast tonight. If she's going to lose ten pounds by January she'll have to start getting serious. But a little butter won't hurt. Only twenty-five calories in a teaspoon of butter, less than people think. There's a tiny mirror on the kitchen wall that Rose sometimes stands in front of, demanding: is this face going to turn into dough like Mother's did? Granny's too.

The news these days always seems to be about Libya or South Africa. When Rose thinks of South Africa she pictures a free-form shape with watery sides way down at the bottom of the map. The Dutch people went there first, she recalls vaguely, or else the English. In South Africa untidy policemen in shirt sleeves are always stopping people, black people, from going to funerals or forming labour unions. Well, Rose thinks, that doesn't seem like too much to ask for, though she's grateful she doesn't have to deal with unions herself. Howie and Jean belong to the teachers' union, but Howie says it's mostly bullshit, just two or three troublemakers trying to stir things up for everyone else. In South Africa there's a man called Nelson Mandela, a family man, stuck in jail. Rose has seen pictures of him on television, and pictures of his wife, too, a handsome woman with a grave face and a kerchief on her head.

From habit she eats slowly, daintily. Then she opens the refrigerator door and helps herself to a scoop of chocolate ice cream for dessert. Tomorrow morning she'll go down to the Red and White and buy a carton of yogurt. Jean and Howie both recommend yogurt, and Jean has even offered to lend Rose her electric yogurt maker. But Rose loves chocolate ice cream. Her mother used to make ice cream out on the lawn on summer evenings — that was when they were still in the house over on Second where the Harts live now. Rose remembers being twelve years old, turning the crank, waiting for the ice cream to form. A little rock salt, a little elbow grease, and the miracle took place. Almost the only miracle she can recall witnessing.

Rose is a happy woman; her routines make her happy. When in the early morning she pulls the sheets and blankets smooth and fluffs the pillow on her bed, she feels hopeful about the day ahead. A parade of minor pleasures — like the lucky coin today — reassure her, let her know she's part of the world. And on Friday nights she gets into her pyjamas early and crawls into bed to read. It's only seven-thirty and still fairly light outside. She cleans her face with cold cream and brushes her teeth and creeps under the covers. Her bare feet stretch out contentedly. She might read until midnight or later. Tomorrow is Saturday; she can sleep as late as she likes.

This is the bed her mother and father slept in, though Rose can't recall anything about her father who was a soldier — his mother was a Nadeau, a descendant of Martin Nadeau — who died at Dieppe. It's a comfortable double bed with a walnut-veneer headboard and has a good firm mattress that Rose bought after her mother's last illness and death; and smooth fitted sheets, cotton and Fortrel, a cheerful checked pattern. When Rose reads in bed she props herself up in the middle so that the pillows on each side embrace and warm her.

Only once has she shared this bed with another. That was two years ago, on a Friday night like this. She was reading as usual. It must have been eleven or later when she heard someone tapping or scratching lightly on her door. Then there was a hoarse whisper. "Rose? It's me, Jean. Can you let me in?"

Big bony Jean with her muscular shoulders and arms protruding absurdly from the lacy sleeves of a pale blue nylon nightgown. Her large feet were bare and her hair was pulled back as always by a heavy wooden barrette. That night her wide mouth gleamed in the dim hall light, a rectangle of anguish. "Oh, Rose. Oh, Rose," she was whimpering.

Sitting in Rose's kitchen she wept helplessly, and while she wept she beat her fist softly and rhythmically on the kitchen table.

Rose made her drink some rye, a good inch, straight, out of a nice juice glass.

"I hate him, I hate him." Jean made a wailing sound and put her head on the table. Rose, sitting beside her, stroked Jean's heavy hair, awkwardly at first, tentatively, and then she got up and made some tea.

"Oh, he's such a fucking bastard, oh Rose, he's a bastard, a first-class bastard, if you knew what he was really like. You don't know how lucky you are. Oh, my God, oh, my God."

Rose herself drank some tea, but poured another inch of rye for Jean. She wanted to say, "Can you tell me what happened?" or "Do you want to talk about it?" This was what people said in such situations. But a lump of stone had lodged itself in the centre of her chest and kept her from speaking. The pain was terrible. What a ninny she was.

Jean's nose burned bright red, and large paisley-shaped

blotches formed on the sides of her face. Rose supposed —
hoped — they were caused by the weeping and the rye
whisky, and not by the force of Howie Elton's fist. With
both hands she passed Jean a box of Kleenex. "Here," she
said.

After a minute Jean blew her nose. The light from the
fluorescent fixture sharpened her somewhat vulpine checks
and lips. She drew herself up and said "What am I going to
do?" Then she said, "He doesn't know I'm up here. He
thinks I ran out the back door."

"You can stay here," Rose said, "as long you want." She
felt heroic at that moment.

"Oh Rose, can I? Really? Are you sure you don't
mind?" Jean began sobbing again. The sobs sounded like
water bubbling up from a deep lake, and Rose put her arms
around her. It seemed to her that Jean was like a daughter or
a sister.

Neither of them mentioned Rose's living-room couch.
They slept together — it seemed perfectly natural — in the
big double bed; or at least Jean slept, her copious kinky hair,
wild and perfumy, loosened from the barette and spread
out wide on the pillow. Rose lay awake most of the night,
staring at the dark softenings in the corners of the ceiling
and feeling herself in a daze of happiness. Her nose twitched
with tears. She had no desire to touch the heavy, humming,
sleeping body beside her. A narrow, exquisitely proportioned channel of space separated them and seemed to Rose
to be a breathing organism. When Jean turned, Rose turned.
When Jean murmured something from the depths of a
dream, Rose heard herself murmuring too, a wordless,
shapeless burr of pleasure. The wonder of it. The bewilder-
ing surprise. So this was what it was like to feel another
human being so close. Inches away, so close she could feel

the minute vibrations that were the sounds of Jean's inhaling and exhaling. Dear God. At almost fifty years old she at last divined that a body was more than a hinged apparatus for getting around, for ingesting and processing food, for sustaining queasy cyclical assaults. The same body that needed to be washed and trimmed and tended, and sometimes put to sleep with the help of a wet finger, also yearned to be close to another. How could she have failed to know something as simple as this? There was nothing to be wary of, there was nothing dangerous at all about this, lying here in bed with Jean Elton beside her.

In the morning Jean was gone. A note on the kitchen table said: "Thanks."

Nothing was ever said. Howie and Jean disappeared to Cornwall for the weekend and came home late on Sunday night; Rose heard them in the kitchen downstairs making coffee, Jean's familiar heavy voice, always on the verge of swelling into horsy laughter.

What had happened? What was it that Howie had done? Rose didn't know, or, more accurately, she *did* know, or at least suspected. Women, other women, opened their bodies trustingly. Howie must have done something unspeakable, something that appalled Jean, something vicious and sexual, something less than human; he must have climbed on top of her and taken some dark animal presumption. What that violation might be, Rose didn't know, didn't need to know. She regarded Howie after that with a certain awe. Jean, she loved.

It didn't happen again, but even now, after two years, Rose spends her Friday nights reading and waiting. She turns the pages of her book slowly, one ear tipped for the sound of Jean Elton scratching on her door. She feels it important to be there if Jean needs her.

Oh, she loves her Friday nights. During the week she's too tired to read, and it's all she can do to keep her attention on the television. But Friday nights: a pot of tea by her bedside, the satin binding of the blanket at her chin, the clean cotton-and-Fortrel-blend sheets moving across her legs, her book propped up in front of her. Amid this comfort she speaks harshly to herself. "Well, Rose kiddo, you're getting to be a real old maid, tucking in here like a hermit Friday after Friday. You should get out, go to a movie in Elgin now and then, the bingo even. What about the Little Theatre in Kingston, you used to go along with the Harts to all the shows. You're getting downright anti-social. Set in your ways and that's a bad sign."

It has crossed Rose's mind that someone should do a survey of what the librarians of small villages read in their spare time. Librarians are, after all, the ones who order new books and the ones who are always recommending such and such to someone else. "You'll love this," they cry, trying to remember who likes thrillers and who goes in for war stories and who opts for heavier things — though only Homer Hart in Nadeau reads books that might be called heavy.

It can't be said that Rose Hindmarch is a narrow reader. At the library, whenever she has a minute, she's dipping into this and that, a little local history, a Hollywood biography, the new mysteries, the new romances, the latest bestsellers, two inches thick — though these are getting so expensive Rose orders only one or two a month — and even the occasional volume of modern poetry

Poetry, though, poses a problem for Rose. Except for Mary Swann's book, she has trouble understanding what it's about, and even with Mrs. Swann she's not always sure. "The rooms in my head are bare/Thunder brushes my hair." Now what's she trying to say in that poem? Of course rooms are a symbol of something, but thunder? "The mirror on the other side/Opens the place where I hide." Who can make heads or tails of that? Mr. Jimroy maybe. Morton.

Poetry, biography, romance, travel — Rose will read anything. But what she craves, and what she saves up for her Friday-night reading binges, are stories of espionage.

She tells herself she should sit down some day and make a list of all the spy stories she's read. There must be five hundred at least. Intrigue, escape, foghorns in the harbour, duty and patriotism. She knocks one back every week or so depending on the number of pages. Ian Fleming — but she scorns him now, his bag of tricks—Ken Follet, John le Carré, Robert Ludlum, these are her favourites. The delicious titles, the midnight blueness of them, and the heroes with their hair curling over their ears, their intricate disguises and quick thinking, the cipher clerks labouring away by night in the back of an electrical supply store, the plump Munich prostitute with the radio receiver strapped to her thigh.

What Rose Hindmarch appreciates in most tales of espionage is the fine clean absence of extenuating circumstances — not that she would put it in those words — and the way the universe falls so sparely into two equal parts, good on one side, evil on the other. There's nothing random about the world of espionage. Evil is never the accidental eruption it is in real life, far from it. Evil, well, evil is part of an efficiently executed plot set into motion by those unnamed ones who possess a portion of dark power. And death? Death is never for a minute left in the hands of capricious gods (the morose, easily offended Ontario God included). Death is a clean errand dispatched by a hired gun. A slender man enters a brilliantly lit room, his wide velvet collar spilling charm, but his right hand moving meaningfully toward an inner pocket.

And Rose is drawn, too, toward that black confusion that pulsates behind the Iron Curtain — the tricky, well-guarded borders, the deep Danube, the cyanide pellets concealed in Polish fountain pens and lipstick cases, the rendezvous in shabby Warsaw bars or under flickering Slavic streetlamps. The swift-running trains that cross Germany and Hungary, always at night, transport her too, her chugging heart, her dry hands, carrying along a carload of ideological passion, none of which matters in the least to Rose, and the obsession to get to the heart of evil, to follow orders, to risk all. Mr. X (greenish skin beneath a greenish suit), a man of no fixed profession but protected nevertheless by hooded guards and German shepherds with open mouths. Why? Rose reads on. Because he is part of a gigantic plot to take over the Western world, that's why. The linkages glow like jewellery below a mirrored surface. Solutions arrive in the final chapters, cleansing as iodine, though Rose has read so many spy stories by now that she sees, halfway through, how it will go for her special envoy. This doesn't prevent her from reading on.

Another chapter, another poisoned gin rickey ("She had only taken a swallow when she realized . . . "), another undelivered message — and an hour has been subtracted from Rose's life. Her eyes intensify and shine. There's no turning back now. "My name is Smith," she reads. "I have been sent to warn you."

Rose's bedside clock says 2:00 A.M. The hour and the grey chill of the room augment the airlessness that enters her throat. Just one more chapter, she promises herself, but she can't stop. Through a crack in her curtains she can see the moon, shaved down to a chip. The tea in her cup has been cold for hours, but she sips a little anyway to relieve her terrible thirst. "You aren't the real Smith, my friend. I happen to know that you are really — " Rose postpones a trip to the bathroom, though her bladder is burning. "Here is an envelope. You will find plane tickets and a small map — "

Then the last page. It's 4:00 A.M. Jacob Smith is really Count Ramouski, as Rose suspected all along, and his double agentry has placed him on the side of good, as Rose hoped it would. He receives a commendation at a small private ceremony, and his nights are only slightly troubled by the number of assassinations the case necessitated. But part of his cover has been blown. A new code name will be assigned. This he accepts with a shrug. *C'est la vie.* Rose turns out the light, expecting to fall asleep immediately.

But for some reason she doesn't, not tonight. Something is nagging at her, making her restless. Then she remembers: the invitation to the symposium. The thought of it flicks on in her head like the burst of a cigarette lighter. (For Rose, who was a smoker before signing up last year for the Elgin Non-smokers Buzz Group, this is an appropriate image.) Click, click, the obedient flame leaps up.

It burns a small bright orange hole in the future. *Symposium. Symposium.* Her blind, sealed bedroom is set floatingly adrift by the single word, and her long night ends with a rush of joy.

A Saturday Night in Nadeau

In Nadeau, Ontario, as in other towns and villages on the continent of North America, and indeed around the world, there is a social structure that determines more or less how people will spend their disposable time. A social historian would be able to plot this leisure factor on a graph. Certain

activities seem suited for certain people, while others seem
inappropriate, even unthinkable. Rose Hindmarch, for
instance, would feel — almost as ill at ease having a drink at
the Nadeau Legion as you would on arriving in town for the
first time and stopping in there for a few relaxing beers.
(Even so, you would not be turned away. You would be able
to find yourself a chair in the damp beery coolness, and
Susan Marland Jones, aged nineteen and sleeping with
young Dick Strayer from Elgin, would bring you a drink
and favour you with one of her vague, loopy smiles.) But
unlike Rose Hindmarch, you will be unable in a single visit
to take in the *sense* of the Nadeau Legion. The faces floating
before you and the brief scraps of conversation you overhear
will be dissociated from any meaningful context, just as
though you were observing a single scene plucked at random
from an extremely long and complex play. For every ounce
of recognition provoked, there would be an answering tax of
bafflement; a glimpse of "Life in Nadeau on a Saturday
Night" conceals more than it reveals. Although you listen
intently (and perhaps take notes), the scene before you never
rounds itself out into the fullness of meaning. Too much is
taken for granted by the speakers — Hy Crombie, Sel Ross,
the Switzer twins, and their large smiling wives — and the
allusions tossed up are patchy and fleeting and are embedded in long, shared histories. True they are careless of
strangers down at the legion, and besotted by beer, but there
is no thought of unkindness and no wish to suppress information. The same thing would happen if you stopped off at
the Buffalo Bingo in the basement of the Nadeau Hotel or
dropped in at one of the gracious old houses on Second
Street where people (two or three or four, the number varies)
have gathered to spend a Saturday evening.

  Fat, tender-faced Homer Hart, for instance, sits in his

living-room shuffling cards and listening to Rose Hindmarch rattle on about the symposium in Toronto. Then he says, "I once attended a symposium. At Lake Placid. I found it very interesting, if I remember rightly."

"What I can't imagine is why they bothered inviting me," Rose says, and looks around the bridge table at the others. She and her mother lived in this house before the Harts bought it, but that seems centuries ago.

"Your cut, Rose," Belle Waterman prompts, sighing and tutting. She's been invited tonight to replace Daisy, who is still in Florida. This happens every year about this time.

"Don't know why the heck they shouldn't invite you," Homer says. "Why, you're the expert, Rose. If anyone knows about Mary Swann, you're the one. The only one who really got to know her."

"Well," Rose allows, "maybe. But when I think about who's going to be there! It gives me the shakes. They're all scholars, and so on."

"Scholars, eh?"

"All of them. Eminent in their field. Morton Jimroy, he writes books, biographies, life stories of famous people. And Professor Lang. He was here in Nadeau once. No, twice. And probably Sarah Maloney will be there."

"Ah, Sarah!" This from Homer who met Sarah Maloney when she came to Nadeau five years ago.

"She's really Dr. Maloney," Rose explains to the others, "I found that out after she was here. The Ph.D. kind of doctor. But you'd never know it."

"What do you bid?" Floyd Sears says. He's a regular at Saturday-night bridge, a man with a red, papery face. His wife, Bea, goes to bingo.

"Two clubs."

"So. We're back in clubs, are we?"

"This isn't my night. Not a good hand all night."

"Well, I think it's absolutely fantastic, Rose. And you deserve it, to get invited, I mean. Look at all the work you did, getting a room set up at the museum."

"Sounds real la-de-da."

"There was Plato's symposium," says Homer. "I remember — "

"Okay, I'm going to four clubs."

"Pass."

"As long as they don't expect me to contribute to the discussion," Rose says. "I wouldn't dare open my mouth if they did."

"I don't blame you a bit."

"Now, Rose, that doesn't sound like you. I've never known you to be shy or hold back."

"Well — "

"Well, if you ask me," says Belle, "you're more of an expert than any of them. Sure, so maybe they write these books and what have you, but you're the one who actually knew Mrs. Swann. Did any single one of *them* ever meet her? Face to face, I mean? No."

"Well," Rose answers slowly, looking around the table. "No, I guess not."

"See! You're the one with the real know-how, the firsthand knowledge. You've got it right over all those professors and book writers. You knew Mary Swann. In person."

"That's true, Rose," Homer says. His tone is fond. His face too.

"Still — "

"Trump."

"Damn. 'Scuse my French."

"It isn't as though I knew her all that well."

"No one knew her all that well when it come to that. I never said more'n two words to her. Well, maybe 'nice day,' something like that, if she happened to come into the post office. Not that she'd say anything back much."

"Wasn't much of a talker, Mrs. Swann, that's for sure."

"She used to make those dolls for the Fall Fair. Remember?"

"Only once, I think."

"Queer in her ways," Floyd Sears says. "That's what Bea used to say."

"I wouldn't say queer exactly."

"Odd?" Rose looks around her. She has known Homer since she was six, Belle Waterman since she was five, Floyd Sears for — she can't remember; she has always known Floyd Sears.

"Well, what the heck, poets are supposed to be odd, aren't they?"

"She didn't seem all that odd to me. Just one of your nervous types. And ashamed of how she looked, those clothes of hers."

"Remember the poem she did on the big snowstorm? When was that, anyways?"

"Good grief, yes, I remember that."

"Fifty-nine, November. Twenty-two inches we got. Boy oh boy, what a dump of snow. I'll never forget that."

"Where's the time go."

"Older I get, the faster — "

"It was a nice poem. Real nice. You know the one I mean, Rose? It was in the paper. All about white — "

"Buried under bridal white," Rose says. "That's how it starts out anyhow."

"Bridal white?"

"Like a bride's dress. She compared it to — "

"Oh."

"Anyone for coffee?" Homer offers, rising heavily. "Or is tea okay?"

"Here let me give you a hand."

"She was kind of shy, I think. Mary Swann, she was one of your shy women. Sort of countrified, if you take my meaning. Didn't take to shooting the breeze."

"Well, she sure is famous now. Wouldn't you say so, Rose?"

"Well — "

"She sure as heck must be famous if all these people're getting together in Toronto for a — what was it again?"

"A symposium."

"Plato's symposium, I can remember — "

"Poor Mrs. Swann. She always looked scared to me, a regular rabbit-type woman. Never had two nickels to rub together. Used to buy her postage stamps one at a time. Of course folks did in those days."

"Those were darn tough times."

"One at a time. Imagine!"

"Sorry, folks," says Homer. "Store cookies is all we've got. Chocolate chip."

"Tasty, though."

"Thanks, Homer, I will."

"Well, she went and put this town on the map, Mary Swann. You never know."

"Nadeau, Ontario, home of Mary Swann."

"World-famous poetess."

"Remember that black coat she used to wear?"

"I remember the running shoes. The poor woman. She'd come into the Red and White in those darned old running shoes."

"Poor old soul."

"She wasn't really that old. I wouldn't call fifty exactly old."

"Not nowadays."

"Not then either."

"Who knows, she might of written a lot more books of poems if she'd lived another ten, twenty years. Boy, that woman could sure write the poems. There was one that really got me. About a calf drowning. Any of you remember that one?"

"That was in the Elgin paper if I'm not mistaken."

"Real sad. But kind of touching, too."

"She had a gift. Writing poems is a genuine gift."

"You never know, do you, when you look at a person, I mean. What kind of talent they're keeping under their bushel basket."

"What was she like, Rose? She must of warmed up to you some. When she came in to borrow books."

"Not all that much. This was when the library was in the church basement. After it got moved out of the post office — "

"Well, what *was* she like? Like in a nutshell, how'd you describe her?"

"Oh, we used to chat about this and that. About the weather. I knew her daughter, Frances, a little at school. I used to ask her how Frances was getting along out in California, that kind of thing."

"A good-looking girl, Frances."

"Still is, probably. Not one of your glamour girls, but a smart-looking girl when she was young."

"And she got the Queen's scholarship. Not bad when you think — "

"Her husband's a big shot, I hear. Goes around telling folks how to invest their money. Wrote a book — "

"Really?"

"She must of had a tough time, Mrs. Swann, bringing up a kid with never two nickels to rub together."

"Frances was always clean. And polite. You could say that for her.

"Poor Mrs. Swann. What kind of life was that for a woman of her talents? Stuck out on that good-for-nothing farm with that good-for-nothing husband — "

"She married him. She must of thought he was okay. In the beginning at any rate."

"Well, she found out different, didn't she?"

"She sure did. The hard way."

"Of course we'll never know the whole story."

"That's true, that's so true. It takes two. That's what Bea said at the time."

"Two to tangle."

"Poor Mary Swann."

"Funny the way things turn out. You just never know what's going to happen in this life. From one day to the next."

Drifting Thoughts of Rose Hindmarch

We no longer care about the lives of the saints, yet we long for a holiness of our own.

This, or something like this, is what Rose Hindmarch is thinking as she bows her head during silent meditation on Sunday morning. And such a lengthy silent meditation! The new minister, Bob Holly, who drives up from Kingston on Sunday morning to conduct holy worship in Nadeau (his young wife sits outside in their Pontiac doing a crossword puzzle, a picnic lunch beside her on the seat) imposes, for reasons of his own, uncomfortably long periods of silent prayer, sometimes as long as five minutes. This morning he directs the congregation to pray for the struggle in South Africa, which is all very well, but Rose is unable to compose her thoughts. Black townships, barbed wire; something swims into the pious hush of the church, an oily substance, green in colour, then slides away. "Our father," Rose begins, and is filled with unrest.

She shouldn't have come, not this morning, not in this condition, nagged by the betrayal of her own leaking body. She likes to sail into this church with the lightness and dryness of a pressed oak leaf. But early this morning she awoke to find a pool of blood between her legs. After eleven months — this! The odour and the stickiness brought tears to her eyes and, rinsing out her sheets in the bathtub, she gave way to a single sharp cry of anguish. This! "You okay, Rose?" Jean Elton yelled up the stairs.

"I'm fine," Rose called down gaily. "Just dandy."

She would stay home from church, she decided. Then changed her mind.

Despite her atheism, or perhaps because of it, she almost never misses church. On those few Sunday mornings when she *has* stayed home, she's sat stiffly on her brocade chesterfield in the front room as though glued there and felt loneliness blow through her body. The longest hour of the week is the one wrenched from the machinery of habit.

Holy, holy, holy, Lord God Almighty,
Early in the morning, we raise our song to thee.

It was better, far better, despite everything, to be seated here in the austere waxy light, head inclined, praying. "Our Father — "

As always Rose leaves her eyes half open and directs her

prayers toward the railing that encloses the pulpit, a railing composed of four pine panels topped with a pretty moulding of carved leaves. The prettiness of the carving, which by rights ought to be neutral, seriously challenges the few moral choices made by Rose Hindmarch in her life. From where she sits, row six this morning, she can see light shining between the leaves, and it is to these lighted spaces that she addresses her prayers, or rather her questions. *Why?* is what she usually asks, the *whys* coming like a bombardment of electrons — why, for instance, is she thinking about Mary Swann this morning instead of Bishop Tutu and Nelson Mandela?

It is a surprising fact that Mary Swann never, at least as far as anyone knows, attended church. Surprising because in every one of her poems there is one line at least that can be interpreted as sacred. It was Morton Jimroy who pointed this out to Rose when he visited Nadeau a year ago. No, it was closer to eighteen months ago. How time flies, Rose thinks. He was extraordinarily kind, lingering in the museum, plainly enchanted by the exhibits, particularly by the two photographs of Mrs. Swann, and asking questions, nodding his head, taking notes, he invited Rose out to dinner at the old hotel in Elgin. "You don't have to do that," she protested. "But I want to," he said. "I really do."

He brought his copy of *Swann's Songs* to the restaurant, a rather battered copy and not very clean, and after they had ordered the double pork chop platter with mashed potatoes, turnip, and a mound of apple sauce, he showed Rose those lines of Mary Swann's that he felt demonstrated her deep religious impulse. "There," he said, pointing with a patient finger, "and there. And there."

"I see what you mean," Rose said after a minute, disoriented.

"Look at this line," Morton Jimroy said. "This reference to water — a stunning line, isn't it? — which clearly expresses a yearning for baptism, for acceptance of some kind. Or even forgiveness."

"You don't think—" Rose began. "I mean, perhaps you know that there's no well out there on the Swann property."

"Of course, of course, but then" — he switched to his instructor's voice — "serious poetry functions on several levels. And in Swann's work the spiritual impulse shines like a light on every detail of weather or habit or natural object. The quest for the spiritual. The lust for the spiritual."

Spirituality from Mary Swann? That rough-featured woman who never once came to church? (Though she had, Rose told Morton Jimroy, always donated some of her handmade crochet work to the Fall Fair.)

"But why not?" he pressed her. He was facing her across the little table, one hand curling a corner of the paper placemat, the other reaching in his breast pocket for a pencil. "Why do you think she stayed away from church so religiously? — if you'll pardon my little joke."

"Clothes probably," Rose said this boldly. She was conscious of a noisy brimming of happiness. She had only once before in her life been taken to dinner by a man, and that had been Homer Hart, years ago, before he married Daisy.

"Clothes?" His pencil moved busily.

"Well, she probably didn't have the right clothes. For church, you know."

"Do you think so? Really?"

She could see he was disappointed. "Yes," she said. "I think that must have been the reason."

"You don't suppose," Jimroy said, "that Swann felt her spirituality was, well, less explicit than it was for regular churchgoers in the area. That it was outside the bounds, as it were, of church doctrine?" He regarded Rose closely. "If you see what I mean."

"I see what you mean, Mr. Jimroy. Morton. But I really think, well, it was probably a question of not having the right kind of clothes."

"She told you this?"

"Oh, heavens, no. It's just a feeling I have."

"Oh?"

"I know it sounds silly, but a few years ago it was different. You just didn't set foot in church without a hat, not in Nadeau, not in the United Church. And gloves. Mrs. Swann didn't have a hat or gloves. Well, just work gloves, and she wouldn't have had a decent Sunday dress or stockings or anything like that."

He put his fingertips together. "I suppose I see her," he paused, "as someone whose faith was exceedingly primitive and mystical. Is that how you saw her, Miss Hindmarch?"

"Rose," she reminded him.

"Rose, of course. Is that how — ?"

"I, well, I think so, yes." She gave a nod, implying tolerance and generosity.

"As in this passage?" He opened the book again and read aloud. (Rose was glad there was no one else in the dining-room.)

Blood pronounces my name
Blisters the day with shame
Spends what little I own,
Robbing the hour, rubbing the bone.

Rose waited, respectfully, her hand touching her brooch.

"Well," Jimroy said, speaking rather loudly. "This seems to be — now you may disagree — but to me it's a pretty direct reference to the sacrament of holy communion. Or perhaps, and this is my point, perhaps to a more elemental sort of blood covenant, the eating of the Godhead, that sort of thing."

Rose said nothing, not wanting to disappoint him a second time. She was unable to utter the word menstruation. She would have died first. It was a word she had always been uneasy with. She nodded, first hesitantly, then vigorously. And chewed away on her meat. She had trimmed away the fat, feeling it would be indelicate to eat it — but it was a sacrifice, she loved it so!

For dessert there was a choice of rice pudding or rhubarb pie. It seemed to Rose that Morton Jimroy shuddered slightly when presented with this choice, but after a moment's indecision, he accepted the pudding, and when it arrived, a formless cloud stuck with currants, he sat pushing it from side to side on the plate with the back of his spoon, still pursuing the substance of Mary Swann's blood poem. "A poet," he told Rose, "is able to speak of those states of consciousness of which he or she has no personal knowledge."

"But how — ?" She waved her arm, a little too gaily.

Jimroy's eyes shot upward to the pressed-tin ceiling as though its patterned squares contained the key to his theory. "This is something I've thought about a great deal," he said. "What sets poets apart from the rest of us — and I'm talking about those rare poets who stand head and shoulders above the simpering 'little mag' people, the offset people — true poets carry a greater share of the racial memory than do we lesser beings."

Rose smiled, not displeased to be cast into the category of lesser being, where Mr. Jimroy, Morton, clearly placed himself.

He went on. "Their actual *experience*, what happens to

them in their lives, is really beside the point. It's their genetic disposition, a mutation, of course, which urges them forward and allows them to be filters of a larger knowledge."

"I'm afraid you're a little over my head," Rose said. This was not strictly true. She was following what he said, yet sensed that humility was called for.

Jimroy continued, his hands jabbing. "This is the central mystery of the poets, Miss Hindmarch. We examine the roots of our poets, their sources, the experiences they draw upon, and it never adds up. Never. There's something that you" — he looked directly into Rose's eyes at last — "that you and I can't account for. Call it an extra dimension if you like. A third eye."

For some reason Rose felt unworthy of this insight. A gust of real humility struck her, and she wished Jimroy would remove his gaze. "I see," she said foggily.

"Take Swann's profound sense of Angst," Jimroy said.

"*Angst?*" Rose looked down, then cut into her pie. She was conscious of Mrs. Ryan in her large apron standing in the doorway to the kitchen. Normally the hotel dining-room closed at 8:00 on week nights.

"Perhaps despair is a better word," Jimroy said kindly. "I don't suppose our Swann read the existentialists, at least there is no concrete evidence that she did, but she was most assuredly affected by the trickle-down despair of our century."

"I think we all are," Rose said. "All of us. I know I have my low moments — "

Jimroy pushed aside his uneaten pudding. He leaned forward. "But you see, Swann had that rare gift of *translating* her despair. She wasn't writing poems about housewife blues. She was speaking about the universal sense of loss and alienation, not about washing machines breaking down or about — "

"Oh," Rose said, "the Swanns didn't have a washing machine."

"I beg your pardon."

"A washing machine. They didn't have one." She felt obliged to explain. "Of course there *were* people in the country who did have washing machines, even then, but the water supply out at the Swann place — "

Jimroy looked tired. "I was using a washing machine as an example," he said. "It was just a metaphor for, well, for all that's nonspiritual in life if you like." Nevertheless he pulled out his pencil and made a brief note. "What I meant was that great poets write from large universalized perceptions, and Mary Swann's blood poem seems to me to be her central spiritual statement." He paused, making sure Rose was following his argument. "The blood, you see, is a symbol. It stands for the continuum of belief, a metaphysical covenant with an inexplicable universe."

"Yes," said Rose, and closed her mouth.

Courage, courage, she said to herself, a word she has learned to unfurl in her head whenever her awful timidity rises up. Her voice immediately grew louder — she hoped not shrill — and her shoulders gathered force. "But you see," she began, "Mrs. Swann was a woman and — "

"Yes?"

"It isn't important."

"Everything's important."

"I can't remember what I was going to say." She looked down at her rhubarb pie and pledged herself not to jeopardize what was left of the evening.

"Our Father," she says on Sunday morning to the carved leaves on the pulpit railing. "Take it away, take it away. When I come out of church today, make it be gone."

Mr. Jimroy wrote a lovely letter thanking her for all

her help. She wrote back "But I'm the one who should be thanking you. It was such a pleasure — "

Such a pleasure. Such an honour. Morton Jimroy — he was a famous author. She hadn't realized how famous he was until later. He was in *Who's Who*. She'd looked him up. He was a world authority. He knew everything there was to know about poetry, including what it all meant. Except for that poem of Mary Swann's — he couldn't seem to get the drift of that. Of course he was a man, an unmarried man at that, or at least separated — he'd mentioned something about a former wife — and perhaps men have a tendency to overlook what is perfectly obvious to women. Or perhaps he found it embarrassing or messy; she wouldn't blame him a bit if he did. It had seemed so clear to Rose, but then she was no authority, and poetry could be so . . . so vague. Still, she was sure, a hundred per cent sure, of what Mary Swann had been talking about. Rose supposed she had made do with old rags as country women still did occasionally. Never two nickels to rub together, poor woman. And no clothes suitable for Sunday service, something else Mr. Jimroy hadn't quite cottoned onto, though in the end maybe he had. At least he'd made a number of notes as she talked and talked.

It was wonderful really, how he listened to her, to every little thing she had to say about Mary Swann, no matter how small or trivial. Sitting there, talking and talking, she realized she didn't really like him. But she wanted him to like *her*. He was too anxious, too greedy somehow, but underneath the anxiousness and greed there was something else, a green shoot that matched her own unfolded greenness. *Courage*, she said to herself, and began another anecdote. "One day Mrs. Swann and I — "

He wanted to hear it all. Tell me what she looked like,

this famous author and scholar had begged Rose Hindmarch, local librarian. How did Mary Swann wear her hair? How did she walk? What was her voice like? Did you ever talk about poetry? What did you usually talk about? And what else?

He was patient, waiting until she found the words and put her recollections in order. His eyes had burned. "Remarkable," he said, and made a note. "Priceless." Then, "Go on."

He filled one notebook and started another. "Now tell me, Miss Hindmarch, Rose, did you ever discuss . . . "

He seemed altogether happy sitting there in the dining-room of the Elgin Hotel, leaning forward so eagerly, his rice pudding forgotten. And she? She felt a happy, porous sense of usefulness, as though joined for once to something that mattered. *Slim-shouldered Rose Hindmarch, local expert on Mary Swann, a woman with an extraordinary memory and gift for detail, able to remember whole conversations word for word, able to put precise dates on . . . episodes that were years in the past . . . and . . .*

He shook her hand in farewell. She wanted him to linger, but his handshake was hurried, as though he could hardly wait to get back to his typewriter before the things she had said faded. A little let down, a little tearful in fact, she had wanted to hang on to his hand and blurt out something more. Anything. "I forgot to tell you about the time Mary and I . . . "

Later, in church, after Morton Jimroy returned to Winnipeg, she begged forgiveness from the pine pulpit rail. She had never meant to be untruthful. She had not intended to exaggerate her friendship with Mary Swann. Friendship! The truth was that she had scarcely done more than pass the time of day with Mrs. Swann. Good morning, Mrs. Swann.

Nice weather we're having, Mrs. Swann. Won't be long till the snow flies.

The two of them had not gone for long walks together. They had *not* discussed — not even once — the books Mary Swann borrowed from the library. Mary Swann had *not* given Rose Hindmarch copies of her poems to read and comment upon. They had *not* — not ever — discussed their deeply shared feeling about literature or about families or about nature. None of this had taken place. It is a myth that people in rural communities are all acquainted with one another and know all about each other's business. Mary Swann had been a virtual stranger to Rose Hindmarch, just as she was to everyone else in Nadeau, Ontario. A woman who kept to herself, that was Mary Swann.

Forgive me, forgive me. Forgive me — the sin of untruthfulness.

Our unlikeliest prayers are answered. Within weeks Rose felt herself to be absolved. Her guilt receded with surprising speed in the days following Jimroy's visit, and before long she felt the balm of complete forgiveness. This came not in the usual way through a cycle of confession and mortification, penalty and pardon, but through the roughly weighted balance of mutual transgression. Human beings are not stainless; this is a fact. Rose is far from possessing moral perfection. So too is Morton Jimroy. Their imperfections, colliding in a blue sky somewhere between Ontario and Manitoba, merged and cancelled each other out.

For Morton Jimroy took — stole, that is, no use to shilly-shally — the photograph of Mary Swann from the Nadeau Museum. There could be no doubt of this. He probably, Rose believes, slipped it under his jacket while she was looking the other way. Yes, she is sure this is what happened. There were two photographs: one rather blurred, showing

Mary standing in the sunshine; the other, much clearer, showing the unsmiling matte face, eyes wide open, a mouth that was intensely secretive; it is this second photograph that vanished. There were no other visitors to the museum that day, not one.

Her first thought was to write Jimroy a letter and accuse him directly. "Dear Mr. Jimroy, I am afraid I must ask you to return . . . "

But the impulse died almost at once. Weeks passed. Months went by. Now, if she thinks of the photograph at all it's with the sense that it is in the hands of its rightful owner. (Just as it is right that Mary Swann's notebook is with Dr. Maloney, Sarah.) Knowing this, she experiences a quiet tide of relief. An act of restitution has taken place, an undefined wrong set right, and as for Jimroy, her fondness for him has increased steadily. His friendship, his *confidence*, is the anointing she has longed for, and the evening in the Elgin Hotel glows like one of those stained-glass birds people hang in their windows, the two of them together, chaste, joyful, the book of Mary Swann's poems between them on the table. There was a moment when his hand, reaching for the bill, brushed hers. It shames her that she should savour this moment, since she knows it is the sort of accident others cast away as valueless. Nevertheless it is hers, and nothing will persuade her to give it up.

Rose Hindmarch Is Visited by the November Blues

The water tower at the edge of town wears a crown of snow, though it's only mid-November. It has been snowing steadily for two days now. The lake is full of snow. The back roads are full of snow, and so are the small straight streets of

Nadeau and the whitely blowing late-afternoon sky that
hovers over the village. A water-colourist attempting to capture the scene would need only a minimal palette: blue,
white, and a slash of violet. The violet, especially in the late
afternoon, carries the power of melancholy.

Coming through the snow is a human form that can
barely be distinguished. Yes, it is female; yes, it is someone
no longer young, a figure bundled against the snow and
walking with an awkward and seemingly painful gait. It's
only Rose Hindmarch with a sack of groceries in her arms.
Wouldn't you think some kind person would offer her a lift?

Now, around the corner, comes a blue Volkswagen van
with its jumpy, nervous little windshield wipers going like
fury. Homer Hart is behind the wheel, a kindly, fat-chested
man squashed into an old-fashioned overcoat. He brings the
little car to a sliding halt, rolls down the window and says in
that quavering tenor of his, "Rose? Is that you? Climb in
and I'll run you home."

Before Homer's breakdown he was principal of the
Nadeau High School. Then the shock treatments wiped
away his Latin and French and left behind only his sputter-
ing, faltering high-pitched English. "This is no weather to
be out in, Rose," he natters. "This is no kind of day to be
walking around out of doors."

"Thanks a million, Homer," Rose says, getting in beside
him. "I needed a few things from the store so I thought
I'd — " Then she stops herself and says, "Any news from
Daisy?"

He takes the corner slowly. "Not a word for two weeks.
You know Daisy when she gets down in the Florida sunshine."

"Didn't she say when she'd be back? In her last letter, I
mean?"

"End of next week, she said, but you know Daisy." He gives Rose a shrewd, unhopeful smile. "Gets a little longer every year."

"It won't be long now," Rose says. Then she adds, sighing, "Just look at all the snow she's missed! Have you ever seen snow like this?"

Homer offers to carry up the bag of groceries, but Rose says no, she can manage. "Thanks anyway, Homer." Then "Let me know if there's anything I can do for you."

A lot of people say this to Homer. It's a natural gesture, offering aid to an older man who's keeping house on his own for an interval and who's lonely and disoriented. Of course Homer is chronically disoriented and, therefore, the recipient of many small kindnesses, which he has learned to accept meekly. This is especially the case when Daisy is off on her annual trip south.

Rose is waiting for Daisy to come home from Florida and feed some life into her. Daisy with her leathery tan will bring her a new fund of stories: the people she's met at her sister's trailer park, the bridge hands she's played, the new restaurants she and her sister have discovered in the Sarasota area. She'll have bought herself two or three new outfits, and for Rose a rainbow-coloured scarf or a shell necklace from St. Armand's Key. Rose is hoping to persuade Daisy to go into Kingston with her for a pre-Christmas shopping spree. Not that Daisy will need much persuading; she loves to go shopping with her friends, taking them by the arm and coaxing them into Eaton's, offering advice and sharing precious threads of information. This'll wear well, she'll say, but this won't. This flatters you, this brings out your complexion, covers your neck, hides your upper arms, conceals the bust. Daisy has an eye. Some say a wicked eye.

Six months ago, just after Easter, Rose received a note in

the mail. There was a local postmark on the envelope. A shower invitation, Rose thought happily; she hadn't been to a shower for ages. Inside was an attractive little hasty note with a blue flower in one corner. The note was printed. "Dear Rose: I am a friend and can't think of any way to tell you this, but there is a little hair growing on your chin. It's been there for a while now, and I thought you might want to know."

Of course the note wasn't signed. Of course Rose knew it could only have been sent by Daisy Hart.

She felt sick. She would never be able to look Daisy in the face again. In the bathroom mirror she peered at herself, tipping her head back as far as she could. There it was, a little grey hair about an inch long, a small wiry hair, curly like a pig's tail. She removed it with manicure scissors and immediately felt better, and also more kindly toward Daisy, and now, every night she looks to see if it has grown back in. She has replaced the bathroom lightbulb with one twice as bright and has also purchased a small magnifying mirror into which she can scarcely bring herself to look, so suddenly present are the colony of pores at the side of her nose and the webby flesh under her eyes. When Daisy comes home from Florida, Rose intends to consult her about buying a new makeup base. She wants to look her best for the Swann symposium, which is now only two months away. She would like to lose her tired, wan look and appear lively and knowledgeable, not exactly a fashion plate, that would be ridiculous, but someone who possesses the brisk freshness of the countryside. *"You're looking just the same, Rose," cry Sarah Maloney, Morton Jimroy, Professor Lang, too.*

At least she's managed to lose some weight. Twelve pounds so far, and without the pain of going on a special diet or eating yogurt. Mysteriously, she seems to have lost her appetite for chocolate ice cream, and has just about given up her evening omelettes, too. Toast and tea are all she bothers with these days. Her blue skirt hangs on her, and she feels tired at the thought of taking in the side seams. When she looks in the mirror she sees only a blur, but accepts the fact that aging means estrangement from one's own face. She's tired most of the time lately, what with the long hours at work and the evening meetings and so on. Of course people slow down at this time of year — Homer was saying something like that not long ago, something about iron deficiency. On top of everything else there's the worry about her periods starting up again.

It's exasperating the way they start and stop, stop and start. Only today, on a Saturday afternoon, she had to go down to the Red and White to buy a new box of pads. Naturally, Stan Fortas was at the cash register with his big hands gripping the box and dropping it into the grocery sack, talking a mile a minute about how he was planning to do some ice fishing this winter, just as though it was Rice Krispies she was buying and not sanitary pads which she required to staunch this new, thick, dark-red outpouring.

She should see a doctor. Women her age are always being told to have annual check-ups. Daisy Hart goes twice a year to a women's clinic in Kingston. She will ask Daisy when she gets home where the clinic is and perhaps make an appointment. She certainly doesn't intend to go back to Dr. Thoms in Elgin, not if she's bleeding to death.

"Just slip off your panties," he said in his crackling young man's voice, "and try to relax." As though anyone could relax with that rubber glove pushing away up inside her. She whimpered a little with the pain, a bleating sound that surprised her, but the rubber glove plunged even farther, twisting and testing the helpless interior pulp of her body. Afterwards he sat her down in the little office and asked, without preliminaries, "Would you say your sex life is satisfactory?" She was tempted to whimper again. Something like a nettle rash came over her larynx. His pen wagged in the air, impatient. She managed to nod. "No pain during intercourse?" he pursued her. She shook her head and he made another check mark. "Libido falling off at all?" He was relentless — to this last question it seemed she could neither nod nor shake her head, so she grimaced stupidly and gave the smallest of shrugs and was rewarded by another check mark on her chart. A moment later he was taking her blood pressure and inquiring about her diet, and she was giving him curt, icy replies, which he seemed not to notice.

For a day afterward, her stomach churned with humiliation. She resolved never to go back. That he was new in the area only made it worse, for he was bound to find out who she was sooner or later, the virgin village clerk, the old-maid librarian. She wondered if he could guess how she put herself to sleep some nights, her finger working.

He pronounced her a healthy specimen, but that was five years ago. What should she do now about this pouring blood?

She's going to have to buck up, she tells herself with a shake of her head. Start taking an interest in things the way she used to. Buck up, Rose girl. Mind over matter. The new John le Carré on the bedside table is only half read, but this one doesn't hold her interest the way the others did. Everything in the story is happening so far away that she has a hard time imagining it. It all seems a little silly, in fact, all jumbled up, though probably it will come together in the end. But the end lies somewhere beyond her strength at the moment. It's such a big book, so many pages. Were his other books this long? She finds it curiously heavy to hold. That's the trouble with a hardcover book, of course. A paperback wouldn't draw the strength from her arms like this, making her shoulders ache and her fingers go numb.

She decides she will abandon le Carré for tonight and browse through her copy of *Swann's Songs*. She's familiar with most of the poems, of course, even if she doesn't understand them, but it's been a while since she's read the book straight through. She has been intending to give it some serious attention before the symposium actually rolls around. She doesn't want to look ignorant. People there will be looking at her — her! — as an expert.

But the little book isn't in its usual place under her magazine rack. Probably it has slipped through onto the floor behind. Well, she'll look for it in the morning. Right now she's too tired to bend over.

Her eyes especially are heavy and tired; sometimes Rose thinks they're like two hard stones perched there on a face that's half dead.

Rose and Homer Take a Sunday Drive

"Feel up to taking a drive over to Westport?" Homer says to Rose two weeks later. It is the middle of a cold, windless Sunday afternoon when he phones. At this moment Jean and Howie Elton are quarrelling loudly downstairs. Some heavy object has been dropped on the floor, an act of carelessness on Jean's part, it seems, and Rose can hear Howie shouting and slamming cupboard doors, and the shrill counterpoint of Jean defending herself. (It has been going on for more than an hour; at first Rose listened with a disabling sense of excitement and eagerness. Then there was another loud crash and the sound of weeping; Jean's of course.) Rose puts her lips close to the telephone and whispers to Homer that yes, she would love a drive over to Westport, that he is a godsend — which seems to please him inordinately.

The road to Westport is clear of ice, and the running glare on the snow-filled fields is so bright that Rose feels herself grow buoyant. "Oh, I love it," she says. "It's a wonderful day for a run. I love it."

People in Nadeau, at least those older people who still subscribe to the idea of a Sunday "run," quite often travel the twelve miles to Westport. Westport is a smaller village than Nadeau, a prettier village. Its white houses with their shining windowpanes and painted doors are arranged not in neat rows as in Nadeau, but charmingly, haphazardly, along the lake shore. In Westport you can stand by the side of the lake next to the old ferry shed and get a fine view of the ice fishing out on the bay. Afterward, if you like, you can stop in at Lou's Antique Barn where blue glass insulators and pink glass relish dishes are arranged on rustic shelves, and then you can warm yourself up with a cup of coffee and a muffin at the Westport Luncheonette.

Homer Hart, buttering his second muffin, is in a merry mood. He has a feeling in his bones, he tells Rose, that Daisy will be home by the end of the week. He is ninety-nine per cent sure that there will be a letter from her Monday morning telling him when she'll be arriving.

Anticipation makes him adventurous, and he proposes to Rose that they go back to Nadeau by way of the back road. He feels sure that the snowplough has been through by now. It's still early, just three-thirty, and the road is prettier that way.

"Well," Rose says, "I don't know." But after a minute she agrees. She's feeling uneasy now about Jean, and wondering if she's done the right thing leaving the house. On the other hand, the back road is prettier, just as Homer says, even if it does take a little longer.

For the first mile or two it follows the lake and then cuts north, wandering back and forth gaily between low rounded hills. Rose often thinks to herself what a pleasure it is, the flash of scenery through a car window, how it infects her with an ancient rush of innocence and holds in abeyance more difficult daily chores and dealings. A tent is thrown over her thoughts. Scenery gliding past the eye doesn't need worrying about. It passes, that's all, quick as a wink, and asks nothing in return.

One by one the old farms come into view, along the back road, and Rose, because of her position as town clerk, is able to put a name to each of them, as well as being able to comment on the acreage and the taxes paid or owing. There's the old Hanna place. And that's where the Enrights used to live. Mainly these are poor farms, though the deep layer of snow gives them a false look of prosperity. The soil beneath is thin and stony, good for nothing but grazing animals or planting a few acres of hay or corn. It's a wonder, Rose observes, that people stay on these farms and continue to eke out a living somehow.

The farm where Mary Swann lived with her husband and daughter is one of the smallest and poorest of the area, though it's encouraging to see that the new owner, a young man from the States who bought the place as a weekend retreat, has at least had the fences repaired and a new roof put on the house. The sight of the dull silvery silo poking up next to the barn always affects Rose. What she feels is some unnamed inner organ flopping in her chest and squeezing her breath right out.

"Poor Mrs. Swann," Homer says, as though reading Rose's thoughts. He slows the car just a bit.

"It's a wonder," Rose says, thinking of the new owner, "how he could bring himself to buy a place where something awful happened."

"Probably never thinks about it," Homer says. "That was a long time ago."

"Not that long."

"People forget. And he's not from the area. Didn't know the family."

"But still." Rose lifts her gloved hands helplessly in the air, then drops them on her lap with a sigh.

"As a matter of fact," Homer goes on, his tender mouth moving, "I don't suppose that young fellow cares about the farm. Probably just a tax shelter. Looks like he's letting the fields go wild."

"A hobby farm," Rose says, "That's what Mr. Browning said when he came into the office. Just for weekends. Not that he ever seems to come."

The countryside around Nadeau is full of weekend farmers these days. Rose, going over her tax sheets, is familiar enough with the phenomenon, but she still finds it strange. She can remember that as a child it was a rare treat to be taken to Kingston. Now people think nothing of driving all the way from Montreal or Toronto or up from the States just for a weekend.

"Well," Rose says to Homer, "he sure couldn't make any kind of living off this place. And the silo. What would he put in it?"

Both Rose Hindmarch and Homer Hart remember the year when Angus Swann amazed his neighbours by erecting a silo on his farm. There was talk. The news travelled fast and met with wide disapproval. There was a feeling that an injustice had been done. Mary Swann had no washing machine and no refrigerator. She cooked the family meals on a blackened wood-burning stove right up until the day she was killed — though it was said she owned a Parker 51 fountain pen with which she wrote her poems. But, the pen aside, she lacked those conveniences that had become common even on the less-prosperous farms, those conveniences that were said to "make a woman's lot easier."

How were these daily domestic deprivations, a washing machine, a refrigerator, to be balanced beside Angus Swann's new silver-clad silo? Because it was obvious even to the disinterested eye that the Swann farm didn't merit such a dignifying emblem. Silos belonged on prosperous dairy farms, keeping company with roomy, wide-raftered barns and graceful rows of elms. But not on the old Swann farm, or rather, the old Swann *place*, for it was an exaggeration to call this tumbledown habitation a farm. The crippled rail fences, the teetering shed, the broken machinery rusting in the weedy, chicken-maddened yard, the sopping clothes perpetually dripping from a sagging line, the shame of cardboard over a broken bedroom window — and all this presided over by a new concrete-and-steel silo paid for, it was said, in cash.

It mustn't be thought that the Swann place resembles in any way those paintings of run-down farms so popular in suburban livingrooms during the late fifties and early sixties, a fad that quickly bankrupted itself, for where can decay go but down toward deeper decay? In the silvery dilapidated farms of popular art there's little suggestion of the real sourness of old back sheds or the reek of privies or the sucking mud between house and barn. Even if you could pry open the door and enter the kitchen of one of these houses, chances are you would get no glimpse of that kind of cheap patterned linoleum that soon flaked underfoot and somehow never got replaced. One of Mary Swann's poems, one of those published by Frederic Cruzzi after her death, and one that is a puzzle to scholars goes:

> Feet on the winter floor
> Beat Flowers to blackness
> Making a corridor
> Named helplessness

Rose Hindmarch has visited the Swann farmhouse twice. The first time was with Sarah Maloney and Homer and Daisy Hart, but they didn't go inside that time, just walked around the yard and stood for a few minutes on the porch. The second time was two years ago when she was setting up the Mary Swann Memorial Room in the old high school in Nadeau. Russell Donegal, the good-natured, semi-alcoholic real-estate agent who operates out of both Nadeau and Westport, drove her out there in his Oldsmobile (a cold Sunday afternoon, much like today) and let her wander at will through the house.

That, of course, was during the time when the house was up for sale, before the new owner came up from the States and bought the place. ("Who the hell wants to buy a house where a murder's been done?" So said Russell Donegal.) Rose moved silently from room to room, walking hesitantly on tiptoe: the verandah (where Mrs. Swann had once stood smiling into a camera), the kitchen with its suspended smell of cold and its torn linoleum, beneath which Professor Lang had found a number of poems that had been hidden away. The sitting-room had plastic sheeting on its windows. There was a crude, railingless stairway leading to two upstairs bedrooms. Russell followed close behind Rose, and she was both flustered and relieved to have him there.

"Well," he said at last in his meaty salesman's voice. "What d'ya think, Rose?"

She waved a limp arm, then asked boldly, "What happened to everything?" To herself she said: What did you expect? The word that floated to her lips, like a child's balloon bobbing crookedly to the ceiling, was not the word *squalor* and not *trash*. Those are middle-class words, heavy with judgement. (And by now you will have realized that Rose Hindmarch lacks the spirit, the haemoglobin, for judgement. She is afflicted with social anaemia — though she does possess something else, which might be termed *acuity*.) *Poor* is the word that came to her, *poor*. A spare, descriptive, forgiving term, thin as a knife blade and somewhat out of fashion. *Poor*.

In Mary Swann's house there were a few straight chairs, a painted kitchen table, another table in the sitting-room with an old Westinghouse radio on it, a single cheap armchair missing one arm, iron pipe beds in the bedrooms, and old cheap bureaus of the kind that are *not* stripped down and sold as antiques at the Antique Barn in Westport.

"Where is everything?" she asked Russell Donegal, and he replied with a level grunt, wagging his broad, empurpled-with-whisky face, "This is it. Such as it is." Then he said, "We've got a saying in the business that a house sells faster when it's furnished. Well, this place is an exception. I'd like to clear the damn place right out."

"I suppose some of the things, the family mementoes and so on, went to Mrs. Swann's daughter in California." Rose ventured this hypothesis with only half a heart. Except for the two photographs and the drawerful of crocheted doilies, there appeared to be no family mementoes. Unless Professor Lang, when Russell had showed him through the house, carted off more than a sheaf of crumpled poems.

"Nope," Russell said. He lit a cigarette with a match struck directly on the kitchen wall. "He just took what he found under the linoleum. This is the way she was. Except" — he gave his goofy laugh — "except for the blood. We had that cleaned up before the place went on the market. Needless to say."

"Of course," Rose said. Then she added with a tincture of shame, "I suppose there was an awful lot of blood."

"The old boy was just about emptied out when they found him. Every last drop. Head wounds are the worst for blood, you know, and he'd put the bullet right through his. So you can imagine the mess. Of course there was no telling how long *she'd* been dead."

A week, the coroner had reported.

And so Rose was forced to use her imagination when it came to furnishing the Mary Swann Memorial Room . She was fortunate that the Nadeau town council had appropriated $300 for acquisitions (she embraced that wonder-word *acquisitions*) and that a second grant from Ottawa brought the amount up to $500. Russell Donegal encouraged her to help herself to anything in the house, saying she was welcome to the lot for all he cared. He'd thank her, he said, to tote off what she could. Rose took the kitchen table, two of the better kitchen chairs (pressbacks, Daisy Hart informed her) and a few cooking utensils, pathetic things with worn handles and a look of hard use. She left behind the bent rusty carving knife and the nickel-plated forks and spoons.

As for the other articles in the Memorial Room, she bought them from the Antique Barn and from Selma's Antiques in Kingston: a pretty wooden turnip masher, a wood and glass scrubbing board, a cherrywood churn, a fanciful, feminine iron bedstead, and a walnut bookcase and the set of tattered dull-covered books (Dickens, Sir Walter Scott) that came with it. At an auction in the town of Lyndhurst she bought three old quilts and a set of blue-and-white china and a framed picture of a cocker spaniel. A measure of pride flowed around her not-quite-secret purchases, and she watched with joy, with creative amazement, as the room took shape, acquiring a look of authenticity and even a sense of the lean, useful life that had inhabited it. Yes, Rose could imagine the figure of Mary Swann bent over the painted table scratching out her poems by the light of the kerosene lamp. (The table had been repainted, and the kerosene lamp she found at a rummage sale in Westport.)

> Redness of cold, circle of light
> Heating the heart when the hour is late

If you suggest to Rose that her room has been wrenched into being through duplicity, through countless small acts of deception, she will be sure to look injured and offer up a pained denial. These articles, after all, belong to the *time* and the *region* of which Mary Swann was a part, and therefore nothing is misrepresented, not the quilts, not the china, not even the picture of the cocker spaniel. She may admit, though, that she has considered, then rejected, the idea of placing a small card in the doorway advising visitors that the contents are *similar* to those found in Mary Swann's rural home. But quite rightly she has decided that such a notice would be a distraction and that it might inject a hint of apology, of insufficiency. (The charm of falsehood is not that it distorts reality, but that it creates reality afresh.) With all her heart Rose would like to have on display the papers found by Professor Lang under the linoleum — and the Parker 51 fountain pen that Mary Swann was reputed to have owned; but this article (according to Russell Donegal who heard it from Cecil Deacon, the trust officer in Kingston who handled the estate) was sent as a keepsake to Frances Swann Moore in California.

The missing pen is a void that sucks away at Rose. A number of times she has been on the verge of writing to Frances in California to ask if she would care to donate or at least lend her mother's pen to the museum. Meanwhile Rose is keeping a lookout at local flea markets for one of a similar vintage.

It is a mystery why Angus Swann hacked his wife Mary to death in December of 1965. Homer Hart and Rose Hindmarch, driving by the old Swann farm, discuss the various theories. Angus Swann was a violent man. No one ever denied that. It was known he butchered his poultry crudely with an axe and bragged about it. Also that he once went into a rage at the Red and White over the price of a ballpeen hammer. Another time Mary Swann was seen in town with a bruise over one eye and an arm in a sling. Some people say he was jealous of her poetry, the little bit of local celebrity that came her way, and that he begrudged her the postage when she sent her poems to local newspapers. But there is no proof of any of this, and other people say that, on the contrary, he was proud of her in his way, that it was he who gave her the fountain pen for a birthday present.

The last person to see her alive — other than her husband and possibly the bus driver — was Kingston publisher Frederic Cruzzi. According to the testimony Mr. Cruzzi gave the coroner after Mrs. Swann's body was discovered, he was sitting quietly at home one wintry afternoon when she suddenly appeared at his doorway. She thrust a bulky bag at him and, kind man that he was, he invited her inside and read through the loose sheets of paper that constituted a manuscript, later to form the bulk of *Swann's Songs*.

It was said he realized at once that the poems were

remarkable. "I'd like to publish these, " he told her, but she seemed ill at ease, puzzled, anxious about getting her bus home. The bus driver, not the regular driver, but a holiday replacement, half remembers dropping her at the side road near the Swann farm, and then, presumably, she walked into her house and was bludgeoned to death by her husband.

Rose came close to telling Homer as they drive along the back road that she sometimes dreams about this scene of horror—mazy dreams of splashing blood and thin-walled vessels hacked open and strewn on kitchen linoleum.

Homer said into the silence, "It must have been something pretty bad to set him off like that. Well, we'll never know."

"No," Rose says, and gazes at the glare-filled hills.

She doesn't tell Homer — she has never told anyone — that it was she who suggested to Mrs. Swann, in their one and only extended conversation, that she should show her poems to Frederic Cruzzi. Rose had read about Frederic Cruzzi and his wife and their publishing company, Peregrine Press, in *Library News*. Peregrine Press was interested in regional poets whose work was not sufficiently recognized. When Mary Swann came into the library one December day in 1965 to return a book, looking feverish and wearing her running shoes and her terrible coat and with her hair matted and uncombed, Rose was stricken by the wish to do her a kindness. She pulled the article about Frederic Cruzzi out of her clipping file and showed it to Mrs. Swann. "You should mail him some of your poems," she urged her. "Or better yet, go and see him."

Mrs. Swann looked dubious, but Rose detected a nervous stirring of interest and cut out the article then and there with her library shears — not without a stitch of regret — and placed it inside the book. It was the last book Mary

Swann ever borrowed from the Nadeau library, *The Ice Palace*, by Edna Ferber.

It might be thought that Rose Helen Hindmarch suffers anguish over this episode and the part she may, inadvertently, have played in Mary Swann's murder. But oddly enough she doesn't. She thinks about it from time to time, and wonders about it, but feels no sense of responsibility.

What protects her from guilt is the simple balm of modesty, of self-effacement. She cannot possibly be the one who set in motion the chain of events that led to Mary Swann's death since she has never been capable of setting anything in motion. Never mind her work in the town office, in the library, and in the museum — she has always known, not sensed, but *known*, that she is deficient in power. So many have insisted on her deficiency, beginning with her dimly remembered soldier father who failed to come back home to Nadeau to take his place as her parent, and her grandmother who told her, moving leathery gums stretched with spittle, that she had the worst posture ever seen in a young girl, and her mother who said looks weren't everything, and a teacher back in the early grades who said she was a silly goose; and then Daisy Hart who noticed the hair on her chin, and Dr. Thoms who slyly inquired about her libido, and the United Church God who deserted his switchboard, and Morton Jimroy who, except for one little letter, has not answered any of her perky little notes or cards, and Jean Elton who has never come back to share her bed, and even Homer Hart who has not had the goodness to inquire about the Swann symposium for some time now, and the seditious blood that is pouring out of her day after day after day, making her weaker and weaker so that she can hardly think — all this has interfered with her life and made her deficient in her own eyes, and it is this that mercifully

guards her against self-recrimination, from believing she is
someone who might possibly have played a part in the death
of the poet Mary Swann. Rose is a person powerless to stir
love and so she must also be powerless in her ability to hurt
or destroy.

Rose Receives a Letter and Also Writes One

Rose very often gets postcards from vacationing friends and
neighbours: cards that come all the way from White Rock,
B.C., or New York City and, of course, from Daisy Hart in
Florida. She also receives a fair number of small, dainty pas-
tel envelopes containing shower invitations or thank-you
notes or the like. And then there's her official mail: from the
National Library Association, from the Department of
Cultural Affairs, from the OATC (Ontario Association of
Township Clerks) or from the CCUC (Committee of
Concern for the United Church).

Seldom, though, does she receive a real letter. The one
that comes for her today, from Professor Willard Lang in
Toronto, brings a mixed flush of pride and apprehension.
"Gotta letter for ya, Rose," Johnny Sears at the post office
calls when Rose pops in after work. "Boy oh boy, you sure
get lots of mail."

Her hand shakes; Willard Lang, his name on the envelope. Writing to tell her the symposium has been cancelled.
Or that her presence is not required after all. Or that some
mistake has been made; she should never have received an
invitation in the first place. Some administrative bungle. She
will understand. He hopes.

Rose opens the letter, cheerfully chatting all the while to
Johnny, how is his mother doing, what about the hockey

game last Friday night, those roughnecks from Elgin, the weather.

"Dear Miss Hindmarch," Professor Lang has written. "We are delighted you are to be with us at the symposium. Will you allow me to ask two very special favours of you."

The first favour is that she bring along her photograph of Mary Swann so that it can be included in a special display the committee is setting up. "As you know, it is the only photograph we have of our poet."

The second request is more complicated. Professor Lang writes:

> The rather elderly Frederic Cruzzi from Kingston, after considerable persuasion, has agreed to attend the symposium and perhaps say a few words about his role as Mrs. Swann's publisher. I am not sure what his travel arrangements are, but at his age there may be difficulties, and it occurred to me that since you live only a stone's throw from each other, and no doubt have met, perhaps you wouldn't mind offering the old fellow a lift to Toronto. He is well past eighty, I believe, and not in the best of shape since his wife died (she was a charming woman, very intelligent). Here, at any rate, is his phone number in case you feel like giving him a buzz regarding travel plans.

Rose would sooner put a sack over her head and jump down through a hole in the ice on Whitefish Lake than give Frederic Cruzzi a "buzz" on the phone. Mr. Cruzzi is the retired editor of the *Kingston Banner*; she once heard him deliver an address at the National Library Association annual meeting. He is tall, angular, has a foreign accent, quotes Shakespeare, and wouldn't be able to make head or tail of a phone call from Rose Hindmarch of Nadeau, Ontario.

Instead she writes him a letter, a long letter, which takes

her all of one evening to get right. She introduces herself: Rose Hindmarch, librarian and former friend of Mary Swann. She will be travelling up to Toronto by train for the symposium, she explains, and she thinks perhaps the two of them might keep each other company. (She apologizes twice for not being able to offer him a ride for the very good reason that she has never learned to drive a car.) She mails the letter in a mood of gaiety, uneasiness, and disbelief, gaiety because she is overtaken by a sense of abandonment, unease because she fully expects a rebuff from Mr. Cruzzi, and disbelief because she is unable now to hold in steady focus an image of herself actually sitting on a train bound for Toronto.

It is not to be. She may go on and on pretending, packing her bag, buying her train ticket and so on, but the blood secretly leaking from her body leaves her a future that is numbered in days now, not weeks. Every morning she wakes up and repeats the cycle: desolation, a brief buoyancy, and again desolation. It is laughable. By the first week of January there will be nothing left of Rose Hindmarch but the clothes in her closet, her row of paperbacks on the TV set, half a carton of cottage cheese in her refrigerator, and her bed with its checked sheets and chenille spread. She could leave a note saying goodbye. But to whom? And for what reason?

Rose Hindmarch Gives a Party

Rose Hindmarch's Christmas Day eggnog party is something of a tradition. Even when she and her mother lived in the Second Street house, they always "asked people in" for a glass of eggnog and a slice of Christmas cake between 5:00 and 7:00 P.M. on Christmas Day. (Christmas dinner is taken at about 2:00 or 3:00 in Nadeau, and so Rose's guests arrive already stuffed with turkey and drowsy from overeating.)

Rose makes better eggnog than her mother did. She's more generous with the rum, for one thing, and she also offers the alternative of rye and ginger-ale to those who prefer it, and most do. Her Christmas cake is store bought, but she has canned baby shrimp in a glass bowl on the table and a plate of Ritz crackers, and she serves her famous Velveeta Christmas Log, full of glittering green pepper bits and slices of stuffed olives.

Despite the fact that she's feeling punk — her word — she has decided to go ahead with the party, and her living-room looks surprisingly merry this dull snowy Christmas day. She has strung her Christmas cards, one of them from Sarah Maloney in Chicago, on a cord over the window, and set up her little artificial tree by the window between the radiator and the television set. Her tree ornaments always bring her pleasure: that little smudged cotton Santa with his beady eyes, the tiny straw donkey Daisy once brought her back from Florida, and the red glass reindeer she herself bought on Markham Street in a store called "Things." She has even put up the string of lights this year, something she hasn't done since her mother died.

The first person to come is Homer Hart, huffing up the stairs, looking bulkier than ever and bearing a box of Laura Secord chocolate almonds, Rose's favourite. He arrives at the party alone; Daisy has, at last, written from Sarasota to say that she and a divorceé called Audrey Beamish, a woman she met in her sister's trailer court, are about to embark on an auto trip to the southern states and that she won't be back to Nadeau before February at the earliest.

Next to arrive are Jean and Howie from downstairs, Jean wearing the dusty-pink velour track suit Howie gave her for Christmas, and Howie the navy blue track suit Jean gave him. Their gift to Rose is an electric yogurt maker and a booklet of instructions and recipes. Other years they've gone to Cornwall for Christmas, but this year, since Jean is three months pregnant, they've decided not to risk the icy roads. Howie seems enormously pleased about the baby. He breaks off in the middle of discussion on the regime in Libya and pats Jean's stomach, saying, "Ha! Won't be long before we have our own little dictator." At this Jean smiles dreamily. She's hoping for a boy, she tells Rose privately, for Howie's sake.

Also at the party are Floyd and Bea Sears. Floyd is in good spirits, winding up his second term as reeve of Nadeau Township. Bea, his wife, a woman often described for want of a more specific title as "an A-one housewife," has brought Rose a gift of a homemade cushion crocheted with ribbon. Belle Waterman, who was widowed years back, has come along with Floyd and Bea and has brought Rose a dried-flower-and-driftwood arrangement to put on her TV. Percy "Perce" Flemming and his wife, Peg, are with their three-hundred-pound son, Bobby, who has twice attempted suicide and cannot be left alone, even for an hour. Joe and Marnie Fletcher are a little late because Marnie was slow getting the turkey in the oven this morning, and for this she takes a good-natured ribbing from her husband and from Floyd Sears. "We just this minute got up from the table," Marnie says, refusing a piece of Velveeta Log. Vic Brower, a lifelong bachelor, huddles with Homer on the couch. Someone once hinted to Rose that Vic frequents a house of prostitution in Kingston, but Rose, when she looks at Vic, his shy eyes and small mouth, doesn't see how this can be. Hank Cleary, his wife, Agnes, and his sister, Elfreda, who is visiting from Sarnia, all get quite merry on eggnog, the three of them, and Hank tells a long Libyan joke, mangling the punchline and getting shouted down by his wife, who then dissolves into a fit of laughter.

Merriment, merriment, Seasonal joy, Time slips away. Rose thinks how glad she is she decided to give her party after all. People come to depend on certain traditions in a small town, and this may well be a farewell to her old friends, a farewell to life.

Happiness seizes her, exhausted though she is by the loss of blood and by the preparations for the party. In recent weeks she has had a feeling that some poisonous sorrow has seeped into her life, and now, this afternoon, from nowhere comes a sudden shine of joy.

What is Homer saying to her? Into her ear he is whispering how he has suffered terrible loneliness in the last month and that he is extremely doubtful whether Daisy will be home before spring. Vic Brower has fallen asleep, resting his head rather sweetly on the new crocheted cushion. Joe and Marnie look at him, winking at each other and grinning like mad, and Marnie laughs her watery laugh and says very softly into Joe's ear, "Let's go to bed early tonight and have ourselves a high old time." Bobby Flemming is telling Floyd Sears about a new diet the doctor has put him on. Starting January first, only three hundred calories a day, mostly lemon juice, club soda and strawberries. Bea Shears is telling Howie that fatherhood should be taken seriously. Her own father, she confides for the first time in her life, never once asked her a single question about herself, not once. Jean is chewing a shrimp and watching Howie and trying to imagine the little shrimp-shaped organism inside her, how she will teach it the meaning of charity and gentleness, how if it is a girl she will not be disappointed.

Elfreda is telling her sister-in-law that the real reason

she's taking early retirement from the post office in Sarnia is because her supervisor hinted that her breath was less than fresh, and she has been unable, for some reason, to absorb this terrible accusation. "Perce" Flemming tells his wife, Peg, about a recurrent nightmare he has, a lion chasing him and nipping at his heels, and Peg pats him on his stringy arm and says, "Next time wake me up and I'll give it a bop on the head." Rose hands Homer a glass of ginger-ale and tells him about the blood that's been pouring out of her for two months straight and of how she refuses to go to the doctor in Elgin because his brisk scrutiny reminds her of how lonely she is, and that she is one of the unclaimed, and Homer responds by taking her hand on his lap and promising that on Monday morning he will drive her into Kingston where they'll head straight to the clinic where Daisy goes and find out what's causing the trouble.

Rose gazes about the room, at her friends, at the table of food, the little tree, and in the corner the television set, its sound off but the screen flickering with the dark, coarse, stiffening face of Muammar Gadaffi, and then, out of the blue, she remembers a line from one of Mary Swann's poems. It just swims into her head like a little fish.

A pound of joy weighs more
When grief had gone before

FREDERIC CRUZZI

The Circuitous Introduction

The world claps its hands for the intellectual nomad: the Icelandic scholar in Cuba, patiently translating his sagas into Spanish, or the Quaker lesbian traveller in Peru with her backpack and her flute and her notebook full of compassionate poems, or the young barmaid in Dubrovnik with a degree in physics who serves rum cocktails with a monologue that dilutes and reconstitutes the seven languages she speaks, or the French existentialist in his Irish cottage, contemplating local flora and folktales and extracting from them a message that will soon convert hundreds, or at least a handful, to a simplified, nourishing vision of the oneness of things. We love these wanderers for their brilliance, their adaptive colouring, their many tongues and tricks of courage; but chiefly we love them for the innocence and joy with which they burrow into the very world so many of us have given up on.

Retired newspaper editor Frederic Cruzzi of Grenoble, Casablanca, Manchester, and Kingston, Ontario, aged eighty, is such a one — equally at home grafting an apple tree or poaching a salmon or reading a page of Urdu poetry or writing one of his newspaper columns on the diabolism of modern technology. Recently he has come out against the telephone. Vile instrument of slander and babble. Rude interrupter of lamp-lit evenings. Purring flatterer, canny imposter, silky lover, sly mendicant, cunning messenger of unwelcome news, of debts, of dinner parties. "We are dialling our way direct to an early death," says the outspoken octogenarian Cruzzi, who has a weakness for alliteration. Buzzed, bashed, kept on hold. Welded to copper wire, bonded to slippery plastic. Recorded, pre-empted, insulted, seduced, and finally, ultimate injury, presented with a bill as long as your femur.

Sitting in an upstairs bedroom of a hundred-year-old house (limestone, creepers) in Kingston, Ontario, F. Cruzzi, who has risen at half-past seven, is typing his weekly column on a 1950 Underwood, a large, muscular office model, solid and unmusical. He leans over the keys, heated to a fine frenzy. By now, although he fiercely believes people must compromise with the history they are born into, he is persuaded by the crescendo of his own history that telephones must go. What a sight he is, surrounded by his hundreds and hundreds of books, with that sail of white hair, that turkey neck, those bobbling shoulders, the stub of a pencil gripped between his strong old teeth. He has a hard humorous face and oaken hands. Down beneath his wine-dark dressing gown his spindly old-man legs poke out, and his long narrow yellowed feet slap away at the dusty floor. A ladder of sunlight climbs his sleeve, reaches the triangularity of bushy eye sockets. Wham goes the carriage, plink-plunk go the keys. It's a wonder steam isn't pouring out of his ancient orifices, a wonder his heart doesn't give way. Sorry, wrong number — O execrable telephone pole, despicable wire and vulgar coin box. The wound the world inflicts on itself is tinged by automatic answering machines. The barbarous disembodied yoking of human voices, the chattering, battering, shattering of pure air. Desecration. Shame. Gossip in the treetops, alarm in the night.

One paragraph to go and he'll have his five hundred words for this week.

His dressing-gown gapes, revealing shrunken testicles and penis. His foot keeps time. A delicate web gathers at the left side of his mouth. He has come to the last sentence, the final word.

He chooses it with care. As always.

Frederic Cruzzi: A Few of his Friends

Frederic Cruzzi of Kingston, Ontario, former newspaper editor, journalist, traveller, atheist, lover of women and poetry, tender son of gentle parents, scholar, immigrant, gardener, socialist, husband, and father — he is also a man who can be said to have been lucky in friendship. His friendships, he sometimes thinks, are all he has to forestall the pursuing chaos of old age. They give him interludes of calm as well as moments of exhilaration and reverence. Now and then he recalls the slightly overwrought words of a nineteenth-century Indian poet describing friends:

> Jewels of uncertain colour
> Flowers of evasive scent
> Stars of shifting distance
> And hands that hesitate never

The opaque ironies of the poet appeal to Cruzzi, since they emphasize the steadiness of friendship and reject the current jejune notion of soul-baring and abandonment of self. There's something devouringly selfish, he believes, about the wish to know someone "through and through."

Of course, by now many of his friends have been taken from him by death: his brother Hilaire, dead at twenty in a climbing accident; Herve Villeneuve, friend from his student days in Grenoble, a suicide at forty-six; Professor Nicholas Guincourt, a colleague of his father, who gave him the gift of the English language: Sami Salah, his Moroccan cousin who travelled with him for a year in the Far East and was later killed in a hotel fire in Cleveland, Ohio; Tante Maleka, his giggling, indulgent Casablanca aunt, a prodigious smoker of cigarettes who worried about bronchitis but died instead of measles; Max Robinson, literary editor of the *Manchester Guardian* in the thirties, a man of bountiful imagination and easy tears; and Max's wife, May, contemplative, spiritual, alluring; Estelle Berger, Jungian therapist, whose plangent voice still visits Cruzzi in dreams; Glen Forrestal of Ottawa, tonsured sybaritic physician, essayist and poet, sanguine sipper of whisky sodas; Monkey La Rue of Kingston, naturalist, fisherman, skier, composer; Barney Ouilette, also of Kingston, amateur painter and brilliant mathematician (despite the tide of vodka between his ears), and many many more, but of all of these dead friends Cruzzi misses most his wife, Hildë, who in fifty years sometimes exasperated him but never once gave him a moment of boredom.

It's true that Cruzzi is at an age when he can count more friends among the dead than the living, but he is still a man who lives in the midst of friendship. More and more, to be sure, he seeks solitude, is out of sorts, is impatient with confidences, feels put upon, feels weary and oddly restless; but he cannot imagine a life in which friendship is not the largest part.

He is slightly in awe of those who manage their lives without friends and wonders where these unfortunates find their strength. In all of Mary Swann's poems, for instance, the word friend is found only once, and even then it is used reflexively and all but buried in a metaphor, pointing, he believes, to a terrifying ellipsis.

> Like a cup on the shelf
> That's no longer here
> Like the friend of myself
> Who's drowned in the mirror
> The hour is murdered, the moment is lost,
> And everything counted except for the cost.

Those things that kept Mrs. Swann friendless — fear, crippling shyness, isolation, drudgery — are as foreign to Frederic Cruzzi as such bodily afflictions as impetigo or beriberi. His life has always been organized, and is *still* organized, so that he is in the midst of people who possess "hands that hesitate never."

Bridget Riordan is one of those friends, even though he has seen her infrequently during the last forty years. Seductive, rangy, managerial, she is master of all the arts of love and all the modes of loving. Only recently retired from the theatre, she lives in a London flat furnished with airy furniture and heavy paintings, and writes endless letters to friends, including Cruzzi — letters full of wit, skepticism, memory, gossip, tact, and cheerful lewdness.

Cruzzi also counts among his friends a man named Bud McWilliam, former linotype operator on the *Kingston Banner*, a man who loves guns, hunting dogs, machinery, hearty food, and speculative conversation. (Some physical provision or deficiency — Cruzzi doesn't know which — has separated Bud McWilliam from the need for women, but he is able, nevertheless, to cackle at the paradoxes his life has held up.) Nowadays he's more or less confined to bed,

and he welcomes Cruzzi's weekly visits. A number of operations have left him with a gnarly larynx and a throat full
of scar tissue, but he steadfastly refuses to indulge in the
quavering warble of the aged. His struggle to overcome his
bodily infirmities strikes Cruzzi as heroic, and he has often
been tempted to remark on it. Last week their discussion
centred on the emergence of certain sprightly neologisms in
the popular press, the week before on the refraction of light.

He loves, has always loved, Pauline Ouilette. Her passion for perfume, pedicures, and expensive underwear gives
an impression of frivolity that is false. Sometimes when the
two of them sit talking, usually in Pauline's pink and grey
sunporch, Cruzzi shuts his eyes for an instant and breathes
in, along with her fragrance, the skirted merriment of her
voice, the way her vowels tumble out, an engaging spill of
music forming little hillocks that signal the beginning of
laughter. If Pauline should see him close his eyes, she would
never be offended or suspect boredom. She is fully conscious
of her powers, appreciates the importance of good food,
knows that books, particularly fiction, form a valuable core
of experience, and believes she can trust Cruzzi absolutely to
understand and follow the intricacies of her observations.

He wonders sometimes how he would manage without
Dennis and Caroline Cooper-Beckman, who live with their
three children in the brick house across the street from him.
Dennis, aged forty, brings him clippings from obscure journals, fresh raspberries, and iconoclastic views on universities
and governments. Caroline, thirty-five, brings the terrible
sincerity of her social concerns and a slightly skewed sexual
ambivalence that suggests faint, flirtatious arcs of possibility
and stirs in Cruzzi memories of buried passion. He would
do anything for Dennis and Caroline, and they for him.

Mimi Russell, otherwise known as Sister Mary Francis,

has won Cruzzi's heart. Not yet fifty, not yet out of a long childhood, she is breezy and articulate and in love with English literature. She can recite most of Keats by heart (except for "Endymion," which she considers a piece of kitsch). In literature she sniffs a kind of godly oxygen that binds one human being to the next and shortens the distance we must travel to discover that our most private perceptions are universally felt. In this, Cruzzi believes, she is right. (They lunch together weekly and speak often on the phone, or did until Cruzzi's phone was disconnected.) Mimi Russell's biography of Laura Jane Oldfeld, the nineteenth-century Ontario pioneer, is impeccable; also lively and suffused with a rare amiability. When Mary Swann's biographer, Morton Jimroy, visited Kingston a year or so ago, Cruzzi arranged a dinner so the two of them might meet and talk shop; never had such sweetness met such sourness. (Cruzzi supposes the sad, sour, spluttery Jimroy will be in attendance at the Swann symposium and mentally braces himself.)

Simone Cruzzi is Frederic Cruzzi's daughter-in-law, not that he attaches that clumsy title to so slim, so blonde, so vivacious a woman. She lives in Montreal, has a neat, organized face and dresses snappily. Often she comes down to Kingston for the weekend, and between visits she writes Cruzzi fond little notes on company stationery. For a number of years she has worked as a travel agent and tour guide, and she is forever setting off for Salzburg or Beijing or Oslo with her "little chicks" in tow. From these distant points on the globe she mails Cruzzi postcards crowded with stamps (which he pretends he collects). The messages scrawled on the back are always in animated counterpoint to the scenes — sunsets, fountains — displayed on the front. She almost never alludes to her husband, Armand (only son of

Hildë and Frederic Cruzzi) who died of a brain tumour at the age of thirty-six.

There is also Frank Hurley who owns Hurley and Sons, Funeral Directors, of Kingston. In his nether-world Frank embalms bodies and sells coffins sheathed in bronze and lined with satin. Otherwise he scours the countryside on foot (five miles is nothing) for wild flowers and grasses. His need to observe and classify operates like a busy little buzz-saw in his brain, and it is partly for this ever-humming busyness that Cruzzi loves him. He has no humour, but is prodigiously kind and something of a metaphysician. Human society, he says to Cruzzi in his soft burr, is distinguished by four manifestations: the existence of tools, the presence of art, a respect for the dead, and a compulsion to give names to natural phenomena. At eighty-four he is Cruzzi's brother in old age.

And one more: Tom Halpenny, who now edits the *Banner*. He is an American by birth and education, is forty-four years old, speaks in a loud voice, sometimes of matters he knows nothing about. He has a quacky laugh, yawns in public, wears a black T-shirt and a gold chain around his neck, and is famous for his explosive farts, manifested most recently while he was addressing the Ontario Bay Jaycees at their annual fall banquet. Two wives have left him. Of his four children, only one is still in touch. His hair, what remains of it, hangs raggedly on the ears. Laziness, or perhaps the withdrawal of love, has caused his shoulders to slope. His roots are in the old New Left which means they are nowhere. New England puritanism runs through him like a scam of coal. He worships Cruzzi, adored Hildë, thinks Kingston is heaven and the *Banner* the banner of heaven.

At least once a month Tom Halpenny tries to bully

Cruzzi into writing his life story. "Before it's too late," he goads wickedly.

Today, a Tuesday in early November, the two of them are eating lunch in Kingston's Old Firehall Restaurant. Cruzzi is part way through a plain omelette, sipping his Perrier, wishing it were wine, and refusing to be bullied. Tom Halpenny, who has just savaged a nine-dollar lobster salad, is gulping cold milk. From the bottom drawer of cleverness he produces what he considers the ultimate argument, which is that an unrecorded life is a selfish life.

Cruzzi shakes his head at this piece of foolishness but says nothing. (Bad enough to be wobbly and squint-sided at his age, but to be encumbered with garrulousness too!) The truth is that except for those of Orwell and Pritchett, autobiography is a form that offends him. The cosy cherishing of self is only part of the problem. There is the inevitable lack of perspective, not to mention hideous evasions, settlings of scores, awesome preciosity, and the appalling melted fat of rumination, barrels of it, boatloads. Most of the people in the world, he tells Halpenny, could write their autobiographies in one line.

"Ha!" Tom shouts, spraying milk. "Impossible."

"One sentence then," Cruzzi concedes.

"Jesus, God," Tom breathes. "The cynicism, the cheap cynicism. You of all people. I don't believe it. And you a humanist."

"Ex-humanist."

"Since when ex?"

"Since . . . " Cruzzi looks evasively to the ceiling.

"You honestly can sit there and tell me that a whole human life can be boiled down to one shitty little fucking sentence?"

"How about one *long* sentence then?" Cruzzi suggests slyly.

Frederic Cruzzi: His (Unwritten)
One-Sentence Autobiography

Frederic Georges Cruzzi was born eighty years ago in
the French city of Grenoble, the second son of happily
mismatched parents (Mohammed Cruzzi, formerly of
Casablanca, a professor of middle eastern languages, and
Monique Roche Cruzzi, a shy, pretty, musically able
woman), and in that exquisite mountain-ringed city, now
bitterly contaminated by the chlorine industry, the young
Cruzzi was educated, formally and informally, by exposure
to languages and to the arts — though not to science — and
to people who were for the most part kind, following which
he spent a number of years travelling and testing the shock
of strangeness in such places as Morocco (a second home to
him), Turkey, India, Japan, and the United States (the world
being in those days, before the invention of work visas and
inflation, more accessible, more welcoming) and acquiring
along the way a taste for women and for literature and
supporting himself by becoming a journalist, a profession
that was continually carrying him to unlikely places, one of
them being, ironically, the French town of Gap, not far from
his home city of Grenoble, where he happened to meet at a
small supper party a young student by the name of Hildë
Joubert, a rather large-boned girl with straight yellow hair
parted in the middle, who had grown up in the hamlet of
La Motte-en-Champsaur (where her father kept goats) and
who was possessed of a shining face in which Cruzzi
glimpsed the promise of his future happiness, though it took
him a week before he found the courage to declare his
love — in the museum at Gap, as it happened, standing
before a hideous oil painting, even then peeling away from
its frame, depicting Prometheus being fawned upon by a

dozen lardy maidens — after which the two of them lived
for some years in England, Hildë finishing her dissertation
on the poet Rilke, and Cruzzi working on the staff of a
newspaper in the city of Manchester, where they bought
a semi-detached suburban house (Didsbury) with a garden
and fruit trees, produced a baby son, Armand, and decided
one midsummer night when the English sky glowed laven-
der in the west and seemed to beckon, that they would
emigrate to Canada (where they naively believed they might
keep a foothold on the French language), an excellent
choice, as it turned out, since a newspaper in the small
(population: 50,000) lakeside city of Kingston (King's town;
the name promised history) was at that time looking for a
new managing editor, a position offering that extremely
rare combination of independence and security, and which
Cruzzi — despite his socialism — was to enjoy for more
than three decades, though the death of Armand came
near to breaking his heart, and would have if he hadn't
had his work at the paper to occupy him, as well as a small
literary venture, the Peregrine Press, which he and Hildë
launched in order that they might print the work of a
number of new Canadian poets who had come to their
attention. Mary Swann of Nadeau Township being perhaps
the most singular, a poet that Hildë found endearingly
"rough" in technique, but as fine a poet in her way as the
great Rilke — a rather extravagant comparison, but one
with which Cruzzi partly concurred, though both he and
Hildë kept their estimation to themselves for reasons they
avoided mentioning even to each other, and that Cruzzi,
now eighty years old, must carry alone.

* * *

Frederic Cruzzi: Some Recent
Invitations and Replies

September 5

Dear Editor Cruzzi:

Once again it's the fall of the year and we of the
Ontario Bay Jaycees are getting together for our annual
blast-off banquet. September 30 is the big day, and as usual
we're going all out for a great evening. It is my special
privilege to invite you to be this year's banquet speaker,
and we hope you'll do us the honours. What we usually
appreciate by way of a talk is something short and snappy
and full of humour. Fifteen minutes is the absolute maxi-
mum. We've found that after turkey and trimmings
nobody's in the mood for deep thoughts. Rumour has it
your after-dinner speeches are a barrel of laughs and
appreciated by one and all. Your own meal will of course
be gratis. Hoping you will reply soon due to the fact that
we have to get our program to the printers pronto.

Yours truly,
J. Wade Hollinghead
(Hollinghead Hardware), Bath, Ontario

September 8

Dear Mr. Hollinghead:

Thank you for your kind invitation, but I am afraid
you and I have both been ill-served by rumour. I am no
longer *Editor* Cruzzi, having retired from the *Banner*
more than ten years ago. Laughs by the barrel have never
been my commodity. I am a strict vegetarian, eschewing
fowl as well as other animal proteins. I am long-winded
and bad-tempered and, since suffering a slight stroke,

unpleasant in appearance. In short, I am afraid I will not "do" for the Ontario Bay Jaycees.

Yours,
F. Cruzzi

September 7

My dear Freddy,

Come and give me some cheer. I promise you roast lamb and a good bottle of wine. Possibly artichokes. Certainly my usual mustard sauce. Any evening will do, but make it soon. Forgive me, Freddy, but you've been alone too much since Hildë died. (I miss her too, and, selfishly, I miss your company.)

Yours,
Pauline

September 8

My dear Pauline,

I've just this minute written a shameful and pompous letter to a Mr. Hollinghead of Hollinghead Hardware in Bath, declining an unwanted invitation and claiming to be a vegetarian and curmudgeon. I hope I can be better company in your presence. Would next Friday do?

Your uncivilized old friend,
F. C.

September 15

Dear F,

I'll come right to the point. I think it's time you stirred yourself and came to Montreal for a visit. Thanksgiving to be precise. Come! I can't bear to think of you in that big house by yourself with time hanging on your hands. And I can't imagine why on earth you had the phone disconnected. What if there is an emergency? What if you need a doctor

or something? And how would I get hold of you? Think
about it. And think about coming for Thanksgiving. You
could take the train. You used to love the train.

Take care,
Simone

October 3

Dearest Simone,

Many thanks for your card. Thanksgiving is impossible, I'm afraid, much as the thought of family tempts me.
I'm loath to leave home for long these days. I seem to require
certain things around me, my books especially. And I still
look in at the *Banner* now and then, and there's the Friday
column, of course. The column is fast becoming a burden,
since (to tell the truth) it is increasingly difficult to be genial
and carping at one and the same time, or even to think of
topics worth rumbling and rambling about. In the last
month I've covered false gentility, technological insult, the
crimes of local politicians and sins against the language —
and now must thrust about for something freshly abhorrent.
I enclose my piece on telephone tyranny, which partly
explains my present state of disconnectedness. (The real
problem, If you insist on knowing, is the press of invitations
from long-lived widows, Hildë's dear old friends, chiefly,
who beseech me daily to come for suppers, lunches, bridge
games, concerts, picnics, whatever. They believe me to be
in need of comfort, and, as you know, comfort has always
been the focus of my deepest skepticism.) And then there are
the antiquarians, *les bouqinistes* (one in particular) who
pester me via the telephone about selling my books and
other oddments — as if I ever would.

Your loving,
F.

October 8

Dear Frederic Cruzzi:

I have been trying to reach you for some time by telephone, but without success. As Chairman of the Steering Committee for the Swann Symposium to be held in January at the Harbourview Hotel in Toronto (tentative details enclosed) I would like to invite you to be our Keynote Speaker. We on the Committee are all fully cognizant of your role as Mary Swann's first (and only) publisher and one who early glimpsed her extraordinary (to my mind) textual genius. It seems, therefore, eminently appropriate to the members of the Committee (unanimous, in fact) that you be given a leading role in this first — though not, we hope, last — scholarly gathering to be held in her honour.

I understand that you have not been in the best of health recently, but we do, nevertheless, hope you will do us the honour of accepting. Will you be kind enough to contact me as soon as possible?

Yours very truly,
Willard W. Lang, Chm, Dept. of Eng.
University of Toronto

P.S. You probably don't remember that we met some four years ago when I was bold enough to knock on your door while passing through Kingston. We had a most interesting (to me) discussion on modern poetics, as I recall, and on the work of Mrs. Swann. Please give my regards to your wife who, I remember, was kind enough to give me a cup of tea and a magnificent slice of walnut cake.

* * *

October 15

Dear Professor Lang,

I am sorry to say I am unable, for reasons of health and temperament, to take part in your "symposium." It has always seemed to me that the glory of Mary Swann's work lies in its innocence, the fact that it does not invite scholarly meddling or whimsical interpretation. As a close reader of her "text," you will remember the lines that conclude her second water poem:

Let me hide.
Let this kneeling-down pain
Of mine
Wait safe inside.

Of course it would be ludicrous to interpret these lines as a plea that we not read her work. Poets, after all, write in order to show others their singleness of heart and mind. But I do believe Mrs. Swann would resist with all her "kneeling-down pain" any attempt to analyse and systematize what came out of her as naturally as did her own breath. I often think of the sage who commented, " Critics are to art as ornithologists are to birds." I remain grateful for the words and rhythms Mrs. Swann left us, and I have no wish to tamper with their meaning. Furthermore, it would cause me grief to hear others doing so.

Yours,

F. Cruzzi

P.S. My late wife would have been pleased, I know, that you have remembered her, *and* her walnut cake. As for me, I do indeed remember your visit and have often wondered what became of the poems you discovered under Mrs. Swann's kitchen linoleum.

* * *

October 20

Dear Freddy,

The flowers are lovely and you are a dear to have
sent them. I'm sure the sight of them will speed my con-
valescence and bring me good cheer. But I can't help
wondering if *you* aren't the one who needs cheering.
When you were here the other evening you seemed somehow quieter than usual, a little sunk in your thoughts. Are
you still dwelling on South Africa? I hope not, for what
can any of us do? Let's you and me have a cheery drink
together next Friday, any time after five. I'm afraid,
though, I'll have to ask you to bring along the gin since I
won't be allowed out on these wretched crutches for
another ten days.

Yours,
Pauline

October 23

My dear Pauline,

Just a note to say I'll be there on Friday with a bottle
of Beefeater. We can console each other. I will question
you about your poor fracture and your insomnia, and you
may pry if you like into my current vexations, most of
which I've brought upon myself. I miss my telephone for
one thing, but hubris prevents me from contacting Ma
Bell. And I've recently turned down, viciously, mockingly,
arrogantly, and with a wide scatter of sneering quotation
marks, an invitation to a symposium on Mary Swann
that I now think I might rather have enjoyed. (What
wickedness makes me so eager to snub the academic
world?) Some of the spiritual poison has overflowed into
my column — don't tell me you haven't noticed — and
certainly my last piece on free-roaming dogs has caused

hard feelings. It was Hildë, you know, who kept my malice under control, her daily innoculations of goodness, something in her more delicately balanced. Ah well . . .

Until Friday,

F

November 1

Dear F.C.,

Bravo and keep it up for crissake. The mail's been raining down steadily since the famous dog piece (pro, con, mid-fence, you name it). And the thing on abolishing the senate got good vigorous waves too. Judy and Fran and I were sitting around the other day going through the mail sack and got to wondering if you'd maybe do us two columns a week instead of the one. Say, Tuesday and Saturday kind of thing. I know it would be a break with tradition, but it's terrific for circulation and gives the poor folks out there something to chew over besides the bloody Middle East. Let me know what you think. I don't suppose there's any chance of your getting your phone reconnected, is there? You might as well be on the moon instead of across town.

A suggestion for a future column!! How about pour-ing a little timely vitriol on pink plastic flamingos? Judy sends her love. Fran too. Also me.

TSH

November 6

My dear Tom,

Your note has just arrived; that's six days for a quarter of an ounce of paper to travel half a mile. The moon indeed!

I'm afraid I must gratefully decline your twice-weekly

column suggestion, since it's difficult enough gathering ire for one. My ability to become incensed declines along with my various other physical parts, and I find that working up a lather even once a week is landing me in difficulties. The fact is, I *like* dogs. I believe, to a certain extent, in the senate. I admire courtesy, false *or* genuine. The majority of politicians *are* well-intentioned, strange as it seems. The English language *must* be kept pliable and open and out of the hands of pedants like myself. And the telephone is one of the world's greatest conveniences. (I intend to get hooked up again in the New Year, as soon as the fuss has died down.) As you can see, my venting of spleen, now that it has become an artificial exercise, is depriving me of those beliefs and pleasures that have sustained my life. Nevertheless I will continue the Friday column for another year at least, a creaky perseverance being the prime disease of old age. But I'm thinking seriously of coming out *in favour* of something next week, just to see if I'm still capable of writing a piece that doesn't "take umbrage."

If I may make a suggestion, Tom, one syndicated column of advice for the lovelorn is quite enough in my opinion. And you may want to think about cancelling that "Advice to Golden Agers" fellow. We're all going down the chute anyway, and that idiot's little rays of sunshine are insulting.

F. C.

P.S. Afraid I cannot throw my heart into a condemnation of flamingos, nor the casual effrontery of garden elves, nor even Black Sambo at the gatepost. I feel quite sure these trinkets are purchased and displayed in an innocent attempt to ornament a bleak world, and how can one attack an impulse so simple and human as that?

November 7

Dear Mr. Cruzzi,

I apologize for bothering you once again with what at
first glance may appear to be a commercial inquiry. You
may remember that we spoke on the phone two or three
times early in the fall and at that time you made it quite
clear that you were not interested in selling any portion of
your personal library, nor were you anxious to avail yourself of the sort of inventory and evaluation services in
which our firm specializes.

This letter is written, frankly, in the hope that you
may have reconsidered and may now want to liquidate
your holdings and enjoy the benefit of alternate investment or disposable income for travel, charity and so on. It
has been our experience that many people wait too long to
dispose of their valuables, so that at the time of settling an
estate, those articles most treasured and revered during a
lifetime become neglected and overlooked by heirs.
Instead of finding their way into the hands of those who
would most appreciate them, cherished collections (books
in particular) are broken up and scattered, or sometimes
even destroyed by careless handling.

The special focus of our firm is the matching of books
with discriminating collectors. While we are happy to consider entire inventories, we also deal in partial collections
and even with individual volumes. At the moment for
instance, we have a buyer keenly searching for first-edition
Hemingway. Another active collector whom we represent
has a special interest in the poet Mary Swann, whose work
you yourself published in the not-so-distant past.

I can assure you that our firm appreciates and pays the
top market price for such volumes. Indeed, in certain
cases, such as Mrs. Swann's rather curious little book, we

are prepared to offer well above the going price, depending on condition, of course.

We invite you, at least, to consider our services and to contact us at the New York mailing address or to telephone the toll-free number indicated in our letterhead.

Yours very truly,
Book Browsers Inc.

November 11

Dear Book Browser:

I address you as such since you offer no other name. Please do not worry yourself further about what will befall my "estate" after my death. I have an extremely alert daughter-in-law who appreciates fully the value of the library that my late wife and I spent fifty years accumulating. What she will do with the collection when it becomes hers is up to her, but while I am still alive, and I expect to remain alive for some time, I intend to see that the library remains intact. My books, dear Book Browser, are a comfort, a presence, a diary of my life. What more can I say?

If it will ease your mind and prevent further communication, I will assure you that nothing of the Hemingway school occupies my shelves. As for the four remaining copies of *Swann's Songs* (all that are left of the original 250 copies my wife and I published under the Peregrine Imprint), I have made provisions in my will that they are to go to the Queen's University Library here in Kingston.

And so I am afraid, Book Browser, that I cannot be of help to you, nor you to me.

Respectfully yours,
Frederic Cruzzi

November 16

Dear Mr. Cruzzi,

My name is Sarah Maloney, and I'm a fellow Swannian. Recently I've had a phone call from Willard Lang, chairman of the Steering Committee for the Swann Symposium, saying you had declined the committee's invitation to be our keynote speaker. I can tell you that we are all downcast at this news.

I'm writing to see if I can possibly persuade you, instead, to take part in an informal question-and-answer session concerning the original publication of *Swann's Songs* by your own Peregrine Press. This hypothetical event might take place on the second or third day of the meetings, after the academic stiffness has been leached from our bones. Those of us in the Swann industry can endlessly speculate, but you're the one who midwifed the original text and the only one to lay eyes (and hands) on the manuscript — which I understand was grievously lost some years ago. What a tragedy.

Speaking selfishly, I'd like very much to meet you and hear your impressions of Mary Swann. To me she remains maddeningly enigmatic, not only her work but herself. How did all those words get inside her innocent head? Perhaps you know. I think you may. I hope you'll tell me. Please reconsider and come to the symposium. We can talk and talk.

With sincere good wishes,
Sarah Maloney (Ms.)

November 26

My dear Ms. Maloney,

Your charming letter arrived today. (Forgive me for suspecting that you make rather a specialty of charming letters. Certainly you flatter me with your suggestion that

I understand the secret of Mary Swann's power; in fact, I am as baffled as the next person by her preternatural ability to place two ordinary words side by side and extract a kilowatt, and sometimes more, much more, from them.) At any rate, I am both seduced and persuaded by your invitation, and feel this crisp fall morning decidedly anticipatory — though I will probably regret my decision in a week's time.

As for my possible contribution, perhaps it would be useful to those at the symposium if I were to talk for a few minutes in a generalized "midwifery" way about how I came to know Mrs. Swann, though I expect the story of her bringing me her poems on that long-ago snowy day is fairly well known. I might also describe briefly, if it would be of interest, the odd clutter of paper, or "manuscript" as you call it, on which the poems were written. I'm not at all sure myself that I would call such a heap of scraps a *manuscript*, and I cannot agree with you that the loss of it is "tragic." (As a matter of fact, my late dear wife used it for wrapping up some fish bones after a particularly fine meal of local whitefish, but I believe that story too is well documented.)

Furthermore, as an old newspaper man, rather than a professional scholar, I may have rather less reverence than you for the holiness of working papers. If you are familiar with Urdu poetry, or indeed with the oral tradition of most of the world's literature, you will know that this cherishing of original manuscripts is a relatively new phenomenon, and one that I find puzzling. A manuscript is, after all, only a crude representation of that step between creative thought and artefact, and might just as usefully be employed as kindling for a fire or in the wrapping of fishbones.

Frankly, the endless checking of one text against another, this tyranny of accuracy that rules the academic world, is all rather tiresome. I have found that it is sometimes better to look at the universe with a squint, to subject oneself to a deliberate distortion, and hope that out of the 'jumbled vision, or jumbled notes if you like, will fall the accident that is the truth. So please, Ms. Maloney, don't "grieve" for the loss of a few shreds of paper. As you surely know, there are other things to spend your grief upon.

> Yours,
> F. Cruzzi

P.S. May I compliment you on your handwriting — the almost engraved quality of your uppercase C's in particular, and the deep whimsical, old-fashioned way you indent your paragraphs — very pretty indeed.

December 7

My dear Freddy,

Let me say first that you have nothing, nothing, nothing to reproach yourself for. I am not, as you suggest in your note, offended, and I am sure Hildë and my own dear Barnie, too, would think it the most natural thing in the world. You are not ready yet for mellow avuncularity, and why should you be? I was only a little startled, that's all — it's been so long. Oh, my dear, I am finding this difficult to put down on paper. What I know is that words are rather pathetic at times and that what we need most is to reach past them and touch each other. That's all that happened, such a little thing, but what happiness it brought me, though you seem to have thought otherwise.

Please come on the 17th. I am going to do partridges with that sauterne sauce you're forever talking about, and with luck there'll be strawberries in the market.

Yours,
Pauline

December 10

My sweet Pauline,

I will be there, bearing a walnut cake, just this minute out of the oven and ready for its brandy bath.

Until then,
F.

December 11

Dear Mr. Cruzzi,

You probably won't remember meeting me at the Library Association meeting a few years back, when you were the guest speaker. We had a little visit afterwards. Maybe it will jog your memory if I tell you that I am the librarian (part-time) out in Nadeau and that I was a great friend of Mary Swann's before she passed away. Wouldn't she be surprised how famous she's got to be? I hope there's some way she knows.

Not so long ago I received an invitation to her symposium in Toronto, and last week I had a nice little note from Professor Lang saying you would be coming too and would be giving one of the speeches, in fact.

To get to the point, Professor Lang suggested that if I was driving down to Toronto maybe I could give you a ride, but the problem is, crazy as it seems, I've never learned to drive a car, and so I'll be taking the bus into Kingston on Monday morning (Jan. 3) and then getting the 10:00 A.M. train. Whenever I go into Toronto, which isn't half as often as I wish I could go, I take the train. Once I took a bus all the way and didn't like it half as much and got bus sick part way there to make matters worse.

This may seem awfully forward of me, but I thought maybe we could take the train together and keep each other company on the way. We could meet at the train station in Kingston about 9:30 or so, in plenty of time to buy our tickets, unless we get them earlier, which I always do. So as you'll know who I am, I'm five feet, four inches, and people say I'm on the thin side these days due to being a bit under the weather of late, though I'm bound to pick up before too long. I've got glasses with blue-grey frames and I'll be wearing a brown suede coat if there's no snow, but if it's snowing, as it probably will be, I'll be in my old down-filled blue coat with a grey fur collar (just artificial).

By now you've probably made other arrangements for getting there, so please don't think my feelings will be hurt if I get there (the train station) and you're not there. It was just that Professor Lang asked if I could drive you down, but as I explained, I don't drive a car. Which is ridiculous living out in the country like I do. But anyway, I love the train, every minute of it, especially the part along the lake.

Sincerely,
Rose Hindmarch

P.S. Merry Christmas

December 18

Dear Ms. Hindmarch,

I expect Lang wrote and told you I was elderly and infirm and muddled and needed looking after, all of which is true or partly true, and so it is with gratitude that I accept your kind invitation to be your travelling companion.

I too love the train, especially at this time of the year. We can gaze out the window and you can tell me all about your good friend Mary Swann, whom I am sorry to say I met only briefly. It has been some years since I've passed through Nadeau, but I have been told that the local museum has a special Mary Swann display.

I send you best wishes for good health and for a happy Christmas.

Yours,

F. Cruzzi

P.S. Since we've met before, you'll recognize me easily, though I am somewhat more tottery than I was when we talked at the Library Association.

Frederic Cruzzi: His Dreams

Everyone is familiar with the Persian poet Rashid and what he has written about the power of dreams, how if all the dreams dreamt by men on a single random night were gathered into a bundle and hurled into the early morning sky, the blaze of it would:

> . . . put to shame
> The paltry shrivelled,
> Fires of the sun.

When Frederic Cruzzi's wife, Hildë, was alive, the two of them occasionally made gifts to each other of their dreams as they moved about in their large old-fashioned kitchen preparing breakfast. Hildë, rhythmically buttering toast, described wild animals, brightly coloured food, sudden nakedness, and misplaced objects, objects that remained stubbornly unidentified.

Cruzzi himself, ever the editor, was sometimes guilty of polishing his disjointed dreams for Hildë's benefit, giving them a sense of shape and applying small, elegant, decorative touches. (There are many modes of estrangement, the poet Rashid has observed, and elegance is one.) Cruzzi's dreams, as conveyed to Hildë, were filled with flowers, with long healing conversations, with the whimsical or heroic defiance of gravity. A lack of linearity lent charm, and still does. He is forever in his dreams bumping his forehead against some surprise of texture or weather or, even at age eighty, watching his hands, which are the symbols, the messengers, of his whole self, travelling across a landscape of undiscovered female bodies, breasts, clefts, thighs, ankles — and all these mountains and vales pinned down by the patient cobalt eyes of his wife, Hildë.

Ever since her death a year ago — a single cataclysmic explosion of the cranial artery — Cruzzi has kept his dreams to himself. He would sooner plunge his hand into boiling water than bore his good friends with his dreams. (Whereas these same friends approach the subject of *their* dreams rather frequently, and whenever they do Cruzzi knows he's in for a dull time of it.)

Nevertheless, his dreams continue, and are, if anything, more varied, more vivid, more Dadaist in their narration, and more persistent in their reaching after odd tossed chunks of history. Their pursuit of him into old age amazes him, and he is perplexed always by their utter uselessness, sometimes comparing their substance to the magically soft, recurring skin of lint he peels from the steel mesh in the door of the electric clothes dryer. (There's a certain pleasure in this peeling, he thinks; but to what use can the clean, gathered handful of fluff be put?)

The idea that dreams are the involuntary poetry of the mind appeals to him, but he rejects it. He is also by nature skeptical of that theory that dreams accumulate and become part of the making and unmaking of the universe, and equally distrusts the notion that dreams exorcise guilt or fear or mend the imagination. He doesn't know what he believes, and remains as baffled as the poet Mary Swann (cosmic cousin to the great Rashid) who felt herself tormented by:

> What seems
> A broken memory that tears
> At whitened nerves
> Like useless dreams
> The night preserves
> In sealed undreamed-
> Of jars.

Early in September, or perhaps late in August, after a short afternoon's walk in the woods that began behind his house, Cruzzi fell asleep in an armchair by an open window, and in his first breath caught a glimpse of his mother's white hand attempting to open a bottle of mineral water and, after making a struggle of it, handing it to her husband. In the foreground, a red cloth is spread on the grass, a picnic is in progress, and the sleeping Cruzzi catches with his second breath the round Muslim face of his father — soft, slightly overripe, as smooth and hairless as a pear, and made even rounder by a wonderful spreading candour. How they smile, the two of them! The radiance of their smiles forms the melody that keeps this dream aloft, even as a fly buzzes in Cruzzi's ear, threatening to whisk the picnic cloth out of

sight and overturn the bottle of mineral water. The smiles of
the two picnickers are directed upward into the leaves of a
small dusty tree, at each other, at the rippling water poured
from the bottle, and at Cruzzi himself who is somehow
there and not there.

Walking through this dream, and through all Cruzzi's
dreams, are the stout, sun-browned legs of his wife, Hildë.
Mahogany is how he thinks of those legs, solid, polished
lengths of hardwood between walking shorts and laced
boots, legs brought to full strength on her annual hiking
tours in the Appalachians or along the Bruce Trail. The
roundness of Hildë's brown thighs on the picnic cloth overwhelms the multiplicity of other forms and gestures and
brings a whimper to Cruzzi's groin, breaking through the
fragile arrangement of sandwiches and fruit and pulling
him slowly and painfully to consciousness. In October, on
that particular Saturday night when clocks are officially
turned back one hour, Cruzzi sleeps soundly, thanks to a
nightcap of warm whisky. It is almost as though the fibres
still strong beneath his aged, flaking skin are fused to those
other fibres that make up the smooth cotton sheets of his
bed.

But toward morning, perhaps because of the dislocation
of the single unaccommodated hour, his sleep is invaded by
violence. The violence comes in the form of a voice that
achieves a loudness rare in dreams. It goes on and on,
booming against the tight weave of the sheets, and Cruzzi,
sleeping, his hands curled into fists, struggles to hear what
the voice is saying, but can hear only a roar of anger and
injury. It is his own voice, of course, and this makes his
inability to distinguish words all the more frustrating. An
oldfashioned clock strikes the hour and announces that the
floor — for a patterned floor has suddenly established itself

in the void — is tilting dangerously. Hildë is running, her strong brown legs frightened, trying to keep her balance; but the voice, loud enough now to tighten a muscle in Cruzzi's shoulder and bid him turn on his side, threatens to pull down the floor along with the slippery tiled walls and the beautiful ceiling tracked with blue-black hieroglyphics, which, because of their astringent colour and configuration, remain maddeningly unreadable.

Cruzzi, still sleeping, shifts the whole of his body and brings a bony thumb into the cavity of his mouth.

Landscapes, earthquakes and sharp cliffs give way suddenly to an Alpine meadow and warm sunlight. (It is a cold night in Kingston, the temperature reaches minus ten, low for this time of year, and Cruzzi gropes in his sleep for the wool-filled quilt he keeps at the foot of the bed.)

Hildë is laughing, pulling away from him, and showing a smile that has turned provisional. Then she is arranging fruit in a bowl, placing the plums carefully so that the soft blue cleft that marks each one catches a streak of lustre from the sun. But no — it's not the sun, but the moon. She dances lightly into his arms, giving him the kind of embrace that promises nothing, then whirls away on legs that are thinner, whiter, that shine from calf to thigh with a strange lacteal whiteness. (Cruzzi wakens briefly, scratches his genitals, acknowledges soreness in his joints, and is carried with his next exhalation through the doorway of a cottage where he discovers a stairway, corridors, a great hall brilliantly lit, a table set for twelve, and stately music.)

The face on the television screen has been talking for several minutes now. The subject is Libya, a hijacked plane, a ter-rorist's telephone call, impossible demands. Gadaffi appears briefly, peers with fanatical eyes into the camera, then wavers and flickers. After a minute his wide retreating image seems to float. Cruzzi can feel his own face begin to fade and dissolve into a miasma of dots — then his brown-speckled hand on his coffee cup and then the length of his arm. He is being eaten up by light. He is a young man standing in the corridor of a train and in his hand is a postcard. Hieroglyphics again, but this time he struggles harder to make them out. The words are in French, written very large, and they promise foolishness, gaiety, passion, love... especially love.

Snow is everywhere, filling up the woods behind Cruzzi's house and the crevasses between the drifts of his breath. From nowhere comes a saving hand, warm, pale in colour, talcum enriched, a gold ring gleaming, a few muffled words that point toward a dream inside this dream, a house-like cave built into a hillside.

But the door is sealed by pressure, his bladder again, then a seizure of coughing, and numbness in the feet, and his loud voice filling the kitchen. Hildë is weeping, her brown arms over her eyes, and he is striking out at her with his voice, with his hand, even his fist, so that she falls under the snow, which is deeper than ever now and so heavy that he must scramble like a madman in his effort to rescue her.

Frederic Cruzzi: His Short Untranscribed History of the Peregrine Press: 1956 – 1976

The *Kingston Banner*, even before Frederic Cruzzi arrived from England to be its editor, had perforce been something of an anomaly as a regional newspaper, its constituency being an uneasy yoking of town and gown, farmers, civil servants, and petit-bourgeoisie. Its advertisers were the owners of such small, conservative family businesses as the Princess Tearoom and Diamond Bros. Colonial Furniture Emporium, but its most vociferous readers were revolutionaries and progressives of the academic stripe. The *Banner*'s editorial policy, as a result, tended to be skittish, gliding between pragmatic waltz and feinting soft-shoe, and for that reason was always, and still is, perused with a knowing wink of the eye. This is accepted by everybody. It is also accepted that the real battles are fought on the Letters-to-the-Editor page, which occasionally spills over to a second page and once — in 1970, with the War Measures Act — to a third. Here, despite quaint temporary alliances and retreats into unanimity, the struggle assumes those classic polarities between those who would stand still and those who would move forward.

The boisterous, ongoing warfare of the Letters page has mostly been regarded by Cruzzi as analogous to a healthy game of societal tennis, both amusing and lifegiving. Sometimes, too, it yields an inch of enlightenment. But warfare abruptly stops at the Entertainment page. Even among those readers who would never dream of subscribing to the Kingston Regional Theatre or the fledgling Eastern Ontario Symphony, and who would rather dive naked into a patch of summer thistle than be caught reading one of the books reviewed in the *Banner*, there is a silent consensus that *art* is somehow privileged and deserving of protection. A dirty book discovered in a school library may raise a brief fuss, but the general concept of art is sacred in the Kingston region, and lip service, if nothing else, is paid to it.

When Cruzzi took over the *Banner* he was bemused, and so was Hildë, by a long-running feature on the Entertainment page known as "The Poet's Corner." A number of local poets, mostly elderly, always genteel, vied for this small weekly space, dropping off batches of sonnets at the *Banner* office on Second Street, as well as quatrains, sestinas, limericks, haiku, bumpity-bump, and shrimpy dactyls, all attached to such unblushing titles as "Seagull Serenade," "Springtime Reverie," "Ode to Fort Henry," "Birches at Eventide," "The Stalwart Flag Old Sadie," "The First Bluebird," "Sailors Ahoy," "Cupid in Action," "The Trillium," "The Old Thrashing Crew," "The Eve of Virtue," and so on. Payment, regardless of length or verse form, was five dollars, but this rather small sum in no way discouraged the number of submissions. Cruzzi, in his first month in Kingston, looked carefully at both quantity and quality and immediately announced plans to terminate "The Poet's Corner."

What a fool he was in those days, he with his heavy tweed suits and strangely unbarbered hair, his queer way of talking, his manners and pronouncements. The public outcry over the cancellation of "The Poet's Corner" was unprecedented and appeared to come from all quarters of the community. He was labelled a philistine and a brute journalist of the modern school. The word foreigner was invoked: Frenchy, Limey, Wog — there was understandable confusion here. Readers might be willing to tolerate the new typeface imposed on them, and no one seemed to miss the old "Pie of the Week" feature when it disappeared from the Women's page, but they refused to surrender Li'l Abner and "The Poet's Corner." Culture was culture. Even the advertisers became restless, and Cruzzi, in the interest of comity and suffering a heretic's embarrassment, capitulated, though he let it be known that there would be a two-year interregnum on seagull poems.

In time, because the Kingston literary community was

small, he and Hildë befriended and grew fond of the local poets. Cruzzi even took a certain glee in the awfulness of their product. Herb Farlingham's poem "Springtime Reverie," for instance ("Mrs. Robin in feathered galoshes/ Splashes in puddles chirping 'O my goshes!'"), gave him moments of precious hilarity that were especially welcome after a day spent composing careful, pointed, balanced, and doomed-to-be-ignored editorials on the arms race or the threat of McCarthyism.

In 1955, toward the end of a long golden summer, Cruzzi opened an envelope addressed to "The Poet's Corner," and out fell a single poem, typed for once, titled "Anatomy of a Passing Thought" written by one Kurt Wiesmann of William Avenue, just two streets from Byron Road where Cruzzi and Hildë lived. The sixteen-line poem possessed grace and strength. Light seemed to shine through it. Cruzzi read it quickly, with amazement. One line, toward the end, briefly alarmed him by veering toward sentimentality, but the next line answered back, mocking, witty, and containing that spacey necessary bridge that in the best poetry joins binocular clarity to universal vision. Extraordinary.

It was 5:30 in the afternoon. He took a deep breath and rubbed a hand through his thick, still-unbarbered hair. Hildë was expecting him at home for a picnic supper with friends. Already she would have set the table under the trees, a red table cloth, wine glasses turned upside down, paper napkins folded and weighed down by cutlery. Nevertheless he sat down at his desk and wrote Mr. Wiesmann a letter telling him why his poem was unsuitable for the *Banner*. It was unrhymed. It had no regular metre. It did not celebrate nature, or allude to God, or even to Kingston and its environs. It did not tug at the heartstrings or touch the

tear ducts and was in no way calculated to bring forth a
gruff chuckle of recognition; in short it was too good for
"The Poet's Corner." He ended the letter, "Yours resignedly,
F. Cruzzi," surprising himself; he had not realized his own
resignation until that moment. (Rationality won't rescue
this scene the way, say, a footnote can save a muddled paragraph, but it might be argued that Cruzzi, by this time,
had acquired an understanding and even a respect for his
readers' sensibilities.)

Kurt Wiesmann, a chemist with a local cooking-oil
manufacturer, was delighted with his letter of rejection, and
continued to send the *Banner* unprintable poems. In a year's
time Cruzzi and Hildë had read close to fifty of them, and
they both urged Wiesmann, by now a friend and frequent
visitor in their house, to approach a book publisher. They
were astonished, moved, and entertained by what he wrote,
and felt he should have an audience larger than the two of
them.

But it turned out that publishers in Canada found
Wiesmann's poems "too European;" American publishers
thought them "too Canadian," and a British publisher
sensed "an American influence that might be troubling" to
his readers. Hildë, exasperated, suggested one night —
the three of them were in the kitchen drinking filtered
coffee and eating cheesecake — that they publish the poems
themselves.

In a month's time they were in production. It was Kurt
Wiesmann who suggested the name Peregrine Press.
He was a restless man, tied down by a family and job, but a
traveller by instinct. His book was titled *Inroads* (Hildë's
idea) and was favourably reviewed as "a courageous voice
speaking with the full force of the alienated." A Toronto
newspaper wrote, "The newly launched Peregrine Press

must be congratulated on its discovery of a fresh new Canadian voice."

Their second poet was the elegant Glen Forrestal of Ottawa, later to win a Governor General's Award, who wrote to the Peregrine Press introducing himself as a member of the Kurt Wiesmann fan club and a veteran of several serious peregrinations of his own. Their third poet was the fey, frangible Rhoda MacKenzie, and after that came Cassie Sinclair, Hugh Walkley Donaldson, Mary Swann, Mavis Stockard, w.w. wooley, Burnt Umber, Serge Tawowski, and a number of others who went on to make names for themselves.

Printing was done during off-hours at the *Banner* and paid for out of Cruzzi's pocket. Hildë, who had set up an office in an upstairs bedroom, read the manuscripts that soon came flowing in. She had a sharp eye and, with some notable exceptions, excellent judgement. "Whatever we decide to publish must have a new sound." She said this in a voice that contained more and more of the sonorous Canadian inflection. To a local businessman, whom she attempted to convert into a patron, she said, "We have the responsibility as a small press to work at the frontier."

Along the frontier a few mistakes were inevitably made. Even Hildë admitted she had been taken in by Rhoda MacKenzie's work, that behind its fretwork there was little substance. And both she and Cruzzi regretted the title they chose for Mary Swann's book — *Swann's Songs*. An inexplicable lapse of sensibility. A miscalculation, an embarrassment.

For twenty years the press operated out of the Cruzzi house on Byron Road. Methodically, working in the early mornings after her daily lakeside walk, Hildë read submissions, edited manuscripts, handled correspondence, and attended, if necessary, to financial matters — though bookkeeping took little time since the Peregrine Press never earned a profit and print-runs were small, generally between two hundred and three hundred copies. Always, in the final stages before the publication of a new book, a group of friends, the official board as they called themselves, gathered in the Cruzzi dining-room for a long evening of plum brandy and hard work: collating pages, stapling, gluing covers, the best of these covers designed by Barney Ouilette, and remarkably handsome, with a nod toward modernism and a suggestion of what Hildë liked to call "fire along the frontier."

Her only agony was the problem of what to do with unsuccessful manuscripts. Tenderhearted, she laboured over her letters of rejection, striving for a blend of honesty and kindness, but forbidding herself to give false encouragement, explaining carefully what the press was looking for. These explanations gave her pleasure, as though she were reciting a beloved prayer. "New sounds," she explained, "and innovative technique, but work that turns on a solid core of language."

Despite her tact, there was sometimes acrimony, once an obscene phone call, several times scolding letters impugning her taste. Herb Farlingham, who would have financed the publication of his *Seasoned Sonnets* if Hildë had let him, wept openly. "I'm so terribly sorry," Hildë said, supplying him with tea and a paper towel for his tears. "It's nothing personal, you may be sure." The Peregrine Press, she explained, thankful for a ready excuse, had very early taken a stand on self-publication and was anxious to avoid even the appearance of being a vanity press.

This stricture was put to the test years later when Hildë herself began to write poetry. She had reached the age of fifty, her waist had thickened, and her hair, which was short and straight with a bang over her forehead, was almost completely white. She had a dozen interests, though her ardour, flatteringly, centred on Cruzzi. There was her schedule of reading, her music, her fling at oil painting, her tennis and her hiking, her work with the blind. She was robust, cheerful, impatient, amiable, always occupied, always determined and passionate in her undertakings, pleased as a child with her successes, and smiling with her round face in her failures. That round face of hers, friends said, was unique in its openness, and yet it was a year before she showed her husband what she had been writing. "Here," she said to him late one evening, thrusting a folder forward. "I want you to be absolutely honest with me."

"Poetry?" His eyebrows went up.

She shrugged. "An attempt." It had been years since they'd spoken French at home.

Her poems, he saw with sadness, had no edges, no hardness. The words themselves were pleasing enough, melodious and rather dreamlike, but there was also a quality in some of the lines that he identified as kittenish — and that surprised him. He was reminded of the year Hildë had leaped into oil painting and how her curious, wild abstractions whirled without regard for line or composition; these canvases, relics of a lapsed enthusiasm, were stacked now in the basement, keeping company with the summer screens and garden tools. He wondered if some natural amiability in his wife's nature blocked the imaginative vision. (He *knew* poets, their ever-expanding egos, their righteousness.)

"Well, what do you think then?" Hildë asked him. She was sitting tensely on a footstool inches from his chair. "I want you to be very, very severe."

"They're quite moving," he said. "Some of them."

She was not fooled. "Do you think the Peregrine might . . . " She let the suggestion drift off. One of her hands smoothed her skirt over a round knee.

He looked at her with amazed pity. A mingling of tenderness and caution dictated his reply. "You remember," he said slowly, "that we decided in the beginning that we would avoid — "

"They're not much good," Hildë said, more baffled than heartbroken. She gave one of her steep, explosive laughs. "I was just trying to express — well, I don't know what exactly. Maybe that's the problem." She got up with an awkward little jerk to make coffee, a gesture so self-protective that it lingered in Cruzzi's mind far longer than her words. "You're right," she said firmly. "We did make that decision, and we must stick to it."

By 1977 Hildë was engaged in the anti-nuclear movement, and the Peregrine Press began to languish. Then she died.

Twenty years, Cruzzi has since learned, is the usual life of a small literary press. The vital juices get used up, energy or a willingness to take risks. The manuscripts — they still arrive from time to time — begin to look creased and not very clean. The corners curl. Some of them bear coffee rings.

It's been quite some time since Cruzzi has seen anything that suggested "fire along the frontier." Every once in a while his conscience gets the better of him, and then he gathers up the accumulated manuscripts, attaches to each one a little printed fiche declaring that the Peregrine Press is no more, and mails them back to their owners. "Good luck elsewhere," he always adds, just as Hildë used to do when she was alive.

* * *

Frederic Cruzzi: An Unwritten Account of the Fifteenth of December, 1965

In his life Frederic Cruzzi has had two loves: the written word and his wife, Hildë. The two loves are compatible but differently ordered, occupying separate berths in his brain and defying explanation or description, something that bothers him not at all.

His own father once told him — and this conversation he now lovingly reviews as he walks in the woods behind his house — the trees bare of leaves, the low junipers underfoot snapping with cold — that love would not exist if the word *love* were taken from the language. At the time he had nodded agreement, happy to be included in his father's solemn abstractions, but destined to outgrow them.

Once in a while, walking like this in shadowed woodland at three o'clock on a winter afternoon, or hearing perhaps a particular phrase of music, or approaching a wave of sexual ecstasy, Cruzzi has felt a force so resistant to the power of syntax, description or definition, so savage and primitive in its form, that he has been tempted to shed his long years of language and howl monosyllables of delight and outrage.

Outrage because these are moments of humility, of dressing down, of rebuke to those, like Cruzzi, who perceive reality through print, the moments when those who are proudly articulate confess their speechlessness. It is as though some enormous noisy motor of which they had not ever been conscious, were suddenly switched off. These moments, and their ability to spring leaks at the edges of language, tend to be exceedingly brief, and Cruzzi has noticed, too, that they are shattered by the least effort to analyse them or extend their duration. Only this morning he stood naked in front of a mirror and regarded the body that both pleased and disgusted him. "Knackers," he pronounced aloud, cupping his balls in a mothy hand, and heard the word slip from its encasement of meaning, and fly, ludicrously, into the air.

Go back to love, he instructs himself, bending stiffly to examine the scars on a young birch. Rodents.

He and Hildë, from the beginning — that convivial evening in the city of Gap, seated around a supper table that was lit by an overhead gas lamp — had felt themselves separated from the others by a narrow arc of privilege. Each, it seemed, at once measured the other's need, though each had been grave, correct, addressing the other with a respectful *vous*, and shaking hands briskly when the party ended. But Cruzzi had not neglected to write down her address in a small notebook he carried, sealing in print that promise he could not have described. He asked if he might see her the following day; a long walk was what he suggested, a walk followed by tea in a café. He determined to take up as much of her day as possible. The cruder stratagems of the *célibataire* wearied him, but he would delight all his life in the miniature theatre of courtship, its gifts and entrances and phrases frozen out of meaning — all this Hildë seemed to grasp. Her response as she stood in the dim foyer had the quality of instinct. By all means a long walk, she told him directly, by all means tea in a café.

Already a brisk adjustment had been made, an understanding reached.

The hold most married people have on each other tends to dwindle fairly quickly, but occasionally accident and temperament, so strangely mingled, keep it buoyant. It might be suggested, in the case of the Cruzzis' marriage, that a curious, possibly shameful need to ameliorate the effects of their foreignness, first in England and later in Canada, was a further bond. Or that the death of their son had the effect of isolating them in their incoherence. Or that the health of the Peregrine Press, in its good years especially, imbued them with a spirit that even close friends judged to be a rebirth of love. Not one of these speculations, however, held much truth.

Their simplicity, their little routines, would always escape others, especially those who thought of passion in terms of appetite and rich, sad sighs of impatience. That even in midlife, and after, Hildë's face was often foolish with affection, that Cruzzi's hand rested frequently on the back of her chair at Kingston concerts or theatricals — these actions falsely signalled to others the devotion of habit that arrives after love's final retreat.

All these supposed mutations and gradations of love Cruzzi would have denied if the question were put to him (it never was), arguing that the regard he and Hildë had for each other was a simple, uncomplicated element like the air he took into his body or the print that swam into his head. Its force, fluctuation, and flavour were not even to be thought of, much less given expression. *They take each other for granted* — that curse hurled at those who embrace their good fortune wordlessly — has always seemed to Cruzzi an unfair challenging of fate. Furthermore, he would have considered it an act of arrogance to believe that he and Hildë had been served with something finer, stronger, and more enduring than the love he has observed between other married people. (A remnant of innocence convinces him that even those who practise public cruelties on each other, are tender in their private moments.)

He did not love Hildë because of her black-currant sherbet or her generous hospitality or her early morning cheerfulness or the way her rounded features took the light, or the graceful, energetic way she leaned over a bed and pounded the air back into a pillow, as though she were doing it a kindness and doing it with the whole of her heart. His range of response did not coalesce around such lists. He was not one to produce an informed rationale about a bond so simple and natural. Such dissection, such *counting of ways*, was frivolous and ignoble. He was, some might think, almost careless of his good fortune.

But just as everyday articles — preserving jars, tea-spoons, loaves of bread — take on the look of sacred objects when seen in exceptional light, so he sometimes looked at his wife and saw her freshly and with the full force of vision. One of these "seizures of the heart," as Cruzzi might describe it (but never did), occurred early in the afternoon of December 15, 1965.

He awakened on that particular morning with a sore throat. Both he and Hildë had long since surrendered their first language, but maladies of the body continued to speak to them with their French names. *Mal à la gorge. Le rheum.* He had gone to bed in good health and wakened like this!

He decided he would spend the morning, at least, in bed. He was still several years from retirement, but not averse to letting the *Banner* run itself occasionally.

Hildë brought him a steaming infusion of thyme. She swore by it, especially for the throat. He drank it, then dozed. He heard her in various parts of the house as she moved about, talking on the telephone, playing the piano, concocting something in the kitchen — he knew before he saw it that it would be a thick soup made with cauliflower, milk, and butter. In times of illness she always made this soup. He ate a bowl of it for lunch, by now dressed and sitting at the kitchen table, and began to feel a little better.

He fished in his pocket for a pencil and wrote down the first paragraph of an editorial that was to be a defence of a new piece of public sculpture. It was an exceptionally cold day. The wind blew hard against the old window frames of the house and, hearing it, he resolved to spend the afternoon, too, at home, sipping his hot tea and working on his column, which was going surprisingly well.

He looked up, slowly, and saw Hildë standing beside him. She was dressed in her warmest clothing — sheepskin boots, woollen ski pants, a bulky parka, her heavy fur-lined mittens, a knitted scarf, and a hat from which wisps of white hair poignantly escaped. "I'm going ice-fishing," she told him, smiling broadly.

She loved to fish at any time of the year, but ice-fishing in particular gave her pleasure, its clumsy paraphernalia and intrinsic paradox — the flashing bitter cold and the calm wait in a warmed hut. Sometimes she went with friends and sometimes alone. Usually she was lucky, bringing home fresh whitefish, which she expertly boned and grilled for dinner; fish never seemed so fresh to her as when pulled miraculously through an opening in the thick ice.

How he had loved her at that moment! More it seemed than at any time in their life together, her strength and imagination and, beneath the impossibly coarse outdoor clothing, her body, all polished wood and knowable clefts. She had removed one mitten, which she held between her teeth, and was bending over, checking the contents of her tackle box, mumbling a little to herself — utterly, endearingly, preoccupied — and the next minute she was gone, the heavy storm door shut behind her, leaving him alone in the house.

It was mostly for this abandonment that he loved her, the unlooked-for gift of an empty afternoon.

The living-room smelled of cold fireplace ashes and (very faintly) of cooked cauliflower. Outside it was dark for so early in the afternoon, a storm coming up, the first big one of the season, but the large, many-paned windows let in enough light to read by. From a bookcase Cruzzi took down his dilapidated copy of Rashid's *Persian Songs* and allowed his eyes to travel over a familiar page.

> On your shoulder a bird alights
> Singing, singing a song without words,
> A song without meaning or wisdom or words,
> A song without asking or giving or words,
> Without kindness or judgement or flattering words.
> On your shoulder a bird alights
> Singing against your loud silence.

He thought to himself, as he had thought many times before, how little he demanded of eastern poetry. The poets of the East lacked western rigour, that ability to build up a universe with the nib of a pen. He conceded that much. The ironies were too slack, the music too rhythmically obvious. But, reading it, he felt himself connected to ancient rhythms that some less ordered part of his brain welcomed. Most of what he knew of love he found amplified in eastern poetry, not its application but its brief transports. Reverberations, he knew, were an aspect of love, which was why, when he picked up a volume of the great Rashid, he asked only for the affirmation of a single moment and no more. The moment stretched; he turned over a page, yawned, glanced out the window at the blown trees and heavy sky, and wondered if Hildë would return home early; he hoped so. After that he may have slept a little in his chair, because when he looked at the clock again it was after three.

The room felt more than usually drafty, and he stirred

himself to organize a heap of kindling and dry wood in the fireplace. He had just got a blaze flickering when he heard the front doorbell. One faint ring, then the stutter of the door knocker, something of entreaty about it that sent him hurrying into the chilly vestibule.

Standing on the stone porch was Mary Swann, though of course he didn't ask her name or even what she wanted. It was far too cold for such preliminaries; later he discovered that the temperature had fallen twenty degrees since noon. He took her arm, murmuring a stream of comforting words, and drew her into the hall, then into the living-room, steering her firmly in the direction of the fireplace.

In those first moments, bewilderment gave her the look of an imbecile. She wore a shapeless black coat, hideous thick fawn stockings and rubber overshoes with buckles. She had no gloves. Around her face was tied a man's plaid muffler. Her face was small, purplish, the mouth working, the eyes squeezed shut as though the room were unbearably bright.

What was the mouth saying, those shrunken lips like rows of stitching? Something grotesquely apologetic. She was so sorry. Sorry to be bothering him. To just drop in like this. To arrive without, without —

He made her sit in a chair, which he drew up to the fire, and he insisted she remove her rubber boots. She drew back, reluctant, and so he leaned over to assist her, feeling like an actor in a fine old play, undoing the buckles, easing them off, ignoring her weak little mew of shame. "Frozen," he said, addressing the feet, now revealed in their thick grey work socks. An obsequious whimper came from her mouth, and he, still relishing his actor's role, continued to rub her feet between his hands, conscious of her acute embarrassment and also of his strange happiness. Under the socks her toes curled tensely; he massaged them, muttering inanities as

one does to children — there, there, it's all right. He was
beginning to drift in his thoughts, to think of the story he
would make of this for Hildë's sake — *a stranger came to the
door and . . .*

"Are you feeling any better?" he asked her.

She nodded mutely.

He offered her sherry, which she refused, shaking her
head and looking at the floor.

Tea?

Her flow of apology began once again, mumbled and
unintelligible. So sorry. Such a bother. She refused to meet
his eyes. Her head bobbed and shook. She was taking up his
valuable time, she said. She should have written a letter
instead of arriving out of the blue like this. It wasn't proper.
It wasn't right.

Tea, he asked again, and she nodded. Her face flushed
with shame. She started to say something, but couldn't go
on. She was so sorry. She never intended —

He fled to the kitchen, put a kettle on, took cups from
the cupboard, giving her time to compose herself, making a
fearful noise with the tea canister, forcing himself to hum a
jaunty little tune, feeling still the shapes of her frozen feet in
his hands. Sugar — he was sure she would want sugar. He
found some fruit cake in a tin and put a large slice on a plate,
then put milk in a little jug. For himself he poured a hefty
brandy, which he sipped as the kettle came slowly to a boil.

He judged her at first to be a woman in her sixties, even
her seventies, something about the hunched sweatered
shoulders and the whiteness of scalp under scanty hair. As
she lifted the teacup to her mouth, he saw that the wrist of
her green cardigan had been mended with grey wool. She
drank the tea greedily, adding milk and sugar and stirring
with terrifying thoroughness, darting little looks in his

direction. He decided at this point that she might be in her fifties, perhaps even her *early* fifties.

Did she behave in a manner that could be described as deranged? he was asked later. Was her speech incoherent? Did she mention any specific fears or threats? Exhibit paranoid signs? Did she at any time mention her husband?

Some of these questions came from the police, some from a reporter on Cruzzi's own paper, Freddy Waggoner, who later drifted off into television work. Other questions arose at the inquest, which was held in mid-January, 1966, and still others came from a Professor Willard Lang of the University of Toronto — this was more than fifteen years later — and still later from the egregious Morton Jimroy, who had recently appointed himself Mary Swann's official biographer.

To most of these questions Cruzzi said no. Signs of instability? No. Not even what you might call eccentricity? No. She was, of course, very, very cold, having walked more than a mile from the bus station in appalling weather. She was perhaps excessively anxious about the time of her return bus and several times asked to be told the time. And naturally, being a timid woman, she was nervous about how she and her bag of poems would be received.

But you say she gradually relaxed?

"Yes, once she had warmed up and had drunk two or three cups of tea, she grew composed.

It was then, Cruzzi said, that he realized she was younger than he had originally thought. (In fact she was forty-nine. She would have been fifty years old the following February.)

Can you describe her physical appearance, her face, her way of wearing her hair? These questions from the indefatigable Jimroy.

The hair could be easily enough described, or rather, not

described, since it was without shape or colour. Skinned
back, the scalp barely covered. He could not, in fact, remember much about Mrs. Swann's hair. Medium brown, he told
Jimroy. Slightly wavy over the ears.

Would you say she was tall or short? Fat or thin?

Difficult to remember. She was seated for most of the
time, remember. Not tall, certainly not tall. Not fat either,
no. She had a look of being wasted. Thin, but thin without
the lankiness that accompanies ease and good health.

Wasted, you say? Jimroy at his most persistent, full of
nerviness.

If the poor woman had had a driver's licence, there
would have been a record of her height and weight. But,
alas, she did not. And there were no doctor's records, none
that could be found, at any rate. Apparently she wasn't in
the habit of visiting a doctor, though once she had seen a
dentist — in Elgin — where she had several teeth pulled.
No x-rays, however.

Surely it's not possible for a person in this century to go
through a life without being measured or weighed or x-
rayed?

It seems it *is* possible. Her only child was delivered at
home — Incredible!

You mean — ?

A doctor, yes, but no records were kept. And one could
hardly ascertain her height and weight after her death.

No, quite. But the colour of her eyes — ?

That, too, would have been on a driver's licence if only
she had had —

But perhaps you noticed?

Afraid not. I usually *do* notice such things, eyes, especially women's eyes, but —

But?

The room was rather dark that day. A storm coming up. And I didn't want to put the light on for fear of —

For fear of what?

Well, startling her. Her face —

She was very ill at ease then?

Only at first. She was not used to . . . to being served tea. One could see that. She was not used to being *served*.

Her face. You started to say her face —

(Rabbity. Rodentlike. Not that I intend to give you that for your tape recorder.) An ordinary face, I would say. No makeup, of course. Nothing like that.

Any distinguishing mannerisms?

Not really.

Nothing?

Well, two or three times she put her fingertips to her earlobes.

Why?

I've no idea. Nerves perhaps.

A nervous mannerism, then?

Perhaps. (And sensual for some reason, this touching of the ears. One kept hoping she'd do it again.) But as I said, after she had some tea she became more at ease.

Did you say two cups or three? Sorry to be so banal, but a biographer —

Three cups. Orange pekoe. Milk. And sugar.

And until then she had not mentioned why she had come?

That is correct.

Then how did she approach the subject of — ?

I believe I eventually asked her if she had come to see me about anything special.

In fact, Cruzzi, who had drawn up a chair beside her, only gradually became aware of the paper bag she clutched on her lap. A white bag, or so he said into Jimroy's tape recorder. An ordinary bag, much folded and creased. At first he had been conscious only of some shapeless object cradled on her knees, which she did not set aside even while she drank her tea. Whatever it was, Cruzzi sensed it had to do with her reason for having come.

"I've come here about my poems," she told him when at last he asked. Her eyes went straight to the paper bag on her lap and stayed there.

"Ah," he said, and almost laughed with relief. She was *not* a madwoman. "So! You're a poet."

She seemed about to deny this, then confided shyly. "I've had some poems printed. In the newspaper. The Elgin paper took one just last month."

"I see," he said gently.

"About the first snow. That was what I called it. 'The First Snowfall.'"

"How pleased you must have been," he said.

"And they sent a cheque — " She stopped herself. Up went her two hands, fluttering to her ears and then back into her lap.

He waited a few seconds, and then, to encourage her, said, "Perhaps you'll send something to the *Banner*. We have a poet's corner once a week — "

She opened her mouth, her expression loose, scattered, full of entreaty. "I've brought these," she said, holding up her shopping bag. "Someone said, someone told me you were looking for... and so I thought, well, I'll get on the bus and bring everything I've got. Well, almost everything. Here." And she handed over her bag.

He looked inside. It was half-filled with small pieces of paper in varying size. There seemed no order. It was a bag full of poems and nothing more.

"Would you like to leave these with me?" he suggested.

"I could read them and give you a call. If there's something we can use."

"We don't," she said, "have a telephone."

"In that case, I could drop you a line."

"I was hoping — "

"Yes?"

" — hoping you could look at them now. I have to get my bus at half-past five, you see, so I don't have much time, but if you could — "

To himself he said: this is absurd. His throat was feeling raw, and the fever he had had in the morning had returned. An image of warmed brandy passed before his eyes. He longed for Hildë's return. He dreaded what he knew would be in Mrs. Swann's paper bag and what he would have to say to her.

"If you would please read a few." She said this in a voice that he found intimate and dignified.

He shook the bag lightly. "Is there any special order?"

"Order?"

"What I mean is, where would you like me to begin?"

Her hands rose again, barely grazing her earlobes. "It doesn't make a difference," she said. "They're all poems, all of them."

He reached in the bag and drew out a piece of lined paper. It had been torn from a spiral notebook and bore a ragged edge. At the top was written, "Thinning Radishes." The writing was in ink, at least, but was scarcely legible. His heart squeezed with pity, but he read the poem carefully, then set it aside and again reached into the bag. "Lilacs" was the name of the second poem. After that he read "Pears." Then "The Silo."

She watched him as he read, her eyes on his face. He thought once to offer her a newspaper or magazine to occupy her, but she shook her head at the suggestion.

After reading the first few poems he became accustomed to her unevenly shaped letters and her strange mixture of printing and writing. The spelling surprised him by its accuracy, but the words were crowded on the little pieces of paper as though an effort had been made to be thrifty. As he read he placed the poems in a little pile on the hearthrug. It took an hour and a half to read them all. Then he gathered them up — thinking how like fallen leaves they were — and lowered them once again into their bag.

"Did you know at once that you had stumbled on the work of an important poet?" Professor Lang had not carried a tape recorder or even a notebook, but he had had the hungry face of a man on whom nothing was lost.

"I knew the work was highly original. It was powerful. There was, you might say, a beguiling cleanliness to the lines that is only rarely seen."

"Did you tell her this?"

"Yes."

"What did she do?"

"She smiled."

"But what did she say?"

"Nothing. Just smiled. A soft, quite lovely smile."

Two of her upper teeth had been missing — Cruzzi found the sight piercingly sad — and slackness at the side of her face suggested the further absence of molars. "You have every reason to be proud of your work," he remembers telling her.

"My work?"

"Your writing. Your poems."

She continued to smile. He smiled back, and they sat together in silence for a minute or two.

"I suppose this was a moment of epiphany for her,"

Morton Jimroy had commented. "Hearing her genius confirmed in such a way."

"I've no idea," Cruzzi said, "what she was thinking."

"Is that when you mentioned publishing the work?"

"Yes."

"How exactly did you phrase this, if you don't mind my asking?"

"I told her I would like my wife to see her work. And that I would like to publish her poems in a book if she were agreeable."

"And she replied?"

"She agreed to leave the poems with me for publication."

"But what were her exact words?"

"Mr. Jimroy, this conversation took place in 1965. I cannot possibly, I'm afraid, reconstruct our conversation in its entirety."

"But she must have expressed some . . . jubilation?"

"If I remember rightly, she was a little confused."

"Perhaps she was overcome. By the suddenness of it. The idea of her poems forming a book, I mean."

"Perhaps."

"Can you remember, I know it's difficult after all this time, but can you remember what she said next?"

"She asked me what time it was."

"And?"

"I said it was a few minutes after five o'clock, and then I insisted on driving her to the bus station."

"And did she resist this suggestion?"

"I was very firm."

"Did she at any point mention having been threatened by her husband?" This was a question that came up several times during the inquest.

"She didn't mention her husband at all," Cruzzi told the court, "but she did express great urgency about catching the five-thirty bus."

"Would you say she was frightened?"

"I would say she showed anxiety. I assured her that I would get her to the bus station in time."

"Is it your opinion, Mr. Cruzzi, that her anxiety stemmed from the weather conditions or from some other unstated fear?"

"I'm afraid I wouldn't be able to say."

"While you were in the car driving to the station did she refer in any way to her domestic situation?"

"She was quite silent. And so was I. The snow was blowing directly into the headlights and visibility was very poor."

"What were the last words she said to you?" Morton Jimroy asked, pressing the release button on his tape recorder. "Before she got on the bus?"

"She said goodbye."

"And what did you say? If you'll forgive my asking."

"I said I would be in touch within a few days."

"And that, of course, was the last time you saw her alive."

"Yes."

"Were you deeply shocked to hear the news of her death?"

"Deeply."

"It is the kind of act," Jimroy said into his machine, "which is beyond the comprehension of ordinary people."

To which Cruzzi made no reply.

Cruzzi returned from driving Mrs. Swann to the bus station and found that Hildë was back home. Still ruddy-faced from the cold and wonderfully pleased with herself, she stood in the middle of the big kitchen holding high in one hand a string of whitefish. "Oh, I was a lucky one today," she cried out as he came through the door. "They came jumping up to meet me, I loved them all. Look! This one is smiling at you, just look at that smile, he's already dreaming about hot butter."

Cruzzi, whose happiness had been building all day, felt his skin ready to burst, and if his wife hadn't at that moment picked up her filleting knife — which she kept killingly sharp — he would have taken her into his arms and danced her through the house. "Something's happened," he said. Then, more quietly, "Something truly remarkable happened while you were gone."

He remembers that he shivered with pleasure thinking how he would tell her about Mary Swann. "I have been visited," he began, "by a beautiful toothless witch. A glorious, gifted crone. She materialized out of the storm — "

She heard the excitement in his voice and turned her face toward him, always quick to catch his mood. "I want to hear it all," she said, and held up her knife. "But from the beginning. Just let me do these beautiful, beautiful fish, and then I can sit down and listen with both my ears."

At the table he told her what Mary Swann had looked like, what she had said. He ate with great happiness. Hildë possessed rare skill with a filleting knife and even greater skill with the cooking of lake fish. It came off the grill redolent of butter, a thin skin of salty gold on the outside, and tender, breaking whiteness within.

Along with the fish they drank glasses of very cold dry white wine, and he told his story as Hildë had requested, from the beginning. "It was about three o'clock. I had drifted off in the wing chair, but I heard the doorbell ringing and . . . "

She listened the way a child listens, with touching expectation, without a single interruption, her eyes rapt. "If only I'd been here," she said when he finished. "If only I'd had a chance to talk to her, too, to ask questions."

"But you will." He took her hand. He had promised, he said, to contact Mrs. Swann in the next week. Meanwhile he would show her the poems.

"She left them all?"

"All of them."

He reminded her, teasing a little, of how she had once tried to persuade the owner of a local gravel pit to become a patron of the Peregrine Press by telling him they only published work that was mysterious and accessible at the same time. "You've never seen anything quite like these poems," he told her now.

"Wait till I make coffee," Hildë said. She loved surprises and loved even more to delay them, letting her anticipation rise and sharpen. It was an old game of theirs, a sexual game too, this greedy stretching out of pleasure.

Cruzzi, euphoric, feeling years younger than his true age, carried the coffee tray into the living-room. The smooth wood tray, the white cups, the small ovalness of the spoons — all these objects appeared that evening to be ringed with light. What he balanced so carefully in his arms, but with such ease, seemed suddenly to be the gathered entity of his life. Outside a storm blew, a blizzard of hard-driven pellets, but here was Hildë, his own Hildë, kneeling at the hearth, poking the fire back to life, reaching now for the little Swiss bellows they kept on a hook next to the fireplace. Her skill with fish, her skill with fires, the generous sorcery of her flashing elbows — what a void his life would have been without her. He could not even imagine it. She ought to be thanked, plied with gifts, as though anything would quite suffice.

He would make a presentation of the new poems. Benefice of the afternoon storm. Mary Swann's bag of poems. Providence from an accidental universe — from Nadeau Township, less than thirty miles away.

This thought, blindingly welcome, immediately blurred with another, the fact that he was staring at Hildë's round back and thinking, a little wildly, that she must be kneeling on the paper bag. Then she stood up, and he saw it wasn't there.

The room seemed to darken, and at first he thought he might faint, something he had never done in his life. His eyes closed, and what crashed in front of him was a boulder of depthless black. It had the weight of nausea. Hildë told him later that he cried out, "No!"

He *knew*, he was *sure* at that moment that Hildë had put the bag into the flames. It was this certainty closing over his head that sent him swirling into darkness.

For Hildë that terrible, involuntary "No!" meant only an arm thrown up in disbelief.

For Cruzzi, though he never came close to admitting it, not even to himself, it was a wail of denial. Because the darkness, or whatever it was that engulfed him, had dissolved for the briefest of moments, and what he glimpsed was the whole of his happiness revealed in a grotesque negative image. He was a man weakened by age and standing in a remote corner of the world, a man with a sore throat, a little drunk, and before him, facing him, was a thickish person without beauty. Who was she, this clumsy, clown-faced woman, so careless, so full of guilt and ignorance? He addressed her coldly as though she were a stranger. "There was a bag there," he said. "A paper bag."

Her mouth opened; puzzlement drifted across the opaque face. Then recognition. His beautiful Hildë, smiling and stepping toward him. "Oh, that," she said. "I put it in the kitchen."

Air and lightness returned. Lightness mixed with love. He lurched his way to the kitchen, unsteady on his feet, hideously giddy with something sour rising in his throat. His body seemed to drag behind him, an elderly man's deceived body that had been shaken and made breathless.

He found the bag on the kitchen table, gaping wide. Inside were the fishbones from their dinner, the ooze of fish innards, the wet flashing scales of fish skin, fish heads raggedly cut, fish tails, all the detritus of appetite, startlingly fresh an hour ago and already turned to a mass of rot.

Under the fish remains, under the wet heaviness of fish slime, were the soaked remains of Mary Swann's poems.

"Christ, Christ, Christ." He was moaning, lifting the stinking mess from the bag, hurling it in handfuls onto the floor. Bones dropped and shattered. Fish eyes glittered from the floor tiles. He was choking back tears. "Oh, Christ."

Hildë, who had followed him into the kitchen, watched this scene of madness. She saw a section of fish vertebrae, delicately formed, fly through the air and strike the wall. Then she saw her husband pulling pieces of soaked paper from the bottom of the bag, pulling them apart and gazing at them with sorrow.

She went to him and put her comforting arms around him.

It was a mistake, though not one she could have foreseen. He threw her off violently with the whole force of his body, and an arm reached out, his arm, striking her at the side of her neck. They both knew it was a blow delivered without restraint. It sent her falling to the floor, slipping on the fish guts, out of control, banging her jaw on the edge of the table as she went down.

The sight of her body on the floor brought Cruzzi back to himself. In an instant he was down beside her, cradling her head on his chest. A bubble of blood seeped from her chin, and he cupped it in his hands. "Forgive me," he said over and over, stroking her hair. The smell of fish rot deepened his sorrow immeasurably. In his arms Hildë was trembling and gasping for breath.

His first thought was a selfish one: he would not be able to live without her forgiveness.

He confessed to her his blindness and madness. He had not, he said, now firmly in the grasp of reason, struck out at *her*. He had struck at some fearful conclusion. Too much had happened in one day, too wide a swing of feeling to be accommodated.

As he spoke he realized this was true. Illness and fever and a secondary fever of happiness, and then the astonishing fact of Mary Swann's visit, the violent improbability of her arrival, the amazing offering of her paper bag. Then shock, followed too quickly by relief, then the sight of the ruined poems. He was not a young man. Something had come unbalanced. Something had snapped.

He knew that phrase — *something snapped*. He heard it every day; he deplored it. It was cheaply, commonly used, even in his own newspaper, in the reporting of crimes of passion. Something snapped. Someone was pushed over the edge. Temporary insanity.

He had never completely understood what constituted a crime of passion.

The bleeding at the edge of Hildë's jaw stopped. It was only a small cut, but he washed it carefully with a clean cloth and insisted on applying an antiseptic. She lifted her hand and, with her fingertips, attempted to steady his. He could not stop begging her forgiveness.

Hildë was never a woman who cried easily — her tears are collector's items, Cruzzi once said — but that night her sobbing seemed unstoppable. She was blind with tears. He was sure this meant she would never forgive him.

But of course she forgave him. She forgave him at once. It was only shock, she said, that brought the tears. An hour later they sat drinking brandy in the living-room, their shoulders touching. She had stopped crying, but she was still shaking.

Mary Swann wrote her poems with a Parker 51 pen, a gift, it was said, from her husband "in happier days." And she used a kind of ink very popular in those days, called "washable blue." When a drop of water touched a word written in washable blue, the result was a pale swimmy smudge, subtly shaded, like a miniature pond floating on a white field. Two or three such smudges and a written page became opaque and indecipherable, like a Japanese water-colour.

With great care, with tenderness, Cruzzi and his wife Hildë removed Mary Swann's drenched poems from the bottom of the paper bag. They by now had exchanged their brandy for coffee, planning to stay up all night if necessary.

First they used paper towelling torn into strips to blot up as much excess water as they could. Some of the little pieces of paper were so wet it was necessary to hold them at the edges to keep them from breaking apart. Some of them Hildë separated with the help of tweezers and a spatula. Then she and Cruzzi arranged the poems flat on the dining table, which they first covered with bath towels. When the table was full, they set up a card table beside it for the over-flow. To speed the drying, Cruzzi brought in from the garage a portable electric heater.

At least half the poems had escaped serious damage, and

these they worked on first, Cruzzi reading them aloud while Hildë transcribed them in her round, ready handwriting. At one point she raised her head and said, "I don't suppose there's any chance she has copies at home." It was a statement rather than a question. Neither believed that a woman like Mary Swann would have made copies. Her innocence and inexperience ruled against it.

A surprising number of poems became legible as they dried. From the puddles of blue ink, words could be glimpsed, then guessed at. If one or two letters swam into incomprehension, the rest followed. Hildë was quick to pick up Mary Swann's quirky syntax, and when she made guesses, they seemed to Cruzzi's ear laden with logic.

By midnight they had transcribed more than fifty of the poems. Cautious at first, they grew bolder, and as they worked they felt themselves supported by the knowledge that they would be able to check the manuscript with Mrs. Swann who would surely remember what most of the obliterated words had been. Already they were referring to Hildë's transcribed notes, and not the drying, curling poems on the table, as "the manuscript."

The seriously damaged poems worried them more. Lakes of blue ink flowed between lines, blotting out entire phrases, and they wondered about Mary Swann's ability to recall whole passages. Would she be able to reconstruct them line by line? They puzzled and conferred over every blot, then guessed, then invented. The late hour, the river of black coffee, and the intense dry heat in the room bestowed a kind of reckless permission. At one point, Hildë, supplying missing lines and even the greater part of a missing stanza, said she could feel what the inside of Mary Swann's head must look like. She seemed to be inhabiting, she said, another woman's body.

The manuscript grew slowly. It helped that Mary
Swann was a rhyming poet — the guessing was less chancy.
It helped, too, to understand that she used in most of her
poems the kind of rocking, responsive rhythm borrowed
from low-church hymns. Her vocabulary was domestic,
hence knowable, and though she used it daringly, it was
limited.

The last poem, and the most severely damaged, began:
"Blood pronounces my name." Or was it "Blood renounces
my name"? The second line could be read in either of two
ways: "Brightens the day with shame," or "Blisters the day
with shame." They decided on blisters. The third line,
"Spends what little I own" might just as easily be transcribed, "Bends what little I own," but they wrote *Spends*
because — though they didn't say so — they liked it better.

By now — it was morning — a curious conspiracy had
overtaken them. Guilt, or perhaps a wish to make amends,
convinced them that they owed Mrs. Swann an interpretation that would reinforce her strengths as a poet. They
wanted to offer her help and protection, what she seemed
never to have had. Both of them, Cruzzi from his instinct
for tinkering and Hildë from a vestigial talent never abused,
made their alterations with, it seemed to them, a single
hand.

It was eight-thirty. The weak winter sun was beginning
to show at the window.

Mary Swann, though they would not know for several
days, was already dead. Her husband shot her in the head
at close range, probably in the early evening shortly after
she returned home. He pounded her face with a hammer,
dismembered her body, crudely, with an axe, and hid
the bloodied parts in a silo. It was one of the most brutal
murders reported in the area, the kind of murder that

makes people buy newspapers, read hungrily, and ask each other what kind of monster would do such a thing. It was the kind of murder that prompts other people to shrug their shoulders, raise their eyebrows, to say that we are all prey to savagery and are tempted often in our lives to wreak violence on others. Why this should happen is a mystery. "Something snaps" is what people usually say by way of explanation.

Frederic Cruzzi: The House in which He Has Lived for the Greater Part of His Life

You sometimes see, driving through small North American cities, those large symmetrical stone houses built years ago. The roofs are almost always in good repair, with chimneys that sit authoritatively; window boxes are painted black or white and in summer are filled with brightly coloured flowers; everything speaks of family and peace and security; and, oh, you think, they knew how to build houses back in those wonderful days! Such a house is Frederic Cruzzi's on Byron Road in Kingston, Ontario. Through those tranced decades, the forties, the fifties, the sixties, the seventies, each rich in weather and economic outlook and modes of music and dress — through all those years Cruzzi and his wife occupied the rooms of this house and persisted in their lives.

It is best if we enter through the wide front door, for this is the way Cruzzi's many friends come and go, and this is also the way the burglar entered on Christmas Eve when Cruzzi, happily unaware, was dining across the street with his good friends Dennis and Caroline Cooper-Beckman and their three children. What an agreeable evening! And what a quaint assembly they formed, they a modern agnostic family, and he, old and widowed, sitting in noisy scented air at a table brilliant with poinsettias and spilled milk, amid platters of sliced turkey and vegetables and the solid cone of a Christmas pudding, then fruit, then chocolates, then the snapping frizzle of Christmas crackers, a final brandy, a morsel of peppermint sucked to nothingness in his old teeth, then home, a little tottery but filled with the resolve to put himself at risk one more time. He entered the house, climbed the stairs, went directly to bed (still happily unaware) and dreamed of Pauline Ouilette, her fragrant flesh, her floury neck and arms.

Outside, the snow had been falling steadily all evening and with such fine driving flakes that the handsome porch was completely covered, even the intricate crevices of the stone balusters that enclose the porch. (*Portico* is the term sometimes used for this architectural feature, with its polite proportions and civilized air of welcome.) The main door of the house is solid and graceful, and the knocker is the kind that fits the hand and kindles hope. Above the brass housing of the door lock, there are several scratches and a deep gouge; these were made by the Christmas Eve burglar.

A clumsy entry, or so a Kingston police constable judged later. Clearly the work of a bungling amateur, yet he succeeded. He would have been assisted in his work by the carriage lamp next to the door, the type of lamp referred to by some area residents as a welcome light and by others, of different disposition, as a safety light. It had been the habit of Cruzzi and Hildë to turn this lamp on during the long evenings in order to greet friends and strangers and to prevent accidents on the slippery stone steps.

Inside the front door is a vestibule, that practical Victorian invention, the means by which the weather of the house is separated from the true weather outside. Beyond the vestibule is the large, high-ceilinged hall, full of the gleam of dark wood and containing a bench where one can sit while pulling on overshoes, a hall-tree of whimsical design, and a very beautiful maple dresser, the drawers of which had been left open by the burglar — though Cruzzi, on his way to bed that night, failed to take note of this fact.

The design of the Byron Road house, like many in the area, is generous, but dictated by strict symmetry, and thus the living-room, leading to the left off the hall, precisely corresponds in size and shape to the dining-room, which leads from the right. In the daytime these two rooms are filled with light, that most precious element in a cold climate. The wide curtainless windows stretch from the ceiling to the floor. Their sills are made of stone, delicately bevelled, and the same stone has been used for the hearth and mantel of the very fine classical living-room fireplace. It was here, in front of the fireplace, that Cruzzi observed the gap-toothed Mary Swann, how she moved her hands to her earlobes, and thought to himself that he had never seen a more seductive gesture. In this room, too, Frederic Cruzzi and his wife, Hildë, spent uncounted hours, hours that, if dissected, would contain billions of separate images, so many in fact that if one or two were perverse or aberrant, it would not really be surprising. The room is filled with modest treasures, a curious set of andirons on charming, ugly feet, four excellent watercolours, a superb oil by the primitive painter Marcus Hovingstadt, two very old brass candlesticks, an eighteenth-century clock with wooden works, and a valuable collection of early jazz records — all these things were mercifully left undisturbed by the Christmas Eve burglar.

The walls of the dining-room are white. The floor is polished hardwood. Overhead a lamp of tinted glass, made by a local craftswoman, sends a soft circle of light down onto

the broad oval table. So many, many meals have been eaten
here. So many conversations, so much clamour of language.
Upraised hands have bridged the spaces between words and
sent shadows up the walls. There have been loud debates
and cherishing looks, the ceremonial cutting of cheeses and
cakes, celebrations and rituals, satisfaction and satiety. Here
at this table more than fifty books published by the
Peregrine Press were assembled, and here in that distant
December of 1965 Cruzzi and his wife, Hildë, worked
through the night in an attempt to rescue Mary Swann's
ruined poems, and here, with rare, unsquandered creativity,
Hildë made her small emendations. The dining-room
contains silver from France, porcelain from Germany and a
set of rare old chairs from Quebec, but none of these things
attracted the attention of the Christmas Eve intruder.

At the back of the house symmetry abruptly breaks
down. There is an oddly shaped sunroom full of plants,
comfortable chairs, and a piano. The kitchen is a hodge-
podge, the various parts worn and mismatched, though the
overall effect is one of harmony. Across uneven kitchen tiles
and scattered fish bones, Cruzzi had looked at Hildë and
watched the best part of himself fissure. Here the atoms of
his wife's face had grown smaller and smaller, retreating
from him in a width of confusion. The kitchen contains the
usual electrical appliances, a blender, a toaster, and so on, but
nothing apparently that tempted the uninvited visitor on
Christmas Eve.

He — the unbidden guest — did, however, mount the
broad staircase, without a doubt running his fingers up the
silky bannister and pausing in the dim upstairs hall. It was
in this hall, between bathroom and bedroom, that Hildë
suffered the stroke that killed her, a thunderbolt many times
the force of the tiny haemorrhage that knocked Cruzzi off

balance for a few minutes last summer, and that he at first thought was nothing but a touch of sunstroke.

Four doors open from the upstairs hall. One, of course, leads to a bathroom, but there is little in a bathroom, even a hundred-year-old bathroom, to excite the interest of a prowler.

A second door leads to the bedroom that Frederic and Hildë Cruzzi shared for so many years. What would catch a thieving eye in such a bedroom? Not the excellent new stainless-steel reading lamp, just two years old, not the wool-filled comforter from Austria, not the marble-topped bureau or the plants by the window or the pine-framed mirror, which can be tipped back and forth, or the comfortable wicker chair in the corner. The scenes that have taken place in this room are unguessable. Memory, that folded book, alters and distorts our most intimate settings so that passion, forgiveness, and the currency of small daily bargains are largely stolen from us — which may be just as well.

The very large room running across the front of the house is where Frederic and Hildë Cruzzi kept their books. (Because this room, forty years ago, was painted a brilliant yellow, it has always been known as the "Gold Room.") There are some chairs here and a desk that holds an old typewriter, but this room is mainly a resting place for books. They line the four walls and reach from floor to ceiling. Other rooms in the house contain odd shelves of books, but Cruzzi's most cherished books are kept here. They number in the thousands, and are arranged on the shelves according to language, then subject or author. Any reasonably intelligent adult entering this room could, in a matter of minutes, find what he or she was looking for. If, for example, a person were looking for one of the various editions published by the Peregrine Press between the years 1957 and 1977, it

could be spotted easily by the logo — a set of blue wings —
on the narrow grey spine. The four copies of Mary Swann's
book, *Swann's Songs*, published in 1966, were in the middle
of the Peregrine shelf, since their publication occurred about
halfway through the life of the press. All four of these books
were stolen by the Christmas Eve burglar, and the books on
either side pushed together, presumably to make the gap less
noticeable.

In the ordinary course of events it might have been
weeks or months before Cruzzi noticed the missing books,
but, in fact, he was alerted to the theft on Christmas Day.
He wakened late after the revels of the night before, made
himself coffee, which he drank sitting on a kitchen chair
and listening to the mutters and rumbles of the house. After
a while he went upstairs and was about to take up a volume
of his beloved Rashid when he remembered that he had as
yet done nothing to prepare for the little talk he had
promised to present at the Swann symposium, now just ten
days away.

He had, however, given it some thought. It was his
intention to keep his remarks simple and tuned to a tolerant
orthodoxy, to discuss the manner in which he had met Mary
Swann, and the decision, not an easy one, of the Peregrine
Press to go ahead with publication after her death. He
planned also to comment, savouring the irony of it, on how
little stir the book had originally caused. The notoriety of
the Swann murder had been brief and confined to the
immediate region. The poems in *Swann's Songs* were passed
over by most reviewers as simple, workmanlike curiosities,
and the 250 copies that the press printed sold poorly, even in
Nadeau Township. In the end he and Hildë gave most of
them away, keeping just four copies for themselves. It was
these four copies that were missing.

Gazing at the shelf, Cruzzi felt pierced with the fact of his old age, his helplessness, and the knowledge that a long-delayed act of reprisal had taken place. It was unbearable; some menacing reversal had occurred, leaving him with nothing but his old fraudulent skin hanging loose on his bones. He felt his vision blur as he made his way to the little back bedroom that Hildë had once used as the Peregrine office. He opened the door. There was nothing in the room but a table, two chairs, and a rather large file cabinet. The drawers of the cabinet were open and the contents were scattered over the whole of the room.

It took him the rest of the day to put things back in order. As he sorted through twenty years of manuscripts and correspondence, he listened to Handel's *Messiah* on the radio and felt a feeble tide of balance reassert itself.

Occasionally he hummed along with the music, and the sound of his voice, creaky and out of tune, kept bewilderment at bay. The music soared and plunged and seemed to coat the little room with luminous, concurrent waves of colour. By late afternoon he was finished. Everything was in place, with only the file on Mary Swann missing. He supposed he should be grateful, but instead found his face confused by tears.

THE SWANN SYMPOSIUM

DIRECTOR'S NOTE: *The Swann Symposium* is a film lasting approximately 120 minutes. The main characters, Sarah Maloney, Morton Jimroy, Rose Hindmarch, and Frederic Cruzzi, are fictional creations, as is the tragic Mary Swann, *poète naïve,* of rural Ontario. The film may be described (for distribution purposes) as a thriller. A subtext focuses on the more subtle thefts and acts of cannibalism that tempt and mystify the main characters. The director hopes to remain unobtrusive throughout, allowing dialogue and visual effects (and not private passions) to carry the weight of the narrative.

Fade in: Full screen photograph, black and white, grainy, blurred, of MARY SWANN, a farm wife, standing on the ramshackle porch of her rural house. She is wearing a house dress and bib apron; her lean face clearly indicates premature aging; her eyes are shut against the sun. TITLES roll across the photograph. SOUND: a sprightly (faintly Scottish) organ tune that gradually grows heavier as the CAMERA concentrates on Mary's face.

Dissolve to: Exterior shot, main street of Nadeau, Ontario. Early morning, winter, still dark.

The darkness gradually yields up a hint of light. Snow is falling. The main street of Nadeau becomes faintly visible. One or two cars pass, then a pick-up truck; their headlights glow yellow through the swirled snow. A Greyhound bus comes into view, then pulls to a stop at the side of the road. The CAMERA picks up a sign, NADEAU.

A woman steps from the shadows and boards the bus. She is small, middle-aged, somewhat awkward, and hesitant in the manner of someone who has recently been ill. This is ROSE HINDMARCH. She wears a too-large padded blue coat with an artificial fur collar and a wool muffler pulled loosely over her plastic headscarf.

CLOSE SHOT of driver's face. He is about thirty, with a fresh, alert face. Seeing Rose, his eyes widen.

DRIVER: Hi ya, Rose. Hey you're up early, aren't ya? You off to Kingston?

He stands up, takes her suitcase and wedges it behind his seat. Rose opens her purse and takes out a five-dollar bill. The bus is nearly empty, with three or four shadowy figures dozing at the back.

ROSE (cheerful, newsy): I'm getting the ten o'clock train. For Toronto, as a matter of fact.
DRIVER (making change): You'll be in plenty of time. You'll be sitting around the station waiting. Couple hours anyways.

Rose, seating herself in one of the front seats, carefully removes her muffler and her plastic scarf and pats at her hairdo. The bus starts up slowly.

* * *

ROSE: Well, I didn't want to . . . you know, take a chance.
And you never know this time of yea

DRIVER: Right you are, Rose. Don't blame you one little bit.

ROSE (still fussing with her hair): Wouldn't you just know
we'd get snow today? I watched the forecast last night.

DRIVER: Yeah?

ROSE: Snow, he said. Of all days, just when —

DRIVER: (shifting gears to climb a hill): S'posed to get six
inches.

ROSE: — and I said to myself, just my luck, the roads closed
and just when I have to get my train to Toronto for —

CAMERA pans open highway and fields. Snow is blowing
across the road, but houses and barns can be glimpsed in
outline. MUSIC, an alto clarinet, makes a jaunty counterpoint
to the rather laconic conversation.

DRIVER: Jeez, yeah, the train's your best bet this time of the
year. I mean, they tell ya six inches, but it looks to me
like —

ROSE (chattily): I'd of worn my good coat, but with this
snow, well, you can't wear a suede coat in weather like
this. Oh, it's warm enough, that's not the trouble, but
suede can't take it, getting wet.

Rose's natural garrulousness is augmented by the excitement of the journey to Toronto, and she sits on the seat
tensely, jerking off her gloves and examining her nails.

DRIVER: So! You're having yourself a trip to Toronto, eh,
Rose?

ROSE (still fussing): Just four days, that's all I can spare, what
with having to shut the library down, and —

DRIVER: Fuck! (He swerves hard, brakes, barely missing a car.) Where the... did he come from? (Relaxing): 'Scuse me, Rose, but that bugger came out of that side road without even —

ROSE (staring dreamily out of the window, not hearing): You know, I do believe it's letting up. The snow. Maybe I should have — (She fingers her coat, questioningly, regretfully.)

The bus stops and a woman with a baby gets on. She greets Rose and the driver and makes her way to the back of the bus.

DRIVER (starting up again, adjusting the mirror): So I suppose you're going to hit the January sales, eh Rose? Go on a spending spree. (His tone is teasing; Rose is by nature a woman who is subject to good-natured kidding.)

ROSE (dreamily): Pardon? Sorry, Roy, you were saying?

DRIVER (louder, as though addressing a deaf person): Shopping spree, I said. You going on a spree?

ROSE (delighted at this show of interest): It's for a symposium. (She loves this word.) In Toronto.

DRIVER (self-mocking): A who?

ROSE: A symposium. (Apologetic now): It's sort of a meeting.

DRIVER (concentrating on road): Yeah?

ROSE: You know, people talking and discussing and so on. It's about —

DRIVER: Makes a change, I guess.

ROSE: It's about Mary Swann. She came from Nadeau, you know. A poetess. You probably never heard of her, but she's —

DRIVER (scratching an ear): She the one whose old man shot

her up and stuffed her in the silo? Way back when?

ROSE (almost proudly): That's the one.

DRIVER: Whaddaya know!

ROSE: She's got real famous now. Not because of . . . that, but on account of her poems, her book of poems that was published. Oh, people'll be coming from all over, the States, everywhere. She's got quite a reputation now. She's real well thought of, people writing books about her and —

DRIVER: Why'd he do it, her husband I mean. Do her in?

ROSE (ignoring the question): It's going to be at the Harbourview. The Harbourview Hotel, that's where the meetings are and that's —

DRIVER: The Harbourview, eh? (He negotiates a curve.) Was there another guy or what? I think I heard my dad saying once . . . anyways, I can't remember the details, but —

ROSE: How *is* your dad, Roy? Better? (Rose knows everyone).

CAMERA pans countryside, buried in snow. There are a few billboards indicating that the bus is approaching Kingston. SOUND of clarinet, cooler now.

DRIVER: Not bad. He's a lot better, in fact. You can't keep the old man down.

ROSE: Your mom? She taking it pretty well?

DRIVER: Oh yeah, you know Mom.

ROSE (regarding snow): Look at that, will you. Definitely letting up. I wish now — (She looks down at her coat mournfully.)

DRIVER: So whaddaya think of all this hijacking jazz, Rose? Real mess over there, people getting roughed up —

ROSE: Terrible. (A long pause.) Terrible. (She stares dreamily out the window as the bus enters town.) Terrible.
(Dissolve.)

Fade to: Interior, the train station. Daytime.
Clearly this is the train station of a small city. There is a
rather old-fashioned air about it: brown wooden benches,
drab posters, and windows through which can be seen the
double train tracks, this morning interfilled with snow. Rose,
her muffler now nearly tucked into the neck of her coat, her
plastic head scarf removed, is standing nervously and looking
through the window to the platform. She looks at the station
clock, which says 9:50, then at her wristwatch. She gazes
about her. A few people come and go carrying luggage. She
opens her purse, takes out a compact and looks at herself, pats
her hair; she is obviously waiting for someone. She checks her
watch once more, and then a voice takes her by surprise.

CRUZZI: Miss Hindmarch? (FREDERIC CRUZZI is a tall, thin,
elderly man, wearing a long dark overcoat and a fur hat,
and carrying a cane, which he clearly needs.)
ROSE (startled): You're . . . are you — ?
CRUZZI (bowing very slightly): Frederic Cruzzi. How do you
do?
ROSE (nervously): How do *you* do? (Her handbag slips to the
floor; they both bend to retrieve it.) Thank you, but . . .
oh dear, I've got such a handful. And that's all you have?
(She gestures at Cruzzi's small carry-on.)
CRUZZI (smiling): A light traveller.
ROSE (rattled): I was . . . was starting to think, maybe you'd
changed your mind, and, well, when I saw it was 9:50
on the station clock, I thought maybe you'd decided
not to . . . meet me, the way we arranged like. (Her

words are drowned by the sound of the train entering the station.)

CRUZZI: Shall we? (He offers his arm, but Rose, juggling her handbag, suitcase, and shopping tote, doesn't have a free arm. She attempts to rearrange things. Cruzzi picks up her suitcase.)

ROSE (alarmed): No! You mustn't. It's very, very heavy. No matter how I try I always end up with too much. And shoes weigh such a lot, and then there's my hair dryer and, well, what I need, I was saying to a friend of mine, is one of those backpacks (laughs) like the kids wear nowadays.

CRUZZI (listening patiently, amused and polite): Ready?

They exit, arm in arm, MUSIC swells, a Scottish air, and the CAMERA follows them through the station window as they walk slowly, almost a matrimonial march, to the waiting train. Dissolve.

Fade to: Interior, SARAH MALONEY's bedroom, Chicago. It is early morning.

A very small bedroom is revealed in half-darkness, a room nearly overwhelmed by a king-size waterbed. The walls and furniture are white. There are books on shelves, plants, one piece of white sculpture. From under a thick white blanket come murmurs and grunts and sighs of sensual pleasure. They are suddenly interrupted by an alarm clock ringing musically.

SARAH (reaching out and shutting off alarm): Morning!

She kisses Stephen's bare shoulder, yawns, slips from the bed, stretches, and tiptoes into the adjoining bathroom. When she returns, she is fresh from a shower, a towel around her body, her long hair wet. In the half-light she dresses: underwear, a suit in a subtle shade of dusty pink, a soft blouse in a lighter shade, shoes. As she dresses she steals smiling looks at her watch and at Stephen, who is observing her from the bed. Her gestures are quick, hurried, absent-minded, though she touches her clothes, especially the silk blouse, with loving attention. She pulls a brush through her wet hair without glancing in the mirror. She applies no makeup. She opens a briefcase, checks its contents, and snaps it shut. For a moment she stands, holding the clasp, and goes through a mental checklist, then sets the briefcase by the bedroom door, puts on a heavy coat of white fleece, hoists up her shoulder bag, and approaches the bed. She sits down beside Stephen and opens her arms.

SARAH: Well?

STEPHEN (sitting up; he is a large, handsome shaggy man, he is wearing no clothes): You want some coffee? I could —

SARAH: I'll get some at the airport. (She starts to rise, but he pulls her down in an embrace more comradely than sexual; for a moment they rock back and forth; still embracing, she checks her watch, and this makes Stephen smile.)

STEPHEN: Time?

SARAH: Time.

STEPHEN: Good luck. With your speech.

SARAH (lazily): Not a speech, a paper.

STEPHEN: Good luck, anyway.

SARAH (pulling away): I'd better go. The cab should be here. You be shiftless and go back to sleep.

STEPHEN: It's still night! (He hoists himself out of bed, reaching for the white wool blanket, which he wraps around him Indian style; he puts an arm around her, and together they go down a miniature staircase, so narrow they bump against the walls as they descend.) This is a crazy hour. You live a crazy life, you know.

Stephen opens the door to a city street; there is no front yard and it is only a few feet to the curb where a taxi waits, its light gleaming in the darkness.

STEPHEN: So long. (He hugs her.)

SARAH (peering at him critically): For a minute there I thought you were going to say "take care." Or "be good." (She is scornful of such phrases.)

STEPHEN: How about . . . (miming) . . . *ciao?*

SARAH (pulling away as she hears the taxi toot): All of a sudden I hate to go.

STEPHEN: Toronto in January. (He phrases this so that it sounds both a question and a declaration.)

SARAH: Not just that. I feel spooked for some reason.

STEPHEN: Four days. (He gives a clownish shrug.)

SARAH (stepping across the snowy sidewalk and getting into the cab): O'Hare. (She rolls down the window and looks at Stephen, who is shivering in the doorway, wrapped in his blanket. She waves slowly; he waves back. The taxi pulls away.)

TAXI DRIVER: Jesus, it's cold. (Good naturedly): Whyn'cha say goodbye to your boyfriend inside?

SARAH (with music-hall rhythm): That's not my boyfriend, that's my husband.

They both laugh. The cab proceeds slowly down the street. Sarah, still waving, rolls up the window. SOUND: a cheerful, piping woodwind.

SARAH (CAMERA close-up on her face): Lord! (Dissolve.)

Fade to: Interior, San Francisco Airport. Early morning.

MORTON JIMROY, a middle-aged man in a cheap light-coloured cotton suit, is waiting his turn in an immigration line. SOUND: the usual hubbub of a busy airport underlain by MUSIC: something symphonic and emotional.

LOUDSPEAKER: Flight 492 for Toronto now boarding. Flight 492 boarding now at Gate 77.

IMMIGRATION OFFICER (bored): How long do you intend to be in Canada, Mr. Jimroy?

JIMROY (testily): Four days. And I happen to be a Canadian citizen, and I am not obliged to stand —

IMMIGRATION OFFICER (mechanically): Business or pleasure, Mr. Jimroy?

JIMROY (annoyed; he is a man who takes all questions seriously): Business. Pleasure. Both. (He pauses; the immigration officer eyes him sharply.) A meeting. A symposium, to be precise. I will be attending a —

IMMIGRATION OFFICER: Nature of meeting? (He holds a rubber stamp in his hand.)

JIMROY: I resent this interrogation. As a Canadian citizen I am not required —

IMMIGRATION OFFICER: Meeting you say? Nature of which is? (He waves the stamp in the air.)

JIMROY (shrugging): Scholarly. Literary. (As though addressing an idiot): Poetry, if you must know. You know, as in "Jack and Jill went up the hill —"

IMMIGRATION OFFICER: Okay, okay. (He stamps the paper and hands it to Jimroy.) Next.

JIMROY (bitterly): Thank you. (CAMERA follows him as he disappears into the crowd. Dissolve.)

SOUND: noise of the airport crowd blends with the rushing sound of the train.

Fade to: Interior of the train. Daytime.

CAMERA focuses on Cruzzi and Rose who sit facing each other on the train. They are drinking coffee out of plastic cups, stirring it with plastic spoons, and behind them flash the snowy, rounded hills of eastern Ontario. The sky is grey and wintry, but the sun struggles through so that the top of the scene is pink with light. The ongoing rumble of the train blends gradually with the sound of Rose's voice.

ROSE: . . . well, you must of thought I was dippy, I mean, writing you a letter and suggesting we, you know, go to Toronto *together,* but, well, it's one thing to travel alone and another, well, I was saying to a friend of mine, *another* thing to have someone to chat with on the way, and, well, it was really Professor Lang . . . I suppose you know Professor Lang —

Cruzzi grunts and nods.

ROSE: Well, Professor Lang was in Nadeau, must of been three, four years back, you lose track of time, don't you, one year sort of blends in with the next one, doesn't it? And anyway, along he came one day, middle of the week I think it was . . . yes, because I remember I was sitting in the library surrounded by cataloguing. Even in a little library like our town has, you always seem to be cataloguing. It's surprising how much work, every time a new book comes in, you have to do. Of course it's different in the bigger towns what with computers and all, but I say it'll be a major miracle (laughs) if

Nadeau ever gets a computer, not that I'm overly fond of mechanical things myself, but anyway, it's not very likely, financial restraint and what have you.

CAMERA close-up of Cruzzi's face; he is nodding, struggling to stay awake, yet something peaceful in his face shows that he finds the garrulous Rose more comforting than irritating. Rose, on her part, is blithely unaware of his inattention.

ROSE: . . . well, anyway, Professor Lang came along, just sort of dropped in, and he said he wanted to get a . . . feel . . . for where Mary Swann lived, her roots and all. You know what he said? He said we should have a sign at the edge of town, you know, like "Nadeau, Ontario, Home of Mary Swann, Distinguished Poet," and I said, Heavens, I didn't know she was *that* famous, and he said, Well, people were starting to take notice of her and in a few years . . . and I said lots of people right in this town maybe remember Mrs. Swann, at least the older ones, but hardly a one of them's ever read her book. Of course there's a copy in the library, at least there was up till recently, we're always losing books, people just walk off with them, kids! A real problem for librarians, the same everywhere I guess . . . Well, Professor Lang was so interested, had all kinds of questions and wanted to look around town real good, even drove out to see the old house where Mrs. Swann used to live before . . . well, you know . . . before! He even went out to the cemetery to see where she was buried, imagine, just a bitty little stone, and well, as I said, this was a few years back, she's a lot better known now, more famous, that is, and Professor Lang, I guess it was his idea, having a symposium about her, and you could of knocked me over with a feather when I got an invitation to come. I mean (laughs) well, this sounds crazy, but I've never been, well, to a symposium, I'm just a librarian, part-time. *And* town clerk, and I never... does that sound crazy to you? Me, never been to a symposium?

CRUZZI (jerking away and blinking once or twice, looks kindly at Rose and speaks gently): No, Miss Hindmarch, not crazy at all.

ROSE (pleased and relieved): Really?

CRUZZI: Not in the least.

ROSE: Whew! Well, I'm glad to hear that. Anyway, I got this letter from Professor Lang, the beginning of December, no, maybe it was the last week in November, I remember it was a Monday, blue Monday, ha, it always cheers me up, getting some mail on a Monday, I guess everyone feels that way, and, well, he said that Mr. Frederic Cruzzi, *you*, were planning to go to the symposium too, and you were going to give a talk and all, after all you were the one that published Mrs. Swann's book, it makes sense you'd be going, and he thought maybe I could give you a lift, but as I explained in my letter, I don't drive a car, just never learned, though a friend of mine, Daisy Hart her name is, says five lessons and I'd pass the test just like that, but I've never... anyway, I thought, it just struck me (laughs) that we could, you know, on the train, we could — (She falters at last.)

CRUZZI (waking up): ... keep each other company.

ROSE (leaping in): Exactly, exactly. And then he also wrote to ask me if I'd mind bringing along the photograph of Mrs. Swann, which, well, you know it's the only one there is now. (She grimaces.) And he wanted —

CRUZZI (wide awake and interested): Ah, you have a photograph of Mrs. Swann?

ROSE: The only one! So they say, anyway. We keep it in the
little museum we have in the old high school, just local
history and so on, but . . . would you like to see it, Mr.
Cruzzi? The picture?

CRUZZI: With pleasure.

ROSE: I'll just — (She stands and reaches for her overhead
suitcase.) I've got it right here, I'll just — (She struggles,
then takes off her shoes and stands on the seat; Cruzzi
makes an attempt to help her, but she holds up a
restraining hand.) Oh, no, Mr. Cruzzi, you mustn't
strain . . . I'll just —

CRUZZI: If it's too much trouble, don't —

Rose stands on her toes in stocking feet to open her case.
She fishes blindly for the photo.

ROSE: I put it in at the last minute, just slipped it in, didn't
want the glass to break. (She continues to struggle, sweating slightly.) Not that it's the best likeness, blurred you
know, just an old snapshot someone went and stuck in
a frame. I'm sure — (She struggles, pulling the suitcase
down; it opens, spilling clothes, a toilet case, a nightgown and, to her shame, a shower of underwear.) Oh!
(Embarrassed, she gathers up the clothes and stuffs them
back.) Oh, what a mess, oh, everything happens to —

CRUZZI: Can I help? (He says this doubtfully.)

ROSE (frantically stuffing clothes away): No! (She steals
looks at Cruzzi and at the passengers at the far end of
the car.) Here! Here it is. (She closes her case, unwinds
the photo from its tea towel wrapping and sits down
again, this time beside Cruzzi on the double seat; she is

breathing hard. The sun can be seen through the window, shining on the fields and lakes and woods.) Here! There she is. Mary Swann!

CRUZZI (taking the photo and regarding it quizzically, then discerningly, as though it were itself a work of art. He reaches in a breast pocket for spectacles so he may observe her even more closely, then says, with an air of pronouncement): Mrs. Swann.

ROSE (rattling on at full speed): As I say, not a good likeness. The sun's in her eyes, but, well, there she is! (She laughs nervously, still panting a little.)

CRUZZI: Of course I met her only once. My impression was — (he waves a hand) — fragmented.

CAMERA close-up of photo.

ROSE (looking on companionably, relaxed now): I'd say this was taken, well, around the mid-fifties, maybe earlier. She never seemed to age. What I mean is, she always, well, looked like *this,* sort of tired out. And old. Sort of sad and worried. But you know, she had, well, a kind of spirit about her, I guess it came out in her poems, like inside she was . . . like a young woman . . . not so, you know, down in the dumps, not so worn out. You can't tell from the outside what a person's really like, even when a person knows a person real well.

CAMERA side shot catches their two profiles side by side; Cruzzi's eyes are starting to close again; Rose, in a trance, talks on, her eyes straight ahead.

ROSE: It's funny. People always say I was the only one who knew Mrs. Swann, personally, but I didn't, not well.

Well, no one really knows anyone *really* well, not the things they're worried about or scared to death of or what they're really thinking, people keep it all locked up like they're too shy or something. I don't know why that should be, do you?

There is no answer from the sleeping Cruzzi; Rose shifts her eyes, takes in his sleeping presence, and continues.

ROSE: Like all fall. (She glances at Cruzzi). With me, ever since September, well, I've had these . . . health . . . problems and, you know, I kept putting off going to the doctor. Next week I kept saying to myself, and all the time I was, well, getting weaker and weaker, just not myself. "You're not yourself, Rose," people were saying, but I just said, "Who, me? I'm fine, just losing a little weight, that's all," and it . . . it kept getting worse and worse. (Rose steals another look at Cruzzi). You know how it is when you're going about your daily life, how you're always getting *ready* for something. Like, for example, a vacation coming up or Christmas or a bridal shower or something? Well, toward the end of November — (She pauses, looks again at Cruzzi; can she trust him?) I guess I got a bit . . . down, feeling so poorly and all, and one morning I woke up, it was after a real bad night, tossing and turning, and I said to myself — I live alone — I said, "Rose, kiddo, you're not waiting for a single thing, unless" . . . well, I'm not the morbid type, lucky for me, but I really did believe that I was going to, maybe . . . and so this dear old friend of mine took me in hand, insisted I got to a doctor, wouldn't take no. Which I did, and she, the doctor, it was a woman doctor, said it was only *fibroids*! and all I needed

was a simple little operation, routine, she said, it's a sort
of woman thing, next month they'll be doing it — I
won't bother you with all the details, but the thing is,
just when I thought everything, *everything* had stopped,
it all of a sudden... just started up again. (She laughs.)
Oh, it was wonderful. I thought, so this is what flying
is like, when we were driving home from the doctor's
in my friend's car, my bones felt... so light, like a little
kid's bones. I know it sounds crazy, Mr. Cruzzi,
but — (Rose turns her head to face him). Mr. Cruzzi!
(Alarmed): Mr. Cruzzi!

For an instant Rose is certain he is dead; she half-rises,
peers at him, passes her hand in front of his eyes, but is
reassured by a low melodious snore. She sits down again
beside him, puts back her head, closes her eyes. CAMERA
focuses on her face, on her lips, which part in a smile, and on
her closed eyes. She is still clutching the photo of Mary
Swann on her lap. Fields and small towns are seen flashing
by. SOUND: the rushing of the train fades into sprightly
organ music. Dissolve.

Fade to: Interior of an Air Canada jet. Daytime.
    SOUND: the music merges with the humming motor of
an aircraft. At the end of the aisle a flight attendant is
demonstrating emergency procedures; she is pretty, blonde,
and possessed of a dead, wooden face. Her monologue is
indistinct; its rhythms are discernible, but the words blend
with the words of one of the male passengers sitting in an
aisle seat next to Jimroy. This man (about sixty) is rangy in a
Lincolnesque way with a thick thatch of white hair. He
wears horn-rimmed glasses, jeans, a neat silk cowboy shirt
with a string tie, and a casual outdoor jacket. His wife, a

heavy woman in a navy pantsuit with glasses on a chain and
enormous diamond earrings, is in the window seat, and
Jimroy, squashed between them and snapping his briefcase
open on his lap, has the look of a trapped, elderly child.

MAN (to Jimroy, speaking loudly): So! You're getting right
    down to work, eh?
WOMAN (wearing a headset, beating out music on her knees,
    and smiling loopily at Jimroy and at her husband): Da,
    da, da dee da.
JIMROY: Hmmm. (An affirmative grunt; he shuffles his
    papers and nods vaguely.)
MAN (clearly anxious to strike up a conversation): I expect
    you're involved in the world of commerce, right?
JIMROY (considering this for a moment): Yes. (He looks
    straight ahead, as though steeling himself, then returns
    to his papers, pencil in hand.)
MAN: I'm retired myself, the wife and myself. (He gestures to
    the woman, who continues to beat out music and smile.)
    Only my wife says I'll never *really* retire. (He chuckles.)
JIMROY: Hmmmm. (He writes something rapidly in the
    margin, not looking up.)
MAN (after a long pause): What kind of business you happen
    to be in?
JIMROY (again considering): Books.
MAN: Books, eh? You mean like to read?

Jimroy nods crisply and turns a page.

MAN: Interesting. (He pauses.) Books. (There is a longer
    pause.) Sales? You in sales? You in the book-selling
    business?
JIMROY (puzzled): Sales?

MAN: Your book business you're in. You sell 'em?

JIMROY: No. (He returns to work, making an elaborate correction on the corner of his paper.)

The man pauses, then folds his arm resolutely, determined to remain silent. But eventually curiosity wins.

MAN: Well . . . what *do* you do with them then?

Jimroy looks up, baffled. The wife is tipping her head back and forth to the music, her whole body bouncing and her earrings catching the light.

MAN (somewhat cross): Your book business you say you're into, What do you do with 'em? (Loudly): Your books.

JIMROY (calmly underlining a phrase in the text): I write them.

MAN (galvanized): Books? You write books?

JIMROY (affixing a note with paperclip, taking his time): Yes.

MAN (grinning): Whaddaya know. (He reaches across Jimroy to his wife and taps her knees.) Honey, this here's a book writer sitting beside you.

WOMAN (loudly): Huh?

MAN (to Jimroy): My wife here's the reader in the family. The books she puts away! (To his wife, who has now removed her headset): Honey, this here's a real author sitting here. Boy, oh boy!

WOMAN: Well, well, you never know who you're going to end up sitting next to. (She floats cheerfully into non sequiturs). You probably think it's pretty weird, us, sitting like this, me at the window like this and my hubby there, in the aisle seat. Well, the honest truth is, I'm not the best flyer in the world. Ron, he takes it in his stride, just like a Greyhound bus, he says, a Greyhound bus that —

MAN (emphatically, an old joke): A Greyhound bus with wings growing out the sides, I tell her.

WOMAN (chuckling): But me, I get queasy, you know? Not scared of crashing, not a bit, but the old stomach doing flip-flops, so it feels, you know, more safe like by the window, probably just psychological, but Ron, with his long legs, he's six-foot-six, he likes to have room —

MAN: Closer to the washroom too. (He winks at Jimroy, as though urination is a male conspiracy.)

WOMAN (confidingly): Oh, but we're forever flying here and there, on account of Ron's investments, he thinks it's only right, even if he's officially retired, to show an interest, and the branch offices just love when —

MAN (leaning over and reaching into his wife's bag): Got any gum, hon? My ears're poppin' again.

Jimroy looks straight ahead. He is unable to fit himself into the scene; his body is rigid and his face has become a stiff mask.

WOMAN (rummaging in large purse, chortling at the weakness of men and speaking with womanly authority): Coming right up. Dentyne? (To Jimroy): Go ahead, I've got lots. I never leave home without. Between Ron's ears popping and my stomach doing flip-flops —

FLIGHT ATTENDANT (in her deadly monotone): Anyone care for a sunrise surprise before breakfast? Champagne and orange —

MAN: Coke for me.

JIMROY: Milk. If you have it?

WOMAN: Glass of juice, please.

FLIGHT ATTENDANT (to woman): Orange, tomato, grapefruit, apple?

WOMAN (with maddening hesitation): Oh, tomato, I guess.

MAN: Oh boy, honey, you and your tomato juice! (He laughs
uproariously at this, leaving Jimroy, milk to his lips,
stunned, lonely, and lost. Jimroy does not "look down"
on these people; he is puzzled by them, and in a curious
way, deeply envious.)

WOMAN (sporting a tomato-juice moustache): So! Well! You
really are a book writer?

MAN: A real one! What d'ya think of them apples.

WOMAN: That's the wonderful thing about travel, you meet
people from all walks of life. Like once we —

MAN (interrupting his wife): Pretty good money in it? I've
seen these authors on Johnny Carson, my wife and I —

WOMAN: Satin suits, covered with sparkles, just chatting
away with Johnny, easy as you please —

MAN: I suppose you use a typewriter? When you're writing
on your books?

JIMROY (looking wildly from one to the other): Well, I
actually —

WOMAN: I expect you get used to it, being on the TV, talking
away about —

MAN (as though struck with inspiration): Say, I guess it's
pretty good publicity, pretty good market angle —
creating the need, that's how the Japanese got us
licked —

WOMAN: That's what that what's-his-name fellow said,
wasn't it, hon? That real nice little man we met in
Yokohama —

MAN: That's what the man said. Little fellow, but real smart;
look to your markets, he said, keep an eye on your
markets.

WOMAN: Only makes sense. (She laughs. To Jimroy): You use your own name?

MAN: On your books, she means. Or like a — ?

WOMAN: Like a pen name? Made up?

MAN: You know something? When I saw you getting on this plane this morning, in the waiting room there, with your newspaper and all, I thought to myself: That fella looks, well, I've seen that fella before —

WOMAN: Ron always stays up for Johnny. Me, I need my beauty sleep. Ha!

MAN: But she's the reader in the family, always reading at something or other.

WOMAN (throwing up her hands, blushing, resisting this compliment with flustered modesty): Well, you see, Ron, he's so darn busy, the business, visiting the branch offices, his volunteer work, he works with the —

MAN: What kind of books you say you write?

JIMROY (determined): Well, my books are really —

MAN: I've thought of writing a book, but you know, I've never learned to use a typewriter and —

JIMROY (relentless): Biography's my field. I write biography.

MAN: Your life story, eh?

JIMROY: Not *my* life story. I'm writing the life of a poet. Her name is Mary Swann.

FLIGHT ATTENDANT: Breakfast! (She briskly hands out three trays.)

MAN: My favourite meal of the day, breakfast.

JIMROY (insistently, gesturing crisply): Actually, my books are about —

MAN: Hon? (He reaches across to take his wife's hand; their hands meet in the vicinity of Jimroy's lap; they bow their heads.)

WOMAN (urging): You.

MAN: No, hon, you.

WOMAN (capitulating): For what we are about to receive, for the blessings of warmth, love, fellowship, and heavenly guidance, we offer humble thanks and beg that —

Her voice fades. The CAMERA focuses on Jimroy, pinned between the praying couple, his mouth open as though he is about to speak. His eyes, bewildered, gaze at the joined hands on his lap. Dissolve.

Fade to: Exterior in front of Toronto Airport. Daytime.

CAMERA follows Sarah Maloney as she emerges from the airport door, her suitcase in tow. The wind is blowing and there is snow on the ground; she tugs her coat closer; then stops and addresses a redcap.

SARAH: The downtown bus? Over there?

She points; the redcap nods and points. Sarah walks over to the waiting bus, and the CAMERA follows her as she boards, pays, stows her case, and settles herself by a window. Other passengers are boarding, and the bus is crowded with luggage. Next to Sarah sits a woman of about forty, snuggled into a fur coat. The bus starts, and the CAMERA follows for a moment as the vehicle makes its way out of the airport area.

FUR COAT (darting looks at Sarah, who is staring out the window and shifting her purse and coat): Sorry. You have enough room?

SARAH: Fine, thanks. (She reaches for a paperback.)

FUR COAT (continuing to steal little glances at Sarah): Excuse me. I . . . I can't stand it any longer, but you look like . . . are you by any chance Sarah Maloney?

SARAH (smiling): Yes, I am.

FUR COAT: I knew it. I knew it. I've got your book at home and of course your picture's on the back — and I've seen you interviewed on TV. Twice, I think. This is surreal. Sarah Maloney. But I had an idea you'd be —

SARAH: Older. (She's heard this before). Everyone does. (She shrugs.)

FUR COAT: You sounded, in the book, I mean, so . . . (she searches for the word) so positive about everything.

SARAH: My wise days. (She smiles.) Actually I'm a little less positive now. About everything. A little more flexible, I've been told.

FUR COAT: You still feel the same way about female power? That a militant position offers our best —

SARAH: Yes. Absolutely. But with certain exceptions —

FUR COAT: What about men?

SARAH: Men?

FUR COAT: What I mean is, do you still feel the same about them? In your book, in the middle part, you talk about men as the masked enemy and —

SARAH (smiling, shrugging, acknowledging a joke on her younger self): I just got married. Last week.

FUR COAT: Ah! So you do believe in love.

SARAH: Love?

FUR COAT: Love and marriage. That they don't necessarily cancel each other out as you said in —

SARAH (with confusion): That's a tough one.

FUR COAT: And what about your idea that marriage is a series of compromises that necessitates —

SARAH: Actually, this is my second marriage. But this time it feels better. (She says this wistfully, her brightness clouded by a drop in pitch that suggests a fugitive sense of fear or uncertainty.)

FUR COAT: What about motherhood? How did you put it? "Motherhood is the only power conduit available to —"

SARAH (shrugging again, confidingly): I'm pregnant.

FUR COAT: Pregnant!

SARAH: Just a few weeks.

FUR COAT: Good God, you shouldn't be sitting in all this smoke. (She waves cigarette smoke away.) Even a small amount is damaging at —

SARAH: Lord! (She tries to open the window but it is stuck.)

FUR COAT: I tell all my patients — I'm an M.D. — that side-stream smoke is just as bad as —

SARAH (trying window again and succeeding): What else? Flying okay?

FUR COAT: As far as we know.

SARAH: I've got a conference here in Toronto. Four days. After that, though, I'm going to sit on my fanny and eat green vegetables and (putting her hand on her belly) feel it grow. You know something? — this is what I've always wanted only I didn't know it.

FUR COAT: But in your book, didn't you say something about childbearing being the — (Dissolve.)

Fade to: Interior of the bus, which is now in the city centre. Sarah and Fur Coat are talking with great concentration and energy and with the intimacy of old friends.

SARAH: Take Mary Swann, for instance. She's the reason I'm here, the one the symposium's all about. Okay, so she had zero power. This woman was a total victim —

FUR COAT: I'm not sure how you define a female victim, but don't you have to —

SARAH: Yeah, I think we over-simplify the whole thing.

Victims get squeezed into corners and they either die
or they invent a new strategy. I think that's why —

FUR COAT: And this woman? Mary? . . .

SARAH: Mary Swann. A classic case. She had a rotten life,
dead end, lived on a marginal farm with a husband who
wasn't even marginal — he was off the map, a bully, a
pig. You know the type, doled out a few bucks every
couple of weeks for groceries —

FUR COAT: And she survived?

SARAH: She wrote these poems. Not many, just over a hundred, but they're . . . there's nothing else like them.

FUR COAT: Is she still writing?

BUS DRIVER (calling out): Harbourview.

SARAH: Oh, I get off here. She's dead. Since 1965. Her husband finally —

FUR COAT: Her husband finally what?

Sarah hurriedly gathers her things together. The two
women start to shake hands, then embrace quickly. Sarah
gets off the bus, turns and waves.

FUR COAT: (shouting through the open window): Her husband finally what?

SARAH: (shouting from the pavement in front of the revolving doors): Shut her up.

FUR COAT: Did what?

SARAH (waving and shouting as the bus starts to pull away):
He shut her up. For good. He —

She realizes her words can't be heard, turns and enters
the hotel through the revolving doors. The CAMERA focuses
on the large notice board. Between "IODE Annual
Reunion" and "Dominion Leather Goods Sales Conference"

there is a line that reads: "The Swann Symposium." The CAMERA lingers for a moment on the sign. MUSIC: fife and drums. Dissolve.

Director's Note: This scene marks the end of film SET UP. All major characters have been introduced and brought to their destination, the Swann symposium, at the Harbourview Hotel. Occasional motivational suggestions will be given to the actors, but it is hoped that directorial comment will remain non-specific.

Fade in: Interior, hotel reception room. Evening.

Overhead CAMERA, wide shot of about fifty heads moving about in the hotel reception room. The room is gracefully proportioned, designed to accommodate medium-sized gatherings. The look is opulent; updated traditional, but rather heavy with swagged velvet and ornate furniture. Waiters can be seen from above, moving among groups of people with trays of drinks and canapés. Lively background MUSIC mingles with the rich sound of conversation and the tinkling of glasses. CAMERA lingers for a minute or two on the assembly. The scene is that well-known cocktail reception that precedes most conferences and symposia. Very gradually the CAMERA lowers, coming closer and closer to the crowd, and the murmur of voices becomes, finally, audible. Random phrases rise and fall in the festive air.

. . . personally, I see Swann as being blinded by innocence, and by that I mean —
. . . no use pretending the woman's a feminist when she makes it perfectly clear she's accepted the values of —
. . . well, when you consider that Nadeau, Ontario, is not exactly the centre of the world —

. . . remarkable, yes, remarkable. I agree, yes, remarkable!

. . . Emily Dickinson never . . .

It's the love poems I'm waiting for.

. . . now this is only a suggestion, but if you look at what Swann does with the stanza and think of it as the microcosm . . .

. . . time for another edition. Past time, if you ask me.

. . . is it true old Cruzzi's here? My God, the man must be a hundred years old.

. . . It's a pleasure, an honour, as I was saying to Mick here —

And this, ahem, is Frederic Cruzzi.

. . . read your article on Swann in the October issue, or was it the September — ?

. . . all these faces. Wouldn't our muse be amazed if she saw all these —

. . . giving the keynote address when it would have been more appropriate for —

. . . when, and if, Lang lets go of those love poems. What in Christ is he doing —

. . . wasn't quite what Sarah Maloney said —

. . . sweet as baby Jesus in velvet trousers!

. . . He's gone electronic, she's gone electronic, even the president has —

It's a good line, but it's not a great line.

Cosy.

. . . sibilance, don't you think?

The fragments of conversation intensify, grow louder, a roar, then once again becomes indistinct; the tinkling of glasses and shrieks of laughter begin to recede, replaced by the insistent sound of a spoon being struck against a glass. CAMERA close-up of a hand striking the glass with a spoon, and then the face of Willard Lang. His is a large, soft face masked with heavy naivety. Achieving silence, Lang raises his glass. He has the air of a man slyly keen to please.

LANG: Ladies and gentlemen. (He pauses for effect). My name is Willard Lang and it is my pleasure to welcome you (another dramatic pause) to the Swann symposium.

DRUNKEN VOICE: Hear, Hear.

SOBER VOICE: Shhhh.

LANG: I would like to extend a special welcome from the Steering Committee, which has worked long and hard to make this symposium possible, and to remind you that tomorrow morning, at nine o'clock sharp, we will be assembling in —

He is suddenly interrupted. The room is thrown into darkness. There is a great deal of evident confusion, and overlapping voices can be heard.

. . . the lights —

. . . power cut or, ahem, else —

. . . someone find the bloody switch . . .

Ladies and gentlemen —

Good heavens!

My God, talk about chaos —

. . . sure that if we remain calm the power will be restored.

Christ!

. . . so if you will be patient, ladies and gentlemen.

Ouch, that's my foot.

Sorry, I didn't mean —

If you think this is a nightmare, remember —

Someone in the crowd strikes a match; someone else

lights a lighter. Gradually the matches and lighters go on
around the room, revealing the assembled faces, buoyant
only a moment ago, now ghostly with shadow and looking
surprisingly frail, a look of having been caught doing something foolish. Very slowly the hubbub begins to build again;
there is even some laughter, thought it is nervous laughter,
ignited perhaps by drink. An instant later the overhead
lights go on, blinding, brighter than before, so that people
are caught off guard, dazed.

. . . at last. I just about —
About time —
. . . talk about timing, I mean he just —
. . . miniature theatre of the absurd —
. . . major power cut, wouldn't be at all surprised —
. . . Mary Swann putting in an appearance —
Ha!
. . . as I was saying, ahem, Swann is a kind of symbolic
        orphan who voices the —
. . . wouldn't you think a hotel like this would have an
        emergency power source, or else —
Remember that time at the St. Thomas in New York —
My briefcase!
It was right here.
. . . Oedipal darkness as symbol of, but only a symbol, let me
        say —
. . . is going to publish those love poems. You know, the
        ones he found under the kitchen floor — the linoleum,
        actually.
It was a black leather briefcase, the standard size and shape—
. . . let's hope that tomorrow will —
It was sitting right here by this table leg before the lights
        went out, and —

CAMERA close up: Jimroy is talking heatedly to two or three waiters. As a crowd begins to gather around him, CAMERA slowly withdraws, rising to overhead position once again. We see the cluster of people around Jimroy increase, and over the murmuring crowd his voice rings out with extreme clarity.

JIMROY: My briefcase! All my notes for the symposium, my talk, the program, everything! I had them in my brief-case. My papers. And a fountain pen, a very valuable fountain pen. It was right here! Someone must have picked up — yes, of course, I'm sure. How could I possibly not know where my own briefcase was? It was right here beside me, you idiot, right here.

Jimroy has started to shout; his face, so smooth and amiable before, has grown red and has a furious boiled look; he is mortally offended, embarrassed, and angry; clearly he sees the blackout and the loss of his briefcase as damaging to his dignity. The CAMERA focuses on the image of his angry face and freezes.

Fade to: Interior of a meeting room. The next morning.

The frozen image of Jimroy's face slowly dissolves into Willard Lang's face, which is genial, smiling, perhaps a little ingratiating. He is eager, despite the catastrophe of the night before, to launch the symposium on the right note. People attending are seated in rows on folding chairs. Some of them have pens in hand, ready to take notes; others sit with books or papers on their laps; many are in conversation with one another. Lang is at the front of the room, standing at a small lectern equipped with a microphone. He clears his throat, but the buzz in the room persists.

LANG: Ladies and gentlemen, assembled scholars. (The voices die.) Good morning. Once again I welcome you to the first, but let us hope not the last, Mary Swann symposium. And let us also hope — (the microphone gives a jarring electronic squawk) — that the electricity will not fail us as it did last night. (Another squawk.)

MAN WITH OUTSIZE AFRO: Hear, hear.

LANG (slightly annoyed): Just two items before I introduce our keynote speaker. I wish to draw your attention to a display that has been set up in the corridor. Some off-prints of recent articles have been assembled, and also, you will be happy to hear, a photograph of Mary Swann, which has been brought along by Miss Rose Hindmarch of Nadeau. Ah, is Miss Hindmarch with us this morning? (There is a brief stir: people turn their heads looking for Rose, who is seated in the last row.) Ah! Perhaps Miss Hindmarch would be good enough to stand and be recognized.

Rose, enormously embarrassed, rises slowly, her shy smile showing pleasure, awkwardness, confusion. She manages a gawky nod, a slight shake of her newly permed head, then sits down again to scattered, somewhat indifferent applause.

LANG: Thank you, thank you. And now for item two. A personal plea, if I may, concerning our mini-disaster (laughs dismissively) yesterday evening. If anyone should find himself, or herself, with an extra briefcase, black leather, initials M.J. on the clasp, Mr. Jimroy would appreciate its speedy return. And now, ladies and gentlemen, fellow Swannians, if I may address you in such a manner, it is my great pleasure to introduce our

speaker. Not that Morton Jimroy, holder of two honorary degrees needs a — yes?

CAMERA picks up Jimroy sitting in a chair a little apart
from the others. He is somewhat tense, a little strained.
Almost bashfully apologetic, he lifts his arms in a shrug; he
is holding up three fingers.

LANG (comprehending): Ah, excuse me, Morton. *Three* honorary degrees, of course! The most recent from
Princeton University, I believe. Everyone in this room is
familiar, I am sure, with Morton Jimroy's esteemed
biography of Ezra Pound, *A Perverse Pilgrimage,* and his
equally fine biography of the American poet John
Starman, entitled *Verse, Voice and Vision* . . . (he becomes
distracted). Yes? (He catches Jimroy's eyes once again.)
Yes, Mr. Jimroy?

JIMROY (quietly, shyly, half-bobbing from his chair): That's
Voice, Vision and Verse, just a small correction. Sorry.

LANG (in tones of pompous injury): I stand corrected. *Voice,
Vision and Verse. As* I was saying, Ezra Pound! John
Starman! Giants of our literature. And now the question might be put — what is it about the obscure
Canadian poet, because we must face the fact, ladies and
gentlemen, that the seminal work of Mary Swann is not
as widely known as it deserves — what is it about this
woman, this writer, that attracted the attention of
the world-famous biographer of Ezra Starman and
John — (A murmur from the audience tells him he
has stumbled again, and he quickly corrects himself.)
Ezra Pound and John Starman. A little early in the
morning, I'm afraid. What was it that drew — but
perhaps it would be best if I let our honoured guest tell

you himself, (He gestures broadly). Mr. Morton Jimroy!

Jimroy rises and allows the applause to die as he stands
at the lectern. He adjure his papers, loosens his tie, lowers
the microphone. He is a man who enjoys teasing his audience, believing it sharpens their attention. But he manages
to appear more fussy than in command, and the audience
responds with restlessness. At last he speaks.

JIMROY: Ladies and gentlemen, I must first ask your indul-
    gence. Because of last night's mishap . . . my briefcase
    caper . . . I am forced today to speak from the scantiest
    of notes, and may be even more rambling than is my
    usual way. (He breathes deeply and plunges into his
    talk.) Why, our honoured chairman asks, have devoted
    my attention for the last two years to the work and per-
    son of Mary Swann, a poet some have compared to
    Emily Dickinson, to Stevie Smith, and also, if it is not
    too extreme a comparison for so early in the morning
    (a sour glance at Lang) to the great romantic voice of
    the —

His voice fades to a murmur, rising and falling with a
somewhat monotonous rhythm, but the words themselves
are blurred. The CAMERA, as he speaks, wanders to various
other faces in the audience, settles for a moment on Sarah
Maloney, exceptionally alert and possessed of an expectant
sparkle. She wears boots, pants, and a beautiful silk shirt,
and is sitting boyishly with one leg drawn up, tuned to every
word. Her look is one of critical appraisal. The CAMERA also
falls on Rose Hindmarch sitting next to Sarah. Rose touches
her hair repeatedly, scratches her neck, tries to remain alert,
but is distracted by the excitement of the gathering. She

looks to right and left, over her shoulder, etc. Jimroy's voice once again fades in.

JIMROY: . . . always referred to as "a Canadian poet," but I suggest the time has come to leave off this modifier and to spring her free of the bolted confines of regionalism. Hers is an international voice, which —

Jimroy's voice again blurs. The CAMERA falls on the bright, skeptical face of Frederic Cruzzi, octogenarian, dressed this morning in a grey suit with a red sweater beneath. He strokes his chin, a little bored, somewhat disapproving of the tack Jimroy is taking. An instant later his eyes begin to close; in recent days he has withdrawn more and more into his memories, a province he likens to a low, raftered attic with insufficient air.

JIMROY (voice fading in again): . . . and who would happily blow Mrs. Swann's past to ashes and make her a comely country matron cheerfully secreting bits of egg money, as well as those who want to force on her a myth she is too frail to support. She was a seer and a celebrant, and in her 125 poems, 129 when Professor Lang agrees to publish the love poems —
MAN WITH OUTSIZE AFRO: Hear, hear.
BLUE-SPOTTED TIE: But when, when?
JIMROY (turning to Lang): You see, Professor Lang, how eagerly we await publication. To continue, who really was Mary Swann?

His face dissolves again. The CAMERA travels across the faces of those in the audience; some take notes, some listen attentively, Cruzzi dozes, Rose fidgets.

JIMROY (again becoming audible): May I suggest further that
    the real reason we have come here is the wish to travel
    (pause) that short but difficult distance (pause) between
    appearance and reality. Who, given what we know, was
    Mary Swann? A woman. A wife. A mother. Perhaps
    a lover. (He eyes Lang, who looks away.) She was poor.
    Badly educated. A woman who travelled only a few
    miles from her home. She had no social security card,
    no medical records. Her only official papers, in fact,
    consisted (dramatic pause) of a library card from the
    Nadeau Public Library.

The CAMERA lights on Rose Hindmarch, who blushes
appropriately and nods. CAMERA follows the faces in the
audience; interest quickens and even Cruzzi jerks awake.

JIMROY: It is a mystery, just as our own lives are mysteries.
    Just as we don't ever really know that person sitting to
    our right or left. (Rose and Sarah exchange small smiles
    at this.) Appearance and reality.

Jimroy ends his talk with a flourish, a crisp nod to the
audience. He bows stiffly, and walks back to his chair.

Director's Note: The repetition of the phrase "appearance
and reality" must be framed with silence and intensity, since
it can be said to define the submerged dichotomy of the film.
The applause, when it comes, must be slightly delayed so
that the words (and implications) will have time to register.
    Lang steps to the microphone and leads the applause,
gleeful as a cheerleader; after a moment he gestures Jimroy
back to the lectern.

* * *

LANG: Our guest has kindly agreed to field a few questions. We have, I believe, just ten minutes before our coffee break. Questions? (Several hands go up at once. Lang, dancing like a marionette, pleased things are running smoothly, points to Dr. Buswell near the back of the room): Syd? You have a question for Mr. Jimroy?

Syd Buswell is a man of about forty, wearing blue jeans and a tweed jacket; he speaks with a nasal, aggrieved whine, employing truncated phrases that give the impression of self-importance.

BUSWELL: The question of influences! Very important as we all know. You mention, Professor Jimroy, that Mrs. Swann was an avid reader. A great borrower of books from the local library. Now I have *been* to the local library in Nadeau, Ontario. I have made a *point* of going there. I am sure you have as well. And I feel sure that you will agree with me that there isn't a great deal offered by the Nadeau Public Library. Pleasant it may be, but —

Director's Note: Another sort of director, distrustful of his or her audience, might employ a flashback at this point. Buswell, clad in a ratty leather jacket, prowling through the innocent shelves of the Nadeau library, or something along those lines.

JIMROY: Ah yes, but —
BUSWELL: For example. There is *no* T.S. Eliot in the Nadeau library. Just an example. Enough said? (He sits down, believing he has scored magnificently with this point.)
JIMROY (clearing his throat): Perhaps you're aware, Professor Buswell, that the librarian of the Nadeau Public Library,

Rose Hindmarch, is in our midst today? (CAMERA close-up of Rose, who looks hideously alarmed.)

BUSWELL: I am perfectly aware that Miss Hindmarch is present. And she would no doubt agree. With me. That this particular library was in no particular position to offer much. Much substance that is. To someone like Mary Swann. Now it is all very well —

Rose has risen to her feet; there are tears in her eyes, and her face wears a mixed look of self-censure and wincing bewilderment; this is not what she expected.

ROSE (quavering): We have a budget. People don't always appreciate . . . a very small budget. Last year it got cut twice, the hockey arena got a hike, but we got —

BUSWELL (lazily): I'm sure you do the best you can, Miss Hindmarch. With a limited budget. I was not imputing (at this Rose blinks) that you run an establishment that is . . . less than —

JIMROY (icily): That is exactly what you did say, Professor Buswell, and —

BUSWELL (unperturbed): It is hardly an accusation to acknowledge that a particular rural library is . . . substandard. No Eliot. No Lowell. I ask you. (He sits down in triumph.)

ROSE (rising again): Every year I tell the council the same thing, we need money, the price of books —

JIMROY: Miss Hindmarch, there is no need for you to defend your —

BUSWELL (rising again): No one said anything about a need to defend. I am simply saying what we all know. That the Nadeau Public Library cannot have provided serious nourishment to the mind of a poet like —

ROSE (on her feet, her terrible garrulousness shifting to its defensive mode): Oh, Mrs. Swann came every two weeks to the library. I don't think she ever missed, not for years and years, every two weeks, like clockwork —

BUSWELL: Miss Hindmarch. My interest is in addressing the question of influences. I assure you, I am not challenging you personally. It is Mr. Jimroy who makes claims for Mrs. Swann's familiarity with certain works in the modern trad —

JIMROY: I suggest only. I do *not* claim.

ROSE (not understanding the focus of the discussion): We *do* have a poetry section. We use the Library of Congress numbering system and you can find —

BUSWELL (to Jimroy, ignoring Rose): You point to parallels between Swann and Emily Dickinson and you suggest —

ROSE (still awkwardly standing): Mrs. Swann liked a good story. For example, Pearl Buck. I remember she liked Pearl Buck real well. And Edna Ferber —

Director's Note: Others in the audience watch the proceedings with distress, humour, annoyance, fascination. There must be a sense of order breaking down and a suggestion that an unwanted revelation threatens.

WOMAN IN GREEN TWEED SUIT: Is this really germane?

MAN WITH CRINKLED FOREHEAD: Of course it's germane. Everything that sheds light on —

WATTLED GENT: Why not let Mr. Jimroy reply? After all, he's the one who —

MERRY EYES: Order.

SARAH (rising, twisting her wedding ring as she speaks): Why can't we just say that Mary Swann was self-evolved and be done with it? Remember what Pound said about Eliot, that he made his own modernism —

GINGER PONYTAIL: And isn't it possible that her influences were general rather than specific —

WIMPY GRIN: The question of influence is oversimplified in most cases. For instance —

JIMROY (to all three comments): Yes. And furthermore —

BUSWELL: All I want to say, and then I promise to pipe down, is that the resources of the Nadeau Public Library *cannot* seriously be considered as an influence.

JIMROY (instinctively dealing in flattery, knowing how efficacious it can be in such a public situation): Professor Buswell, from previous discussions you and I have had, I know you to be a man of wide reading and sensitivity. Of course I understand that you are anxious to establish a link between Mrs. Swann's writing and her grasp on modern poetics —

BUSWELL: I only ask —

JIMROY: — and I can tell you that Mrs. Swann's daughter, whom I have interviewed in depth in recent months, has confided that her mother was familiar with that genre of verse commonly known as Mother Goose —

BUSWELL (with an appalled laugh): Nursery rhymes! Surely you're not serious —

JIMROY: I see no reason to dismiss —

MAN WITH OUTSIZE AFRO: Bloody rude son of a —

BIRDLADY: . . . snobbish approach to —

JIMROY (leaning on lectern beseechingly; he has clearly lost control, but will not admit to it): If you will allow me to enlarge —

LANG (stepping nimbly forward): Perhaps, ladies and gentlemen, it might be more profitable to continue this most interesting discussion over coffee, which I now believe — (he peers over the heads of the audience) — yes, I can see coffee is ready and . . .

Lang's voice fades; all around him people are rising to their feet and heading toward the coffee urns. They can be seen chatting, stretching, moving.

Rose rises hurriedly and heads for the door into the corridor. There are tears standing in her eyes, and her nose is red. She is a woman who can never speak coherently when her emotions are stirred, and for this reason she is anxious to escape.

SARAH (attempting to catch up with Rose): Rose, wait a minute. Excuse me, I want to — Rose! (She follows Rose into the corridor, looks right and left and sees nobody.) Rose! (She sees a door marked "Ladies," decides Rose is there, and enters. The CAMERA follows, focusing on three stalls, the door to one of them closed.) Rose, you there? (Sarah leans on a washbasin and folds her arms, prepared to be patient.) Okay, Rose, I know you're in there. Now listen to me. You trust me, don't you? Buswell's a shit. Everyone in that room knows what he is. An asshole. Insecure. That's what the tenure system does to the insecure. The man's paranoid, Rose. Can you hear me? You can't stay in there all day, you know.

She continues talking while turning and glancing in the mirror; her face has the kind of seriousness that throws off energy. From her deep bag she takes a hairbrush and begins brushing her long hair, an act performed with a kind of distracted sensuality.

SARAH: I can tell you, Rose — I was on the Steering

Committee — that, that twit, Buswell, is one hundred per cent on the defensive. He's running for the bushes. This is confidential, Rose, but I can tell you this much — he was supposed to be giving a paper himself, something idiotic and desperate on vowel sounds in *Swann's Songs,* and he's been working on it for two years (gives her hair a yank) and then he suddenly writes to the committee, this was in October, to say his notes had been stolen. Stolen! Everyone knows he's the most absent-minded nerd. (She puts the brush away, turns sideways, observes the curve of her abdomen and runs her hand over it.) He's the sort of crazy creep that loves to put the blame . . . well, they all are, the bunch of them, it makes me wonder if I want to spend my life hanging out with — Rose? (She sees that the collar of her pink shirt is standing prettily away from her neck, careless and controlled at the same time in a way that makes her happy.) Rose? Rose! (She pushes open the door, which swings in to reveal nothing but a solitary toilet.) Rose. (Softly, hands on hips): Rose?

Dissolve to: Interior, meeting room. Late morning.

Members of the symposium are enjoying a coffee break. People are milling about, relaxed, standing in groups of three or four, and there is a pleasing sense of animation. In one corner Jimroy, Buswell, and Cruzzi are conducting a cheerful but guarded discussion. CLOSE-UP on Lang, he scurries from group to group sociably, then joins Jimroy and the others; his look is amiable and conciliatory. A nearby group consists of Wattled Gent, Wimpy Grin, Ginger Ponytail, and Sarah, who joins them belatedly and is handed a cup of coffee by Silver Cufflinks.

* * *

SILVER CUFFLINKS: Well, you might say Jimroy managed to capture the attention of —

GINGER PONYTAIL (earnestly): Threw some light on the early poems which you have to admit are . . . but it's the love poems we're all waiting for —

WIMPY GRIN (to Sarah): I suppose you must have met Morton Jimroy —

SARAH (distracted, looking over her shoulder for Rose): Met who?

WIMPY GRIN: Morton Jimroy — you must have met —

SARAH (focusing, but still distracted): No. I decided not to go to the reception last night. All that smoke —

GINGER PONYTAIL: So you don't know him at all?

SARAH: We've been corresponding. For about a year or so, but I haven't actually met —

LANG (approaching and taking Sarah by the elbow): Sarah, may I interrupt? I'd like very much to present you to Mr. Jimroy —

SARAH (detaching herself from the group and following Lang through the crowded, noise-filled room): Willard, have you seen Rose Hindmarch? She seems to have disappeared. I've looked in the —

LANG: Oh, she'll turn up. Probably in the loo. Unfortunate. Tactless bugger, Buswell. Utterly paranoid, still says his notes were stolen —

SARAH: Any news about Morton Jimroy's briefcase?

LANG (his face falling): Not yet. I can't understand who — (He steers Sarah over to where Jimroy is holding court.) Morton, sorry to interrupt, but you expressly asked earlier to meet Sarah, and I've managed to snatch her away from — Sarah Maloney, Morton Jimroy.

JIMROY (offering his hand and looking suddenly timid): How do you — ?

SARAH (smiling broadly, unprepared for such formality): At last! (She embraces him warmly and plants a kiss on one cheek; she is a naturally demonstrative woman.) At last!

Jimroy, gratified but confused by so spontaneous an embrace, instantly draws back, squirming. CAMERA close-up of his face reveals a twisted scowl of mingled pain and desire.

JIMROY (muttering coldly under his breath): So good to meet you.

Sarah, interpreting Jimroy's cool behaviour as an act of rejection, steps back and attempts to explain to him, to the others, and to herself.

SARAH: After all the letters we've . . . I just felt, you know, that we were —
JIMROY (aloofly): I assume you've met Professor Buswell?
BUSWELL (carelessly): Old friends. We go way back.
JIMROY: I see.
SARAH (still puzzled by Jimroy's snub): I've been looking forward to —
LANG (recognizing an awkward situation and anxious to deflect it): And have you met Frederic Cruzzi? Mr. Cruzzi, Sarah Maloney.
CRUZZI (also trying to relieve the tension): We have met. By letter. A charming letter if I may say so.
JIMROY (blanching, pierced to the heart by this information): You must be very busy, Ms. Maloney, with all your letter writing.
LANG (rattling on expansively): It was Sarah who managed to persuade Mr. Cruzzi to attend our gathering.

CRUZZI: A most persuasive letter. How could I possibly refuse?

LANG: Actually we're very, very fortunate to have Sarah with us. Perhaps you know her happy good news?

JIMROY (icily): I'm afraid not.

LANG: Just newly married. Christmas Eve, wasn't it, Sarah?

BUSWELL (breezy, bored): Congrats.

JIMROY: Married. (There is more exclamation than query in this outburst.)

SARAH: To someone — (shrugs nervously) — someone I've known for some time.

JIMROY: My congratulations. Excuse me, won't you? I see someone I must have a word with. (He starts to leave.)

SARAH (perplexed): We *will* have a chance to talk later, won't we, Morton?

JIMROY (cringing at the sound of his name): I expect that *might* be possible —

SARAH: There are dozens of things I want to ask you about —

JIMROY (dismissively as he leaves): We must do that some time.

SARAH (to others): Did I by any chance say something wrong? Put my foot in it or what?

LANG (smoothly): I'm sure Mr. Jimroy is just tired, his long journey, and then speaking for — and without notes —

SARAH: No, not just that, Willard. I've been (she pauses) snubbed.

LANG (looking at his watch): Good god, we're running late. Completely lost track of time. You ready, Sarah? (To Cruzzi and Buswell): Sarah's on next.

SARAH (staring at Jimroy's back): I can't understand it. In his letters he was so — maybe he's brooding about his brief-case, or —

LANG: I'm afraid . . . mustn't fall behind, you know. (He

firmly takes the coffee cup away from her and steers her to the front of the room.)

SARAH (still mulling over the snub): I must have done *something*. Or *said* something. Or —

WOMAN WITH TURBAN (grasping Lang's hand): Just want to let you know, Willard, that I'm looking forward to the love series. I've done some work —

LANG: Five minutes late! I don't know how we —

SARAH: Maybe I came on a bit strong. I do that sometimes.

WOMAN WITH TURBAN (clinging): I think all of us are —

LANG (at the lectern): Ladies and gentlemen. (People drift to their seats with looks of expectation.) Ladies and gentlemen. I am particularly happy to present our next speaker, Sarah Maloney, who is the person — and I think I can say this without exaggeration — the person most responsible for the rediscovery of Mary Swann, who, in her article a mere five years ago, pointed to Swann's unique genius and to — well, perhaps I should now turn the microphone over to Ms. Maloney herself. (Applause.)

Sarah squares her shoulders: whatever she says she knows it must be delivered with authority. Her eyes search the audience. She sees Morton Jimroy and sends him a tentative smile, then begins.

SARAH: Mr. Jimroy, in his keynote address this morning, raised a number of interesting points, particularly the notion we have of regarding Swann as a kind of curious cultural hiccup isolated from any sort of cultural tradition. It is a compelling belief but shaky in my opinion, to think of Mary Swann's work as a miniaturized, spontaneous, virgin birth, but —

* * *

Her voice fades, becomes indistinct. The CAMERA pans
the audience. Wattled Gent furiously scribbles notes; Rose,
her nose red, listens dully from the back row; Jimroy sits
with hooded eyes, looking trapped and betrayed, much as he
looked on the airplane, Sarah continues, her voice very gradually becoming audible again,

SARAH: . . . And I'd like to state in conclusion that, like
    other self-generated artists, Mary Swann had the ability
    to state her truths with a sharpness and slant that lit
    up what had become stale by traditional use. It's this,
    more than anything else that gives her work its power.
    Ladies and gentlemen, thank you. (There is a pleasing
    roll of applause, and a number of hands immediately
    go up.)
LANG (stepping to microphone and holding up a hand): Just
    a few questions, I'm afraid. Lunch is ordered for 12:30
    sharp. (He looks into the audience, spots Woman With
    Turban, and points.)
WOMAN WITH TURBAN: Dr. Maloney, I found your remarks
    about the resonance of the primitive imagination inter-
    esting —
SARAH: Actually, I didn't use . . . I deliberately avoided the
    word *primitive*.
WOMAN WITH TURBAN (waving this objection aside):
    Untutored then. Self-nurtured. Whatever. You seem to
    feel, if I understand you properly, that it is impossible
    for a twentieth-century being to escape the — what was
    the exact word — ?
SARAH: Matrix.
WOMAN WITH TURBAN: Matrix, yes. That even at the edge of
    the social matrix, certain cultural ideas are absorbed.
    Even the social outcast —

SARAH: With respect, *outcast* is another term that I rather rigorously —

WOMAN WITH TURBAN (patiently): Even those at the *fringe* of the, shall we say, prevailing communal structure, are open to general patterns of cultural thought — have I quoted you correctly?

SARAH (recovering some of her combative sparkle, but fearful of where this line of questioning is leading): Yes and no. It is, of course, very difficult to pin down what Swann may have perceived about the direction and . . . (searches for word) *shape* of modern poetry —

WOMAN WITH TURBAN: But isn't that, in fact, exactly what we *must* do? Look beyond the work to some other form of documentation that reinforces —

SARAH: Ideally, yes, but we all know how rare the ideal situation is. In Mary Swann's case —

JIMROY (standing suddenly and interrupting; his tone is peculiarly aggressive): If I may interrupt our questioner — whose name I'm afraid I don't know —

WOMAN WITH TURBAN: Professor Croft. From Tulane.

JIMROY: Thank you, Ms. Croft. If I may interject . . . a special plea on my part, I'm afraid . . . that is to say, we are all anxious to discover *anything at all* that may illuminate the . . . character of Mary Swann's special muse. And we all lament, I am sure, that there is so little apparent light. Mrs. Swann, alas, left us no transcribed manifesto. She did *not* write scholarly articles or essays elucidating her poetic theories. She did not enjoy the pleasure of an extensive correspondence. But she did, and perhaps this is what my distinguished colleague . . . Ms. . . . sorry, I'm afraid —

WOMAN WITH TURBAN (crossly): Croft. From Tulane.

JIMROY: — what Ms. Croft (pause) of Tulane . . . was alluding to. The fact is, Mary Swann did keep a journal. I wonder, Dr. Maloney, if you, as the one person privy to the contents of this journal, might be persuaded to say a few words about it today? (He sits.)

SARAH: Well, I —

JIMROY (rising again): I am particularly interested, and I'm sure my colleagues at this symposium are equally interested — (he waves a hand airily) — in knowing when you intend to make Mrs. Swann's journal available to the public. (He sits.)

MAN WITH OUTSIZE AFRO: Hear, hear.

WOMAN WITH TURBAN (also rising): And while we're on the subject, maybe we should ask Professor Lang when he intends to publish Swann's love poems. We've waited for —

SARAH: I'm afraid —

LANG (half-rising): We seem to be straying from the original question —

JIMROY (rising): The question is really quite simple and can be answered in one word. When, Dr. Maloney, do you intend to publish Mary Swann's journal?

WOMAN WITH TURBAN: Surely the public, or at least those who have an academic investment, should be allowed access to the journal.

MAN WITH OUTSIZE AFRO: Hear, hear.

SARAH (nervously, rubbing her hair and taking a deep breath): The Swann journal . . . as you call it . . . which was given to me by Rose Hindmarch — (CAMERA close-up of Rose, who smiles in a vague and friendly way, apparently recovered from the earlier session) — given to me . . . precisely *because* there was so little of importance in it —

WATTLED GENT (rising): But there must be something. That

is to say, the journal surely contains *words* and words contain *meaning* and so there must be, perforce, some . . . shall we say, value to even the most . . . cursory document. (He sits. There is an uneasy stirring in the room; people move in their chairs, murmur, clearly demanding an explanation.)

SARAH (at a loss): The journal . . . as you call it — and perhaps I should never have used that term in my original article — covered a period of just three months, the summer of 1950. This was, as you all know, before Mrs. Swann began to write her poems —

JIMROY (on his feet, jabbing the air): All the more reason, if I may say so, Ms. Maloney, that the journal holds interest for —

SARAH (regarding him directly; from this point the debate is between the two of them: the Woman With Turban and Wattled Gent fade away): But it is *not* of interest, Mr. Jimroy. I sincerely hoped, when I first looked at it, that it would be. But there is nothing —

JIMROY: Surely, Dr. Maloney, there is *something*.

SARAH (close to tears): There's nothing. Absolutely nothing that would interest —

JIMROY: Then why not demystify the document by allowing others to —

SARAH (exasperated): Shopping lists, Mr. Jimroy. That's what's in the journal. Comments about the weather. Once, once, she mentioned a door latch that was broken. Not a symbolic door latch, either. A real door latch. Anyone could have written the stuff on those pages. That's the tragedy of —

JIMROY (fiercely, but trying for control): Nevertheless, this material, marginal as it may be, and I suppose I must take your word for *that*, Dr. Maloney, this marginalia does offer a glimpse of that private person behind —

SARAH: But I am afraid it does *not*. Offer a glimpse, Mr. Jimroy. Otherwise I would have —

JIMROY (trying for a statesmanlike approach): I can't, of course, speak for my fellow scholars (he gestures broadly), but for the biographer (he claps a hand to his heart), for the biographer, that which *seems* trivial —

SARAH: This journal, Mr. Jimroy, is not even particularly legible —

JIMROY: Ah, that may be, but you see, even the illegible nature of the work offers a kind of comment on —

SARAH (flustered): It's really just . . . I can assure you . . . it is utterly lacking in meaningful —

JIMROY: Dr. Maloney, I am what you might call an old hand in this business of . . . shall we say, uncovering the core of personality. I know perfectly well what most journals are like. They are tentative documents at the most. Provisional. Rambling. Uncommitted to structure. I'm not, you know, such a novice as to presume exegesis. But the feebleness you suggest is attached to Mrs. Swann's journal is surely balanced by the fact that it is, after all, a privileged communication and —

SARAH: I would agree with you in most cases, Mr. Jimroy. (She bears down on his name with bitterness.) But this is a special case —

LANG (stepping forward briskly, anxious to keep the proceedings genial): Awfullly sorry, ladies and gentlemen, but the time —

JIMROY: One question, one question only. A simple yes or no will do. Do you intend, Dr. Maloney, do you intend, at any time in the future, to publish Mary Swann's private journal?

SARAH: Well, I —

LANG: I'm really terribly sorry, but time —

JIMROY: Yes or no?

SARAH: (pausing, waving her hands weakly; her voice is unsteady, almost a whimper): No.

The announcement is greeted by an angry murmur; people turn in their seats and talk openly to their neighbours. In a moment the room is filled with an indignant uproar. Jimroy's voice booms from the back of the room.

JIMROY: And may I inquire (raising his voice in order to be heard) — may I inquire of our speaker why she has decided not to publish Mary Swann's private journal?

LANG: Lunch is now ready, ladies and gentlemen. If you will find your way to the LaSalle Room adjoining this room. I now declare this session adjourned —

JIMROY: (over the uproar): — as to *why* Dr. Maloney has taken it on *herself* to withhold —

SARAH: (whispering into microphone, the kind of whisper that brings instant silence): Because I can't. (She pauses.) Because . . . I am unable. The jounal has been . . . I am sorry to have to say this . . . the jounal has been . . . lost.

She holds out her hands in a gesture of helplessness and shakes her head. The audience stirs; people begin to speak from every corner of the room. SOUND is reinforced by the echo effects of the faulty microphone, so that the noise is crushing. Sarah can be seen mouthing the words again. "The journal has been lost."

Fade to: Interior, the LaSalle Room set up with tables for eight. Noon.

CAMERA focuses on buffet table where there is a large

wet-looking salmon on a platter, several bowls of salad, an immense basket of rolls, plates of cheese and fruit, glasses of wine already poured. The members of the symposium are cheerfully filling their plates, then finding their way to the various tables. The room is loud with social chatter.

CRINKLED FOREHEAD: . . . seems damned unlikely in this day and age, what with storage systems —

WIMPY GRIN: . . . when you think of Willard Lang hoarding the treasure trove —

SILVER CUFFLINKS: . . . fresh salmon. I get so sick of looking at salmon, you'd think —

GREEN TWEED SUIT: . . . think Jimroy was a bit thrown off by the whole thing, first losing his briefcase and then —

ROSE: . . . was so embarrassed, I don't know when I've been so —

GINGER PONYTAIL: Frankly, the man is a tyrant, I don't care what you say, he's —

SILVER CUFFLINKS: How does that line go? From "Lilacs," starting with —

MERRY EYES: A terrible disappointment, and I'd been counting on —

BIRDLADY: I wonder if I could possibly have a glass of water?

WIMPY GRIN: . . . hair of the dog —

GREEN TWEED SUIT: . . . the way she just stood there and took —

WATTLED GENT: May I present Herbert Block.

BLUE-SPOTTED TIE: . . . delicious —

WIMPY GRIN: ...all owe a great deal to the Peregrine Press, you know, and you have to give Mr. Cruzzi credit —

MAN WITH OUTSIZE AFRO: . . . mostly subsidized, of course, but without regional presses —

SILVER CUFFLINKS: . . . piece of fishbone in my throat —

GINGER PONYTAIL: . . . drenched with this rancid olive oil and then absolutely —

JIMROY: We are after all a community of scholars, and —

CRINKLED FOREHEAD: What the hell's wrong with the word *primitive?*

WATTLED GENT: . . . hasn't found it yet, his briefcase that is, but evidently he hopes —

BIRDLADY: . . . the giggle-and-tease school of criticism —

MERRY EYES: . . . spontaneity, always say spontaneity's just another name for shoddiness —

BIRDLADY: . . . was in Nadeau twice, I think, but there wasn't —

SILVER CUFFLINKS: . . . the way he had her pinned there, like a butterfly —

MAN WITH OUTSIZE AFRO: . . . bastard —

CRINKLED FOREHEAD: Would you mind if I join you?

WOMAN WITH TURBAN (turning her attention to Wimpy Grin, seated beside her): Well, of course I'm disappointed. Waiting two years for the love poems and now —

WIMPY GRIN: I'm more than disappointed. I'm thinking of—

WOMAN WITH TURBAN: I felt so sure the journal would serve as a kind of gloss, that is to say, enlarge the meaning of the Water Poems in particular.

WIMPY GRIN: Yes, the Water Poems. Especially those. Not that there's anything obscure about them.

WOMAN WITH TURBAN: Obscurity's not the point. Not at all. I'm talking about reference points. The journal would have expanded the number of reference points — and the love poems will —

WIMPY GRIN: But at least she —

WOMAN WITH TURBAN: Who? Maloney? Or Swann?

WIMPY GRIN: Sarah Maloney. She was very firm about that. That there was nothing in the journal of interest.

WOMAN WITH TURBAN: And you believe that! You honestly believe that? Maybe *she* was unable to see any connections, but —

WIMPY GRIN: Hmmmmmmm.

The CAMERA moves to another table and focuses on Rose Hindmarch in conversation with Syd Buswell.

ROSE (daintily picking at her food): Well, as for myself, I was kind of disappointed. You see, I'd been thinking I might ask her if, well, if she'd care to donate the journal to our little museum, and maybe the rhyming dictionary, too, but I don't want to be an Indian giver —

BUSWELL (chewing and gesturing with his fork): Dictionary?

ROSE (rambling): Since you were in Nadeau we've got ourselves a new room in the museum, a real nice display of, well, you'll have to come and have yourself a look. It's up over the library —

BUSWELL: I'm sure you understand about my comments this morning. Just wanted to point out —

ROSE: Oh well, I'm pretty proud of our library. You see, in the old days, when it was in the post office, we didn't even have —

BUSWELL: . . . just wanted to make the point about the idiocy of influences. Jimroy did the same thing in his Starman book, said Starman's work had been influenced by *Moby Dick*. He exaggerates. Romances. The bugger should have been a novelist, not a bloody biographer —

ROSE (applying sauce to salmon): I haven't actually read —

BUSWELL (ramming a roll into his mouth): He's all talk. He talks documentation, but lives in fairyland —

ROSE: Oh, he's very famous. I looked him up in *Who's Who*—
BUSWELL: Inflated reputation. Happens too frequently. Conjecture. Ha! What about proof! The straight goods.
ROSE: Well, of course, Mrs. Swann and myself . . . we used to talk about . . . we were friends you know. We used to discuss this and that and sometimes we —
BUSWELL (bored): Yeah?

The CAMERA moves to another couple at another table: Merry Eyes and Blue-Spotted Tie.

MERRY EYES: . . . hard to understand how a thing like this can happen —
BLUE-SPOTTED TIE: . . . valuable documentation like that, well, should have been archived of course. I always make sure prime materials are duplicated and archived —
MERRY EYES: It's only common sense.
BLUE-SPOTTED TIE: Especially when you take the view, as I do, that this kind of documentation belongs to the whole scholarly —
MERRY EYES: . . . and not to any one individual. That's certainly the view I take. And as for Professor Lang sitting on the love poems —
BLUE-SPOTTED TIE: . . . really no excuse —
MERRY EYES: Even my working papers I keep in a little fireproof safe we have —
BLUE-SPOTTED TIE: Sense of responsibility.
MERRY EYES: Exactly!

Fade to: Interior, lecture room. Same time as above.
    The CAMERA focuses on the empty lecture room. MUSIC: clarinet, a few repeated phrases. CLOSE-UP of Sarah, on the platform gathering together her lecture notes. Sadly, almost

in a trance, she replaces a paperclip and puts the papers in her briefcase. Her air is one of defeat. In the empty room she appears suddenly small and vulnerable. She can hear the murmur of voices from the adjoining room, and this reinforces her feelings of abandonment. She pauses, looks out over the rows of empty chairs. "Well, that's that," her look says. Then her eyes (and the CAMERA) fall on Frederic Cruzzi, who has remained seated on the far side of the room, very nearly obscured by shadows.

CRUZZI (rising slowly with an old man's stiffness; his voice, too, creaks): Ms. Maloney?

SARAH: Mr. Cruzzi! I . . . didn't see you there. I thought you'd . . . you'd gone in with the others, for lunch.

CRUZZI (pulling himself erect): I was hoping to speak to you alone. If you can spare —

SARAH: Of course. (She descends the platform and, somewhat tentatively, approaches him.)

CRUZZI: May I suggest that, instead of joining the others, we escape for an hour. There's something I'd like to discuss with you, and — there's quite a good restaurant downstairs. Or perhaps the coffee shop might be quicker.

SARAH (pausing, smiling): Yes, let's. I'd like to get away for an hour. Especially after . . . (She gestures toward the platform.)

CRUZZI: Well, then. (He offers his arm in a rather old-world manner.) I don't move very quickly, I'm afraid.

SARAH: In that case (takes his arm), we can take our time.

The CAMERA follows them out of the room and into the corridor. Together they pause for a moment and regard the glass display unit in which can be seen a few off-prints and, in the centre, the photograph of Mary Swann.

CRUZZI (tapping the glass softly): Our woman of mystery.

SARAH: Yes. (She smiles at Cruzzi, and then the two of them proceed slowly down the corridor toward the elevator. MUSIC: organ, the upper ranges; dissolve.)

Cruzzi and Sarah are seated at a corner table. A waiter has just placed a large leafy salad before Sarah, a golden omelette in front of Cruzzi.

CRUZZI (relaxed and talkative, a man who expands in the company of women): This really is very pleasant — to escape. I'm not sure why it is, but I find that a roomful of "scholars" tends to bring on an attack of mental indigestion. That Delphic tone they love to take. And something chilly and unhelpful about them too. I'm speaking generally, of course.

SARAH (smiling; she too is beginning to relax): What I can't understand is Jimroy's attitude. To me, I mean. The antagonism.

CRUZZI (eyeing her keenly): Can't you?

SARAH: I've never met him before this morning. (She chews a piece of celery thoughtfully.) Not face to face. But we've been corresponding, writing back and forth . . . for more than a year now.

CRUZZI: I see.

SARAH: And (continuing to chew) to be truthful, he's a good letter writer. Very amusing, if you appreciate ironic edges — and I do. And surprisingly intimate at times. Open. He must have written me half a dozen times to say how much he looked forward to our meeting. (She puts down her celery branch.) But today — I can't figure it out. He was . . . baiting me. He was . . . today he was — (She stops herself, bites her lip.)

CRUZZI (patiently prompting): Today?

SARAH: Today — well you were there when Willard Lang introduced us. At first Jimroy seemed scared to death. Went all cold-fish. And during the question time, after my presentation, I had the feeling that he — this may be putting it in a bit strongly, but I had the distinct feeling... he actually... hated me.

CRUZZI (calmly): Hmmmm.

SARAH: And... I don't know why. That's the scary part. The minute Willard Lang mentioned that I'd got married — did you see his face, Jimroy's? As though I'd smashed him in the stomach. I suppose, well, maybe I should have mentioned in my last letter that I was getting married, but... I didn't decide... the wedding was sort of a sudden decision. I'd been seeing someone else, another man, and that didn't work out and... Why am I blathering away like this?

CRUZZI: I wouldn't worry about Jimroy. Some men, you know — forgive me if I sound like a wizened sage — but some men only relate to women in the... abstract. And not in the actuality. A letter, even an intimate letter, is still somewhat of an abstraction.

SARAH: I hate to be hated. It's a failing of mine. Especially when I don't know what I've done to earn it.

CRUZZI: It's just a thought, but — (he pours mineral water into a glass, with deliberation) — could it be that you have something he wants?

SARAH (looking up abruptly from her salad): Like what?

CRUZZI: Perhaps — (he shrugs elegantly) — perhaps something he imagined to be in Mrs. Swann's notebook. Her journal.

SARAH: But I told him... you heard me... I told everyone in the room, and it's the truth, that there's nothing *in* the

notebook. I know it sounds as though I'm making
excuses. I did lose it. Okay. I'll never know how it happened, but I have to take responsibility for *that*. One day
I had it, and the next day I didn't. *Mea culpa*. Eeehh! But
I'm *not* concealing anything. There's nothing *in* the
journal.

CRUZZI: Not what you hoped.

SARAH: I thought I was going to get a look right inside that
woman's head. That she'd be saying the unsayable, a
whole new level of revelation, you know what I mean.
Instead I found "Tire on truck burst," "Rain on Tuesday,"
"Down with flu." Nothing.

CRUZZI: Yes, but —

SARAH: But?

CRUZZI (taking his time): As I understand it, you *did* have
the notebook for some time. Three, four years? And
you've steadfastly resisted the idea of publishing it.

SARAH (shrugging, regretful, but grinning): I know, I know.
I kept reading it over and over. I kept thinking —
there's just got to be *something* here. Like maybe she's
got a symbol system going. Or maybe it's written in
some elaborate, elegant cipher that . . . but (she shrugs
again) in the end I had to conclude that there just wasn't
anything! I hated like hell to admit she was so . . .

CRUZZI: Ordinary? (He swirls his drink and looks upward.)

SARAH (sending him a shrewd look): You know, Mr. Cruzzi,
you are looking just the slightest bit doubtful. As
though . . . you think I might be withholding something when I say there was nothing there.

CRUZZI: No. I believe you. Mrs. Swann, in my judgement,
was an ordinary woman. Whatever that word means.
Of course you were disappointed.

SARAH: And maybe, I have to admit it, a little protective.

About her . . . ordinariness. Sometimes I've wondered if that's why Willard Lang hasn't published the love poems. He's had them long enough.

CRUZZI: You're suggesting they might be of doubtful quality?

SARAH (shrugging): Sentimental, maybe. Soft-centred. Valentine verse. You probably know how he found them? He bribed the real-estate agent at the Swann house, and then found these papers under a loose bit of linoleum.

CRUZZI: You may be right. Of course we have only his word that what he found were love poems.

SARAH: And *you* may be right, too, that Jimroy wants something.

CRUZZI (thoughtfully): Whatever I may think of Morton Jimroy personally, I am forced to admit he is a thorough biographer. You've read his books. I think he, quite simply, wants it all.

SARAH: All what?

CRUZZI: He wants Mrs. Swann's life. Every minute of it if he could have it. Every cup of tea that poor woman imbibed. Every thought in her tormented head. And what's more, he wants her death. Or some clue to it.

SARAH (looking puzzled): The notebook was written in 1950. And Mary Swann was murdered in 1965. Does he actually think he's going to find —

CRUZZI: . . . that there might be a hint? A portent? A scrap of prophecy? Yes, I *do* think so. I met the man —

SARAH: Jimroy?

CRUZZI: Yes. I met him only once. He paid me a brief visit in Kingston a year ago, and we spent some time talking. To be honest, I found him a dry stick, but I do recall some of our conversation. And I remember how hard he pressed me about Mrs. Swann's death. Did I have any "theories?" (Sardonically): He was, I thought, more than a little obsessive about the *cause* of Mrs. Swann's death.

SARAH: The cause?

CRUZZI: He feels . . . he made it quite clear that he'll never be able to understand Mrs. Swann's life until he understands her death.

SARAH: He actually said that?

CRUZZI: I find it a whimsical notion myself.

SARAH: Romantic.

CRUZZI: But then, he has a somewhat romantic view of a human life. Sees it as something with an . . . aesthetic shape. A wholeness. Whereas — whereas the lives of most people are pretty scrappy affairs. And full of secrets and concealments. As I'm almost sure you will agree.

Director's Note: The very long silence that follows Cruzzi's speech signals, to the audience, an abrupt shift of mood. LIGHTING also changes, and the CAMERA loses its sharpness of focus. A few bars of MUSIC (a single oboe) fill in the void. The gazes of the two characters, Sarah and Cruzzi, seem directed inward, rather than at each other.

SARAH (suddenly): I'm pregnant.

CRUZZI (smiling): Splendid.

SARAH: I just wanted you to know. What *I* was concealing. (She lifts a glass of milk to her lips, as though giving a toast.)

CRUZZI (also lifting his glass): And *I* am in love.

SARAH (pleased): Ahh.

CRUZZI: With a seventy-five-year-old widow. In love, but somewhat frightened of it.

SARAH: I *was* in love.

CRUZZI: And now?

SARAH: It didn't work out.

CRUZZI: Do you mind? Much?

SARAH: Terribly. I think he loved me too. But he loved a lot of other things more.

CRUZZI: Things?

SARAH: Money, chiefly. He never seemed to get enough. He didn't want to end up like his father, a working stiff.

CRUZZI: So you understand — *why*, I mean?

SARAH (pausing): Yes. And (patting stomach) this seems more important.

CRUZZI: Probably it is. In the long run.

SARAH: And what will you do? About your love? Your widow?

CRUZZI: Think about it a little. Try to get used to it. To be calm about it.

SARAH: Is that why you decided to come to the symposium? To give yourself time?

CRUZZI (nodding thoughtfully): Mrs. Swann *is* a puzzle, and puzzles are . . . (he shrugs) diverting.

SARAH: Her *death* is a puzzle? Is that what you mean?

Director's Note: The moment of intimacy has ended. MUSIC, LIGHTING and CAMERA focus and sharpen.

CRUZZI: Her *life* is a puzzle. Her death, as far as I'm concerned, is just one of those . . . random accidents.

SARAH: An accident! Mr. Cruzzi, you surprise me. (Her voice takes on heat.) That monster, her husband, shot her. Point blank. He hammered her face to mush — I've read all the newspaper reports. And cut her up into pieces and stuck her in a sack. That sounds pretty deliberate to me. And you call that an accident? Without any motive behind it?

CRUZZI (buttering a roll): And what would constitute a "motive"? Probably her "monster" of a husband was hungry and his supper was late. (Cruzzi is a man who speaks often with quotation marks around his words, a manifestation of his growing crustiness.)

SARAH (incredulous): You honestly think a man would hack his wife to death for *that*?

CRUZZI: He *was* a man of violent temper. That much came out in the inquest.

SARAH (gesturing wildly): So supper's a little late and he decides to shoot and dismember his lifelong mate. Show her who's boss.

CRUZZI: Or maybe she gave him a black look. Or talked back. Or burned the potatoes. Or ran out of salt. Or wasted three dollars on bus fare into Kingston. We'll probably never know.

SARAH (her face alight, one finger raised): But what if . . . what if she *did* have a lover . . . a secret . . . it's not impossible . . . and *he* found out about it somehow?

CRUZZI: Can you believe that? That exhausted woman? As you may know, I saw her the same day she was killed. She delivered the poems to my house.

SARAH: But there were the love poems. Under the linoleum. Maybe —

CRUZZI: In matters of love — (his face wears a self-mocking smile) — I have to admit that all things are possible. You've just told me about your own situation.

SARAH: I shouldn't have.

CRUZZI: Don't worry, please. I won't mention it again. But Mary Swann and a lover? Certainly it is what many would *want* to find. A thread of redeeming passion —

SARAH: — in a world that's mainly made up of compromise.

CRUZZI: I would imagine that even Jimroy yearns to discover

it — a love affair for Mary Swann. It would provide specific motivation for the murder, and perhaps he hoped you'd be the one to give it to him.

SARAH (taking this in with a nod): If I ever do find the notebook — and I still haven't given up hope — if I ever find it, the first thing I'm going to do is send Jimroy a photocopy so he can see for himself that there's nothing, *nothing* that points to a love affair —

CRUZZI: I don't think, Sarah, that you are very likely to recover the journal.

SARAH (startled, especially by Cruzzi's ominous tone): And how can you be so sure?

CRUZZI: Because . . . well, one of the reasons I was anxious to talk to you was to discuss — but first, let me ask you something. How exactly did the loss of the journal occur?

SARAH (throwing up her hands, bewildered): Just what I said before — one day I had it, the next day I didn't.

CRUZZI: But where did you normally keep it?

SARAH: I've got a little shelf over my bed. What a perfect fool I was to trust —

CRUZZI: And one day you looked at this little shelf and the journal was gone?

SARAH: I must have picked it up by mistake, thrown it away. It wasn't very big, you know, and —

CRUZZI: Or perhaps someone *else* picked it up —

SARAH (stopped for a moment): No. No one else would have done that. (She shakes her head vigorously.) No!

CRUZZI: Why not?

SARAH: Because . . . who would want to?

CRUZZI (speculatively; it is his nature to be speculative): There are any number of reasons that . . . certain individuals might want access to Mary Swann's journal. Scholarly greed for one. Or the sheer monetary value of —

SARAH: Mr. Cruzzi. I don't know if I'm understanding you
or not. Surely you're not saying that someone might
have *stolen* the journal?

CRUZZI: Yes. That is what I am saying.

SARAH: That's — (she regards him closely, then laughs) —
that's a little wild, if you'll excuse my saying so.

CRUZZI: Do I appear to you to be a crazy person?

SARAH (embarrassed): No. No, of course not, I —

CRUZZI: "Senile" perhaps? "Screw loose?" "Bats in the bel-
fry"? Paranoid delusions?

SARAH: Mr. Cruzzi, I keep my doors locked. You know where
I live? The south side of Chicago. I've got triple locks on
my doors, back and front. On the groundfloor windows
I've got iron bars, and I'm thinking of installing —

CRUZZI: Perhaps . . . perhaps someone you know. Someone
who just happened to be in your house and saw —

SARAH (laughing, but only a little): Light-fingered friends I
don't have. The people I know don't give two beans for
Mary Swann. As a matter of fact, they're sick to death of
hearing me talk about Mary Swann — they actually put
their hands over their ears when I start to —

CRUZZI (interrupting, speaking with even-tempered deliberation; this is what he has been wanting to say to her all
along): On Christmas Eve — are you listening, Sarah
Maloney? — my house in Kingston was burgled. I was
out for a few hours, and when I returned — I, too, lock
my doors by the way, even in Kingston — and when I
returned home I found certain items missing. I wonder
if you can guess what they might be?

SARAH (alarmed by the gravity of his tone; she puts down
her knife and fork quietly): What?

CRUZZI: For one thing, a file relating to the publication of
Mrs. Swann's book, and . . .

SARAH: And?

CRUZZI: And four copies of *Swann's Songs*. The only copies I possess, by the way. We — my late wife and I — published only 250 copies of Mrs. Swann's book. That was the usual print run for a small press in those days — and I am told that only about twenty of those still exist.

SARAH: That's true. A friend of mine, well, more than a friend . . . the man I mentioned earlier —

CRUZZI: The man you loved?

SARAH (after a pause): Yes. He's in the rare book business and he says that's the norm, that books, especially paperbound books just . . . (gestures skyward) disappear.

CRUZZI: I'm sure you can imagine my distress when I discovered the books had been stolen.

SARAH: You're saying — ?

CRUZZI: Nothing else in the house was touched.

SARAH (shaking her head in disbelief, unable to imagine what this means): But it must be a joke — maybe a practical joke.

CRUZZI (shaking his head): And naturally, with the thought of this symposium coming up, I was anxious to acquire a copy of *Swann's Songs*, simply to refresh my memory. With my own copies gone, I tried the Kingston Public Library. And then the university library. In both places the copies seem to have been, shall we say, "spirited away."

SARAH (first shocked, then solemn, then doubtful): But look, libraries are notorious for misplacing their holdings. Or else they've got lousy security systems and with all the petty vandals around — it happens all the time. Even in the university where I teach . . . (she pauses) . . . the university archives . . .

CRUZZI (sitting patiently with laced fingers; he senses what she is about to say): Go on.

SARAH: . . . even there . . . well, they've been known to . . .
   lose . . . quite valuable papers, whole collections even —

CRUZZI: The Mary Swann collection, for example?

SARAH: How did you know?

CRUZZI : I made a phone call. When I began to suspect that
   something was going on.

SARAH: Surely —

CRUZZI: I've also phoned the National Library in Ottawa,
   the University of Toronto library, the University of
   Manitoba —

SARAH (shaking her head over the absurdity of it all): And
   you began to suspect a worldwide conspiracy? Is that it?

CRUZZI: I can see . . . I can tell from your expression . . . that
   you believe me to be quite insane.

SARAH: I just —

CRUZZI: You have one of those transparent faces, I'm afraid,
   that gives you away. You observe this ancient gent
   before you. One eye asquint, the casualty of a recent
   stroke. Voice quavery. He has been babbling about love,
   of all things. Love! And now it is paranoid accusations.
   Academic piracy.

SARAH: But surely —

CRUZZI: I don't blame you for suspecting imbalance. I was
   of the same opinion. What kind of old goat was I getting
   to be? — that's what I asked myself. And then I talked
   to Buswell.

SARAH: Buswell! That self-pitying misogynist . . .

CRUZZI: Yes. Exactly. I do agree. But he has a similar story to
   tell. His notes for an article on Swann *and* his copy of
   Swann's Songs, he tells me, were removed from his desk.
   He had left the office for only a minute, he claims, and
   when he returned —

SARAH: It still seems a little —

CRUZZI: Fanciful? I agree with you there. As a matter of fact, it wasn't until this morning, when you yourself announced the loss of Mrs. Swann's notebook that I became persuaded that there was a rather remarkable, not to say alarming, pattern to all this. If you know anything about the laws of probability, you will quickly see —

SARAH: It's a little hard to see who would want . . . and for what reason? (The waiter puts the bill down on the table, and both Sarah and Cruzzi reach for it.) Please, Mr. Cruzzi, let me. Please. It's been my pleasure. (She places bills on the plate, and rises.)

CRUZZI (rising stiffly; his speech, too, is stiff, containing the awkwardness of translated words): I think, rather, that I have *not* given you pleasure. I have given you my own troubling concerns, and I am sorry for that. But I do feel . . . that this his gone far enough. And that something will have to be . . . (His voice fades and blends with the general noise.)

Sarah leaves the coffee shop, walking slowly by Cruzzi's side. CAMERA follows them into the hotel lobby; they can be observed talking, but what they say is drowned out by the general noise of passers-by and by MUSIC: a swirling organ tune that holds an element of agitation. They stand waiting before a bank of elevators, gesturing, conferring, questioning, shaking their heads; one of the elevators opens, and they step inside.

Cut to: Interior of an identical elevator. Same time as above.

Jimroy is alone in the elevator. The doors spring open, and he is joined by Rose Hindmarch who steps aboard in sprightly fashion.

JIMROY: Ah, Miss Hindmarch. Enjoying the symposium?

ROSE (laughing): Please, it's Rose. You remember — Rose!

JIMROY: Rose. Of course.

ROSE: Oh, I'm having the loveliest time. Everyone's so nice
and friendly, well, almost everyone. (She makes a face,
thinking of Buswell.)

JIMROY: I think you'll find the afternoon interesting. A number of papers on various —

ROSE (nervously): You don't think we'll be late, do you? I went
up to my room for a little lie-down after lunch. I haven't
been awfully well of late, and then all these new faces,
well, it's tiring. And the trip down from Kingston, and the
elevators—elevators always give me a funny feeling in the
tummy. I'd of taken the stairs, but I didn't want to be late.

JIMROY: They can be tiring, meetings like this. (The elevator
doors open. Politely he allows Rose to exit first, then he
follows; they are about to pass the glass display case
holding Mary Swann's photograph when Rose suddenly
grasps Jimroy's arm.)

Director's Note: Jimroy must cringe at Rose's touch. It is
important that the actor playing this role reveal, by facial
expression and bodily contraction, that he finds Rose's touch
repellent and that he regards the photograph of Mary
Swann as vaguely threatening.

ROSE (girlish, garrulous): There she is! Don't you wonder
what she'd think of all this fuss. I mean, she'd be just
bowled over to think . . . (CAMERA focuses on Mary
Swann's photo.)

JIMROY (speaking socially, composing himself): Good of you to
bring the photograph along, Miss Hindmarch. Rose. Some
people like to have a visual image to reinforce — (His
manner implies he himself is not one of these people.)

ROSE: Oh, well, of course it's a terrible, terrible likeness. Out of focus, you know, and too much sun, that was the trouble with those old box cameras, you couldn't adjust for the light —

JIMROY (anything to shut her up): Well, as I say, it is most fortunate to have even a poor likeness. I don't suppose we can expect anything —

ROSE (suddenly courageous, seizing her opportunity): Mr. Jimroy. Morton. There's something — if you don't mind — something I'd like to ask you about.

JIMROY (gesturing at the open door of the meeting room where people are beginning to assemble for the afternoon session): Perhaps we might converse a little later. I believe (he consults his watch) it's nearly time for the next —

ROSE (not about to let him escape): It's just, well, I don't want to seem impolite or anything, but, you see, there's something I've been wanting to mention to you. Ever since that time you visited Nadeau. I almost wrote you a letter once—

JIMROY (his expression is one of pain): I believe we *are* going to be late if we don't —

ROSE (pursuing): You remember when you came to Nadeau, that you wanted, you wanted to see everything, you were so interested in every last little thing?

JIMROY: A most pleasant visit as I remember. Most interesting. But really, we must —

ROSE: Oh, we talked and talked, I remember how you asked all about —

JIMROY: I believe, yes, we had a most interesting —

ROSE: You took me out for dinner. To the Elgin Hotel, remember? We had the double pork chop platter. With apple sauce. I'll never forget that. That evening. But do you remember the next day, I'm sure you do, visiting the

museum, the Mary Swann Memorial Room, that's what
I want to ask you about . . . Morton.

JIMROY (attempting once more to extricate himself): Most
fascinating exhibition. A credit to your community, yes.
Perhaps we can chat later, but now —

ROSE (doggedly): I showed you those two photographs of
Mary Swann, the ones they found in a dresser drawer
after she was . . . Do you remember that? There were —

The voice of Willard Lang can be heard from the meeting room.

LANG: Ladies and gentlemen, the afternoon session is now
called to order and —

JIMROY: I really am awfully afraid — I don't want to
miss . . . (He makes a helpless gesture toward the door.)

ROSE: There was *this* photograph *here* (points to display case)
and then there was the *other* one. A much better likeness. Not so fuzzy. Her eyes, Mrs. Swann's eyes, were
wide open, remember? You picked it up and said how
her eyes showed feeling. Do you remember, Mr. Jimroy,
how you picked up —

JIMROY: I'm afraid not. I don't really remember there being
another — and I certainly never picked up —

ROSE: But it's true, I remember things like that. People are
always saying what a memory I've got. Like a camera!
You picked up the picture and —

JIMROY (attempting unsuccessfully to get around her): If you
don't mind. This is really —

ROSE: — and afterwards, the very next day when I went into
that room . . . I was showing a bunch of school kids
around and —

JIMROY (dully, with desperation): Please!

ROSE: — and I was just about to show them the two photographs, and one of them was missing. The good one with the eyes open. It was gone, Mr. Jimroy. And now — I hate to say this, but facts are facts and you were the last person to . . . (gasps for breath) and I think it's only fair for you to —

JIMROY: This is outrageous! (He speaks loudly, not just to Rose, but to Merry Eyes and Wimpy Grin, who are arriving late, stepping arm-in-arm off an elevator, followed a second later by Sarah and Cruzzi.) I did not come all the way from California, Miss Hindmarch, to listen to . . . dim-witted *ravings*.

ROSE: Oh! (She covers her face with her hands.) Oh! (At the word *ravings,* she rushes in tears to the EXIT stairway, blindly pushing open the door and disappearing.)

JIMROY (shrugging to Merry Eyes, Wimpy Grin, Sarah, and Cruzzi, who stand in stunned bafflement before him): Poor soul. She's been ill apparently. Very ill. Under a strain. I'm not sure she's . . . (winces) . . . afraid she's not quite . . . (He taps his forehead meaningfully.)

Sarah's mouth drops. CAMERA close-up. She is taking in Jimroy's behaviour, which is close to hysterical. Her eyes move sideways and meet Cruzzi's.

Again the voice of Lang is heard from the meeting room.

LANG: And so if you will kindly take your places we will commence with —

Director's Note: The next few TAKES are fragmentary; their purpose is not to illuminate the film's theme or to advance the action, but to suggest the passing of time. The symposium has moved into its second stage; the atmosphere

is calm, hard-working, serious, even somewhat plodding,
and the faces of the actors must reflect this shift.

Fade to: Interior of the meeting room. Afternoon.

Blue-Spotted Tie is standing at the lectern, winding up
a paper entitled "Regional Allusions in the Poetry of Mary
Swann."

BLUE-SPOTTED TIE: And now, to sum up my main points
of departure: the non-specific nature of the geo-socio-
logical references in Mrs. Swann's universe, and the
mythic and biblical implications of place names and
allusions. . .

Cut to: Interior of small seminar room. Afternoon.

A workshop is in progress. Eight men and women are
seated around a table. The discussion leader is Woman With
Turban.

WOMAN WITH TURBAN: . . . would sincerely like to thank
you all for your participation, especially Professor
Herbert Block, who has been so kind as to give us his
ideas concerning a post-modernist interpretation of
Swann's Water Poems. (Polite applause.)

Cut to: Interior of meeting room. Late afternoon.

WATTLED GENT (at lectern): . . . and I do apologize for going
over time, but I want to express my thanks to you all for
your enthusiastic reception of — but I see I'm getting a
signal. Thank you. (Applause.)

Cut to: Interior of the LaSalle Room. Early evening.

The members of the symposium are mingling in a cocktail atmosphere. There is a sound of glasses, ice clinking, and blurred talk.

WISTFUL DEMEANOUR: . . . not a bad day, all in all —

WOMAN WITH TURBAN: . . . but it's the love poems we really came for —

MAN WITH OUTSIZE AFRO: The love poems, ha! I'll eat my neck-tie if Lang —

GINGER PONYTAIL: . . . splitting headache —

CRINKLED FOREHEAD: . . . was a trifle disturbed by his remarks regarding —

BIRDLADY: . . . blatantly sexist —

GREEN TWEED SUIT: Slash, slash —

GINGER PONYTAIL: Jesus, the smoke in here's thick enough to —

WOMAN IN PALE SUEDE BOOTS: . . . and the noise —

SILVER CUFFLINKS: . . . sorry, I didn't catch —

The noise escalates, loud, indistinct, overwhelming.

Cut to: Interior of the banquet room. Evening.

Dinner is over; coffee cups litter the long white tablecloths. Members of the symposium are relaxed at their places, some smoking, lolling in their chairs, only partly attentive to the speaker. Rose Hindmarch, dressed in a harsh red lace dress, sits between Cruzzi (in a dark suit) and Sarah (in dark green silk with a lace collar).

LANG (at head table): . . . his been a most profitable first day, ladies and gentlemen. Just a reminder before we adjourn—we will be meeting at nine-thirty sharp tomorrow for our session on Swann's love poems. Thank you.

People begin to rise from the tables. There is the sound of chairs being pushed back, spontaneous conversations springing up. The crowd begins to surge into the corridor and disperse. MUSIC: dense, lyrical.

Cut to: Interior of the hotel corridor, between the display case and the bank of elevators. Evening.

The crowd thins out; there is continuous chattering as people enter elevators, call good night and disappear. A small group stands in front of the display case.

ROSE: Well, I've had it for this day. I don't know when I've been so dog tired.

WOMAN WITH TURBAN: Gawd, morning's going to come early.

MERRY EYES: Anyone for a nightcap? I've some gin in my room and a little —

BLUE-SPOTTED TIE: Don't mind if I do. How 'bout you, Mr. Cruzzi?

CRUZZI: Ah, well, perhaps one —

WISTFUL DEMEANOUR: Why not?

CRINKLED FOREHEAD: Onward!

SARAH (to Merry Eyes, Blue-Spotted Tie, etc.): Good night.

CRUZZI (tapping on display case): Good night, Mrs. Swann.

SARAH (extending a hand to Cruzzi): Good night. I'm glad . . . very glad we've had a chance to talk. And you, too, Rose. (Her tone is weighted with meaning.)

Director's Note: There is a shaking of hands all around, a sense of people going off in their separate directions, and a sense, too, of a change in mood, a gathering of tension. MUSIC: begins slowly, a combination of strings and organ. Frederic Cruzzi, Rose, and the others enter the elevators and disappear, leaving Sarah alone in the corridor. Her hand moves to touch the elevator button, then hovers in the air uncertainly. Her face wears a look of intense concentration, and her wandering hand goes first to her mouth, then becomes part of a salute in the direction of the display case.

SARAH (softly whispering): Good night, Mary Swann. Sleep . . . tight.

Fade to: Interior of the same corridor. It is approaching midnight, and the corridor is in total darkness.

MUSIC: alto clarinet, very soft. Complete darkness gives way to partial darkness. Light in the corridor is provided by the red EXIT sign over the stairs and by the illuminated panel above the bank of elevators. A portion of this dim light reaches the glass display unit and shines on its mitred edges. SOUND: clarinet diminishes until the silence is total; this lasts for a few beats; then the silence is broken by a small swishing sound. The door to the EXIT stairway opens, and the figure of a man slips quickly through. He is only faintly visible, but CAMERA picks him up in silhouette as, quickly and quietly, he approaches the display case, glancing catlike over his shoulder. From his pocket he takes two or three small keys and begins to tinker with the lock of the case. His first attempts fail, he then takes out a small knife and works it into the lock. There is a sharp sound as the locking mechanism breaks and the lid of the display case opens. At this moment, as he is about to reach for the photograph, a sudden beam of light falls on him, causing him to jerk with surprise.

SARAH (emerging from behind the coffee vending machine with a flashlight in her hand. The beam of light catches the man on his arm, which he quickly raises to cover his

face. Sarah's voice is shaky but determined): Hello, Mr.
Jimroy. I thought I might find you here.

The intruder jumps, letting the lid of the display case
crash heavily. It breaks. He runs for the stair exit, pursued
by Sarah, who has difficulty keeping the beam of light
directed on him.

Sarah follows, but arrives at the stairwell in time to
see only his fleeing back in a maintenance man's uniform,
disappearing down the stairs. She turns back to the display
case and, as she does so, her light picks out the figure of
Morton Jimroy, his back pressed to the wall at the doorway
of the meeting room. The LIGHTING increases slightly, but
only enough to suggest eyes growing gradually accustomed
to the darkness. Seeing Jimroy, Sarah gasps.

JIMROY (sardonically, arms crossed on his chest): Well, well,
    Dr. Maloney. Prowling the corridors. And with a flash-
    light I see. A regular Girl Guide on patrol.
SARAH (glancing back at door): And what are you doing
    here, Mr. Jimroy? If I may ask.
JIMROY: The same thing you're doing, I would guess.
    Guarding (gestures toward the display case) our high
    priestess from thieves and rogues.
SARAH: Who? . . . (She is shaken and confused.) Who *was*
    that? (She gestures toward the exit.)
JIMROY: I'm afraid I didn't see *its* face. Not having equipped
    myself with a handy flashlight.
SARAH (holding up the flashlight): I borrowed it from the
    front desk. (She laughs nervously.) I told them I was . . .
    afraid of the dark. Who *was* that?
JIMROY: It looked like one of the maintenance men. At
    least he wore the garb. I gather from your . . . your

outburst . . . that you thought it was *I* who was busying myself with the burglar tools.

SARAH: Do you think, Mr. Jimroy, that you might speak to me, just for once, in a normal voice. Not quite so loaded with venom.

JIMROY (continuing in sardonic tone): I was almost sure I heard my name ringing out in the darkness. Well, I don't have to ask you who planted the ugly seeds of suspicion in your head. I suppose our dear MissHindmarch has been spreading her libellous little tales. Which have no foundation, let me tell you.

SARAH: You *were* in Nadeau. She *did* show you the photo — she told me. And it disappeared the same day. I don't pretend to understand what you're up to, Mr. Jimroy, but — quite a number of things seem to be disappearing . . . as I think you know.

JIMROY: Including, if I may remind you, my own briefcase. During our little power break yesterday evening.

SARAH: Someone probably . . . in the confusion —

JIMROY (interrupting decisively): Do you know what was in that briefcase? Let me tell you. My notes for my lecture. All right, those notes are of little importance. I'm quite accustomed to speaking without notes. But I also had with me my copy of *Swann's Songs*. And need I tell you, it was my only copy. Can you imagine my . . . grief.

SARAH (softening): I'm sorry about that. Really. But about the photograph, the *other* photograph —

JIMROY: Would you kindly stop shining that light in my eyes? Your Miss Marple act is less polished if I may say so, than your . . . letters.

SARAH: And will you kindly stop addressing me with that accusing tone. Has anyone ever told you that continual sarcasm can be offensive?

JIMROY (always a man to take a question seriously): My wife.
SARAH: Your wife?
JIMROY: My ex-wife, I should say. Her daily complaint. Sarcasm.

Cut to: Interior of the stairwell. Same time as above.

 The stairway is dimly lit and pin-droppingly quiet. Very gradually the sound of slow, trudging ascending footsteps is heard. CAMERA focuses on Rose Hindmarch, still in her red party dress, climbing the stairs. She is breathing with difficulty, clutching at the rail, resting occasionally. She is alerted suddenly by the sound of descending footsteps, rapidly approaching. Her look changes from exhaustion to fear, and she stops, listens, then flattens herself against the wall in the shadows. The footsteps continue to approach.

INTRUDER (coming into view, startled to see Rose crouched against the wall): What — ?
ROSE (relieved somewhat at the sight of the maintenance uniform): I was just . . .
INTRUDER (attempting to get around her): Excuse me.
ROSE: Good heavens. Why — aren't you? . . .
INTRUDER (trying again to pass Rose): I'm in a hurry, sorry.
ROSE: But, don't I know you? You look so — I'm Rose. From the town clerk's office. In Nadeau. Wasn't it you — ?
INTRUDER: Sorry, I don't know you.
ROSE (drawing back): Unless . . . maybe I've made a mistake.
INTRUDER: Must be, I've never —
ROSE: You could be his twin brother, do you know that? He just bought a farm in our area . . . A hobby farm, he calls it. He's the spitting image —
INTRUDER: Sorry. I've got work to do.
ROSE: I feel such a fool. Usually I remember faces. Names now, I have trouble with —

INTRUDER: I'm afraid I have to — (He succeeds in getting past Rose, and continues down the stairs, running, taking them two at a time.)

Rose shrugs, mystified, then continues puffing her way up the stairs. At the eighteenth floor she pushes open the door into a dark corridor and sees two shadowy figures, one of them holding a flashlight. She rubs her eyes with a bewildered hand, still panting from the exertion of the climb. Her voice shaking, she calls out.

ROSE: Who's there? Is someone there?

SARAH: It's me, Rose. Sarah. And Morton Jimroy.

ROSE: For heaven's sake. What are you doing — ?

SARAH: It's all right, Rose.

ROSE (seeing the broken display case): I knew it! I knew it! I got back to my room and was about to get ready for bed, and I got to thinking — (she shoots Jimroy a baleful look) — that I didn't trust —

JIMROY: Good God, is she going to start up all that again!

ROSE: . . . so I said to myself, I'll just go see if everything's safe. I would of taken the elevator but my tummy always . . . so I walked all the way up to . . . and here he is. I knew I should have had it out with him right away when the other photograph —

SARAH: Now look Rose —

JIMROY: There is such a thing as professional ethics, you know. (To Sarah): If you could please explain to Miss Hindmarch here that —

ROSE: . . . the very day it was gone I should have done something, maybe called the police, but I —

SARAH: Rose, he says he didn't —

ROSE: . . . and then to say I was ranting. *Ranting*, when all I wanted was to get the picture back. For the museum. That museum means an awful lot to me, you know.

JIMROY: Dear God, I've had about enough for one day.

SARAH: Rose, we've been talking, the two of us, and —

ROSE (snatching the photograph out of the broken case and tucking it under her arm): I'll just keep this in *my* room tonight.

SARAH: Rose, will you listen?

JIMROY: . . . ranting and raving —

SARAH: Rose, it was someone *else* who broke the case. M . . . Mr. Jimroy and I just happened . . . to be here when —

ROSE: I have to think about the museum. (She clutches the photograph.) I'm the one who's responsible —

SARAH: There was someone *else* here. Maybe you saw . . . on the stairs just now. Did you see someone? A man?

ROSE (calming down): One of the maintenance men. But it was so dark that . . . I couldn't see him real well. I thought —

SARAH: We saw him in the act of breaking into the case. Another minute and —

ROSE: A maintenance man at the Harbourview Hotel? What would he want with? . . . I still think — (She glares at Jimroy.)

JIMROY: I am not in the habit of —

SARAH: It's someone *else*, Rose. *Everyone's* losing things all of a sudden. I've been talking to Frederic Cruzzi, and it seems all sorts of people have lost —

JIMROY: Including, if I may interrupt, myself. You will remember, I'm sure, that my own briefcase was stolen right here in the hotel. And there have been one or two other items as well.

ROSE: I thought — (puzzled) — naturally I thought —

SARAH: Frederic Cruzzi thinks — he and I had a long talk

about it — he thinks all these disappearing objects are
somehow connected. It sounds farfetched, but —

JIMROY: Too much for me, I'm afraid. I'm going to say good
night. This day has been altogether too long. (He glares
at Rose, then presses the button for the elevator.)

SARAH: Maybe we should all talk more tomorrow. See if we
can resolve —

ROSE: I still don't understand why —

SARAH: None of us does, Rose.

JIMROY (as the elevator arrives): Until tomorrow.

Sarah shrugs and looks at Rose, who shrugs back.

Fade to: Interior of Sarah's hotel room. Midnight.

Sarah is in bed, propped up reading a paperback book,
She holds a pencil in one hand and occasionally makes a
mark in the margin. The small table lamp is her only light.
Her concentration is interrupted by a knock on the door.

SARAH (getting out of bed and moving, with some hesitation, to the door): Who is it?

ROSE: Me. Rose. Rose Hindmarch.

SARAH: Rose? (She immediately undoes the triple lock and
takes the chain off.) Rose!

ROSE: Can I come in? For just a minute? (She is wearing a
robe belted over pyjamas, slippers, and is holding the
photograph in her hands.)

SARAH: Come in, Rose. Sit down.

ROSE (entering and sitting gingerly on the unoccupied bed):
I'm just . . . I don't know where to start . . . I got back to
my room and I just . . . I just started to feel . . . scared to
death, just got a case of the shakes, you know. I don't
know what I'm scared of. (She holds the photograph of

Mary Swann at arm's length.) I looked at this, at her, and all of a sudden I just got scared to death. Of her. (Tears come into Rose's eyes.) And I'm so tired out I don't know what to do.

SARAH (reaching for photo): Would you like me to keep it here, Rose? For the night?

ROSE: Would you?

SARAH: I'll take good care of it. (She carries the photograph to the dresser and sets it up. leaning it against the wall.) Now look, Rose, why don't you stay here tonight, There's an extra bed, plenty of room, and you'll be asleep in two minutes. (She briskly turns down the bed for Rose.) Come on, now. You'll sleep better here. Okay? Why not?

ROSE: I couldn't — (She touches the belt of her robe.) Are you sure? Sure you don't mind? My nerves are so jangled up and —

SARAH: In you go. (She pulls up the covers.) There. Warm enough?

ROSE (relaxing): Fine. Better.

SARAH: Everything'll look better in the morning. (She gets into her own bed and reaches over to turn out the light.)

ROSE: My mother used to say that. It's one of the things mothers say, I guess.

SARAH (yawning): And it's usually true.

ROSE: I guess it's because —

SARAH (almost asleep): Because why, Rose?

ROSE: Well, at night we . . . (She yawns.) We feel the most . . . lonely. At least I do.

SARAH: I was feeling lonely just now. Just before you knocked on the door. (She breathes deeply, almost asleep.)

ROSE: I feel lonely . . . almost all the time. (Her voice blurs, and sleep comes.)

Fade to: Interior of Sarah's room. An hour later.

The two women are asleep. Rose's face wears a look of intense happiness. Sarah's face is more troubled, and she is curled into a tight knot. The sound of knocking at the door gradually causes her to stir and waken, while Rose sleeps on. Sarah rises, slips on a robe, and goes to the door.

SARAH (speaking through the door): Yes? Who is it? (Her voice is groggy with sleep.)

CRUZZI (softly): Frederic Cruzzi.

SARAH (undoing locks and chain): Hello. (She stares at him, puzzled.)

CRUZZI: I hope you weren't asleep. (He sees she *has* been sleeping, and glimpses the second bed, occupied.) I do apologize. I took a chance —

SARAH: It's all right. Come in. What time is it, anyway?

CRUZZI (looking at his watch): One A.M. Hardly an hour to come calling, but — (He stops and glances uneasily at the second bed.)

SARAH: It's Rose. She's . . . keeping me company.

ROSE (hearing her name and opening her eyes): Why, it's Mr. Cruzzi!

CRUZZI: I wanted to let you know —

SARAH: Here. (She offers him an easy chair.) Sit down. (She climbs back into bed and sits with the covers pulled up over her lap.)

CRUZZI: I suppose this could have waited until morning, but . . . I've been down the hall, talking to a few of the others. Professor Croft and that Kramer chap, and what's-his-name with the blue-spotted tie?

SARAH (all attention now): Yes?

CRUZZI: They got into a bit of a discussion — they were all pretty well into their cups by this time — over Block's

interpretation of the Water Poems. I don't know if you
were there —

SARAH: I heard about it —

ROSE (propping herself up on one elbow and reaching for
her glasses): He thinks —

CRUZZI: I wasn't entirely clear about his theory. Thinks the
poems are purely reactive rather than symbolic, something like that — (expresses impatience) — and then
someone, the gentleman with the hair (holds up hands
to describe Afro), suggested we settle the discussion by
consulting the text itself.

SARAH: Yes?

CRUZZI: The long and the short of it was that nobody *had*
a text. There were ten, twelve of us in the room, and no
one had a copy of *Swann's Songs*. Professor Croft —
from Tulane, you remember — went to her room to
get her copy but came back a few minutes later to say
she couldn't find it. She was rather . . . rather frantic, as
a matter of fact. Hysterical. Kramer and the gentleman
in the blue-spotted tie and the other, with the hair, they
all admitted they'd . . . that they'd recently *lost* their
copies.

ROSE (fully awake now): Why, that's what happened to me.
I had my copy, it was sort of falling apart, I had it in a
magazine rack, in my suite, and when I looked for it —

SARAH (to Cruzzi): Then what?

CRUZZI: Well, the emotional temperature in the room began
to rise. Of course, as I say, they were well down in the
bottle, and at that point I thought I might see if you
were still awake and what you made of all this.

SARAH: It certainly does seem as if — (She stops, hearing a
knock at the door.) Who can — ?

ROSE (cheery): Grand Central Station!

SARAH (again undoing the locks, but leaving the chain on.
    She opens the door an inch and peers out): Mr. Jimroy!
    Morton.
JIMROY: I was afraid you might have gone to bed. (He is
    wearing wrinkled pyjamas with a suit jacket over top.)
SARAH: As a matter of fact —
JIMROY: May I come in? For just two minutes.
SARAH (signalling him to enter with a sweeping gesture):
    Won't you join our late-night party?
CRUZZI (with coolness): Good evening, Jimroy.
ROSE (with gawky shrug): Hello again.
JIMROY (pained): I seem to be interrupting —
SARAH: Not at all. Do sit down. (She removes Rose's dressing
    gown from the desk chair to make a place.)

Director's note: This scene, in which the four main characters assemble their separate clues, may be played with a very
slight parodic edge.

JIMROY: I've had a thought, something I thought might
    interest you. It was after we said good night. By the way
    (he looks around), this is entirely confidential.
CRUZZI: Of course.
ROSE: Naturally.
SARAH: After we said good night? (prompting).
JIMROY: I returned to my room and got, as you see, ready for
    bed. But for some reason I was unable to sleep.
ROSE: Exactly the way I felt! Full of the jitters.
CRUZZI: We've all had a long day.
JIMROY (annoyed at the interruptions): *At any rate*, I started
    to turn over the events of the day, and quite a few things
    began to fall into place.
CRUZZI: A "pattern" more or less.

JIMROY: More or less. And I began to wonder if — now this may surprise you, Sarah (he says her name with a break in his voice, as though testing it for substance), but I began to wonder (pauses) if the notebook, Mary Swann's notebook that is, the one you *say* you lost —

SARAH: Yes?

JIMROY: Well, at the risk of sounding . . . ludicrous . . . I wonder if it ever occurred to you that the notebook might have been —

ROSE (pouncing): Stolen!

JIMROY: That was my thought.

SARAH (smiling toward Cruzzi): What a coincidence! Mr. Cruzzi had the same idea.

JIMROY (deflated): Oh.

CRUZZI: It does seem to fit the —

ROSE: The pattern!

JIMROY: Mary Swann is in a most peculiar position. As a literary figure, I mean. She has only been recently discovered, and her star . . . as they say, has risen very quickly. Too soon, for example, for her book to have been reprinted. Too soon for those who admire her work to be sufficiently protective about those artifacts that attach —

CRUZZI: What you're saying is, the situation may have attracted an unscrupulous —

ROSE: You know what I think? (She is terribly excited.) I think it's an inside job. (She looks eagerly at the others.)

CRUZZI: I agree.

SARAH: Someone here? Attending the symposium?

JIMROY: Yes. Most certainly possible.

SARAH: But why would anyone — ?

JIMROY: Someone who wants to corner the available material. Cut us out, all of us, as Swann scholars.

CRUZZI (musing): I'm not sure scholarly acquisitiveness ever goes to quite such extremes. I think it's more likely to be —

ROSE (waving an arm in the air): Money!

JIMROY: Money?

CRUZZI: Yes, I would agree, money.

JIMROY: I still don't see how —

SARAH: I don't either. Whoever is cornering the market won't have any market to sell to. I mean, there's no Swann industry if there are no Swann texts.

JIMROY: I couldn't have said it better.

ROSE: Blackmail! (She speaks with wonderful deliberation.)

CRUZZI: I beg your pardon.

ROSE: Not really blackmail. What's the word! (She attempts, and fails, to snap her fingers.) Like when someone has something you want — like hostage taking!

SARAH: You mean ransom? Extortion?

JIMROY: We don't want to get *too* fanciful about this.

CRUZZI (mulling): And do you think that —

ROSE: It happens all the time. In books. I read quite a lot of books — mysteries, espionage, that sort of thing. You see, Nadeau isn't a big place and there's not a lot going on —

SARAH: So what do you think will happen, Rose?

ROSE: I think whoever it is, well, will try to contact us. Sell us back what . . . used to belong to *us*.

CRUZZI: For an inflated price, of course.

SARAH: Of course.

JIMROY (addressing Rose, now, with respect): And you think it's someone here? One of us? In this hotel?

SARAH: What we could do is go through the symposium list —

JIMROY: Precisely my idea. As a matter of fact, I've brought

along the registration list, and, well, if it's not too late —

SARAH: We're all awake now anyway.

ROSE: I'm wide awake.

CRUZZI: What are there — sixty names?

SARAH: Sixty-seven. Take away the four of us, *and I think we might safely do that,* that's sixty-three.

JIMROY: Shall we begin? (He waves the sheets.)

ROSE (thrilled): Yes. Begin.

CRUZZI: Might as well.

JIMROY (reading in alphabetical order): Aldington, Michael J.

CRUZZI: Afraid I can't quite place —

ROSE (without a moment's hesitation): The one with the pink shirt. Lovely silver cufflinks and the —

SARAH: From Alberta. Michael's straight as an arrow, can't be Michael.

JIMROY: Cross off Aldington. (He gropes for a pencil, then remembers he is in pyjamas.)

SARAH: Here. (She holds out a pencil.)

JIMROY: Thank you.

Director's Note: The handing over of the pencil must be done so that the audience understands that Sarah and Jimroy have broken through to some sort of understanding. Jimroy's voice has lost its hostility; he has surrendered his privately held fantasy of Sarah, as well as his perverse anger at the loss of his fantasy. His hand, grasping the pencil, trembles; Sarah's smile, at first provisional, indicates a measure, at least, of this transformation.

SARAH (meaningfully): You're welcome.

ROSE: Who's next?

JIMROY: Anders, Peter. He's the one with the jowly face. A bit of a schemer.

CRUZZI: Anders. I think he was one of the ones involved in the discussion tonight. He seemed most indignant, and that might indicate —

SARAH: I guess we can cross him off then.

ROSE: Of course, you can't be absolutely sure, just because he was a little —

CRUZZI: What do we know about him?

SARAH: Not much.

JIMROY: I'll put a question mark for Anders. Barcross? Susan Barcross.

ROSE: She's the one with the suede boots.

JIMROY: Feisty.

CRUZZI: Pleasant woman.

SARAH: Bright.

JIMROY: Cross her off?

SARAH: Might as well.

JIMROY: Herb Block. I suppose he's safe. He's only been working on Swann since last summer.

SARAH: You can cross him off.

JIMROY: Sydney Buswell?

SARAH: Buswell! That paranoid —

CRUZZI: Nevertheless it would be ludicrous —

ROSE: True.

JIMROY: Cross him off

SARAH: Yes.

JIMROY: Off. Butler? Jane Butler?

SARAH: Jane Butler. Isn't she the one —

ROSE: Green tweed suit. Little orange scarf. Lots of blush.

CRUZZI: The one who asked about semi-colons?

JIMROY: Right. From Montreal.

SARAH: She'd never —

JIMROY: Off?

ROSE: *Maybe* a question mark. Sometimes the most innocent —

JIMROY: Question mark? All right, question mark. Byford.

SARAH: Tony Byford. With the hair. (She holds up her hands to suggest an outsize Afro.)

CRUZZI: Charming man. Not the sort at all.

ROSE: Awfully polite. He complimented me on —

SARAH: Cross off Tony. Who next?

JIMROY: Carrington, Richard. Isn't he from — ?

SARAH: I vaguely remember. In my workshop —

CRUZZI: Moustache? I can't quite place —

JIMROY: Question mark? We can always go back . . .

Director's Note: The voices become indistinguishable, but the scene continues a few seconds longer. The late hour and the curious impromptu nature of this mini-symposium demand a surreal treatment. MUSIC overrides the voices, almost drowning them out. A burst of laughter comes through, indicating the charged air. Jimroy is seen, stroking off names, his mouth curved into a smile. Rose, cross-legged on her bed, is slicing the air and expressing reservation. Sarah gestures, makes a point, laughs. Cruzzi, his legs elegantly crossed, shrugs, speaks, smiles ruefully, signals to Jimroy to continue. VOICES grow increasingly indistinct, then fade completely. Dissolve.

Fade to: Interior of Sarah's room. Early morning.

A few bars of light enter the bedroom. Sarah is seen sleeping on her side. Rose is sprawled on her back, asleep, her mouth wide open. Cruzzi sleeps in the armchair, his collar unbuttoned, his tie loose, one foot on the end of a bed. Jimroy is curled on the floor with Rose's dressing-gown pulled over him. The registration list, covered with pencil markings, is spread on the floor beside him. SOUND: a telephone ringing.

SARAH (jerking awake, she gropes blindly for the telephone and croaks into the receiver): Hello. Hello. Yes this is... Stephen!... Yes... No... Fine, honestly... Yes. (She slides languorously down under the covers with the phone cradled next to her face.) Of course!... No, she's fine, just fine. (She pats her stomach, smiling.) Not complaining one bit. She loves travelling. No... no... yes, it's... lonely here, too. I know. (She looks around the room, takes in Cruzzi, Rose, Jimroy.) No, really... Yes... Me too, you know I do. (She laughs.)... What can I say? I know... me too... I promise, yes... Bye. (She replaces the phone. Across the room Cruzzi is seen smiling with his eyes closed; Rose is attentive, at attention, but pretending to sleep; Jimroy shuts his eyes grimly.)

CRUZZI (rising from his chair, almost crippled with stiffness, and stepping across Jimroy on his way to the bathroom): Good morning, comrades.

ROSE (singing out): Good morning.

JIMROY: It's morning. (He regards the sun coming through the window with pleasure.)

SARAH: Anyone for breakfast? (She reaches for the phone.)

ROSE: I could eat a horse.

SARAH (into phone): Three full breakfasts. The Bay Street Specials, orange juice, bacon, eggs, toast, coffee. One wheat cereal with double milk, also double orange juice. (She sits up and stretches.)

Cut to: Interior of Sarah's room. Breakfast time.

Sarah and Rose sit on the edge of the bed with the breakfast table in front of them. Across from them, seated on the other bed, are Jimroy and Cruzzi. Jimroy, with a smudge of egg adhering to his chin, is rechecking his list.

* * *

JIMROY (businesslike): A quick rundown then. With single question marks we've got Anders, Carrington, Gorham, Loftus, Norchuk, Oldfield, Skelton, and Tolliver.

ROSE: Urbanski? What happened to Urbanski?

JIMROY: Who?

SARAH: The one from Los Angeles. With the short socks. I think we decided he was okay.

CRUZZI: I must have drifted off at that point.

JIMROY: And — with *double* question marks we have — Crozier, Hall, and Webborn.

SARAH: And?

JIMROY: *Triple* question mark — Lang.

CRUZZI: Willard Lang. I *did* drift off.

JIMROY: I've never trusted the man. One of us — today — should ask him if he still has *his* copy of *Swann's Songs*.

SARAH: I'll volunteer.

ROSE: Wouldn't it be funny if —

SARAH: If what, Rose?

ROSE: Well, if here we were, all sixty-seven of us. All of us here to talk about Mary Swann's poems, and what if — what if not a single one of us has a copy of her book?

SARAH: That would be strange all right.

JIMROY: Statistically speaking . . .

CRUZZI: It's possible, I suppose.

JIMROY (bitterly): Of course some of us *came* here with a copy and —

CRUZZI: Well, my four copies are certainly gone. All four.

ROSE: And mine. I don't know how I could have —

SARAH (spooning up cereal): Luckily I've got mine.

CRUZZI (delighted): You do! I hadn't realized that you —

SARAH: Well, not with me. I didn't bring it, as a matter of fact. I've lent it to a friend, and he hasn't returned it yet.

Director's Note: Sarah's face — and her voice — must convey the warmth of affection. She stretches, smiles, bites her lower lip on the word *friend*.

CRUZZI: You're sure he *will* return it — your friend?

SARAH: Oh, Brownie would never lose a book. He's in the business, rare books. Books — (she stops to think) — books to Brownie are holy. Other things he's careless about, but books, well, with book's he's —

JIMROY: Where is it? The copy he borrowed? (He asks this in an abrupt, almost rude tone.)

SARAH: Where?

JIMROY: What I mean is, can you get your hands on it? Today?

SARAH (doubtfully): He works out of Chicago, my friend. Well, more than just a friend, actually...

JIMROY: I wonder if you should warn him. Make sure it's safe with him. It may be the last copy we have.

CRUZZI: A good idea.

SARAH: I suppose I *could* phone him. (She smiles at the thought.) Just to make sure. I could phone him at work. (She looks at her watch.) He's always there by eight o'clock, a real workaholic, that was part of the . . . he was always working.

ROSE (handing Sarah the phone): Here.

SARAH (looking around at the others): Maybe . . . maybe I should . . . make it a private call. He's sort of . . .

ROSE: I'm going back to my room anyway to get dressed. It's getting late.

CRUZZI (tactfully): I should be going too. (He rubs his chin.) A shave, perhaps, is in order.

JIMROY (gathering up papers): I'm going to have to duck my way back. (He gestures at his pyjamas.)

ROSE: Me too. (She laughs. Jimroy flinches, then follows her
    out.)

The instant they are gone Sarah takes up the telephone.
She makes an effort to compose herself, strokes back her
hair, breathes deeply, then dials with almost childish deliberation.

SARAH: Hello. Hello, it's Sarah Maloney. May I speak to
    Brownie please. Mr. Brown. Yes...Oh...(Disappointed):
    Well, what time will he be in?... Are you sure?...
    Well, do you know when he's expected back? I was anx-
    ious to get hold of him today. Something's come up,
    business... No, I don't think so, I have to speak to
    him confidentially, because... You don't happen
    to know where he is at the moment?... No, I'll be
    happy to hold on... (She hums while she waits, taps
    her fingers on the table, smiles.) Yes. But *someone* there
    must know where he is. I mean, hasn't he left some kind
    of... I see. Yes. But he must have something written
    on his appointment calendar... Yes, I'll hold... (She
    rubs nervously at her hair, twirling a strand around a
    finger.) Yes. Is that all?... Just that one word... I see.
    Symposium. (She puts down the phone and for a minute
    sits on the edge of the bed, unable to move.) Symposium.

Fade to: Interior of the meeting room. Morning.
    Members of the symposium are taking their seats.
The mood is congenial and relaxed, with a distinct sense of
anticipation.

BUTTER MOUTH: ... running a bit late this morning —
MERRY EYES: ... not like Lang to be —

TOP KNOT: What a night! I'm so goddamn hungover —

SILVER CUFFLINKS: This is what I've really been waiting for —

CLIPBOARD: . . . and this is why I came, if you want to know the truth —

CRUZZI (to Jimroy who is sitting next to him): Well, do you think it's really going to happen?

JIMROY (deeply skeptical): He's promised to *talk* about the love poems, but as far as actually *giving up* the poems themselves —

ROSE (sitting beside them): There's Sarah now. (Calls): Over here. I've saved you a seat.

SARAH (dazed): It's a quarter to ten. I thought I'd be late.

ROSE (conspiratorially): Did you get through? To your. . . friend?

SARAH: No. (Her face is stiff with incomprehension, and she speaks as though in a trance.) He's . . . out of town.

ROSE: You can always try later.

SARAH: No. (She pauses, gives a violent shake of her head.) I don't think so.

SILVER CUFFLINKS (loudly): Hey, what's up? I thought Willard was supposed to start at 9:30.

CRINKLED FOREHEAD (at lectern): Ladies and gentlemen, fellow scholars. Professor Lang appears to have been delayed. If you'll just be patient, I'm sure he'll be along in a minute or two.

WATTLED GENT: . . . bugger slept in —

GINGER PONYTAIL: . . . not Lang, he's always right on the button —

GREEN TWEED SUIT: Personally, I can't sit too long in these chairs —

WISTFUL DEMEANOUR: What's a love poem to one ear is just a—

WIMPY GRIN: . . . bird calls and mating dances —

CLIPBOARD: . . . a tad elitist, but he's managed to trash those elements most cherished —

GREEN TWEED SUIT: Almost time for the coffee break —

CRINKLED FOREHEAD (stepping up to lectern again): We've just telephoned up to Professor Lang's room, and since there's no answer, we assume he's on his way. Please bear with us for a few minutes longer.

As though a signal has been given, the meeting room falls silent. All eyes are fixed on the empty lectern and on the clock behind it. The only sounds are throat clearing, coughing, sighing, and shuffling of feet. It is now 10:00 A.M. There is some rustling of papers, an air of expectancy. The clock does not actually tick, but there is a distinct *sense* of a clock ticking. The seconds pass, then the minutes. It is now 10:02. Crinkled Forehead once again approaches the lectern.

CRINKLED FOREHEAD: I'm sure any minute now —

WOMAN WITH TURBAN: Has anyone looked in the coffee shop?

CRINKLED FOREHEAD: He's not there. We checked.

SARAH (rising): Perhaps one of us should go to see if —

JIMROY (on his feet): I'll gladly volunteer. I think we've been sitting quite long enough. (He heads for the doorway.)

ROSE: I'll go along with you. Mr. Jimroy. Keep you company.

SARAH: Maybe I will too. Might as well.

CRUZZI: I'll just —

CRINKLED FOREHEAD: Well, I'll just tag along too, perhaps.

WOMAN WITH TURBAN: Might as well join in —

BLUE-SPOTTED TIE: Why don't I come along — ?

CRINKLED FOREHEAD: He may be ill.

A group of ten or twelve rapidly assembles and walks

along in lock step toward the bank of elevators. MUSIC: a skirling tune, strings mainly, with some bagpipes. The small, silent swarm squeezes through the corridor. An elevator arrives, and the group, acting almost as a single being, pours itself inside. CAMERA then picks up the group inside the elevator, where there is total silence except for:

JIMROY (in vice-admiral's voice): Twenty-fourth floor, I believe. Right down the hall from my room.
CRUZZI: Right. (He presses the button, and the elevator swiftly rises.)
ROSE (gasping): We're here.

The group exits, with Sarah in the lead. Long CAMERA shot of the silent march down the corridor.

SARAH (stopping before the door): This is it. (She knocks. There is no response.)
WOMAN WITH TURBAN: Try again.
SARAH (knocking again): Nothing. (She puts her ear against the door, listening and knocking again. She motions to Cruzzi to listen too.)

Cruzzi presses his ear to the door, listens, and nods, then steps aside for Crinkled Forehead who repeats the procedure.

ROSE (pushing forward, placing her ear to the door): I hear something. (She holds up a finger for silence.)

Director's Note: From the distance comes the strangled sound of Lang beating on the wall and calling out. His cries gradually grow louder and more wild, but they are also faintly theatrical and subtly exaggerated.

LANG: Help! Help!

ROSE (to others): Did you hear that? Someone said help. (She
    tries the door.)

LANG: Help! Get me out of here!

ROSE: It's Professor Lang.

Cut to: Interior of Lang's hotel room. Same time as above.
    CAMERA close-up of the bathroom door, which is tied
with a curtain cord, the doorknob looped and secured to the
knob of the clothes closet next to it.

LANG (from inside the bathroom): Get me out of here!

Director's Note: Because the employment of the curtain
cord, a staple in crime films, is intended here to be an ironic,
self-referential nod in the direction of the genre, the CAMERA
lingers on the subject for several seconds before moving into
the room and focusing on the intruder in his maintenance
uniform. He is a short man, agile, with curly hair, busily
stuffing papers into a pillowcase, the same man Rose
Hindmarch encountered on the stairway the evening before.

Cut to: The corridor. Same time as above.

ROSE: I think we should force the door.

CRUZZI (in reasonable tones): I'm sure we can get a key from
    the desk —

CRINKLED FOREHEAD: Someone telephone down. I'll just —

WOMAN WITH TURBAN: What's he saying in there?

JIMROY (Always a man to honour questions): He's still saying
    "Help," I believe.

ROSE: The only thing to do is break the door down.

SARAH: Rose has a point —

BLUE-SPOTTED TIE: If we all leaned together —

JIMROY (vice-admirally): One, two, three, push. (Though they all push at once, it is a poorly executed move, almost comically clumsy, and the door fails to give way.)

LANG (muffled): Help! Help!

ROSE: One more try. One and a two and a three —

Crinkled Forehead returns with three bellhops, one of them carrying a key. MUSIC: a loud orchestral crash, the sort of music that, in western films, traditionally accompanies the arrival of the posse.

Cut to: Interior of Lang's room. Same time as above.

CAMERA close-up of intruder who hurries with papers, hearing the commotion in the corridor. He looks to left and right, goes to the window and wedges it open. For an instant he regards the street twenty-four storeys below. He pushes the bag through the window and reluctantly lets it drop just as Jimroy, Cruzzi, Sarah, and the others crowd into the room. The intruder ducks neatly behind the curtain, the same curtain from which the cord has been taken.

LANG: Help! I'm in the bathroom!

ROSE: He's in the bathroom. Look, a curtain cord!

LANG: Get me out of here.

Director's Note: The excitement as the members of the symposium cluster around the bathroom door is intense, and not one of them notices the faintly stagy sound of Lang's voice. Everyone is talking at once, and Jimroy is tugging at the curtain cord.

Cut to: Exterior of building. The CAMERA picks up the pillow case as it falls through the air; some of its contents fly out as it descends, mixing with the snow and carried by the wind into the street.

Cut to: Interior of Lang's room. Same time as above.

LANG (staggering from bathroom; he is wearing undershorts and a towel and appears agitated): I was just having a bath and . . .

CRUZZI (looking around): Looks like a burglary.

ROSE: Check the closets. Under the bed —

LANG (growing hysterical). For God's sake, never mind that! My papers . . .

SARAH: What exactly's been taken?

LANG (wildly histrionic): My papers! My years of work!

JIMROY: . . . got everything I suppose.

ROSE: The pillow case . . . a pillow case is missing!

CRUZZI: . . . made the most of his moment —

LANG: The love poems. Don't tell me the love poems — (He is waving his arms extravagantly and wailing, but his face is watchful.) I had the love poems over there, on the dresser. The originals!

GINGER PONYTAIL: Take it easy, fellow, take it easy.

BLUE-SPOTTED TIE: Give the man breathing room.

MAN WITH OUTSIZE AFRO: Jesus, he's in shock, we'd better get a medic up here.

ROSE: *And* the hotel detective.

CRINKLED FOREHEAD: Water! Get him some water.

WOMAN WITH TURBAN (to Lang): Here. Take my raincoat. I insist.

Director's Note: It is important that the confusion in this scene (which lasts less than a minute) be palpable; it must obscure and animate at the same time, filling the room like a blizzard and numbing the perceptions of those who are acting and reacting. The Swannians have gathered around Lang, and they are all talking at once. Not one of them observes the intruder as he slips from behind the curtain and walks nonchalantly past them, into the corridor, glancing back over his shoulder just before he disappears. Only Willard Lang, struggling into the raincoat and babbling incoherently catches, and holds, the intruder's gaze for the briefest of moments. The look between them is shrewd and culpable — and ambiguous enough to puzzle the sort of reflective movie-goers who like to dissect the variables of a story over a cup of coffee on their way home from their local cinemas.

Cut to: Corridor. Same time. Long shot of intruder running toward exit stairs. CAMERA close-up on Sarah, stepping into corridor, regarding running figure.

SARAH: Brownie? (She whispers his name, and then repeats it more loudly, even recklessly.) Brownie.

Director's Note: The intruder — it is uncertain whether or not he hears his name — dives through the exit door, leaving CAMERA on Sarah's face. She looks first puzzled, then wistful, then knowing. Her mouth opens a final time, mouthing the word "Brownie," then closes abruptly. She closes her eyes, sways slightly, then opens her eyes widely. One hand goes to her mouth, rests there.

Fade to: Interior of meeting room. Later in the day.
    A meeting is in session, but there is no one at the lectern and no one, seemingly, in charge. People are seated in a sort

of circle, speaking out, offering up remembered lines of poetry, laboriously reassembling one of Mary Swann's poems. Sarah is writing, a clipboard on her knee.

Director's Final Note: The faces of the actors have been subtly transformed. They are seen joined in a ceremonial act of reconstruction, perhaps even an act of creation. There need be no suggestion that any one of them will become less selfish in the future, less cranky, less consumed with thoughts of tenure and academic glory, but each of them has, for the moment at least, transcended personal concerns.

BUSWELL: We all agree, then, on the first line.

WATTLED GENT (quoting): "It sometimes happens when looking for"

MERRY EYES: Yes, that's it. Did you get that down?

SARAH (writing in notebook): "It sometimes happens when looking for." Are you sure?

MAN WITH OUTSIZE AFRO: Second line?

WISTFUL DEMEANOUR: It's a run-on line, I'm almost sure. "It sometimes happens when looking for/ Lost objects, a book, a picture or"

CRINKLED FOREHEAD: That's it, I'm positive.

SARAH: Close, anyway. What comes next?

WOMAN WITH TURBAN: "a book, a picture or/ A coin or spoon."

GREEN TWEED SUIT: Wait! Is that "spoon or coin" or "coin or spoon"?

BUTTER MOUTH: "Coin or spoon" I think. Yes.

JIMROY (quoting): "That something falls across the mind—"

CRUZZI: "Not quite a shadow but what a shadow would be."

SARAH (looking up): "In a place that lacked light."

MUSIC: an organ, dense, heavy. The words of the poem grow indistinct; only the rhythm remains strong.

BUSWELL: "As though the lost things have withdrawn/ Into themselves — "
PALE SUEDE BOOTS: "books returned — "
JIMROY: "To paper or wood or thought"
CRINKLED FOREHEAD: "Coins and spoons to simple ores"
WOMAN WITH TURBAN: "Lustreless and without history"
BLUE-SPOTTED TIE: "Waiting out of sight."

MUSIC continues; CAMERA shot of photograph of Mary Swann; CREDITS roll across the photo as the voices continue.

SARAH: "And becoming part of a larger loss"
CRUZZI: "Without a name"
WOMAN WITH TURBAN: "Or definition or form"
JIMROY: "Not unlike what touches us"
CRUZZI: "In moments of shame."

LOST THINGS
By Mary Swann

It sometimes happens when looking for
Lost objects, a book, a picture or
A coin or spoon,
That something falls across the mind—
Not quite a shadow but what a shadow would be
In a place that lacked light.

As though the lost things have withdrawn
Into themselves, books returned
To paper or wood or thought,
Coins and spoons to simple ores,
Lustreless and without history,
Waiting out of sight

And becoming part of a larger loss
Without a name
Or definition or form
Not unlike what touches us
In moments of shame.